Alaskan
MIDNIGHT

Four Romances Quilted from the Pieces of Broken Lives

JOYCE
LIVINGSTON

BARBOUR
PUBLISHING

ISBN 1-59310-432-4

Cover image © Corbis

All Scripture quotations, unless otherwise noted, are taken from the King James Version.

Published by Barbour Books, an imprint of Barbour Publishing, Inc., P.O. Box 719, Uhrichsville, Ohio 44683, www.barbourbooks.com

Our mission is to publish and distribute inspirational products offering exceptional value and biblical encouragement to the masses.

 Member of the
Evangelical Christian
Publishers Association

Printed in the United States of America.
5 4 3 2 1

Dear Reader,

Alaska! What a beautiful place! How near and dear it is to my heart. Although I have never lived in Alaska, as a travel escort it has been my privilege to visit there a number of times. I've cruised the inland passage, traveled the highway from Anchorage to Fairbanks, taken the wonderful riverboat ride, ridden the domed train through the gorgeous wildlife areas of Denali Park, walked the trails of Earthquake Park, ridden up Juneau's fabulous Mt. Roberts tramway and stood at the top, in awe of the spectacular city spread out below, watched the salmon swim upstream, and way too many other things to mention here.

As I wrote these four stories, in my mind's eye, I could see all of the above places, and I wanted so much to share them with you. I hope you enjoy the stories of Victoria and Buck, Glorianna and Trapper, Tina and Hank, and last of all, Jackie and Sam, as they struggle to overcome the obstacles in their lives and find that one true love. It may sound silly, but I laughed and cried with each one as I wrote their story. They became so important to me, I didn't want to the book to end and bid them a final farewell.

My husband, Don, and I live on a little lake in the middle of our good old USA, in the cabin he built for us. Our six children are grown, doing wonderfully well, and have families of their own, so I am able to spend many hours each day at my computer. Don is supportive and is a tremendous help. I am truly blessed. A number of years ago, God called me to be an encourager to women—women of all ages. It is my prayer that, through my books, you and other readers will be encouraged to face life head-on, finding answers by seeking God's will and trusting in Him.

I hope you enjoy *Alaskan Midnight*. I'd love to hear from you. Visit my website: www.joycelivingston.com, or email: joyce@joycelivingston.com

In HIM,
Joyce Livingston

Northern Exposure

Chapter 1

"Hi, Jason, it's me. I'm in Seward, Alaska, waiting for Mom. The cruise ship anchored about an hour ago. She should be getting off any minute. Any word from the bank?"

Victoria Whitmore leaned her head to one side and braced the phone against her shoulder, then shuffled her notebook under her arm, nearly dropping it when she heard her brother's answer. "They did? They approved our loan? Yippee! That means Mom and I are going to be able to open our gift shop after all. Everything hinged on that bank loan. I can hardly wait to tell her. How soon can we get the money?"

The smartly dressed young woman wearing a victorious smile listened intently to her lawyer brother. "Three weeks, huh? That's not bad, Jason. I was afraid it'd take much longer. Oh, this is exciting. Mom's gonna be so pleased." Victoria checked her watch. "We're really going to do it—open our own shop. I'm glad you and the boys agreed with me that Mom needs something challenging. She's gone through some pretty tough times since Dad died. I can't believe I got that stupid three-day flu and couldn't go with her on this cruise. I'm amazed she went alone."

Victoria glanced toward the double doors. "I'm not sure where we'll be in Alaska. Mom just said to pack a suitcase and meet her in Seward. If I get a chance, I'll call you again in a few days and let you know where we are. We should be home a week from today. Well, better go now. I want to greet Mom with the good news when she gets off the ship. Bye, Jason, and thanks for everything. And say hi to Jonathan for me."

After hanging up the phone, Victoria moved to her seat, pulled her ballpoint pen from her purse, and flipped through her notebook. She checked and rechecked the figures for the new gift shop.

This week in Alaska will probably be the last vacation Mom and I will have for a very long time. Victoria entered a new idea in the notebook. *With the responsibility of opening a new shop, we're both going to be stuck in Kansas City.*

At least until we get it off the ground and into a paying proposition. I'm going to make every minute count while we're in Alaska.

"This seat taken?"

Startled, Victoria looked up at a man clad in a western-cut leather jacket. She shifted her position and surveyed all the empty chairs in the room. Why did he have to pick one near her? Cautiously she answered, "No, it's not."

"Good." The stranger extended his hand and a warm smile. "I'm Buck."

Reluctantly she accepted his hand, flinching at his firm grasp. She watched out of the corner of her eye as the attractive, bearded man in faded jeans lowered himself into the nearby chrome and vinyl chair.

It was not her policy to carry on a conversation with a stranger, especially a male stranger. His unsolicited friendliness made Victoria uncomfortable, and she found herself pulling back into her shell, the shell she'd created for herself eight years ago. With a second glance about the room, she wondered why he'd selected that particular chair, when he probably had another hundred from which to choose. Hopefully, her mother would be coming through those doors soon and they'd be on their way.

What a hard time she'd had convincing her mother to go on the cruise alone! But the tickets were nonrefundable, and Victoria and her mother had too much invested to let two tickets go unused. One unused ticket was bad enough. She was hoping the cruise line would relent and at least refund part of her money since she'd been too ill to take the trip. She just hoped Abigale had made a few friends and not stayed to herself. Good thing she'd taken her cross-stitch project, along with some books.

"Meeting someone coming in on the ship?" Buck asked, interrupting Victoria's thoughts.

"My mom."

He gave her a big grin as he stuffed his thumbs through his belt loops and settled his long frame into the uncomfortable chair. "Oh? Your mom, huh? I'm meeting my dad. He won this cruise in a drawing on the local radio station. I hated for him to come by himself, but he said he didn't mind. He's probably spent the week trying to avoid a shipboard romance. For an old geezer, he's good-looking and too smart to be taken. I reckon he's made it through unscathed."

Their eyes met. "You don't believe those things really happen, do you?" Victoria asked. "Shipboard romances? I think they only happen in fiction." She frowned. Surely situations like that only happened on television, never in real life. Not often anyway. She'd never heard of it actually happening to a real person. You would have to be pretty desperate to fall for a total stranger onboard a cruise ship.

"I don't know." A hearty laugh boomed from somewhere within his broad chest. "I've heard some pretty good stories. All those widows looking for rich old men. What better place to look than on a cruise ship?"

Victoria winced as he pulled a knife from a leather sheath on his belt and began carefully whittling on a frayed fingernail.

"Hey, my mother's a widow and she'd never do anything to encourage a shipboard romance," she responded defensively. She tucked an errant strand of hair behind her ear and turned her attention back to her notebook. She didn't want to talk, not after getting the good news from her brother. What she really wanted to do was think about the shop that would soon be a reality and plan how she would arrange the shelving, counters, and racks in the building they hoped to lease.

"Some women do strange things when they're lonely," Buck teased. He folded the knife and placed it back in the case. His eyes sparkled with mischief.

A frown creased Victoria's brow as she eyed him suspiciously, not sure exactly how to take his comment. "Some women? How about some men?"

He grinned, crossed his arms over his chest, and thrust his long legs into the narrow aisle. "Aw, come on now. Those cute little silver-haired ladies bat their sexy blues at a lonely guy, and bingo. Matrimony! Before the guy knows what hit him, the knot's tied and he's committed for the rest of his life. And so is his money!"

Victoria stiffened, her female feathers slightly ruffled, not sure if he was serious or just putting her on. "Maybe your father's the one who's on the prowl for a lonely, rich widow. Ever think of that?"

He crossed his ankles and spread his long arms across the adjoining chair backs. After a loud chuckle, he said, "Hey, I'm only kidding. My dad would never do that."

"You had me going there for a minute," she declared with relief, wishing this conversation had never started. "I know my mother would never be a party to a shipboard romance."

"Then I guess both our parents are safe. We can feel sorry for those who are more gullible." He smiled and winked. "I'm an old worrywart where my dad's concerned. Don't know why. He's taken good care of himself since my mom died six years ago. He's my best friend and sort of my business partner. I don't want any woman taking him away from me." Buck grinned. "We're getting along just fine the way things are. You know, the parent becomes the child and the child becomes the parent thing?" He made a gesture as if he were tipping his hat. "Sorry if I offended you. I didn't mean anything by my words, just making friendly conversation. Guess we Alaskans never see a stranger. We'll talk to anyone that'll listen." He glanced around the sparsely filled room. "I'm sure your mother behaved as a perfect lady on her cruise."

Victoria's brows lifted and she snickered. "That's because she is a perfect lady. The last thing she'd want to do is seduce your father and move to Alaska."

"Hey, Alaska's not such a bad place to live. Ask any Alaskan."

"Well, that may be true. But my mom and I have plans."

She watched as a uniformed security guard moved toward the double doors. Surely the passengers would be unloading soon. How long could it take to get through customs?

"Plans?" he asked, apparently interested in her comment.

She closed her notebook. Deciding he looked harmless enough, she answered,

"When we get back to Missouri after this vacation, we're going to open a gift shop together. It's been our lifelong dream. I'm an artist, and I plan to sell a lot of my work there." She smiled triumphantly, her good news still fresh on her mind, and closed the notebook in her lap.

"Artist, huh? I'll bet you're a good one. You don't paint any of those funny things that look like the guy poured paint on canvas and then stepped in it barefooted, do you?"

She had to laugh at his description of abstract art. "No. I'm more the Thomas Kinkade type of artist. You know, landscapes, trees, flowers, country settings. But what I enjoy the most is portraits."

"Well, I do want to apologize—about the way I talked about your mother. I'm sure she's a very nice person."

"Your apology isn't necessary. I understand about your dad. I do the same thing with my mom. Protect her, that is. She's my best friend, too. We're fortunate to still have our parents. Many of my friends have lost their parents." Victoria pushed back the sleeve of her jacket and checked her watch. "Shouldn't they be coming soon?"

The words had barely passed her lips when the security guard opened one of the double doors. Disembarking passengers began elbowing through the narrow opening, pushing overflowing carts laden with bulging suitcases.

"Mom!" Victoria jumped to her feet and waved her arms wildly. "Over here!"

A tall slender woman clad in a coral pantsuit smiled and waved back. "Victoria, hi. You made it! I wasn't sure you would."

"There's my dad. Been nice visiting with you," Buck volunteered and nodded. He pushed past Abigale Whitmore and her daughter. "Dad! Dad! Over here."

The two women embraced.

"Mom! I just talked to Jason, and he heard from the bank. We got the loan. Aren't you excited?"

Abigale threw her arms about her daughter and squeezed her tight. "Oh, honey, this is such good news for you—"

"For us, Mom, for us. We're going to be partners. It's our gift shop." Victoria clasped her mother's hands in hers and stepped back for a better look at the woman. "You must've had a good trip, you're positively glowing. I'm so sorry I had to cancel at the last minute. I really wanted to go on that cruise with you. But it looks like you had a good time without me."

"I did, Victoria. I had a wonderful time. I can hardly wait to tell you all about it," Abigale exclaimed, her green eyes bright and shining. "The most amazing things happened!"

It was good to see her mother excited like this. Even with silver hair, no one would guess Abigale was sixty-two. Victoria smiled to herself, remembering Buck's comment about silver-haired women. The past year had been a difficult one for Abigale. Losing the husband she'd married as a teenager had taken its toll. She'd withdrawn from nearly everyone, even her best friends. Victoria and her brothers had worried about their mother. They were surprised when she agreed to go on the Alaskan cruise, the same cruise she and Guy Whitmore had planned to take on their forty-fifth wedding anniversary.

"And I want to hear every little detail. I hope you took lots of pictures," Victoria rattled on, unable to contain her enthusiasm. "The family has planned a welcome home party for us when we get back, so we'd better get your film developed before we head to Kansas City." She paused thoughtfully. "By the way, where are we going from here? Your message just said to pack for a week in Alaska and meet you here in Seward. Are we going on a tour bus? Or the domed excursion train?" Victoria glanced around at the crowd pressing in around them. "You didn't leave much information on my answering machine when you called from the ship."

"Not at fifteen dollars a minute, I didn't. That's the cost of a ship-to-shore phone call. You're the one who offered to meet me at the end of the cruise so we could have some time together after you had to cancel. Remember? And besides, I need to—"

"Sure I remember, and I meant it. I might have missed the cruise, but I'm well now and ready to see Alaska, if you're not too tired after a week on the ship." The young woman took stock of the area with a concerned look. "Mother, where's your luggage?"

"Dear, that's one of the things I want to tell you—"

Victoria frowned as her palm moved swiftly to her cheek. "Oh, no. They didn't lose your luggage, did they? Oh, Mom, surely not."

A man's deep voice boomed from behind them, "Dad, where are you going? I'm parked in the other direction."

The two women turned to find Buck following a tall, slender man who Victoria decided was Buck's father.

"Oh, I see you found your dad," she acknowledged, noting he seemed rather perturbed by something.

He nodded his head toward the man. "Oh, hello again. Yes, I found him."

The older man abruptly stopped the cart beside the two women.

Victoria smiled, feeling rather awkward, not knowing if she should try to introduce them to her mother or just turn away. "I found her, but not her luggage. I guess it didn't—"

"It's right here. I have it on my cart," Buck's father declared proudly. He motioned toward the floral tapestry suitcases standing alongside his. "See? All safe and sound."

Buck stopped in his tracks with a puzzled look on his face. "You have her luggage on your cart? Maybe I'd better try to run down another cart, Dad. I'm parked in the lot on the east side of the building. The ladies may not be going that direction."

"I'll get a cart for her, you needn't bother," Victoria volunteered quickly. She gestured toward an empty chair. "Just put her luggage there so she can sit down while I go after the cart. That way you two won't be delayed. And thank you for bringing it for her," she added with a nod. "I'm glad she didn't have to juggle it herself."

"No, I'll get it. You three stay here. It'll only take me a minute." Buck slid his hand under his father's elbow and motioned him toward a chair. "Sit down, Dad."

Ron Silverbow pulled free of his son's grasp. He stood straight and tall. "No need, son. I'll handle Abigale's luggage myself. Right, Abbey?"

"Right, Ron," Abigale agreed. Smiling, she moved to stand beside the older man and slipped her hand into the crook of his arm.

Buck shot a quick look at Victoria as if to say, *Do you have any idea what is going on here? Because I sure don't.*

She returned the look with a shrug of her shoulders.

The older man, quite handsome with his silver-gray hair and straight, chiseled features, gestured toward the questioning young woman. "You must be Abigale's daughter, Victoria. You're just as pretty as your mother described you. And you're almost as pretty as your mom. You've already met Buck. Right?"

Both Victoria and Buck nodded and glared at one another in stunned silence.

"Well, Abigale," Ron said as he wrapped his fingers over hers and patted them gently, "you haven't met him. This is my son, Buck. He's a good kid, but he tries to keep me on a short rope sometimes. He has a tendency to forget I'm the senior here."

Abigale snickered and reached toward the younger man. "Nice to meet you, Buck. I've heard so much about you and Micah. I've looked forward to meeting both of you."

Victoria quickly moved to her mother's side. "Who's Micah?"

"My son," Buck answered bluntly; his glare fixed on his father.

"Did you bring the minivan like I told you, son?"

Buck nodded. "Just like you said on the telephone. But I still don't understand why it had to be the minivan. You didn't buy that many Alaskan souvenirs, did you?"

"Not hardly. I live in Alaska, remember? As a matter of fact, I didn't buy any souvenirs at all. Not a one," Ron admitted. He chuckled, then winked at the lovely gray-haired woman standing beside him. "But I am bringing something special home with me."

"Then why the minivan, Dad? Why not my pickup?"

Ron Silverbow looked first to Buck, then to Victoria, and then to Abigale.

"Why don't we sit down while the crowd thins out and the parking lot empties a bit?"

"But—" Buck started.

"Just sit, Buck. We're in no hurry."

The three took seats while Ron stood before them, tall and proud.

"I'm sure you two kids have figured out by now that Abigale and I met on the ship. First night, actually. I was sitting at a table on the open deck, wishing your mama had lived long enough to take this cruise with me, and feeling sorry for myself, I might add, when the music started to play and the cruise director announced a line dance."

He paused and stepped aside to allow a pregnant woman and her cart to pass.

"Well," Ron continued, "he instructed his staff of attractive young ladies and gents to fetch themselves partners from the audience. When one of them approached me, I backed off, but she wouldn't take no for an answer and pulled me onto the deck."

"Same thing happened to me," Abigale interjected excitedly, never taking her eyes off Ron's weathered face. "A young man in a blue blazer and white slacks took my hand and pulled me onto the deck with the other dancers. At first, I was mortified. Then, I thought, I'm on a cruise, and this is what they do on cruises. And I actually learned to line dance."

The young woman cupped her hand over her mother's sleeve. "Mother, you didn't! You and Daddy never danced. You never wanted to."

"Oh, but I did," her mother confessed. "Your father was the one who never wanted to."

"It was fun, wasn't it, Abigale?" Ron asked, his handlebar mustache tilting upward as he spoke. "Even though I was all feet till you came to my rescue."

Victoria watched in horror as she caught her mother's new friend winking at her mother a second time.

Abigale grinned. "You were very graceful, once you caught on. I was proud of you."

"So, if you were each dancing with a staff member, how did you get together?" Victoria asked. She found it nearly impossible to believe her timid mother would actually do the line dance, or any dance, with a stranger.

"Well, when the first number ended, I was going to leave the dance area, but my partner swung me around and said she was going to get another partner and for me to dance with the lady next to me, who happened to be Abigale. I'll tell you, I was embarrassed. So was she. But that instructor took Abbey's hand and placed it in mine. What could we do? Right, kid?"

"Right, Ronnie." Abigale blushed.

Kid? Victoria thought. *He called my sixty-two-year-old mother kid?*

"Dad!" Buck chastised as he quickly rose to his feet.

"Let me finish, son." Ron clasped his hand firmly over Buck's arm. "That happened the first night. Me and Abbey danced that line dance thing till most of the others dropped out, then we went into the lounge and talked about our families till it got dark." He gave a good belly laugh. "And in Ketchikan, Alaska, this time of year it's about one in the morning before it gets dark. And since the sun was coming up in a couple of hours, we stayed up for the sunrise too."

"So, didn't you meet anyone else onboard?" Victoria asked. As soon as the words came out of her mouth, she wished she hadn't asked.

"Sure, honey, lots of nice people. You'd be surprised how many people our age take cruises. And they have so many activities you could be busy every waking hour. I'm so sorry you got the flu and couldn't go at the last minute. But if you'd gone, I might not have met Ron."

That was a fine thing to say, Victoria thought, surprised at her mother's candor. *Sounds like she didn't even miss me.*

"And I'm sure glad that didn't happen," Ron said. "Your mother and I had a great time. Spent every minute of every day together. And like I said, in Alaska. . . the days last into the night."

"Way into the night," Abigale added with a raise of her brow. "Ron took good care of me, Victoria. Your fears about me going on the cruise alone were foolish. I was perfectly safe, and rarely alone."

"So it seems," Victoria muttered. *Safe and rarely alone? Oh, dear. What has she gotten herself into? She's not old enough to be senile.*

Buck checked his watch nervously. "This is interesting, hearing how you two met, but shouldn't we be going, Dad, and let the ladies be on their way? I'm sure they have plans. And we've got a long way to go."

"No hurry, son. Park it." Ron pointed to the chair formerly occupied by Buck. "The story gets more interesting as it goes along. And I'm not finished yet."

Victoria shot a questioning glance at her mother who seemed to have no concern about where they were going from here.

"Like I said, we spent every minute together. I've lived in Alaska all my life, but seeing it through Abigale's eyes was like seeing it for the first time. Her enthusiasm for its beauty opened my eyes to things I'd never seen or appreciated."

He stepped forward and placed his hand on Abigale's shoulder. "And we talked for hours and hours."

He turned and let out a slight chuckle. "Why, Victoria, I know you and your brothers so well I could probably tell you things even your closest friends don't know about you."

He returned his gaze to his son. "And Abbey knows everything about my family. We swam together in both the indoor and outdoor pools, sunned on the decks, played bingo, shuffleboard, and even batted a few tennis balls. We ate at the midnight buffet every night, we rode the tram up Mount Roberts in Juneau.

We did it all together. We even prayed together. She loves our Lord as much as I do."

Abigale gave him a smile of approval. "I sure do."

Ron Silverbow removed his hand from Abigale's shoulder and extended his open palm as a smile lit up her face. She placed her hand in his and rose to stand by his side. He slid his arm around her waist and pulled her close. "And together we've decided to stay. Victoria, Buck, Abigale and I are getting married!"

Chapter 2

Y ou're what?" Buck hollered loud enough that the passersby stopped and turned to see where the commotion was coming from.

"Married? You and my mother?" Stunned and confused, Victoria instinctively reached for her mother's hand and pulled her away from the man who had just made his ridiculous announcement.

A uniformed officer left his post by the door and hurried over. "Anything wrong here, folks?"

Ron shook his head and smiled pleasantly. "Everything's fine, Officer. Just having a few family words. Sorry if we got a little carried away. We'll try to knock it down a few decibels."

The man looked from face to face, then moved away slowly with a backward glance over his shoulder. The passersby moved on, their attention once again turned to finding the right bus.

Victoria wanted to say something, anything, but the words refused to come. Surely, she'd misunderstood. "Oh, Mom," she stammered, "wh–what about the plans to open our shop?"

Abigale took her daughter's hand and squeezed it affectionately. "We'll talk about that later. Just the two of us. Okay, dear?"

Victoria nodded, temporarily appeased.

"Dad?" Buck questioned in a hushed but firm voice. "Do you know what you just said?"

"I said exactly what I intended to say, son. Abigale and I are getting married. Right, sweetheart?" He gently tugged Abigale away from Victoria's grasp. "I don't think our kids believe us."

Abigale smiled and stood by Ron. "Then we'll just have to convince them, Ronnie." She leaned into his side and beamed into his face. "Give them a little time. After all, I'm sure this is the last thing they expected to hear when they met us here."

"Mother!" Victoria blurted out, surprised to find her voice in working order once again. "This has to be a joke! And I'm not laughing. This isn't funny."

"Yeah, it's a joke, right?" Buck moved in. The frown eased from his face and he let loose a relieved chuckle. "You two had us going there for a minute. Married? That's pretty funny. Good joke."

Ron leaned over and planted a kiss on Abigale's forehead. "No joke. Is it, honey?"

Abigale blushed as she turned toward her daughter. "I'm sorry, Victoria. I wish there was some way I could have warned you, given you a chance to get to know Ron and what a wonderful man he is before I told you we were planning on getting married. But we talked it over, and the best way seemed to be to tell you right up front."

Frustrated, Victoria threw her arms in the air. "But, Mom!"

"Dad!" Buck interrupted before Victoria could continue. "You're crazy! You can't meet a lady on a cruise ship, know her for seven days, and marry her!"

Ron wrapped his arms protectively around Abigale. "Oh, but I did. And I am! I love this woman, and we're going to spend the rest of our lives together. Aren't we, sugar?"

"And where, may I ask, are you going to live?" Victoria questioned, wondering if they'd even considered that currently they lived eons apart. "In Alaska, Mother? Or are you planning to bring him to Missouri?"

"Dad could never survive a year in Missouri!" Buck reasoned aloud with a white-knuckled grasp on the luggage cart.

"And Mother couldn't take the Alaska cold," Victoria added convincingly, allying herself with a stranger.

"Why don't you two let us decide that for ourselves. After all, we're quite capable of making our own decisions." Ron turned his attention to his son. "Buck, stack Victoria's luggage on top of ours, and we'll all head to the minivan."

"Mother! Where are we going? What about our trip?" Victoria stood with her hands on her hips. "What about our gift shop? Our dream?" She needed answers.

"We're going with Ron," Abigale replied softly, as if to cushion the blow they'd just dealt their children. "We're going to spend the next week at his place, the place I'll be living once we're married. We want the four of us to get to know one another."

"But, Dad!" Buck said with exasperation.

"Mom, you can't!" Victoria argued.

The pleas went unheeded by the newly engaged couple. The parents were already walking arm in arm toward the exit doors, leaving their children to bring the cart.

Victoria shot Buck a questioning look and accused through clenched teeth, "You knew about this, didn't you? You knew your dad was going to find himself a wife on that ship! You knew it all the time, and you didn't stop him!"

Buck gave her a frown. "Your mom went on that cruise alone. What does that tell you? She had her sights out for a good man and she found one. My vulnerable old father! I hope you're satisfied. Or were you a part of the plot?" He grabbed her suitcases and flung them on top of the others, then motioned to her. "Come on. Looks like their plans are all made. Guess we'll have to go along with them. For now!"

Victoria adjusted the strap on her shoulder bag and followed the big man toward the parking lot. "For now is right. We've got to talk them out of this!"

"You drive," Ron ordered Buck when the last piece of luggage had been loaded into the minivan. "Victoria can sit up front with you, it'll give you two a chance to get acquainted. My honey and I will sit in the back."

Victoria watched as Ron ushered Abigale into the seat, then climbed in after her as she slid across. *He might as well have pulled her onto his lap, he is sitting so close,* Victoria thought.

Buck stood impatiently while Victoria climbed into the front seat, and then he closed her door with a slam. He went around and sat in the driver's seat. "Since I'm driving, don't you think it'd be nice if you'd tell me where I'm supposed to drive?" he asked sarcastically.

Ron leaned forward and placed his hand on the seat back behind his son. "First, let's find us a nice little restaurant and get us something to eat. My little sweetie and I are famished, and I'll bet you two kids are too. Right, Victoria?"

"Um, I guess so," Victoria muttered. She felt as out of control as a baby bird who'd just fallen out of its nest. "At this point, whatever the rest of you want to do is fine with me." She lifted her arms in defeat.

Ron continued. "After lunch, we'll take the beautiful drive up the coast to Anchorage. We'll be home by five or six tonight. That'll give us plenty of time to have an early dinner, and you ladies can get a good night's sleep."

Buck shoved the gearshift to neutral and turned to face his father, who was already deeply engrossed in conversation with Abigale. "All four of us?"

Ron stopped pointing and seemed surprised at his son's question. "Of course, all four of us. I already told you that. We're taking the ladies with us to Anchorage."

"But, Dad—"

Ron gave his son a pleasant but I-don't-want-to-hear-anymore-about-this grin. "Just do it, son."

The minivan leaped forward as Buck shoved the gearshift into drive, pinning the foursome to their seats. Victoria was sure she heard Buck mumble something under his breath.

"Your dad always like this?" she asked softly, not wanting to interrupt the conversation in the backseat.

He sent a quick glance her way. "No. Sometimes he's worse."

"Parents. You think you know them, then they pull something like this." Victoria shrugged.

Buck pulled around a slow-moving car. "Tell me about it. I sure never expected this from my dad. He's always been so levelheaded."

"My mom too. She didn't even want me taking modern dance in gym class. Now she's line dancing with a total stranger from another country."

"Alaska isn't another country, Victoria."

"I know that! What I mean is—a place so far from home."

He gave a snort. "That stranger happens to be the father I thought I knew. Mr. Straight-laced himself. I don't even know that man sitting in the backseat making out with your mother."

Victoria crossed her arms indignantly. "I warned you your father may have been playing Casanova with the ladies on the ship, but you wouldn't beli—"

"My father? How about your mother? The baby blue eyes? Remember? I'll bet your mom made the first move. My dad sure wouldn't!"

"Oh, he wouldn't? Well, he's doing a pretty good job of it right now! Just listen to him sweet-talking her in the backseat."

"Hey?" Ron asked as he leaned over the seat and lightly tapped Victoria's arm. "You two getting acquainted? You're gonna be related soon, you know."

"Yes, Victoria," Abigale volunteered as she leaned up beside Ron. "I do want the two of you to get along. Soon you'll be brother and sister. Isn't that sweet?"

The young woman in the front seat did a quick double take. "Brother and sister? Just what I need, another brother."

"Sure," Ron confirmed quickly. "Well, stepbrother and stepsister. But that doesn't make any difference. We'll be one big happy family. I can hardly wait to meet the rest of your clan."

He reached forward and slapped his son on the shoulder. "Just think, Buck. You're gonna have five brothers."

Buck groaned. "That'll be fun," he replied coolly. "If there was anything I ever wanted, it was five brothers." He nodded toward Victoria. "And a sister."

"Well, you got them now!" Ron added proudly. "Soon as Abigale and Victoria have a good rest at our place, I'm gonna fly back to Kansas City with them to meet the boys. Want to come along, son?"

Buck turned his shoulders toward his father but kept his eyes on the road. "I'd just love to make a trip to Missouri to meet my new kinfolk, Dad; but in case you have forgotten, I have a practice to run. I don't think my patients would appreciate it if their doctor didn't show up at the office for their appointments."

Victoria brightened. "You're a doctor? I thought you and your father were partners—in some sort of business venture."

Ron leaned over the seat again. "We are. We jointly own The Golden Nugget Lodge in Anchorage. His sainted mama left her half to Buck when she died."

"Oh," Victoria said, feeling the man's grief betrayed in his voice. "I'm sorry. About your wife, I mean."

"It's okay, Victoria. I'm sure everyone was wondering if I was gonna grieve myself to death. It's been a long time." He flung an arm around Abigale and hugged her close. "But I'm not grieving anymore. Not now that I have my Abbey to love."

Victoria cringed.

"Buck had just started his practice when his mama left us," he continued with a quick kiss to Abigale's forehead. "He helps me out when I need him. And he gives me financial advice. He's much better at figures than I am."

Ron reached across Abigale quickly and pointed toward the deep green foothills that rose majestically at the edge of the road. "See them, sweetie? A couple of Dall sheep clinging to the side of that cliff. Up there! See?"

The two women leaned toward the windows.

"Sure they aren't mountain goats, Dad?" Buck chided, apparently relieved at the change of subject as he maneuvered the minivan around a sharp curve.

"Hey, son. This old guy knows a sheep from a goat. Next, you'll be telling me that eagle over there is a raven," Ron returned good-naturedly.

"Whoops, you're right," his son admitted as he took his eyes off the road long enough to sneak a peek at the two sheep moving slowly across the cliff's surface. "I should know better than to question you when it comes to Alaska's wild animals."

He turned to Victoria. "My dad has been hunting since long before I was born. He makes a great guide. Guess now that he's going to get married, his guiding days are over."

"You really think they'll go through with it?" Victoria whispered with her hand to her mouth. "Get married?"

Buck's face became serious, and Victoria could see the little vein in his temple ticking nervously. "I don't know, Victoria. I've never seen him like this. I don't know what to think. I only know—if they are serious—there are going to be plenty of adjustments in all our lives. We may be in for a bumpy ride."

Victoria thought about what he said as she gazed at the beauty of the bay. The blue water sparkled like a million dewdrops after an unexpected spring shower. The afternoon sun shone brightly in the cloudless sky. The lush green mountains rose out of the sea as if reaching to God Himself, each peak commanding attention with its pristine white frosting. The scene was more than Victoria had imagined it would be, better than the pictures in the travel brochures. Purple mountain majesties. She beheld their beauty as they rode along the highway. *No wonder the writer had coined such a phrase. Majestic is the perfect word to describe them.*

"I never tire of seeing them." Buck's words broke into her thoughts. "Alaskan mountains are like no others in the world."

"I can see why. They're beautiful," she conceded.

"Bet Missouri doesn't have anything like this." He smiled and raised a bushy brow.

"No, but I love Missouri. Is Anchorage pretty?"

"Sure is," he answered with pride. "We don't have the coastal beauty of some of the cities like Ketchikan and Juneau, but we have the snowcapped mountains nearby. All of Alaska is beautiful country."

"You ski?" she asked, truly interested in the country in which her mother claimed she was going to live.

"Sure. You?"

She screwed up her face. "Some. I'm not very good at it. We usually only get to Colorado a couple days each year. But I enjoy it. So does my son."

He frowned and turned his head slightly toward her. "You have a son?"

"Sure do. Jonathan. He's seven. He's staying at home with my brother and his wife while I'm on this vacation with Mom. I work for my brother as a research assistant, so Jonathan is used to being around his uncle. I miss Jonathan, but I'm sure he'll be fine. They love spoiling him. Probably enjoying his break from his doting, overly protective mother." She rolled her eyes.

"Micah's a little older than Jonathan." Buck shook his head ruefully. "If things go the way our parents plan, I guess those boys will be step-cousins."

"What are you two talking about up there in the front seat?" Ron asked, his arm still wrapped around Abigale.

"Just getting acquainted, Dad."

A big smile curved across the elder man's face. "Good. Abigale and I want our kids to be friends. Carry on." He gave a mock salute and turned to his seatmate.

"Guess that means you're married, if you have a son. Your husband didn't come on this vacation with you?"

Victoria blinked her eyes and swallowed hard. Why did everyone always assume she had a husband? She did not have a husband, and she did not want to talk about it with this man, or anyone. "We live alone. The two of us."

He paused. "Sorry."

"For what? That I don't have a husband? Or that we live alone? We do just fine, thank you." She regretted the intonation in her voice.

He raised his brows and backed away from her and toward his door. "Wow. Sorry! Didn't mean to wake up sleeping dogs. Guess I touched a nerve."

She forced a slight smile. "You didn't. Wake up the dogs, I mean. It's just that—well, I'll explain it sometime. If—we become kinfolk, as your dad says."

"Well—if it's any consolation, my son and I live alone too. Guess you'll find out sooner or later, so I'll tell you myself. My wife and my mother were killed in a car-train accident six years ago. I should have died with them."

His words cut through any false pride of self-defense she had built up.

"I'm so sorry," she said sincerely. Her fingertips lightly touched his hand. "But why would you say such a thing? That you should have died with them? You have a son to raise. Surely you wouldn't want him to be without both parents, would you?"

"No." His answer was barely audible. "Of course not."

"You mustn't say such things. Life is too precious to wish for death." She was fumbling for words and she knew it. But what could you say to a man who had just told you the deepest hurt he'd ever had in his life? A hurt most people would never experience. Somehow, her predicament paled in light of his comments.

He straightened. "Oh, I didn't mean I wish I'd died with them. I'm thankful I didn't. For Micah's sake. I meant I should have been in the accident with them. I was supposed to drive them to Nenana that day; but I had a patient about to deliver her baby, so my wife drove the car instead." His eyes clouded and he blinked several times before going on. "Maybe if I'd been at the wheel, maybe if—"

"You can't do that to yourself, Buck. Blame yourself like that. God—"

He turned to her sharply. "God? God what? God wanted to add angels to His heaven? My wife and mother had fulfilled their purposes on earth? I've heard all those flowery explanations, and they're all a bunch of bunk."

"Now, Buck," Ron warned as he caught the anguish in his son's voice. "You know you can't blame God for what happened to your mama and Claudette."

"Yeah? Then who shall I blame, Dad? If not God, who? He could have prevented that accident. He could have made that train cross the intersection one minute later. He could have caused a flat tire or mechanical breakdown so they wouldn't have been there at that exact moment. If God shouldn't be blamed, I guess there is only one person who should be blamed—me!" Buck's voice had risen to such a level it filled the minivan and frightened the occupants.

No one answered. There seemed to be nothing to say. The group rode along in silence. Soon Abigale's head was bobbing and Ron pulled her over onto his shoulder. Then he leaned his forehead against the window glass and stared outside. No doubt he was remembering the accident and the horrible loss of his wife and daughter-in-law.

After what seemed to be hours, Victoria gently placed her hand over Buck's. He turned his head slightly and in his eyes she could see the open wound still lingering after six long years. "I'm sorry, Buck. I know it doesn't help, but in some ways I understand what you're going through. My son was born with a twisted foot."

He took his eyes off the road. "I'm sure he's had surgery to correct it. Is he doing better now?"

She nodded. "I guess you could say that. He's been through so much, but it's been worth it. He limps, but his foot is nearly normal. He gets along fine."

"Guess he's got some more surgeries coming up in his future."

"Yes. Several."

"Hey, look. I'm a doctor and although I'm not an orthopedist, I'd like to hear more about his condition and take a look at that leg." He smiled. "When—and if—he becomes my nephew."

A feeble smile met his. "Sure. When—and if."

She shifted nervously in her seat, weighing her words before she spoke, wanting to say just enough and no more. "The rest of my story is different from yours too, and although I love God and He is Lord of my life—"

She lowered her head and added in a near whisper, "I'm as angry at God as you are. For several reasons."

With a raised brow, Buck did a quick double take.

She quickly looked into the backseat, making sure her mother was sleeping and Ron wasn't paying attention. She hadn't shared her feelings on this matter with her closest friends. "Oh, I live life on the outside like a good little Christian girl, but on the inside I'm filled with anger too. I've never told this to anyone, and I don't know why I'm telling you. I guess it's because I think you'd understand, going through all you have. I just wanted you to know that, and I hope we can become friends. Especially since we're apparently going to become relatives."

Buck slid his hand from beneath hers and placed it on top, then gave a little squeeze. "I'm ready to listen, whenever you want to talk about it."

Chapter 3

Ron Silverbow twisted a lock of Abigale's silver hair around his finger as she lay sleeping in the backseat, her head leaning against his broad shoulder. *Abigale.* He repeated her name in his heart as he watched the even rise and fall of her breathing. *She is so beautiful. How could I be this lucky?*

He glanced at his son and Abigale's daughter. He hoped the two of them would get along. And he hoped they could understand the love he and Abigale felt for one another. He smiled to himself. *Love at my age? No wonder these kids were skeptical when Abigale and I told them we planned to get married.*

Abigale stirred slightly as she nestled closer to Ron. He grazed her hair lightly with his chin. *Well, no matter what the kids say, we're going to get married. Time is passing, and we don't intend to miss a minute of it.* He and Abbey had decided that before they had gotten off the ship. Since the first minute he had seen this woman, he knew she was something special; but little had he dreamed she would pay him any attention. She was soft and gentle. He was rugged and tough from years of guiding hunting trips through the wilderness. She was cautious and slow to speak. He was bold and ready to speak his mind, even if it went against other folks' grain. They were like opposites on the color wheel; but from his viewpoint, they complemented one another. *Yes,* he told himself with a grin of satisfaction, *Abbey and I belong together. And together we're going to be, no matter what our kids say.*

❧

"Dad?"

Ron stiffened. "What? You say something, Buck?"

Buck laughed as his eyes caught his father's in the rearview mirror. Even though his father was handsome for his age, the thought of the crusty old man sweeping a lovely, sophisticated woman off her feet on a cruise was ludicrous. Buck hoped he would be able to talk some sense into his father's head when they could be alone. "I was just telling Victoria how beautiful Alaska is up around Anchorage."

Victoria twisted in the seat so she could look at Ron. "I've heard it gets really cold in the winter. Did you tell my mom that?"

Ron nodded. "Now, Victoria, don't worry your pretty little head about that. We keep the Golden Nugget Lodge as warm as a sauna in the wintertime. Your mama won't even have to wear her longies unless she goes outside."

"Longies?" Buck repeated as he peered into the mirror. "She'd better wear her longies or the woman will freeze to death. If you're planning on keeping that woman in Alaska, the least you can do is be honest with her and get her some long underwear."

Victoria's eyes widened. "Really, Buck? It gets that cold?"

"Cold enough to freeze spit in midair."

"Buck!" Ron gave his son a shake of his finger. "Mind your manners. You're talking to a lady."

"Just being honest, Dad."

"Mom gets goose bumps when the temperature drops to thirty degrees in Kansas City."

Buck grinned to himself. *Thirty degrees? Wait until she sees how low the temperature can drop on the thermometer by the lodge's front door.*

"You two just never mind. I'll make sure my little buttercup doesn't get too cold," Ron said.

"Mr. Silverbow, I—" Victoria began.

"Ron. Call me Ron."

"Ron," she began again. "Are you sure this isn't infatuation? I mean—seven days on a ship—"

Ron leaned forward, his quick movements waking Abigale. "Now listen to me, both of you. We're old enough to know the difference between love and infatuation. We've both been there, done that. We both loved our deceased spouses. That love will never change, and we'll never forget them. But—"

"But, Dad. Mom and—"

"Son! Will you put a sock in that mouth of yours and listen to your father for once in your life?"

Abigale rubbed at her eyes and stretched her arms. "What? What's going on? Have I been asleep long?"

"Not long, sweetie." Ron patted her shoulder, then turned his attention back to the couple in the front seat. "I was just telling these two kids of ours how much we love each other. If they're as smart as I hope they are, they'll both shut up and be happy for us."

Buck shot Victoria a look of defeat.

"Of course they'll be happy for us," Abigale sweetly assured the silver-haired man whose arm cradled her shoulders. "Won't you, children?"

Good thing she slept through our discussion, Buck mused as he eyed the young woman in the seat beside him. She appeared to have decided to abandon her argument rather than upset her mother. Perhaps he'd better do the same. He cast a look in the mirror and caught his father staring at him, as if waiting for his response to Abigale's request.

"Victoria?" Abigale questioned.

"Ah—sure. I'm happy for you, Mom. At least I will be if you're happy."

"Buck?" Ron asked.

Buck gulped hard. He hated to agree, but he didn't want to upset either his father or Abigale any further. Besides, his argument didn't seem to have any weight with either of them. "Sure, Dad. Like Victoria said, if the two of you are happy, I'll be happy."

Victoria gave him a look that seemed to be saying, *Liar.*

And Buck felt like one.

The two in the front seat rode along silently while the couple in the backseat chattered on endlessly about their cruise and their plans for their future.

Oh, boy. Now what? Victoria wondered as she looked out the window. *Does this mean an end to the plans for our gift shop?*

"What?" Buck asked.

Victoria turned her head quickly. "Did you say something?"

Buck relaxed his hold on the steering wheel and grinned. "Not really. Just curious. Your eyes may have been looking at our beautiful scenery, but I get the feeling you weren't really seeing it. Am I right?"

The confused young woman sighed. She rotated her fingertips on her temples. "Guess I'm hurt. No, I'm mad! How could Mom do this to me? We've been planning to open this shop for over a year. Surely she doesn't think I'll go on and do this by myself. I could never manage it on my own."

"Look," Buck said quietly. "Don't give up yet. I don't know much about the shop you keep talking about, but if you and I work together, maybe we can convince our ditsy parents—"

"Ditsy?" she broke in.

His eyes darted to the rearview mirror, which reflected the pair in the backseat. They were caught up in their own conversation and paying no attention to their children. "Yeah, ditsy. I think that pretty well describes them, don't you?" Buck smiled.

Victoria thought it over and decided he was right. Ditsy was a good name for the way their parents were behaving. "Ditsy."

They snickered like two kids sharing a secret.

"I interrupted you, Buck. What were you saying? About us working together?"

He checked the mirror again. "Like I said, if we work together, maybe we can make them see how foolish this whole marriage thing is at their age."

"It's more than their age. Mom will be giving up her home in Kansas City, the home she shared with my father for over twenty-five years, to move—"

"Whoa, little lady. My father doesn't exactly live in an igloo. That lodge of ours is pretty nice."

Victoria twisted in the seat belt. "I didn't mean your father's place wasn't nice. It's just that Mom's the one who'll be making all the changes—new home, new friends, new surroundings. Looks to me like he's expecting her to give up everything while he's giving up nothing!"

Buck maneuvered the minivan around two cars and pulled in behind a truck loaded with logs. "What about his independence? His money? His freedom?"

"His independence? His money? His freedom?" Victoria echoed, finding it difficult to keep her voice down, as her blood pressure rose. "Seems to me she's giving up all of those and much more. I don't hear him volunteering to move to Kansas City!"

He seemed surprised. "Kansas City? Move from Alaska to Kansas City? Now why'd anyone want to do that?"

"Buck?" Ron reached over the seat back and rested his hand on his son's shoulder. "What's wrong?"

Buck sent a quick look at his companion. "Nothing, Dad. Victoria and I were just talking about—" He paused. "Alaska."

The elder man gave his son's shoulder a pat. "Good. Abigale and I want the two of you to get along." His other hand reached out and touched Victoria's shoulder. "After all, you're going to be kinfolk."

The young couple sat quietly, forcing smiles until Ron settled back in his seat and continued his conversation with Abigale.

"Kinfolk," Victoria muttered.

"Not if we work together. Look, Victoria, I don't like this situation any better than you do."

She had to agree. Neither of them wanted this marriage. Maybe if they worked together. . .

The car behind them honked several times, then whizzed past the minivan. Buck hit the brakes and pulled quickly to the right, miraculously keeping the van under control. The four watched in horror as the offending car swerved into the lane in front of them, missing their front bumper by mere inches as the semi in the oncoming lane braked and pulled onto the paved shoulder. The car then swerved back to the left, nearly clipping the semi's back end before leveling out only a hair's width behind the log-laden semi in front of them.

Buck leaned on his horn, then shook his fist. "Stupid guy. That's how accidents happen! I hope he's ready to meet his Maker."

"That was close." Victoria took a deep breath and slumped back in the seat, trembling.

"Too close," Buck agreed, his eyes still riveted on the car ahead of him, anger blanketing his face.

Ron cradled Abigale in his arms. "Good defense driving, son. Can you imagine a guy taking a chance like that? Where was his brain?"

"Sometimes people do stupid things without thinking them through!" Buck retorted.

Victoria winced. She was sure his answer had a double meaning. And as much as she wanted to turn and see if Ron and her mother had caught it too, she didn't.

❧

"Now that wasn't so bad, was it, Victoria?" Abigale asked as they stood in the lovely master bedroom at the Golden Nugget Lodge.

Victoria tossed her handbag onto the table. Then she plunked herself down beside her mother on the edge of the king-size bed. "Mom, it took us forever to get here! Do you realize how far we are from Kansas City? Have you even looked at a map?"

Abigale's eyes twinkled as she took her only daughter's hand in hers. "No, have you?"

Victoria had to admit she had no idea where Anchorage was located, only that it was in Alaska. She had long forgotten her geography lessons.

"Isn't this just the loveliest place you've ever seen, honey? Those lush green pines, the flowers, the heavy timbers—"

"The long, dark winters, the wild animals, the isolation!" Victoria countered. "Mom! You'll die here."

Her mother laughed. "Don't you think that's a bit melodramatic? Die? I think not. I'm going to love it. Ron says—"

"Ron says! Ron says!" She pulled her hand away from her mother's grasp and stood. "You barely know the man, and you're talking like he knows you as well as—"

"As your father did? Oh, Victoria. Your father and I talked many times about doing something very much like this, when our children were all grown and out of the nest. We never had the money to take the adventurous trips we talked about, not when you kids were all at home. That's why we planned our anniversary trip. We wanted to do something totally different from the routine lifestyle of our forty-five-year marriage. We even talked about going to the Holy Land next year. And Africa the year after that, to visit those missionary friends of ours."

Victoria kicked off her shoes and sat down beside her mother again. "Really? Even Africa? You were both such homebodies."

"Just shows how little you really know me." She patted Victoria's cheek. "Some of us keep our dreams inside us. I guess because we fear we'll never have the opportunity to live them, and we don't want to be disappointed."

"But the trips you are talking about were visits. Marrying Ron Silverbow would mean living in Alaska. Permanently! That's a whole different thing."

❧

Abigale rose and walked to the bay window that overlooked the circle drive leading into the Golden Nugget Lodge. She watched Buck pulling their luggage from the open door at the back of his minivan and handing the bags to Ron, who placed them on the cart. The two men were so much alike it was uncanny. Both well over six feet and straight, despite Ron's additional years. Where Buck's shoulder-length hair was dark, Ron's was heavily peppered with silver. *If only Victoria could know the side of Ron I know. How can I explain this to my daughter? How can I tell her how lonely I've been since her father died? How can I reveal my fear of facing the future and old age without a husband by my side? And most of all, how can I convince her of my feelings of love for a man I met only a few days ago? I knew Ron and I were meant to be together the minute I saw him bow his head in prayer at our first meal together.*

Victoria followed her mother to the window. "Mom, look. I don't mean to be difficult. It's not that I don't want you to get married again. I'm sure Dad wouldn't want you to spend the rest of your life alone. But Alaska? With Ron Silverbow?"

"Victoria, I know you love me and want the best for me. But please, give Ron a chance. Get to know him. We have so much in common. He's a fine Christian man who loves God, like your father did." Her eyes misted over as she thought about her wonderful husband. "We'll be here most of the week, and I'm asking you, as a favor to me, try to keep an open mind. It may be difficult to believe, but Ron is everything I could want in a husband, and I want to marry him. Just try, please? For me?"

"Here's your luggage, ladies," Buck said. The two men, weighted down with suitcases, stood grinning in the doorway.

Buck pulled a face at their guests. "With all this stuff, you two could probably stay a month and never have to do laundry! Did you leave anything in your closets in Kansas City?"

❧

Ron placed his napkin on the table and leaned back in his chair. "That was a great dinner, Wasilla."

"Yes, sure was. And from the looks of Miss Victoria's empty plate, I'd say she enjoyed it too," Buck added. The woman with sleek black hair cleared the table.

Victoria shoved her plate away with a smile of contentment. "I didn't even know I liked salmon."

"I love fresh salmon," Abigale admitted. "We had some on the ship, and Ron told me about all the fresh salmon they serve here at the Golden Nugget dining room. They catch much of it themselves. Did you know that, Victoria?"

The young woman shrugged her shoulders with a slight smile. "Why am I not surprised?"

"When you come and visit your mom, Buck and I'll take you salmon fishing." Ron waved his empty coffee cup toward their waitress.

"Wasilla? That's your name?" Victoria asked as she held out her cup for a refill.

"Ask them two." The woman nodded.

Ron and Buck snickered.

"No. Her real name is too difficult to pronounce. She's from Wasilla, a little town down the road. Buck started calling her Wasilla the first day she hired on, and she's been Wasilla ever since," Ron said.

"How long have you worked here at the Lodge?" Abigale lifted her cup to her lips.

"Too long." Wasilla grinned.

Once the coffee was consumed and the dishes removed from the table, Ron took Abigale's hand in his and leaned toward her. "Sugar, how about taking a walk with me?"

Abigale nodded and the two took off, arm in arm, leaving Buck and Victoria seated at the table.

"You want to take a walk?" Buck asked.

Victoria stifled a little yawn. "Not me. I'm still on Kansas City time. I think I'll turn in early if it's all right with you."

He nodded.

"Maybe I'll think better after a good night's sleep," Victoria said.

"Don't forget to pull down the blinds and close the drapes. It won't get dark until nearly two in the morning, and then it only gets to what you folks would call twilight. Makes it kind of hard to sleep when you're not used to it."

She grinned. "Thanks, I will."

"Plan on seeing the place in the morning. I'll be your guide."

"Sounds good. I hate to admit it, but this place is lovely. I'm anxious to see more. But you said you're a doctor. Don't you have to go to your office?"

"Not on Monday mornings." He fingered his thick mustache. "I only see patients in the afternoon on Mondays."

"Oh, I see. Did you have something else planned for tomorrow morning? We could take the tour later. I don't want to be a bother."

"No bother. I'm happy to show off the Lodge and the grounds."

Victoria was hoping a tour of the place would give her more ammunition to use in convincing Abigale that Ron was not the husband for her and Alaska was not the place for her to live.

"I think we've got our work cut out for us, Tori," Buck warned with a sigh. "Those two are gonna be hard to break up."

Tori? He called me Tori? No one has ever called me by that name.

"What do you think?" he added.

She traced the rim of the empty coffee cup with her fingertip. "Ah—I think you may be right. I tried to talk to my mom when we first got here, but you can chalk that conversation up to her side. I came out the loser."

"I know what you mean. I tried to talk to Dad when we unloaded the luggage. I didn't have any success either."

"I'm at my wit's end. I'm wondering if I should call my brothers and ask them to come up and try to talk some sense into her."

Buck shook his head. "I'd hold off on that. You're only going to be here a week. It'll probably take them that long to get their affairs in order so they could be gone and get their airline tickets. Let's see what the two of us can do."

"So, what's the plan?"

Buck dipped his shoulders and stared at the ceiling. "I haven't a clue."

Surprisingly, Victoria slept quite well and found herself rested and eager to meet the day when she awoke the next morning at eight, Alaskan time. After a hearty breakfast in the dining room with her mother, Victoria wandered around the lobby of the Lodge waiting for her guide. He arrived about nine and seemed surprised to see her ready to go.

"Did you think I'd sleep till noon?" She smiled. Without waiting for an answer, she added, "I'm ready for my tour. Are you sure you can spare the time this morning?"

Buck smiled and reached out his hand. She hesitated a bit, then took it.

"It's a great morning, I thought we'd walk. Is that okay with you?" He took a quick look at her feet.

"Wore my tennies," she quipped and stuck out one foot. "Lead on."

Victoria had been so weary and upset when they arrived the evening before she hadn't really noticed all the colorful flowers in full bloom around the Lodge's exterior. But now in the light of day, she was fully impressed with their beauty. "I've never seen such large geraniums!" She cupped a huge blossom between her hands. "How do you grow them like this?"

Buck broke off one of the larger red flowers and handed it to her. "We can't take all the credit. Over twenty years ago the city developed a program to put more blossoms and greenery around the area." He broke off a smaller white flower and sniffed it before handing it to her. "When we go into town, I'll show you the flowers they have along Fourth Avenue. They're part of that program. I think you'll be impressed."

Victoria lifted the white flower to her nose and inhaled deeply, taking in the sweet-smelling fragrance. "That's where you get these flowers?"

He laughed. "No, but once the Anchorage citizens started seeing the flowers around town, they all wanted some for their homes. So now we have huge commercial greenhouses that start the plants every year. In fact, during the dark days of winter, folks go up there just to sit on the wooden benches and enjoy the bright lights and the flowers. Then when it's warm enough, we all transplant them into our hanging baskets and gardens. With all the sun we have every day all summer, they grow pretty good."

"Pretty good? I'd call these more than pretty good. Folks back home would never believe the size of these flowers. And they're so healthy. Do you have a gardener to take care of them for you?"

Buck pulled his knife from the sheath on his belt and cut away a sagging branch on a small pine tree. "Gardener? No, not a regular one anyhow. We have a service that comes and plants them, but Dad and I do most of the upkeep of the baskets and gardens. Kind of a hobby with us."

Victoria eyed the flower-filled baskets hanging on a series of iron posts. The posts staked out the big circle drive leading to the Lodge's front door.

Buck folded his knife and slipped it into its sheath. "Like those posts, Tori? I welded them myself."

She turned quickly to face him. "What don't you do, Dr. Silverbow?"

With a shy grin as an answer, he took her hand and they began their walk. She couldn't believe the lushness of the trees and bushes, or the size of the Lodge as they circled its exterior. "How many rooms does the Golden Nugget have?"

He scratched his bearded chin. "Well, let me see, twenty on the first floor, twenty on the second, and ten cabins down by the creek. Plus Dad and Mom's suite." He looked embarrassed. "I mean—Dad's suite. Then we have the bunkhouse for the help. I reckon there's maybe sixteen or eighteen people living there during the busy season."

She frowned. "Where do you live? I assumed you lived at the Lodge."

He kicked a rock off the path with the toe of his worn boot. "Me? Live at the Lodge? No, I have my own place." He pointed up into the trees where you could barely see the tip of a roof peeking through. "Up there."

"I'm afraid my mother will find Alaska as beautiful as I'm finding it," Victoria confessed reluctantly. "I was hoping it'd be barren and ugly."

He stopped walking and picked up a chunk of wood from the path. "You fail geography?"

She laughed. "No, but I must have been absent when they studied the chapter on Alaska."

He motioned toward a little gazebo nestled in an overgrowth of trees, and they sat down on a weathered bench. "Alaska will grow on you if you give it a chance."

She watched as he again pulled his knife from its sheath and began to whittle on the chunk of wood he'd picked up. "But I don't want to give it a chance. Don't you understand? I want to take my mother and go home."

He sat silently. The only sound was the swoosh-swooshing of the blade as it made each cut.

Victoria bowed her head and folded her hands in her lap. "Ever since I was a senior in high school I've had plans to open my own gift shop. Now, just when we get the news our loan has been approved and we can go ahead with my dream, your dad comes along and rips it all apart."

"Well, I'd say your mother had an equal part in that rip, Tori. It takes two, you know."

She watched the chips fall away as he deftly moved the blade. "I know. It's not that I'm laying the whole blame on him—"

He looked up through dark, heavy brows. "Just the major part?"

"Not fair, huh?"

"Not quite. Let's blame them both."

She grinned.

"There." He brushed the chips from his lap and extended his hand toward her. "A flower for a lady." He placed a tiny carved blossom in her hand.

Her eyes widened with appreciation at his talent. In just a matter of minutes he'd carved what looked like a columbine blossom. "Buck, it's beautiful."

He grinned and placed the knife back in its sheath. "I like carving. It's my hobby."

"I'd like to see more of your carvings. Do you have any at the Lodge?"

"No. Most of my carvings are big. I'm talking huge. I carve totem poles."

"You mean real totem poles? Like ten feet high?"

"Some taller than that. They're a kind of therapy for me."

She looked puzzled. "Therapy?"

"Yeah." He glanced at his watch. "If you want, we can walk up to my place and I'll show you."

Ten minutes later, after a rather steep climb up a rocky path, they reached a slight clearing. Victoria caught her breath as she stared at the lovely house nestled into the thick foliage. "You live here?"

"Yes and no. It's my house. I lived here with my wife before. . ." His voice trailed off and he turned away from her. "I don't live here anymore. No one does. I live in the little bunk house over there." He pointed to a small cabin off to one side and slightly higher up than the house.

She wanted to ask more questions, but there was something in his tone that forbade it. When he offered his hand, she took it. They walked around the house and up the path to the bunkhouse.

"Sorry it's so messy up here," he apologized as they neared the cabin. "But the chips from my carvings make a good cover for the path. I just put them here rather than gather and burn them."

When they made the final turn, they were greeted by four magnificent totem poles, standing as if they were guarding the little cabin.

"You carved these?" Victoria asked, impressed with the detailed carving of the intricate yet grotesque faces staring down at her.

He nodded. "Yes, carved these a number of years ago, right after my wife and I were married. Up here in Alaska, totem poles have a special meaning. There's even a park dedicated to them here in Anchorage. Visitors come from all over the world to see them, even think of them as an art form."

Victoria glanced at the freshly cut chips that lay at their feet. "But you're still carving them, right?"

He seemed a little hesitant. "When I need to."

She didn't understand his answer. "When you need to? Do you sell them? Take custom orders?"

His face grew serious. "No. Never sell them."

She wanted to know more. "You're not working on one now?"

He swallowed hard, and even with his well-trimmed beard she could see his Adam's apple move. "Yes. Sort of."

"May—may I see it?"

He smoothed his mustache and appeared to be thinking over his answer. She wondered if her request had somehow invaded his privacy.

"Okay." He offered his hand once more and led her around to the far side of the cabin. There on a stand made of two Xs lay a partially carved totem pole with the most grotesque faces she could imagine. Just the sight of them made her shudder, and she turned away.

"I know they're ugly. You don't have to tell me."

There was something so vulnerable in his voice. He was like a child who'd been caught stealing, or cheating on a test.

She mustered up her courage and asked, "But why? The others are like works of art. This one is—excuse me for saying it—hideous!"

He picked up a long-handled ax and gave a hearty swing at an uncarved section of the big pole. A huge chip flew through the air. "Remember I told you I use my carving for therapy? You have no idea how much frustration I can get rid of by cutting away at this awful thing."

He stepped back and held out the ax as he motioned toward the log. "Here, have a swing."

Her palm went to her chest as she backed away. "I couldn't. I might ruin something."

His laugh echoed through the hills. "Ruin it? That's impossible. The worse you can make it look, the better. Go ahead, give it a whack."

Reluctantly she took the ax. With both hands, she raised it high over her head and slammed the blade into the hard wood. A small, ragged chip joined his on the pile as she grinned awkwardly. "I guess I didn't hit it as hard as I thought I did."

"Good enough for a beginner, and you haven't had the practice I've had. But still, you have to admit it did feel good, didn't it?" He picked up a handful of chips and tossed them into the air with a hearty laugh.

But to her, his tone seemed sad. "Not really." She handed back the ax.

He took another huge swing, and the blade cut a second deep wedge into the seasoned wood. "I do this when I'm angry." He watched the chips fall onto the pile with the others.

34

"When you're angry?" Victoria asked. Her eyes grew round with question. "At who? Or what?"

Buck stared at her, and she almost wished she hadn't asked. She watched as he lifted a booted foot and let it rest on one of the crossbars that held the long pole. After a long, uncomfortable silence, he answered, "I've already told you. God."

Chapter 4

"You mean because your wife and mother died?" Victoria asked.

Buck stood straight and tall, his face raised toward heaven, and his eyes took on an intensity that almost frightened her. "Exactly. He had no right to take them that way. Even if He was unhappy with me, He had no business taking Micah's mother and grandmother. And my dad sure didn't deserve to lose his wife. He's a good man."

"But," Victoria offered in feeble defense, "I'm sure it wasn't because He was unhappy with you. He had a plan—"

Buck swung around, his eyes blazing. "Don't give me that rot about His plan. If I've heard that excuse once, I've heard it a hundred times. That's what folks say when anyone dies. God had a plan." Buck's large hand tightly cupped her shoulder and she nearly winced. "A good God would not deliberately take a man's wife and a boy's mother."

"But did He?" She felt her voice wavering, her hurt and confusion welling up inside.

"Did He what?" Buck's voice boomed. "Take her deliberately? Looks that way to me! You got another answer?"

She backed away slightly and Buck released his grasp. "No. I'm not the one to begin to explain God's plan to you. He failed me. . ." Her voice trailed off and she wished she had been silent.

Suddenly Buck seemed drawn back from his anger and into reality. "What'd you mean, failed you?"

Victoria knelt, picked up a handful of chips, and flung them into the air before answering. "I—He—I'd just as soon not talk about it."

"Got your own baggage, huh?"

She took a deep breath and let it out slowly. "Yeah, you might say that. But it all happened long ago."

A sympathetic smile tilted his lips. "Hate to tell you this, but it doesn't get any better with time."

"Tell me about it." Unwilling to tell more to this near stranger, Victoria turned and headed back down the path. "Our parents probably wonder where we are. Perhaps we'd better get back."

Buck picked up the ax. With one mighty swing, he nearly buried its head in the pole, and left it there. "Good idea."

Abigale and Ron were sitting in the hotel dining room sipping coffee, giggling like two teenagers, Ron's fingers entwined across the table with his new fiancée's. "You two have a good walk?" Ron asked, rising long enough to greet them before sitting down and again twining his fingers with Abigale's.

"Nice. I never realized how beautiful Alaska is," Victoria conceded. She slipped out of her jacket and into the empty chair next to her mother.

Buck pulled off his jacket and seated himself opposite her. "All you need, lady, is a good solid dose of northern exposure. And I intend to give it to you. I've arranged to go in a little late tomorrow morning. I'm going to take you on a tour of Anchorage, and I want to show you Cook's Inlet. And before you and your mom head back to the mainland, maybe Dad and I'll take you two up into the mountains."

"Look, Buck," Ron reminded him firmly, "Victoria may be going back to Kansas City but Abigale's here to stay. We are getting married, and don't you forget it."

Buck flashed his father a frown. "Aw, come on, Dad. You can't be serious."

"Serious as a heart attack, Bucky, my boy. And the sooner you realize it, the better." He signaled to Wasilla, and she hurried to their table. "Now, I suggest we all tell Wasilla what we'd like for lunch."

Buck glanced across the table to Victoria and shrugged. Although Victoria was glad the confrontation had stopped, she hoped his shrug didn't imply he was giving up. They had to change their parents' minds.

After they enjoyed a pleasant lunch of salmon salad, croissants, and a fresh fruit cup, Ron suggested Victoria and her mother spend some time together while the men folk took care of their chores. Abigale took her daughter's hand. They made their way up the dramatic, log-railed staircase to the second floor suite where Abigale was staying.

The rooms were beautifully decorated. Although Ron's deceased wife was not there, her presence was everywhere. Victoria sensed it the moment she entered. Abigale hurried to the massive stone fireplace and took down a large framed picture of Regina Silverbow. "Look, Victoria. Isn't she beautiful?"

The young woman stared at the picture. It was as though she were seeing a reflection of Buck in the woman's lovely face. The same dark eyes, the long sooty eyelashes, the dark wavy hair. She even had the same single dimple on her left cheek. The likeness was uncanny, and Victoria felt a twinge of sorrow pierce her gut. Each time Ron Silverbow looked at his son he had to be reminded of his wife. What agony that must be.

"Ronnie loved his wife. His life was centered around her," Abigale whispered somewhat wistfully. "He tells me he has never changed a thing in these rooms since her death. Even her clothes are still hanging in her closet."

Victoria placed the frame back on the mantel and dropped onto the sofa with a heavy heart. "Do you actually think you can take her place, Mom?"

Abigale sat down beside her. "I know I can. Ronnie has assured me of that. He said since Regina's death, many women have made a play for him. He jokes it's because he's one of Alaska's only two available males. Buck being the other."

"Well, it looks like none of them were able to capture him, Mom. What makes you think you're any different?"

Abigale pulled a lovely marquise diamond out of her pocket and placed it on the third finger of her left hand, next to the wedding ring Victoria's father had given her forty-five years ago. "Because of this. Ronnie and I went to the jeweler's this morning and picked it out. He wanted to place it on my finger, but I told him I wanted to talk to you first. Because once I take off your father's ring and Ronnie places his on my finger, I'm never taking it off again."

Tears flooded the young woman's eyes as she thought of her father and how happy her parents had been all those years they were together. "But, Mom—"

Abigale's fingers rose to touch her daughter's lips. "Shh, Victoria. I don't want to hear another word about this. My mind is made up. Just be assured that Ronnie and I discussed every bit of our lives during the seven days we had on that ship. Believe me, honey, we know what we're doing."

"But Alaska is so far—"

"I know. But by plane, I'll only be a few hours away from you, and Ronnie has promised me I can go home for a visit whenever I want. And, of course, you and the rest of the family will always be welcome here anytime you can come."

Victoria bit her lip. She had so much to say—words she knew her mother didn't want to hear.

Abigale went on. "We're going to completely redo our living quarters here at the Lodge. Ronnie says I can do anything I want with this place. Change everything, if I desire." She moved to the fireplace and once again took down Regina's picture. "He even said we'd take down all of his wife's pictures and store them away." Abigale smiled and her fingers gently ran over the glass covering Regina Silverbow's likeness. "But I told him that was not necessary. I'm as happy that he shared that part of his life with such a wonderful woman as he is that I shared my life with a wonderful man. Neither one of us ever wants to forget those precious times or the spouse we loved. Your father's pictures will go on the mantel right beside Regina's."

Victoria swallowed at a lump in her throat. It seemed Ron and her mother had discussed many more things than she'd realized. But the idea of losing her mother to Alaska and this man was no less agonizing.

"It seems you have your life with Ron all planned out, Mom, but what about my life? Have you so easily forgotten our plans? Yours and mine? Plans to open our gift shop? The shop we've been planning and working so hard to bring to fruition?"

Abigale placed Regina's picture back where it belonged and walked slowly toward her daughter, her face void of the smile. "That's the only hurdle I haven't been able to solve, sweetie."

"How could you let me down this way, Mom? You know how much that shop means to me. It's been my dream since before my son was born. I'm an artist, Mom. I don't want to work for my brother the rest of my life. That's why I was so pleased when you agreed to be my business partner. You and I have taken the Better Business Bureau classes in preparation. We've researched a location. We've studied all the wholesale catalogues. We've done it all." The young woman paced across the floor, throwing her arms up in defeat. "And now, just like that," she snapped her fingers, "you're walking out on me? Right after the bank has agreed to give us our loan."

Abigale quickly rose to her feet. "I'm not walking out on you, Victoria."

Eyes flashing, the young woman turned to face her. "Then exactly what do you call it?"

"I'm marrying the man I love."

"Love? You call it love to marry a man you've only known seven days?"

Loving arms circled the young woman's shoulders. "I hate to say this to you, honey, but you've never known real love. It takes over your life. You have no other choice but to link up with the man God has sent to you. Remember what the Scriptures say? A man shall leave his father and mother and be joined to his wife?"

Victoria gave an indignant snort. "Where does it say you should leave your daughter and marry a second man? I've never read that in the Bible."

Abigale's face softened. "I want you and your brothers to understand, to realize I love Ron and want to become his wife. We don't know how many years we'll have together, but whatever amount we do have, we want to spend them with each other. Neither of us wants to be a burden to our children. When and if the time comes, we'll be there for one another, to care for each other. Yes, until death do us part."

"And what am I supposed to do?"

Abigale's arms tightened about Victoria's shoulders. Then Abigale kissed her daughter's cheek. "Be thankful your mother and Ron are both so happy, and go on with your life. You're young, you have a wonderful son, your brothers are all there for you in Kansas City, and the bank has approved our loan. It's all there for you. Reach out and grab your future with both hands."

Victoria pulled away. "The bank will never let me have the loan alone."

"They will if I'm your silent partner. Nothing has to change as far as they're concerned. As long as my name is on the dotted line and the monthly payments are made on time, they'll be quite happy."

Victoria was getting nowhere trying to talk her mother out of this ridiculous marriage. In fact, every argument she'd brought up against it, her mother had had an answer to defeat it. Perhaps, at this point, the best way to combat it was to let time take its course. Let her mother live in Alaska for a few days and see how different it is from Kansas City. Maybe as soon as the newness wore off and Ron Silverbow let his true self shine through, Abigale would see how very different the two of them were and come to her senses.

"I don't want to open this shop without you, Mother. If necessary I'll put off the opening and give you time to change your mind." Victoria straightened her shoulders, confident things would change.

"Don't count on it, sweetie. I'm staying in Alaska as Ron's wife. Now you can either help me with my wedding plans or continue to sulk and try to upset me. Which is it going to be?"

"I'll try, but—"

"No buts, Victoria. I'm tired of hearing negatives."

"But the boys will be furious—"

"I'm sure, initially, your brothers will respond just as you have. But in the end, they'll want what's best for me. Once they meet Ron and see how in love we are, I'm confident they'll come around. Are you with me or against me?"

Victoria knew she was defeated. At least for now. "I'm with you, I guess."

"Good. Let's get started with the wedding plans."

∂๑

Buck looked up from the computer. "Look, Dad. I know you're attracted to Abigale, any red-blooded man your age would be, but—"

"My age? You think my life is over, do you?"

The hinge on the computer chair squeaked as Buck leaned back and locked his hands behind his head. "You know I didn't mean it that way. You could probably take a man twenty years younger than you if you had a mind to."

"Well, then. What did you mean? That I'm too old to have another wife? You think I should spend the rest of my days living with the ghost of your mom? God rest her soul."

Buck considered his father's words. "No, I wouldn't expect you to do that. But what about all the women right here in Alaska, women that love the land like you do?"

"Easy to answer that one. I don't love any of them."

"But you think you love Abigale?"

Ron grinned as he leaned over Buck's shoulder and peered at the entries on the computer screen. "Nope, I don't think I love Abigale."

Buck brightened. "Good, I knew you'd come to your senses."

"Senses? That's not it at all. I don't think I love Abigale. I know I love Abigale!"

The chair squeaked once again as Buck leaped out of it and faced his father. "Dad! What has gotten into you? You've always been so levelheaded. How could you even consider such a foolish thing as marrying a woman from Kansas City? That woman has no idea what she is getting herself into. Do you think it's being fair to her, to convince her to pull up stakes and move to Alaska? Things are different up here. People are different. Life is different. What about the long, dark, cold winters? Do you think she can survive that?"

Ron twisted the tips of his graying mustache. "Son, I think you're the one who isn't thinking straight. I've worked hard all my life. I've made wise investments. I've been careful with my money. I'm not exactly poor. Actually, I think Abigale and I will enjoy those long, cold winters snuggling up by the fire, being with one another. But, if she gets cabin fever, we'll fly down to the Caribbean. Or spend time in Kansas City with her children. Or vacation in California. You're borrowing trouble, son. We are more resilient than you think."

Buck shook his head woefully. "Is there anything I can say or do that will persuade you to put off this wedding for awhile? Give you time to reconsider your options? Make sure this woman is for you?"

Ron rose to his full height of six-foot-four. "Not a thing, son. Not a thing. This old man is gonna marry Abigale Whitmore as soon as possible, with or without your consent."

"But, Dad—"

"Are you for me or against me?"

A deep sigh of defeat escaped Buck's lips. *Arguing is accomplishing nothing. Maybe time will work out things.* "With you, I guess."

❧

"Hey, Tori. Sleepyhead, you ready?" Buck yelled up the stairs early the next morning. "I've got to be in my office by one o'clock. I have patients to see."

Victoria bounded down the staircase dressed in a red corduroy pantsuit, her long hair tied up in a ponytail and banded in red. "Sleepyhead? I've showered and had breakfast already." She smiled. "Where we off to?"

"That'd be telling. You'll just have to wait and see. Does your mom want to come with us?"

She stopped on the bottom step where she could look him eye to eye. "Mom? Go with us when she can stay here and make goo-goo eyes at your father? No way."

"Bat those baby blues, huh?" He grinned.

A few days before, Victoria would have been incensed at his comment, but not now. Now, although she would never admit it to Buck, she wondered if her mother had batted her baby blues at Ron on that ship. Otherwise, why would the man have fallen so deeply and so quickly in love with her? "Let's leave that remark alone," Victoria admonished. "We'll never know which one initiated the first flirtatious smile."

"You're right about that. I'm as surprised at my old man as you are at your mother. I'd have never guessed he'd do something so foolish. At his age!"

Victoria swept on past him with a flourish of her hand. "I hope I'm not that senile when I'm their age."

"Me either," Buck agreed as he turned to follow her. "Call your son?"

She nodded. "He's doing fine. He loves staying with my brother and his wife. They spoil him rotten."

"You actually have five brothers?" He opened the door and they stepped out into a beautiful, sunshiny morning.

"Yes, five. I'm the only girl. And the baby of the family."

Buck opened the door on the passenger side of the minivan. "I'll bet you are."

She scooted in. "Are you implying I'm spoiled?"

"I'm smarter than that." He winked, closed the door, and circled around to his side. Once inside the minivan, Buck said, "My mother didn't raise a dummy."

Victoria leaned against the headrest and folded her hands in her lap. "She must have been a lovely woman. Mom showed me her picture. You look just like her."

Buck inserted the key in the ignition and the minivan's engine roared. "I'll take that as a compliment."

"I meant it that way. Does your son look like her? By the way, when am I going to meet him?"

"He looks like me, so I guess he looks like her. Micah's been at a church retreat. He'll be home in a few days."

She frowned. "Church retreat? I—"

"You thought I was mad at God, right?" The car started down the hill and toward town.

She nodded.

"I am. But I've got a son to raise, and I figure being around church and church people won't hurt him. Raising kids alone is a tough proposition, and I need all the help I can get." He turned and gave a sheepish grin. "Guess you know all about that, you having a son and raising him alone."

"Yes, I do," she said simply.

"Well, I may be mad at God, but I know in my heart my wife would have wanted our son raised in the church. I guess folks around here don't know about God and me not being on speaking terms anymore. I put up a good front. And then there's my dad. He's one of those devout Christians, takes everything to God in prayer. You'd think he'd be mad at God too, after He took my mom like that."

"But he's not?"

Buck glanced in the rearview mirror, then made a left-hand turn. "Nope, not at all. Says it was God Who got him through the whole ordeal. Doesn't blame Him at all. Dad attends church and prays like nothing ever happened. Sits in the same pew he and my mom used to sit in. I think he finds comfort in it."

"Your father seems to be a good man. I'm glad to hear he goes to church regularly. So does my mom. I don't ever remember hearing her blame God for my father dying so young."

"You ever consider remarrying?"

His question came out of the blue and caught her off guard.

"I—no—it. . ." She stared out the window, avoiding his eyes.

"Hey, Tori. I get the feeling you're avoiding my questions—about your husband. Really, I don't mean to pry, but if we're going to be stepkin—"

She flung her head around, still reeling from his question. "But we're not going to be kin. Buck, we have to talk them out of this foolish marriage idea. For everyone's sake."

"I already tried and ran into a brick wall with the old guy. He's as bullheaded as that stubborn horse of his. I'm open to ideas if you got any." He waved at a passerby.

"I've tried too." She sounded defeated. "Mom is as stubborn as your dad. She even threatened me. Said I could either accept it and help her with her wedding plans, or continue to sulk and upset her. Didn't leave me much choice, did she?"

He offered a slight chuckle. "About as much as my dad offered me."

"Back to your question."

He frowned. "My question?"

"The one about me considering marrying again."

"Oh, that one. You don't have to answer, you know. I guess I was prying into something that's none of my business."

She bit her lip. "Jonathan's father and I parted years ago."

Buck's eyes widened. "Oh?"

"I don't want to say anything more about it, Buck. I hope you understand."

He stared straight ahead. "Your privilege."

"I have considered marrying a man back home. Morton Pendergast. I've known him since I was a teenager. He's a few years older than me. Goes to our church. He has a very nice house, and a great job, and he thinks the world of Jonathan."

Buck's hand slipped over hers and he gave it a gentle squeeze. "But you don't love him, do you?"

Her eyes widened and she jerked her hand from his. "Why would you say that?"

"A woman in love doesn't talk about her man like that. Sounds like you're only considering marriage as a way to secure a good life for you and your son. I get the impression there's no love for the man."

Her eyes flashed with fire. "That's a rotten thing to say. You make me sound like a—"

He broke in. "A woman who'd say yes out of need?"

"I'd never do that!" Victoria retorted defensively.

"Well, you just said you were considering marrying the man, but not once have you mentioned love."

They rode along in silence, Victoria's heart pounding with outrage.

"I think I could love him," she confessed finally. "In time."

"That's a lousy way to start a marriage, Tori. I think we both know that."

She had to change the subject. He was getting much too close to reality. She was afraid in another two minutes she'd blurt out her life story, and she wasn't ready for that.

"Let's get back to our parents. How are we going to stop this wedding?" Victoria tried to make an unnoticeable dab at her eyes.

"Got me. But we have to find a way. And quick."

They spent the morning touring the city. Buck took her to the cultural sites and through the downtown area where she was able to admire the beautiful blue and yellow flower baskets hanging on all the light posts. Next, they went to the place where all the fishermen went to fish during the salmon run. They passed the statue of Captain Cook, and Buck took time to explain how Captain Cook was the same Captain Cook who explored the Antarctica and many other areas of the world. Eventually they ended up at Cook's Inlet.

"You don't ever want to go walking out there." Buck pointed to the rim of muck left along the edge by the low tide. "It's nearly high tide now. But when the tide goes out, the biggest part of this inlet is nothing but that heavy brown muck."

She frowned. "Why? From what I can see, it looks pretty solid."

"That's what many people think. When they get out there, their feet slowly start sinking. The first thing you know, it's too late and they can't get their feet out. One woman got stuck out there and by the time her husband got back to shore to get help, she was stuck so hard and so deep they couldn't pull her out. One of the firemen even tried to hold her up as he stood on a piece of plywood, but he couldn't. Eventually they had to leave her there when the water rose above her head."

Victoria shuddered. "How awful."

"Yeah," Buck agreed. "It was awful. Next morning a crowd gathered to watch as the water went down. And there she was."

"What a gruesome story."

Buck's arm circled her waist as they stood there. "It's part of Alaska, Tori. Like everywhere, we have the good, bad, and the ugly. That's the ugly."

"But why would she and her husband go out there?"

"People do it all the time. Finally, our fire department was able to get some special equipment that enables them to free people with a powerful hose that washes away the silt from around their feet and legs. Every year they rescue dozens of people."

"But there are warning signs everywhere." She turned and leaned into his chest, hating to even see the scene where such a tragedy could happen.

"We don't always heed the warning signs in life. That's what I'm afraid our parents are neglecting to do now. They're avoiding the warning signs. We have to make them see them, Tori. You and I. Will you help me?"

She looked up into his eyes and felt reassured. "Of course I'll help you."

He laughed. "Otherwise, you're going to have six brothers, you know."

"We can't let that happen," she chortled. "Sometimes, five is four too many. And," she added as she slipped out of his arms, "you'd make an awful brother!"

"Yeah, but I'm a great doctor. And if I don't get to my office soon—"

Victoria turned and raced toward the minivan, calling back over her shoulder. "Beat you!"

Buck let her get a good head start, then darted after her, catching her just as she reached for the door handle, pulling her away. "You cheated. You had a head start."

"Did not," she told him, laughing and trying to catch her breath at the same time. "You're just slow, old man."

He pulled her to him and held her fast. "Old man, eh? I beat you, didn't I?"

"No, you didn't beat me."

"Okay, then, we tied. That satisfy you?"

She struggled to pull herself free, to no avail. "You're worse than a brother." She pushed him away.

"And you're too pretty to be any man's sister," he chided, finally relaxing his grip. "But you'd make some man a great wife."

She grinned shyly. "Got anyone in mind? If the right man came along I might decide to stay in Alaska myself."

Buck winked. "I think you'll recognize him—when he comes along."

His words echoed in her mind all the way back to the hotel. Would she recognize true love when—and if—it came along? Hopefully, she'd have the opportunity to find out. Someday.

Chapter 5

"We're no closer to breaking them up than we were two days ago," Victoria reminded Buck as they lingered over breakfast coffee. "In fact, if anything they're even closer."

He stared into his cup as Wasilla filled it to the brim. "All that lovey-dovey stuff almost makes me sick. I wonder if I was ever that foolish when my wife and I were courting."

"I—" Victoria stopped and her face took on a slight flush.

"You what?" Buck questioned softly, apparently realizing the thoughts that had gone through her mind were private.

"I—" she began again. "I can remember when I was in college and dating a man. I thought I was in love. I was even more foolish than my mother."

"Jonathan's father?"

She lowered her head and stirred at her coffee, which contained neither sugar nor cream. "Yes, Jonathan's father. I was sure I was in love with him and he with me."

"But he wasn't?"

"No. And now I can see that even with me it was infatuation. I was in awe of one of the big football players showing an interest in little old me, a mere freshman. A gullible, misguided freshman. He broke my heart."

His hand slipped across the table and circled hers. "I'm sorry, Tori. Honest I am. Some guys were born jerks."

She tried, but she couldn't stop the tear that wound its way down her cheek. "Like I said. It was a long time ago."

Buck's grip tightened on her hand as his other hand found its way to cup her chin and lift her face to meet his. "But you're still suffering from the unhappiness he caused, aren't you?"

She nodded and began to weep openly. Buck scooted across to the chair next to hers and wrapped her in his arms, cradling her head against his shoulder. "Let it out, Tori. It's not good to hold something inside for so long. Go ahead, cry."

His voice was gentle, his concern so genuine, she found herself leaning into him and crying as if her heart would burst unless it found relief.

After she had had a good cry, she lifted watery eyes and found a look of compassion she never expected. Even though he didn't know her story, she felt as if he understood her misery. She was grateful. Back home in Kansas City,

Victoria found it impossible to open up to anyone, even her mother, about the hurt and abandonment she felt when she gave birth to Jonathan and left the birth certificate blank where she should have listed the father. Instead, Victoria had put up a brave front and tried to let people think it didn't matter, claiming many single women gave birth to children every day. But in her heart, she wished there'd been another way. Oh, there'd been the abortion choice, but she couldn't do that.

"Sometimes life's the pits," Buck whispered. He pulled a red bandana from his pocket and wiped her tears.

"Yes, it is."

"Well, I'm here for you, Tori." He wrapped her securely in his arms. "You can count on me. I'd never let you down."

And she knew he meant those words. She'd come to greatly respect Buck in the short time she'd known him.

He wiped her tears again, then slipped back over into his chair. "I've got to go into the office early this morning and will be there most of the day. My patients are expecting me. What are your plans?"

She swallowed hard and fought to gather her wits, glad for a chance to put Armando out of her mind and get on to other things. "Gonna go shopping with Mother—for the wedding," she said without enthusiasm.

Buck became serious. "You know, Tori, I've been watching my dad and Abigale pretty closely these past few days, and I'm not sure we're doing the right thing trying to break them up."

She jumped to her feet, her hands on her hips as she glared at him, finding it difficult to believe she'd heard him right. "What? How can you say that, Buck?"

He took her hand in his, as if to calm her down. "Hold it, Tori. Let me have my say before you take me on. I'm beginning to think our parents are in love and just might make it together."

The room became icy silent as she continued to stare at this man whom she'd come to think of as her friend and ally.

"I mean it. My father has tried to convince me they can make it work, and I almost believe him. I haven't seen him this happy since Mom died. And since in a way it was my fault he lost her, who am I to try to take your mother away from him?"

Her arms crossed over her chest defensively. "So—out of guilt—you are asking me to sacrifice my mother to soothe your father's sorrow?"

"I wouldn't put it that way. But face it, your mom loves my dad. It's written all over her face. I honestly think they can make a great life together," he argued.

"And live in Alaska?" she asked snidely.

He nodded. "Yes, in Alaska."

"Even when it's dark twenty-four hours a day? And cold? And snow is up to the roof?"

"Come on, Tori. You know that's an exaggeration; it never gets that high." His lips formed a teasing grin. "Well, not often anyway."

She plopped into her chair and downed the last swig of coffee that'd been left in her cup, not even noticing it was cold. "I never thought I'd hear this coming from you, Buck Silverbow. I thought we were in agreement that we should do all we could to break them up before they did something foolish."

"Well, we'll have to finish this conversation later. My first patient is due in ten minutes, and I have a reputation of being on time."

Victoria watched as Buck took his last bite of toast, then pulled on his jacket. Even Buck had turned against her. It was beginning to seem as if marriage between Ron and her mother was inevitable. Victoria felt totally helpless. The only place she knew to turn was to God. But would He hear her after all these months she'd ignored Him?

"Morning, sweetie," Abigale's voice sang out as she entered the dining room. "Sleep well?"

"Sleep? Knowing my mother is going to marry a man she barely knows and stay in Alaska? Sure, sleep came easily, about as easily as an A did in my college finals."

Abigale poured herself a cup of hot, steaming coffee and seated herself beside her daughter. "Wow, a little testy this morning, aren't we?"

Victoria decided to give it one more shot. "Why don't you give up this foolish dream and go home with me, Mom? Surely you've realized by this time marrying Ron would be a mistake. Admit it. No one back home has even heard what you planned to do. I'm the only one who knows, and I promise I'll never remind you of it again once we're back in Kansas City where we belong."

Abigale blew into her cup and sipped her coffee. "I'm going to forget you said that, dear. I know this is hard for you to believe, but I do love Ron and I want to spend the rest of my life with him—in Alaska. And since we've been here nearly a week, Ron and I have decided it's time for us to go back to Kansas City and tell the boys and their families. He's made plane reservations for us for six tomorrow morning, so you'd better get a good night's sleep tonight. We're going home."

"But—"

Her mother lifted her hand. "No more, Victoria. It's settled, and you'd best get used to it."

"Micah's here!" Buck's voice ricocheted through the lobby. "Victoria, Abigale, come and meet my son."

Victoria and her mother hurried across the now empty dining room, anxious to meet the boy his father had talked so much about.

"Micah, this is Mrs. Whitmore. She and your grandfather have decided to get married. She'll be your new grandmother."

Although noticeably surprised by his father's announcement, Micah reached out and vigorously shook Abigale's hand. "N—nice to meet you."

"And this is Victoria, her daughter. She'll be my stepsister, so I guess that'll make her your aunt. And she has a son just a year or two younger than you. You'll finally have a cousin."

Victoria wanted to scream. Everyone was being so cordial. Well, they might want this union, but she sure didn't, and she would do everything in her power to stop it. And she was sure once she was back in Kansas City, she'd have plenty of help. Her brothers would never stand for such a ridiculous marriage. Maybe her mother would respect their feelings about this more than she did her only daughter's. For the young boy's sake, Victoria put on her best face, masking the feelings that were tearing at her heart. "Hello, Micah. Your father has told me all about you. He's very proud of you."

"Thank you, ma'am." The boy smiled toward his dad. Victoria was surprised by Micah's well-mannered behavior.

That evening, the entire group settled in the comfortable lobby area and visited for nearly an hour. Finally, it was Ron who stretched and yawned as he said, "Well, it's nearly nine o'clock. If we're going to catch that six o'clock flight in the morning we'd best hit the hay."

"Wish you could come with us, Buck," Abigale said as the group started up the steps.

"I tried to talk him into it, but he says he can't get away from his clinic," Ron answered, a sad note to his voice.

"I'm so anxious for you to meet my sons," Abigale added. "And for them to meet you."

"Guess you'll have to meet them in two weeks when they come for the wedding." Ron's arm found its way around Abigale's waist.

Victoria listened, but she wasn't happy. All this talk about meeting family members infuriated her. After her mother went into the suite where they were staying, Victoria hesitated in the hallway. With one final look toward Buck, she said, "Well, guess we won't be seeing one another again. Once my brothers get hold of my mother, the wedding will be off, I can assure you. Up here, I've been the only sane voice. But once we reach Kansas City, there'll be eleven of us to open Mother's eyes. Me, my brothers, and my brothers' wives. So don't rent a tuxedo, Buck. You won't get a chance to wear it."

Buck leaned toward her, his hand resting on the wall, his face so close she could feel the warmth of his breath on her cheek. "Don't count on it, Tori. You can't fight true love." And with that he planted a brotherly kiss on her cheek.

She ducked under his arm and opened the door, turning only long enough to say, "Good-bye, Buck. It's been swell." But the remembrance of that kiss lingered on her mind all night.

~❧

Early the next morning, Buck drove the group to the airport. Victoria avoided eye contact with him, although she rode in the front seat with him. Their conversation was friendly but strained. She wished they could part under better terms; but since Buck had taken his father's side, that was impossible.

"Dad, you take Abigale and Victoria into the lobby, and I'll get a porter to bring in the luggage," Buck instructed once they'd reached the unloading area. "I'll park the minivan and join you in a few minutes. I'll meet you at your gate."

Ron nodded. "Okay, son. But hurry. We'll want to say our good-byes before we leave."

Buck grinned. "I'll be there in plenty of time."

The three made their way to the ticket counter, and soon the porter appeared with their luggage. After producing their drivers' licenses and getting their boarding passes and instructions, the three headed to the appointed gate and seated themselves in a corner of the waiting area.

"Plane's on time," Ron told them after checking the big board that listed the departing flights. He glanced at his watch. "Wonder what's keeping Buck?"

"I'm sure he'll be here in plenty of time, Ron. Our plane doesn't leave for nearly a half hour."

"But they'll be calling for us to board any time now," Ron reminded her. "I wouldn't want to leave without seeing him."

"Flight Number 333 now boarding at gate 12 for Chicago," a voice boomed from a speaker. "Will all passengers please present your boarding passes at the gate for immediate boarding."

Ron scanned the area. "Where's Buck?"

"Probably got tied up in the parking lot," Victoria said, as she slipped an arm about her mother. She was feeling a little sad that she wouldn't have the opportunity to see Buck one more time and feeling a little guilty at the way she'd treated him the night before.

"Hey, you'd better get on board, I heard them call your flight," a familiar voice said as the three turned to see Buck hurrying toward them.

"Couldn't leave without saying good-bye." Ron reached out to hug his son.

"No need for that," Buck returned with a broad smile. "I'm going with you."

Victoria couldn't believe what she was hearing. "But you said you couldn't get away. How—?"

"Called old Doc Richards and talked him into coming out of retirement long enough to cover for me while I'm gone. The patients will love him."

"Oh, Buck. I'm so glad," Abigale said, reaching out to pat his hand. "Your father so wanted you to go."

"And you, Tori? How do you feel about me going?"

"Outnumbered," she answered, afraid of the influence Buck might be on her brothers. "Why didn't you tell us last night?"

He grinned as he took her arm and hurried to catch up with their parents who had already disappeared into the skyway. "Didn't know then. Old Doc Richards was at a concert and I couldn't reach him until nearly ten, and by then you were asleep. I called, got my ticket, and here I am. Micah was invited to stay with a friend, so he's happy as well."

Victoria smiled despite herself. It was nice to have Buck by her side.

❧

Eleven sets of eyes trained on the four people walking two by two through the doorway as the Whitmore men and their wives waited for their mother and sister.

"Mom!" It was Sam, Abigale's eldest son, and with him was Jonathan.

"Oh, come here." Victoria rushed to hug her son.

Abigale grabbed Ron's hand and hurried toward Sam, her arm outstretched. "Oh, Sam. This is Ron. I've told him all about you. And that's Buck, Ron's son."

Sam frowned. "Ah—nice to meet you, Ron," he murmured as if confused as to who Ron might be, then bent to kiss his mother's cheek. "And Buck."

Abigale kissed each son and daughter-in-law, telling each one, "This is Ron. And that is Buck."

After she greeted each one, Victoria could stand it no longer and spoke up loudly. "Mother, don't you think it's about time you told them who Ron is?"

All eyes riveted on the lovely gray-haired woman in the black pantsuit who was positively glowing. Abigale's eyes brightened with excitement as she leaned into Ron's side and laid her head against his broad shoulder. "Ron and I are going to be married. In Alaska, two weeks from today. And we want you all to come!"

It was as if every passenger in the crowded area became part of the Whitmore-Silverbow family as the area suddenly became silent and everyone turned toward the happy couple. The Whitmore men stood staring at their mother.

Sam finally spoke. "Is this some sort of joke?"

"No, it's true," Abigale decreed joyfully. "We met on the cruise ship and fell in love. I'm going to be Ron's wife. See?" She held out her left hand, the marquise diamond sparkling in the light.

Sam turned to his sister. "Victoria, what's going on here?"

Victoria shrugged, her arms still wrapped around her son. "You got me. I've been trying to talk her out of this for a week, but she's determined. I'm hoping you and the other boys will have more influence than I have."

Abigale stood proud and tall, looking much younger than her sixty-two years. "Look here, all of you, I'm your mother and quite old enough to make up my own mind about my life. You can accept my decision and be happy for me, or you can fight me and we'll all be miserable. Right now, all I want to do is get home and have a hot bath and a nap. My body is still on Alaskan time. If someone would be good enough to help us with our bags at baggage claim and show us to a car, we'll be on our way."

Five men nodded silently and followed their mother and her group to baggage claim.

Buck tapped his father on the shoulder as they stood waiting for their bags to arrive on the carousel. "Looks like you've got a tough bunch to convince."

Ron turned to face his son. "No convincing to do, son. Abigale has already made up her mind. They either accept it, or they don't."

The next day the family met again. It was Saturday, so the whole clan assembled for a welcome-home lunch at Sam's house, which was the largest and could accommodate the most people. After a barbecue of ribs and hamburgers, the group gathered in the family room, sending the children outside to play.

Sam, who seemed to have been appointed by the others as spokesperson, looked at Ron as Abigale sat on the sofa entwined in Ron's long arms. "All of this came as quite a surprise to our family, Mr. Silverbow. I'm sure you can appreciate the predicament this puts us in. We love our mother and want the best for her. And—" He paused. "And we're just not sure marrying you and moving off to Alaska is the best thing."

Ron's voice was sure and confident. "I can understand every word you're saying, Sam. If I were in your shoes, I'd feel the very same way. But let me assure you that I, too, want what is best for your mother. And I intend to do everything in my power to provide that best for her—financially, spiritually, materially, and with more love than you could possibly imagine."

His words hung in the air, as each family member seemed to assess the words.

"But Alaska—it's so—far," one brother said.

"And cold," another offered.

"You'll all be welcome to visit your mother and me whenever you want. And don't worry about your mother." He gave Abigale a wink. "I'll keep her warm, I promise."

"But we'll all miss her," a daughter-in-law said. "We usually see her every day or so."

Ron grinned, his handsome face filled with the love he felt for Abigale. "My little sweetie can phone you as often as she likes. I promise to never complain about the phone bill. Whatever makes Abigale happy makes me happy."

"But—" Jason, the next eldest, began as he gestured toward his sister. "What about the gift shop you and Victoria were going to open? I got the bank to approve your loan."

His mother slipped her arm through Ron's. "We've already talked about that.

I'll be Victoria's silent partner. That'll keep the bank happy, and she can go on with her plans."

Victoria broke her silence. "But it won't be the same without you. I'm not sure I can handle it by myself."

Abigale smiled toward her youngest child. "Of course you can, dear. You're a smart woman, you can learn anything you need to. After a few months you'll have everything in hand, and you'll be glad you're running your own business by yourself, without me."

Sam spoke up. "We can all help Victoria, that's no problem. It seems to me the problem at hand is—will our mother be happy marrying again and living in Alaska?"

"She thinks so," Victoria said quickly, still hoping for a change of her mother's mind. "But I'm not so sure. It's different up there."

"Okay, sis. You've been there, tell us about it. Have you seen where Mother will be living?" Jason asked.

She nodded. "Yes, I have."

"What's it like?" one of her sisters-in-law asked.

"Well, I have to admit it's beautiful where Ron's lodge is."

Sam broke in. "Ron's lodge? Explain."

Abigale's eyes sparkled. "Let me tell you. The Golden Nugget Lodge is quite large and very attractive. He has a wonderful staff working for him. It's surrounded by trees and loads of flowers, and the air is so clear you actually want to take deep breaths."

Everyone laughed.

"The nights are cool this time of year, but the sun is bright and warms both the earth and your spirit. Ronnie and I will be living in his suite on the second floor of the Lodge, and Ronnie wants me to redecorate the entire suite any way I choose." She gave them a sheepish grin. "And I won't even have to cook or do laundry, unless I want to. His staff will do all of that. Even clean our suite. So you see, I'll be just like a queen, living with my king." She reached upward, cupped Ron's chin with her hand, and kissed his cheek.

"Sounds good to me," Jason's wife said with a laugh. "Any vacancies in that lodge for our family?"

"Whenever you want to come. Just say the word and your rooms will be ready," Ron said. "That's the advantage of owning a lodge. You always can make room for visiting relatives. And we both want you to come."

Victoria could feel her mother slipping away from her as one by one her brothers seemed to favorably consider their mother's announcement. "But you know Mom won't be happy living that far away from us. She's always lived in Kansas City, in the same house, for the past twenty-five years. You've got to talk her out of this." Victoria felt her voice quiver as she spoke, but she couldn't help it.

"Relax, sis," Jason said with a reassuring smile. "We all want the best for Mom." He turned to Buck who had been silent. "How do you feel about all of this, Buck?"

Buck stood to his feet and surveyed the group seated in the family room. "Well, like Tori, at first I was as against it as she is. In fact, the two of us agreed to try and break up this pair." He glanced her way. "But after spending the week with your mom and my dad, and seeing them together and how happy they made one another, I kind of changed my mind. I'd like to see them get married, if they want to. They have my blessing."

Victoria glared at Buck. *Traitor*, she thought.

Abigale pulled away from Ron and walked to the center of the group, turning slowly, eyeing each person. "You know, you're all talking about me as if I weren't even here. Or worse than that—a senile old woman who doesn't know her mind. Well, family, let me assure you neither of those things are true. I'm sixty-two years old, fit as a fiddle, mentally alert, financially stable, and in love. I don't need your permission to marry Ronnie, although I prefer to have your blessing, even as Buck has given his. Now, go into a powwow or whatever you want to do. Ronnie and I are leaving. I want to take him to your father's grave and introduce them to one another." She turned to Victoria. "I'll see you and Buck at home later." Abigale took Ron's hand and they slipped out the door, leaving a befuddled family.

"Well, I guess your mother set that record straight," Jason's wife said quickly. "What are we all going to do about this?"

Buck stood to his feet again. "I feel like the fifth wheel in all of this. If you don't mind, Tori, I'll take your car and go on to your mom's house while you all talk."

"You don't need to leave, Buck," Sam responded with a warm smile. "You have as much stock in this as we do."

"Thanks, Sam, but if it's all the same to you, I'd rather bow out. I've already said my piece."

"I'm ready to cast my vote right now," Jason said. "For months I've watched Mother go downhill. Since Dad's death she's been like a hermit, walled up in that house of hers. It's been years since I can remember seeing her this happy. She's like a schoolgirl. I know Alaska is a long way away, but like Ron said, we can visit her anytime we like and she's only a phone call away. I hate to lose her as much as you all do, but can we be selfish enough to keep her from marrying Ron, if she loves him the way she says she does? Looks to me like he's a good man. I can't blame them for wanting to spend the rest of their years together."

Sam stood to his feet. "I agree with Jason. This has come as a shock, but to refuse to give our blessing would be pure selfishness on our part."

In turn, the other three brothers rose to their feet, voiced their opinions, and all agreed with Sam and Jason.

"Well, it looks like we're all in agreement. Let's tell Mom," Sam said proudly as he looked from one brother to the next.

"Oh, no you don't!" Victoria shouted, jumping to her feet. "I don't agree. I think it's wrong to encourage Mom to move to Alaska!"

Jason pointed his finger at his sister. "Sorry, Victoria. You're outnumbered. We all understand your feelings, you're Mom's only daughter. But majority rules."

Victoria called for Jonathan then headed toward the door, her face etched with anger. "I thought I could count on all of you to do the right thing. But you've all let me down. Buck included."

"You're getting your shop, sis. What more do you want?" Sam asked, his fingers drumming the table, his impatience with his sister showing.

"You may forsake her, but I'm not. The shop can wait. If Mom goes to Alaska, I'm going with her. And I'm not leaving until I'm sure she's happy living there."

"You're going back to Alaska?" Jason's wife asked as she shifted her baby to her shoulder.

"You bet I am." Victoria jerked open the door, then turned to Buck. "You can ride home with Sam. Jonathan and I are going over to Morton's."

With a shrug of his shoulders and a quick smile toward the family he'd just met, Buck nodded. "Fine with me. I'll just stay here and get better acquainted with these good folks. Seems like we're all going to be related."

Chapter 6

Victoria kept her distance on the night flight back to Alaska. It was dark, and since most of the passengers slept, there was little excuse for talking. She was glad she and Jonathan were seated across the aisle from Buck, Ron, and her mother. It made it easier to ignore them. Victoria was still upset with her brothers. Was she the only one who sensed impending doom for their mother's marriage?

She and Jonathan chattered on endlessly from the minivan's backseat as she pointed out various sights along the way to the Lodge from the airport, sites she'd visited with Buck only days before. When they reached the Lodge, Micah was waiting in the doorway and hurried out to meet them.

"Jonathan, I want you to meet my son, Micah," Buck said proudly. "I think you boys are going to be good friends."

"Want to see my knife?" Micah asked, his eyes shining with little-boy excitement. "My dad got it for me."

"Sure," Jonathan answered quickly, his eyes round with curiosity.

"Knife?" Victoria moved forward quickly, latching onto her son's arm. "Jonathan doesn't play with knives."

"They'll be fine, Tori. Kids in Alaska grow up with knives. Micah knows better than to take his knife out of its sheath unless I'm with him. Give the boy some space."

"Just make sure you don't touch it, Jonathan." She released her grip slowly. Perhaps she was being a little overprotective. Everyone told her so. Even her father had said she coddled her son.

The two boys ran through the lobby.

Buck grinned. "Boys."

"I don't know about the rest of you, but I'd like to take a shower and a nap." Abigale yawned. "Sleeping on a plane doesn't give much rest."

Ron patted her hand. "Now you go on up to your room, my little sweetie, and get your shower. I'll have your bags up in a jiffy."

Buck looked toward Victoria. "You look like you could use a nap too."

She bristled at the suggestion. "I slept on the plane."

"You never told me how your visit with old Morton came out."

She leaned against the desk and crossed her arms. "Didn't know I was supposed to tell you."

"He still after you to marry him?"

She nodded.

"Bet he was thrilled when he heard you were coming back up here to stay."

Victoria glared at Buck. "Not to stay, Buck. I'll only be here until I'm sure my mother is happy, or better yet, until she comes to her senses and decides to go back with me."

"You think you could be happy?"

She frowned. "Taking my mother home? Of course."

He shook his head. "No, I mean being married to Morton Pendergast."

"Of course I could. He's a fine man."

"But you don't love him."

"How do you know?"

"You can't fool me, Tori. A woman in love doesn't talk about her man the way you talk about Morton. Did he kiss you when you went to see him?"

Again, she bristled. "Of course he did."

With a mischievous grin, he moved right up into her face. "Like this?" He gave her a slight peck on the cheek.

She blushed but didn't answer.

"Or was it like this?" He quickly took her in his arms and planted a deep lingering kiss on her lips.

She tried to pull away, but he wouldn't let her.

"Let me go." She pushed against his chest and tried to free herself. "What do you think you're doing?"

Buck let loose with a robust laugh. "Just trying to show you how people in love kiss. Hey, Tori, bet old Morton didn't kiss you like that."

She ran the back of her hand over her mouth. "Did too."

"Liar."

"You—you make me so mad—I'd—I'd like to—"

"Kiss me back?" Buck smiled.

Ron came in carrying his and Abigale's bags. "Buck, what are you two doing? Victoria looks like she'd like to take a swing at you."

"We're just having a little fun, Dad. Nothing serious going on, is there, Tori?"

Knowing nothing would be gained by complaining to Ron about his grown son, Victoria mustered up a fake smile. "Yeah, fun. Nothing serious that I can't handle."

"Good. I'd hate to have any hard feelings between you two." Ron headed for the stairway, whistling as he went, then called out over his shoulder as he reached the landing. "Because in just two weeks you'll be related. Brother and sister."

"Guess I'd better get the rest of the bags," Buck said. His finger reached out and touched the tip of Victoria's nose. "Go take a nap. You're gonna need your strength."

During the next ten days Victoria saw very little of Buck. He had his patients to take care of and spent long days at his clinic and several late nights at the hospital with accident victims. She and her mother shopped, met with the pastor, the caterer, the florist, and everyone else it would take to pull off the wedding she and her husband-to-be wanted. Ron had encouraged Abigale to wear the wedding gown she'd worn when she married Victoria's father, which greatly pleased Abigale. At first the idea upset Victoria, but after talking to her mother and seeing how happy she was with her decision, Victoria resigned herself to it.

Ron was busy running the Lodge, and Micah and Jonathan were occupied playing with the myriad of electronic toys Buck had bought for Micah, or exploring the foothills around the Lodge. It seemed everyone was busy—and happy—about the upcoming wedding. Except Victoria. And each day, as the wedding drew nearer, she became more depressed.

Finally, the big day arrived. Victoria's brothers had all arrived along with their wives and many children, and along with them came Morton Pendergast and several other close friends of the family. Ron had reserved plenty of rooms at the Lodge for all their guests and even had special tables reserved for them in the dining room for all their meals.

"This is some place your father has here," Morton told Buck as the two men visited in the lobby. "Like Victoria, I'd sure never want to live in Alaska. But if I had to live here, this is the kind of place I'd want to live in. I hate cold weather and snow. I'd probably never leave that massive fireplace."

Buck smoothed his mustache, allowing his fingers to cover his smile of amusement. There wasn't much about Morton he liked. "I take it you don't ski. Or hunt."

"No!" Morton said. "I'm not much of a sportsman. And I could never slaughter an animal. Give me a good book and I'm happy."

"Victoria tells me you've never married. That so?"

"Absolutely. Never found a woman I'd want to marry. Until Victoria, that is."

Buck crossed his long legs, his weathered boots a sharp contrast to Morton's highly polished wing tips. "Oh? You're gonna marry her?"

"Well, she hasn't exactly said yes yet. But she will."

Buck hated the man's cockiness. "What makes you think so?"

Morton's fingers moved to check the knot on his silk designer tie. "I make a good living, have a beautiful home, and I can be a father to her son. And I'm a good catch. What more could a woman ask?"

"Something missing in that scenario, isn't there, fellow?"

Morton appeared thoughtful. "Don't think so."

Buck squared his shoulders as he glared at the irritating little man in his

Armani suit. Men like this drove him crazy. "How about love? I didn't hear you mention that word."

The man laughed, and Buck found him arrogant. "Love? A little old-fashioned, aren't you? You're forgetting Victoria and I aren't starry-eyed teenagers with raging hormones. I'm sure at this point in her life she's more interested in security and companionship than she is hearts and lace." He scrutinized Buck from head to toe. "Actually, you don't look like the romantic type. I'm surprised to hear you mention such things."

Buck settled back into the sofa's cushions, having a hard time understanding why this man he'd barely met aggravated him so. "Just goes to show you how looks can be deceiving."

"Well, take it from me, the last thing Victoria is interested in is romance. She's not the kind of woman who wants some guy hanging all over her."

Buck raised a brow. "How do you know? Have you tried it?"

The man's face flushed with anger or embarrassment. "Of course not. I'm a gentleman."

"Um." Buck stroked at his mustache again. "Gentlemen come in all types of packages."

"You two getting acquainted?" Victoria asked as she entered the lobby and seated herself beside Morton.

Buck stared at the two as they sat side by side. *If I were interested in that woman, I sure wouldn't take old Morton's approach. I'd show her what love is like—Alaskan style, and I don't mean rubbing noses.*

❧

Victoria stood at the back of the chapel, her bouquet of white camellias held in her lace-gloved hand. She waited for the music to signal it was time for the wedding party to move down the long white carpet runner. She had to admit her mother never looked lovelier. Being engaged to Ron had taken years off Abigale's age. Despite her gray hair, she looked young, vital, and positively glowing. The wedding gown she'd worn forty-five years ago still fit perfectly. And although the white satin had turned to a cream color, it was as pretty now as it was in the photograph of her parents. Watching Abigale made Victoria's heart swell with pride.

And yet, her heart was also filled with sadness. And she wished she could turn the pages of time back to her freshman year. If she'd had her eyes open and hadn't been so enamored by Armando's good looks and popularity, her life might have turned out very differently. She might have married a nice boy and had a beautiful church wedding much like her mother's, rather than being a single mom raising a child by herself, without a husband or a wedding ring.

"Ready?" the handsome man in the black tuxedo standing beside her asked as he took her hand and tucked it into the crook of his arm. "Looks like the wedding is going to come off despite your efforts."

She gazed up into the sympathetic eyes of Buck Silverbow and returned his smile. "Seems I lost, doesn't it?"

He gave her hand a squeeze. "Well, she hasn't said I do yet. Want to give it another try?"

She gulped and then exhaled slowly. "No, I'll just tuck my tail between my legs and run away and hide once the ceremony's over."

He seemed surprised by her response. "Oh? That mean you're going back to Kansas City and marry that stuffed shirt of yours?"

"I haven't decided."

"To marry him? Or to leave?"

The organ began to play, leaving both Victoria and Buck to wonder what her answer might have been.

The wedding party moved down the aisle and ended up at the flower-laden lattice arch at the front of the church. Buck gave his partner's hand a gentle squeeze and a quick wink as their hands separated. The pair moved to stand on either side of the arch, Buck by his father, and Victoria beside her son who held the heart-shaped pillow containing the wedding rings.

And then the bride appeared, her face vaguely covered by a fingertip veil of white illusion, which didn't even begin to mask her blissful smile. Victoria's heart leaped. Her mother was so radiant, so alive. Victoria felt a pang of jealousy. Why couldn't she find the same happiness her mother had found? Twice!

She caught a glimpse of Morton Pendergast and found him looking at her. She sent a weak smile his way. Would marriage to Morton be so bad? Couldn't she learn to love him, in time?

As she turned away from Morton and back to the happy couple, her eyes locked with Buck's and her heart seemed to skip a beat. But why?

As the vows were exchanged, Victoria found herself repeating them along with her mother, wondering all the while if she would ever have a chance to repeat them to the man she loved. A slight smile tilted at her lips. What man?

The soloist sang, the rings were exchanged, and soon the ceremony ended. Everyone was smiling and happy. Even Victoria felt the joy that permeated the air. In the revelry of the moment, she'd lost sight of Buck; but she knew he was more than okay with the way things had worked out for his father and Abigale.

A delicate hand clamped over her wrist. "It's over! I'm Mrs. Ronald Silverbow. Please be happy for me, Victoria." Abigale's face beamed with delight.

Victoria forced a smile. "I am happy for you, Mom. I just hope you've—"

"Don't even say it, sweetie. I don't want to hear any negative words. This is my wedding day!"

Her daughter donned her best smile, for her mother's sake. "You're right. You've chosen to marry Ron and live in Alaska. I guess I'll have to learn to live with it whether I like it or not." She planted a kiss on her mother's flushed cheek.

"Congratulations, Mrs. Ronald Silverbow."

Abigale beamed. "I knew I could count on you." She began to search the crowd. "Do you know where Buck is? Ronnie's trying to find him. He seems to have disappeared."

Victoria scanned the crowd but Buck was nowhere to be found. "I haven't seen him since we left the chapel."

"Well, if you see him, tell him his father and his new stepmother are looking for him." Abigale's eyes sparkled as she lifted her bouquet. "Be sure you're there when I toss my bouquet, you just might be the one to catch it."

"I should be so lucky," Victoria mumbled as Ron whisked away Abigale.

The reception line formed and the wedding party began greeting the wedding attendees one by one—all but Buck. He seemed to have disappeared. No one knew where he was, not even Micah. Victoria kept an eye out for him but to no avail.

"Get ready," Abigale told all the women who'd gathered at the foot of the steps outside the church. "I'm going to toss the bouquet."

Victoria joined the group but felt nothing like catching her mother's bouquet, a constant reminder of her mother's decision to leave her and marry an Alaskan man. In fact, she was barely paying attention when the bouquet left her mother's hands and flew through the air and headed straight for Neva Wilson, the mother of six.

But instead of reaching up to catch the lovely camellias, the woman ducked and the bouquet continued its flight and dropped into Victoria's hands. Aghast, Victoria hurriedly tried to hand it to one of the ladies standing near her, but they all refused.

"It's yours." Neva Wilson laughed. "You caught it fair and square."

"Looks like you're going to have to say yes to me after all," Morton said as he moved through the crowd and joined her. "Catching those flowers must be an omen." He took her hand in his. "What do you say? Will you marry me?"

Victoria stared at the man she'd known so long. She wondered, when Morton kissed her, why she felt different than when Buck kissed her. "I have too many things on my mind right now, Morton," she said, backing away from him. "We'll talk later. Right now I have something I have to take care of."

"Don't put me off too long, Victoria. There are plenty of other women out there who'd jump at the chance to marry me." His confidence irritated her.

Without answering, she headed for the little car Ron had rented for her to use during her stay in Anchorage.

She parked near the back door of the Lodge and took the path up the hill, struggling to hold up her long skirt to avoid tripping on the rocks as she moved. It was a beautiful day, much like a spring day in Kansas City. The sky was a clear blue with only a small occasional cloud.

Up ahead she caught sight of a tall male figure dressed in a black tuxedo, moving up the path a few minutes ahead of her. Sure he hadn't seen her, she hurried to catch him, the bouquet still clutched in her hand. By the time she reached the clearing, he'd seated himself on a fallen tree and was staring off in space, his black cummerbund dangling in his hand. Caught up in his thoughts, he didn't even notice her as she walked up to him. "Buck," she said softly.

He jumped and dabbed at his eyes with his sleeve. "What are you doing up here? I supposed you were still at the church."

"I—" Why had she come there? She wasn't sure herself. All she knew was that she wanted to find him. Right now, he was the only one who might understand her feelings. "I'm not really sure. Guess I wanted to escape. Guess you did too." She seated herself beside him and kicked off her shoes. "These aren't exactly for hiking. My feet hurt."

He laughed and she felt those butterflies again.

"You're right about the escaping. I did fine until they got to that 'death do us part' line. All I could think about was my own wedding and how beautiful Claudette was in her wedding gown. She looked like an angel." The laugh disappeared and an unsteady smile took its place.

"I'm sorry, Buck. I never thought—"

"It's okay. I don't say much about it to folks, but the hurt is still there. There's never a day goes by that I don't feel her presence near me." He gestured toward the home he'd built for Claudette, the one that had remained unoccupied since her death. "I come up here and talk to her. Foolish, huh?"

"No, not foolish at all! She was an important part of your life." Victoria wished she were gifted with words. Right now they seemed to fail her.

With the toe of his black leather boots, Buck kicked the wood chips that surrounded his feet. "Not a part of my life, Tori. She was my life! A part of me died when she did." The big man's hands flew to his face and he began to weep openly, his sobs racking at his chest.

Victoria wasn't sure exactly what she should do to comfort Buck. Finally, she gathered courage to slip her arms about his neck and cradle his head against her breast. Her fingers stroked his hair, much like she did Jonathan's when he needed comforting. "It's okay, Buck. Go ahead. Cry it out. It'll make you feel better."

He tried to pull away, but she held fast. When he relaxed a bit and his chest quit heaving, she lifted the hem of her long skirt and wiped his tears. The two were so close she could feel the beat of his heart as he agonized there beside her.

"You must think I'm a real pantywaist," he said softly. He sucked in a deep breath. "Macho men don't cry."

"They do if they've lost a loved one," she said, trying to console him. "I'd say it takes a real man to cry. You must have loved her deeply."

He pushed away a bit. "I did. Guess I still do. My biggest regret, other than for myself, is that Micah was so young when she left us. He barely remembers her."

"Have—have you ever considered marrying again?"

"No."

His answer was spoken with such firmness she wished she'd never asked.

"I'd never find another woman like Claudette. When she died, I told myself I'd never marry again. In fact, the day she was buried, I put my hand on her casket and promised her I'd never let another woman take her place."

"And you closed up your house?"

"Yes. I couldn't go back there to live without her."

"I think I can understand that."

"Most folks don't. Some think I'm crazy. Others have tried to set me up with some pretty, nice women, but I wouldn't have any part of it. I'd rather spend the rest of my life alone."

"Do you have a picture of her?"

A smile crept across his tear-stained face as he reached into his pocket for his wallet. "Oh, yes. Always carry one with me." He pulled the picture out and handed it to her.

"She's beautiful," Victoria said, meaning it. The woman staring back at her looked much like Buck. Same dark hair, dark eyes, and a smile almost as beautiful as his. "She looks enough like you to be your sister."

His grin shook up those butterflies once more. "That's what everyone used to say. Guess it's our genes. We both have Athabascan Indian ancestors."

Victoria's face sobered. "Honestly, Buck. I'm so sorry about your wife. It must have been terrible losing her like that. And your mother too. I wish I'd have had a chance to meet them both. They must have been very special people."

"They were," he said with a note of overwhelming sadness as he took back the picture. After one last look, he placed it back in his wallet.

Victoria shivered and wrapped her arms about herself. Buck noticed and quickly tugged off his jacket. "Here, take this. Gets cool pretty quick in the evening."

She backed away and held up a palm between them. "No, I couldn't. Besides, it's time I left you alone. I'm sure you didn't plan on having company when you came up here."

He slipped the jacket over her shoulders and pulled her back down beside him. "Please stay. I like having you here."

She knew she should go, but in her heart she wanted to stay. There was something so comforting about being near this man. Knowing he would be close to her mother in some way helped. It made leaving her in Alaska somewhat bearable. "If you're sure—"

"I'm sure. After all, you are my sister now." He slipped an arm about her waist and drew her close. "That better?"

She smiled. "Much better, thank you. But I don't want you getting cold."

He gave her a slight squeeze. "Hey, are you forgetting? Me tough Alaskan man!"

"Seriously, Buck. I don't know what to do about Mom."

He lifted a brow. "Not much you can do now—she's married."

Victoria leaned into him. His body made her feel warm and secure. "I know, silly. I mean about leaving her. I'd vowed I would not leave until I was convinced she was happy living here."

"So, what's the problem? Don't leave."

She gave him a look of surprise. "You think I should stay? Won't your father resent my presence?"

"Why should he? You heard him say whatever makes Abigale happy makes him happy. I'm sure she'd want you to stay as long as you'd like." Buck grinned. "And I would too. I've never had a sister before. I kind of like the idea. But what about that shop you were going to open?"

"I guess I could put it on hold."

"Good. So, do it."

A look of trouble clouded her face. "I'd have to get a job. I won't take charity. And Jonathan and I would have to have a place to live."

"Plenty of room at the Lodge. And I'm sure there are plenty of people who'd like to hire a good-looking, talented, smart girl like you."

"Flatterer. Seems you have all the answers."

"I also have a question."

"Oh?"

"What about old Morton?"

"Guess he'll have to wait until I make sure Mom's settled."

"Think he'll wait?"

"Morton? Oh, yes. He's a very patient man."

"I can think of a few other words to describe him. Stuffed shirt. Arrogant. Egotistical. Want to hear more?"

She shook her head and cocked a brow. "No, that's plenty. Why do I get the feeling you don't like him much?"

"Perceptive little thing, aren't you? I just don't happen to like men who think the world revolves around them."

She pursed her lips. "He's a good man, Buck. Jonathan and I would want for nothing if I married him."

"Except the thing you need the most."

"And just what is that?"

He stood awkwardly, shifting from one foot to the other before lifting his eyes to hers.

"Go on, you can tell me. I'm your sister, remember?"

"You're sure you want to hear this?"

"Yes. Say it. What is the one thing I'd be missing if I married Morton, Dr. Silverbow?"

Pulling himself up to his full height of six-foot-four, he answered with one word.

"Love."

Chapter 7

Look, Victoria, I understand your concern for your mother, but don't you think you're being a bit foolish staying here in Alaska with her? Do you plan to go along on her honeymoon?" Morton Pendergast pulled a boarding pass from his coat pocket and waited for her answer.

"Morton, I have no intention of going on Mom's honeymoon with her. As a matter of fact, they're not going on a honeymoon. Not for awhile anyway. Ron wants to take Mom to the Caribbean when the Alaskan weather turns cold."

"Well, I'll ask you one more time. Come home with me and let's set a wedding date. I have an important convention coming up in France next spring, and it would help my professional image if I had an attractive wife to attend with me."

She frowned. "That's why you're asking me to marry you? For business reasons?"

"That's not the only reason, Victoria. You're pretty, you're smart, you're talented. You and I would make a great team," he stated without hesitation. "And think of all the social functions you'd be able to attend as my wife."

Victoria stared at him. She couldn't believe what she was hearing. Why was it each time she saw Morton now, Buck's words came back to her. Stuffed shirt. Arrogant. Egotistical. She'd never really thought of Morton that way before, but now that Morton had spelled out his reasons for wanting to marry her and Buck had called his ways to her attention, it was all she could think about when she was with him.

"I'm sorry, Morton. But for now, I'm putting my own life on hold. Perhaps after Mom is settled and I'm back in Kansas City, I'll—"

Morton tossed his jacket over his arm and picked up his briefcase. "Don't wait too long, Victoria. You'll never do any better than me, you know."

"So you've told me." Anger tainted her voice. "Have a pleasant flight."

Buck was climbing into the minivan when she arrived back at the Lodge. "Get old what's-his-name off okay?"

"Yes, he's gone."

"Good. Glad he's gone. I didn't like that guy." With that, Buck took off down the road toward the hospital.

Early the next morning after enrolling her son in school, and with the classified section of the newspaper under her arm, Victoria searched for a job. Several days of filling out forms and enduring endless interviews yielded nothing other than a few minimum-wage jobs, paying much less than she felt she and Jonathan could live on. She had her savings to fall back on, but that was earmarked for the new shop she planned to open back home.

"How's the job hunting going?" Buck asked at the dinner table one evening after a particularly frustrating day for Victoria.

"Not good. I thought I was preparing myself for a real world occupation when I majored in graphic arts. No one wants to hire me. I may end up having to go home after all."

"Aw, Mom. I don't want to go home," Jonathan complained. Wasilla poured him another glass of milk. "I like school and Micah, and Buck promised to take me and Micah to a ball game Saturday."

"If I don't find a job soon—"

"Now, dear," Abigale said, laying down her fork, "I told you I'd help you out in any way I can. I still have the money your father left me and—"

Victoria shook her head. "No. If I can't make it on my own, I'm leaving. I'm not going to be a burden to anyone. I don't want to leave, but I may have no choice. I've made up my mind. If I don't have a job by this weekend, we're going home. It's time I stood on my own two feet."

That night as she made ready for bed, her eyes were drawn to the Gideon Bible on the nightstand. It'd been weeks since she had read a Bible, but tonight she felt the need to seek its comfort. Someone had placed a marker in the book of Philippians and had used a green highlighter to mark verse 19 of the fourth chapter. Victoria read aloud, "But my God shall supply all your need according to his riches in glory by Christ Jesus."

All my needs, God? Victoria's fingers traced the words. I've been separated from You for a long time. But for my son's sake, for my mom's sake, if You want us to stay in Alaska, please provide me a job.

❧

"Hey, Tori. You'll never guess what happened," Buck said as he arrived at the Lodge unexpectedly for lunch the next day. "When I got in the office this morning, my head nurse told me she and the others had decided to quit if I didn't hire someone to help get caught up in the office and to act as my assistant when we get overloaded with patients. It's only a temporary job. I told them I knew just the woman for the job. They want you to start tomorrow. Can you make it?"

She eyed him suspiciously. "Really, Buck? You're not just creating this position, are you? Do you really need someone?"

He let loose a robust laugh. Then he grabbed his napkin and spread it across his lap. "Hey, would I lie to my own little sister? Ask Dad. He knows how the women in my office are always grumbling about being overworked."

Ron tore himself away from his new bride long enough to answer. "He's right, Victoria. Complain, complain, complain. That's all they do."

"Well, if you're sure—"

"You bet I'm sure. Will you take the job or am I going to have to run an ad in the paper?"

"No! I'll take it, and thanks."

Buck raised a hand. "Don't thank me yet. You don't know what a tough taskmaster I am. I'm a bear to work for."

"A teddy bear." Ron winked at his son.

"You won't be sorry, Buck. I promise," Victoria said, relieved she didn't have to leave her mother yet.

"My pleasure," Buck said. "I like having you here."

❧

The next few weeks flew by. Jonathan loved his new school, he and Micah were inseparable, and Victoria was happy in her new job. She'd never realized how important Buck was to the community until each day she watched as he treated dozens of patients, some only with tender, kind words. His patience never ceased to amaze her. The man was tireless. She especially liked the way he was with the babies and young children. They all loved him and trusted him right from the start, letting him examine them and give them shots with little or no complaint. She was especially impressed when Jean, the head nurse, told her how many patients Buck treated who were never able to pay him.

"He sends them a bill marked paid in full. That's the kind of man he is," Jean told Victoria one day when they were having a late lunch together. "Never seen a man like him. He could be making good money in Vancouver or Seattle. But you think he's interested? No way. He's an Alaskan through and through."

As his assistant, Victoria learned much about Dr. Buck Silverbow. His kindness toward his elderly patients, his gentleness with those who were ill, his generosity to those who could not pay, his concern for those who were hurting—his virtues were endless. Victoria developed a high respect for him both as a man and as a doctor.

If I could ever learn to trust a man again, it would be a man like Buck Silverbow, she admitted to herself one night when she was with him at the hospital. She was assisting him with a man whose car had been sideswiped by a truck. Although Buck didn't say anything, Victoria was sure he was reliving his wife's accident. Buck did everything he could, but the man died. Victoria cried when she watched Buck's compassion as he told the man's family.

On the way home, Buck and Victoria stopped at an all-night café for coffee and rolls. Although their talk was light, inwardly each was filled with deep sorrow at the loss of their patient. Finally, Victoria could no longer stand the chitchat. "How do you do it, Buck? Day in and day out you're faced with misery and death, yet you seem to revel in being a doctor. The demands on you and your life are unbelievable."

His hands cupped hers. "Easy. I just look into their faces and see their pain and anguish. And knowing I might be able to help them gives me great gratification. I don't always succeed, but I know I've tried. I can't find words to describe it. I just know it fills me with satisfaction."

"I can see that. It's written all over your face. You're quite a man, Dr. Silverbow."

"Hey, you're gonna turn a guy's head. Let's change the subject. How about renting a movie tonight, something the boys will like? You can come up to the cabin and we'll pop it into the VCR."

"Great. I'm sure the kids will love it."

"Good. How about I have Wasilla box up a pizza for us, and we'll eat while we watch the movie? That way the boys can get to bed early."

"Terrific idea. Let's do it. I'll try to get back to the Lodge a little early and see if Wasilla will let me bake a batch of my famous peanut butter cookies."

Buck smiled. "You know how to cook?"

"A few things, but I'm best at baking sweets, of course."

Victoria, Jonathan, and Micah enjoyed the movie, but Dr. Silverbow fell asleep as soon as he'd finished his pizza. Victoria watched the sleeping man, his head pressed against the recliner back, his long legs dangling over the end of the footrest. She wondered what it would be like to be married to a man like Buck, living in a house with two sons, like normal married couples. Then she thought of Morton. Debonair, sophisticated Morton. Somehow he didn't fit into her picture of the perfect family. But Buck did.

The next few weeks Victoria was happy. In addition to spending time with her mother and new stepfather, she spent wonderful times as she joined Buck on his early morning walks before going into the clinic. One morning they met one of Buck's patients, a young woman pushing her baby in a stroller. Buck stopped to introduce them, then made baby sounds to the adorable baby girl all wrapped up in a pink snuggly. The baby smiled at Buck immediately and grasped his thumb.

"You have quite a way with children," Victoria told him as they made their way on up the path.

"Claudette and I had planned on having a house full of kids. I love them. At one time I even considered being a pediatrician. But how about you? You want more kids?"

She bit back feelings of hurt and disappointment. "Oh, yes. I'd love to have a little girl. When I was a child playing with dolls, I used to visualize having a little girl, tying bows in her hair and dressing her in frilly little dresses. But it looks like that'll never happen."

"Why not? Doesn't old Morton want kids?"

She could tell Buck was slowing his pace for her benefit. His long strides made it difficult to keep in step. "No, he doesn't. He's made that very clear to me. Although he's good to Jonathan, I think he only tolerates him because of me."

"And what does your son think about old Morton?"

She rolled her eyes. "He hates him."

"Ah, a perceptive kid." Buck winked and quickened his pace. "We'd better be heading back if we're going to get to the clinic on time."

The clinic was filled with patients when they arrived. Buck had a habit of allowing people to walk in without an appointment if they had a problem, and many of them seemed to abuse that privilege.

About ten o'clock a pregnant woman elbowed her way through the waiting room and demanded to see Dr. Silverbow immediately. Jean, the head nurse, seemed to know the woman and tried to calm her down. Victoria's efforts to calm the woman also failed.

Finally, in order to keep peace, Buck came into the waiting room. "Well, hello. We haven't seen you for a long time. I'm sorry I don't remember your name. What can I do for you?"

The woman waved her finger in his face as she patted her extended stomach. "You better remember me. You're the father of my baby!"

Chapter 8

Buck reeled backward. Those in the crowded waiting room fell silent as every eye zeroed in on Buck and the woman.

"Look, I don't know what your game is, but I'm certainly not that baby's father. Now, if you'll excuse me, I have patients to see." His voice was calm, but everyone could tell her words had upset him.

The woman grabbed his sleeve and pulled him around. "Oh, no you don't, I'm—"

"If you have something to say to me, I suggest you come into my office," Buck told her in a controlled voice. He motioned to Victoria. "And you come with us."

Victoria followed the two of them, her heart broken. The only man she'd ever felt she could trust had just been accused of fathering a child outside of marriage.

Buck motioned to the woman and Victoria to be seated, then circled his desk and dropped into the high-back leather chair. "Now, I don't even know your name."

"Bonnie. Bonnie Connor," she said simply, her hand still on her large stomach.

"How far along are you?" the ever-present doctor asked.

"A little over eight months."

"Have you been under a doctor's care?"

"No. I couldn't afford no doctor."

"Well, I will be glad to examine you and provide you with vitamins, free of charge. Or, I can recommend you to another doctor in the area. But—I am not that baby's father."

Victoria wanted to run, to get as far away from Buck as possible. There was no reason a woman would accuse a man of being the father of her baby if it weren't true. Especially if that man was nearly a stranger to her.

"Oh, yes you are," the woman said in a near scream. "Don't try to deny it. This is your baby and you're going to have to take care of it. I don't want no baby. Never did!"

Once again, in that calm voice that had come to irritate Victoria, Buck told the woman, "I am not the father, Bonnie. There is no way I could be. You and I have never been together except right here in this office, and I have a policy of never examining a woman patient without one of my nurses present." He rose to his feet. "Now, why don't you just go and we'll forget about this whole thing.

I think you're just overwrought. You need to take care of both yourself and that baby. I'll have my nurse fix you up with some vitamins, and I suggest you take them regularly from now until time for the birth."

How can he be so matter-of-fact? Victoria asked herself as she watched the scene. Either he's innocent or he's very good at covering up his actions.

But the woman wasn't so easily appeased. "Either you admit your paternity, or I'm going to make sure everyone in Anchorage knows you're the father of my baby and you've refused to help me."

Buck had obviously had it. He took the woman by the arm and ushered her out of his office and out the side door. "Look, I'm not about to be conned. I don't know why you're doing this, but I am not the father of that child, and I refuse to take the responsibility for it. Tell anyone you want. If necessary, I'll meet you in court. Now, get out of here and don't come back!" Buck slammed the door.

"Are you?" Victoria asked, still not convinced the woman was lying.

Buck seemed surprised. "The father? Of course not. I can't believe you'd even consider that I am."

Victoria had to get away. After telling the head nurse she was leaving for the day, Victoria headed for the Lodge. Fortunately, both Ron and Abigale were out, and she was able to go directly to her room without talking to anyone. Her tears were just beneath the surface, and it was only once she'd locked the door behind her that she was able to let them free.

Bonnie Connor was a fairly attractive woman, as attractive as any woman could be at nearly nine months pregnant. And she seemed relatively intelligent. Why would she make up such a story? Her story haunted her and she could feel the pain and agony Bonnie was suffering—if she were telling the truth. Victoria's memories of her lover's denial filled her mind, and although it hurt her deeply, she found herself mistrusting Buck more than the woman, as her sympathy leaned toward the woman so great with child. *Oh, Buck, like Armando, you've let me down. Just when I was beginning to—to love you.*

❧

A rap sounded on her door at five o'clock. "Tori, are you in there? Open the door, I have to talk to you. Tori?" The rap sounded again. Louder this time.

The last thing she wanted to do at that moment was talk to Buck. "Go away."

"No, I'm not leaving until you open this door."

"Go away, Buck."

"You open this door right now or I'll break it down."

"You wouldn't dare."

"I'm going to count to three, Tori. One. Two—"

She hurried to the door, twisted the safety bolt, and flung it open wide. "All right, the door's open. What do you want?"

He pushed past her, his eyes blazing. "I want to know why you left like that.

If I hadn't had a waiting room full of patients I'd have come after you. Surely you didn't believe that woman's story."

She slammed the door. "Why shouldn't I believe her? You think women go around accusing men of fathering their children without just reason?"

"She did. She's crazy," Buck shouted in his defense.

"She's desperate, Buck. Can't you see that? Men should take responsibility and face up to it instead of leading a woman on and then deserting her after—" She stopped, afraid if she said one more word, she wouldn't be able to hold back her tears any longer.

"After what?"

"After—after—oh, you know what I mean. Don't make me spell it out for you."

Buck shook his head in exasperation as he paced about the room. "I can't understand how you can take the side of a woman you don't even know."

"Because I've been there, Buck!" The words slipped out before she could stop them.

He stopped dead in his tracks. "Been where? I don't get it."

She had to figure out a way to explain her words. She couldn't let him think she'd been promiscuous. "I mean, I have a friend whose boyfriend left her when he found out she was pregnant. She—she stayed with me for awhile. I saw how miserable she was, facing her pregnancy alone."

"The rat didn't help her at all?"

She bit her lip. Lying had never been easy for her. "He denied being the father."

"The jerk."

She moved to the door. "I'd just as soon you'd leave, Buck."

He followed her but paused in the doorway. "You don't believe me, do you?"

"I—I don't know what to believe at this point. Please just go. I'd like to be left alone."

An angry look covered Buck's face as his hand grasped the doorknob. "Look, I don't have to prove myself to anyone. Not even you. Believe what you want." And he stormed out.

≈

Victoria gave Buck her two weeks' notice at the clinic. She decided she would leave Anchorage at the end of the month and return home to Kansas City, despite Jonathan's pleas that they stay. Her mother and Ron seemed quite happy, and Victoria knew her mother was in good hands. Abigale loved Alaska and, more importantly, she loved Ron. And he loved her. Their marriage was good.

Victoria kept her distance from Buck, her illusion shattered. As far as she knew, Bonnie Connor had left him alone.

Exactly one week before she was scheduled to leave, Buck invited her and

Jonathan to go along with him and Micah on his monthly visit to the bush country. She refused, not wanting to be anywhere near the man. But when she saw her son's disappointment, she relented.

It was the first time she'd ridden in Buck's little seaplane and she had to admit he was a good pilot, although she white-knuckled the skinny armrest all the way.

It seemed hundreds of Indian people were there to greet them when they landed, all with smiling faces, all glad to see Dr. Silverbow.

"I could use your help," he told her as he pulled box after box from the cargo area of the little plane. "Sometimes my nurse comes along to help."

She nodded, not knowing exactly what she was getting into, but willing to lend a hand.

"We'll set all this stuff up on the little table over there by that hut," he instructed. "And bring that small metal case from behind the front seat."

Within fifteen minutes Buck was examining people, giving them the medicine he'd brought with him, administering shots to newborn babies, listening to the elderly complain about their rheumatism, and checking pregnant women. In exchange for his services, some people gave him beads, another a handmade leather belt, one a hand-carved statue of an eagle. Several others gave him animal pelts, and some gave him nothing but a toothless smile of thanks. Even Victoria received a gift—a colorful bead necklace one of the Indian woman had woven.

"They're a proud people," he told her when they had a slight break. "I don't expect any pay. I've told them that, but they want to pay for my services even though most of them have little of this world's goods. To refuse to accept these things would insult them."

Victoria helped where she could while Micah and Jonathan played with the Indian boys. She smiled as she watched them dart between the humble dwellings. Even the language barrier didn't keep them from having fun with the Indian children.

Watching Buck amazed her. His dedication was tireless. He greeted patients as if each were most important, taking time to listen to them, encouraging them, and being their friend. Is he living a double life? Or is Bonnie Connor falsely accusing him, and he's as honorable as he appears on the surface?

When it was time to board the little plane and head for home, Micah and Jonathan were nowhere to be found.

"They said they was gonna go exploring," an Indian boy who looked to be about fourteen said. He pointed toward a huge mound of boulders off in the distance. "I told them they better hadn't go, but Micah said it'd be okay."

Buck looked quickly at his watch. "If we don't get out of here within the next hour, we won't make it until morning. Too dangerous to take off after dark in a seaplane."

"Normally Jonathan would have asked my permission to go off like that," she told Buck. "This isn't like him."

"Don't panic," he said calmly. But Victoria saw the concern in his eyes. He was as frightened as she was.

She bit her lip. Her heart pounded with alarm. "I'm trying not to panic, honest I am, but where could they have gone? And why aren't they back? You'd told them what time you had to leave, and both boys were wearing watches."

"Don't know, Tori. But I'm going after them. You stay here with—"

She grabbed onto his sleeve. "Oh, no you don't. I'm going with you."

"No," he said firmly, pulling from her grasp. "They may still be here in the village. I'll take some of the men with me, and you find a couple of the women to help you go door to door. They may be in one of the huts playing with some of the children."

His idea seemed best at the moment, and already women in the group were beginning to volunteer to help her.

Victoria's voice quivered. "All right, but hurry, Buck. Our boys may have lost their sense of direction and be wandering around trying to find their way back."

"And they may be right here," he assured her as he moved away, signaling several of the men to join him. "Don't worry, I'm sure they're fine."

Fine? In this strange place? Victoria watched Buck issue orders to the men, telling them to move off in different directions.

The door-to-door search yielded nothing. No one had seen the boys in over two hours. Victoria was frantic. Even though several women invited her to come into their homes, she refused. She had to stay by the little plane in case their boys came running back.

By ten, there had been no sign of the boys. The night air had become quite cool, and an older man, whom Buck had treated earlier that very day, had built a small fire at the edge of the clearing where she could warm herself as she sat on a log and waited.

I should've gone with him. She fingered the bead necklace the woman had placed about Victoria's neck and listened to the night sounds crowding in all around her. *Why do I always let a man dominate my thinking?*

Suddenly male voices pierced the eerie silence as Buck and the members of his search party stepped out of the darkness.

"Did you find them?" Victoria screamed as she ran toward him, searching the group for the two small boys.

Buck didn't have to answer. The look on his face said it all as he shook his head sadly.

She flung herself into his arms and began to cry. "Oh, Buck. What are we going to do?"

His shoulders slumped in defeat. "Not much else we can do tonight, except keep the fire going and hope they find their way back."

After giving words of encouragement, one by one the others left for their homes, leaving the couple alone by the fire.

Her eyes widened and she began to beat upon his chest with her fists. "This is all your fault. If you hadn't insisted we come up here—"

He grabbed her wrists and held them tightly in his big hands. "Okay, Tori, blame me if it makes you feel any better. But right now it really doesn't make a whole lot of difference whose fault it is that we're here. What is important is that our boys are missing."

She quit struggling, knowing he was right. And she knew it was no more his fault than it was hers. She was the one who had said yes when he'd invited them. She could have said no. "I'm sorry. It's just that I'm so worried."

He loosened his grip and pulled her into his arms. "Me too. Micah has never done anything like this before. He's older. He should have known better."

"Is there nothing we can do?" Victoria asked with frustration as she leaned into the strength of his warm body.

"Nothing but wait for dawn. The terrain here is too dangerous to search at night."

"But the boys—"

"Remember, Tori, Micah is an Alaskan. He's hunted with me many times. Hopefully, he'll remember the things I've taught him, and he'll find a secure place for them to spend the night. He knows we'll be looking for them at dawn."

"Secure place?" she asked, her eyes damp with tears. "Out there?"

"Like between a couple of old logs or in between big rocks. He knows what to look for to keep. . ."

Again, panic set in. "Keep what?"

Buck looked as if he wished he hadn't started that sentence. "W–warm," he stammered. She knew that was not what he intended to say.

She pushed away from him. "Away from wild animals! That's what you were going to say, wasn't it?"

"Yes. I was going to say wild animals, but it isn't likely they'll meet up with any."

She knew he was trying to cover up the danger the boys might be in, for her sake. "I know they're scared, and they only had on sweaters. They'll freeze out there."

"Now, Tori," he said, his voice low and soothing, "don't worry so much. They'll probably huddle together, maybe even cover up with some pine branches. They may be asleep even now."

Her hands rubbed at her forehead. "But Jonathan is only seven. He's never—"

Buck wrapped his long arms about her and rested his bearded chin in her hair. "But Micah has. He and I have camped out many times. He knows what to do."

She relaxed a bit and leaned against Buck. Only moments before she'd felt chilled to the bone, her nerves jangled with fright. "He's all I've got," she explained as the two stood there in front of the fire, their silhouettes reflecting on the little plane parked in the middle of the clearing. "I don't know what I'd do if I lost him."

"Shh, none of that kind of talk. The men will be back at the crack of dawn and we'll find them, I promise you."

She let out a big sigh. "Don't make promises you might not be able to deliver. That's what people have been doing to me all my life."

"Well," he said in a hushed tone as he planted a kiss on her forehead, "Buck Silverbow doesn't make a practice of making promises he can't keep. You have to trust me, Tori. We'll find them."

"I'll try, Buck. But my luck with men who've made promises hasn't been too good."

He took her hand and led her to a huge log near the blazing fire. "I'm going to get the little blanket I carry in my plane. Sit here. I'll be right back."

She dropped onto the ground and wrapped her arms about her legs and watched as he walked to the plane and back, so tall, strong, and confident. Perhaps he was right. Perhaps the boys would be all right until dawn.

He sat down beside her and wrapped the blanket of red, green, and blue about both their shoulders, cocooning the two of them.

Neither felt sleepy as they stared silently into the flames of the fire. They watched it flicker and sparks spiral into the air.

"You must be frightened too, Buck. You've already lost your wife and your mother. . ." Victoria's voice trailed off. She gulped as words failed her.

"I'm not losing Micah," he said in a soft, but firm voice. "Don't even think like that."

"But it could happen. There are a dozen things that could have happened to the boys. Aren't there bears up here?"

"Sure, there are bears, but the boys probably didn't have any food with them. Or if they did, they probably ate it earlier. That's what attracts bears—food."

"How about wolves?"

"Yes, there are wolves, but they aren't interested in two little boys," he told her, as if she'd asked a foolish question.

"You're not lying to me, are you?" she asked, her eyes misty with concern. "Just to make me feel better?"

He pulled her closer. "Cold?"

"Don't change the subject."

"No, I'm not lying to you. How many stories on the news have you heard about bears or wolves attacking little boys?"

She thought about it a bit, and he was right, she hadn't heard any. But then, she lived in Kansas City. Would news stories of that sort reach all the way from Anchorage, Alaska, to Kansas City?

"There's more bears and wolves up around Denali National Park than there are near here," he assured her. Buck nestled his chin in her hair. "At least there are no snakes in Alaska."

"Do you suppose God is punishing us?"

Buck appeared thoughtful. "Could be. What makes you say that?"

"Because I deserve punishment, I guess."

"No more than I do."

"But you're a fine man, Buck. You're a good father and a great doctor. Just look at all the good you did today for these people. Other than trying to be a good mother, I'm of no value to anyone."

The tip of his finger lifted her chin. "I'd say that's about the most important job in the world, and it looks to me as if you're doing a mighty fine job of it. That Jonathan's a great kid. You should be very proud of what you've accomplished with him. And alone, to boot."

"But, you don't know the real me. I've made such a mess of my life."

"I find it hard to believe that, Tori."

"I broke my parents' hearts by deceiving them when I was in college. I dated a boy they knew was trouble, but would I listen to them? No. I sneaked around behind their backs and lied about where and with whom I was going. Just to be near him," she confessed tearfully.

"You're not the first girl to do that."

"But I'd never defied my parents before. I was always that good little girl, the one that never did anything wrong. Until I met Armando."

"Is he Jonathan's father?"

She nodded. "Yes."

"Ah, you two had to get married?"

She sat up straight. "No, it was nothing like that."

"Then how was it?"

She blinked her eyes and swallowed hard. "Guess you deserve to know the truth, now that we're related. Since you and Ron are part of our family now, it'll all come out at one time or another."

"I got plenty of time to listen." He leaned back onto the log and pulled her back with him, cradling her in his long arms.

"I'll leave out all the gory details. I'm sure you don't want to hear those."

He grinned. "Suit yourself. It's your story. Tell it any way you like."

She sucked in a deep breath and let it out slowly. "When I went off to college, my parents reminded me of the usual things. You know, the birds and bees story and how I should be careful and not get into any compromising situations; that sort of stuff. And I believed them and fully intended to take their advice. At first I only dated the guys with whom I'd gone to high school. But one night as I was walking back to my dorm, this car pulled up beside me, and I immediately recognized the man who was driving. Everyone on campus knew him. He had come to the States from Acapulco to attend college. His dad was some kind of ambassador or something, and very wealthy. Armando was the star tackle on our football team. Well, anyway, he offered me a ride, and I was so flattered by him paying attention to me, a little freshman, I accepted."

"Not a smart move, huh?"

"Things were okay then. And next, he invited me to a movie. I really thought I was big stuff, and again I accepted. We had a great time. He was funny, attentive, and polite. When I told my folks about him, my dad immediately asked me what the man saw in me that made me special. It was a fair question, only I took it as an insult. Both Mom and Dad tried to tell me it was a little unusual for a star football player to be interested in a freshman girl, unless he was looking at her as an easy target. They told me to stay away from him."

"Wow, your dad didn't pull any punches, did he?" Buck whistled. "Bet that set up your dander."

She offered a feeble laugh. "Sure did. I stormed out of there and decided I'd date Armando and never let them know. Well, to make a long story short, we dated constantly for the next few weeks. He drove a brand new Mercedes convertible; believe me, all my friends were envious. I really thought I was something. I practically deserted my friends. Everything in my life revolved around Armando."

"I think I know where this is leading."

"I wish I'd been that perceptive." She sighed. "Well, to go on—I had visions of standing by Armando's side at his graduation, then the two of us going off to Acapulco to be married in wedded bliss the rest of our lives. I thought I'd live in a fine home—you get the picture."

"Didn't quite work out that way?"

"No, not at all. One night after we'd been to a party where Armando had had a bit too much to drink, he drove us to a deserted spot and began to kiss me. I loved his kisses, but that is as far as we'd ever gone. Even though I was in awe of him, I'd made it clear from the beginning I was a virgin and intended to stay that way until I was married."

"And he went along with it?"

She paused thoughtfully. "Yes. I thought he respected me for it. But that night, he came on strong, and I tried to tell him to stop—"

"But he wouldn't?" Buck interjected.

"No. I told him no over and over, but he was like an animal and way too strong for me. He—" She wiped her eyes. "He forced me, Buck. And he really hurt me."

Buck's fingers stroked her hair. "I'm so sorry."

She continued. "Afterward, he acted like it was all a joke and said I'd seduced him. He warned me if I said anything to anyone, he'd deny it and all his buddies would back him up on his story. They'd all say they had—" She began to cry uncontrollably.

"You don't need to say it. I get the message. What a bunch of scumbags. It's guys like them that make it hard on the rest of us. No wonder women don't trust men when they hear stories like that."

"After that night, Armando totally ignored me. It was like he didn't even know my name. And all his buddies made snide, sexy comments to me. And then I realized I was pregnant."

"And you two had to get married and then got a divorce later?"

"No. I wish that was the way it turned out. He spit in my face and called me awful names. He said he was going to go back to Acapulco to marry his high school sweetheart, and he never wanted to hear from me again. He refused to even acknowledge he might be the father of my baby. He even accused me of being with a lot of other guys. But honest, Buck, he was the only one, and it was only that one time. I wanted to die."

"Oh, you poor thing. What did your parents say?"

She twisted at the little ring on her pinkie finger. "Of course, they were devastated and Daddy said, 'I warned you.' But they stood behind me. Some of my relatives suggested abortion, but I couldn't do that. I was a real embarrassment to my parents, I know. And I was so ashamed, I could barely hold up my head."

"So, you had little Jonathan?"

She nodded. "I'd considered letting him be adopted by a couple in our church. I was so young, naïve, and certainly not equipped for motherhood. But the closer it came time for him to be born, the more I felt I would be the best one to raise him." She sighed. "Someone else might have made another choice. But that seemed to be the best way for me. It wasn't easy, though."

"Tough, huh?"

"At times."

"And he was born with that twisted foot? That must have made it even harder."

"To this day I think Jonathan's foot was God's way of punishing me." She blotted her tears on the edge of the fluffy blanket.

Buck stared into the fire. "I understand that feeling. That's the way I felt when Claudette drove our car onto the track in front of that oncoming train."

"It's not the same, Buck. You hadn't done anything to deserve that kind of punishment. I went against everything my parents had taught me, and against all the things I'd learned from the Bible since childhood."

"You didn't know me then, Tori. All I could think about was success—as a doctor. I had plans to move to Vancouver and open a large clinic, then on to Seattle to open a second one. I wanted my clinics to be on the cutting edge of medicine. I wanted the name Dr. Buck Silverbow to be a household word. I loved my family, but I rarely spent any time with them. I was too busy attending this conference and that convention, rubbing elbows with some of the great names in the field of medicine."

"I didn't know. I assumed you'd always wanted to be right where you are."

"Well, shows how much you know about me. When we were first married, I was a deacon in the church, on the board, the man everyone called when there was a need. Then I got this dream and I left it all to go after it. When Micah was born, I told myself I was building this medical empire for him, the son who would follow in my footsteps. I planned to leave him a legacy. But I left him and my wife behind, alone, while I put in endless hours at my little clinic and worked at being a big shot."

"And how did your wife feel about that?"

"She hated it. She never wanted any more than what we had right here in Anchorage. She begged me to forget my dream. But old smarty-pants me, I ignored her requests and forged ahead. I missed a lot of Micah's growing up years, years I now regret."

A frown of confusion clouded her face. "Do you regret the Bonnie Connor thing?"

His eyes narrowed as his voice boomed into the darkness and she knew immediately she'd said the wrong thing. "You mean fathering her baby? What do I have to do to make you believe me? I had nothing to do with that woman. At any time."

"Too bad we can't see the future before we make our mistakes, isn't it?" she said sadly, refusing to answer his question, still not convinced he was telling the truth.

He bristled. "Look, I don't have to prove my innocence to anyone. Not even you. I did nothing wrong. And I have to be honest with you, Tori, it makes my blood boil to think you'd even consider that I might be that baby's father."

"She'll probably insist on a paternity test," she shot back defensively. "Then what'll you do?"

He stared into the fire, its red glow reflecting the anger in his eyes. "That'd be a ridiculous move. She knows I'm not the father." His eyes suddenly riveted on her face. "Unlike some people I know."

His words hurt. She really wanted to believe him, but she couldn't shake the lump of doubt that still lingered in her heart.

"Look," he said with a sigh as he tucked the blanket closer about her neck, "for now, let's forget about Bonnie Connor. We need to focus on finding Micah and Jonathan."

"Oh, Buck, we can't lose our boys," she said with deep emotion, she, too, wanting to put their differences to rest.

"I know."

"I wish there was something we could do tonight. I can't bear the thought of them out there, alone in the dark."

Buck's hand stroked at his mustache. "I guess if we were on praying ground, we could pray."

She lowered her head, her voice barely audible. "I've tried to live as a Christian, attended church and all, but I haven't honestly prayed for years. I've been too mad at God."

"Seems we're two peas in a pod." He let out a long, low whistle. "I'd pray, but I don't think He wants to hear my prayers."

"Same here. How did I ever get so far from God?"

"You know, Tori, I remember standing at that altar when Claudette and I were married and thanking God for such a beautiful, Christian woman. I promised Him I'd take care of her and be the kind of husband she deserved. Then I broke that promise."

She allowed one finger to idly scrawl her son's name in the dirt as they sat on the ground. "And as a teenager I promised God I would serve Him as a missionary. I sure goofed on that one."

"I remember Dad telling me God is a forgiving God. All we have to do is ask. Wonder if it's really that simple?"

"That's what Mom told me when I told her about my pregnancy. She said God would forgive anything if we ask. But—"

"But what?"

"I never asked. I felt too unworthy."

"Me neither. I'd sunk too low. I knew a just God would condemn me for failing Him and my family."

Buck rose to his feet, poked the fire with a stick, and added new logs. The fire crackled and snapped. "We could try."

She stared up at him. "You mean it? Pray?"

"Guess it's worth a try."

"Do you think He'll be interested in hearing from us?"

"Got a better idea?"

She shook her head. "One of the verses I learned as a child said if we confess our sins, He is faithful and just to forgive them and to cleanse us from all unrighteousness, or something like that. I haven't confessed my sin to Him—the sin of disobedience to Him and to my parents, and the sin of dating a man I knew I should not be dating."

"And I never told Him I was sorry for turning my back on Him and being so angry with Him for taking Claudette and my mom from me."

"I think we have to do that before we can even begin to ask Him to protect our boys and safely bring them home to us."

Buck nodded. He extended a hand and pulled Victoria to her feet. "I'll start, but you have to jump in and help me if I need it. I haven't talked to God in a long time. I'm not sure if I remember how to do it."

"I think it'd be best if we knelt." Victoria smiled and she felt a certain peace.

The two knelt by the fire, wrapped in one another's arms as Buck lifted his face skyward. "Lord, this is Buck. I never did tell You how sorry I am for acting the way I did, putting everything in the world before You. Sometimes when I'm unable to sleep, I think things over. I don't know why You allowed Claudette and Mom to die, but I'm sorry for blaming You for their deaths. Folks have told me You have a plan and every right to do what You want. There's no reason You'd share that plan with me. But please, God, forgive me for being such a sinner and for turning away from You.

"And now," Buck squeezed Victoria's hand, "I'm coming to You to ask a favor. Be with my boy and with Jonathan—wherever they are. Protect them from anything that would harm them. Most of all, God, keep them from being scared. I love You, God, and I promise I'll read Your Word and talk to You more often.

"And now Tori wants to talk to You. She's a good woman, God. Please listen to her and grant her prayer. She's a great mom."

Moved by Buck's prayer, it was all Victoria could do to keep her composure as she began. "Lord, I'm such a sinner. From the time I was a small child, I've loved You and wanted to serve You—on the mission field, as a teacher, or wherever You wanted to use me. But I failed You. I turned away from You, and look where it got me. And as much as I love my son, each time I look into his precious face I see my sin staring back at me. He looks so much like his father. But I must confess, Lord, if I had to do it all over and go through all I've gone through just to have Jonathan in my life, I'd do it. Sin and all, because I love him so much." She took in a gulp of air and let it slowly escape. It helped her to keep from crying.

"You had a Son. You have to know how I feel about mine. He is the result of my sin, God. The sin I have never confessed to You. I was too proud and too ashamed. Please forgive me of my sins as You promise in Your Word.

"And now, please bring Jonathan and Micah safely back to us." She felt Buck's fingers tighten over hers once again. "And be with Buck. He's lost his wife and mother, and he needs comforting. Make Yourself real to him. To both of us. I'm not much good at praying, but I want You to know I do love You, God, even though I've acted like a spoiled brat. Thank You for listening. Amen."

"Amen," Buck echoed. He threw his arms around Victoria in a big bear hug. "I think He heard us. What do you think?"

"I know He heard us," she said with renewed confidence. "Now I guess we just have to trust that one way or another our boys are in His hands."

"I agree."

"So, now what do we do?" She surveyed the darkness around them.

"We wait until morning, which is only a few hours away."

"But the boys—"

Buck sat down against the log and motioned for her to join him. "I'll bet our boys are hunkered down somewhere wondering what we're doing. They'll be fine, Tori. We've placed them in God's hands now."

Chapter 9

The men began gathering even before dawn, carrying pickaxes, ropes, and other items that might be needed to find the boys.

"I'm going with you." Victoria rose to her feet, stretched, and ran her fingers through her hair. Her whole body ached from her sleepless night in Buck's arms, leaning against the log. She could only begin to imagine how he felt, but to look at him you could never tell he, too, had spent a sleepless night. He was a bundle of nervous energy, anxious to get started.

"No, it'd be better if you stayed here. We'll be walking on some pretty uneven terrain, and I have no idea how many miles we'll walk before we find them."

She perceived his advice to be an outright order, and she straightened her shoulders. "Oh, no you don't. You're not leaving me behind. I have as much at stake in this as you do. My son is out there too."

An understanding smile curved Buck's lips. "Okay, but stay close to me, and be careful. I wouldn't want anything happening to you. You're too important to me—and Micah."

She fell in step behind him, her eyes scanning the approaching horizon for any sign of the two children.

"Don't worry, missy," a toothless old man told her as they moved along. "We'll find them. For Doc."

They walked for nearly two hours before stopping to rest. Victoria was exhausted, but she'd never admit it.

❧

Buck knew Tori was tired, and he wished they could linger longer, but they had to move on. He'd never let her know, but he was greatly concerned for the boys' safety. There were dangers out there she'd never even imagined. Most of the night, after confessing his sins to God and asking for forgiveness, he'd spent in silent prayer. It felt good to pray again. He'd forgotten the comfort prayer could bring.

"Here, take a drink of water." He passed his canteen to her and watched as she took large gulps.

"We'd better go on," one of the Native American men told him in a whisper.

Buck assembled the group, but before they continued the search he invited them to pray with him. Some bowed their heads, but most stared at him in disbelief, as if wondering why a man would take time for such foolishness when his boy's life was at risk.

He pulled off his hat and reached for Victoria's hand, then lifted his face heavenward. "Father God, it's me again. Once more I bring our request to You for our children's safe return to us. Wherever they are, comfort them and make them know we're coming to find them. Please, God, lead us in the right direction. And we'll praise You, I promise. Amen."

The smile on Victoria's face melted his heart as he forged ahead, her hand in his.

An hour later, Buck lifted his hand and the party came to a halt while he prayed a second time.

A little farther up the trail, they found Jonathan's backpack hanging on a tree branch. "They probably knew they were lost and left that as a sign to us they'd gone this way," Buck said excitedly as he handed the bag to Victoria, his faith renewed. "This is the first clue we've found."

She held it close and took it as a sign from God.

They continued on, slipping and sliding on the jagged rocks. One of the men took Buck aside, and although Victoria was too far away to hear their conversation, from the look on Buck's face she could tell he was worried.

"What? What did he say?" she asked as she worked her way over the rocks to his side.

"Better you don't know."

She tugged on his shirt. "Tell me this instant!"

He lifted both palms toward her. "Okay, I'll tell you, but promise me you won't get upset. Remember, we've turned our children over to God."

"I promise. Just tell me."

"He said we are heading in the direction of a deep, jagged crevice. That if it was dark when the boys reached it, they—"

She gasped and looked as though she were going to faint. Buck grabbed her and held her close. "Tori, don't. We're not even sure they came this way. They may have taken a turn where we found Jonathan's bag. God, Tori, trust in God."

His words were consoling, but inwardly, he was even more frightened than she. He'd flown over that area, he knew how treacherous it was. If the boys—Buck willed himself to forget about the what-ifs.

Finally, they reached the area above the menacing crevice, but the boys weren't there.

"We'd better turn back and go the other way," one of the men told Buck. "The boys aren't here."

"Hold on." Buck fell to one knee and bowed his head. "God, I need Your help. Give me wisdom and guidance. Show me the way to go."

"Better hurry," the man said. "Those boys are probably hungry and cold."

"Not yet," Buck told the man with a glance toward Victoria, who was standing a few yards back where he'd told her to stay. With that, he lifted his head high, put two fingers in his mouth and let out a loud shrill whistle that seemed to split the sky. And then he listened. "If Micah hears that, he'll whistle back. It's kind of our code."

Nothing.

Again, he whistled.

Again, nothing.

"Oh, Buck," Victoria cried out as her hands flew to cover her face. "Where are they?"

One more time, Buck lifted his fingers to his mouth.

Somewhere off in the distance a faint sound echoed back, an exact repeat of the sound Buck had made.

"It's him!" Buck shouted with joy. "Tori, we've found them!"

"Which way did the sound come from?" the Native American asked as he turned his head from side to side.

"Oh, Buck, whistle again," Victoria pleaded, her face aglow with happiness that they'd located their sons.

Again, Buck whistled.

This time the sound that echoed back was a little stronger.

"Son! Where are you?" Buck hollered, his big hands cupped around his mouth.

"Down here," the answer came back faintly but clearly.

Victoria let out a loud gasp and grabbed onto one of the men for support.

"Dear God, they've fallen into the ravine," Buck exclaimed as he moved quickly toward the edge, trying to look over the side.

"Buck, be careful," she shouted, reaching toward him. "I can't lose you too!"

"Toss me a rope," he called, and one of the men quickly pulled a long coil of rope from his shoulder and threw it toward Buck. Three other men moved as close to the edge as they dared and held onto one end while Buck tied the other end about his waist.

"I'll go. You stay," a short muscular man told Buck as he cautiously climbed across the rocks and tried to take the rope from Buck's hand. "I'm used to climbing on rock. You're not."

But Buck wouldn't hear of it. It was his son who was down there.

"Ask him if he knows where Jonathan is," Victoria called out, afraid her son might be down there with Micah and possibly hurt.

"Is Jonathan with you?" Buck called out as he began his descent over the rocks at the head of the crevice.

"Yes, I'm here," came a frightened seven-year-old voice.

"Oh, are you all right?" Victoria called as loudly as she could.

"My arm hurts really bad," the child answered.

"How about you, Micah? Are you all right?" Buck yelled out as he began his descent, disappearing over the edge of the ledge as the three men held onto the rope.

"I think I broke my ankle," he answered back weakly. Everyone who heard him could hear the pain in his voice.

"Pull me up," Buck shouted from over the ledge. "Quick!"

From the look on his face as he appeared, it was obvious there was a problem.

"Rope's not long enough. They're way down there, on a ledge." He stood to his feet, giving the men a well-deserved rest from holding his weight.

"I've got a rope." The muscular man hurried forward, taking the loop of rope from his shoulder and tossed it to Buck.

Buck smiled and carefully knotted the new rope to the one that was tied about his waist. "Let's give it another shot."

"Could you see them?" Victoria asked, relieved they were alive.

"Yes, but they're a long way down there. Good thing that ledge was there or they'd be—" He stopped. "God was with them, Tori."

She smiled at him. "I know. I've been thanking Him."

A fourth man joined the others in holding the rope and Buck disappeared over the side again, this time descending hand over hand.

If only I could get near enough the edge to see them, Victoria reasoned as she warily moved forward.

"You stay there," the fifth man said firmly. "It's too dangerous."

She yielded to his command, knowing it was for her good.

It seemed an eternity before Buck surfaced again. "Any more rope?"

They all shook their heads.

"You still can't reach them?" Victoria asked as panic froze her to the spot.

"No, the rope is a good twelve feet too short." He dropped onto one of the flatter-topped rocks, his head in his hands. "Oh, God, show me what to do."

The search party stood staring at the man. No one had any suggestions. Suddenly, Buck stood to his feet and pulled his belt from his trouser loops, the belt one of the Native Americans had given him in exchange for his medical services the day before. "Anyone else have a strong leather belt?"

A taller man who had pretty much remained silent offered his. Buck fastened them together and slung the looped belts over one shoulder. "Hang on tight, men. I'm going to bring them up."

"How?" Victoria hollered as he was about to disappear over the edge.

"Just have faith in me and pray."

She breathed a frantic plea to God. If anyone could rescue the boys, she knew it would be Buck. Even if he had to lay down his life to do it.

❧

Buck reached the end of the rope, his feet dangling a good thirteen or fourteen feet over the boys. With one foot he kicked away from the rocky surface and swung himself nearly three feet to the left where he caught hold of a small tree growing out of the rock and held onto it. Once he was securely latched onto the tree, he let go of the rope.

"Dad, be careful," Micah called up to him.

Buck turned to look down at the boys who were perched on a small ledge, maybe six feet square, and beneath them lay the deep crevice yawning out at them like a hungry bear. One slip and he could drop past the ledge that held them and into that waiting vee of jagged rock. He lifted his face heavenward. "God, if I ever needed strength, it's now. Be my strength as You've promised."

Adjusting the looped belts that hung from his shoulder, Buck began to make his way down the jagged wall. He stepped on small bits of rock protruding out of the rocky surface, and his fingertips clung to other rocks.

Once, a rock holding his foot gave way and it bounced onto the ledge and ricocheted into the crevice. Buck held on with his fingertips and one foot, until he located another small rock on which to place his foot. The terrified boys covered their eyes.

"I'm okay, boys. I'm coming to get you. Don't be afraid." He tried to sound as if getting them would be an easy task, but at that point he wasn't sure his plan would work or that he would have the strength to carry it out. Unless God intervened.

At last, he reached the ledge and the arms of two little boys circled his neck and held on for dear life. "I'm gonna get you out of here, but first I want to check out each of you. That was quite a fall you had." It didn't take him long to realize his son's ankle was broken. And although Jonathan was in great pain with his arm, Buck was fairly confident it wasn't broken, just badly sprained, with much of the skin ripped off.

"Hey," he said, forcing a smile of encouragement, knowing much was going to be required of the two young boys in the next few minutes, "you're both going to be fine, but you're going to have to do exactly as I say. We'll be on top soon, and we'll get some food in those empty bellies of yours. I'll bet you're hungry."

Both boys nodded, their dirty faces streaked with tears, their clothing torn and tattered.

Buck stopped long enough to catch his breath and survey the path he must take to scale the steep cliff. Finally, he took hold of Jonathan. "Look, Jonathan, I'm going to take you up first since you're the lightest."

He slipped an arm about his son. "Micah, I promise I'll get you out of here. Just be patient and don't move until I get back down for you. I'm going to take Jonathan up, then take a minute to catch my breath, and I'll be back. Understand?"

Micah shook his head, his round eyes filled with fright.

"I love you, Micah. I don't tell you that often enough, but things are going to be different from now on. You're my special boy. Never forget it."

Buck turned to the younger boy. "Jonathan, I want you to climb on my back.

I'm going to wrap these belts around your waist and mine and I want you to put your arms around my neck and hold on as tight as you can. I know your arm hurts but you have to do it. Whatever you do, don't let go."

Jonathan did as he was told, but Buck could feel the little boy's body tremble. "I know you're in pain, but this is the only way I can get us all out of here."

With the little boy strapped to his back, slowly Buck stood to his feet. He placed his hands and feet on the rocks he had selected to carry them up to the little tree protruding from the rock.

Each step was agony. The rocks looked secure, but he felt them pull away and roll down the face of the crevice. "Don't look down," he told Jonathan. "Look up. Your mom is up there waiting for us."

"I will," the young voice answered.

Finally, Buck and Jonathan reached the tree. Buck leaned out as far as he could, but he couldn't reach the end of the rope. "Hey, up there. Swing the rope a bit so I can grab hold."

The men responded immediately and on the third swing, Buck grabbed it. The top looked miles away, but one look down told him he had no choice. He had to make it.

"Here we go. Hang on," he told the child one last time and began to ascend the rope, hand over hand, pulling them both up with sheer brute strength, occasionally finding a niche or a rock where he could get a momentary footing. Finally, he reached the top and was greeted with cheers from the men and tears of joy and thankfulness from Victoria.

"Oh, Buck, you did it," she said as he made his way toward her and unstrapped her son from his back. She threw her arms around Buck's neck and smothered him with kisses. "I love you, I love you, I love you!" Then she gathered Jonathan in her arms and held him close, tears flowing down her cheeks.

"What about Micah?" she asked, finally realizing he'd left his son down on the ledge to bring up her son.

"Be careful with his arm," Buck told her. Then he added with a grin, "I'm going after Micah now."

"I'll go," the muscular man told him. "You're tired. It's too much to go again."

Buck stood proud and tall, his face scratched and bleeding from his climb. "He's my son, I'll bring him up. You men hold the ropes."

"But are you sure you have the strength to make the trip again?" Still cradling her son, Victoria knew she would never forgive herself for allowing him to bring Jonathan up first if anything happened to Micah. Buck has already lost his wife and mother—could he survive losing Micah? She shuddered as she considered the possibility. Or what if neither of them makes it back to the top?

The determined man drank water from the canteen he'd given to Victoria, slung the leather belts over his shoulder, and began his trek down the face of the steep cliff.

"He'll make it, missy," the toothless man told her as he helped the other men hold onto the rope. "Doc's a good man, and he's as strong as an ox."

Buck rappelled himself as far down the crevice's evil face as he could, then slowly lowered himself to the near end of the rope. His breathing was labored; he'd expended more energy than he'd realized hauling Jonathan up on his back. Once again, he pushed off the wall with his foot and swung to the left until his hand was able to grasp the tree. He wrapped his leg over the sturdiest branch and turned the rope loose, lingering only long enough to catch his breath before scaling the remaining distance, one scary step at a time. It became more and more difficult to find places to secure himself as rocks shifted beneath his feet.

"Dad, be careful," Micah called up to Buck.

Buck could hear the fear in Micah's voice and it chilled his heart. "I'm coming, son. Dad's almost there." He chose to not look down, knowing the deep canyon below would only unnerve him. Finally, his foot reached the ledge, and he hurried to wrap his arms about the boy he loved more than his life. "How's the leg?"

"It's okay," Micah said, pain written all over his face, despite his smile of relief that his father was once again with him.

Buck took his knife from his pocket and slit the boy's trouser leg to the knee, revealing a nasty gash he knew required stitches. Further examination told him the ankle was fractured. He had to get Micah to the top and back to Anchorage as quickly as he could. The boy was close to shock from the break and the length of time in the cold night air. "I'll have us up to the top before you know it," he told his son with great assurance, despite his fears. He used the knife to cut the sleeve off his shirt, then wrapped it about the boy's leg. "There, that ought to help protect your leg."

"Are you sure you can carry me, Dad? I'm heavier than Jonathan."

"Sure, I'm sure. Trust me," he said with a hug around the boy's trembling shoulders. "Just give me a minute to rest and we'll be on our way."

Buck's eyes scanned the wall. Many of the rocks he had used were now gone, dislodged to the bottom of the deep crevice. If he weren't extremely cautious in his selection of strongholds, he and Micah also would be at the bottom. Buck carefully planned the route that looked best, then gently lifted his son onto his back, securing the belts around their waists. "Listen to me, Micah. What I'm about to say is very important. I know your leg hurts, but you must wrap your legs around my waist and hang on tight to my neck. And whatever you do, don't look down. Do you understand me?"

Micah nodded, his dark eyes misty.

Buck leaned against the rock wall and lifted his face. "God," he called out in a loud voice that echoed through the canyon, "You know how much I love this boy, and I can't do this in my own strength. Help me, show me the best way up. I promise I'm going to be the father You want me to be. Just give me another chance, please."

Micah cradled his head against his father's back. "Do you think God heard you?"

Buck's face brightened as all fear seemed to vanish. "I know He heard me, Micah. Let's go!"

Despite Micah's additional weight, Buck made it to the little tree with no more effort than it had taken with Jonathan. But when the men tried to swing the rope over to him, it lodged itself between two rocks.

Again, Buck lifted his face heavenward. "God, are You there? Help us. Don't abandon us now. Give me wisdom. What should I do?"

Chapter 10

H ey, Buck, can you hear me?" He recognized the voice of the tall, quiet
man.

"Yeah, I hear you."

"I'm coming down to free the rope. Can you two hang on there for a bit?"

Buck breathed a quick prayer, *Thank You, Lord.* "Sure. Come on down, but
be careful."

The man slowly lowered himself on the rope until his foot reached the place
where it was snagged, then looped it around his leg and gave it a jerk.

But it didn't move.

"Hang on, let me give it another try."

Buck held his breath and stared at the man as he worked to free the rope
with the toe of his boot.

"Is he going to get it loose?" Micah asked, his eyes round with trepidation.

"Of course, son," his father said with assurance, though inwardly he was a
bundle of nerves.

The man kicked at the rope several times. "Hang on. I'll get it," he shouted
down to the pair.

"I know you will," Buck called back to him.

"There she goes!"

"Yeeooww!" Buck shouted as the rope swung free. "Praise the Lord!" He and
Micah watched as the man climbed back to the top. Then Buck grabbed the rope
as it freely swung toward him. "Got it. We're coming up!"

Victoria dropped to her knees and bowed her head. *Thank You, God. Thank
You he was able to free the rope. Now, please, give Buck the strength he needs to bring
them both up safely.*

Complete silence took over the group on top, both those holding the rope
and those watching, each knowing if Buck was able to pull both himself and his
son up that rope simply by brute strength and willpower, they would be witness-
ing a miracle. Most of the men had been on a number of dangerous rescues, some
without success, but none so treacherous and none so far down the side of such
a deep crevice. And since they couldn't get close enough to the edge to see him,
no one was able to tell how far down the rope he was. They only knew as long as
they could feel his weight on the rope, he hadn't fallen.

Buck could feel the flesh tearing away from his hands as he laboriously pulled both his weight and that of his son up the rough surface of the rope. But what did it matter, if he was able to make it to the top? Sore hands were a small price to pay for the life of his son. "Hang on," he told Micah with great effort. "We're almost there."

Hand over hand he climbed, each thrust more difficult than the last, as he could feel his strength waning. *God, it's so far to the top. Help me,* Buck pleaded in a whisper that only God could hear.

A Scripture in Isaiah Buck had learned as a child flooded his mind, giving him the burst of strength he so desperately needed. *He giveth power to the faint; and to them that have no might he increaseth strength.* Buck shouted, "Micah, God answers prayer. Never forget it!"

He felt two small hands tighten about his neck.

Each pull brought them one step closer to safety. Finally, they reached the top and Buck was able to pull the two of them onto firm ground. The men dropped the rope and rushed to take Micah from his back as Buck staggered toward them. They'd made it! They were safe.

Buck scooped up his son, being careful with his injured leg, and carried him to Victoria who stood weeping with little Jonathan. The four stood together, their arms around one another. Buck, breathless and in agonizing pain from his ripped hands, thanked God for answered prayer.

The long walk back to the village seemed to take forever. And although Buck wanted to carry Micah himself, the men carried Micah and Jonathan all the way, leaving Buck and Victoria to walk arm in arm back to the little seaplane that would take them home.

꙳

It was nearly midnight before they all arrived at the hospital in Anchorage. Jonathan's arm was stitched up while X-rays were taken of Micah's ankle.

"Sorry, son," Buck told his son as he and the emergency room doctor evaluated the results of the X-rays. "Looks like you're going to have to stay off that ankle a couple of days until the swelling goes down. Then, old buddy, we'll have to put a cast on it."

"Aw, Dad, are you sure?" Micah asked with a groan, his skinned face wearing a frown. "I've got a game Saturday."

"No more soccer for you this season," the doctor told the boy. "From what I've heard about your adventure, I'd say you're lucky to be alive."

"If it weren't for that little tree that broke their fall, who knows what would have happened to those boys." Buck shuddered at the thought.

Everyone agreed it would be best for Micah to spend the night in the hospital. The doctor on duty gave him something to make him sleep through the night, and Buck promised to be there first thing in the morning. Buck even allowed the doctor, the same doctor who stitched up Jonathan's arm, to dress and bandage his hands after a number of protests about how they were fine and needed no attention at all.

"You were a brave little man, Jonathan," Buck said as Ron drove them back to the Lodge. "You've proven you're quite mature for a seven year old. I think it's time you have your own knife, and I'm going to get you one."

"No, Buck, not a knife," Victoria protested as she slipped an arm around her son protectively. "He's much too young."

"Now, Mother, don't be such a worrywart. I'm going to teach him everything I taught Micah when I gave him his knife." He tossed a smile her way. "You can even keep it for him until you're convinced he knows how to handle it."

"Please, Mom?"

"Well, if you promise to let me keep it for you until—okay, you can have the knife, but only under my conditions," she agreed hesitantly, wishing Buck had never brought up the subject. "But the first time I find you using it without my permission—"

"I know," Jonathan broke in with a frown, "you'll take it away from me, right?"

"Right."

"You were pretty brave yourself," Buck added with a grin. "I'll even get a knife for you."

Victoria smiled. "Now why would I want a knife?"

"Oh, there are many uses for a knife."

"Name one."

"To cut up vegetables, meat, fish. That sort of stuff. You'd love one, and I'll even teach you how to use it too. All the Alaskan women use them. I've even seen your mom use one."

"Okay, but I'm not promising I'll like that funny-looking thing. That's the weirdest knife I've ever seen."

"Weird? Don't knock it till you try it."

Victoria tried to tell Buck good night at the door, but he wouldn't hear of it, wanting to make sure Jonathan was tucked in for the night before leaving.

Once Jonathan was settled and asleep, Victoria and Buck lingered over Jonathan, watching the rhythmic rise and fall of his little chest. Victoria stood on tiptoe and slipped her arms around Buck's neck. "How can I ever thank you for what you did today?" Her heart was so filled with gratitude, she was barely able to utter the words. "I'm indebted to you forever."

Buck's arms circled her waist and he pulled her close. "God did it, Tori. To be real honest, that last climb—I wasn't sure we were going to make it."

She lifted misty eyes to his as her fingers stroked his cheek. "I was praying for you every second."

"Believe me, I was praying too. And you'd never guess what happened."

"Oh? What?"

A bandaged hand rose and cupped hers as it caressed his cheek. "I actually remembered a Scripture I'd learned when I was about Micah's age. Shot right through my mind as we hung there on the side of that crevice. Hadn't thought of it in years. Had to have been God made it surface to my memory when I needed it most. I think it's in Isaiah."

"Say it for me."

Buck's brow creased as he tried to remember where in Isaiah the verse was found, but it wouldn't come to him. "He giveth power to the faint; and to them that have no might he increaseth strength."

"And He did, didn't He? Increased your strength when you needed it most?"

Buck nodded, then kissed Victoria's forehead. "I knew you were praying for me. I could feel it."

His kiss trailed to her cheek, then slowly as she lifted her face toward his, he found her lips. It wasn't more than a brotherly kiss, at first. But as he looked into her eyes, it took on a different meaning, and he found himself unable to stop as his lips pressed against hers in a way they had when he had kissed his wife. Buck realized his feelings for this woman were more than that of a friend or a stepbrother.

Victoria pushed away slightly. "I—ah—we—"

But Buck pulled her to him, this time taking her into his arms and smothering her face with kisses. "Tori, I—"

Her fingers covered his lips. "Don't, Buck. Please."

"But—"

She pushed him away. "It's late, you'd better go. You promised Micah you'd be there early."

Buck didn't want to go. He wanted to stay there with her, never leave her again. Was he falling in love with this woman? Or was it only the life-threatening day they'd experienced that was bringing them together in a way they'd never known before? He didn't have answers. He only knew he wanted to be with Tori. Tonight. Tomorrow. Forever.

"Please, Buck. Go. We're both tired."

He bent and kissed the top of her hair and caught the scent of their campfire still lingering there. "Try to get a good night's sleep, and I'll check in with you tomorrow after I see my early morning patients."

"You're not going into the clinic tomorrow, are you?" she asked with surprise, knowing all he'd been through.

"Sure, why not? My patients are expecting me."

"But—your hands."

He held up the two bulky bandages with a teasing grin. "Think a few scratches are going to stop me? No way, I've got things to do."

96

She shook her head. "You're incorrigible. If you're going to the clinic, so am I. I'll see you there in the morning."

He frowned. "But what about Jonathan?"

"Mom will look after him, and thanks to you he's fine. That arm of his was a small price to pay for his disobedience."

"Yes, as soon as the time is right, I think our two boys had better face up to all the trouble they caused. You in agreement?"

"Absolutely. Now go on home."

Although exhausted, Victoria had a difficult time going to sleep. Buck had kissed her! And despite her vow to never let a man get that near to her again, she found herself wanting him to stay, to continue to hold her in his arms. And his kisses were different than Armando's. Buck's were tender and loving. Armando's had been rough and domineering. At times, he'd even made her lips swell from the pressure he'd put on them. Morton's kisses, on the other hand, were always dry and passionless. She'd never experienced kisses like Buck's before, and she liked them. Craved them.

Stop, you stupid woman. Haven't you learned your lesson? she asked herself in the darkness of her room as she lay staring at the ceiling. *You thought Armando was in love with you and look what happened. Sure, there're some fine men in this world, but are you smart enough to know which are the good ones and which are the bad ones? And who would want a woman like you? A woman gullible enough to allow herself to be compromised. Couldn't you see what was coming? Were you that naïve? Why would Buck be interested in you, a single mom with a young son? A woman with—what did Buck call it—baggage?*

She flipped onto her stomach and buried her face in the pillow. *Oh, God, I've been fooling myself all these years, telling myself I didn't want or need another man in my life. I do! And I want him to be a man like Buck.*

Victoria sighed. *But Buck is so in love with the wife he lost, he'd never even look at another woman. I've seen the way he stares at her picture, the loving way he talks about her. He has that woman on a pedestal, and no one will ever take her place. I've got to wake up and smell the coffee! He'd never be interested in another serious relationship. I can't let myself be hurt again.*

And then, another thought crossed her mind. A very disturbing thought. Bonnie Connor.

❧

Buck arrived at the clinic a few minutes after Victoria. "Micah slept all night, and the swelling in his ankle seems to have gone down a bit. In a day or two I'll be able to put a cast on it and he should be feeling better. He's not going to run any races for a while, though. He was concerned about Jonathan. How's he doing?"

"Whining a bit, but thanks to you, he's fine. Mom is spending the day with him."

"I told you not to come in—"

She shook a finger in his face. "Look at those hands, Doctor Silverbow. If you can work with those, surely I can handle a few hours in the office. Besides, Mom is spoiling Jonathan, and he loves every minute of it. He won't even miss me."

Buck and Victoria worked together until noon. "One more patient and I suggest we take a half hour for lunch. Do you want pizza? Does that sound good to you?" He reached for the doorknob to the next examining room.

But before Victoria could answer, Bonnie Connor came bursting into the clinic. Her face was flushed, and she was holding her stomach with both hands.

Chapter 11

I'm in labor. You have to help me!" the frantic woman screamed at Buck.

"After what you've accused me of, you expect me to help you?" Buck put his hands on his hips.

"You're the baby's father, you'd better help me." Bonnie braced herself against the doorway, her face racked with pain. "Do something! I can't stand this much longer."

Buck shot a questioning look at Victoria.

Brokenhearted by this turn of events, Victoria threw her palms in the air. She had hoped Buck would never hear from Bonnie again. "Don't look at me."

Buck looked from one woman to the other, then motioned Bonnie toward the examination room. "There's a gown on the table, get yourself into it."

He turned to Victoria who stood staring at him, confused by Bonnie's sudden appearance. "I need your help—Jean's at lunch."

She turned away. "Me? No way. Forget it, Buck!"

"Tori, I'm a doctor. I don't have a choice." His tone was pleading.

"But—"

"I always have someone with me when I examine a patient. I need you. There's no one else here."

Bonnie Connor screamed out again, apparently from another labor pain. "Get in here!" she ordered between groans.

"Tori?" Buck asked.

The young woman bit her lip. She could turn and run out the door, and Buck could do nothing to stop her.

"Please, Tori." His voice was kind, but anxious. "Please."

"Oh, all right!" She pushed past him and into the little cubicle where Bonnie Connor was doubled up on the side of the paper-covered examination table. Her arms were folded over her abdomen, and her white face was covered with perspiration.

Buck checked his watch, then stood waiting until the pain stopped. "Lay back. Let me check and see how far along you are."

Victoria cringed as she watched Buck pull the bandages from his mangled hands, wash them, and slip them carefully into rubber gloves. She knew he was hurting. "What should I do?"

"Let her squeeze your hand when the next pain hits. And you might put a cold rag on her forehead."

"Oh, another one is coming!" Bonnie doubled up again.

Buck turned quickly toward Victoria. "Delivery time." Buck moved quickly and assembled a few items from the wall cabinet and put them on a tray. Then he moved to the little sink and began to scrub his hands again, totally ignoring the wounds. "Scrub your hands. Use that little bottle to disinfect them. I need you to help me into my gloves and a clean gown. And put one on yourself. That baby won't wait."

Victoria did as she was told.

"There're some sterile, paper-wrapped packages of towels and blankets in that cabinet. Get several. We'll need them to wrap the baby."

Bonnie screamed again and Buck hurried to her. "Baby's coming, Bonnie. I need your help. Try to relax and—"

"Relax?" Bonnie grabbed his sleeve, her face writhing with pain. "I hurt! Can't you do something? Give me something?"

"Not if you want a healthy baby," Buck explained as calmly as he could. He stood at her feet, staring at the tip of the baby's head. "Don't push until I tell you. Have you had any Lamaze classes?"

The woman shook her head. "Don't even know what they are. Oh, I can't stand this. Do something!"

Victoria listened to Buck's every command, obeying them to the letter, afraid she might make a mistake that would hurt the baby.

The hands on the clock seemed to crawl as Buck issued orders to the woman and reported on the baby's progress. Finally, with one mighty thrust, the perfect form of a baby girl emerged.

"You've got yourself a girl," Buck told the new mother as he proudly held up the newly born infant for Bonnie to see. "And she looks perfect."

The relieved woman dropped back onto the pillow, totally spent, her breath coming in short pants, her hair wringing wet with perspiration. "Good. I couldn't take much more."

Buck placed the baby in the sterile blankets Victoria was holding and turned to her with a victorious smile. "We did it. Wrap her up and put her under that lamp. I've already turned it on. She'll be fine until I can tend to her. Right now, I need to finish up with Bonnie."

Victoria took the precious bundle in her arms, carried her to the little basket under the heat lamp, and carefully placed her there. She was feeling a euphoria she'd never experienced before.

The baby was beautiful. Her tiny pink face, her hair thick and dark. Victoria winced. Buck's hair was thick and dark. Could he be—?

"Victoria, I asked you to bring me another blanket. I don't want Bonnie to get chilled."

Victoria pulled her attention from the little basket and immediately went to the cabinet. She took another sterile package from the shelf, ripped it open, and covered the woman who'd just given birth to the baby Victoria feared might be Buck's. Then she stood idly by as Buck finished up with Bonnie and moved to the baby, deftly cleaning the precious child before wrapping her tightly in a fresh blanket and slipping the tiny little cap onto her head.

"Looks like Bonnie has left us. She's sound asleep. I gave her something to make her rest." He pulled the gloves from his hands and dropped them into the waste bin. "You did great. I couldn't have done it without you."

Her impulse was to slap him. The thought of a man denying his paternity made her sick. But what if he were telling the truth? Again, that old question surfaced. Why? Why would Bonnie lie about such a thing? What did she have to gain? Support money? And from a near stranger? None of it made any sense. And, after all, hadn't Buck saved Jonathan's life? Didn't she owe him the benefit of her doubts?

"She is beautiful, isn't she?" Buck whispered as he leaned over the basket and smiled at the baby he'd just delivered.

"Yes, she is," Victoria conceded as she joined him. "I'd love to have a baby girl. All I ever wanted out of life was to get married and have babies. And while I'm thankful for Jonathan, I wish I could have had a little girl too."

"Too bad she's coming into this world like this. Apparently her father doesn't want her any more than Jonathan's father wanted him." His voice was filled with sympathy and compassion.

His words brought tears to her eyes but she pushed them back. "I can't imagine a father denying his child." She gazed at the delicate infant in the funny little hat.

Buck's arm slipped around her shoulder. "Neither can I, Tori. If that baby were mine, I'd claim her in a heartbeat."

And for that one moment, she almost believed he was telling the truth.

"What do we have here?" Jean asked with raised brows as she entered the little room. "Looks like you two have been busy while I was at lunch."

Buck put his fingers to his lips and pointed to Bonnie, now strapped onto the narrow table. "Whew, am I glad to see you!" Buck whispered to the woman who'd assisted him through many births. "Take over, will you? And you'd better call the hospital and have them send over an ambulance. I don't want any complications. Not with this woman."

"Gotcha." Jean gave an understanding wink.

"Then I'm out of here. I owe my assistant some lunch."

"As if I could eat after what I've just seen," Victoria whispered. "I feel a bit lightheaded."

She felt Buck's arm circle her waist as he helped her out the door and into the outer office.

"You okay? You're not going to faint on me, are you?" he asked, genuinely concerned.

She shook her head, then leaned into him. "I hope not. I think I just need some fresh air."

The two walked to the little café across the street.

"I'll bet you didn't have breakfast this morning," Buck told her as he pushed open the door.

She shook her head. "No, I didn't. But I'm hungry now, and you were right, the fresh air helped. I'm feeling much better."

They'd barely been seated when an ambulance came down the street and stopped in front of the clinic. Two attendants pulled a gurney from the back, lowered the legs, and hurried inside. Within minutes they returned with Bonnie Connor strapped to the gurney with Buck's nurse close behind, carrying a little bundle wrapped in white.

"Hope that's the last we see of that woman," Buck said resolutely as he forked a bite of salad.

"I'm not so sure. She seemed pretty determined."

"To name me as the father of her baby? Well, let me assure you, I am not."

"What if she takes you to court?" Victoria avoided his eyes.

"Then I'll demand a paternity test. That'll end this once and for all. That woman's crazy!"

"Well, for your sake and for Micah's, I hope she leaves you alone."

Buck dropped his fork and stared at her. "You still believe her, don't you?"

"I—sort of."

"Well, do you or don't you? Be honest with me, Tori."

She lifted both palms. "Why would she make such accusations if there wasn't any truth to it? It doesn't make any sense."

He leaned against the chrome back of the chair. "You're right about one thing. It doesn't make any sense. I've tried to reason this out, but nothing about it gels. All I know is—I am not that baby's father. I don't care what Bonnie Connor says."

They finished their lunch in silence, and then Buck insisted Victoria go home and spend the rest of the day with Jonathan.

"I'm going to see the rest of my patients, then head to the hospital and spend some time with Micah."

❧

It was nearly seven o'clock before Buck pulled past the Lodge and on up the trail toward his little cabin. As he passed the home he and Claudette had shared, he felt compelled to stop and go inside. He made his way through the house, ending up in their bedroom. He sat on the side of the bed. He ran his fingers over the stitches on the beautiful burgundy and white sampler quilt. It was one of many quilts his wife had made, and Buck remembered the day she finished hand quilting it and placed it on their bed. He smiled. "I miss you, honey," he told her picture as he lifted it from the nightstand. "We almost lost our little boy, but I guess you know all about that."

He stood to his feet and paced about the room, the picture in his hands. "And today I delivered Bonnie Connor's baby. Can you believe the gall of that woman? Trying to name me as the father? I'd never cheat like that. You know that, don't you?"

The picture back in its place on the nightstand, he dropped back onto the bed. "I do have a confession to make." He rubbed at his forehead with a bandaged hand. "This is hard for me to say. I–I have feelings for Tori. Feelings I don't understand." He stared at the picture. "Now, don't get mad. Hear me out. I could never love another woman the way I loved you, but—I'm lonely, Claudette. And Micah needs a mother. I try, but it's just not the same."

He gulped and swallowed hard. "Tori's a single mom and she has a great kid. He and Micah are friends. You should see them together. I'm not even sure Tori would want me. But if she would, I think I'd like to spend the rest of my life with her. But I want your approval. Isn't that silly? As if you could talk to me and tell me it's okay. I've asked God's forgiveness for turning away from Him. And now I'm asking for your forgiveness, for breaking my promise. Can you forgive me?"

He lay back on the bed and closed his eyes. *God, am I being selfish? Am I betraying my wife? Am I asking too much?*

Buck didn't hear God's voice, nor did he see visions of his wife, but an over-whelming sense of peace came over him. Buck knew his prayer had been answered.

He leaped from the bed and flung open the drapes, allowing the security light in the yard to filter in. *I've been keeping this house as a shrine, making my son live in that little cabin while our home sat here unoccupied. But no more.*

He moved from room to room, snapping up shades and flinging open drapes. *As soon as I can air out this place and get the dust out of here, Micah and I are moving back.* He could hardly wait to tell his son.

And tomorrow I'm going to ask Tori out on a real date. No kids. Just the two of us. Who knows what'll happen after that?

Victoria spent another sleepless night as her thoughts kept returning to Bonnie Connor and her new baby. If a man fathered a child, would he be so intent on having a paternity test done? Or was he just saying that to throw off everyone?

Why, oh why did Buck and his father have to come into their lives? Things were going along so well before her mother went on that cruise and met Ron.

Chapter 12

I've been doing a lot of thinking lately, and I've come to realize I've been pretty foolish," Buck said.

Victoria appeared puzzled. "Foolish? About what?"

"Let's just say I'm making some major changes in my life. The first one has to do with you. How about a date? Just the two of us. No kids."

"A date. You mean like—"

His smile was infectious. "Like a movie."

"Sure. I'd love it. When?"

"How about tonight?"

"Maybe stop for a soda afterward?" she gave a shy grin.

"I'll even pop for a hot fudge sundae."

They were quite busy the rest of the day, with Victoria acting as Buck's assistant in his nurse's absence. Just before four o'clock, with only two more patients to be seen, a messenger arrived with a manila envelope in his hands. He handed it to Buck and left.

"Wonder what it is?" Buck ripped it open and pulled out an official-looking paper. His face fell and a heavy frown creased his brow.

"Buck, what is it?"

He dropped onto a chair and buried his head in his hands. "Bonnie Connor's baby's birth certificate, naming me as the father."

Victoria thought she was going to be sick. She'd just begun to trust Buck and now this. She grabbed her jacket and headed for the door.

"Tori, wait. It's not true! You have to believe me."

"Give me one good reason why," she retorted as she pushed against the heavy glass door.

"Because—because I love you!"

Her eyes turned to fire. "Is that what you told Bonnie before you got her pregnant?" The door slammed behind her.

All the way home she thought of nothing but Buck, Bonnie, and Armando. Victoria could empathize with Bonnie. Buck was treating the new mother exactly as Armando had treated her, and all the old hurts she'd worked so hard to bury had surfaced. Yes, she loved Buck. She knew that now. But life with him would be impossible. How could she be around a man who lied and evaded his responsibility? She'd loved Armando and he'd taken advantage of her love and trust. Wasn't Buck doing the same thing? Well, this time she refused to be a victim. How could she have let down her guard? She had no other choice but to get away from Buck and back to Kansas City as soon as possible.

❧

"I'm leaving, Mom. Jonathan and I are going back to Kansas City," Victoria said that night.

"But, Victoria, you and Buck were getting along so well. Ron and I had hoped the two of you would get together. Nothing would make me any happier than to have my daughter and grandson living with us here in Alaska."

"I thought we were too, but—" Victoria didn't want to be the one to tell their parents about Buck's suspected paternity. If he wanted them to know, he could be the one to tell them. "But there are complications."

The next morning, she reminded Buck that he would need to find a replacement for her. Her two weeks' notice was nearly over. "And I'm not going to work as your assistant in the meantime," she told him. "You can get one of your other employees to help you. I'll work on the files so they'll be in good shape when I leave. But keep your distance, Buck, or I'll be out of here as quick as I can move. Understood?"

He nodded. "Understood. But I'm not happy about it."

❧

Her third and final day, Buck took a call from an attorney who said he had to see him and would be right over. "I'm pretty busy," Buck told the man. "Can you make it tomorrow?"

After being told he had something of great importance to discuss with him, Buck finally agreed and told him he'd make time for him.

When the man entered the clinic, Victoria got up to leave the room, but Buck motioned for her to stay.

"I got a call from the Anchorage Police Department," the man told Buck after they shook hands. "Seems some woman deliberately ran her car into a tree and killed herself."

"So, what does that have to do with me? Was she one of my patients?"

The man pulled a pad from his pocket. "The woman's name was Bonnie Connor."

Buck dropped into a chair, his head cradled in his hands. "Oh, no. Now why'd she go and do that?"

"No one knows, but an observer said they were sure she did it deliberately."

"What about the baby?" Victoria asked with concern for the little girl she'd helped deliver.

"I understand the baby was at the sitter's house at the time of the accident. Seems Bonnie Connor left an envelope with instructions that the baby should be taken to you if anything happened to her," the man explained.

Buck jumped to his feet, his face red with frustration. "How many times do I have to tell everyone? I am not that baby's father!"

"Well, I guess that's for the court to decide," the man told him as he shoved the little pad back into his pocket. "Until then, since your name is on the birth certificate, I guess you'll have a baby to care for. The social worker will be here with the baby within the hour."

"But—" Buck moved after the man to protest.

"Sorry. That's all I know. If I hear any more, I'll let you know. Call me if you have any questions. I'll be representing the baby's rights in all of this."

Victoria watched from her place behind the desk. If Buck weren't the father, why would the woman plan to kill herself and claim Buck as the father? What would be the purpose?

Little was accomplished in the clinic for the next hour as everyone waited in anticipation of the baby's arrival. Sure enough, just as the man said, exactly one hour to the minute the social worker arrived with a tiny bundle in her arms. "You Dr. Silverbow?"

He nodded. "Yes, but I'm not that baby's father."

"Well, my papers say you are. Here's your baby." She thrust the child into Buck's arms, then turned to Victoria. "Here's a bag with a few things that baby will be needing—formula, diapers, the usual stuff. But only enough for a day or two. You'll have to get more."

Victoria took the bag and watched the woman turn and march out the door. Victoria was thankful that she would soon be leaving Buck Silverbow and his duplicity. She'd been deceived by this man, and this was the final straw.

She watched as Buck pulled the blanket off the baby's face. And although she knew he was upset by the baby's arrival, she respected him for not taking his wrath out on the child. His demeanor with the precious little girl was gentle, which only led her to mistrust him even more. "What are you going to do with her?" Victoria prodded, wondering how a man could care for such an infant child.

"I have no idea," he answered honestly. "Think Abigale will help me?"

"My mother? That's asking quite a bit of her, isn't it? To take care of your illegitimate child? She's already helping your dad with Micah."

His eyes were imploring. "Got a better idea? How about you?"

"Me? Isn't it pretty nervy to ask me to take care of your baby? What do you take me for, Buck? A sucker, like Bonnie?"

"Look, Tori, I need help. This baby needs help. Have you no compassion? Even if you hate me, do you want to take out your anger on this innocent baby?" He held out the infant toward her. "Look at her."

She couldn't resist the invitation and walked over to Buck. The baby was beautiful, and her arms longed to hold her. "But I'm leaving tomorrow."

"I can't run a practice, do all the legal work this mess will require, and take care of Micah all at the same time. Please stay on for a few days, until I get this settled. I need you."

Victoria could refuse Buck, but not that precious baby. "Okay, but only for a few days. No more than a week. Then I'm leaving, and you can find yourself another sitter if things aren't settled."

"Thanks, Tori," he said gratefully, his face showing signs of relief. "That's all I ask. Jean can take care of the baby until I'm ready to go home. I'd appreciate it if you'd take the minivan and go over to Barnes Department Store and buy anything the baby needs. You can charge it to my account. Dad will unload it for you when you get back to the Lodge, and I'll meet you there later."

"Anything the baby needs? Do you have any idea how many things that will be? And what it will cost you?"

Buck pulled his credit card from his wallet. "Anything she needs."

❧

The next few days were some of the happiest Victoria had ever spent as she set up a nursery in her room and cared for the dark-eyed, pink-cheeked angel. The feeding, bathing, dressing, and rocking were all tasks Victoria enjoyed.

"This baby needs a name," she told Buck as he walked the room with the baby in his arms.

"Name? I guess you're right. You choose."

She pondered the thought. "How about Rachel? Or Serena?"

"Um, no, she doesn't seem like either of those names."

"You have a better idea? After all you are the—"

He shot Victoria a daggered look. "I am not the father."

"Touché! That hasn't been proven yet. So what are you going to call her? She needs a name. We can't just keep calling her Bonnie's baby."

Buck placed a finger under the baby's delicate little chin. "A little angel like this deserves an angelic name. How about Angela?"

Victoria nodded. "Or how about Angelica?"

"Perfect." Buck smiled as the baby grasped his finger. "See, she likes it. Angelica it is."

"Well, it's been three days since we brought Angelica to the Lodge, and it seems you're no closer to a solution than you were the day she came to stay with you. I think you'd better start looking for another baby-sitter. I'm going home at the end of the week."

"But I need you—"

Victoria backed away. "Sorry. As much as I love caring for little Angelica, I have to move forward with my own life."

"You're really going through with this?"

She nodded.

"If you insist on leaving, would you at least find a sitter for me? I'm still looking for your replacement at the clinic." He handed the baby to her. "You do want to make sure I hire a good one, don't you?"

She thought over his words. He was right: She was concerned about who would take over her jobs when she left. "Okay. But I'm leaving at the end of the week, baby-sitter or no baby-sitter. I'll get on it first thing tomorrow."

The ad she placed in the paper yielded nothing but a bunch of women she wouldn't trust with a Barbie doll, let alone a flesh-and-blood baby. And the sitters the service sent over were no better.

"What is Buck going to do with the baby when you leave?" Victoria's mother asked when the last applicant left.

"I have no idea, but I warned him. I told him I was leaving, baby-sitter or no baby-sitter, and I meant it."

"I guess I could take care of Angelica until Buck finds someone," Abigale said, but Victoria could tell her newlywed mother did not want to offer.

"No, I've already told Buck that was not an option."

The day of Victoria's departure arrived. "Well, I'm off," she told Buck as she wrapped little Angelica in her blanket, "and here is your baby."

"I don't want you to leave. I hope you know that." Buck tried to slip his free arm around her waist.

"Because you need a baby-sitter?" Victoria asked him sarcastically.

"No, it has nothing to do with the baby. I love you, Tori. I think I've loved you since the day I met you when we were both waiting for our parents to get off that cruise ship. I was too stubborn to let go of my past life with Claudette."

She breathed a sigh of resignation. "Well, it's too late now. I've loved you too, Buck, but we could never build a life on deceit. I tried that once before and I couldn't take it again. The pain is too severe and it never goes away."

"You have to believe me, I love you—"

She backed away. "That's exactly what Armando told me. Then he took advantage of me and deserted me."

"I'd never do that, Tori."

"You already have, Buck. Not to me. Bonnie Connor. She needed you and you deserted her. She faced her pregnancy alone, just as I did. I could never forgive a man who does that to a woman." She turned away, afraid she might weaken and be tempted to stay if she looked into his eyes one more time.

"I have to get to the airport. Your father's taking us. Thanks for everything, and thanks for nothing. It's been swell." And Victoria walked out of Buck's life, her heart bursting.

Chapter 13

A disillusioned young woman and her son arrived in Kansas City unannounced and without fanfare. The last thing she wanted was a pity party from her relatives.

Victoria threw herself into her work, the research job she'd had with her brother before leaving for Alaska. Jonathan, happy to be back with his former classmates but missing his new friend Micah, started school. Victoria was comfortable living in her mother's house. She and Jonathan quickly fell into their old routines.

"You okay?" Jason asked as Victoria placed a pile of case studies on his desk. "You've been pretty low since you got home. Anything wrong?"

She shook her head and dabbed at her nose with her hanky. "I'm fine, just coming down with a cold, I think."

He gave her a skeptical look. "Couldn't be missing that Alaskan stepbrother of yours, could you?"

"Of course not. Why would you say such a thing?"

Jason jabbed at her arm. "I kind of thought you two had something going there."

"For your information," she said briskly, "I'm considering marrying Morton. He's asked me again and I just might accept."

"What's he think about you opening your shop?"

She shrugged. "He wants me to wait until after the wedding."

"I wouldn't hold my breath on that one. I doubt you'll ever see that shop if he has his way about it," Jason said with a snort. "What's Jonathan think about having old Morton as a stepfather?"

Victoria picked up a book and thumbed idly through the pages. "You know he doesn't like him, but he'll come around. Morton is a fine man."

"A fine, arrogant man, if you ask me," Jason retorted.

"That's your opinion." She slammed the book on the desk. "Yours and Buck's."

"Take your time making a decision like that, sis. Till death do us part is a long, long time."

I have to forget about Buck, she told herself as she walked into her office. *I could never give myself wholly to a man who denies his child. Even if he wanted me, which I'm sure he doesn't, I could never let him touch me or make love to me. Oh, Buck, how could you? I loved you and you let me down.*

One week later on a Saturday morning, the doorbell rang just as Victoria was ready to go to the grocery store for milk. Hoping to get rid of her caller, she grabbed her purse and hurried to the door.

There stood Buck, holding little Angelica in his arms. "She wanted to come and see you." Buck smiled an easygoing grin, the one that always made Victoria's heart skip a beat.

She flung the door open wide and eagerly took the baby from him. "She can speak already?" Victoria smiled and motioned Buck toward the sofa.

"We've learned to communicate," Buck said.

"Is she wet?" Victoria sat next to Buck. She tugged the blanket from the baby's legs.

Buck laughed and pulled a disposable diaper from the bag he'd had slung over his shoulder. "Is she ever not wet?"

"I can't believe how she's grown," Victoria said, lifting the baby's plump bottom and removing the wet diaper. "Look at those chubby little legs. You must be feeding her well."

"Any credit for her well-being goes to your mom. I tried to find a baby-sitter, but she didn't like any of them and finally decided to take on the job herself. She's quite a lady."

Victoria returned his smile. "That she is. I'm not surprised she stepped in. She's never let me down, not once." She paused. "Except when we didn't get to open our shop."

"And I let you down?"

Victoria ignored his question as she tended to Angelica.

"I've been miserable without you, Tori." Buck slipped his arm around her shoulders, but she pretended not to notice.

"And one night, after you left, I was reading my Bible and came across a Scripture I'd memorized after Micah was born. Actually, it's in the book of Micah, in the seventh chapter. I claimed that verse as my own that night. It said, 'Therefore, I will look unto the Lord; I will wait for the God of my salvation: my God will hear me.' "

Victoria remembered how she learned that verse as a child. She thought of the many times her father had reminded her that even if God didn't seem to answer her prayers, He always heard them.

"I love you. I've looked to God and asked Him over and over to give me some way to show you and to prove to you, once and for all, I am not Angelica's father."

With a victorious grin he pulled an envelope from his pocket and waved it at her. "And, in His time, He provided that way."

Her eyes scanned the innocuous envelope. "That's your proof?"

"Yes, open it. And notice the seal has not been broken. I wanted you to be the first one to take a look at it." He offered it to her.

She held back. "Why do you want me to see it before you? I don't understand."

"It contains the results of the paternity test I decided to have taken. To prove my innocence once and for all."

She pursed her lips. "But what if it says you are—"

"It won't. Because I'm not Angelica's father. I've told everyone that from the beginning. There is no way I could be." His voice was filled with confidence. "Open it, please."

Slowly she took the envelope from his hand, examined the seal, then forced open the flap. But as she reached inside, she was reminded of a Scripture she'd read that morning. *Trust in the Lord with all thine heart; and lean not unto thine own understanding.* Her understanding had led to nothing but confusion.

"Look, Tori. I know I hurt you, but I didn't do it intentionally. After all you'd been through with Armando, it's easy to understand why you'd believe the worst about me—especially when there was so much evidence against me. I'm not mad at you for mistrusting me. I love you. I want to spend the rest of my life loving you and taking care of you. I'd never willingly hurt you in any way. You should know that. Now, go ahead, open it. Please."

She fingered the brown envelope, each of Buck's words replaying in her mind, torn between truth and trust. "No, Buck. I have to tell you some things first. Hear me out, please." She bit her lower lip and let out a long, slow sigh. "All my life I've prayed if ever another man came into my life, he'd be a man after God's own heart. You've turned back to God and have promised to make Him the center of your life. And I've wanted that man to love my son and be the father Jonathan's never had. In so many ways you've shown your love for Jonathan, and you have even put your own life at risk to save his. Most of all, I've wanted that man to love me more than himself. Buck, you've proven your love for me time and time again."

Buck placed his hand on her shoulder. "I can see why you'd doubt me. That woman's—"

"Don't make excuses for me." She pushed his hand away, struggling to hold back tears of regret that ached for release. "I've denied your love by allowing little seeds of doubt to grow into straggling vines of distrust. I know I've hurt you. I've seen it in your eyes. I've heard it in your voice. I'm so afraid you'll never be able to forgive me for even considering you could have fathered that baby."

"Tori, it's okay. There's nothing to forgive." Again he tried to comfort her, but she pushed him away.

"I've held something back from you, Buck. Something I should have told you a long time ago, when I told you about Armando."

Buck smiled. He held Victoria's hand and began to stroke it with the pad of his thumb. "It can't be very important. You've told me all about that skunk. What could be any worse than that?"

"You may not feel the same about me when you hear what I have to say." She paused, biting her lower lip until it almost bled. "I—ah—because of my difficult pregnancy with Jonathan, I—"

He looked at her expectantly. "Yes?"

"I know you want a house full of children, and I—the doctor said I can't have any more." She turned away, sure this would put an end to any relationship they might have had.

"Is that all?" Buck snickered. "Sweetie, this world is filled with children who need good homes."

Finally, Victoria handed the unopened envelope to him. "Here."

"You're not going to open it? You hate me that much?"

"No, Buck. I love you that much. I no longer need a paternity test to prove your innocence. I know you. You'd never do such a thing. I should have realized it long ago. But old wounds don't heal quickly." She began to weep. "Can you ever forgive me for doubting you?"

He wiped her tears with his thumb. "Nothing to forgive." He pulled her to his shoulder and kissed her while the baby snuggled between them.

Victoria pulled away suddenly and stared into his eyes. "But what about the baby? Since that paper will say you're not the father, what will happen to Angelica?"

He touched the tip of the baby's round little nose, and she wiggled ever so slightly. "I thought about that all the way here, and I've come up with two choices. One, I can show these results to the court, proving I'm not her father. She will become a ward of the court and probably be sent to a foster home until she can be adopted."

Victoria shuddered at the thought. "Little Angelica in a foster home? Adopted by strangers? What's the second choice?"

"Or we can tear up the paper and let the world think I'm her father, and we can keep her as our own. That is, if you'll consent to marry me and accept another woman's child as your own."

She beamed as she considered his words. "Marry you? Oh, Buck, I never expected to hear those words. Yes, I'll marry you." She bent and kissed the sleeping baby. "And of course I'll accept Angelica as my own. Micah, too. I love you, Buck."

Buck shifted the sleeping baby into the crook of his other arm and reached into his shirt pocket. "I just happen to have an engagement ring with me—hoping you'd say yes."

Victoria found herself breathless as he slipped the ring on her finger.

"This means you're mine, you know," he said, love filling his eyes.

She lifted her hand and gazed at the sparkling diamond. "I know. Marriage is a sacred thing, Buck. God's Word is very explicit about that. This is a lifetime commitment. Are you sure you're ready for it?"

"Ready for it? How about eloping right now?"

She leaned into him and laughed. "And deprive all of our family members from seeing us tie the knot? They'd never forgive us."

He rested his chin in her hair. "You name the day."

Two weeks later, Victoria stood before the mirror in the church's dressing room and adjusted her veil. In a few minutes she would become Mrs. Buck Silverbow.

"You make a beautiful bride," Abigale said to her only daughter. Abigale held little Angelica who was dressed in an adorable pink gown. A tiny pink bow was tucked in her thick black hair.

The young woman in the white satin gown stared at her reflection. "Oh, Mom, is that happy woman really me? Am I dreaming? Am I actually going to marry this wonderful, caring man?"

Abigale grinned. "I don't want to say I told you so, but I knew Buck was the right man for you the day you told me you were staying in Alaska until you were sure I'd be happy married to Ron. You may not have realized it at the time, but I did. You wanted to stay not only for me, but you didn't want to leave Buck."

"You really knew it?"

Her mother smiled as she adjusted little Angelica in her arms. "So did Ron. We tried to make sure the two of you spent plenty of time together. Without being too obvious, of course."

A knock sounded at the door. "Tori? Let me in." It was Buck.

"No!" she said firmly. "It's bad luck for the groom to see—"

"This is important, Tori. I think you'd better let me in."

Chapter 14

Victoria opened the door a crack and peeked through. There was Buck, looking dashing in his black tuxedo, standing with a woman she didn't recognize. From the look on his face, Victoria knew something was wrong. "Give me a second, I'll slip out of my gown and into a dress."

He nodded. "Hurry."

Less than two minutes later, she was standing beside him, her heart pounding.

"This lady is a friend of Bonnie Connor. She says she has a message for me from Bonnie. As my wife, I wanted you to hear whatever she has to say."

"I went to Dr. Silverbow's office to deliver this letter. Before Bonnie died, she asked me to make sure he got it by the baby's third-month birthday. His nurse thought I should deliver it to him here, before the wedding," she told Victoria. The woman handed the letter to Buck. "The nurse even arranged an airline ticket for me and gave me some money. I told her it was too expensive to send me all the way to Kansas City, but she insisted."

The woman turned to Buck. "She said you'd want me to come. I'm sorry I wasn't here earlier, but I missed plane connections in Seattle."

Buck took the letter from her. "She was right, I'm sure whatever is in that letter is important. Maybe it'll answer some of my questions." He slipped a finger under the flap and ripped open the envelope. He unfolded a letter penned in a woman's scrawling handwriting and began to read.

Dear Dr. Silverbow,

First of all, I have to apologize for all the trouble I've caused you. I hope when you hear why I had to do it, you will understand and forgive me. Perhaps you've learned to love my baby after living with her these past few weeks. I hope so. Loving her will make it easier to hear what I have to tell you.

Buck smiled at Victoria, knowing they already loved little Angelica. He continued reading:

Rocky, the baby's real father, is in prison for killing a security guard during an armed robbery and may be facing death row. He hasn't told anyone yet, but I was his partner. I helped plan it and drove the escape car.

114

A friend of his has already told me Rocky is threatening to implicate me because I haven't come to see him. But I've been too scared. I know it's only a matter of time before I'm arrested since the police have already questioned me.

Even Rocky doesn't know he's the baby's father. I told him I was raped by a stranger. I knew if the police ever found out Rocky was the father, I would be caught. So I had to make sure another man was named. I've spent eight years of my life in prison, and I can't face going back. I don't want my child to be a ward of the court and raised by a long line of foster parents like I was.

I decided the best thing I could do for my baby was to find a fine, upstanding man and name him as the father. And you were so good to me when you treated me last year. You probably don't remember, but your son was in the office that day. I watched the loving way you were with him, and I knew you'd be good to my baby.

Buck blinked several times, then continued:

I'm sorry for causing those scenes in your office, but I knew I had to take drastic measures; otherwise you'd never be interested in taking the baby of a woman you barely knew. I hope I didn't ruin your reputation. That's the last thing I wanted to do. But I was desperate. All I could think about was my baby's future.

As soon as I leave my friend's house, I'm going to take the baby to her baby-sitter, then I'm going to drive my car into a tree. I already have the one picked out. I'll drive fast enough that I'll be sure to die. I want to go quick. It's my only way to escape prison.

Please, Dr. Silverbow, keep my baby. Your name is already on the birth certificate. As far as the law is concerned, she's already yours. That's the way I planned it. And if you have it in your heart to raise her as your own, I have one more favor to ask. Never let her know her father and mother were involved in that robbery, or that we both have prison records. She's so sweet and innocent. She doesn't deserve this.

I wish there were something I could do to make up for all the trouble I've caused, and in some ways I guess I am. I'm giving you the most precious thing I've ever had in my life—my baby.

Thank you,
Bonnie Connor

Buck wiped his eyes with the back of his hand. "That poor woman. If I had only known—"

Victoria leaned into Buck and buried her head in his chest. "Jus—just think what she went through, living a l–lie, going through her pr–pregnancy all alone, planning her d–death," she said between heaving sobs.

"What's going on out here?" Abigale asked, still holding little Angelica.

Buck rushed to take the sleeping baby and cradled her close to him. "We'll tell you all about it later."

"Have you two been crying?" she asked as she looked from Buck to Victoria, then to the stranger.

Victoria smiled through her tears. "She brought good news, Mom. At least part of it is good. We now know the whole story behind Bonnie Connor's strange actions. I'll tell you all about it later." She touched Angelica's little chin, then stood on tiptoe and planted a kiss on Buck's cheek. "But right now I have to get ready for my wedding."

Minutes later Buck Silverbow, accompanied by his bride and two little boys dressed in black tuxedos, stood at the altar holding a sleeping baby girl.

After the traditional wedding music, the pastor gave a Biblical challenge to Victoria and Buck. Then the pastor told the audience, "Buck and Victoria have chosen to say their own vows. Buck."

The big man shifted Angelica to the crook of his other arm and took Victoria's hand in his. He looked into Victoria's eyes. "Tori, I take you as my wife, to love and cherish for the rest of our lives. I promise I'll be the husband you deserve. I'll be faithful, and I'll take care of you through sickness and in health. And I promise to be the best father I can be to your son, Jonathan, who is now my son. To my son, Micah, who is now your son. And to our baby, little Angelica. I make these vows in God's presence, and I thank Him for bringing us together. Together, we'll make Him the head of our home. I love you, Tori, and I'm going to spend the rest of my life proving it to you. Thank you for becoming Mrs. Buck Silverbow."

Victoria found it hard to speak after hearing Buck's words. She forgot all the words she had practiced. She felt Buck's fingers squeeze hers and that made it a little easier. She looked up into Buck's eyes. "Oh, Buck, how can I ever tell you how much I love you? How can I put into words the joy of being with you? Just knowing you has changed my life. I promise to be the wife you deserve. Although I know I can never be the wife you lost, I promise to try to be the best wife I can be. I'm so proud Micah wants to accept me as his mother, and that you want to be a father to my son. Together, we'll raise Angelica. I'll take care of you in sickness and in health. And I'll be faithful to you."

She swallowed at the lump in her throat. "Oh, what else can I say, except I love you with my whole heart?"

Buck turned to the pastor. "May I say something else?"

He smiled and shrugged his shoulders. "It's your wedding, you can say anything you like."

"I just want to add that because of all Victoria and I have been through, we've turned back to God. He's going to be the center of our home, and with His help we'll do our best to raise our children according to His Word. Because without Him and answered prayer, we might not be standing at this altar right now."

"You may place the ring on your bride's finger," the pastor said.

Micah stepped forward and handed the ring to his father. Buck slipped it onto Victoria's hand. "This ring is a token of our love. Wear it always, my love."

Jonathan handed a gold band to his mother, and with a trembling hand she slipped it onto the third finger of Buck's left hand. "Wear it always, my love."

Buck reached into his pocket and pulled out two small gold rings and handed them to Victoria. "These are for Micah and Jonathan. We're going to be a family now and these are to remind you boys we'll always love you. Each of you is as special to us as the other. And as soon as Angelica is old enough to wear one, we have a ring for her too."

Victoria placed the rings on the fingers of two beaming boys, kissing each one on the cheek.

"I now pronounce you husband and wife. You may kiss the bride."

Slowly, Buck lifted Tori's veil, his eyes never leaving hers. He could see love reflected, love that would last a lifetime. His lips pressed hers, and he knew in his heart that Claudette was in heaven smiling her approval. He was finally at peace. Their lips parted. "I love you, Tori," he said.

The couple turned to face the many well-wishers assembled to sanction their wedding. The pastor said proudly, "I'd like to introduce you to Mr. and Mrs. Buck Silverbow and their family."

And the audience applauded.

❧

After the long flight to Alaska, Victoria and Buck and the children were tired. Once the children were all tucked in bed in the Lodge, the newlyweds sat alone in the tiny living room of Buck's cabin. He took Victoria's hand and pulled her toward the door. "Leave your jacket on and come with me. I've got a wedding present for you."

"Really? What is it? Tell me."

His eyes sparkled with mischief, but he didn't head for their little bedroom as she had supposed he would. Instead, he led her outdoors and down to the clearing where he had been carving the ugly totem pole.

"My present is here?" Victoria asked in surprise.

Buck flipped the switch on the big yard light, and there, standing alone, was the most beautifully carved pole Victoria had ever seen. "Oh, Buck. I love it." She moved to examine the magnificently carved pole more closely. "But where are the others, the ones with the grotesque faces?"

"Gone. I took them all down." He strode up behind her and slipped his arms around her waist. "They represented everything ugly in my life. They no longer belong here, not since I met you."

Her eyes scanned the tall pole from its tip to its base. "I've never seen anything like it, all those delicate flowers and vines. Where did it come from?"

"I carved it for you while you were in Kansas City." He paused. "Well, I had a little help from my carver friends, but I designed it." He pointed to the top. "See what it says?"

She took a few steps backward, where she could see it better, and read aloud: "To Tori, with love." Her hands flew to cover her face as she began to cry.

Buck's face grew grim. "You don't like it?"

She brushed aside her tears as she ran into his arms. "Oh, Buck, I love it. It's the sweetest thing anyone has ever done for me."

"If ever you doubt my love, look to the pole, Tori. It will stand here as a constant reminder to you. I'm sure, like any other married couple, there will be times when we won't agree, but my love for you will never waver."

"How could I ever doubt your love? Your love and God's love have changed my life."

"I wanted you to see it on our wedding day." He flipped off the light and they walked arm in arm back to the cabin. "And another thing, I'm going to build us a new home. One that will be all ours, yours and mine, with no ghosts in it."

She stopped and stared at him. "I don't need a new house. The cabin is fine."

He let out a robust laugh. "For me and Micah maybe. But for five of us? I don't think so. Give me till spring and—"

Her face filled with concern. "But what about the beautiful home you and Claudette shared? You can't sell it. It's filled with too many memories."

He kissed the tip of her nose. "I'm going to save it for Micah. Someday he'll get married, maybe eventually take over my practice. I'd like for him to have it. Nothing would please me more."

"You think of everything," she said as she slipped her hand into the crook of his arm and they began the walk back to the cabin.

He bent and kissed the top of her head. "And right now I'm thinking of the love we're going to share tonight."

She wanted Buck to make love to her. More than anything else, Victoria wanted to become one with him, the husband she had vowed to love until death parted them. But old memories died hard and suddenly all she could think about was the last time a man touched her in that way. Armando. She shuddered.

"Don't worry, Tori. I'll be gentle. There's no rush. We have a lifetime."

And with his tender words, she knew the memories of Armando and the fear she'd felt all these years since that horrible night were now behind her, never to haunt her again.

As she gazed at the handsome man beside her, she knew that this night was going to be the most special night of her life.

Epilogue

How was school today?" Victoria asked the dark-haired child who stood at the table dipping her mother's famous peanut butter cookies into a glass of milk.

"Wish I was in first grade," Micah said. He groaned as he poured himself a tall glass of cold milk. "First grade was easy. I have to study history, grammar, and other dumb stuff." He grabbed one of his sister's cookies, broke it in half, and stuffed it into his mouth. "Who cares who was president during the Civil War?"

The little girl yanked her plate away and made a face at her brother. "Mom, he took my cookie."

Victoria playfully shook a finger at the boy. "Micah, there's plenty in the cookie jar. Leave your little sister alone."

"At least you get to play on the soccer team." Jonathan flipped Micah's cap from his head. "Just wait until next year. One more operation and the doctor said I could play on the team. Then I'll show you how to kick a ball."

"You'd be better off butting it with your big head," Micah teased. He picked his cap off the floor, tossed it onto a kitchen chair, and headed for the cookie jar.

"Okay, you boys stop that. Your dad will be home any minute. You don't want to ruin our anniversary with all that squabbling, do you?"

"Yeah, it's Mama and Daddy's versery. You'd better be good," Angelica warned her brothers. She took another bite of cookie.

"Hey, what's going on here?" Buck sniffed the air as he came into the room, hugging each child. "Mmm, is that peanut butter cookies I smell? Looks like Mom's been busy in the kitchen today."

"Happy versery," Angelica said and shoved a big piece of milk-soaked cookie into her father's mouth.

Buck finished chewing. "Thanks, I love your mama's cookies." He pulled Victoria away from her place at the sink where she was washing cookie sheets and wrapped her in his arms. "Six glorious years I've had with your mama. And she still says she loves me."

Victoria reached a damp hand to cup his chin. "And I love you more each day, Dr. Silverbow."

Buck squeezed her hand, then knelt to pick up their daughter. "You kids are gonna spend the night with your grandparents. Your mama and I are going out on the town to celebrate. God has given us six years together and—"

"Why can't we go with you?" the little girl asked as she twined sticky fingers through her father's hair.

"Yeah, take her with you," Jonathan said. He grinned at his brother. "She always messes up our video games."

"Do not!" Angelica retorted, her chin sticking out defiantly.

"Do so," both boys accused in unison.

Buck held up a hand. "No more of this. You boys need to be nice to your little sister." A horn sounded. "Now get your things. Grandpa Ron is waiting."

The children ran through the house and out the door.

Buck dropped into a kitchen chair and folded his hands. "Just you and me, babe."

"Yeah, quiet around here now, isn't it?" Victoria sat down on his lap and gazed into his dark eyes as her arms slipped around his neck. "Think you can take another six years of being married to me?"

"How about eternity?" He rubbed his forehead against hers. "I wish I was a poet or a writer. I have a difficult time expressing myself sometimes. I'd like to present you with flowery words, words that would adequately describe my love for you."

She kissed the tip of his nose. "You tell me everyday with your gentleness, your loving ways. You're my hero, Buck."

He grinned. "Hero, huh? That sounds pretty good to me."

"I have an anniversary present for you," she said. With an eager smile, she stood, pulled a large flat package from behind the pantry door, and placed it on his lap. "Open it."

Buck popped the string with his pocketknife and pulled off the colorful paper. "Tori, I love it." He held up the beautiful oil painting of himself, Victoria, and the three children. "You did this from the snapshot Dad took last summer at Earthquake Park?"

Victoria nodded with a look of satisfaction. He liked her gift. She smiled. "I guess I haven't lost my touch." She leaned over his shoulder and admired the family portrait she had worked on for months.

Buck's fingers moved over the uneven surface appreciatively, touching each likeness. "I don't see how you do this. The kids look just like themselves."

"You really think so?"

"Sure do. Just look at Angelica's little button nose. The likeness is uncanny. You are one talented lady. Too bad you have to waste that talent staying home and taking care of us. You should be doing commission work, or have your own studio." He braced the painting against the wall and took her hand and pulled her into his lap again. "Sorry you haven't had much time to paint—with the kids and all. But now that Angelica's in school all day—"

"I love to paint, Buck, but I wouldn't exchange one minute I've had with the four of you." She snickered. "I didn't even mind the dirty diapers. And besides, the art classes I've been teaching part-time at the college have helped keep me in practice."

Buck smiled, as if he knew something she didn't. "I have a present for you too. But you'll have to come with me to see it."

She nudged him. "Another beautiful totem pole?"

"You'll have to wait and see. Go get your coat."

Victoria was puzzled as the car headed toward downtown. "Is it bigger than a bread box?" she asked and scooted closer to him. "That's what my mother used to ask us on her birthday."

"Yes, I'd say so. Quite a bit bigger."

"Is it a new bread machine? The one we got as a wedding gift is getting pretty sluggish."

He frowned, but kept his eyes straight ahead on the road. "Now, would I get you a bread machine for an anniversary gift? What kind of a husband would do that?"

She poked him in the ribs. "The kind that likes fresh, homemade bread."

"I can promise you it is not a bread machine." He pulled the minivan onto Fourth Street and parked along the curb. He took a small gift-wrapped box from his jacket pocket and handed it to her. "Here."

"This is it? You said it was bigger than a bread box!"

"Part of it is. Open it," he instructed her with a look of anticipation.

"Here? Now?"

He nodded.

"But why here? Why not at home?"

"Tori, open it."

She carefully untied the ribbon and placed it in her lap.

"You're not going to keep that ribbon and use it again, are you?" Buck asked.

"I'm going to put it in our scrapbook." She gently pulled the paper off, folded it, and slipped it beneath the pink satin ribbon.

"You'd better hurry or we'll be celebrating our seventh anniversary by the time we eat and get home," he teased. "Want me to help?"

"I can do it by myself." She smiled back at him. She removed the lid and found a single brass key inside. "A key?" she asked.

"You don't like keys?"

"I don't make a habit of collecting them." Victoria spun the little key in her fingers.

"Look in the bottom of the box."

She lifted the lid again. Folded in the bottom beneath the tiny layer of tissue paper was a photograph of a building. She recognized it immediately. "This is that building over there!" She pointed her finger to a large two-story building across the street from where Buck had parked the car. "The old Wilson building."

"It's not the old Wilson building anymore. It's Tori's building. I leased it for you, for that art and gift shop you've always dreamed about opening—the dream you had to put aside when you agreed to marry me. Now that Angelica's in school all day, there's nothing to stop you."

"But how—"

He pulled her close. "I've already contacted an architect, and I have a construction crew lined up waiting to remodel it any way you want. Happy sixth anniversary, darling."

Tears trickled down her cheeks. "I'll bet you think I'm a crybaby. It seems since I met you I've done nothing but cry."

He nestled her head against him. "You're my crybaby. And besides, we've been through a lot these past few years."

"Oh, Buck, this is the most wonderful present you could give me. My very own shop." She sat up and stared at the building that would soon house her dream. "What shall I call it?"

"I've been giving that some thought. I have a suggestion, but it's your shop. You can call it anything you wish."

She brushed a lock of shiny black hair from his brow. "And what do you think I should call it?"

"You really want to know?"

She nodded.

He took a deep breath and exhaled slowly. "I think my suggestion for a name would be appropriate under the circumstances."

"What circumstances?"

"That once you had a chance to see Alaska, you came to love it almost as much as I do."

"That's true. So what name would you suggest?"

"How about—"

Her eyes sparkled. "Yes?"

"How about—" Again he paused, enjoying this game he was playing with her.

"Buck, say it!"

"Tori's Northern Exposure Art and Gift Shop."

She repeated the words several times, then planted a kiss on his lips. "It's the perfect name." She looked again at the building. "I love it."

Buck grinned. His dream had come true too. "Remember what I told you when you first arrived in Alaska?"

She slid across the seat and snuggled in close to him. "How could I forget?"

"And what did I say you needed?"

Victoria sighed. Contented, she rested her head on Buck's broad shoulder. "How well I remember your exact words. You said all I needed was a little northern exposure. And oh, how right you were!"

Hand Quilted
with Love

Chapter 1

Quilt shop? In Juneau, Alaska? Me?" Glorianna frowned and clutched the phone tightly with both hands. Surely she'd misunderstood the attorney.

"That's right, Mrs. Kane. Your aunt left it to you," the male voice answered succinctly. "In her will."

"Why? I don't remember ever seeing my aunt Anna. Why would she leave me anything?" Glorianna's eyes narrowed with suspicion. This had to be someone's idea of a cruel joke. Either that, or God was answering her prayer in a strange way.

"She had no children of her own and you were her sister's only child. Perhaps she thought that was reason enough," the voice answered indifferently. "She didn't owe me any explanations. I'm simply her attorney. I do as I'm instructed."

"Well, ah—I do know how to quilt. I learned when I was in 4-H in junior high, but I don't know anything about running a business," she reasoned aloud, more to herself than to the stranger at the other end.

"Seems to me, if you plan to run a quilt shop, you'd better learn."

She pulled the phone from her ear and glared at the receiver, trying to ignore his inconsiderate remark. "Even if I could learn how to run a business, why would I want to move to Alaska? It's cold up there!"

"Your option. Perhaps your aunt suspected you'd feel this way. She arranged for everything to be passed on to her best friend, Emily Timberwolf, if you refused to accept your inheritance," he explained in a near monotone.

A gamut of emotions rushed through her confused mind. He did sound official. Perhaps his call was on the up-and-up. "Ah—she must have wanted me to have it or she wouldn't have left it to me, would she?"

"It's not for me to say. My clients rarely discuss their reasons with me." He cleared his throat noisily. "I'd suggest you come up here at your earliest convenience. Time is of the essence."

"To Alaska?" She nervously twisted the phone cord around her fingers. "Can't I just turn the business over to a real estate company and let them sell it for me? With my financial condition, I could sure use the money it'd bring."

"Sorry, Mrs. Kane, that is not an option." The voice on the phone took on an overly authoritative air. "Your aunt was afraid you might want to do something like that. In her will, she stipulated that in order for you to claim your inheritance, you have to personally live in Juneau, run the shop yourself, and keep it in full operation for at least two years. At the end of the two years, you may do with it whatever you wish. She was very specific about that."

Glorianna gulped hard. "Stay two years? In Alaska?"

"That's what she said."

The young mother needed time to think. After all, the call had come out of nowhere. Surely the man didn't expect an answer at this moment, and she needed time to check him out, to see if he was really who he said he was. "Let me think it over and I'll call you back when I've made my decision."

"Fine. In the meantime, I'll send you a copy of the will. I'd suggest you let your attorney take a look at it."

"My attorney?"

"Yes, your attorney. You do have one, don't you?" His voice sounded agitated. "If not, I'd suggest you find one. I'll be waiting for your call."

Frazzled, she had to have him repeat his phone number twice before she got it right and hung up the phone. Totally confused and wondering if she'd imagined the whole episode, she dropped into the worn chair next to the desk with a plop, one leg draped awkwardly over the armrest, her fingers massaging at her temples. It'd been a lousy day. First, Todd, her nearly seven-year-old son, had spilled his glass of milk all over the kitchen floor. Next, the washer wouldn't agitate. Then the checkbook wouldn't balance and the new shoes she'd hoped to buy for her son had to be put off 'til next month. Now, this! At times, she felt like God had forsaken her, although she knew He never would.

She kicked off her shoes and wiggled her puffy toes. Her feet were swollen. Not bad, but enough to make them feel weird. She'd been on them most of the day.

Alaska? Run a quilt shop? Why not? What do I have to lose?

Chapter 2

Glorianna stood on the dock in Vancouver, waiting, feeling like a stranger in a foreign land, her luggage piled at her feet. She stretched, then splayed her fingers across the small of her back, pressing hard. Why had the attorney arranged for her to meet her escort here, of all places? On a dock? She checked the address on the paper again, the fourth time since the taxi she'd taken from the Vancouver airport had dropped her off there.

Yep, this is it, she assured herself confidently as she folded the paper and slipped it back into her pocket. *He said my aunt's best friend, Emily Timberwolf, would be in Vancouver on business and would be happy to accompany me to Juneau. We were to meet by the bronze statue of Vancouver's famous Captain George Vancouver.* She shifted her weight from one foot to the other as she smiled up at the likeness of the courageous captain.

She checked her watch. Ten minutes of eleven. She was early. They weren't to meet until eleven. Why wasn't there some place she could sit down? Her shoes pinched her feet and her head was killing her. She considered sitting on her suitcases, but they looked none too stable.

"You Glorianna?" a male voice asked from somewhere behind her. "Glorianna Kane?"

She spun around to find a bearded, dark-haired, blue-eyed stranger clad in faded jeans and red plaid shirt walking toward her, and his presence unnerved her. Her impulse was to turn and run, but she stood her ground. "Y–yes, I'm Glorianna. How did you know my name?"

The tips of his handlebar mustache tilted upward as he gave her a broad grin and stuck out his hand. "I'm Trapper. Trapper Timberwolf," he told her as he pulled off his hat.

The man towered over her. Timidly, she accepted his hand, then quickly backed away.

"My mom wasn't feeling too good, and since I was coming down to Vancouver on business anyway, I offered to take you back to Juneau," he explained as he eyed first her, then her pile of luggage. "From the look on your face, you're disappointed I'm not my mom, right?"

"We–well, now that you mention it," she stammered, her voice unsteady and wavering. He was right. She was definitely disappointed it wasn't Emily Timberwolf, and somewhat afraid. "Y–yes, I am. I mean—well—I was looking

129

forward to meeting your mother."

"And you're not sure I'm who I say I am?"

His friendly smile eased her fears a bit, but she still didn't trust him.

"It's not that—exactly—"

His well-tanned hand reached into his back pocket and retrieved his wallet. "Mom was sure you'd feel that way when I showed up instead of her. She told me I'd better show you some identification. I guess a woman can't be too careful these days." He presented her with his Alaskan driver's license, which bore the name Trapper Timberwolf and a picture that hardly did justice to his handsome features. "Satisfied?"

She offered a weak nod. "Sorta."

A brow lifted as he shrugged. "I guess you folks in the lower forty-eight are afraid to trust any stranger. Gettin' to be like that up here too."

"Yes," she agreed, "it pays to be cautious."

He fished around in his wallet and proudly displayed a picture of him with his arm wrapped around an attractive elderly woman. "Here, this ought to do it. Mom said you'd feel better about going with me if I made sure you realized I was her son."

She reached for the picture, her eyes still riveted on the stranger with the intriguing clear blue eyes. A welcome wave of relief swept over her as she immediately recognized Emily Timberwolf from the picture the attorney had sent to her.

"Me and my mom," he said proudly as his finger tapped the photograph. His hands were long and slender, with well-trimmed nails, but she could tell they'd done their share of honest work.

She focused on the picture. "Yes, I see that now. You do resemble her."

"I'm harmless, Mrs. Kane. Honest, I am." He slipped the picture into its place, then the wallet into his back pocket. "But if you're hesitant about riding with me, there are some commercial carriers around. We can probably get you on one of those. I promise I won't be offended, but my mom'll sure be upset with me if I don't bring you back to her like I promised. Your call."

She stared at the man. He appeared to be who he said he was. But what did that mean? Just because he was Emily Timberwolf's son didn't mean he wasn't an axe murderer. What did she know about any of the Timberwolfs? Only what a voice on the phone had told her. Yet, here she stood—stranded on a dock in Vancouver, with no idea what to do next.

"You wanna call my mom? I've got my cell phone right here in my pocket."

She couldn't dawdle on the dock all day. She had to make a decision, and she certainly didn't want to appear ungrateful if he was on the up-and-up. *Oh, God, be with me, please.* "N–no, I think I'd better go with you, since that's what your mother expected," she said feebly, still not totally convinced she was doing the right thing.

His responsive grin was reassuring. "My mama raised me to be a gentleman. You're in good hands."

She hoped he was telling the truth. If he wasn't. . . She shuddered to think of what sort of predicament she might be getting herself into. She'd trusted her husband, and look where it'd gotten her. Even after living in the same house and sharing the same bed, she hadn't really known him or what he was capable of doing to their family.

"Hungry? My mom packed a little something for us to munch on," he told her as he grabbed up her bags and they began to move forward. "Some crackers, a jar of cheese spread, some chips, a couple of pieces of fruit—that sort of stuff. We'll eat it on the plane."

"Plane? I thought we were going by train or maybe the bus." She stopped abruptly, her eyes rounded with fright. "It's not a small plane, is it? I'm terrified of small planes!"

He threw back his head and let loose a hearty laugh. "Train? You thought we were going on a train or a bus? Lady, don't you know the only way you can get into Juneau is by plane or ship?"

"No," she confessed with a deep sigh, feeling utterly stupid. "I didn't know. I just assumed—since it's the state capital—"

"Well, you're in good company," he said as he motioned her along. "Most people don't know that. Really, it's not as bad as it sounds. Actually, being isolated from the rest of the world is kinda nice."

"For Eskimos," she grumbled under her breath as she allowed herself to be catapulted along the dock while trying to keep up with his long strides. *What have I gotten myself into? Coming to this place, and without any business experience? I must have been crazy to even consider this whole fiasco!*

"You'll love it," he said with a wink. "Or you'll hate it. It's up to you."

She shifted the strap on her shoulder bag. "How far is it to the airport?"

"Airport?"

"Yes, where your plane is."

Another vigorous laugh boomed from somewhere deep in his broad chest.

"What's so funny?" she asked, hating jokes at her expense, especially when she didn't understand them.

"Lady, my plane is right there." He motioned to the end of the big dock just ahead of them. "The blue one with the eagle painted on the side. Isn't she a beauty?"

Glorianna gasped as her palm rose to flatten itself against her chest. "That's a seaplane!"

"Sure is. What did you expect? A DC-9?"

"I'm afraid—"

He gave her a mimicking frown. "Of what? That little plane's safer than a

131

bicycle, if that's what's worrying you."

She gulped hard, attempting to swallow the fear that welled up in her throat as they moved forward and he opened the door on the little seaplane. Then, frozen to the spot, she watched as he carefully placed her suitcases inside the compartment.

He held out a hand. "You're next!"

Looking heavenward, she breathed a prayer. *Oh, God, don't desert me now! I've got to do this. I have to be brave. There's no other choice.* Gripping Trapper's hand tightly, she cautiously placed her foot on the little step. "Have—have you been flying long?"

A grin tilted his weathered face as he squinted against the sun's rays and helped her inside. "Want to see my pilot's license too?"

She felt a sudden flush rise to her cheeks. "No, it's just—"

"Just that you're scared to death?" he asked with the lift of a brow. "You're not only afraid of me, you're afraid to fly with me!"

She nodded her head toward the pontoons on the sleek blue plane. "Oh, no. Not you. I'm afraid to fly with anyone in one of these—"

He lifted both palms toward her. "Okay, lady, I'll be the first to admit seaplanes aren't for everyone. I've had full-grown men break out in a cold sweat at the thought. But trust me. I know how to fly this thing and I'm a good pilot. You'll be perfectly safe."

Chagrined, she gulped and accepted the foolishness of her fears and made every attempt to relax. The dock was lined with seaplanes. Dozens of them. Apparently, up here in the North Country they were as common as SUVs were in Kansas. She was headed for Alaska now. Things were different up here. If she was to fit into her new life, she'd have to be ready to make adjustments, and it looked as though riding in a seaplane was one of them. With an uplifted chin and willing herself to sound courageous, she slipped into the seat and fastened the seat belt before white-knuckling the armrest. "I do trust you, Mr. Timberwolf. I'm—I'm sure you're a very good pilot."

He climbed in through the little door behind her and slammed it securely, placing his Stetson on a box before crossing over and sliding into the pilot's seat. "Then, we're off!" He snapped his own seat belt in place. "We've got quite a few miles ahead of us." He grinned. "And by the way, call me Trapper."

Glorianna's eyelids pressed tightly together and her heart pounded wildly as he revved up the engine. When he seemed satisfied with the pitch, she felt the little plane inch away from the dock and begin to pick up speed. She let out a gasp, then held her breath.

"Aren't you gonna watch us take off? It's pretty exciting."

She wished he hadn't asked. They'd barely left the dock and already her stomach was churning. "No, I'd prefer not to." One hand weakly flattened against her abdomen. The antacid tablet she'd taken hadn't helped at all. "I'd rather not."

"Well, you'll get a second chance when we refuel," he said matter-of-factly. "In Ketchikan."

She opened her eyes and swallowed hard, wishing she'd brought the motion sickness pills her mother had suggested for her flight from Kansas. But she'd opted to leave them behind. *Well, too late now. Probably wouldn't have been a good idea anyway.* Flying on big planes had never bothered her much, but flying on seaplanes was a whole other category. Something she hadn't anticipated.

"You sure you should be here? I mean, taking over your aunt's quilt shop? It's a big responsibility," he asked over the engine's drone as he gave her a sideways glance. "You okay? You look a little green."

She wished he'd look away and leave her alone. She was beginning to feel a bit queasy. *Maybe I shouldn't have taken those antacid pills on an empty stomach.* "I'm fine," she lied, wishing she were anywhere but in that plane. "And, believe it or not, I do know how to quilt. Even won a blue ribbon or two," she bragged to impress the man and to remind herself she wasn't a complete novice when it came to quilting.

"Like I was saying, I love Alaska, wouldn't live anywhere else. . .but a woman from Kansas moving here with a young son? I'm not sure it's a good idea. Alaska is different from the lower forty-eight. Most sourdoughs can't make it through the first year. They—"

She watched the clouds disappear as the tip of the plane nosed toward the heavens and her stomach sank into her shoes. "Sou—sourdoughs?"

"Yeah," he responded with a chuckle. "That's what they used to called the people who came to Alaska to seek their fortune. They soured on Alaska their first winter but couldn't leave because their dough was all gone. Happens to folks nowadays too. Maybe it'll happen to you."

"That's a fine thing to say," she retorted as she forced herself to look out the window again and wished she hadn't. "I—"

Her hand flew to cover her mouth as her stomach flip-flopped, gave one final lurch, and spewed forth. With her free hand, she grabbed the wadded-up paper napkin the flight attendant had given her when she'd served the soft drinks on the flight from Kansas and wiped her hand as best she could, sure there was more to come.

His nose wrinkled up as he grabbed a paper sack from a box on the floor and thrust it toward her. "Here, use this."

She quickly separated the top and stuck her face into the narrow opening, feeling lightheaded and nauseous, the world spinning behind her closed eyelids.

"I've got a box of tissues when you're ready for them," he offered with a sympathetic voice. "And water in a bottle."

She kept her head buried in the sack until her stomach calmed down. When the worst was over, she stuck out a hand to receive the tissues.

"Don't be embarrassed. It's not uncommon for folks to get a little airsick on a small plane. You'll be fine in a minute or two. Just try to relax."

She felt the cool of his hand rest on her arm. "Th–thank you."

He pulled a clean rag from a bag in the box and moistened it with water from the bottle. "Wash your face. It'll help."

She took the cloth and rubbed it gently across her face. The cool of the water was soothing. "You're right, it does help," she conceded in an almost whisper, hoping her nausea had passed.

He reached into the box and pulled out a small package of soda crackers, much like she'd find on a restaurant salad bar, and handed them to her. "When you feel like it, nibble on these. When you're ready, I'll pour you a cool cup of water. Okay?"

She managed a forced smile. "Thanks, again."

I must look a mess, she reasoned with a stolen glance at his strong profile as she smoothed her wrinkled jacket and adjusted her rumpled skirt beneath the seat belt. *What an impression I'm making on this poor man, after he was nice enough to fly me to Juneau.*

"Feeling any better?" His voice was kind and his eyes showed great concern.

"A–a little," she murmured with a fake smile as she blinked and swallowed hard. "You were right. The crackers helped."

They flew along in silence, the roar of the plane's engine filling the cabin with a rhythmic hum.

"Take some deep breaths," he suggested, breaking the silence. "We'll be landing in Ketchikan in about thirty minutes and you can get out and walk around a bit in the fresh air."

Fine time to get sick, she babbled to herself as she leaned against the headrest and gazed out the window. Her stomach had settled down some and she was actually feeling a bit more like herself. "You mean you're going to land this thing on the water?" She shuddered, touching her cheek to the cool of the window glass. "I can hardly wait."

"Unless you have a better idea," he teased with a smile as he checked the instrument panel. He turned his face toward hers and added convincingly, "I promise I'll make a smooth landing. You'll hardly know when we make contact."

"I'll hold you to it," she said, hoping to believe him. The odd thing was, she did trust him.

"I won't let you down. I've landed this baby hundreds of times. She never disappoints me. She knows who's boss," he said with a pat to the multi-windowed instrument panel. "The only gal I can trust."

"She? You call your plane she? You sound a bit cynical."

"Me? Cynical? Never."

"You sound like it. That comment about your plane being the only gal you can trust. And about you being the boss."

He gave her a puzzled look. "Didn't mean it to sound that way. But, now that you've accused me of it, I guess I am. In some ways. How long were you married?"

His question toppled her off guard. They hadn't discussed personal things until now, and she wasn't sure she was ready to discuss the topsy-turvy events in her life with this stranger.

"Nearly nine years." She bit at her lip.

"Mom said when she phoned you, you mentioned your husband died in a hunting accident. How long ago?"

She nodded, her eyes misty. "Midsummer."

"Oh," he sympathized, turning to her with a frown. "I'm so sorry. I can't imagine losing a loved one like that. You must have been devastated."

"I was," she answered simply, remembering the horrible way in which she'd found out about her husband's philandering the day after the funeral. His death was hard to take, but learning of his infidelity nearly killed her.

"You are making some major changes in your life, aren't you?"

She nodded. *Some changes?* That was putting it mildly. A whole new life was more like it.

"How old's your boy?"

Her face brightened. "Todd? He's nearly seven. I miss him already, but he's coming in a week or two. Right now, he's staying with my mom."

"Your mom, eh?" He gave her a sideways glance, a brow cocked. "I'll bet she's thrilled with the idea of you two moving to Alaska."

That's an understatement, she mused, shaking her head. "No, she was anything but thrilled when I got the call from Aunt Anna's attorney, and she's not much better now. She was furious with my aunt for leaving me the shop and even more furious with me for accepting it, but I look at it this way: It's a great opportunity to start a whole new life—kind of an adventure. Know what I mean?"

"Yes, but I can't say I blame her. If I were a mother—" He grinned. "Which I'm not, nor obviously ever will be—I'd do everything I could to keep my daughter from moving so far away."

"But I need something new in my life. Something to take away all the trauma I've been through. Owning this shop will be a whole new thing for me. Like I said, an adventure. I think an adventure will be good for Todd too."

"It'll be an adventure alright." He gave her a sly grin. "By the way, does that son of yours have your beautiful blue eyes?"

She wiggled uncomfortably in the seat. "I'm not sure about the beautiful part, but yes, his eyes are blue. I wish he'd inherited his father's blond hair, but his came out mousy brown, just like mine."

"If he looks anything like his mother—"

"He does, but I'm sure he'll be tall, like the Kane side of the family."

"What does he think about coming to live in Alaska?"

"Oh, he's excited about the move. He's a great kid. I promised him a puppy as soon as he gets up here, probably a poodle."

"How's he taking his dad leaving him so suddenly? Losing a father at his age has to be hard on the boy. I can't imagine losing my dad."

The shrug of her shoulders fairly well answered his question. "It's been hard on him, but his father was never home much. They weren't really close." *But oh, how I wish they had been. Maybe if Jim had spent more time with his family, things would have worked out differently, she thought with a grimace. He hardly said boo to Todd these past two years. And here I thought he was working overtime to get us out of debt. Boy, was I dumb!*

He turned away and gazed at the blue sky ahead. "Tough raising a kid. I sure wouldn't want to do it."

"Oh? Why not?" His comment surprised her. She felt being trusted with a child was one of God's biggest blessings, and he seemed like the kind of guy who'd want a house full of kids.

"Too much trouble. Kids tie you down. I've seen it happen with my friends. Me? I like my independence." He tapped one of the little round windows on the instrument panel with the tip of his finger, leaned forward a bit to check its numbers before answering, then shook his head. "Nope, kids aren't for this old guy. A wife either. A woman and kids would hamper my lifestyle. I'm sort of a vagabond. I like things the way they are. I value my freedom too much. Besides, I'd be a bear to live with." He gave her a slight grin. "Guess your husband didn't mind being tied down. He married you."

She winced and he noticed.

"Whoops, sorry. I didn't mean any disrespect. Guess it's still too soon for you to talk about him. I meant that as a compliment."

This conversation was getting way out of hand and was certainly going in a different direction than she'd prefer. "You're right. It is too soon. I'd rather not discuss it, if it's all the same to you."

"Suit yourself. Just making small talk."

Once again, other than the monotonous roar of the engine, silence filled the cabin. Glorianna was feeling almost like her normal self. The clamminess had disappeared, her stomach had settled down, and she could look out the window without feeling queasy. Since they'd stopped discussing her husband, she found herself able to think of more pleasant things.

For the first time since takeoff she could actually enjoy the beauty of the Alaskan scenery with its lush green growth and heavily snowcapped mountains. She'd visited Colorado, but it wasn't the same. The mountains were different, and the trees were different. There was an awesome quality to the Alaskan mountains, an ethereal dimension she'd never before experienced. They seemed to go on and on forever, one white peak tucked behind the other, as if there were no beginning and no ending.

"Never been to Alaska, huh?" Trapper asked, breaking into her thoughts as once again he checked the instrument panel.

"Ah—no. Well, actually yes."

He gave her a quick, friendly wink. "Which is it?"

"I was born in Anchorage, but my parents took me to Kansas when I was a week old."

He gave her an incredulous look. "Why would they ever leave Alaska?"

"Long story," she answered with a deep sigh as she remembered things long forgotten.

He gave first one long arm a stretch, then the other. "Well, I've got lots of time, and I'm sure not goin' anywhere. That is, if you don't mind talking about it."

She leaned into the slim seat back and gave Trapper an appreciative look, glad he'd been willing to let the subject of her husband drop when she'd asked him. "Well," she began, "as my mother tells it, my aunt lived in Anchorage and invited my parents to come and visit her. My dad was out of work and she said there were lots of jobs in Alaska, so they packed up and came up here. Neither Mom nor Dad liked it, so as soon as I was born, they headed back to Kansas."

"That's not a long story," he quipped.

"I left out all the boring details," she added with a grin, finding him surprisingly easy to talk with.

"You never came back to visit your aunt?"

"Nope. And she never came to visit us. I never saw her again. Oh, she and my mom exchanged Christmas cards, but that was about it. They never talked much about her. I don't even remember seeing a recent picture of her."

"Really?" He ran a finger over his heavy beard thoughtfully. "Well, your aunt Anna must have remembered you, to leave you all her worldly possessions like she did. She and my mom were close friends. She was a nice lady. Wish you could have known her. You'd have liked her."

"I'm sure I would've liked her," she said politely. "I'm named after her, you know."

"The Anna part? I'm amazed I hadn't figured that out. Umm, interesting."

She nodded. "Yeah, the Anna part. I've always been surprised they named me after an aunt who never even sent me a birthday card."

"She didn't? That doesn't sound like the Anna I knew."

"Never sent a single one."

"Well, that's some business you've inherited. Wait'll you see the shop. Your aunt was quite successful," he told her with a slap to his knee. "You're one lucky woman!"

"Lucky?" she repeated with a defeated shrug. She'd been married to Jim nearly nine years and had thought she'd known her husband well. Apparently, she hadn't known him at all. She remembered the feelings of shock and betrayal when she discovered all the bills he'd run up entertaining his girlfriend, charges she'd found when she'd gone through his desk after the funeral. No wonder they were in debt and there never seemed to be any extra money to put into a savings account. "I wouldn't exactly say I'm lucky."

"Yeah, I see your point, losing your husband so suddenly. But you have to admit, this inheritance of yours came at the right time in your life. After what you've gone through, sounds to me like a change would be just the thing."

She tucked a wayward curl behind her ear and blinked away a tear of regret as she thought over his words. He was right. That had been her thought exactly, although her mother hadn't been able to see it. This was the perfect time in her life to make major changes. *It's time things start going my way. Maybe Juneau will be the answer to my prayers.*

With a renewed spirit, she turned to the stranger sitting beside her. "You know, you're right, Trapper. I am a lucky woman. I have a wonderful son, an awesome God, and I'm heading for a new life. What more could I ask?"

"Look down there," he said, apparently not noticing her tears or her newly found resolve, his attention focused on their destination as the little plane banked deeply to the right. "There's our gas station. I'm gonna set her down. You ready?"

She stared out the window at the tiny red speck along the waterfront, sucked in a deep breath, and sat up straight in the seat. *I should be very thankful for an aunt who saw fit to leave me her worldly possessions.* Shoulders squared, she lifted her chin determinedly. She was getting a second chance at life. Inheritances of this magnitude didn't drop into your lap every day. Why had she been so apprehensive about coming to Alaska? This was exactly what she needed. Hadn't she asked for God's leading?

She dabbed at her eyes, using one of the little tissues Trapper had given her, and turned with a smile toward the gentle man piloting the little seaplane. "Yes, Trapper. I'm ready. Set her down."

Chapter 3

Well, you two finally made it. Dad and I were getting a little worried. I've kept supper waiting for you." She gave them each a hug, then motioned them into a warm, inviting kitchen. "Glorianna, I'm Emily. I'm sorry I couldn't come pick you up. You're every bit as pretty as I thought you'd be."

Without waiting for a response, she began issuing orders. "Glorianna, take your coat off and find yourself a chair. Trapper, put down that suitcase and help her with her coat. Dyami, throw another log or two on the fire. We want our guest to be comfortable."

After a sly wink from Trapper, Glorianna slipped out of her coat and moved into one of the chairs at the heavy round oak table in the center of the big room, watching as the tall, slender woman scurried about.

Trapper hung the coat on the rack, then briskly rubbed his hands together. "What am I smelling, Mama? Couldn't be venison stew, could it?"

Venison? Glorianna recoiled at his words and certainly didn't share his enthusiasm. She'd never eaten venison in her life!

"I don't know why it'd surprise you, son. Your doting mother fixes it for you at least once a week. I can't get her to fix any of my favorites."

A damp sponge hit the man squarely on the cheek. "Now, Dyami, you know better'n that! Don't you go lettin' our guest get the wrong idea about me. Livin' with you two is like livin' with a circus."

Trapper pulled the butter dish from the top shelf of the refrigerator and put it on the table alongside an uncut loaf of what appeared to be freshly baked bread. He gave Glorianna a quick wink before moving up behind his mother, wrapping his long arms about her waist, and giving her a noisy smackeroo on her cheek as she gave the stew one final stir.

"You'd better be kind to your mama if you want any of this stew," Emily warned him as she grabbed two hot pads, lifted the pot, and headed for the table.

"Yes, Mama." Trapper pulled the big ladle from a drawer, then seated himself on a chair between his father and Glorianna.

"Dyami, you pray."

Glorianna's heart soared as the members of the little group joined hands, forming an unbroken circle.

Praying and asking God's blessing on their meal had been a regular part of hers and her son's routine. Unfortunately, her husband had wanted no part of it.

How many years had she attended church without Jim, begging God to change his attitude about Christianity? Instead of seeing answers to her prayer, things had only gotten worse. Jim had begun to spend more and more evenings away from home, drinking and carousing with his buddies, going on those long hunting trips. He'd even forbidden her to speak God's name in front of him, though it'd been fine for him to, to use God's name in vain, and in front of their son.

She listened carefully as Trapper's father lifted his face upward and praised God for His blessings on them before thanking Him and asking His blessings on the food. She was amazed at how easily he talked to God.

"Trapper take good care of you today?" Emily asked as she picked up the salt and pepper shakers and added generous shakes to both her plate and her husband's.

Glorianna smiled. She'd never seen anyone salt and pepper another person's food like that. Somehow, the gesture was endearing and spoke worlds about their close relationship.

"Very good, thank you," she responded with a sheepish grin toward the man eagerly devouring a bowl of his mother's stew.

"She was a model passenger, Mama," he said between gulps. "Hard to believe she'd never flown in a seaplane before."

"He didn't try that dead stick trick on you, did he?"

Glorianna turned to his father, her brows lifted. "Dead stick trick? What's that?"

"Just a little trick he likes to play on first-time seaplane flyers."

"Dad!" Trapper swatted at his father's wrist playfully. "Gimme a break. I'd never do that to a lady."

"Dyami. Trapper. Let the girl eat her supper in peace," Emily told them sharply as she gestured to Glorianna's untouched bowl of soup.

Glorianna swallowed hard, filled her spoon, and braced herself. What if she didn't like it? Would she be able to eat enough of it so as not to offend her host?

"Go on, eat up."

She felt as though she were on stage as three pairs of eyes focused on her, waiting for her to make her move. With one quick motion, she shoved the spoon into her mouth. Much to her surprise, the stew was good. Actually, it had a bit of a sweet taste to it. "It's delicious!"

Trapper grinned. "Did you doubt it would be? Because it was venison?"

"Sorta."

"You've never eaten venison before?" Emily refilled her husband's bowl without him asking.

"No, never."

"Well, your Alaskan adventure has begun," Trapper said with a smile only the two of them understood.

The rest of the meal went pleasantly as the four enjoyed exchanging small talk, mostly about Juneau itself and, of course, Todd. When they'd each consumed a generous wedge of warm pumpkin pie and the last drop of coffee had disappeared, Emily motioned toward her son. "Take Glorianna's suitcase to her room so she can get settled. I'm sure she's had a long day and would like to get a good night's sleep. We'll talk more tomorrow."

"Room at the end of the hall?" Trapper stood, suitcase in hand, waiting for his mother's direction.

She nodded before bidding their houseguest good night and waving them off.

"I like your folks," she told him as they stood in the lovely room.

"Me too." Trapper put the suitcase on the foot of the bed. "Sure this is the only suitcase you're going to need? I can bring in the others. Just say the word."

She shook her head. "Thanks, this one's plenty. I packed everything I'd need for my first night in this one."

"The rest are downstairs in the truck. I'd be happy to get them."

He moved to the windows and pulled down the shades. "It'll take you awhile to get used to the sun shining this time of day. The shades will help."

"I'm so tired, I wouldn't notice if the windows were wide open." She sat down on the foot of the soft bed and kicked off her shoes.

He noticed. "Feet hurt? Sometimes flying makes folks' feet swell."

"They're fine. Just a bit tired. A nice warm bath will do the trick."

One look at her puffy ankles said otherwise. He braced himself in the doorway, marveling at how beautiful she looked in the dim light of the dresser lamp. You'd never guess she'd left Kansas in the wee hours of the morning and had been traveling all day. "Anything else you need?"

"No, thanks. You and your family have been more than kind. I can't thank you enough."

"Too hot in here? I can turn down the furnace. Or, are you too cold?"

She gave him an appreciative smile. "I'm fine. Your mother put several quilts on the foot of the bed."

"Well, if you need anything—"

"I know. Just let your parents know."

"I'm sorry if I offended you when I said you might be making a mistake, pulling up stakes and moving to Alaska."

"You didn't offend me in the slightest. In fact, I've had those same misgivings. I guess only time will tell."

"I really hope things go well for you here in Juneau. You do know that, don't you?"

She nodded with a bit of a yawn. "Yes, I do."

"Well, good night. See you in the morning."

"Good night. And thanks again."

"Don't worry about getting up early. Sleep until you're rested."

"I will."

"Good night."

"Good night."

❧

Her watch showed nearly ten when she awoke the next morning. She'd been afraid she'd be too excited to sleep and was surprised to find she'd slept an hour later than usual. The house was deafeningly quiet. No TV. No radio. None of the boyish laughter she was used to hearing from her son. Nothing. A quick glance at the clock on the dresser reminded her it was several hours earlier there than it was in Kansas. No wonder she'd thought she'd slept late!

After pulling out the stem on her wristwatch and resetting the time, she slipped quietly out of bed and made her way into the little bathroom off her bedroom. In minutes, she'd brushed her teeth, applied her makeup, and combed her hair. She slipped into her blue jeans and topped them with a long-sleeved cotton sweater, stuffed her feet into her too-tight shoes, and headed down the hall toward the kitchen, her repacked suitcase in hand.

Trapper sat at the round table where they'd eaten supper the night before, sipping coffee and reading the paper.

"Morning."

He slowly lowered the paper and peered over the top, his damp hair looking as though he'd just stepped out of the shower. "Morning. Sleep okay?"

"Wonderfully well. You?"

He motioned toward a chair as he grabbed the insulated coffeepot and poured her a cup. "Great, although my house was a bit cold when I got home. I'd forgotten to turn up the heat before I left for Vancouver."

She frowned. "Home? Don't you live here? With your parents? I assumed—"

"Nope." He took a last swig of coffee, then pulled a napkin off a plate of doughnuts sitting in the middle of the table before continuing. "I have my own place. I bought it just before. . ." His voice trailed off.

Before what? she wondered.

"Have a doughnut. Mom left these for us. And there's a pitcher of juice." He grinned, motioning to a small yellow pitcher. "They're already prayed for."

She decided to pass on the doughnuts, poured herself a glass of orange juice, and took several sips before picking up the coffee cup he'd filled. "Good coffee."

"Can't beat a good, hot cup of coffee to get your blood circulating in the morning." He poured himself another cup of coffee and took a swig. "Mom said to tell you to plan on having dinner with us at the restaurant tonight. It's baked salmon night at The Grizzly Bear."

"Oh?"

"Yeah. The place'll be packed, but you'll enjoy it."

She hadn't realized they'd expected to do anything special for dinner. She'd hoped to be settling herself into the little apartment her aunt had left her by that time. Maybe call for a pizza, if they had such a thing as pizza delivery in Juneau. "Your family doesn't have to entertain me, you know. You've done so much already."

"Hey, I know you're anxious to get moved into your place, but you have to eat sometime. Besides, my mom doesn't take no for an answer from anyone when she's made up her mind."

"What time are our reservations?" she asked, hoping the restaurant wasn't far from her shop.

He leaned back in the chair with a hearty laugh. "You don't need reservations when you own the place! Did you see the sign just before we turned up the hill?" He refilled their coffee cups and reached for another doughnut. "My folks own The Grizzly Bear. Have since I was a toddler."

No, she hadn't seen the sign. She'd been too busy thinking about the shop. "That's why it's so quiet here this morning? Your parents are at the restaurant?"

"Yep," he said, rising to his feet. "They start serving breakfast at six."

"And I kept them up late last night? Why didn't they tell me? I could have gotten a room at a motel."

He put the juice pitcher in the refrigerator. "My mom would never hear of it—you being her best friend's niece. Are you ready to go?"

"Ready and eager."

He picked up her suitcase, pulled open the door, and followed her down the steps to his waiting truck. While he was putting the suitcase in the back, she moved to the door and reached for the handle. What she saw inside made her heart lurch and she screamed, backing away quickly, ramming her body into his as he stepped up behind her.

"There's a big dog in your truck!" she screeched out, as if he didn't know it.

He moved to open the door, but she grabbed his arm. "No, don't!"

He gave her a puzzled look. "Why? Meeto won't hurt you."

"I—I'm a—afraid of d—dogs!" she sputtered out, her voice trembling with fear.

"Ah, come on. He's a nice dog, a Siberian husky. All the kids around here love him." His hand moved toward the door handle again.

"No, I ca—can't," she mumbled, panic contorting her face. "I just ca—can't."

"Look, you're in Alaska now. You'd better get used to seeing dogs. Most folks have them." His voice betrayed a slight impatience. "Why don't you let me roll down the window and you can pet him? Get acquainted with him."

Her startled expression answered his question. "Never!"

"I'll have him ride in the little backseat. There's plenty of room for the three of us in the cab."

"The three of us? You expect me to get in there with—that—that monster?"

"So? What do you want me to do? Leave him here?"

143

"Can't you put him in the back?"

Trapper shrugged. "Guess I could, but he always rides in front with me."

"Then call me a taxi." Glorianna crossed her arms defiantly, then wished she hadn't, feeling much like a spoiled child.

"A taxi? You can't mean it."

Her face softened as she touched his arm. "I'm sorry, Trapper, but you don't seem to realize how afraid I am of your dog. When I was about six, I tried to pet a strange dog and he bit me." She extended her arm and pulled up her sleeve. "There. See?"

He examined the jagged scar carefully. "Not all dogs are like the one that did this."

"But how do I know that? How can you be sure which dogs bite and which ones won't?" She pulled her sleeve back down over her wrist. "I can't help it. I've been afraid of dogs all my life. That's why I've never gotten one for my son."

Trapper warily slipped an arm about her waist. "Sometimes the little ones are the worst, but if you're that afraid of Meeto, I'll put him in the back." He grinned down at her. "Even though he'll probably never forgive me."

She watched as he moved around to the driver's side, opened the door, and let the big dog jump out. "Meeto. Here," she heard him say firmly, and instantly the big dog jumped over the tailgate and into the back. "Sit."

Trapper circled the truck and opened the door on the passenger side and motioned her in. "That better?"

She felt like a fool, being so demanding, but she couldn't help it. "Yes, much better, thanks."

She put one foot inside the cab and backed out. "You've got guns in there!"

"Of course, I've got guns, but they're in the rack with the safety on. What's the problem?"

"I'm afraid of guns."

"You want me to take them out of the truck and put them in the back with Meeto?" he asked with a look of disgust.

"I'm sorry, I can't ride in there with guns."

Trapper let out a long gush of air. "Okay, I'll move them."

For a number of blocks, they rode along in silence.

"I'll bet your dog is much happier back there than being cooped up in the cab of your truck," she finally said.

He gave her a half-hearted grin. "Not my dog. He belongs up here with me and he knows it. Where I go, my dog goes. You're in the North Country now, Glorianna. We do things differently here. If you're as smart as I think you are, you'll make allowances for our differences."

His words weren't spoken in an unkind manner, but she knew he was passionate about every word. Had she made a mistake thinking she could

144

adjust to life in Alaska?

Ten minutes later, they were driving down Eagan Drive and onto Franklin Street, along the myriad of docks that flanked the waterfront. Glorianna stared out the windows in amazement. "I can't believe how many businesses there are along this street."

"You ain't seen nothin' yet," he told her with a grin and a quick glance back at Meeto, as if to make sure the big dog was riding comfortably.

"I–I never imagined Juneau was anything like this."

"Look over there."

Shifting slightly in her seat, she could see dozens of colorful little seaplanes bobbing up and down along a wooden dock behind a well-kept building, bearing a sign, SEAPLANE RIDES. SEE THE GLACIERS.

Her eyes widened. "You mean they actually fly over the glaciers in those little planes? Isn't that dangerous?"

Trapper flipped the turn signal, slowed the truck a bit, and moved closer to the curb. "No, of course not. In fact, you can take a helicopter ride and the pilot will land on a glacier so you can actually get out and walk on it."

"Not me!" She pushed back in her seat, her fingers splayed across her chest.

He shrugged. "Too bad. I was hoping to take you and your son on one when he gets here. He'd love it."

A gasp caught in her throat at the thought. "Thanks, but no thanks. I'd never let him do such a thing."

"That's a shame, it's a real thrill."

Suddenly, she leaned toward the windshield, her finger pointing dead ahead. "That's a cruise ship!"

"Yep, sure is. One of the last of the season." He tossed her an easy grin. "And behind it are two more."

Her mouth gaped open. "They park that close to the town?"

"Yep, only a few hundred feet from the hundreds of little shops on Juneau's waterfront. The passengers love shopping here, as you'll find out soon enough."

He slowed down again and pointed out the huge ropes mooring the ships to the heavy posts mounted on the concrete dock. "They'll be here most of the day."

Shielding her eyes from the brilliant morning sun, Glorianna's attention went to the rows of outdoor balconies on the first ship. Several people leaned over the railings, waving to those on the docks. "That ship is huge. How many people does it hold?"

"Oh, that one, probably two thousand, with maybe seven or eight hundred crew members." He leaned forward a bit, his hands and forearms circling the steering wheel. "The two behind it are a bit smaller. Maybe only seventeen hundred passengers."

She shook her head. "I'm impressed. I had no idea they were this large."

Trapper reached over and laid a hand on her arm. "The best is yet to come. Look!"

She turned in the direction he pointed, and there, among the many shops that dotted the opposite side of the street, was a huge, white two-story building. The large sign spanning its entire width said, in big letters no one could miss, THE BEAR PAW QUILT AND GIFT SHOP.

"There she is. She's all yours!"

Speechless, Glorianna stared at the building.

"I'll make a turn at the corner and pull in behind the place." He flipped on the left turn signal and waited for oncoming traffic.

As the truck moved forward and made a long, slow curve, Glorianna craned her neck, keeping the quilt shop in view as long as possible. Her heart pounded with both joy and trepidation.

"I've got to get a car of my own," she told him, as they pulled in behind the building that housed her shop. "I can't expect you to go carting me around all the time."

He tossed her a grin. "Did anyone say I minded?"

After settling the truck into a parking place, he switched off the key and turned to face her. "See what's painted on the wall? Right there where that white minivan is parked?"

She leaned toward him for a better look. "Yes, it says Anna Moore, Proprietor."

"See what's parked in that space?"

"The white minivan?"

"Yes."

"Yes, I see it. Whose is it?"

His smile broadened and he looked like a child with a secret. "Yours."

Her hand flew to her chest. "Mine? Really?"

"It was your aunt's. She left everything she owned to you, including her car. It's all yours." He pulled a small key ring from his pocket and handed it to her.

A sob of gratitude caught in her throat. "I'm—I'm overwhelmed. How could she be so good to me?"

"My mom said it was because your aunt loved you. But, hey, I know you're anxious to see your shop. You can look at your car later."

"Ah—sure." Her eyes were still fixed on the sparkling clean minivan. She'd always wanted a minivan—especially now that Todd was getting old enough to play baseball. She'd envisioned having a car like this one to drive him and his friends to practices and games. When she was a child, her parents rarely went to her games, and she'd vowed to be there for her son.

He took hold of her elbow but stopped before opening the door. "Want a bit of advice?"

She nodded.

"Just remember, even though most of your employees have been working here for a long time and know all the ropes, you're still the boss. I think it'd be best if you let them know that up front."

"But I'm going to need their help. I don't know—"

He patted her shoulder. "Help? Yes. Control? No. There's a big difference. Without Anna around, they're like sheep without a shepherd. They need leadership. That's where you come in."

Before she could respond, Trapper opened the door and jumped out, leaving her with her thoughts. With a nod from his master, Meeto hit the ground, leapt into the cab, and made himself comfortable in the seat just vacated by Trapper, his pale blue eyes focusing on Glorianna. Involuntarily, she screamed.

Trapper pulled open her door, grabbed her arm, and nearly jerked her out. "He won't hurt you, Glorianna," he reminded her firmly, a bit of frustration in his voice.

She leaned into him and buried her face in his broad chest. "I'm sorry. I didn't mean to scream like that. He scared me."

His hand stroked her hair as he held her. After a few moments her heart slowed down to a reasonable rate and she could breathe normally. "Trapper, I'm sorry. I know how fond you are of your dog. You must think I'm a real baby."

"A pretty baby." His tone was gentle, yet teasing. "Are you ready to go in, or do you need a few minutes to collect yourself?"

Her palms flattened against his chest as she pushed away slightly and stared up into his handsome face. "I know you have other things to do, rather than spend all this time carting me around. I just want you to know how much I appreciate it."

" 'Nuff said. It's my pleasure." He motioned toward the heavy steel door marked DELIVERIES. "Welcome home, Miss Shop Owner."

Chapter 4

Glorianna stepped through the door and into a huge stockroom filled with rows of racks laden with colorful shrink-wrapped bolts of fabric, batting, and all sorts of quilting supplies. To her, it looked like a quilter's paradise, and she couldn't help but voice an emotional, "Ohh!"

"Hello," a pleasant voice called out from somewhere between the racks.

The two watched with interest as a small, gray-haired woman emerged, barely able to see over the five bolts of fabric she carried. "Oh, Trapper, it's you."

She dropped the fabric onto a huge worktable and, with a gigantic smile, stuck out a hand. "And you must be Glorianna, Anna's beloved niece. Welcome."

Glorianna liked the woman immediately. If this was any indication of what the other employees were like, she was sure things were going to be fine. "Yes, I am, and you're—"

"Sarah. Nice to meet you." Sarah motioned toward a curtained archway. "The rest are anxious to meet you too."

"Let's go on up front." Trapper's hand moved to the small of her back. "Sarah can show you the stockroom later."

Despite his hand urging her forward, Glorianna took her time, eyeing the spaciousness of the big room and its wall-to-wall shelves that bulged with goodies. *This is all mine.*

When they finally entered the sales part of the shop, a row of six employees stood in a line, waiting, apparently alerted that she'd arrived.

"Well, gang, here she is," Trapper announced before leaning over and whispering in her ear. "Remember, you're the boss. They work for you."

She gave him an appreciative smile and confidently stepped forward. Although her knees were shaking, she thrust out her hand to them, one by one, asking their names and giving each a warm smile. She'd barely reached the end of the line when the front door opened and a lovely, dark-haired, slender woman came bustling in, a bank deposit bag in her hand.

"Ah, there you are." Trapper moved forward, took the woman's hand in his, and led her to where Glorianna stood with the others. "Glorianna, this is your manager, Jackie Reid."

Although the woman returned her smile and was gracious enough, Glorianna detected a slight aloofness in her manner—nothing she could put her finger on, but nonetheless, it was there.

"Good morning, and welcome to Alaska."

Glorianna extended her hand. "Thank you, Jackie. I'm glad to be here. I'd appreciate it if you'd show me around. I guess you, being my aunt's manager, should know this business better than anyone here."

"Happy to," she said, turning to glance out the front window, "but not now!" She clapped her hands together loudly. "Ladies, take your places. They're coming!"

Everyone scattered, leaving Trapper and Glorianna standing alone.

"Who's coming? What did she mean?" she turned and asked Trapper, upset by the woman deserting her like that after their brief introduction.

"You'll soon see." He'd barely gotten the words out when the front door burst open and customers began pouring into the shop, fanning out in all directions.

"But where—"

He gave her an impish grin. "From the cruise ships we saw on our drive here. It takes awhile to get clearance once the ship docks, but when those gangways go down, the passengers flock off the ship and do what they like to do best—next to eating—of course: shopping!"

Glorianna muttered, "Oh, my," as she watched the hustle and bustle going on before her. Soon, each of the three cash registers buzzed loudly with sales as people stood in line to pay for their purchases.

"It'll be like this until about four, when they start boarding again. By five, this place will be like a ghost town, and you and your employees will be ready to drop."

She moved a little closer to one of the checkout areas to watch the mayhem.

"I just love coming here," she overheard one of the customers telling her friend as she pulled a charge card from her big purse. "The Bear Paw has the best selection of fabrics I've seen anywhere. And their gifts, well, they're just the greatest. None of that cheap souvenir stuff. Their items are top quality. I'm coming back this afternoon and buying some things for Christmas gifts. I tell all of my friends who cruise about this place."

Glorianna couldn't help but smile as the woman leaned toward her and asked, "This your first time shopping here, dear?"

Startled by the question, she paused, searching for words. "I—I—"

"She owns the place," a strong male voice declared over her shoulder.

The woman's eyes grew wide. "I'm so pleased to meet you. I just love your shop."

A sense of awe filled Glorianna. "Nice to meet you too. Thank you for shopping with us. I hope you're having a pleasant cruise."

"Well done," Trapper whispered softly so only she could hear. "You're off to a fine start."

Glorianna whispered back, "Thank you," then moved behind the counter and began helping her employees by putting the merchandise into bags as they rang it up.

By noon, the lines were no shorter, and she still helped and thanked customers for shopping with them.

"You need some lunch." Trapper took her by the arm and led Glorianna out the back door to his truck.

"But I'm not hungry. And they need me to—"

"They can get along without you for a while." After putting Meeto into the truck bed, he motioned her in and they drove to a small café several blocks away from the docks.

The place was busy but not crowded, and they quickly found a table for two near the front window.

After making sure she was seated, Trapper sat down across from her and placed his dark Stetson on his knee. "They have a great soup and sandwich special each day. That sound okay?"

She nodded.

He gave her a mischievous grin. "You're not going to ask me if the sandwich is made with venison or something else Alaskan?"

She gave him a little shrug. "When in Alaska, do as the Alaskans, I always say."

Trapper laughed as he reached for her hand and gave it a squeeze. "That's my girl. With that attitude you'll have no trouble making it."

The waitress took their orders, then brought their drinks. Once she'd moved on, Glorianna turned to him. "When am I going to get to see my apartment? I need to get moved in."

"Hey, Glori, surprise! Your bags are already there."

"When did you do that?"

"While you were playing sales clerk." He winked. "If you want, I can take you there as soon as we finish our lunch."

She brightened. She'd been anxious to see her shop, but she was even more anxious to see the place she'd be calling home. "I'd like that." In appreciation, her hand covered his as it rested on the table. "But don't feel you have to spend the entire day with me. I'll get along fine, and I know you have things to do."

He pulled his hand out from beneath hers and placed it on top, adding a light squeeze. "Don't you go worrying about me. Wild horses couldn't drag me here if I didn't want to be here. Once you finish eating, we'll be out of here."

As they drove down the busy street, she smiled at her companion. "This is so exciting I have goose bumps."

Trapper reared back and laughed. "Goose bumps, eh? That's a good one."

As they passed The Bear Paw, Glorianna scanned every detail, this time noting the sparkling clean plate glass windows with colorful quilts arranged attractively on long oak racks. Other items, both quilting items and gift items, filled the displays enticingly. *This is really happening!*

Trapper turned the corner and pulled in behind the shop. Once the truck's doors closed behind them, he took hold of her arm and led her up an outside stairway she hadn't even noticed earlier that morning. At the landing, he reached into his pants pocket and pulled out another little ring of keys and handed them to her. "The one with the red cap."

She found the proper key, stuck it in the lock, and gave it a turn. "Here goes."

What she found was not at all what she'd anticipated. The apartment was beautifully decorated and much larger than she'd expected, with a long row of windows across the back facing the alley, the part that housed a huge living room, dining, and kitchen area. On the walls hung a variety of hand-quilted art-quality pieces, no doubt made by her aunt Anna.

The kitchen, too, was spacious with nearly new appliances, oak cupboards, a stainless steel sink, a large round table, and a walk-in pantry.

"I love it," Glorianna cried as she stood in the middle of the room and twirled about, trying to take in everything at once.

"Check out the rest of the place." Trapper nudged her toward a wide hall.

The first bedroom they came to was definitely the one she'd give Todd. The walls were painted royal blue and held a heavy oak bedroom suite with simple straight lines and boasted two closets—one for his clothing and one for his toys. It was perfect for her boy. A nautical theme quilt in shades of royal blue, red, and white with small touches of yellow and green covered the bed. "Todd will love this!"

The bedroom just across the hall was definitely hers and must have been her aunt Anna's. With soft pink walls and eyelet curtains and bed skirt, a to-die-for Bear Paw quilt in pastel shades on the bed, and white wicker furniture, it said feminine as loudly as if it had a painted sign. Several big bounces on the bed told her she was going to enjoy her new surroundings.

As she turned, she caught Trapper's reflection in the cheval mirror, and her cheeks heated with embarrassment at her childish antics. *What must he think of me?*

"Did anyone ever tell you how pretty you are when you smile like that?"

Her hands rose to smooth her hair. "No. At least, not for a long time."

He tilted his head appraisingly. "Not even your husband?"

She turned away and pretended to be checking out the lamp on the dresser. "Not even him."

Trapper stayed by the door.

She held her breath. *I don't want anyone up here to know how bad my marriage was.*

"I was proud of you this morning, down there in your shop."

Glorianna mumbled an incoherent "Thanks." She managed to slip past him and move into the hall. "Is there another bedroom?"

"Yep, two more, but your aunt used one of them as a workroom, as if she didn't get enough work downstairs."

He took her hand and led her to a small bedroom next to her son's. Although it had a daybed with a lovely sampler quilt, it was more like a parlor, with a small, armless white rocker and a floor lamp placed by the window. A huge round hand-hooked rug in shades of peach, turquoise, and plum complemented the furnishings.

"She used to quilt in here," Trapper explained as he flicked on the lamp by the rocker, "while she watched TV."

Glorianna stood silently as Trapper moved to a pine armoire along the wall and opened its doors, revealing a small color television set, complete with VCR.

"I can almost see my aunt there," she said, sounding melancholy. "Even though I've never met Anna, somehow I feel like I know her, almost like her presence is still here."

"You missed a real treat. Anna was a one-of-a-kind woman. Everyone loved her, and she loved everyone. I never heard her say an unkind word about a soul."

"I'm going to leave this home just as she left it," she said more to herself than to him. "Everything's perfect just as it is."

"Wanna see the johns?"

Brought to her senses, she reeled around and stared at him. "Of course. I was so taken up with the rest of the rooms, I nearly forgot about bathrooms. You mean there are two?"

He grinned. "Yep, you hit the jackpot—two bathrooms, one with a shower and one with a tub. I know because when I was putting up a ceiling fan for Anna, I got filthy dirty from the dust when I crawled around in the attic. I had to wash up in the hall bathroom. Then later, she had me put a new faucet in the tub in the master bath."

Her brows lifted. "There's one off that bedroom? I never noticed."

"Cause you were too busy bouncing on the bed," he teased, amusement quirking his lips. "The door is right next to that dresser thing."

She gave him a coquettish smile. "Sounds like you know the place pretty well, Mr. Handyman. I'll know who to call when I have repair problems."

He chuckled as he propped himself against the doorframe, his arms crossed over his chest. "You bet, and I'm on call twenty-four hours a day."

"But do you work cheap?" She ducked past him and into the hall.

"Lady, my price is a home-cooked meal. I get tired of eating in my parents' restaurant, and I'm sure not going to eat what I cook! Yuck!" He gave a false, exaggerated shudder.

"I know better than that. I heard your mom say she made venison stew for you every Thursday!"

He flashed her a dazzling smile, his white teeth shining between his well-waxed mustache and neatly trimmed beard. "But did she tell you all she does is pull a container of that stew from her freezer and heat it in the microwave?"

She gave a playful jab to his arm. "I'm never sure when to believe you, Trapper."

In search of the bathroom he'd mentioned, she moved back into the room he intended to call her own. Sure enough, right beside the big dresser was a closed door.

She turned the knob and stepped into the most inviting bathroom she'd ever seen. Even Martha Stewart would have been proud. Besides a corner tub with a half-circle shower rod and a gorgeous shower curtain, it featured a lovely hand-painted ceramic sink framed by a long marble countertop and topped by a wall-to-wall beveled mirror. There was a light bar containing five frosted lampshades above it, and next to the vanity was a lovely stained glass window depicting a woman in a lush garden. On the other side were more shelves and racks than a person could wish for. Off in a little alcove was the toilet with its own reading lamp and magazine rack. She had to laugh when she saw it.

"Did I mention your aunt was an avid reader of romance novels?"

"No, I don't think you did." Her answer was accompanied by a giggle, despite her attempt to contain it.

She peeked into the towel cabinets, lifted lids on the jars filled with scented soaps, opened drawers and doors while Trapper watched. "I feel like a voyeur," she finally said, shyly backing out of the room.

"You shouldn't. She wanted you to have everything."

"But it's all so neat and tidy, as if she expected company. Was it always this way? Did she never make a mess and leave it?"

Trapper's smile disappeared. "At the last, she couldn't do much of anything. Mom stayed here with her nearly every day. She said your aunt made her promise she'd make sure everything was ready for you before you came." Glorianna stared at him. "You mean your mother cleaned it all up like this? Everything is spotless. Every towel in that cabinet is folded perfectly."

"Guess that's what friends, true friends, are for. Those two would have done anything for each other. I know Anna would have done the same thing for Mom. God's Word says 'a friend loveth at all times'—not just the good times. Mom was even with her when she died. It nearly killed her too."

Glorianna carefully lowered herself onto the bed and let out a sigh of deep regret. Her fingers idly traced the lovely quilting stitches her aunt had painstakingly applied to the lovely fabric. "And I didn't even get to meet her."

Trapper came to stand beside her. "She loved you, even if she hadn't seen you since you were a baby."

"I'm amazed she didn't have children of her own." She gazed up into his kind eyes. "Did she ever marry?"

"Mom never mentioned a husband. I think it was when she was pretty young. I don't know whether he died or they divorced."

Glorianna felt a surge of overpowering emotion course through her as she looked about the room and thought about the woman who'd lived there such a short time ago. She felt like crying, for mourning the woman who'd only been a name in a will to her until now.

Trapper must have sensed it. He took her hand in his and lifted her to stand beside him. "You couldn't have known the pain she was in. No one told you. Apparently, not even your mother knew."

"But she was my mother's sister, Trapper. Whatever could have happened between them to separate them like it did? My mom, not yours, should have been here caring for Aunt Anna."

He pulled her into his arms and nestled his chin in her hair. "Mom wanted to do it."

Words failed her as she buried her head in his broad chest. He smelled good, soapy clean. Jim had reeked of beer and cigarettes. Even laundering with strong soaps and bleaches, she hadn't been able to get that repugnant smell out of his clothing.

She couldn't even remember a time, other than an occasional embrace or a rare night together, when Jim wasn't hung over.

Trapper slipped a finger under her chin and drew her face up to meet his. "I get the feeling you've had a lot of pain in your life. If I could take it all away, I would."

She blinked hard. "But you can't. No one can."

"God can," he said softly.

"If He wanted to, I guess. I've certainly asked Him often enough."

How many times had she asked God to do that very thing? But He hadn't. The pain and misery and rejection were still very much a part of her, gnawing at her day after day, making her feel inadequate. . .like a nobody in a world of some-bodies. If it weren't for her son. . .

Rubbing at her eyes, she pasted on a happy face and backed away from Trapper. "I think it's time for me to get back to work and you to get back to what-ever you'd have been doing if I hadn't monopolized your day."

"I'll pick you up for dinner about seven?"

She nodded. "Seven will be fine."

Chapter 5

Although the customers had thinned out a bit, all of the clerks were still busy and seemed to barely notice when Glorianna entered.

She almost felt like an intruder as she moved among the aisles, checking out the merchandise, fingering the lovely precut quilt blocks, and straightening the counters, yet she also felt a great sense of gratitude. The shop was lovely, with huge colorful quilts mounted on the walls, giving the entire place a wonderful, homey feeling.

"Excuse me. Can you tell me where I can find the size twelve quilting needles?" someone asked from behind her.

An attractive lady, probably in her mid-forties, undoubtedly from one of the cruise ships, stood waiting for her answer.

"I—ah—I'm not sure," Glorianna mumbled, feeling very stupid. *How would I know? I just got here myself.*

The woman gave her a quick pat to her shoulder and an apologetic smile. "Oh, I'm sorry, I thought you worked here." With that, she turned and went off in search of a sales clerk.

Glorianna grinned. *Give me a week, lady. By then, hopefully, I should be able to answer your question.*

By late afternoon, just as Trapper had promised, the shop nearly emptied as last-minute shoppers scurried up the gangways to reboard their ships. All the sales clerks, Glorianna included, breathed a sigh of relief.

"What a good day," Jackie Reid said as she closed the cash register drawer and leaned against the counter.

Glorianna smiled at the woman. "Is it this busy every day?"

"During tourist season, which is just about to end."

"What about the rest of the year?"

Jackie slipped onto a nearby stool and shrugged. "Pretty dull, actually—except for the locals. They come out for the classes. But most of the shop's business is during the tourist season."

"Classes?"

"Yes, Anna taught most of the classes. She was a great instructor."

The woman seemed to catch the surprised look on her new employer's face and added, "I suppose you'll be taking her place."

Me, teach? Oh, boy. I never even thought about classes. "Ah—not at first. I'll—

155

I'll need time to settle in, familiarize myself with the business, get my son moved up here, that sort of thing. Surely, my aunt wasn't the only teacher."

"Oh, my no," one of the other clerks inserted. "Several of us are qualified. But none of us were ever as good at it as your aunt."

Glorianna gave her a grateful smile. "I'm sure I'll be calling on each of you to take a turn until I'm ready. We'll have a meeting sometime soon and discuss it."

She tried to spend a little time with each person, learning her name and how long she'd worked at the shop. All of them seemed glad to visit with her and offered to do everything they could to help her—except Jackie, who remained aloof. Glorianna wondered if it was her imagination.

At exactly five-thirty, Jackie dimmed the overhead lights, moved to the door, twisted the deadbolt, and flipped the OPEN sign around to read CLOSED. The clerks gathered their purses and jackets and said good night, leaving Glorianna and Jackie alone in the shop.

As Jackie busied herself closing out the registers, Glorianna moved up beside her. "Would you please explain what you're doing as you go along?"

"You mean closing out for the day?"

She nodded. "Yes, I have so much to learn and I'm sure this is a vital part of it."

"This is my job," Jackie said, rather curtly. "I always close out the day's business."

"I'm sure you do a very good job of it, but as the new owner, I'd like to learn every phase of my new business."

"Your aunt never stood over me and watched. She trusted me."

What is going on with this woman? "I'm sure she did, and in time, when we get to know one another better, I'm sure I will too. It's not that I don't trust you, Jackie. I need to know how things work around here. Closing out for the day is part of it. Surely, you understand my position." The last thing she wanted to do was alienate the shop's manager.

"You insert the key in the side of the register and turn it to here," the woman said with a slight look of disgust, pointing to the place with her finger. "The register will print the entire day's receipts and payouts, giving you a copy of each individual transaction."

The two stood silently as the register methodically did its thing.

"Now what?" Glorianna asked, amazed at the speed and the completeness of the long roll of tape that had printed out.

"The same information is stored in the computer memory bank, but your aunt always wanted a printed copy each night to take to her apartment and review." Jackie ripped off the tape and began to roll it up.

"I'm sure I'll want to do the same thing. At this point I have no plans to change the procedure," Glorianna told her as she stood watching. "How long have you worked for my aunt?"

"Almost seven years."

"Are you married? Do you have a family?"

Jackie stopped rolling and frowned at her. "What difference does that make?"

Though somewhat surprised by her curt response, undaunted, Glorianna continued. "No difference at all. I just want to get to know each of my employees. I'm interested in them and the things that affect their lives."

After the young woman finished rolling the tape, she pulled a rubber band from a small container on the countertop and secured it tightly before handing it over to her new boss. "I'm a widow."

Glorianna placed a gentle hand on the woman's arm. "Oh, I'm sorry, I—I didn't mean to pry."

With her new boss following closely at her heels, Jackie finished closing out the other two registers, counted the money in each drawer, placed it in separate money bags, and handed them to Glorianna. "I'm sure you're anxious to get out of here, since you have a date with Trapper."

Glorianna stiffened at the terse sound of the woman's voice. "A date with Trapper? His mother invited the two of us to have dinner at his parents' restaurant. I'd hardly call it a date. I barely know the man, but he's been extremely kind to me, as have his parents. Whatever gave you such an idea?"

"From the way he looked at you, I just supposed—"

"Well, you supposed wrong. Looks can be deceiving. There is certainly nothing going on between Trapper and me."

The young woman gave an indignant shrug. "It's none of my business anyway."

The two moved through the stockroom and out the heavy, steel door. Glorianna checked to make sure the lock had engaged, then moved to the outside stairway. "Good night, Jackie," she called out to the woman who was already crawling into her late model sports car. "See you in the morning."

Jackie gave her a slight wave and slammed the door.

Glorianna watched until the little car moved out of sight, shaking her head. Although Jackie seemed quite pleasant to the customers and got along fine with the sales clerks, at times during the day, Glorianna felt the woman's behavior toward her was downright rude. Had Jackie behaved the same way with Aunt Anna?

When she opened her door at seven, the man who stood on her doorstep bore little resemblance to the one who'd left her several hours earlier. Instead of jeans and a plaid shirt, he wore a pale blue sweater and camel-colored trousers. The Stetson was nowhere to be seen, his short curly hair was gelled to perfection, and he smelled good. Although she'd dressed in a plum-colored silk tank dress and matching jacket, she felt underdressed and dowdy. Carrying extra pounds always made her feel that way no matter what she wore. She was glad she'd taken time to touch up her hair with the curling iron and add a bit more blush.

Trapper smiled and listened while she chattered about her day as they drove to the restaurant. "Sounds like you're settling right in."

"Oh, I am. Everyone was so helpful. What a nice, capable staff Aunt Ann had working for her."

He steered into the restaurant's parking lot and turned off the engine. "Well, if anyone knows how your aunt operated that shop, it's Jackie. I'm sure she explained everything to you in great detail."

As soon as Trapper motioned Meeto out of the truck bed and into the cab, they made their way to the big glass door leading into The Grizzly Bear.

Emily greeted each of them with a hug before leading them to a small table in the back of the room. "Trapper knows everyone in town. Maybe if I put you two off in the corner like this, you can eat your dinner in peace. Since you said you wanted salmon, would you like a salad first?"

She scurried off after both had agreed to skip the salad and start on the baked salmon special.

"I thought your parents were going to have dinner with us," Glorianna said, watching the woman disappear through a swinging door she assumed led to the kitchen.

Trapper chuckled as he unrolled the napkin from about his silverware and placed it in his lap. "Hey, even when I'm alone and my mom invites me to have dinner with them, she doesn't sit down with me. Her version of joining them for dinner means eating in their restaurant!"

She laughed at the way his eyes lit up when he talked about his mother and wished she'd had that same kind of relationship with her parents.

"We rarely ate together as a family when I was a kid. That's why I think it's so important for Todd and me to have all our meals together."

"You really miss that son of yours, don't you?"

"Yes, he's the light of my life." She gave him a shy grin. "Is it that obvious?"

Trapper responded with a teasing smile. "Only because you show me his picture every five minutes."

Glorianna blushed. "How dare you say that? I have not!"

"Yep, you're right, I exaggerated a bit. Maybe it was only once an hour."

"Well, what can I say? I love my son."

Trapper pulled a roll from a napkin-covered basket and began to smother it with butter. "Not to change the subject, because I like hearing about your son, but have you heard from Anna's attorney yet?"

"Not yet. I called his office. They said he was out of town for a few days, but he'd get hold of me when he got back."

"In the future, you might want to ask Mom about Hank Gordon. He's also from the same firm, but we've found him far more personable."

Their waiter brought their meals and they delved in, but only after Trapper had blessed their food, much to Glorianna's delight. She loved hearing a man pray.

"Tell me more about your work, Trapper." Glorianna reached for her water glass.

His eyes twinkled. "You mean my job?"

She nodded.

"Well, most of my time is spent as a commercial seaplane pilot. I have contracts with several major companies in the area, so I ferry both people and supplies for them. It's a nice, steady income since I'm on retainers."

"And the rest of your time?" she asked with interest. "Any hobbies?"

"Ah, that's my favorite part. I fly medical supplies and goods into the bush country several times a month and I usually spend a couple of days with the people. I guess you could call me a self-supporting missionary."

Glorianna's fork stopped midair. *Trapper is a missionary?*

"Don't look so surprised," he said with a hearty laugh as he forked a bite of baked potato and popped it into his mouth. "You don't think I look like one? Missionaries come in all shapes and sizes, you know. And some are pilots, like me."

No wonder he and his family pray so easily.

"After you get settled and the tourist season is over, you and your son will have to come with me sometime. It's a beautiful flight and I know you'd love the people. How's the salmon?"

"Very good. I've never had fresh salmon before. Ours always came out of a can," she admitted dolefully, wiping her mouth with the tip of the napkin. "My parents didn't care for fish, so we rarely had any."

"How'd you like to go salmon fishing with me sometime?"

"Are you trying to turn me into a sportswoman with these invitations of yours? First, to go flying with you. Now, fishing. When are you going to invite me to snow ski?"

"That," he said, pointing his finger toward her, "was going to be my next question."

She had to smile. He kept such a positive outlook on life. She wondered if anything ever went badly for him. So far, she hadn't heard him complain about anything.

He smiled back.

Why isn't this handsome, funny guy married? Or, at least spending his evening with a girlfriend, instead of an old widow like me?

"Pie or ice cream?"

"Thank you, but I'm not sure I have room for either."

"Of course, you do. Vanilla? Or do you want to live dangerously and let me order my favorite flavor?" His brows wiggled above his infectious smile.

"I shouldn't, but—"

He motioned to their waiter and instructed him to bring two dishes of lemon crunch ice cream.

"Well, what do you think?" he asked after they'd devoured their dessert. "Thumbs up or thumbs down?"

She twisted her face and touched a finger to her cheek thoughtfully, then held up a single thumb. "Very good."

Although it was nearly nine when they reached her apartment, it seemed much earlier. "Will I ever get used to these long days?" she asked, inserting the key into the lock.

Trapper chuckled as he moved inside and closed the door behind him. "You'll be wishing for all this daylight when winter comes, which won't be long now."

"Trapper," she began after motioning him toward the sofa, wondering if she should bring up the subject at all. "Is Jackie always standoffish?"

"Jackie? No, not at all. Why would you ask such a thing?"

She lowered herself into a chair and broached the subject carefully. "I got along fine with everyone today. But Jackie—well, she kind of kept a little distance between the two of us. And tonight, when it came time to close out, I actually got the impression she resented me being here."

"That doesn't sound like the Jackie I know. Are you sure you didn't imagine it? From the looks of the crowd coming off those ships, you must have had a big day at the shop. Maybe she was tired."

Eyeing him levelly, she asked, "Have you and Jackie ever dated?"

"Sure, a few times. Why?"

"Did you tell her you and I were having dinner together tonight?"

He stroked his well-trimmed beard. "Yes, I guess I did. Jackie mentioned a new movie showing in town, one she thought I'd like, and asked me to go with her tonight. I explained you and I already had plans. That's all. Why?"

"She mentioned it, and I got the feeling she was none too happy about us being together."

"Look, Glori, I've dated a number of women in this town since—" He stopped and shifted his position on the sofa. "Since Judith and I—well, since she left me. But I haven't been serious with any of them. Not even Jackie."

Does Jackie know that? "It's really none of my business and I didn't mean to pry. I am concerned about her attitude toward me and wondered if the two of us having dinner together gave her the wrong idea—you know, about our relationship."

"You're not prying."

"I explained to her we barely knew one another. I hope that put an end to her suspicions. I certainly didn't want her to have any mistaken ideas. Not that you'd ever be—"

"Interested in you? Why not? You're a beautiful woman, Glori."

"Who'd want to spend time with a widow with a nearly seven-year-old son? Not many men, I assure you. Most would run the other way."

"Only if they didn't know you."

She found herself fumbling for a response. "You're only being kind, but thanks anyway."

She felt his fingers curl over her hand as it rested in her lap.

"I'm not being kind, Glori. I meant every word."

She pulled her hand from his grasp and smoothed out her hair, eager to change the subject. It'd been years since a man had complimented her like that and she didn't know how to respond. She felt like a teenager on her first date. "Tell—tell me about my aunt Anna. Anything you can remember."

He leaned back into the sofa's soft cushions and locked his hands behind his head, sticking his long legs out in front of him.

"Well, she was one of the nicest ladies I've ever known. Real salt-of-the-earth gal. She attended the same church we do and took an active part in the women's ministry. Every Thursday afternoon, for as long as I can remember, she and Mom and a number of women would gather in one of the classrooms at her shop—" He paused and nodded toward her with a smile. "Your shop. They'd make little quilts for the police department and the hospital auxiliary, to give to injured children or kids who had something bad happen to them or their family. Sometimes, when children had to be taken away from their parents because of abuse or neglect, they got a neglect quilt. Occasionally, I helped Mom and Aunt Anna make their deliveries. You should have seen the work the women put into those quilts. I used to ask them why they went to so much trouble to make them so fancy."

She gave him a tentative smile. "How did she answer?"

"They said those children deserved the best."

Glorianna stared at one of the lovely quilts on the wall and let out a deep sigh. "I never knew. I always thought of Anna as some stuffy old lady who never even cared she had a niece in Kansas. You make her sound like an angel."

"As a little kid, I thought she was an angel. And you know what? I still thought of her in that same way after I grew up."

Her head dropped to her chest as her hands rose to cover her eyes. "I don't deserve any of this."

"Apparently, she thought you did." He slipped his arm about Glori's shoulders and drew her close. "Otherwise, why would she have left it to you?"

Misty eyes lifted to his. "Tell me more about her, please."

Long after Trapper had gone and she'd crawled into bed, she lay in the darkness assessing her first full day in Alaska. Mostly, she thought about the man who'd been so kind to her. There was something about him that made her feel special. His positive outlook on life, his sense of humor, a respect for his parents, and a love for God. He seemed to love life and squeeze the most out of it every day.

She flipped onto her side and pressed her eyelids shut tightly. *So, Trapper is a missionary.*

Trapper knelt beside the bed in his parents' house, his hands folded, his head bowed, and smiled as he thought about the scripture he'd read that very morning as part of his daily Bible reading. It commanded that widows and orphans should be cared for.

"Sorry, son, I didn't mean to interrupt." His mother walked into the room and laid a hand on his shoulder.

"That's okay. I was finished." He smiled up at her. "For now."

"It's nice to have you sleeping in your old room. Thanks for spending the night with your old mother and dad."

"Nice to be here, but I'm staying for one night. The guy is putting the new pump on my well in the morning."

"Well, you know you're always welcome. Your daddy and I like having you around." She sat down on the bed beside him and stroked his hair. "She sure is pretty, isn't she?"

"Who?"

Her hand playfully ruffled up his hair. "You know very well who I mean. Glorianna."

"Oh, her."

"Seems to me you've kind of taken a shine to her," she said bluntly. "It's about time you started paying some real attention to a woman. It's been a long time since—"

"Since Judith took a hike? Yeah, I know. I goofed once, and I'm sure not going to do it again." He hoped his eyes didn't reflect his feelings of loneliness and disappointment.

"Don't sell yourself short, honey. Judith had us all fooled, even her parents. They were as surprised as the rest of us when she left you right before the wedding. She just wasn't what we all thought she was. You were lucky to find out when you did."

His hand cupped hers as he smiled into her wrinkled face. "I think Dad got the only honest woman around, not to mention good-looking, nice, and talented. They don't make them like you anymore."

She slapped at his shoulder as she rose to her feet and kissed the top of his head affectionately. "The woman who gets you will get a fine man. Just be open enough to recognize her when God sends her to you. Night, baby."

As he watched her slip out of the room and close the door behind her, his thoughts turned back to Glorianna.

162

Chapter 6

Two weeks had passed since Glorianna arrived in Alaska. She'd spent nearly eighteen hours a day on the shop, working during business hours and way into the night after closing. While she still didn't know every phase and needed to depend on Jackie more than she wanted, she was beginning to feel like she might actually make it as a business owner.

She hadn't seen much of Trapper. As a favor to one of his clients, Trapper temporarily took on a big delivery job, flying supplies between Anchorage and Fairbanks, until they could find someone to take over for him.

Glorianna had dinner with his parents a few times, but most of the time, she kept herself tied to the shop, taking hold of the ropes and trying to learn the quilting business.

When someone rapped on her door late one evening, she peeped out the small hole to find Trapper standing there, a small white sack in his hand.

"Hi. I had a yen for lemon crunch ice cream and thought you might share it with me."

She pushed the door open wide. "Umm, how did you know I was hungry for ice cream? Especially lemon crunch?"

"Lucky guess?" He moved past her into the kitchen and pulled two bowls from the cupboard and two spoons from the drawer. "Where do you keep the scoop?"

She shook a teasing finger in his face. "You mean you don't know? I thought you knew everything about this place." She reached into a ceramic pitcher containing wooden spoons, rubber spatulas, and other types of frequently used kitchen tools, pulled out a shiny scoop, and handed it to him.

He served two large helpings, then walked to the refrigerator and stuck the ice cream carton into the freezer compartment. "Anna kept a few secrets," he said with a smile as his arm slipped about her waist. He led her to the table.

"I've missed you," she confessed as she twirled the spoon in her dish, almost wishing she hadn't told him.

"I've missed you too. Seems like months since I've been home. I hated to run out like that, but when duty calls, gotta answer. Are things going okay?"

"Pretty well. I'm actually beginning to get the hang of things. But don't feel bad about running out on me. You've already done more for me than most men would. I've monopolized way too much of your time."

"Well, if it's any consolation, the new quilt shop owner was constantly on my mind."

She rotated the spoon absentmindedly in the bowl. "What a nice thing to say."

"Well, you were. Pulling up stakes and coming to Alaska, leaving Todd behind, taking on a new business—I'm not sure I could have done it."

"The fearless, adventuresome Trapper Timberwolf? I find that hard to believe. But seriously, you picking me up in Vancouver and being such a good friend to me after we got here really helped. Because of the Timberwolfs, I've never really felt alone. I'm so anxious for Todd to meet your family."

When he finished his ice cream, he licked the spoon and set his bowl to one side. "When is your son coming?"

She grinned, unable to suppress the joy she felt at the mention of Todd. "Tomorrow. My dad's bringing him."

"I'm anxious to meet that son of yours, if he's anything like you."

Her brow creased slightly. "He is in some ways; other ways he's much more like his dad."

"Oh, how so?" he asked, apparently catching her change of expression.

She fidgeted with her spoon and avoided his eyes. Todd had been a real concern to her these past few years. He'd picked up many of Jim's habits, habits that really upset her.

"Glori?"

"He—he's a nice little boy, but these past few months—"

His hand cupped her wrist gently. "Hey, I was a kid once. I remember pushing my folks to the limits. He's probably just spreading his wings. I'm sure I caused my mom and dad some anxious moments when I was seven."

"He's—he's gotten belligerent, mouthy, disrespectful." The ache in her heart nearly choked her.

"Probably just upset over the loss of his dad. Losing a father has to be tough on a kid." The pad of his thumb stroked the back of her hand.

She tried to rein in her emotions, but failed. A tear trickled down her cheek. "It's more than that, Trapper. This attitude of his was going on long before Jim died. I hate to say this, but my husband was a bad influence on Todd. There was so much I didn't know about Jim. We'd only dated a few weeks when we ran off and got married, much to my parents' dismay."

Trapper listened silently.

Glorianna hung her head in shame. "How could I have been so gullible? I never knew the man. Not really. Not once during those few weeks did he so much as say a swear word or drink a beer. Then, on our honeymoon, he guzzled down a six-pack and got into a fight with a man in the motel parking lot. He used words I'd never even heard before. They both ended up spending the night in jail. I—I couldn't believe it. I ended up spending our wedding night alone."

Scooting his chair closer to hers, he slipped an arm about her shoulders, patting her as if consoling a child who was hurting. "I'm so sorry. I had no idea."

"You know, Todd barely shed a tear when I told him his father had been killed in that accident. He actually seemed happy about it. His response certainly didn't seem normal to me, but as cruel as Jim was to him. . ." Watery eyes lifted to his as she gulped hard. "I don't know why I'm telling you this."

"Because I'm a friend, that's why. Did your husband straighten up after being arrested and spending a night in jail?"

She shuddered through her tears. "No, that was only the beginning. Right from the start, if he wasn't out with his beer-drinking friends at a bar, they were at our house drinking. I thought once Todd was born, Jim would face the responsibilities of fatherhood, but he didn't. I often wondered why he even married me. Once, I actually caught him giving sips of beer to my baby." She shuddered again as she said it, the thought almost making her sick.

Trapper wrinkled up his face with disgust. "I can't imagine any man giving beer to a baby. The guy must have been nuts."

"Sometimes, I think he was," she said between sobs.

"Did he ever hurt you? Physically?"

She rubbed at her wrist. "Not really, although he did shove me around a bit. One time, I thought he'd broken my arm, but it was just badly sprained."

"What about your dad? Didn't he deck the guy? I know I would have!"

"My dad?" She scoffed, "All he did was say, 'I told you so.' He said I'd made my bed and now I'd have to lie in it. He never was too understanding." She grimaced. "In fact, in many ways, my father was very much like Jim. Not abusive physically, but his words hurt every bit as much as if he'd hit me. I never was good enough. I could never please him or Jim. Even though I tried, I never measured up."

"I'm so sorry." His finger trailed down her cheek. "Sweet, sweet, Glori, you deserve better. I had no idea you'd been through so much. Did you ever consider leaving him?"

She shook her head sadly. "When I made those vows before God, to stay with him for life, I'd meant them. I'd have done almost anything to work things out. At times, though, when life was unbearable, I have to admit I considered divorce."

"Tough, when only one partner honors the commitment. It takes two people to make a good marriage."

"I knew when I married him it wasn't God's will. But I was determined to get out of my father's house, and Jim was my way out. You must think I'm terrible."

"Terrible? No, hardly. Thanks to my fiancée running out on me just before our wedding, I was saved from the kind of marriage you had. She was never right for me. I was looking for my will, not God's. I admire your commitment. It seems few people these days take their marriage vows seriously."

"Apparently, our vows meant nothing to Jim. We'd married right out of high school. I had no skills or work experience of any kind. All I knew how to do was be a wife and mom. He always told me no one would hire me if I left him. Even if I'd thought I could make it on my own, I'd worry about what would happen to Todd. What if Jim fought me for custody? Even part-time custody? I couldn't stand the idea of my boy spending time with Jim and his drunken friends. At least, by staying married to him, I had a small amount of control."

"I see your point." Trapper carefully wiped away her tears with his thumb.

"I–I—"

"What?"

She bit at her lip. "Although I still loved him, I–I was almost relieved when he died. Isn't that an awful thing to say?"

"Not considering the way he treated you."

"Well, he brought on his own death. He was stone drunk when he had his accident. They think that's why he stepped in front of his buddy's gun." She began to weep openly, the memory of that awful night flooding through her, filling her with remorse.

He pulled her close, his chin grazing her hair.

She leaned into him, absorbing his strength. There had been so little touching between Jim and her and rarely any caressing unless he was drunk. Although feeling guilty for having such feelings so soon after her husband's death, she found herself enjoying the closeness she and Trapper were sharing.

"I felt like the whole world had turned against me. My mom came to the funeral, but my dad didn't."

"I'm so sorry. Life's been pretty rough on you." His words were kind, sympathetic, exactly what she needed.

"That's not all. I—" She stopped midsentence.

Trapper felt her body stiffen. *And I thought I had problems when my fiancée walked out on me. At least we hadn't said I do. And there were no children involved.* He brushed a lock of hair off her face as he gazed into her eyes, thinking how beautiful she was. Her story broke his heart and all he wanted to do was hold her and kiss her hurts away. "Glori," he whispered as his lips brushed over her eyelids, loving the sound of her name.

A long sigh came from deep within her chest. "I–I shouldn't have told you all of this. It's not your problem."

"I'm glad you told me." He pressed a kiss lightly to her cheek.

"Oh—"

"Shh." His arms wrapped around her and drew her against him. "Let me hold you."

She pushed away and turned her back on him. "No. We can't do this." Moving quickly across the room, she put distance between them. "Please, go. I—Todd will be here tomorrow and I have a few more things to do to get ready for him."

His hands dropped to his sides. "Is it too soon, Glori? Since your husband's death? I meant no disrespect. Honest."

"Just—just go—please."

He moved toward her, tried to take her hand, but she pulled away. "I'm sorry, I—"

She broke in. "I appreciate your concern and your support, but I have to learn to stand on my own two feet."

He backed away awkwardly, wishing there was some way he could take the hurt away from her. "Can I take you to the airport?"

"No, I'm driving Aunt Anna's car. I think I can find the airport okay. I'll leave plenty early."

He moved to the door, opened it, and stood gazing at her. For some reason, he didn't want to leave her. "It's your car now," he reminded her.

With a slight smile, she fingered at the gold chain about her neck. "Yes, my car."

"Will I see you tomorrow? Get to meet Todd and your dad?"

"Yes, your parents invited us to have dinner at The Grizzly Bear tomorrow night. I'm sure they're expecting you too."

"Good, I'm looking forward to meeting them."

Slowly, she moved to stand beside him, one hand on the doorknob. "Thanks, Trapper, for being such a good friend. You've made my start in Alaska much easier than I dared hope." Standing on tiptoes, she lightly kissed his cheek. "You're a very special man. Good night."

He stood on the landing until she'd closed the door, touching the spot on his cheek where she'd kissed him, until he heard the deadbolt move into place.

All the way home, he mulled over the things she'd told him about her husband. How could that man, any man, treat a woman that way, especially a woman he'd thought enough of to ask to marry him? Yet, in some ways, his life paralleled hers. He'd been so in love with Judith, and he was sure she'd loved him; but when her old boyfriend returned to Juneau months after they'd broken up, she'd forgotten all about Trapper and the wedding plans they'd made and walked out on him.

Both he and Glorianna had been spurned by those they loved and trusted. He could only imagine how much she ached. Though he'd never admit it to anyone, his feelings of hurt had turned to hatred for Judith. It gnawed at him day and night, and he wanted to somehow even the score with her.

He wondered if deep in her heart, Glorianna was as angry at Jim as he was with Judith?

≈

"Oh, Todd, you're here!" Glorianna rushed to hug her son as he bounded down the plane's steps and into her open arms. "I think you've grown at least two inches since I've seen you."

"Hello, daughter."

Momentarily pulling her attention away from her boy, she looked up. "Hello, Dad. Thanks for bringing Todd." Smiling, she stood on tiptoe and kissed his cheek, still holding on to her son's hand. "Did you have a pleasant trip?"

"A long one. I'm exhausted."

Circling her arm about Todd's shoulders, she pointed toward the parking lot. "My car's right over there. We'll pick up your bags and get right home. It's not far, then you can rest."

He eyed the pristine white minivan. "You must have paid a pretty penny for that thing. You'd have been smarter to have bought a used sedan. You never were wise when it came to money. How'd you finance it with all the bills you owe?"

She sucked in a deep breath and rolled her eyes. "I didn't have to finance it, Dad. Aunt Anna left it to me, free and clear, along with enough money to pay off my bills."

The man gave a snort in response, then headed toward the baggage claim. "We brought that stupid cat of yours."

The cat. In her excitement to see her son, she'd forgotten all about Fireball, the cat she'd given Todd for his last birthday. What he'd really wanted was a big dog—a German shepherd like his friend's—but he'd finally settled for a cat after she'd explained her fear of dogs and their lack of space.

In no time, they were making the turn off Main Street and into the area behind The Bear Paw. "This is it."

"You live in this big, old building? Wait'll you get your heating bills this winter."

"We'll see. I understand Aunt Anna had it heavily insulated when she remodeled the shop."

He trudged up the stairs behind her, grumbling all the way about the number of steps they had to climb. "It seems to me this is no place to raise a boy Todd's age. Too much traffic."

"The school is well within walking distance, Dad. It's a good school. I've already checked it out. I know Todd's going to like it." She was hopeful, once he'd seen the inside of her apartment, he'd change his tune.

"Couldn't be as good as the schools in Kansas. Why you'd want to move up here is beyond me. You're as crazy as that aunt of yours."

"Aunt Anna was far from crazy, Dad. She built her business from scratch and it's doing very well. She didn't owe a penny to anyone. Not on her business, building, apartment, the furnishings, her—car—any of it."

She put the key in the lock and pushed open the door, going in ahead of him to turn on the lights—not that the apartment was dark, with the long daylight hours they enjoyed, but because she liked the warm, homey glow the lighting gave to the lovely rooms her aunt had created.

She waited, hoping he would have some complimentary things to say about her new home.

"Where do you want me to put these bags?"

Stunned, she motioned toward the bedroom wing. "You can put yours in the bedroom at the end of the hall. Todd's go in the first room to your left."

"Hey, Mom, this place is really cool." Todd opened the cat carrier and darted from one room to the next, checking out every detail, before rushing into the kitchen, throwing open the refrigerator door, and snatching the milk carton. "Have you seen any bears?"

She turned her attention to her son, her heart aching with disappointment from her father's lack of interest. Though he had never been free with flowery words, at least she'd hoped he'd say her place was nice. "No, no bears. But Trapper says they're plentiful in Alaska."

Todd pulled open several cupboard doors in search of a glass. Finally finding one, he poured himself a glass of milk and settled down at the kitchen table with Fireball wrapped around his ankles. "Trapper? Who's Trapper?"

Pouring herself a small glass of milk, she settled down beside him and tousled her son's hair. "A friend of my aunt Anna's. You'll like him. He flies a seaplane and has offered to take you for a ride."

His eyes lit up. "Really? In a seaplane? Wow!"

"This some guy you've picked up since you've been here? I hope you don't let your boy go riding in one of those dangerous things with some irresponsible stranger," her father inserted as he plopped down in a chair beside them. "You never were a good judge of men, as I recall."

"No, Trapper is not some guy I've picked up, as you so poetically put it. You'll meet him tonight. We're having dinner at his parents' restaurant. His mother, Emily Timberwolf, was my aunt Anna's closest friend."

He ignored her explanation. "Where's the coffee?"

"I'll make some," she answered quietly through gritted teeth, moving to the sink and filling the glass pot.

"Well, have you had your fill of Alaska yet?" His tone was harsh and ridiculing.

After spooning the coffee into the paper filter, she flipped the switch and moved back to the table. "No, and I doubt that I will. I like it here."

For the first time, his eyes scanned the spacious room. "You'd best be thinking about that boy of yours."

Glorianna bit her lip. She felt like a petulant child. "I am thinking of Todd, Dad. This is a new start for us. Aunt Anna—"

His fist hit the table. "Aunt Anna! I'm sick of hearing her name. That woman was never anything but trouble to this family."

Anger ripped through her as she tried to remain calm. How dare he say those things about the woman who'd been her benefactor?

"I wish none of us had ever heard her name!"

"Why? Why would you say such a thing? She was kind enough to leave me this property without even knowing me. Surely you can appreciate that."

"She only did it to cause more trouble."

"I don't understand. What kind of trouble?"

He stared at her levelly. "You and that boy of yours would still be living in Kansas if it weren't for her. I never did like that woman."

"I know you love Todd, but I'd think you'd be happy to be rid of me. I've never been able to do anything that pleased you."

He harrumphed. "Because you've done stupid things all your life. Running off and marrying that no-good husband was the clincher."

"Go start unpacking your suitcase, Todd. And take Fireball with you." She gave her son a slight nudge and motioned toward the hall. "I'll be in to help you after I've given Grandpa his coffee."

When her son disappeared down the hallway, she turned to her father, her heart pounding with rage. "That remark was uncalled for, Dad. Granted, Jim turned out to be everything you and Mom predicted. But he was also Todd's father. I'd appreciate it if you'd keep your comments to yourself. Todd has enough to deal with, losing his father so suddenly and now making this move to Alaska. He needs all the comfort and support we can give him." She swiped the back of her hand over her eyes. "So do I."

"I don't know how you can talk to me like that, missy. I've provided a roof over your head and food for your stomach since you were born. You owe me some respect."

The coffee finished dripping. Glad for the diversion, she busied herself by pulling a mug from the cupboard and filling it. "I hope I can do more for my son than simply seeing to his physical needs. You never even said you loved me! Not once!"

He snatched the cup from her hands, dumped in a spoonful of sugar, and glared at her. "Shouldn't have had to. If I didn't love you, I wouldn't have provided those things."

"I—I needed to hear it."

He blew into the cup and took a big swig. "I did the best I could."

Knowing it was futile, she turned away, blinking at the tears that threatened to erupt. He'd been a hard man to live with, criticizing her at every opportunity. Why should she expect anything different from him now? "How's Mom doing?"

"Your mother is having a hard time of it right now, trying to explain to people why her only daughter would pull up stakes and move to Alaska, of all places."

"Why don't the two of you come for a visit? There's so much to see and do and—"

He reared back, his brow furrowed. "Come here for a visit? Now why would we want to do that when there's so many places right there in the good old USA to see?"

"Dad," she said, trying to mask the impatience in her voice, "Alaska is in the United States."

Rising, he moved to the sink and poured out the remaining coffee from his cup. "Too weak."

She glanced at the wall clock. Four-thirty. "Would you like to see my shop now?"

He leaned against the counter and crossed his arms over his chest. "I suppose now is as good a time as any."

Glorianna called for Todd to join them. After instructing him to put Fireball in his carrier, the three made their way down the steps and through the big steel door.

"What's all this stuff?" her father asked as they passed by aisles filled with racks full of merchandise. "Looks like a bunch of junk to me."

"This junk," she told him curtly, her patience nearing its end, "is expensive merchandise. My customers are happy to buy it at good prices."

"Oh, this must be Todd." Sarah hurried over and gave him a hug.

Glorianna had to laugh as she watched Todd stand like a wooden Indian, allowing the stranger to hug him. "Yes, this is my son. And," she added turning toward her father, "this is my dad, Horace Porter. Dad, this is Sarah. She's one of Aunt Anna's wonderful employees."

"Your employee now," the woman added with a pleasant grin, turning back to the man. "How long are you staying?"

"Going home day after tomorrow," he stated matter-of-factly.

"So soon?" His daughter couldn't believe what she was hearing. "Dad, you just got here. There's so much I want to show you."

"Already got my ticket. I need to get back to Kansas."

Arguing with him was pointless. She'd learned that years ago.

After showing her guests around the large, well-lit stockroom, she led them into the shop itself. A brisk business was going on as last-minute shoppers from the cruise ships crowded around the cash registers with their purchases.

"Having a big sale?" her father asked, his eyes fixed on the long lines.

Glorianna grinned triumphantly. For the first time in her life, she was out from under her father's intense scrutiny, free of her husband's domination, on her own. Her newfound independence felt good. "No, Dad. It's like this every day."

"Can I have a hamburger and fries?"

Glorianna grinned at her son as the four of them sat in the booth at The Grizzly Bear Restaurant. How good it was to have him with her again. She couldn't keep her eyes off him. "I think that can be arranged."

"It was nice of you to bring Todd to Alaska," Trapper told her father with a warm smile.

"Didn't have much choice. It was either that or send the boy on the plane alone."

Glorianna interceded. "Now, Dad, that's not true. You know I'd never allow Todd to fly alone. When I offered to send you a roundtrip ticket, you immediately agreed to bring him. I even offered to send Mom a ticket."

"Did your daughter tell you how hard she's been working?" Trapper interrupted. "She's at that shop from early in the morning until way past closing time every day. I keep telling her, she needs to take a little time off. It's good the two of you have come."

Glorianna gave him a grateful smile, glad for the change of subject.

"That's hard to believe." The man gave Glorianna a surly frown, then turned back to Trapper. "What do you do for a living?"

"I'm a seaplane pilot. I contract with a number of major companies in the area, but my first love is being a missionary. I fly into the bush country a couple of times a month with medicines and supplies. I usually stay a few days and help out where I can."

"Missionary, huh? That sure can't pay you very much. Good thing you've got a steady job."

"Actually, they don't pay me anything. The gas for my plane and most of the supplies I take are my gift to the Lord."

Mr. Porter cocked his head to one side and wore a skeptical smile. "Young man, you must have more money than you've got sense."

Agitated with her father's insolent behavior, Glorianna pushed a menu into his hands. "What would you like for dinner? The fish here is excellent."

The meal was strained, especially when Trapper thanked God for their food. It seemed everything Glorianna said, her father contradicted. Everything Trapper said, he questioned. She found herself almost thankful her father was going home.

Both of Trapper's parents stopped by their table to enjoy dessert with them. To Glorianna's relief, her father was actually halfway pleasant to them.

"I'll call you later," Trapper whispered into her ear as the group exited the restaurant.

It was nearly ten by the time she was able to sit down at the little desk in her bedroom and go over the day's receipts. Exhausted from their trip and the time change, both Todd and her father had drifted off to sleep as soon as they'd hit their beds, despite the long slits of light coming in around the edges of the room-darkening shades.

Even though she was expecting his call, the ringing of the phone startled her. "Hello."

"Hi."

"I'm glad you called. I could use a friendly voice." She picked up the phone and carried it to the bed.

"Rough day, huh?"

"You could say that, but I'm glad Todd is here. Seeing him made it bearable."

"He seems like a nice kid. Wish I could say the same for your father. What's with that man? Does he ever smile?"

Twisting the cord around her finger, she laughed into the phone. "Not often. At least, not where I'm concerned."

"You looked beautiful tonight. I liked your hair. I've never seen it pulled back that way."

"You have no idea how welcome your nice words are. I felt kind of beat down after a few of my dad's tongue-lashings."

"Well, excuse me for saying it, but he's full of bologna. I think you're terrific! And you're going to be a big success with your aunt's business. You're already off to a good start. Seems to me, you're catching on to things real fast."

"Tell that to Jackie. She's still riding my tail, criticizing everything I do. I can't seem to please her any more than I could my father."

"Don't let Jackie get you down. You may have to have it out with her, you know—show her who's boss. Stand your ground, like you did with your father."

She mulled over his words. "What would I do if she walked out on me?"

"You're a survivor. You'd make it without her."

"I am a survivor, aren't I?"

"You bet you are. Well, I'd better let you go. I'm sure you have bookwork to do. I just wanted you to know I think you're a classy lady and I'm glad you're here."

She clutched the phone tightly. "Thank you, Trapper. I don't know what I would have done without you. Good night."

"Mom."

She turned quickly, surprised to see her son standing in her room, the sleepy black and white cat at his side. She'd thought, as tired as he'd been, he wouldn't waken until morning. "What, son? Aren't you feeling well?"

He crossed the room and stood beside her, his mouth drooping, with a look of sadness in his eyes. "Is Trapper your new boyfriend?"

Chapter 7

My boyfriend? Whatever made you say such a thing? Of course not. I barely know the man, but he has been a good friend to me since I arrived in Alaska. He and his parents."

"I heard what Grandpa said about him."

She pulled the child onto her lap. "Sometimes Grandpa says things without thinking."

"My friend Billy said my daddy had a girlfriend. Did you know he had a girlfriend?"

Wondering just how much she should tell him, she chose her words carefully. "Yes, I knew. It wasn't right for him to have a girlfriend. He was married to me. It's alright to have girlfriends before you're married, but once you make a marriage commitment to someone—"

His trusting eyes looked up at her with an innocence only a child could have. "But my daddy's dead now. Doesn't that mean you can have a boyfriend? Billy's daddy doesn't live with them anymore, and his mom has a boyfriend."

She thought about it for a minute before answering. He was right. She was no longer married to Jim. According to God's Word, it would be perfectly permissible to have a boyfriend. . .if she could ever find one. But right now her life was so full, a boyfriend was out of the question.

"Could you?"

"I–I guess so. At least, it would be legal."

"What's legal mean?"

She conjured up a weak laugh. "It means me having a boyfriend would be okay."

"Even if I didn't like him?"

Her arms wrapped around her son protectively. "Oh, honey, I'd never date a man you didn't like, let alone marry him. You don't need to worry about it, anyway. I have no intention of doing anything that would upset you or not be right for you. You're the most important person in my life."

He seemed satisfied with her answer since he turned and padded slowly back toward his bed with Fireball following close behind.

Finally finished recording the day's receipts, she crawled beneath the pastel Bear Paw quilt and closed her eyes. For the first time in months, she felt snug and secure.

❧

Trapper arrived early the next morning, carrying a big bag of sweet rolls from the

174

local bakery and a sack containing two quarts of chocolate milk. "I thought Todd would like them," he explained as he brushed past Glorianna.

Although she was still in her robe and without makeup, he thought she was beautiful. "I hope I didn't come too early, but I've got a flight this morning and won't be back until late afternoon."

"I was just about to hop into the shower." She gestured toward the hall. "I haven't heard a sound from those two." She smiled as her mind went back to her son's late-night question.

"What's the smile for? Did I say something funny?"

"No, I just remembered something Todd said." She sat down at the table, pulled one of the sweet rolls from the sack, and took a small nibble.

"Tell me. I could use a good laugh." He sat down beside her and she handed him the sack.

"It was an inside joke."

He nodded and pulled out a heavily frosted cinnamon twist. "I like inside jokes. Try me."

She blushed and avoided his eyes. "He asked if you were my boyfriend."

He let out a chuckle. "What did you tell him?"

"Of course I told him no, but his question really caught me off guard. I think my little boy is growing up."

"Why not?"

Her eyes narrowed. "Why not, what? Have a boyfriend?"

He nodded. She had so much life ahead of her. Surely she didn't want to spend it alone. But as he stared at her, he thought about himself, of the distance he'd always put between himself and any woman who wanted to get close to him, and he understood her resolve. Once burned, it was hard to get close to a fire again.

She gazed off in space. "I guess I won't be able to answer that question unless Mr. Perfect comes along and sweeps me off my feet. Even then, I think I'd question the wisdom of doing the marriage thing over again. Unless, of course, the man was a Christian with Christian principles. Then I might consider it—if the guy'd have me."

He watched as she broke off a bit of her sweet roll and popped it into her mouth, then licked the frosting off her fingers. *If he'd have her? What man wouldn't want a woman like Glori?*

Suddenly, he felt a sneeze coming on and was barely able to pull his bandana from his pocket before it hit. Before he could recover from that one, another hit. And another. And another, sending him into such a sneezing fit, he could barely catch his breath.

Glorianna dropped her roll and rushed to his side. "Trapper! Trapper! Are you okay? Is there anything I can do?"

He shook his head, but continued to sneeze.

"Is he okay, Mom?" a sleepy voice asked as Todd joined them in the kitchen, Fireball in his arms.

"I'm not sure, Todd," she answered.

Doubled over, Trapper struggled to catch a breath in between sneezes.

"Has this ever happened before? Do you want me to call a doctor or an EMT?"

"No! Not since I was a kid and our neighbor brought over his—" For the first time, he looked at Todd. "Cat!" he added quickly before the next sneeze hit.

"Todd," she said as she hurried to turn him around and point him toward his room, "get Fireball out of here now! Take him to your room and close the door. Trapper must be allergic to cats!"

Wide-eyed, Todd rushed from the room, clutching Fireball.

As the door slammed behind him, Glorianna doubled over with laughter.

With the cat gone, Trapper's sneezing fit eased up a bit, but his face was still red, his eyes were watery, and he had to gasp for air. "What's so funny?" he asked with irritation, slightly miffed that she could laugh when he was in such misery.

One hand across her abdomen, she pointed her finger at him. "You!"

He straightened up and glared at her. "Me?"

"Yes, I'm the one who said animals belonged outside and not in the house. Remember? But Mr. Macho Man of the North Country didn't agree, as I recall."

"I think I said dogs, not cats," he said defensively, wiping at his face with his handkerchief.

"No, you said animals. Period."

He gave her a sheepish grin. "Guilty as charged. Guess I did say that, didn't I?" Suddenly, he had the urge to reach out to her, to pull her close to him. He moved forward with outstretched arms, and for a second he thought she was going to come to him.

"What's going on in here? How do you expect a fellow to sleep with all this racket?" Her father stumbled into the kitchen, wearing a wrinkled T-shirt and boxer shorts, a scruffy beard shadowing his frowning face. "You mean you haven't made coffee yet?"

"I'll do it now." Like a chastised child, Glorianna moved away from Trapper and began to fill the glass coffeepot with water.

The man eyed the rolls on the table. "Is this what you give your son for breakfast? This stuff isn't good for him. Fix him some bacon and eggs."

Trapper couldn't believe what was happening. No wonder Glorianna felt so inadequate. She'd been lorded over by both her parents and her husband. Even now, way up here in Alaska, her father was still trying to control her.

He stepped forward. "I brought the rolls, sir. I thought you and Todd would enjoy them, and I knew Glorianna had stayed up late working on the books. I wanted to help out."

The man eyed him suspiciously. "Seems to me you're making yourself right at home with my daughter. Is there something going on here I should know about?"

"Dad!"

"No, sir, nothing is going on; but I can tell you this: Your daughter is one fine woman. She's beautiful, intelligent, and quite capable of running her own life and that of her son. If I ever decide to marry, I'd want a woman just like her. You should be very proud of her and her accomplishments."

Mr. Porter stared at him for a moment, grumbled something under his breath, and plopped down at the table.

"Maybe you'd better go, Trapper. He's not in a very good mood."

He gave the man's back a disgusted look, then whispered to Glorianna, "Is he ever in a good mood? Maybe it's best if I stay away until after your father is gone. Think that'd break his heart?"

Before she could answer, Todd's bedroom door opened and the cat ran toward them, choosing Trapper's legs as a place to rub itself. Immediately, he went into another sneezing fit.

Mr. Porter jumped up and began swearing, Todd raced around the kitchen chasing the frightened cat, and Glorianna stood speechless, watching the fracas, as Trapper sneezed his way to the door. As he closed it behind him, he heard Glorianna tell her father and son, "Welcome to Alaska."

Trapper sat in his truck, wiping his nose, thinking about what just happened. He'd come so close to taking Glori in his arms and kissing her. Next time, he would.

❧

Glorianna hopped out of bed early the next morning, excited about preparing breakfast for her father and Todd.

Dad's exaggerated yawn echoed through the apartment like a freight train as he entered and glanced at the kitchen clock. "I'm going back to bed. I'm still on Kansas time."

Looking sleepy, Todd gathered his cat up in his arms and sidled up to Glorianna. "Can Fireball have some milk? I think she's thirsty."

Glorianna slipped an arm about her son and pulled him close, one hand patting the cat. "Of course, she can. Oh, and I bought Fireball some of that dry cat food she likes, but it's still in the car. Want to get it for me? My keys are on the coffee table. Be careful when you open the door. We don't want Fireball to get out."

"Okay, I will." Todd picked up the keys and carefully opened the door.

She pulled the carton from the refrigerator, filled a small white dish, and placed it on the floor. Glorianna barely turned to look when she heard the outside door open, but a painful meow and Todd's loud scream quickly caught her attention as the cat pushed its way through her son's hands and bolted down the stairs.

"Catch her!" Glorianna screamed as the two of them raced down the stairs and out onto the deserted street. "Don't let her get away!"

"She's going through the fence," Todd yelled, his face contorted with worry. "I can't get her! Mom, help!"

But Mom couldn't help. Fireball managed to get through the only hole in the high cedar fence, one barely big enough for a frightened cat.

Doing the only thing she could think of, Glorianna ran up onto her neighbor's porch and pounded on the door, hoping he would let them into the backyard to search for the cat. No one answered. After returning to the apartment and donning their coats, the frantic pair searched the neighborhood for Fireball. But she was not to be found.

"That was a stupid cat," Todd's grandfather told him when they returned to the apartment. "I'd say you're good to be rid of her. I only wish she'd run away before I went to all the trouble to cart her to Alaska in that ridiculous carrier."

Todd quit crying and stared at him. "I hate you! I hate you! You're a mean grandpa!"

Todd's words didn't seem to bother him, but they bothered Glorianna, even though in her heart she wanted to say the same thing. Her father was a mean old grandpa and had been since Todd's birth. Even though Todd had every right to be upset, there was no excuse for a child to speak disrespectfully to his grandfather.

"Todd! You tell Grandpa you're sorry."

Todd crossed his arms and defiantly jutted out his chin. "No."

"Todd! Now!"

"No!"

Her father picked up the morning paper and dropped into a chair at the table. "Aw, let the kid alone. He's just like his pa. No respect for no one."

Glorianna's heart ached for her son. He'd not only lost his beloved Fireball, he was taking a real put-down from his grandfather. If anyone needed a scolding, it was her dad.

"We'll talk about this later," she told her son in an even tone. "I have to get to work. Why don't you come spend the day with me, and we'll do some calling around to see if anyone has seen Fireball? Maybe we can even put a few "Missing Cat" signs up in the neighborhood.

❧

When Trapper stopped by early two days later, he found Glorianna dressed and ready for work. "You don't look very happy. Old Dad hand out any more guff after I left?"

She let out a sigh. "You don't know the half of it. We had a real catastrophe. Todd accidentally let Fireball out the door and she ran away. We've looked everywhere and haven't been able to find her. Todd's so upset, I hate to tell him that I doubt we'll ever find her."

He grimaced. "Would I be an awful friend if I said, other than my concern about Todd's pain, that I'm not sorry? It seems Fireball and I aren't too compatible. I was afraid I'd have to either put this apartment off limits or come to see you wearing a HazMat uniform."

"I'm sorry about your cat allergies, Trapper, but Todd loved his pet. And my father! You should have seen how he behaved when Fireball disappeared. He said some very cutting words."

"I hate to say this, and I mean no disrespect, but I'll bet you're glad your dad—"

"Glad my dad is gone?" He detected a sadness in her eyes. "Yes, I guess I am. I've always loved my father and tried to please him, but I found out long ago it was impossible. He expected too much from me. All my life, I've been a big disappointment to both my parents. At times, I even doubted they loved me."

"The way he talked to you—well, I had a rough time keeping my mouth shut." He glanced about before dropping onto the kitchen chair and pulling off the black Stetson. "Todd still in bed? I've got an idea. Maybe I can cheer him up."

She nodded. "I think his body is still operating on Central Time."

"I'm awake," a sleepy voice called out as the six year old padded down the hall and rubbed at his eyes. "But I don't feel very good. I miss Fireball."

"Hey, fellow, since it's Saturday and you don't have school, how about spending the day with me and Meeto while your mom works in her shop?"

Todd blinked a few times, then scooted into a chair at the table and eyed the leftover sweet rolls. "Who's Meeto?"

"My dog," Trapper said proudly with a slight glance toward Todd's mother. "I think you two will like one another."

Glorianna frowned over her cup. "I–I don't know. I haven't had much time with—"

"Look, I know Todd just got here; but since you have to work today, I thought maybe your son would like to spend the day with me. I promise I'll look out for him. No boy wants to spend his day in a quilt shop with a bunch of gabby women."

Todd covered a giggle.

"Well—"

"I'll have him home by five. Come on, say yes."

Thirty minutes later, Trapper and Todd sat side-by-side in the cab of the shiny pickup as it wended its way up Franklin Street. Todd kept his arm wrapped around Meeto's neck.

"I think my dog likes you," Trapper said with a nudge toward the small boy's ribs.

"I like him too. I wanted a dog, but Mom said I have to have a cat instead. That's when we got Fireball, but she ran away. Now Mama says I can have a puppy, but I think she wants to get me one of those yappy little dogs. I want one like Meeto."

"Moms don't always understand the bond between a boy and his dog. Be patient with her. She's doing the best she can. Her plate's pretty full right now."

Todd frowned and gave him a confused look. "What plate?"

"Never mind. Just a figure of speech. Look, there goes a Mt. Roberts tram car. We're going to ride it to the top of the mountain. Would you like that?"

By four o'clock, the nearly seven year old was sound asleep, sprawled across the seat, his head in his new friend's lap, with Meeto riding in the jump seat. The two had been on the Mt. Roberts tram, visited the Gastineau salmon hatchery, the state capitol building, the Alaska State Museum, ridden the downtown area in the trolley, lunched on hotdogs and chili, and made plans to fly and land on a glacier.

Trapper smiled at the sweet child snuggled up against him. "Hey, little buddy, time to wake up. You're home."

"It's about time the two of you got here," Glorianna called out from the little balcony at the top of the stairs.

Todd stretched, then scooted out of the driver's side behind Trapper with Meeto at his heels and called up to his mom. "I had a great time with Trapper, Mom. Can Trapper and Meeto stay for supper?"

"Can't," Trapper interjected quickly, tousling the boy's hair. "I promised Dad I'd play dominoes with him tonight. Maybe another time. Catch you two later." Inwardly, he wished he'd never made that promise to his father. Todd's impromptu invitation had much more appeal.

≈

Four days later, Glorianna, Trapper, and Trapper's parents sat around the big round table in Glorianna's kitchen. They sang "Happy Birthday" to Todd, the guest of honor. One by one, Todd pulled the wrappings from his presents in little-boy fashion, ripping the paper to shreds. The Timberwolfs gave him a pair of snowshoes, which they insisted every North Country boy should have. Glorianna gave him a number of small presents, then expectantly handed him a big box tied with a bright yellow ribbon. "Indirectly," she said with an emotional smile, "this is from your great aunt Anna." Everyone watched as Todd lifted the lid and pulled out a magnificent twin-sized quilt in tones of blue and brown. "She made this. I found it in one of the closets. It'll be perfect for your room, so I finished quilting it for you."

Todd thanked her, but it was obvious a quilt was not on his list of wanted birthday presents.

"You haven't opened my present yet," Trapper said with an impish grin.

The boy looked around the room, but no more presents were to be found. "I—I don't see another present. Where is it?"

Trapper jumped to his feet. "I had a hard time wrapping it, so I left it down in the truck. Sit on the sofa and close your eyes. I'll bring it right up."

Todd did as he was told, and in seconds Trapper appeared with a huge cardboard box, which he sat on the floor at Todd's feet. "Okay. Open your eyes and lift the lid."

Todd opened his eyes and peered into the box. A giant grin stretched from ear to ear. With a quick thrust of his arms, he pulled his present from the box. "He looks like Meeto! Oh, Trapper, thank you, thank you, thank you!"

Glorianna gasped as she watched her son pull the roly-poly puppy from the box. "You cannot keep that dog!"

Todd's expression sobered. "Why? Trapper gave him to me."

Her eyes shot daggers at the man as her hands flew to her hips. "You should have asked first, Trapper. You know I'm afraid of dogs. What if that dog grows up and bites someone—maybe Todd? Then what?"

"Missy," Dyami Timberwolf said, gently touching her arm, "that dog is a thoroughbred Siberian husky, a true Alaskan dog. Any boy'd be lucky to have a dog like that."

"I don't care what breed he is or who'd want him. I do not want my son to have such a big dog. Meeto scares me to death!" By now, Glorianna was next to tears.

"Give him to me," Trapper said evenly as he reached out to take the dog from the boy. "Your mother is right. I should have asked her permission first."

"No! I won't give him up. He's mine! Trapper gave him to me!"

"Todd," Glorianna said sharply, pointing at her son. "Give that dog to Trapper and go to your room."

"You're a mean old mother! You're ruining my birthday! I won't give him up! You can't make me!" Todd squeezed the puppy tightly to his chest and ran down the hall, crying all the way, and slamming his bedroom door behind him.

Glorianna ran to Trapper, her fists flailing at his chest. "Now, look what you've done!"

Dyami pulled his wife to his side and motioned toward Trapper. "I think it's about time the three of us headed for home. Come on, son."

Trapper slowly backed away from his emotional assailant, his hands up in defeat. "I'm sorry, Glori. Honest, I am. Todd said he didn't want a yappy little dog and he loves Meeto. I thought I was doing the right thing."

"Well, you didn't do the right thing! You've caused a rift between me and my son. I hope you're proud of yourself."

"I—ah—"

Dyami pulled him to the door. "I think you've said enough for one night. Come on. Give Glorianna some space."

The three left quietly, closing the door behind them.

Glorianna stood gazing after them, the blue-and-brown quilt crumpled up on the floor, shredded wrapping paper scattered here and there, and let her tears flow unchecked. What a mess she'd made of things. Tomorrow she'd apologize to Todd and tell him he could keep the puppy. After all, all she was concerned about was her son's happiness.

❧

Glorianna spent a fitful night. How could she have been so cruel to Trapper? The man had done nothing but befriend her since she'd arrived in Alaska, asking nothing in return. *It's about time I grew up,* she told herself as she dabbed at her eyes and watched the red numbers slowly change on the clock on the nightstand. *Instead of taking on Alaskan ways, I'm expecting everyone to conform to my Kansas way of living. I can't keep behaving like a spoiled child. What kind of an influence is that on Todd?*

She flipped onto her side and squeezed her eyelids tightly shut. *I should be grateful that Trapper wants to spend time with my son. He needs a male influence in his life. If a godly man like Trapper wants to befriend him, who am I to complain? I should be praising the Lord. Instead, I'm jealous!*

Think, dummy! All your life you've used Jimmy as an excuse for not attending church regularly. For not reading God's Word. For not being the wife you should be. And you've blamed him for your tragic marriage, the marriage you knew God would never have sanctioned in the first place. Isn't it about time you faced up to reality? Jimmy wasn't the only one who was separated from God. You were too. You just put on a pretty front so folks wouldn't know. You've played at being a Christian long enough. Miss Goody-goody, all sweetness and smiles. A real martyr.

The phone rang, breaking into her thoughts.

"Good morning," a male voice she recognized immediately said softly. "I hope I didn't wake Todd."

She sat up in bed and pulled the covers about her, eyeing the room. "No, I don't think so. His door is still shut. I haven't heard a word from him since he stormed in there last night with the puppy."

"I couldn't sleep. I'm sorry, Glori. My brain doesn't function like it should when it comes to women. I never meant to cause—"

"I realize that," she said quickly, breaking in. "I'm the one who needs to apologize. You gave Todd exactly what he dreamed of. I should have known what you understood after spending only one day with him. I wanted him to have what I wanted him to have because of my own insecurities, not what he longed for."

"Well, I'll come and get the puppy this morning before church. I promise I'll never do another thing where Todd is concerned without asking you first."

She smiled into the phone. "Trapper, could we go to church with you?"

He seemed surprised. "Sure. I'd intended to ask you, but after yesterday's fiasco—"

"Please, could we just forget about yesterday? And you can forget about taking the puppy back. I've decided to let Todd keep him."

"You have? Really?"

"Yes, and he's going to stay in the apartment with us and sleep in Todd's bed, if he wants him to."

There was silence on the other end of the phone.

"Trapper? Are you there?"

"Yes, I'm pinching myself to see if I'm really awake. Or is this a bad connection? I thought I heard you say you were letting Todd keep the puppy in the house."

"I did. I'm turning over a new leaf. What time does church start?"

Todd stood in his open doorway, the Siberian husky clutched in one pajama-clad arm, wearing a frown and a belligerent face. "I don't want to go to church. I want to stay home with my puppy."

"Too bad," Glorianna said easily, which seemed to surprise her son. "I was going to let you keep the puppy, but if you want to be difficult, I guess I'll have to call Trapper and tell him to come and get him."

The young face perked up. "You mean it? I can keep him?"

"Yes, but I expect you to take full care of him. He'll be your responsibility."

Suddenly, the brightness disappeared. "But where can we keep him? We don't have a yard or a dog house."

Carefully, Glorianna reached out to pet the ball of fur, knowing if the animal was to live with them, she'd have to get used to him being around and get over her fear. "How about right here in the apartment? He can sleep in your bed with you."

The boy's eyes widened in surprise as a smile replaced the frown. "Really? In my bed? And you won't get mad at him?"

Her fingers crossed her heart. "I promise. Now hurry up and pop into the shower. Trapper is picking us up for church in an hour."

As the boy scurried off to the bathroom, the puppy still clutched in his arms, she leaned against the wall, crossed her arms, and lifted her eyes heavenward. *God, please tell me I'm not making a big mistake. Being a mom is not an easy task.*

After making sure the little puppy was still deposited safely in the cardboard box in the back of the pickup and had plenty of slits for air, Trapper led his two guests to the pew where his family normally sat, greeting friends and fellow worshippers along the way. Todd insisted on sitting between them. Glorianna had to admit it felt good to be back in church. The music was wonderful, and even Todd seemed to enjoy the sermon. Afterward, everyone shook hands and made them feel right at home.

"I hope you'll come every Sunday," Trapper told them as they exited the church. "I'm sure you'll like the people, even though most of them are typical Alaskans."

Glorianna smiled. "I'm an Alaskan now too. Remember?"

"Hey, Trapper, guess what I'm going to call my puppy?" Todd asked as he tugged on his coat sleeve.

"I give up. What?"

"Samson. Like the man in the sermon. The strong guy with the long hair. Don't you think that'd be a good name for him?"

"I think Samson is the perfect name," Trapper agreed with a questioning glance toward the boy's mother. "That is, if your mother likes it."

Glorianna slipped her hand into Trapper's. "I think it's a fine name."

After a wonderful lunch at The Grizzly Bear, Trapper drove the pair back to their apartment with Samson planted firmly on Todd's lap in the jump seat.

"I can hardly wait to introduce Samson to Meeto," Todd said, chattering on and on about the new puppy.

"I have an idea." Trapper turned to Glorianna, as if to ask her permission to state it.

She let out a slight chuckle. "And what is your idea?"

"I promised Todd I'd take him fishing. If you're not too tired, why don't we do it this afternoon, and you can come with us? Meeto can meet Samson."

She frowned. "I don't know. I really should spend the day at the shop. I've got—"

Trapper grabbed her hand. "Glori! You spend every day at that shop. I can't even get you to take time off for lunch! Come on, you deserve a break."

"But fishing?"

His glance went from her to Todd and back again. "Only for a couple of hours. I've heard the fish are biting real good lately. Come on, it'll be fun. I know a great place. I'll run home, change my clothes, grab the gear, stock the ice chest with a few soft drinks, grab a bag of potato chips, and be back in an hour. Whatcha say?"

"Oh, please, Mom. We can take Samson and teach him how to fish. Please! Dad always promised to take me fishing, but he never did. Can we go? P–l–e–a–s–e?"

She pursed her lips and tilted her head in thought. "Okay, but only for a couple of hours. I have laundry to do."

Trapper arrived exactly one hour later and drove the three to a spot about ten minutes from The Grizzly Bear. "This is it. Come on, let's unload."

He and Todd carried the things to an area beside the pond while the two dogs scampered about, playing as if they were old friends. Trapper pulled a blanket from the pickup and started to spread it on the ground.

"What's that for?" Glorianna asked with a teasing grin.

"I thought you'd want to sit on it while we fish."

"While you fish? What about me? I want to try too."

A deep frown creased his forehead. "You know how to fish?"

She bent and selected one of the poles he'd placed on the ground. "Nope, never fished in my life, but I've always wanted to. You can teach me."

Trapper's mustache arched with a big smile. "Lady, you got it. I'll be happy to teach you."

The next two hours were filled with giggles and wiggles and laughs as Todd and Glorianna got their lines either tangled in a tree, caught on a weed, lost their bait, or scared the fish off with their laughter. Two dogs getting drinks at the water's edge didn't help. Still, Trapper couldn't remember when he'd had a better time fishing—not even when he'd caught the biggest fish of his life.

"Look," he told her after finally getting Todd settled on a big rock with his line in the water, "let me show you. You're holding it all wrong." He walked up behind her and put his arms about her, his hands covering hers as they held the pole. "You need to relax. Let the pole do the work. Let the fish come to you."

She took a deep breath and leaned into him. "Like this?"

"Exactly." His close proximity allowed him to inhale the sweet fragrance of her freshly shampooed hair. "You're doing fine," he said, fully aware of her every breath. "Easy. I think you've got a nibble." He rested his chin on the top of her head. "Easy. Give him time to get more interested. Tease him a little."

"Am I doing it right?" she asked in a whisper. "Do you think he'll take the bait?"

"I'm sure I—he—will. Gi–give him time." He shook his head to clear his mind. Why were his thoughts on her instead of the fish?

"When I tell you, reel him in quickly. Don't give him a chance to get away."

"But what if he doesn't want to get caught?" she asked, smiling up into his eyes, her face shining with mischief as she leaned against him. "What if he likes his life just the way it is? Perhaps it's the only life he's ever really known and he's used to it? Maybe he's missing another opportunity by staying in this same little pond."

"I guess only the fish knows the answer to that one," he said, feeling like he was the one who was being caught, the one who was having trouble resisting the bait dangling before him—bait that would change his life forever.

"Can I reel him in yet?"

"I think you've already started," Trapper confessed in a nearly inaudible tone. "He's nearly hooked."

"Look, you guys!" Todd said, rushing at them excitedly with a tiny fish dangling limply from the end of his line. "I caught one!"

"So you did," Trapper said, backing away from Glorianna, "and just in time."

Chapter 8

Glorianna lay in bed, as restless as the night before, but for a totally different reason: Trapper. Only this time, she wasn't mad at him and wishing him off the face of the earth.

I never thought I'd ever be close to a man again. Or trust one. Not after my marriage to Jim. If I hadn't seen how happy my cousin and her husband have been all twenty years of their marriage, I might have thought all men were creeps. But now, after meeting Trapper, I know better. I just happened to pick one who was a creep. If only I'd listened to my parents, maybe I wouldn't have had to endure such an awful marriage. How could I have been so blind? I used to think our problems were all my fault. That I wasn't a good wife. Or I didn't keep the house clean enough. Or I said the wrong things. Somehow, I convinced myself I got exactly what I deserved.

She smiled in the darkness. *But if I hadn't married Jim, there wouldn't be a Todd, and he's worth anything I had to go through.*

She flipped to her side, her hands steepled beneath her chin. *Things are different now. I'm learning to live on my own and doing a fairly decent job of it.*

Sometimes I wish I could spend the rest of my life with Trapper, as his wife, giving him all the love stored up inside of me.

Being so close to him at the fishing hole, feeling his warm breath on my neck, the touch of his chin nestling in my hair, his hand on mine. I haven't felt like that in a long time. Maybe never. Jimmy had a harshness about him, a way of making me feel I owed him something. A domineering, demeaning way of treating me that made me feel uneasy. Used.

But being with Trapper is nothing like that. Despite his size and ruggedness, Trapper is gentle, caring, sweet, putting my feelings and emotions first. Never trying to upset or unnerve me.

With Jimmy, I felt like a victim; with Trapper, I feel like a queen.

As she lay there, she thought of other differences. Jimmy rarely bothered to be honest with her. Trapper was brutally honest. Right from the start he made it perfectly clear he liked his life exactly the way it was and had no intention of changing it—for her, for anyone. He loved the independence his flying gave him. He also loved his work as a missionary. Both took him away from home for long periods. He didn't intend to give up either. Dare she think she could ever find a life with Trapper? Could love really come this soon after losing Jim?

Eventually, she drifted off to sleep, her arms wrapped around her pillow.

Trapper left town on an unexpected rush job early Monday morning. The week went by quickly as Todd entered school and Glorianna worked with her staff. Now that the cruise ships no longer came, she had time to implement many of the changes she'd wanted to try.

"I can't see why you want to switch things," Jackie told her one day when they were moving one of the cutting counters to a new location. "It worked fine the way it was."

"I think change is good," Glorianna said, giving the counter one final shove. "Keeps the shop looking fresh."

"When Trapper and I stopped for ice cream the other night, he told me you had a lot of new ideas you wanted to try."

Glorianna stiffened. "Trapper told you that?"

Jackie began rearranging things on the counter. "Uh huh. He tells me lots of things. We're very close, you know."

"No, I didn't know. He never mentioned it." She turned away, afraid Jackie would read the hurt in her eyes at the thought of Trapper with another woman.

"I'm not surprised. He's a very private man. I doubt he'd kiss a lady and tell." She hurried off to the stockroom, leaving Glorianna's imagination to run wild.

Although the week flew by, each day Glorianna found herself brooding over Jackie's words. Kiss a lady and tell? What exactly did that mean? Was Jackie just trying to yank her chain or was there really something going on between them? Not that she had any claims on him, especially not with the things going on in her own life.

Was that the real reason Trapper didn't want commitment? He wanted to date every woman around? He certainly didn't seem like that kind of man. . .but what did she really know about him or his past?

By the time he arrived on Friday night, she had conjured up all kinds of scenarios, from Trapper and Jackie simply going to the movies as old friends, to the two of them having a torrid love affair.

"Just how involved are you with Jackie?" she asked as he appeared at her door with a small bouquet of fresh flowers.

"Hey! Can't you at least say hello? I've been gone for nearly a week." He crossed to the kitchen, pulled a glass from the cupboard, filled it with water, and inserted the bouquet. Then turning, he asked, "Now, let's start over, okay?"

Moving back through the living room, he stepped outside, shutting the door behind him.

"Hello," he said brightly as he reentered the room. "I've missed you. I could hardly wait to get home."

Glorianna hung her head in shame. "I've missed you too."

187

"Now," he said, taking her hand and leading her to the sofa, "what's all this about Jackie?"

Thoroughly embarrassed by her bad behavior, she decided to tell him about the incident between her and Jackie. "Not that I have any claims on you, but it was the way she said it. I guess I—" She paused and looked up slowly, locking eyes with him. "I guess I overreacted."

Trapper slipped an arm about her shoulders and drew her close. "Did Jackie explain that she was already in the ice cream shop when I stopped in for a cone on the way home from your house?"

Her eyes rounded. "No, she let me think—"

"That's the trouble," he said, chucking her under the chin with a smile, "you think too much."

"She said the two of you are very close."

His finger traced her brows. "We've known each other since we were in diapers. I guess you could call that close, with a stretch of the imagination."

"She said something about you not being the kind of man who would kiss and tell."

A finger touched her lips. "And she's right! Since I've never kissed Jackie, how could I tell about it? But if I kissed you—"

She closed her eyes as his sweet breath fell on her face. "You—wouldn't tell?" she whispered, a weakness settling in her stomach.

"Never." His lips caressed hers. Gently at first, then tenderly, emotionally.

"Mom, Trapper's kissing you! Yuck!"

The two quickly separated as Todd bounded into the room, Samson yelping at his heels.

"He was—I had—there—" Glorianna stammered, turning away from Trapper, embarrassed, but at the same time enjoying the unexpected moment.

"Yep, I was kissing her alright." Trapper smiled at her son. "Your mom's a pretty woman. She deserves to be kissed."

"Yeah, I guess it's okay," Todd said, pulling two cookies from a plate on the table and giving one to Samson, who swallowed it in a quick gulp. "It's legal."

Trapper frowned, looking quickly toward Glorianna. "Legal?"

"Yeah," the boy said matter-of-factly, apparently no longer concerned by the kiss he'd witnessed. "You know, legal means it's okay for her to have a boyfriend, as long as I like him. And I like you. That's what Mom said."

Trapper let out an uproarious laugh. "Oh, you do, do you? Well, I like you too, so I guess it's doubly legal. Eh, Mom?"

Glorianna nodded behind her hands and hurried off to her room to freshen up, totally embarrassed, yet amused.

That Sunday, after church, Trapper escorted the two to another one of his favorite places, a clearing in the woods not far from town, where he and his friends had played as boys.

"I have something for you, Todd," Trapper said as he pulled a long box from the pickup bed. "This belonged to me when I was about your age. I want you to have it."

"Wow, what is it?"

Glorianna frowned. "You're spoiling my boy with all these presents, Trapper."

"I'm only passing something on. I don't have any sons and I likely won't be having any. I want Todd to have this."

His words cut into her heart. *No sons? Not even a stepson?*

Todd watched expectantly as Trapper opened the well-worn box and pulled out a highly polished bow and a quiver full of arrows. "Wow! Will you show me how to shoot it?"

Glorianna rushed toward them, pulling Todd to her and burying his face in her bosom. "Put that dreadful thing away. I will not have my son killing innocent animals like his father did!" *Trapper doesn't understand! I'm in charge now and I refuse to have my son grow up with the same careless attitude toward life as his father.*

"He doesn't have to kill animals. Not even birds. He can shoot at targets!" Trapper said quickly in defense of his gift. "Glorianna, you're coddling that boy. Let him breathe, or one day you're going to have a sniveling baby on your hands instead of a man."

"What right have you to talk? You've never had children, and from what you say, you never will!" Glorianna felt her temperature rising. "Don't try to raise my child to satisfy your fatherly whims. Raising children is not a part-time job you do when the mood strikes you!"

"I'm only trying to help. That boy needs a man in his life!"

"If I ever feel he is lacking in male companionship, I'll find a man who will want to be a full-time father, not someone who only does it when he needs masculine stroking to his own ego!"

"Is that what you think I'm doing? Stroking my masculine ego?"

"Aren't you?"

Trapper stuffed the bow back into the box along with the arrows and threw them in the truck bed before ramming himself beneath the steering wheel and slamming the door.

"Now see what you've done?" Todd said, picking up Samson and crawling in beside Trapper. "I hate you."

The words burned themselves into her heart, and she felt she was going to die right there on the spot.

"Get in," Trapper said in a controlled voice, his eyes straight ahead. "You know he doesn't mean it."

"I do too, and I hated my dad."

Glorianna wiped at her eyes with her sleeve and slowly crawled into the pickup, keeping to her side of the cab.

The three rode along in silence with Todd leaning into Trapper, separating himself from his mother.

"Tell her you're sorry for what you said and you didn't mean it," Trapper told the boy, his eyes trained on the road ahead. "Now."

"But I did mean it," Todd answered firmly. "Mom said I should tell the truth and that's the truth."

"It's not the truth and you know it. Sometimes, in anger or when we're feeling hurt, we say things we don't mean and we have to apologize. Your mother loves you, Todd. More than life itself, and you'd better see that you revere her."

"What's revere mean?"

The man's eyes locked with hers. "It—it means when someone deserves respect—"

"What's respect?"

"Respect?" A soft smile revealed itself beneath the mustache. "Respect is what you have for someone who is the kind of person you'd like to be. Someone you can depend on when you need them. Someone who would never do you wrong. And when you treat them with reverence—" Trapper gnawed at his lip. "And when you treat them with reverence, you give them the kind of love and honor they deserve. Your mother deserves both reverence and respect. She's a real lady. She loves you and wants only the best for you. I have a feeling your mother would lay down her life, if necessary, for you. You're a mighty lucky young man to have her and don't you forget it."

"Guess that means I have to say I'm sorry, 'cause I really don't hate her. I was just mad."

"You got it."

Todd scooted close to his mother and leaned his head against her arm. "I'm sorry, Mama. I don't really hate you."

"Tell her you love her."

"I love you, Mama. And that's the truth."

Glorianna fought against the countless tears struggling behind her tightly closed lids as her heart melted. "I love you too, honey. Although your words hurt, I knew you didn't mean them."

"I love you, Mama, but I hated Daddy. He was mean."

"Sometimes, when we're angry with someone we love, we think we hate them, but we really don't. When we get over being mad at them, we realize we didn't hate them at all," Trapper told the boy.

"I wasn't mad at him, I hated him," Todd said with a scowl.

"If that's the way you feel, don't you think you'd better talk to God about it? God isn't happy when we think we hate someone."

Trapper's words ricocheted back and hit him squarely between the eyes. *What right do I have to dish out this kind of advice? If hating someone makes God unhappy, then I'm afraid I have to plead guilty.*

Todd stared at Trapper, then with a shrug said, "I guess. Sometime I will."

Still caught up in the thoughts of his intense hatred for Judith and his own unwillingness to ask for God's forgiveness, Trapper nearly missed Todd's comment. "Well, it's too late to apologize to your dad, but you can ask God to take these feelings away from you. I'm sure you and your dad must have had some good times together."

"Yes, Todd, do try to remember the good times," Glorianna added, wiping away a tear.

"I—" Trapper swallowed hard as he gave her a sideways glance. "I–I need to apologize to your mom, for letting my anger get the best of me. I should have realized the bow would frighten her, knowing what a gentle woman she is. I seem to barge ahead without asking, like I told her I would."

She bit at her lip and wiped at the tears with her hand. "I apologize to both of you. I've been behaving like a child. And you're right, Trapper, I have been coddling my son, but only because I love him so much. He's all I've got—a real gift from God."

"Okay, we've all apologized to one another. I think we need to seal this with banana splits!" Trapper said, breaking the solemn mood with his humor. "Anyone who's game, shout 'whipped cream!'"

In unison, his two companions shouted, "Whipped cream!" as the truck headed toward town and the ice cream shop.

Before they parted, Trapper talked Glorianna into accompanying him and Todd on his next flight into the bush, on the upcoming Saturday, to take some needed medical supplies. The trip would only last a few hours since the days were growing shorter and Trapper had to land while it was light.

Dr. Buck Silverbow, his wife Tori, and their three children were waiting for them when the plane landed. Trapper and Buck had been friends for many years, both sharing their love of flying and their love for the bush people. It was Buck who had first interested Trapper in helping him with his unusual ministry. Many times Trapper had assisted Buck as he'd either treated or operated on those who were sick and injured. Each man was self-supporting and saw his service as a calling from God. Now, Buck's wife was involved in the ministry as well. As owner of Tori's Northern Exposure Art and Gift Shop in Anchorage, she had encouraged the bush women to share their crude artwork with the customers who frequented her gift shop, bringing in much needed income for the people with so little of this world's goods. She'd even taught them to make little quilted dolls she could sell. The women looked forward to her visits and the fabrics and supplies she lovingly brought with her.

"So how was the flight?" Tori took Glorianna's hand.

She rubbed her tummy and smiled. "I didn't get sick, so that's an improvement. Looking out the window didn't feel awful, either. Trapper made me feel pretty safe."

"Would you help me with the crafts today, Glorianna? I'm teaching the women how to make fabric beads and I could really use an assistant," Tori said as she whisked her new friend off to meet some of the bush women who had already gathered.

"Sorry," Dr. Silverbow told Trapper with a shrug of his shoulders. "You know Tori. No one is ever a stranger very long with her. She'll keep Glorianna busy all day."

"Come on, Todd." Buck's son, Micah, grabbed Todd's arm. "I want to show you the hut my friend lives in. It's really cool. Better than any old tent."

"Guess that leaves you and me, old buddy," Trapper said, pulling supplies out of the little plane. "What do we do today? Build a hut or sew up an arm?" The two men loaded up their supplies on a crude skid one of the bushmen had brought to them and headed for their day's work.

At noon, everyone stopped and enjoyed the very simple meal the native women had prepared. Afterward, Dr. Silverbow opened his Bible and shared God's Word with the people.

By three o'clock, Trapper was trying to assemble his troop, eager to start back before darkness was upon them. "Would you two women quit gabbing so we can get out of here? Todd is already in the plane."

Glorianna gave Tori a big hug as she whispered in her new friend's ear. "I hope Trapper will bring me again. Today has been a milestone in my life. It's made me see how important this ministry is to Trapper and how valuable his visits are to these people."

"You know, you're the first woman he's ever brought. In fact, the first woman he's ever talked about."

"Really?"

"Yes, really. I get the feeling you're pretty important to him."

"Umm, interesting. I loved helping you today. Those women are so sweet, I had no idea how much I'd enjoy being with them. I even learned a few Athabascan words. And what an experience for Todd! Your boys were so good to him, and— Angelica—what a precious little doll. I wish I could have a little girl just like her."

"Maybe you will someday." Tori kissed Glorianna's cheek. "Please come back—"

"Enough!" Buck said, pulling his wife to him. "You two will never find a place to end this conversation and these folks have to get back to Juneau." He turned to Trapper with a grin. "Next time, bring your p.j.'s and we'll have a jammie party. Isn't that what you girls call an overnight?"

"Oh, that'd be fun," Tori said, clapping her hands with glee. "Let's do it!"

"In the plane!" Trapper ordered, taking Glorianna's hand and leading her to the door. "We gotta get outta here. We'll talk about the jammie party later."

As the plane took off, Glorianna gazed with new admiration at the man sitting at the controls; and while she wished he felt otherwise, she could almost understand Trapper's determination to maintain his independent lifestyle. Without ties to anyone, besides his loving parents, he was free to hop into his plane at a moment's notice and soar into the skies to nearly unreachable places and perform a service that God Himself had called him to do. He was as free as the very animals he loved so much. The great outdoors was his home. The Athabascan blood running through his veins, the same blood that ran through his father's veins, made him see the world in a different light than others did. Then she saw it: As much as she admired Trapper and longed to share her life with him, she knew their differences would always keep them apart. Trapper Timberwolf would always be free.

"What a wonderful day," Glorianna told him as he stood at the door, saying good night. "I had no idea how needed your ministry was. I'm very proud of you. This trip has made me see you in a different way. I'm beginning to understand you a bit better."

"Originally, this ministry was Buck's idea. He needed help and I had the time, strength, and the plane—not to mention the money. That man is a saint and so is his wife."

"And so are you. I saw you work with those people today."

"Saint? Me? Hardly. You're one of the few people who've seen me at my worst. Remember the little temper tantrum I threw when you wouldn't let me give Todd my bow?"

"I helped cause that little temper tantrum. You can't take all the credit."

"You were pretty special today yourself, pitching in like you did. The women loved you."

"Will you take me back sometime?"

His brows rose in surprise. "You mean it? You really want to go?"

"You bet. I actually felt I was helping, in a small way, of course. And I have a few ideas about things the women could make. I have gobs of fabrics and supplies in the shop I'd like to contribute."

Trapper bent and kissed her cheek. "Why am I not surprised? I'll be by to pick you up for church. Afterward, if you'll agree, I want to drive up into the mountains. It's going to be a beautiful day and I'd like to get in one more afternoon of fishing before it gets too cold. That is, if you're not exhausted from today's trip."

"Gets too cold? I'd say it's cold already. I kept my heavy jacket on all day, and the sun was shining."

His finger tapped the tip of her nose. "Well, you can wear it again tomorrow.

I'll even throw a couple of blankets in the truck so you can cover up if you need to. Whatcha say? You know Todd will want to go."

"I am a bit tired—but—well—maybe."

"Aw, come on. I know a neat little restaurant along the way. I'll have the lady pack us each a box lunch we can take along."

"Okay, but next weekend, I have to stay home and get some bookwork done. Promise you won't come up with any brilliant ideas and will let me stay home?"

"I promise. Just say yes."

"Umm. Okay. Yes."

It was nearly two before they reached the area Trapper had told her about, and it was as beautiful as he'd promised. The three had changed from their church clothes into jeans and flannel shirts at the little roadside café where Trapper had picked up their boxed lunches.

"Wait here in the truck. Todd and I want to get our fishing gear rigged up before we eat our lunch, don't we, Todd?" Trapper handed the boy a tackle box from the truck bed.

"We won't be gone long." The two gathered up their poles and remaining gear and headed down the path for the lake.

Glorianna spotted a small clearing not far from the truck, grabbed up a blanket, and, noticing the lunch boxes on the jump seat and feeling a few hunger pangs, decided to take her box along and maybe take a few nibbles to tide her over.

The sun was warm on her face and felt good. She opened the box and found a wonderful barbecued beef sandwich, coleslaw, a still-warm baked potato wrapped in foil, and a generous wedge of chocolate layer cake. She took out half a sandwich, and pulling a portion of the blanket over her, began to eat. It tasted good and was seasoned just right. Soon, she found herself feeling quite lazy in the warmth of the sun. After placing the remaining portion of the sandwich on top of the box, she curled up beneath the cover and soon fell fast asleep.

A strange noise wakened her, a sound she'd never heard before. Assuming it was either Trapper or Todd returning and feeling slightly embarrassed she'd fallen asleep, she jumped to her feet.

But the noise hadn't been made by Trapper or her son. Something was moving about in the thick underbrush of the dense forest—something big!

Glorianna froze to the spot as she strained to see who or what it was. A bear! Fear gripped her heart and she had no idea what to do. He must be after her food. Should she throw it toward him? Run for the truck? All sorts of scenarios passed through her mind as she stood there watching the bear, terrified it would attack.

"Don't panic. Don't move. Sing." Trapper's gentle, quiet voice came from somewhere beside her, but she was afraid to turn her head. "Sing any song you can think of."

Although she didn't understand why he would tell her to do such a strange thing when her instinct was to run, she began to sing the only song that came to mind, "Rock-a-bye Baby." The bear watched her with beady eyes that seemed to penetrate her very soul.

"Keep singing and begin to move toward me slowly. I'm about twenty feet to your left. No sudden moves!"

Her heart pounded furiously. She felt sure the bear could hear it, but she did as Trapper instructed and began to move as the bear watched from his place in the trees.

It seemed like an eternity before she reached Trapper. She had sung "Rock-a-bye Baby" at least three times and was starting on her fourth when she felt his hand on her shoulder.

Slowly, he pulled her to him, whispering in her ear, "Move slowly to the truck, get inside, and shut the door quietly. Todd is already there, waiting for you." He gave her hand a squeeze. "I'll take over the singing."

Although she wanted to run as fast as she could, she continued to move slowly, looking from the bear to Trapper and back to the bear. Despite her panic, she had to smile as she heard a deep baritone voice begin to sing "The Bear Went Over the Mountain." As soon as she was safely in her seat, Trapper began to move slowly toward the truck, still singing softly, never taking his eyes off the bear, and leaving the reason the bear was there: the open lunch box on the blanket on the ground.

At last, he reached the truck and crawled inside. The three let out a sigh of relief. After they'd held hands and thanked God for bringing them all through safely and the crisis was over, Glorianna lit into Trapper.

"How could you do such a stupid thing? Bringing us into bear country?"

"Me? Stupid? I wasn't the one who left the truck or was fool enough to leave an open food container there to attract him! You did all of that on your own, without my help!"

"That bear could have killed us all!" she said between sobs. "And why did you have me sing that stupid song? To further embarrass me and show how gullible I am?"

Todd looked from one to another as the angry words shot back and forth above his head.

"That stupid song, lady, is what kept that bear from attacking you!"

"The bear likes songs?" Todd inserted.

Trapper took a deep breath and put a hand on the boy's arm. "No, he's probably never heard a song before, and certainly not sung by a pretty woman like your mom. You see, son, bears don't like surprises. If you confront one, you have to let him know you're there. Singing does that. In some ways, it confuses him. He's not sure what you are, but at least he knows you're there. He didn't want your mom; he wanted the lunch he smelled. That's what drew him to this spot.

195

Otherwise, he'd have gone on about his business of finding food. Remember all the stories you've heard about bears in national parks tearing into cars to get something to eat?"

"I think I saw it in a TV show once," Todd said, taking in every one of Trapper's words.

"Well, posted all around the national parks are signs telling folks they should never leave food unprotected. They even tell you not to put leftovers in the trash containers, to take it with you. Otherwise, it attracts bears. And the worst part about it is, if the bears can find our food to eat, they lose their natural instincts to hunt for themselves. God made a plan for each species, to provide the food they need to prosper and grow. Human food was not designed for bears. Do you understand what I'm saying?"

Todd nodded. "You're pretty smart, Trapper. I want to be just like you and know all about the animals. Will you teach me?"

Trapper shot a quick glance at Glorianna. "That might not be too good an idea. Your mom—"

"Mom's a girl. Girls don't understand us boys."

Trapper let out a laugh. "You're right about that! You're a smart little kid."

Glorianna stared out the window, watching the passing scenery without really seeing it. Her heart had calmed down some but was still not back to normal. She listened as Todd chattered, asking all sorts of questions about animals and the types of foods they ate to sustain them.

In no time, they were back home. Todd rushed off to retrieve Samson from the little fenced-in area Trapper had built for him under the stairway.

"I'm sorry about today," Trapper said as Glorianna inserted the key in her front door. "I had no idea that bear was in the area or I would never have left you alone in the truck. I should have cautioned you about the food. I would never intentionally put you or Todd in danger."

"Let's forget about it. It happened. It's over. We're home safe. What about your fishing gear?"

"No problem. I'll pick it up next time I'm out that way, if it's still there. Otherwise, maybe the guy who finds it will catch some great fish. It was mostly old stuff anyway."

"Well, I hope you can forgive me for screaming at you like that, but I was really scared. I've never seen a bear without the bars of a zoo separating us."

Cautiously, Trapper pulled her close and wrapped his arms about her. "Try to forget it. Pretend it never happened."

Glorianna slipped her arms about his neck and stared into his clear blue eyes, eyes the color of the Alaskan sky. "I'll try, I promise."

"You are so beautiful, even when you're mad."

She closed her eyes as his lips brushed the tip of her nose, hoping, waiting.

hen, as they moved to her mouth, she found herself leaning into him, her arms ghtening about his neck, her mouth pressing against his. She didn't want this moment to end.

Finally, he pulled away and leaned his forehead against hers. "Wow."

"Yes," she said softly. "Wow."

"I'd better go."

"Can you come by in the morning for an early breakfast?"

"You bet. Seven okay?"

"Perfect."

Has Trapper been so entrenched in his love of nature that he had thrown caution to the wind and put our lives in jeopardy? Or is my history magnifying every event that happens? she asked herself as she lay awake in the darkness of her room long after Trapper had gone.

How stupid can one woman be? Is he toying with me, with my affections? The man has no intention of giving up his freedom and ever settling down. Not once has he led me to believe otherwise. Yet I keep setting myself up for heartbreak. Why? Is it because I'm in love with Trapper, or merely fascinated by him and his kindness toward me and my son? Will he soon tire of us and move on to someone else who needs a shoulder to lean on? And when he knows— She shuddered, no longer wanting to second guess the future. *I have to tell him. He deserves to know!*

Trapper showed up at exactly seven, and they enjoyed a leisurely breakfast together.

"I've got things to do and I know you do too."

She followed him to the door.

"I got a phone call late last night."

"Oh?" She pulled her sweater about her to ward off the cool morning air.

"I should have told you about it as soon as I got here."

"Why do I get the feeling I'm not going to like this?"

"Remember that mining job I told you about? The big contract I bid on just before you arrived?"

"Yes, I remember."

He opened his coat and pulled her inside, next to his warm body. "I got it! It's by far the largest contract I've ever been awarded. Even though I'd prayed about it, I thought for sure they'd give it to one of my competitors. Some faith, huh?"

"They must've known you'd do the best job." She snuggled against him. "I'm very proud of you."

The victorious smile on his face turned to one of sadness. "Here comes the bad part. I'll be gone for nearly eight weeks."

"Eight weeks?" Her mind reeled at his words.

"I'll be leaving tomorrow."

"Tomorrow?" she repeated, staring at him. "That soon?"

"They need me right away. That was one of the conditions of the contrac They've got an important rush job." He glanced at his watch. "You're the first or I've told. I knew you'd be happy for me."

"I am happy for you." Wanting to congratulate him, but feeling more lik crying, she bit her lip and forced a smile. "I know this is something you'v wanted. Congratulations, Trapper."

"Thanks, Glori. I knew you'd be glad. Well, I'd better be going. I've got a to of stuff to do. I'll have to rely on you to tell Todd good-bye for me. I've got a bus day ahead of me."

She followed him onto the little porch at the top of the landing and stoo there, gazing at him, trying not to cry. Eight weeks without Trapper? "Whei will you be?"

"I'll be headquartering out of Fairbanks, but most of the time, I'll be in m plane." He bent and kissed the top of her head. "I'll call you as often as I can."

She blinked hard. "I—we'll miss you."

"I'll miss you too. I hate to leave you guys. I nearly told the man to give th contract to someone else. I've gotten used to being around you and—" With on quick swoop, he gathered her in his arms and lifted her face to his. "And, I— Suddenly, his lips were on hers, and their kiss, although sweet and warm, was passionate kiss, like the kiss of two people madly in love.

She leaned into him, loving the feel of his arms around her as she melte against him.

What am I doing? I have to tell him. Now!

Coming to her senses and gathering up all the strength she could muste: and despite the feelings she'd chosen to ignore, with both hands she pushe against his chest and shoved herself away, tears flowing from her eyes. "We can' Trapper!" she shouted at him as she continued to back away. "You must never kis me like that again! At least, not until you hear me out!"

❧

He stood in the open doorway, watching her, unable to believe what was hap pening. He'd been wanting to kiss her like that since the first evening whe they'd had dinner together. He was sure she'd felt the same way, although she'c never really said anything to encourage him. Why this radical behavior? Was sh still mad about the bear?

Unsure what to say or do next, he slowly reached out a hand, lightly touch ing her arm. "Why? I don't understand."

Pulling away from his touch, she lowered her head and began to weep, he: sobs wracking at her body. "I—I—" Her voice trailed off as she turned away fron him, her hands cupping her tear-stained face.

He wanted to take her in his arms, to tell her whatever was bothering her would be okay. He'd never felt so helpless. Why was she behaving like this? Had he done something to offend her and hadn't realized it? They'd been getting along so well. "Glori, why? Tell me. I need to know."

With a look of anguish, she drew in a deep breath. "Because—" She paused, as if the words were too painful to speak. "I–I've been feeling weak and have been having stomachaches. I didn't know what was wrong with me. Friday, I went to the doctor—"

A look of panic on his face, he asked, "What did he say? Please, Glori, tell me!"

She gulped hard. "This is so hard to say, but there's no other way than to just tell you." She dabbed at her eyes with her sleeve. "The night before Jimmy died in that accident, he begged me to forgive him for the awful things he'd done. I doubted he meant a word of it, and it turns out I was right, because he broke all of his promises and went hunting with the guys the very next day. But that night, I desperately wanted our marriage to work out, for Todd's sake. We—well, you know, we sorta made up and he ended up back in my bed."

Trapper's face turned ashen. "You mean—"

She nodded. "Yes. I'm—I'm pregnant!"

Chapter 9

The door slammed in Trapper's face as Glorianna turned and rushed back inside. "You're pregnant?" he shouted and pounded his fists on the closed door. He waited, listening, fearing another round of knocking would waken Todd, but there was no response from inside. Confused, upset, and bewildered, he turned and moved slowly down the steps, grasping the railing for support. *She's pregnant? I was trying to kiss a pregnant woman?* Suddenly, the whole situation seemed repugnant.

The following week was a struggle for Glorianna. Turning Trapper away like that had been one of the hardest things she'd ever done. No man had treated her better or with more respect than Trapper. Yet, under the circumstances, it was the only thing she could do. For both their sakes, she'd had to tell him. What man in his right mind would want to take on a pregnant widow with a seven-year-old son? Especially a free-spirited man like Trapper, who'd made it very clear he wasn't interested in a wife or children? She just wished she would have told him sooner, before they'd gotten so close.

But how could she? She hadn't even suspected it until the doctor had given her the results of his examination. No, she did the right thing for everyone. There could never be anything serious between the two of them. She was sure of that. She just hoped she hadn't lost Trapper as a friend.

"Mrs. Kane? Glorianna?"

For some reason, the handsome, sandy-haired man standing at her door was much younger than she'd expected. "Yes? You're right on time, Mr. Gordon. Come in and, please, call me Glorianna."

"Only if you'll call me Hank." His warm smile set her immediately at ease.

She motioned him to the sofa, then sat down across from him. "I have many questions. As you know, I'm new to business ownership, and while I think I'm getting the hang of things, I know nothing about the legal aspects of my business. Emily Timberwolf recommended you."

He pulled a few papers from his briefcase and handed them to her. "I've tried to gather up what past records and information I felt would be helpful to you. Perhaps after you take a look at them, I could come back over and explain things to—"

"Mom!" Todd yelled out loudly from the bathroom off the hall. "Come quick! There's water all over the floor."

Glorianna ran down the hall, her guest at her heels. Sure enough, water was pouring out from under the vanity, soaking everything in sight. "Oh, no!" she called out excitedly, feeling at a total loss as to what to do. "Todd, get me the phone book!"

Hank Gordon rushed in behind her and squatted down to have a look. When he opened the vanity's doors, a heavy stream of water came shooting directly at him from a wide crack in the pipe, hitting him squarely on the chest, soaking him from head to toe. Within seconds, he located the shutoff and the water stopped flowing, but the damage was already done. "There, that should take care of it for now." He stood, wiping at his face with his wet sleeve, his drenched shirt and pants clinging to his body.

"Oh, I'm so sorry!" Glorianna cried out, assessing the damage the water had done to his pristine white shirt, gorgeous designer suit and tie, and his exquisite Italian loafers. "Oh, my. Everything is ruined!" She grabbed several towels from a cabinet and thrust them toward him. "I—"

"Don't worry about it." He wiped at the wet shirt, jacket, and trouser legs with the towel and gave a reassuring laugh. "I didn't like this suit much anyway. Guess I must look pretty funny."

"I feel just terrible. I'll be happy to pay for your cleaning bill, and—" she said, looking at his water-drenched feet, "replace your shoes."

With a winsome smile, he took a second towel from her hand and began wiping at his damp hair. "I'll tell you what. Say you'll go to dinner with me tomorrow night, and we'll call it square."

"Dinner?" What a strange request, she thought as she stood gaping, watching him take this catastrophe in stride without a hint of anger. "With you?"

His smile broadened as he stepped into the hall and pulled off his shoes and socks. "Yes, it's one of those social dinners with a client. I hate being there without a spouse or a date. Say you'll go with me."

One more glance at his dripping clothing and shoes, and she knew she was obligated to this man. "Well, my son is going to spend the night with a friend, and I don't have any plans for the evening. I guess I could—"

"Say no more. I'll pick you up at seven and we'll call it even. Now, I'd better get out of here before I leave a bigger puddle on your carpet."

She followed him back down the hall and opened the outside door for him. "I guess I should tell you I'm pregnant."

"You are? Well, congratulations!" He patted her shoulder, then moved out the door.

"Are—are you sure you won't be embarrassed to be seen with me?"

He gave her a surprised look. "Why would I be embarrassed? Isn't pregnancy a normal part of life?"

Relieved, she nodded. "What should I wear?"

"Your choice," he called back over his shoulder as he made a hasty exit. "I'm sure you'll look great in anything you choose. Even a maternity dress. Been nice to meet you, Glorianna."

"You too." She watched him climb down the stairs, barefooted, and crawl into a silver late model sedan. The fact she was pregnant hadn't shaken him at all. *Think, stupid! Why should it bother him? I'm barely showing, and we're only going to a business dinner.*

Hank arrived right on time the next evening, dressed in a charcoal suit with matching shirt and another pair of Italian loafers. "Wow, you look gorgeous! Maybe we should bypass that old dinner and go to the Country Club instead. I'd like to show you off."

She gave him a demure smile, fearing her blush nearly matched the red silk suit she'd been saving for some special occasion. "Thank you. I still feel terrible about what happened to you yesterday. The plumber came out this morning and fixed the leak. I don't know what I would have done if you hadn't been here."

"You would have called a plumber and everything would have been fine." He gave her a smile as he opened the passenger side on his luxurious car. "I have a feeling you can handle just about anything that comes your way."

"Have you lived here all your life?" she asked as they drove up Franklin and turned onto Second Street.

"Yes, except for the years I was away at law school. I can't imagine living anywhere else. Since I asked you to attend this dinner with me, I guess you've figured out I'm not married." He gave her a shy grin. "I lost my precious wife several years ago and have never found another woman who'd put up with me."

She was surprised when he pulled into a circular drive and stopped the car in front of a beautiful, stately, old three-story home and turned off the engine. She'd noticed the lovely, well-kept home when Trapper took her on a tour of the city. "Are we picking someone up here?"

"Nope, this is where we're having dinner. This man is one of my biggest clients, Mr. Calhoun. They invite me at least once a month." He opened the door and hurried around to her side. "They were pleased when I told them you were coming. They're anxious to meet you."

Mrs. Calhoun met them at the door. "Oh, Hank, so nice to see you, and this must be Anna's niece. I'm so glad Hank brought you with him. Come in."

She ushered the two through a grand foyer and into the spacious living room, all done in monochromatic shades of white, with massive plate glass windows affording a breathtaking panoramic view of Gastineau Channel. "Charles, they're here."

A distinguished man who looked to be in his mid-sixties rose from his chair and extended his hand. "Glorianna, how nice to meet you. It's about time Hank brought a lovely woman to our home. Usually, he comes alone."

Despite the elegant surroundings, Glorianna immediately felt at home. With the wonderful food and their warm acceptance of her, she found herself enjoying the evening immensely and was glad she'd come.

"They liked you," Hank told her later when they reached her door. "This has been fun. I hope you'll let me take you out again soon."

She put a hand on his arm. "Look, Hank, I've had a wonderful time tonight, but please don't feel like you have to humor me. I know there are dozens of beautiful, intelligent women here in Juneau who would love to date a handsome attorney. Thanks for boosting my morale. It's nice to be asked."

He took her hand in his and stroked it gently. "I don't care if you're pregnant, if that's what's bothering you. Actually, I think it's sweet. A living memorial to the husband you've lost."

She grimaced. *Memorial? This "memorial" is the result of the only night Jim and I were together in months. I still find it hard to believe I could be pregnant.*

"I—I have to admit, it did come as a surprise," she said, swallowing at the lump in her throat and avoiding his eyes. "I love being a mom and always wanted to have more children. My son is ecstatic at the idea of having a little brother or sister."

"You're carrying quite a load, aren't you, Glorianna? Recently widowed, mother of an active seven year old, new business owner, and moving to Alaska. I not only admire you greatly, I envy you. I've always wanted kids, but Sheila wasn't able to have children. If there's ever anything I can do for you, please don't hesitate to let me know."

His voice was kind and she could tell by his sincere expression he meant every word. "Thank you, Hank."

He braced himself in the open doorway, letting in the cold night air. "How about letting me take you and your son to dinner tomorrow night? I hate eating alone. We'll go to a pizza place."

His impromptu invitation really surprised her. *Why not? Todd misses Trapper. It'll be good for both of us.* "Thank you, Hank. We'd love to go."

As soon as she heard his car drive off, she hurried to check the answering machine, hoping for a message from Trapper. But the red light wasn't blinking.

❧

"I like Hank," Todd told her when she tucked him in after their evening at the pizza place. "He's nice."

"Because he played video games with you all evening?"

Todd giggled. "He's almost as nice as Trapper."

The smile left Glorianna's face. "I don't think we'll be seeing much of Trapper from now on."

"Is he mad at you?"

Her hand cupped her son's chin and she kissed his forehead. "Mad at me? Goodness, no. Whatever gave you that idea?"

"I heard you yelling at him."

She hadn't realized they'd wakened him the morning she'd told Trapper she was pregnant, and she wondered how much he'd heard. "We had a little argument, nothing serious. It's time for you to get to bed, young man."

For the next few weeks, Hank was a regular visitor to the Kane apartment. He helped Todd with his homework, did handyman jobs, even assisted Glorianna with her bookwork. Still, she didn't hear from Trapper.

"Glorianna," Hank said one evening after they'd had a wonderful day snowmobiling out at his ranch, "why don't you marry me and let me take care of you and Todd and that baby of yours?"

Glorianna stared at him, sure she'd either misunderstood his words or they'd been said in jest.

But Hank's face said otherwise. "I'm serious, Glorianna. Look, I've worked day and night to build up my law practice, and for what? Sure, I have a nice home and a great ranch, but I want to share them with someone—with you and your children." His fingers linked through hers. "I know I'd make a good husband, and I love spending time with Todd. I think I'd make a good dad." He carefully splayed his hand across her widening stomach. "This baby is going to need a father too."

She backed away slightly, not wanting to offend him, but pulling her hand from his. "Hank, you're a wonderful man, and you'd make any woman a fantastic husband; but I know you don't love me—not like a man should love the woman he wants to marry. And—I don't—love you. Not in that way."

Again, his hand reached out for hers. "I remember my mother telling me about my great-great grandparents' marriage. Grandma was a mail-order bride. And you know what? Those two ended up deeply in love and lived to celebrate their fiftieth wedding anniversary. I think two people can learn to love one another. How about it? I really want to marry you. I know I'm a little older than you, but no one will take better care of you or treat you half as well as I will. Promise me you'll think about it, okay? I won't pressure you. Take all the time you need. I'm a patient man."

She lay awake until nearly two. What an unexpected turn the evening had taken. Hank proposed, knowing she didn't love him, knowing she was pregnant, offering her the kind of devotion she'd never experienced. *God, I need Your direction. I think I'm in love with Trapper, but he doesn't want a wife and child to mess up his lifestyle, and he sure doesn't want to be burdened with a new baby. Hank wants to marry me and take care of me and my children. I know he'd make a wonderful, devoted husband and he's a fine Christian man. I don't want to spend the rest of my life alone. Show me what to do. Give me a sign. I want to do Your will.*

"Trapper seemed surprised when I told him you were dating Hank Gordon,"

Jackie said nonchalantly several days later while the two women were checking in some new merchandise.

"You told him about Hank?" Glorianna retorted, upset that Jackie had heard from Trapper and she hadn't. "When did you hear from him?"

"Last night. I ran into him at the ice cream parlor. He was with that cute little waitress from his mom's restaurant. Seems he came to town to pick up some tools he needed and planned to leave first thing this morning."

The rest of the day, all Glorianna could think about was what Jackie said. So Trapper was in town long enough to date some woman, yet he made no time to—or didn't want to—call her. Learning she was pregnant must have been too much for him. *God, is this the sign I asked for? Are You telling me to forget about Trapper and move on with my life? To marry Hank?*

❧

"Glorianna, I have something for you," Hank told her several days later while they were having dinner at the Country Club. "I hope you'll like it." At his command, the maitre d' brought over a big box. "Open it."

She smiled at the caring man opposite her. "Hank, dear Hank, you've given me several presents already. I can't keep accepting them."

"I love giving you presents. Please don't deny me that pleasure. Now open your gift."

Carefully, she untied the big silver bow and pulled off the wrapping paper. Inside was what looked to be a blue fox parka, lined in cream-colored satin.

"It's not what you think," Hank asserted quickly. "It's a faux fur. Knowing you and your gentle ways, I was sure you would never wear a real animal fur. But this one will keep you warm as toast and shed off the Alaskan winds. And—" He gave her a sheepish grin. "It's a maternity jacket, so you'll be able to get several months of good wear out of it before that precious baby of yours is born."

His thoughtful gift melted her heart. "I love it, Hank. How can I ever thank you?"

"I think you know the answer to that one. Reach into the pocket." His face bore the expectancy of a child on Christmas morning.

Inside, she found a small, leather drawstring pouch.

"Check inside," Hank said, wearing a broad grin.

She gasped as she pulled open the bag and took out its contents. It was a lovely marquis diamond set on a wide band of gold. It took her breath away. "Oh, Hank, I've never seen such a beautiful ring."

He leaned across the table and took her hand in his. "Say yes to my proposal, Glorianna. Let me put that ring on your finger as a symbol of our engagement. We can set the wedding date as early as next week or as late as after your baby is born. I want to marry you and make you my wife. What's your answer?"

The horrible look on Trapper's face when she'd told him she was pregnant flashed before her eyes, followed by visions of the kind of life she and her children would have if she married Hank. It'd been weeks since she'd heard from Trapper. Apparently, what she'd mistaken for love had only been a sense of obligation to her aunt on his part. If she turned Hank down, would she have to spend the rest of her life alone?

"Glorianna? Will you say yes?"

"I—I don't love you, Hank. Not in the way you deserve to be loved."

"I'm not asking you to, Glorianna. But I love you and have from that first day, when I walked into your apartment and got showered from head to toe with your faulty plumbing. I'm hoping, with the years and God's help, you'll be able to say you love me as much as I love you. I'm asking you to share my life and my worldly goods with me. I promise I'll do everything within my power to provide the kind of home you and your children deserve. I'll be a good husband and a good father. I'll treat your children as if they were my own. Don't you want that for them?"

"Yes, of course I do."

"Is there someone else? I know you've spent a lot of time with Trapper Timberwolf."

She searched her heart. "No, there is nothing going on between Trapper and me. He's merely a very dear friend who has seen me through a difficult time in my life."

"So? What's your answer?"

Heavenly Father, I pray I'm doing the right thing. "Yes, Hank, I'll marry you."

"When, Glorianna? Anytime you say is fine."

"Spring. Yes, in the spring."

"Spring it is! I promise you won't regret this. We'll have a fine marriage. How soon can we tell Todd? I'm anxious to start spending time with him. I'm hoping he'll help me get ready for the Annual Juneau Sourdough Nightshirt Dogsled Race. I'm hoping to win this year."

❧

Trapper arrived home four weeks later, his contract fulfilled. Deciding to stop at his parents' house later, he headed for Glorianna's apartment, pausing at the gas station to fill up the truck's tank on the way.

"Well, if it isn't Trapper Timberwolf," a voice said from behind him.

Trapper turned to see Hank Gordon putting gas in his big sedan at the next pump. "Hi, Hank. How goes it?"

"Fine. I'm a happy man. I'm going to be married in a few months, but I guess you've heard."

"Nope, just got in town late last night. Been pretty well isolated for the past four weeks. Haven't talked to a soul. Who's the lucky girl? Anyone I know?"

Hank placed the nozzle back in the pump and pulled out his credit card. "I'm sure you know her. Glorianna Kane. She told me you two were close friends."

Trapper's eyes widened. Glorianna, engaged to Hank? How could that be? Pregnant women didn't go around dating in their condition, let alone become engaged. "Ah—congratulations. She's a wonderful girl."

"That she is." Hank stopped and turned back to Trapper. "I have an idea. Since you two are such good friends, will you be best man at our wedding?"

Chapter 10

Trapper did a double take. "Be—best man? I don't think so. Maybe that's not—"

"I'm sure Glorianna would like that. Well, you'll have plenty of time to think about it. We haven't set an exact date yet. I'd like to see us get married before the baby comes, but I'm leaving that up to Glorianna. Well, catch you later. Been nice seeing you."

Trapper watched as the big sedan pulled out onto the street, then paid for his gas, and headed down Franklin.

"Just what do you think you're doing?" Trapper demanded ten minutes later as he pushed past Glorianna and into the apartment. "You don't love that man, and you know it."

"What difference does it make to you what I do? I haven't heard from you since the morning I told you I was pregnant!" she shot back. "He's a good man. He'll make a wonderful husband and a good father, and he's not repulsed at being seen with a pregnant woman."

"Did I ever say I was repulsed?"

"Did you ever say you weren't? You sure disappeared when you found out I was carrying Jimmy's baby."

He dropped onto the sofa and pulled off his Stetson. "Your news hit me like a bombshell, Glori. I'd never kissed a pregnant woman before. I felt like I was intruding on another man's territory. To be real honest, I didn't know what to do, say, or how to behave."

"You weren't obligated to behave in any way. Other than a few kisses, you've never shown any interest in making the things going on between us permanent. I need someone in my life I can count on to be there in both good times and bad. I need someone who really loves me and wants to be with me—not someone who shows up when they have nothing else going on. And certainly not someone who wants to play house one minute and be the great white hunter the next!"

"Do you know Hank asked me to be the best man at your wedding?"

She stared at him in amazement. "He did? What did you say?"

"I didn't give him a direct answer. He said he wanted to marry you before the baby is born."

"We haven't set a date yet. Maybe it will be before then."

His eyes narrowed. "You're actually going through with this charade, aren't you?"

"Yes, Trapper. I am."

Late that night Trapper sat at the big round table in his parents' kitchen telling them about Glorianna's engagement.

His mother patted his hand tenderly. "Oh, son, Hank is a fine man, but I think Glorianna is in love with someone else."

"Surely not me! We're more like good friends. I've been there when she's needed someone. She's come to depend on me, that's all. Trust me, Mom. I'm not the marrying kind. I love my life just the way it is. I'm happy doing what I'm doing."

"Are you, son?" his father asked. "There's nothing like the love of the right woman. Just because of what Judith did, sure, I can understand distrust of other women, but blocking them out of your life is a mistake—especially a fine gal like Glorianna. Only an idiot would let her get away if he was in love with her. Any fool can tell she's captured your heart."

"Take on the responsibility of a wife, a seven-year-old son, and a new baby? Is that what you think I should do?"

His mother rose and slipped an arm about Trapper's shoulders. "If that's the way God and your heart lead you, then yes."

"And God's not talking," Trapper retorted, stuffing his hat on his head and walking out the door into the fresh Alaskan air he loved so much. "So how am I supposed to know?"

Glorianna pulled open the closet door in the guest room, the one where her aunt Anna had stored all kinds of odds and ends. When she'd first discovered it, it seemed to be filled with nothing but old, broken picture frames, mirrors that needed resilvering, out-of-date magazines, newspapers she'd kept for one reason or another, and all kinds of other things too numerous to be concerned about. Nothing of value, she was sure. Now, with the baby coming, she wanted to store some things of her own and needed the space. Today was the day she'd set aside to clean it out and have Todd carry things downstairs to the Dumpster.

The two turned the work into a game. She'd pick up an item, give it the once-over, say yes or no, and Todd would put it in the "keep" pile or the trash container, whichever was appropriate. They were nearly halfway through when Glorianna found a huge box of pictures tucked away under an old jewelry chest.

"I'm tired," she said, standing and rubbing at her rapidly expanding abdomen. "Let's call it a day. I want to go through these pictures and my back is killing me."

Todd grinned. "You're getting fat, Mama."

"I know, but you don't have to remind me. Be a good boy and carry this box over to the table, will you?"

Todd nodded and lifted the big box from the closet.

She washed her face, took her vitamins, and settled down at the table, hoping to make quick work of the box. The very first picture she picked up made her gasp. "It's me! And look, here's another. And another!"

There were hundreds of photographs in the box. Nearly every one of them was of her, taken at all stages of her life—at every holiday, birthday, and event of any significance, from when she was born to right before Jimmy's death. "But how? And why?" she asked aloud as she stared at the collection. "Most of these, I've never even seen before. Mom and Dad rarely even mentioned my aunt Anna. Why would they have sent her all these pictures?"

Needing answers to her questions, she pulled on her coat, grabbed Todd by the hand, and headed for The Grizzly Bear. If anyone knew the answers, it would be her aunt's best friend, Emily Timberwolf.

The woman heard her out without a word, finally motioning her to sit down. "I have something for you, Glorianna. I'm sure your aunt would want me to give it to you now."

Emily left the room and came back with a large box. Taped to the top was a beautifully hand-lettered envelope bearing Glorianna's name. The letter inside was written by her aunt.

Dearest Glorianna,

It's time you knew the truth. I ran away from home when I was fifteen and ended up in Alaska. At sixteen, I discovered I was pregnant. My boyfriend, an Alaskan fisherman, didn't want the responsibility of being a father. He ran off and left me alone and penniless. Without a job and no one to turn to, I called my older, married sister. She lived in Kansas and had been unable to have children. I offered to give my baby to her, rather than have it adopted by a stranger. She and her husband finally agreed, but only on certain conditions: The child was never to know it was adopted, and I was not to have any contact with the baby, ever. No presents, no birthday cards, nothing. With no other option, I agreed; and with their financial help, I was able to carry the baby to full term.

When the baby was one week old, they flew to Anchorage and took her back to Kansas. The only stipulations I asked were that the baby would bear my name,—Anna—the only thing of mine I could give my child. I also demanded my sister send pictures of that child monthly, of everything going on in her life. They did as I asked, but instead of naming the baby Anna, they named her Glorianna. Yes, dear one, I am your mother.

Tears dropped onto the pages as she read. The letter explained many things. If only she'd known years ago. If only she'd known her real mother.

I love you, my daughter.

Words can never describe how much I love you. So many times, I wanted to tell you I was your mother; but a promise is a promise, and my word had been given. I've worked hard all these years, in hopes of leaving you a legacy. If you are reading this, you have already taken over The Bear Paw—the business I created for you. It was my hope that you'd accept it and move to the Alaska I've loved these many years and find you love it too. Now, open the box and see what I have made for you. It is a small symbol of my love.

Your mother,
Anna Moore

"She loved you so much," Emily told her as she offered her a fresh tissue to wipe away her tears. "She was a lovely woman and a wonderful friend. I wish you could have known her."

"So do I," Glorianna said between sniffles. "How she must have suffered, giving up her baby like that. It explains a lot. I'm beginning to understand why my parents hated my aunt so much. She was a constant threat to them."

"You have no idea how she looked forward to receiving those pictures." Emily patted her hand. "Open the box."

Carefully untying the satin ribbon, Glorianna lifted the lid and reached into the box, pulling out the most beautiful quilt she had ever seen. It was a sampler pattern in shades of white and ecru, and quilted with the tiniest, most perfect stitches any quilter could hope to achieve. And in the corner, handwritten in a beautiful script, were the words, *Hand quilted with love, Mother.*

Emotion filled Glorianna's heart. "My mother made this quilt for me. For me!" She ran her fingers over the stitches and tried to imagine Anna Moore sitting up at night, in the little rocking chair, working on the quilt, perhaps shedding tears over the child she'd given away. She found a tiny brown stain near the L in the word Love and realized it was a bloodstain, her mother's blood, caused by the prick of a needle. *If only I could thank her for giving me life and for sacrificing to make sure I was well provided for.*

Glorianna kissed Emily's wrinkled cheek. "Thank you, Emily, for being my real mother's friend. I know she loved you too."

Chapter 11

The day of the big Annual Juneau Sourdough Nightshirt Dogsled Race finally arrived. For weeks, Hank, with Todd's help, had been working with his team of three dogs. They'd spent hours going over the course, analyzing the speed they should take the turns, pondering the forecasted weather. Other men in the community were working equally hard with their dogs, endeavoring to train them to function together as a well-organized team, in hopes of winning the trophy and the coveted prize.

"This is going to be so much fun," Glorianna cried out as the drivers and their dogs lined up at their starting places. "Look, there's Hank. He's waving to us," she called to Todd above the cheering of the crowd.

Glorianna had worked tirelessly on the quilt she'd volunteered to make for the winning driver, a log cabin pattern, done in shades of mauve, turquoise, and beige. For over a week she'd had the finished quilt displayed in her shop window, and every driver entered in the race had coveted winning that quilt. Trapper vowed he'd be the winner, and he had the team and the experience to back his words; but many times, she'd seen him gazing in the window at the quilt and what she'd seen in his eyes was more than determination. He wanted that quilt. "And I'm gonna be the one to win it," he'd told Glorianna through the window when he found her watching him. "Not Hank. You'll see."

Additional snow had been hauled into the quarter-mile race site from Fourth and Main Street to Fifth Street, across Fifth to Seward, down Seward to Fourth Street, across Fourth Street back to Main Street, and back up Main Street to the starting line, creating a good solid bed for the festive occasion. Every year, nearly every Juneau resident turned out for the race.

"I don't understand what this event is about," a small woman, bundled from head to toe, who looked to be in her upper eighties told the tall, younger man standing beside her. "Seems like a bunch of foolishness to me."

The man reared back with a hearty laugh. "Aunt Martha, it is foolishness. That's half the fun. These guys aren't really dogsled racers. Most of them are businessmen, just out to have a little fun and raise some money for a good cause."

"Well, why do they have those sleeping bags?" The little woman craned her neck for a better view. "And why are they wearing those ridiculous nightshirts?"

The man gave Glorianna a smile before answering, as if he was sure she was overhearing the conversation. "The rules say the mushers must lie down in a sleeping bag, wear nightshirts, and have their boots off. Then at the crack of the starting pistol, they have to get out of the bag, pull the nightshirt off, put on another shirt, pull on their boots, untie the dogs and harness them, then hook them up to the lines. Then he has to pack the sleeping bag and the nightshirt onto the sled and be the first one to cross the finish line, which is only around the one block. Of course, the rules say he can throw on a parka, but no man is going to take time to do that. With all that adrenaline flowing, he'll never notice the cold."

Glorianna gave the man an approving nod to commend him for his good job of explaining the race to his aunt.

"Mom! Look at Trapper!" Todd said excitedly, yanking on his mother's coat sleeve.

She had to laugh when she saw him. He was wearing the ugliest purple-and-white-striped nightshirt she'd ever seen. When he caught her looking at him, he gave her a slight wave, then turned away.

"Did you see the nightshirt Hank and I picked out?" Todd asked, his voice shrill with the thrill of the moment. "It's red!"

"I saw him, honey. He really looks cute. You did good."

"Two minutes!" the man with the starting pistol announced loudly. "Time to get into those sleeping bags!"

Each entrant scrambled to complete his final checks and make sure his boots were close by, before scooting into the bag and trying to settle down.

"Thirty seconds," the man shouted as a hush fell over the crowd.

He lifted the pistol in the air and Boom! The race was on as twenty-two men struggled back out of their sleeping bags and began pulling their nightshirts over their heads, exposing a wide variety of bare chests.

"Wow, look at Trapper!" Todd called out with a giggle. "He's really hairy!"

Glorianna took her eyes off Hank just long enough to catch a glimpse of Trapper's muscular chest, which was nearly covered with a dark matting of curly black hair. Although her gaze quickly returned to Hank, her mind retained the vision.

Hank was the first one to get into his flannel shirt and his boots. He had a bit of trouble harnessing his dogs faster than Trapper but was well ahead of the other mushers.

By the time the two men packed things onto the sleds and hooked their dogs to the lines, they were running equal in time with four other racers.

Trapper's experience and close relationship with Meeto set him off just seconds before the others. He waved to the crowd as he took off in first place, singling out Glorianna alone for a wink. Hank's dog, Ryan, was nipping close at his heels.

Twenty-two drivers and sixty-six dogs thundered up Main Street, past the state capitol building, each wanting to win the coveted Sourdough Nightshirt

Dogsled Race, and the beautiful Log Cabin quilt. The last team rounded the corner and disappeared from sight.

Todd frowned. "Can I chase them, Mama?"

She put an arm about his slender shoulders and pulled him close. Her little man was growing up. "No, since they're only going around the block, they'll be back in no time. We'd better stay right where we are."

"I prayed and told God I wanted Hank to win. But then I remembered how nice Trapper had been to me, giving me Samson and all, and I told Him it was okay with me whichever one won."

A loving smile tipped at Glorianna's lips. "I'm sure both Hank and Trapper appreciate your prayers, Todd."

"If Hank is going to be my daddy, maybe God will let him win."

It seemed an eternity before the approaching drivers and dogs sounded as they rounded the corner of Seward and Fourth and headed back toward Main Street. Wild cheering broke out. It wasn't long before the first three teams made the last corner and headed up the home stretch.

"Look," a man standing near Glorianna shouted out, "it looks like ol' Moki Paco is in the lead."

Her heart sank. Hank wanted so much to win the race and claim the quilt. Of all the entrants, she'd hoped either he or Trapper would win. But, whoever won, it was for a good cause.

"No, that's not Moki, it's that other fellow—the lawyer," the man said, stepping out onto the track.

"It's Hank!" Glorianna clapped her hands together.

"But another team is right beside him now. It's Trapper!" the man called out to the crowd as he scurried back to safety.

Oh, no! Trapper will never forgive Hank if he beats him. And Hank will be so disappointed if he loses.

Eight teams thundered toward the finish line, their dogs struggling beneath their load.

But the first two teams were several yards ahead of the others.

"Meeto! Go!"

"Faster, Ryan, faster!"

Chapter 12

It was hard to tell who was in first place. The two teams were running side-by-side, coming full-speed toward the big banner hanging over the finish line.

"I think Trapper's gonna be first," someone called out.

"No, I don't think so. Looks to me like that Hank Gordon is gonna take first," another yelled.

Glorianna, now well into her ninth month, wore the snuggly faux fox maternity jacket Hank had given her. She put a hand on Todd's shoulder to stabilize herself and stood on tiptoes, vying for a better view.

The two leaders were nearly upon them, the finish line only inches away. Trapper spotted Glorianna, and with a wave and one mighty shout to Meeto, spurred ahead and passed through the finish line only inches ahead of Hank.

"Trapper Timberwolf and his lead dog, Meeto, have done it again, folks!" the announcer yelled out excitedly into the microphone. "With Hank Gordon and his dog, Ryan, taking second place, and Moki Paco and his dog, Thunder, coming in third! Congratulations to each of these men and their fine teams!"

Cheers and whistles came from the excited onlookers as they crowded around the racers, congratulating the winners and consoling the losers.

As soon as he'd taken care of his dogs, Trapper walked directly to Glorianna, who was holding the folded quilt in her arms. Without a word, he took it from her, wrapped it about his shoulders, and paraded around for all to see.

"I'm sorry, Hank," she told her fiancé when he joined her at the finish line. "I thought for sure you were going to win."

Instead of looking defeated as she'd thought he would, Hank was wearing a victorious smile as he pulled her into his arms, kissed her cheek, and declared loudly for all to hear, "Trapper may have won the quilt, but I got the girl who made it. I'm the real winner here. Not him!"

Glorianna felt like a queen—until she saw the hurt look on Trapper's face.

❧

When someone tapped on the door late that night, Glorianna supposed it was Hank. But it wasn't. It was Trapper.

"I've come to try to talk some sense into you," he told her as he brushed past and plopped onto her sofa. "You and I both know you don't love Hank. Why are you marrying him?"

"What concern is it of yours?" She chose a chair opposite him and carefully lowered her rounded body into it. "You're not interested in taking on a family, are you?"

"Well, no, but I hate to see you make the biggest mistake of your life. You've got Todd and that baby to consider."

"I am considering Todd and my baby. Hank is a wonderful, caring man, and he's dedicated to me and my children."

"But you don't love him, do you?"

She couldn't lie. Trapper knew her too well. "I think I can, in time. The mail-order brides learned to love their husbands." She bit at her lip.

"But you love me."

She turned away. "Why would I? You've never given me reason to love you. You're like a brother to me, that's all."

"You wouldn't tell an untruth, would you?"

Using both hands to lift herself off the chair, she moved to the door. "I resent that question. I think it's time for you to go. Anyway, I would never want a man who wouldn't commit to me. Are you willing to do that? To give up your independent lifestyle?"

"That's impossible."

"That's exactly what I thought. Trapper, I'm marrying Hank in less than a week. Now go." She pushed open the door and watched him as he rose and marched toward her. "I hope someday you find a woman who can change your mind. You're a fine man. Just pigheaded."

"Don't come crying to me after you've made this mistake. Remember my warning."

"Even if I did find I'd made a mistake, I wouldn't give you the satisfaction of knowing it. Good night, Trapper."

"Good night." But as he brushed past her, his lips found hers and he kissed her. Hard. Almost recklessly.

She closed the door and propped herself against it. *Oh, Lord, forgive me, but I still love Trapper.*

Chapter 13

The afternoon of the wedding was bright and clear. Glorianna peered out the church window at the parking lot, hoping, yet fearing, Trapper's truck would be there. She couldn't walk down that aisle knowing he was in the church. But the truck wasn't there. She hadn't heard from him since the night he'd visited her apartment. Emily told her he'd been called out of town on another long-term job.

The music sounded and a very pregnant bride began her slow walk down the aisle toward Hank, who stood with Clarence, a close friend who'd agreed to be his best man. Hank looked handsome in his black tuxedo and heavily starched shirt, like the bridegroom from the top of a wedding cake. She looked down at her rounded tummy. How funny she must look in her pale blue satin wedding dress with its full train flowing out behind her. Lifting her eyes heavenward, she asked, *Please, God. If this is not right, if this is not in Your will, let a thunderbolt come down—something, anything, to let me know. I want to do Your will. Although I'm fond of Hank, You know I don't love him.*

I love—

Suddenly the front doors of the church burst open and Trapper rushed in, grabbed Glorianna up in his arms, and bolted toward the exit. With a back glance over his shoulder toward the bewildered groom, he mouthed the words, "I'm sorry," before heading for his waiting pickup.

"What are you doing?" she screamed as she struggled to free herself. "I'm getting married!"

"What am I doing?" he shouted back as he shoved her into his pickup, and with squealing tires, drove right across the church lawn. "I'm doing what I should have done months ago. Telling you I love you. Telling you I can't live without you and Todd and that precious baby you're carrying! That's what I'm doing! Now shut up and hang on. I don't want you going into labor on me!"

Glorianna stopped struggling and leaned back in the seat. In the door's side mirror she could see Hank in his black tuxedo running after the truck with dozens of people following close behind him. "You can't do this to Hank. It's not fair!"

There was a sudden jolt as the truck ran over a curb and headed down the paved street well over the speed limit. "I'm doing the guy a favor. You know you love me. You think he'd want to marry you if he knew that?"

"What do you know about love?" she snapped back. "And where are you taking me?"

"Just relax. You'll see soon enough."

They rode along in silence. She wasn't about to jump out of a moving truck, and it appeared he wasn't about to stop until he reached his destination. "You said you can't live without me. Does that mean you're ready to marry me and give up your crazy lifestyle? Simply loving me is not enough, Trapper. You know that."

"We'll talk about it later. Now scoot over close to me or do you want me to pull you over?"

Warily, still unable to believe what was happening, she gathered the long train about her legs and slowly did as she'd been told. Trapper's arm slipped about her shoulder and pulled her close to him. "How's that baby doing?"

"Fine. Moving quite a bit, but that's normal."

"Good."

He turned up a mountain road, one she'd never been on, and soon they reached a clearing where smoke was rising from the chimney of a beautiful log cabin home. The truck came to a sudden stop in front of the porch.

"Whose place is this?"

"Yours, if you want it. Been mine up 'til now." He jumped out of the truck and rushed around to the passenger side, once again swooping her up in his arms.

She looped her arms about his neck and allowed him to carry her, thinking how strange it must be for him to be carrying a pregnant woman when he'd been too embarrassed to even kiss one.

Once inside, Trapper carefully placed her on the long sofa in front of the fireplace, then, without a word, opened the screen and tossed a log onto the dwindling fire.

"How long are you planning to keep me prisoner? Hank and the sheriff are probably already on their way up here, you know," she said, watching his strong back as he added another log and poked at it with the fire iron.

"Guess I'd better get a hurry-on then." He dropped on one knee before her and took her hands in his, his blue eyes once again capturing her heart. "I love you, Glorianna. I guess you never expected to hear me say those words."

"No—no, I didn't—"

He put a finger to her lips to silence her. "Today, with God's help, my head told me what my heart has known all along. You are the most important thing in my life. More important than flying, more than fishing, and yes, more than the missionary work I do with the bush people. I know now, if I lost you, I'd lose everything worth having. I can't believe I was blind for so long."

"You—you—love me?"

"Oh, yes, more than my poor selection of words can ever tell you." He paused and swallowed hard. "I never told you much about Judith. Two days

218

before our wedding, she and Charlie—the man I'd thought was my best friend—took off together. Left, just like that. They were long gone by the time I found her farewell note. I'll never forget how embarrassed I was, having to explain to everyone what had happened, having to return all the gifts. I think I could have strangled her if I'd gotten my hands on her. I've never been so angry in my life."

"Or so hurt?"

He squeezed her hand. "Yes, hurt. The only one I could really talk to about it was God, and boy, did I let Him have an earful. I couldn't believe He'd let such a thing happen. And to be real honest, I still can't. In some ways, I've blamed Him for years. I remember telling Him if that's the kind of matchmaking He does, I wanted no part of it. I figured I'd be better off alone than getting attached to some woman and have her take off on me again. I—" He bowed his head with a slight chuckle. "I thought all women were alike."

With feelings of love swelling up in her heart, she reached over and caressed his cheek. "We're not. But I understand what you're saying. I felt the same way. Jimmy was not at all the husband I thought he'd be. He was cruel, Trapper. Mean. I doubt he ever loved me. The only use he had for a wife was someone to pick up after him, do his laundry, and cook a few meals. A maid could have easily replaced me. Worst of all, he was a terrible father. Poor little Todd spent most of the time Jimmy was around cowering in his bedroom, hoping his father would leave him alone. He was terrified of him."

"Poor kid, that must have been hard on him."

"It was. I'd been so anxious to get away from home I wouldn't listen to anyone—not my parents, not my friends. I figured I could reform him. What a joke! It seemed the more I prayed, the worse he got. I blamed God for the mistake I'd made. I was actually angry at God. Can you believe that?"

"Looks like we've both made plenty of wrong choices, but Glorianna," he lifted her hands to his lips and kissed them tenderly, "you were about to make another mistake. I couldn't let that happen. I knew you didn't love Hank. At first, I thought I was merely doing the noble thing by coming to your apartment and warning you not to go through with the marriage; but I lay awake all night last night, wrestling with God. He was telling me it wasn't you who was being the fool, but me! I loved you, and yet I was almost forcing you to marry another man because I wasn't being honest with you, myself, or God. I really do love you! I've always loved you. I was—" He struggled for the right word, then it came. "Pigheaded—just like you said I was."

"Trapper, don't you see? I don't want you to give up the things you care about! I want to share them with you. Your joy of those things is what drew me to you in the first place. It just took me awhile to get used to them. I enjoy flying with you. I love fishing with you. I love going into the bush with you and working with the people you love. I'm thrilled by the way you love our Lord.

But most of all—I love you!"

"I want to marry you, Glorianna. Please say you'll have me. I want to be a father to Todd and this baby. Can you ever forgive me for being so stupid? So—pigheaded?"

Too overcome with emotion to speak, all Glorianna could do was nod.

"I've already evicted Meeto from my pickup and my bed, and I'm going to lock all my guns and knives securely away, where there is no danger of the children finding them."

"Oh, Trapper," she said between sobs, "of course I'll marry you. You're the only man I've ever truly loved." As Trapper reached to kiss her, she let out a sudden gasp. "What about Hank?"

Trapper stood and pulled her up to him, cradling her in his arms. "Hank is a fine man. I don't think, if he's honest with himself, he'd want to marry a woman who was in love with someone else. I'll go to him and try to explain myself to him. I wouldn't blame him if he took a swing at me. And if he does, I won't even duck."

"I don't want there to be any trouble," she said with great concern.

"There won't be, I promise. Now, there's only one thing left to resolve. When shall we get married? I'd like it to be before the baby comes so I can be its father right from the start."

"I'd like that too. I love you, Trapper Timberwolf."

"I love you, Glori."

The screeching of tires in the driveway told them Hank had arrived, and together they went out to face him, hand in hand.

❧

"You're a good man, Hank," Trapper told his best man two days later as they stood at the front of the little chapel. "For years I've hated Judith and my cousin for what they did to me, and now I've done the same thing to you—taken away the woman you loved. Not many men would have been big enough to forgive me like you have."

Hank shrugged. "I won't pretend I'm not still upset, but I knew all along there was something going on between Glorianna and you. I knew she didn't love me, but I hoped, in time, she would learn to love me. I knew better, though. She's always loved you. Any fool could see that—even this fool, if I'd been man enough to admit it. I knew marrying her was wrong, but women like Glorianna don't come around very often. Can't blame a guy for wanting to make her his."

"I know. If I'd had my wits about me, I would have laid claim on her early on. I guess it was the idea of taking on both a wife and a child that scared me. Then, when I found out about the baby, well, I freaked out," he said in a low whisper. "Guess I was a coward."

"Funny you should say that. The things that repelled you most were the very things that attracted me to Glorianna. Ever since my wife died, I've wanted to remarry and have children. Now I'm alone again, and you're about to become a family man."

"I owe you, buddy. Big time. I'm gonna find you a woman—and that's a promise!"

The music began, and down the aisle came the most beautiful bride Trapper had ever seen. His eyes clouded over as she walked slowly toward him, love shining on her sweet face. How could he ever have been so blind? How could he so long have denied the love that now filled his heart to overflowing? *God, I adore this woman. With all my heart and soul, and with Your help, I'll cherish her until death do us part.*

❧

Glorianna blinked back tears of joy, her gaze fastened on Trapper, the love of her life, totally unaware of the hundreds of relatives and friends sitting in the chapel. *I love you, Trapper,* she said in her heart. *God has brought us together, and I promise both Him and you I'll be the best wife I can be. With God as the head of our house, our marriage cannot fail.*

When she'd nearly reached the front of the church, a hand reached out and touched her arm. She turned, and there, to her surprise, sat her adoptive parents, Horace and Wilma Porter. Glorianna bent and kissed each one on the cheek, whispering, "I love you."

The only one missing from the family circle was Anna Moore, her birth mother. But somehow, she knew Anna was watching her from heaven. After all, wasn't she the one who planned this wedding?

Chapter 14

Glorianna dressed carefully for bed, wearing the lacy white maternity nightgown Emily had given her as a wedding gift. "I look like a blimp," she said aloud to her reflection in the mirror. "How can I ever let Trapper see me this way—on our wedding night?"

"Aren't you about ready for bed?" he called to her from their bedroom.

She opened the bathroom door with trepidation. "I–I'm ready."

Trapper, dressed in a brand new pair of plaid flannel pajamas and smelling of aftershave, crossed the room and took her into his arms, planting a kiss on her cheek. "Are you feeling as awkward as I am?"

She leaned into the strength of his shoulder and rested her head. "Yes, very awkward."

"I know tonight should be our honeymoon, but under the circumstances, I think it would be best if we postponed—things, until after that baby is born. What do you think?"

For the first time since she'd said I do, Glorianna felt herself relax. "Yes, I think we should postpone—things. Thank you for being so considerate."

Trapper lifted her into his arms and carried her to their bed, lovingly placing her on the soft white sheets his mother had put on the bed that very afternoon. "Is it okay if I crawl in beside you? I don't want to crowd you. I could sleep in the other bedroom."

She held out a hand. "You're my husband now. I want us to share a bed. And someday very soon—"

"I know."

His fingers snapped loudly. "I nearly forgot. Mom gave me a box and said Anna wanted you to open it on your wedding night." He quickly crossed the room and lifted a large box from a chair and placed it on the bed beside her. "Open it, or Mom will never forgive me."

Lifting the envelope from the top, she opened it and began to read aloud.

My precious daughter, Glorianna,

If you are reading this, I know you have married my beloved Trapper, the boy I loved as if he were my own son. You see, my sweet, my sister whom you have called Mother all these years, confided in me that she had discovered your husband, Jim, was cheating on you. It was only a matter of time until you found out. I knew you would be devastated and would no longer be able to live with a man who wasn't faithful to you. According to what I read in God's Word, I don't think He would expect you to spend the rest of your life alone. I don't condone divorce, my dear one, but I also don't condone cheating.

I have watched Trapper grow up from a mischievous little boy into a fine young man. I saw the hurt in his eyes when Judith walked out on him. I heard the resolve in his voice when he vowed he'd never let another woman get close enough to hurt him again. But, I knew from the time you turned thirteen and I saw the love of life shining in your eyes in the photographs Wilma sent me, you two were meant to be together. So, this romantic woman and her dearest friend, Trapper's mother, devised this scheme to get you two together. I only wish I could have been there to help Emily play Cupid.

I love you both and want only the best for you. I release you, my darling daughter, from your commitment to run The Bear Paw Quilt Shop for two years.

I have a feeling you'd rather be a stay-at-home mom, and that's fine with me. Sell the shop, keep it, do whatever you wish. You have my blessing. And, Trapper, you take care of my precious daughter and her family. Give her all the love you have stored up inside you.

Now—open the box and cover yourselves with this double wedding ring quilt I have made for you and do whatever newlyweds do on their Honeymoon night. As you are kept warm by this quilt, please remember always,

It has been hand quilted with love.

Mother

Together, Glorianna and Trapper opened the box.

"It's beautiful," she said in a mere whisper, overcome by her mother's sweet words and dedication to her happiness.

"Such tiny stitches. How did she ever do it?" Trapper spread the quilt over them and tucked it beneath Glorianna's chin and kissed her cheek. "Good night, sweetheart."

She let out a sigh of contentment. "Good night, my dearest."

The cozy room became silent as the two lovers lay wrapped in each other's arms beneath the quilt.

Suddenly, Glorianna sat straight up in bed.

Chapter 15

W hat happened?" Trapper leaped out from under the covers, his pajama bottoms wet and sticking to his long legs.

"My—my water broke," Glorianna answered with a sheepish grin.

Trapper rushed around the room in circles. "Don't move! Whatever you do, don't move! I'll call the doctor! Do you hurt? Are you in pain?"

"I didn't want to tell you, but I've been having little twinges of pain since early this morning. I knew you wanted us to be married before the baby came. I–I think it's on its way."

In his rush, Trapper tripped over his boots, knocked the phone off the nightstand, and couldn't locate the phonebook, which lay on top of the table in plain sight.

"Drive her to the hospital. I'll meet you there," the doctor told him after asking a number of questions. "Just be calm. I don't want you fainting on her. She needs you."

By the time Trapper located a suitcase, threw a few of Glorianna's personal items into it, and located the keys to his pickup, she was having contractions, one right on top of the other, sweating, and gasping for air.

"I thought women spent hours at the hospital!" Trapper yelled accusingly during one of her contractions. "How can you have a baby that quickly? My mom said she was in labor for hours!"

"It's exactly the same thing I did with Todd! Once my bag of water broke, he was born an hour later," she screamed back at him before she doubled with pain again. "Ohh! It hurts!"

"Stop! You can't have that baby now!" he told her, dropping to his knees beside the bed, a frantic look on his face.

"Oh? You think not?" She quickly drew in another cleansing breath. "Tell that to the baby! It's coming! Now! You'll have to help me!"

"What do I do? Boil water?"

She clutched onto his hands and gripped them tight. "No! Get some clean towels, then call the doctor back and tell him we won't make it. He'll have to come here!"

"I love you, Glori! Don't die on me, please!"

She laughed between her tears. "I'm not going to die; I'm simply having a baby! Now go! Call the doctor! Quick!"

By the time the doctor arrived, a tiny, pink baby girl was resting comfortably in her mother's arms and a proud new father was sitting on the edge of the bed, sweaty, nervous, and looking totally exhausted.

"You did well, Trapper. You two have a beautiful baby daughter. I've called an ambulance. I want to take these two to the hospital to be checked out, just to be on the safe side. I'll wait out front and give you a little time alone with your wife and baby."

The two men shook hands as the doctor left the room.

"I'm a father," Trapper said, wiping his brow and leaning over the tiny baby. "A real father. Do you think Todd will like her?"

Glorianna reached out and stroked his tired face. "I know he'll like her. And you delivered her. Not every father gets to deliver his baby, you know."

"Seeing that baby being born was watching a miracle take place. God's hand at work. How can anyone witness a birth and not believe in God?"

"You want to hold your daughter?"

"Can I? I mean, I won't give her germs or anything, will I?" He held out his arms and Glorianna placed the little bundle in his big hands.

"No, silly, you won't give her germs."

He stared at their baby with her tiny button nose and sweet little lips. "What shall we name her?"

"I've been giving that a lot of thought. How do you like Emily Anna, after both our mothers?"

Trapper repeated the name. "I think it's perfect."

She smiled up at the man, love shining on her weary face. "Then Emily Anna it is."

Trapper held the baby close and nestled his cheek against the fuzzy hair covering her perfectly round little head. "Glori, this might not be the best time to ask you, but could we have another baby sometime? Not right away. But I'd like to have at least two more. What do you think?"

Her smile erupted at his comment. "We'll see if you still feel that way when you're up at two a.m., walking the floor with Emily Anna."

She pulled the quilt about her shoulders, a look of peace and contentment on her face as she whispered to her heavenly Father, "Thank You, God, for Trapper, for Todd, and for little Emily Anna, all three miracles from You! And forgive me for ever doubting You and Your love for me."

Epilogue

Five years later

C hip, get those dogs out of my kitchen!" Glorianna shouted as her three-year-old son chased after Meeto, Samson, and Delilah, the Siberian husky puppy Trapper had given Emily Anna on her third birthday.

"I put all the napkins on the table like you told me, Mommy," Emily Anna told her mother as she entered the big kitchen. "What else can I do to help?"

Glorianna handed her the salt and pepper shakers. "Put these on the table. Where's your father? I'm ready for him to mash the potatoes."

"The baby spit up on him. He's changing his shirt."

"What's Grandpa doing?"

"He's holding the baby."

"Then tell Todd to come in; he can do it."

"That's some family you and Trapper have," Emily said as she pulled salads from the refrigerator. "Whoever thought Trapper would be the proud father of four? Those kids mean the world to him. Dyami and I are proud of both of you. You're great parents."

Glorianna pulled the corn casserole from the oven. "Oh, Emily, do you really think so? Sometimes I wonder. Raising kids these days is no easy task. I don't know how people do it without turning to God."

"Me either, honey. I'm still amazed at the way God worked in your lives. When Anna came to me with that crazy scheme of hers to match you two up, well, I knew it would take nothing short of a miracle for it to happen. Guess her faith was much stronger than mine. It worked!"

"And mine. I came so close to marrying the wrong man. If Trapper hadn't stopped—"

"Umm. Lemon meringue pies! And pumpkin pies! My favorites." A good-looking man dressed in starched jeans and a pristine white shirt entered the big kitchen. "Anything I can do to help?"

"Oh, Hank, I'm glad you're here. Could you mash the potatoes?" Glorianna asked, handing him the stainless steel potato masher.

"Sure, I've never done it before. You'll have to coach me."

"Never mashed potatoes?" Trapper asked, coming into the kitchen, buttoning his freshly laundered shirt.

"Never," Hank responded with a grin, "but I'm willing to learn. Who knows? I may get married someday, if I find another girl like the one I almost married—" He stopped and kissed Glorianna on the cheek.

"Get away from my woman," Trapper told him with a grin. "She's mine."

"I know. Lucky you."

"Hey, I vowed I'd find you a woman almost as good as mine, and I'm not going to back down on my promise. I just haven't found her yet. But I will. I still owe you."

"You'd better hurry, buddy. Time's running out for this old guy."

"You two menfolk quit your jawin' and get everyone around the table," Emily told them as she pulled a basket of hot bread from the microwave. "Trapper, you carry the turkey platter. Hank, you take the ham."

"You tell them, Emily," Glorianna said with a laugh, picking up the two remaining casseroles and heading for the dining room.

When the family had all gathered around the table and joined hands, Trapper began to pray. "Lord, how can we ever thank You for the blessings You've bestowed upon us? You've blessed Glorianna and me with four beautiful children, You've kept my mother and father in good health so our children can enjoy having wonderful, godly grandparents, and You've given us a good friend in Hank Gordon. Lord, we know not many men would have forgiven Glorianna and me for what we did to him, much less given his blessing on our marriage, but in his graciousness, Hank did, and we'll be forever grateful to him. We ask You to forgive us for the many times we break Your heart by sinning against You.

"Now, God, bless us on this Thanksgiving Day as we partake of this bounty You have provided for us, and bless the hands that so willingly prepared it. Keep us close to You, and may we never forget all good things come from You. Bless our nation and those in authority and give them wisdom and guidance. In Your name we ask all these things."

In unison, everyone at the table said, "Amen."

"Wait," Glorianna called out, rising to her feet. "I have an announcement to make. In a few months we'll be adding another blessing to our little love nest."

Trapper's jaw dropped. "Really, babe? We're going to have another baby?"

She threw back her head with an uproarious laugh. "No, sweetheart! The vet said Samson and Delilah are going to have pups!"

Be My Valentine

Chapter 1

Which nightgown would you prefer, sir?" The clerk held up a lacy, low-cut, ultra-sheer number in a slinky vibrant red. "One something like this, perhaps? Most women love this gown."

Hank Gordon couldn't remember a time in his life when he'd been more embarrassed. In all the years he and Sheila were married, not one time had he ever been in the women's lingerie section of Beck's Department Store. "Ah—no, nothing like that. You don't understand." He swallowed hard, sure his face was as red as the gown. "Actually, what I wanted was the same gown I'm returning, but in a smaller size."

The shake of her head and the shrug of the woman's narrow shoulders said it all. "I'm sorry, sir, but we sold out of that particular gown weeks ago. It was a very popular model. Are you sure your wife wouldn't like something a little more—"

Hank's eyes widened. "Oh, it's not for my wife—"

The sales clerk raised a brow. "Well, then, your girlfriend would probably—"

"I don't have a girlfriend," he inserted quickly, though why he owed her an explanation was beyond him. It wasn't exactly the kind of thing you'd discuss with a stranger.

"Look, my friend asked—I—he—" He frowned and sucked in a deep breath before continuing. *This woman must think I'm a total loony.* "It's this way. My best friend bought this gown for his wife." He opened the bag, pulling out the lacy, shimmering nightgown. He was embarrassed just touching it. "It was way too large and, since they were called out of town, he asked me to return it and exchange it for a smaller size."

"I'd definitely take the slinky red one. Your wife will love it!" a pleasant female voice called out from somewhere behind the pair. "Hi, Hank."

Hank spun around, a big smile replacing the frown. "Tink! I'd recognize that chirpy voice of yours anywhere. What are you doing back in Juneau?"

Tina Taylor stood on tiptoe and kissed the big man's crimson cheek. "Long story. If you've got time, after you decide which gown to buy for your wife, I'll treat you to a cup of coffee, and we can catch up on old times. I'd heard you got married. Maybe she'd like to join us. I'd love to meet her."

The broad smile vanished as he drew his breath in sharply. "Sheila died, Tink. Nearly eight years ago."

Hank felt her fingers touch his arm, as her sorrow for him spelled out on her face. "Oh, Hank, I feel terrible. I didn't know."

The clerk took the gown from his hand and cleared her throat noisily. "Sorry to interrupt, but I have other customers who need my attention. Have you made your decision yet?"

"Ah—actually, no, I haven't." Hank fished around in his coat pocket and pulled out a slip of paper. "But I have the sales receipt. Why don't you just credit my friend's charge account, and he can pick out something later, after he gets back in town."

The woman nodded, took the receipt, and headed for the checkout counter.

"Well, do you have time for coffee, or is that lawyer business of yours demanding all your time?" Tina gave his arm a playful pinch. "You are still playing attorney, aren't you?"

Grateful for the change of subject, Hank nodded. The middle of the lingerie sales floor was not exactly the most conducive place to discuss the details of the death of your beloved wife. He was sure Tina sensed that and had come to his rescue. "Yep, sure am, but by your big city standards, I'd say my routine business is pretty boring. How come you're back in Juneau?" He held up a palm between them. "Wait. Don't answer." He signed the refund slip, then grabbed Tina's arm and headed for the elevator. "Let's get out of here. I feel like a voyeur among all these scantily clad mannequins."

The two old friends decided on a small nearby café, walking the short distance in the cold, brisk air, their arms linked.

Hank smiled down at her as he gave her arm a squeeze. "Did your husband come with you?" She had gloves on, but he couldn't remember seeing a wedding ring on her finger at the department store.

Tina Taylor shivered and yanked up the zipper tab on her jacket, pulling it to the top. "Husband? Not yet." A heavy frown momentarily creased her brow. "How about you? Have you remarried since Sheila—" Her unfinished sentence hung heavily in the brisk Alaskan air.

He smiled as visions of Glorianna, the woman he'd nearly married two years after his wife's death, flooded his mind. "Nearly did, once. But it didn't work out."

"Brrr, I'd forgotten how cool it can get in Juneau this time of year." Tina shivered and pulled the collar up about her neck.

Once again, Hank was sure Tina had changed the subject to spare him the misery of having to talk about something that was obviously painful to him. Her renewed smile pulled his thoughts away. The woman still seemed to have a sixth sense. Her melodious laughter brought back joyful memories long forgotten.

"Do you remember when Mr. Halston gave us flashlights for Christmas? I think we were eight years old. We sat on your mom's steps shining their beams at the passing cars?"

"We sure thought we were doing something naughty, didn't we, Tink?" He slipped his arm about her waist and ushered her through the door of the little café fronting Gastineau Bay. "We had some great times growing up."

"I always wished my mother could be like yours."

"My mom loved you, Tink."

She grinned over her shoulder as they made their way to an empty table in a far corner. "You're the only one who ever called me Tink." With a melancholy sigh, she unzipped her jacket and pulled it from her shoulders. "I've missed being called by that name."

Hank took it from her and pulled out a chair, motioning her to be seated. "Well, you'll always be my Tinker Bell." Once she was settled, he slipped off his stylish black cashmere overcoat and placed both garments on an empty chair. "Remember how my mom would read Peter Pan to us when we'd been good? We both loved that story."

"And we made paper wings for me to wear and a green paper hat and cape for you."

"And a wand from a stick and a Ping-Pong ball. Tinker Bell and Peter Pan. What imaginations we had back then." Hank handed her a menu and began to peruse his own. "We made our own fun, didn't we?"

"We were quite a pair, weren't we?" Tina asked, laughing, still holding the unopened menu.

"That we were." Hank closed his menu and leaned across the table, taking Tina's hand in his. "Remember when we rigged that rope from the rafters in the barn and swung from it, playing like Wendy was there with us? It's a wonder one of us didn't break an arm."

She giggled, her free hand cupping his. "Or a leg! We were pretty daring, as I recall. Especially you!"

"We were more than daring. More like stupid! But what fun we had."

"Oh, Hank, you were always my very best friend. I loved those days."

"Me too. We were really a couple of dreamers, you and me, with big plans for our futures. We were going to have it all."

"Yes, we certainly were dreamers." A heavy sigh emitted from deep within her chest as her smile disappeared, and she gazed into his eyes. "Sometimes I wonder if I should've stayed in Juneau, instead of going off to make my fortune in the big city. Things were always so peaceful here. Maybe if—"

Her sudden change of attitude gave Hank cause for concern. "So? Did you?"

The wistful look disappeared, and she gave him a blank stare. "Did I what?"

"Make your fortune in the big city. Chicago? Isn't that where you went?"

"A fortune? Hardly!" She grimaced as she pulled her hands from his. "Even after all these years, all I have to show for my time and effort is a partially paid-for condo, a broken-down car, and a bunch of monthly bills. Living in the big city is not cheap, and my life didn't exactly pan out the way I'd planned. Things happen"—she snapped her fingers—"and your life changes in an instant."

The waitress brought two large coffee mugs to their table and filled them to the brim without asking, placing two packets of creamer beside Hank's cup.

Tina covered her cup with her palm and shook her head.

"You ready to order, or you need a little more time?"

With a wave of his hand toward the waitress, Hank picked up his menu again. "Give us a few more minutes."

They sat silently as the woman gave them an impatient nod and moved on.

"So what're you doing back in town? Juneau's a long way from Chicago. Or anywhere," he added, forcing a big grin, Tina's comment still niggling at his mind.

She stretched first one arm, then the other, as she settled back in her chair and folded her hands in her lap. "Tell me about it! If I sound a bit flaky it's because my body is still on Chicago time. I may have trouble adjusting to Alaska's long, dark winter days. It's never dark in Chicago. Not with all the lights and all the activity going on twenty-four-seven. And it's never quiet. Cars, trains, planes, the El. But you adjust. I guess I'll adjust here too, but it may take me awhile. I'll probably have to sleep with the lights on and a radio blaring." She raised her brows. "But then, there's the flip side. Those wonderful long, lazy summer days filled with sunshine!"

He brightened. "You make it sound like you'll be staying for a while."

She picked up her cup and blew into it, eyeing him over the rim. "Looks like I'm here to stay."

"Permanently?" He stared at his old friend. Although she was smiling, he detected a note of sadness in her tone.

"Umm, not exactly permanently."

"You two ready to order?"

The pair had been so engrossed in their conversation, they hadn't noticed the waitress standing beside them again, with her pad and pencil in hand.

Hank nodded toward Tina. "The soup and sandwich special okay with you? It's usually pretty good."

"Fine."

Hank took their menus and stuffed them into the little holder mounted on the wall before turning his attention back to his guest. "Okay, tell me what you meant by that comment about being here permanently, for a while. Somehow those two terms don't jibe."

A sadness covered her face as she lowered her eyes, her fingers methodically tracing the edge of the cup. "It's my grandmother. She's not at all well."

"Oh no. I'm so sorry to hear that, Tink. I remember how much you loved her."

Her lips began to quiver and she blinked hard. "She's dying, Hank."

"Harriett Taylor is dying? I don't understand. If she's dying and she's in

Chicago, what are you doing back here in Juneau? Knowing you, and how close you two were, I'm surprised you didn't want to stay there with her."

He watched as Tina blinked and rubbed at her eyes, as if to fight back tears. He knew firsthand how important her grandmother had always been to her. He well remembered how her mother had abandoned her less than six months after her father had committed suicide and taken off with one of her surly boyfriends, who didn't want a teenage girl tagging along. Although Hank had only been a junior in high school at the time, he'd wanted to hunt the woman down, make her come back, and face up to her responsibility.

"We—we're both moving back here. The doctor said it's only a matter of time for Gram. After that—" She paused. "I guess I'll be heading back to Chicago."

The pitiful look on Tina's face made him want to pull her into his arms and comfort her, but he sat quietly and listened, offering her his handkerchief instead.

She dabbed at her eyes before going on. "She's never complained, but I know she's hated living at the care home. It's depressing. I wanted to keep her with me, but with working, commuting, and being away so many hours each day, it was impossible. She's been so good to me. I've felt awful about her living there, but we had no other choice."

"I'm sure she understood." Hank's hand again cupped hers across the table. "She knew you had obligations."

"I—I hope so. I've tried to spend as much time with her as I could, but I'm afraid it hasn't been enough."

"You had your own life to live."

She lowered her gaze and dabbed with the handkerchief again. "I—I know. I've tried to tell myself that same thing. For the first few years, I rushed home from the office each day to be with her. But then, I guess I coaxed myself into believing I had my rights too. I—I've left her alone way more than I should have. Now—"

"Surely she's made friends at the care home."

"She has, but I know it isn't the same as having family with you. Many of the ladies who room around her are much worse off than she is. It's heartbreaking. Some are like—I hate to say it—like vegetables. The lights are on, but there's no one at home. It's been hard on her. Unlike them, her mind is as sharp as ever. It's her body that's giving out."

"She's getting old, Tink. That's what happens. It's inevitable. It'll get us too, eventually."

The two sat silently sipping their coffee, watching as the waitress brought their orders.

"You didn't explain about moving back here," Hank pressed easily once the woman had moved on. From the weary look on Tina's face it was obvious the whole situation was stressing her out.

She picked up her spoon and stirred at the steaming soup in her bowl. "I work for a huge parts company and have since the first year I moved to Chicago. They ship parts all over the world."

He ripped open a bag of oyster crackers and dumped them into his bowl. "Even Juneau?"

A faint smile curled up the corners of her mouth. "Even Juneau. Times have changed, Hank, and unlike some companies, my company has changed with those times. We were one of the first major corporations to move our enormous catalog onto the Web. It nearly doubled our business that first year. I was one of the ones who got the catalog up and running. Because of it, and the whopping increase in sales, I got a nice promotion."

Hank did an exaggerated applause. "Good for you! I'm sure you deserved it."

"Not long ago, I was promoted to senior design technologist and became part of the distribution management team. Most of my work now is done independently, using the Internet. Makes me pretty much a loner, but I like it."

"Well, belated congratulations. I hope your promotion meant more money!"

She nodded and took a bite of her sandwich before going on. "It did, but it also means a bit of traveling too, when our team gets together face to face. I've only had to leave Gram maybe two or three times so far, but I'm always worried I'll be in Dallas or New Orleans or some other faraway place when she really needs me. Especially now."

Hank motioned for the waitress to refill their cups, then picked up his sandwich, waving it toward her. "Tink, that still doesn't explain why you're back in Juneau. Now I'm really confused."

With a slight grin she held up a hand between them. "Patience, Peter Pan. I'm coming to that. When the doctor told me he didn't think Gram would last another year, I knew I had to find some way to spend more time with her."

"That sounds like you."

"I had to get her out of that care home. All she's talked about, since she's taken a turn for the worse, is how much she'd like to come back home to die. Back to Juneau."

Hanks brows rose quickly. "You're bringing her here?"

"Yes, she's already here! I called ahead, and they had a vacancy in a nice facility not far from her house. I took her there as soon as we got off the plane. I'll move her into her home as soon as I can get it ready. I knew she'd never be able to take the dust and the noise while I'm cleaning up her place and doing a bit of remodeling. Not to mention the paint fumes. Right now her place is a pretty big mess."

"Sounds like you have your work cut out for you. I guess you'll be looking for a job after that."

"No, I convinced my boss I can work from here. The majority of what I do is on the computer and the Internet anyway, so it won't make any difference where I'm located."

"That's great!" Hank frowned. "I didn't know she still owned that old house. I figured it'd been sold years ago."

"No, she still owns it. She's kept the taxes paid on it. I tried to talk her into renting it out, but she wouldn't hear of it. She's had herself convinced from the time we left that someday she'd come back to it."

"Now she's here."

Tina nodded. "Yes, she's here."

"Thanks to you."

"It's the least I could do for her."

Hank finished off his sandwich and took a final sip of coffee. He hated to bring it up, but the question plagued him. He'd driven by the old house several months earlier and hoped Tina's expectations weren't set too high. "Have you seen her house lately? It's looking kind of shabby."

"I know. After I got Gram settled, I had the taxi driver take me past. You're right. It is in pretty bad shape, at least the roof is, and it needs painting and a general cleanup. But it seems structurally sound. I'm sure the inside needs remodeling from top to bottom. But Gram thinks she has enough money to do it, and she's thrilled with the idea. You're probably wondering why she'd want to go to all the trouble and expense of fixing up her home when she has so little time."

"It had entered my mind."

"Not only is it filled with precious memories for her, she's never liked the idea of me living in Chicago. Particularly after she's gone."

He watched as she blinked a few times.

"She's always said Juneau is a much better and safer place for a single woman to live. Gram is hoping, once the house is fixed up, I'll stay on and live in it. After she——" She paused, as if the words stuck in her throat. "I've taken a temporary leave to get the place ready."

Figuring it'd probably be best to not pursue that subject, seeing how much even the thought of losing her grandmother upset her, he asked, "What about your condo?"

She shrugged and let out a sigh. "I've sublet it."

"Sounds like you've thought of everything." He wiped at his mouth, then placed his napkin on the table. "By the way, where are you staying until you get the house fixed up?"

She crossed her arms over her chest as she stared into the half-eaten bowl of cold soup. "I stayed at a motel last night. I'd hoped I could stay at Gram's house, but until I can get a plumbing and heating man to check out that old furnace and see if the hot water tank needs replacing and get someone to reroof the place, I guess I'll still be staying at the motel."

Hank stood, offered his hand, and pulled her up beside him. "Oh no, you won't. You're staying with me. I've got plenty of room."

She backed away and stared at him. "Stay with you? Impossible! How would it look, a reputable man like you moving a strange woman into his house?"

"You're not strange—" Hank paused and gave her a sideways grin. "Well, not very, anyway. You're an old friend. And besides, I have a housekeeper who lives there full-time. It'll be perfectly proper." He picked up her coat and held it open for her as she slipped into it with a smile that warmed his heart.

"The motel is fine, Hank. Honest. I can't ask you to go out of your way for me."

He put on his overcoat, picked up the ticket, looked it over, and left several dollar bills on the table. "Look, Tink. I've been rattling around in that big old house of mine for more years than I care to count. I'd welcome the company. Maybe I can even offer you a helping hand. I swing a pretty mean hammer and could sure use the exercise."

She gave him an incredulous look. "You're serious!"

"Serious as a dog with a bone. Tell me the name of your motel, give me a few more hours at the office, and I'll pick you up and take you to my place. I'll even call Faynola and tell her to put on a pot of spaghetti." He gave her a friendly wink as his hand went to the small of her back and he ushered her toward the cashier. "As I recall, spaghetti is your favorite dish."

"Faynola? Who's Faynola?"

"My housekeeper." He handed the cashier the ticket and his credit card, signed his name, and in seconds they were on their way out the door. "Faynola's getting pretty old, but she's still a great cook and a terrific housekeeper. You've got to promise not to tell any of my friends, or they'll try to hire her out from under me. I keep her talents a big secret."

"I'm amazed that you remembered my spaghetti fetish. Even after all these years, it's still my favorite."

Hank wrapped his coat about him to ward off the chilling winds coming off the bay. "Of course I remember, Tink. And I'll have her chop some fresh onion and grate plenty of parmesan cheese. As I recall, that's the way you like it."

"You're still the same old sweetie." She reached her gloved hand up and cupped his cheek. "My very own Peter Pan."

Chapter 2

"Hank, this really isn't necessary, you know. The motel was fine." Tina took her small suitcase from his hand and placed it on the bed.

He pressed a finger to her lips. "Enough. Not another word. This is your home until you're ready to move into your grandmother's house. You hear me?"

She took a couple of bounces on the bed, testing its softness, and smiled up at him. "Peter Pan, ever to my rescue."

"Hey, stop. You're making me blush."

"I appreciate your invitation, but fixing Gram's house is going to take awhile, and I'll want to spend some time with her each day. I can't impose upon you for that long. If you'll let me stay for a week or two, at least until I get my bearings, I'll either move into Gram's house or find another place to stay."

"My answer to you about finding another place is an emphatic no, but if it will make you happy, we'll worry about that later. Right now you need to get settled in here."

"Thank you, Hank."

"You're welcome. *Mi casa es su casa.*"

"Wow! Who is that?" Tina asked as a beautiful Siberian husky came bounding into the room.

Hank leaned over and stroked the dog's head. "Hey, Ryan, old boy, I wondered where you were."

"Ryan? What a great name." She scooted off the bed and moved cautiously toward the pair. "Can I pet him?"

Hank grinned. "Sure."

She ran a hand over the dog's soft fur, then patted him on the head. "You're a real beauty."

"The two of us took second in the annual Sourdough Dogsled Nightshirt Race several of years ago. He's a born leader. I really should give him to someone who races dogs on a regular basis, but I couldn't bear to part with him. He's a great companion." He let loose a slight chuckle. "But a poor substitute for a good wife."

Tina stared into his kind face as she continued to pat the dog. "Hank, how did you know Sheila was the one for you? I mean—how can you tell when you're in love? Truly in love?"

He appeared thoughtful. "Boy, you're asking a tough question. Well," he began slowly, his gaze drifting to the picture of his deceased wife on the dresser, "I can't say lightning bolts split the sky or rainbows appeared in the north, but—I knew. The moment I held her in my arms that very first time, I knew we were destined to be together. It was a feeling—no, not just a feeling—an assurance deep in my gut—I was hers, and she was mine. No rockets went off, no blaring horns, no shooting stars, but I knew. Sounds crazy, doesn't it? I think God puts that special feeling in your heart when you've met the one He has planned for you, and you just know. That's the best way I can explain it. Sorry I'm not more eloquent."

"But—what if you're not sure you're feeling that special feeling? I mean, do you think you can learn to love someone?"

He let out a long, slow gush of air. "Now that one is a toughie. In Bible times marriages were arranged, and I guess those people learned to love one another. That, or they accepted their fate and learned to live with it."

"Could you? Learn to love someone?"

"Umm, no. I don't think so. I'm kind of a romantic guy at heart. I believe in the romantic kind of love between a man and a woman. Why?"

Tina bit at her lip and avoided Hank's eyes. "Just curious."

"How about you? Do you think you could learn to love someone who couldn't sweep you off your feet with his smile? Or his touch?"

"I'd like to think I could learn to love him. In time. If there were reason enough."

He frowned. "Reason enough? What reason could there ever be that would make you marry a guy you didn't love?"

"This is a beautiful room," she commented casually, looking around for the first time, hoping he wouldn't pursue his question. "I'll bet your wife decorated it."

Hank's expression became even more somber as he, too, looked around the meticulously decorated room. "She did. Right after Sheila learned she had cancer, she was like a wild woman. Everything she'd ever wanted to do she tried to crowd into those last few months before the weakness set in. Redecorating this room was one of the projects she'd had on her to-do list for several years and had never gotten around to it. This room was one of the guest rooms, but it ended up being her room when we had to bring in the hospital bed. She couldn't manage the steps up to our bedroom." He turned away, and she almost wished she hadn't mentioned Sheila's name.

"Go, Ryan," he said pointing toward the door. "I'll bet Faynola has a treat for you in the kitchen."

Tina's heart went out to Hank as the two of them watched the big dog obey his master and saunter out of the room. What an ordeal he'd been through. Losing a loved one to death had to be one of life's most difficult, hard-to-bear experiences. Now that she was about to lose her grandmother, the person she loved more than anyone else in the world, she could only imagine the pain and suffering she'd be facing in the not-so-distant future. She stood up beside him and kissed his cheek. "I'm sorry. I know how much you must have loved her."

Blinking, Hank took her hand in his and stared into her eyes. "I always held onto that tenuous thread of hope, praying constantly, but God must have had other plans. He didn't answer."

"Gram says God always answers our prayers. Just not always the way we want them answered or when we want them answered. But it's sure hard to understand why he'd take Sheila away from you. Were you—" Her voice trailed off.

Hank backed away a bit, but still held onto her hand. "Was I what? Angry?" She nodded.

"At first I was. I even tried to bargain with God. I actually threatened Him, telling Him if He took her I'd know He wasn't real, and if He wasn't real, there was no reason I'd ever pray to Him again. But after awhile I got over it and realized I was being childish."

"I'm having a hard time dealing with Gram leaving me, and she's old. I can't imagine losing someone as young and vital as Sheila. She had so much to live for."

Hank let loose of her hand, turning his back to her. "We both wanted children, Tink. We thought she was pregnant. That's when we found out about her cancer. When we went for the pregnancy test."

"Was she?" Tina asked, keeping her voice barely audible.

He nodded. "Yes. One of the happiest days of our lives turned out to be the saddest."

Tina stepped forward, looped her arms about his waist, and pressed her face against his back. "The baby?"

"He didn't make it. He never had a chance. She miscarried in her second trimester." Tina could feel the sobs wracking at his body as she pulled him close. "I not only lost my wife, I lost my son."

"I—I wish I'd known her."

"You would've loved her, Tink. Everyone did. We had some wonderful times together those last few months. Times I'll never forget."

"I guess you can be thankful for that much. At least she wasn't taken from you suddenly." She wished she had the proper words to console him, but somehow they didn't come.

"I know. I told myself that a hundred times, but it didn't lessen the pain when the final day came."

"I'm sorry about the baby. You'd have made a terrific daddy."

"I sure would've tried. I wanted to be as good a dad to my son as my dad had been to me."

"Your dad was the best. I used to look at him and fantasize that he was my father. I'd have given anything to have had your dad for a father, instead of the poor excuse of a man my mother married. Of course, she wasn't much better than he was."

Hank pulled away from her grasp, turned, and wrapped his arms about her, pulling her close. "I can't tell you how many times I wanted to go to your house and kick your father's shins. Seems funny now that I'm a grown man, but as a young boy, that was the worst thing I could think of to do to him. I never figured out exactly what I would do to your mom, but I hated the way she neglected you."

Tina let out a slight giggle. "Kick him in the shins, eh?"

"Uh-huh. And I had a second plan."

"Oh? What?"

"Promise you won't laugh, if I tell you?"

"I promise."

"I–I planned to get you to run away with me, and I was going to marry you and take care of you. I think I was about eight at the time. Your dad had just given you a hard whipping for knocking over his can of beer."

"You actually thought of marrying me when you were eight years old? You never told me."

He grinned sheepishly. "I know. It was one of my boyish dreams. I wanted to be your hero. But I figured you'd say no, so I kept my mouth shut."

She tapped the tip of his nose with her fingertip. "You should've asked me. I might've said yes. But then both our lives would've been different. You wouldn't have married Sheila, and I wouldn't be—"

He harrumphed, apparently not even realizing she'd quit talking midsentence. "I'm not sure they would've given a marriage license to a couple of eight year olds. You were my very best friend. I wanted to protect you."

"I knew that, Hank. You were always there for me. And believe me, it helped."

"And I'm here for you now." He backed away and pointed to the huge suitcase standing in the middle of the floor. "Now unpack. Faynola will have dinner on the table at seven." He spun around on his heels and headed for the door. "I'm going back to the office for a couple of hours to catch up on a few things. If you need anything tell Faynola."

Tina watched as he shut the door behind him. Hank may have thought their relationship had been platonic, but that's not the way she'd seen it. She'd loved him from the time they were children right on up through high school, but she'd never felt worthy of him. Hank had been the brainy one, always excelling in academics. The athletic one, the football captain, the point guard, the distance runner, lettering in all the sports. The popular one, the one the girls all wanted to date, and the guys looked up to. What had she been? An uninteresting girl with mediocre grades, from a dysfunctional family who lived constantly in poverty, with a job after school that made it impossible for her to go out for sports. Although she'd had many friends, she was never elected prom queen or to any class office. She'd been the one sitting on the sidelines, cheering loudly, while Hank had been the center of attention. But Hank, dear, sweet, lovable Hank, had never turned his back on her, no matter how popular he'd been. She'd always remained his best friend, and she'd never told him how much she loved him, for fear it would end their relationship.

Slowly, she dropped down on the bed, kicked off her shoes, and picked up the phone, dialing the number from memory.

A sleepy male voice answered on the fifth ring.

"Hi. It's me. I'm in Juneau. But my plans have changed."

Tina unpacked, putting her things in the guest room's empty drawers and hanging her clothing in the spacious closet. It was a beautiful room, the kind of room she'd always dreamed of having one day. It was burgundy, green, and white, with a very feminine rose motif and thick, plush burgundy wall-to-wall carpeting. She wondered about the woman who had so painstakingly decorated it and tried to visualize the room with a hospital bed, instead of the magnificent rice bed that now stood in its place.

After a leisurely shower, she dressed in a soft slip-on sweater and jeans and pulled her shoulder-length brown hair up in a ponytail. It was still only five. She accepted a cup of steaming hot tea from Faynola and wandered into the den, pleased to find several bookcases. After letting her finger trail across the titles of at least fifty books, most of them on law, she located one shelf that harbored books on art and interior decorating. She selected several that dealt with remodeling, took them back to her room, and seated herself on the rose-colored chaise lounge in front of the big bedroom window that overlooked Gastineau Bay.

At seven straight up, Hank rapped on her door and led her into the cozy kitchen, where the big round table was set for two.

"I didn't hear you drive in."

He grinned. "Faynola said you were reading. You were probably too engrossed in some sappy romance novel."

She elbowed him. "I would've been if I could've found one, but apparently you don't keep a good selection on hand."

Hank pulled out her chair, then seated himself opposite her. "Did you find everything you need? If not—"

Her hand rested on his. "Hey, you don't have to take care of me, you know. I'm a big girl now. I've grown up."

He gazed at her for a moment before answering. "I know. I can see that, and you've turned into quite a woman."

She tilted her head and lifted a brow. "Is that a compliment?"

"You bet."

After Hank thanked the Lord for their food, they devoured delicious dinner salads, topped with the best dill dressing Tina had ever tasted. Hank explained it was made from one of Faynola's secret recipes.

"Here you are. Spaghetti, just like you requested, Mr. Gordon." Faynola placed the steaming platter of spaghetti and meatballs in the center of the table. "I've chopped plenty of onion and grated the Parmesan, just like you said."

Tina took in a deep breath. The spaghetti smelled divine. Usually she prepared the meatless kind in the tiny kitchen of her condo, and it was nothing to brag about. She couldn't remember the last time she'd had spaghetti that looked, or smelled, this good. "It looks wonderful, Faynola. Thank you. I hope you didn't go to a lot of trouble. Hank didn't give you much notice."

Faynola gave her employer an adoring look. "For Mr. Gordon, I'd do anything. He's the nicest man in the world." The older woman beamed at him in a motherly fashion.

Hank shyly ducked his head and blushed as he pointed his finger toward the sink. "Faynola, go, before you give me a big head. Compliments won't get you a raise. I keep telling you, you're overpaid as it is."

Tina grabbed the woman's arm before she could get away. "Don't pay any attention to him, Faynola. I want to hear more about this man. I haven't seen him in years. Surely he isn't the nicest man in the world! He has to have a few flaws. Like leaving his dirty socks on the floor? Or spattering shaving cream on the bathroom mirror?"

With a quick glance toward her smiling employer, Faynola shook her head. "Oh no, ma'am, he never does anything like that. When I—"

Hank smiled but put up his hand to silence her. "No! Not another word. You've said enough already."

"But I want to hear all—" Tina began.

"No more, ladies. Let's just let this subject drop."

Tina turned the woman loose. "You can tell me when Mr. Grumpy is away, Faynola. Okay?"

The woman grinned, nodded, and backed away toward the sink again. "Yes, ma'am, enjoy your dinner."

"A terrific dinner and good company, what more could a woman ask?" Tina placed her fork on the plate, took the last nibble of garlic bread, and leaned back in her chair, touching the corners of the napkin to her lips.

Hank folded his own napkin slowly, his eyes never leaving hers. "What more? Let me see if I can take care of that question." He called for Faynola, and she came over with a tray bearing two large crystal dishes, which she placed in front of Tina first, then Hank.

Tina stared at the bowls, then lifted her eyes to meet Hank's. "You remembered. Raspberry sherbet. My favorite."

"I wasn't sure if it's still your fave. It's been a long time."

"Well, it still is." She spooned up a big bite and slowly placed it on her tongue, savoring the robust flavor. "This brings back so many memories. Evenings sitting on your parents' porch, swinging on the porch swing, listening to the radio. Actually, I think it was your mom who got me hooked on this stuff in the first place."

"It was always her favorite too. But be careful, that stuff is cold! It'll go to your head in no time."

"Umm, this is fabulous." She twirled her spoon through the deep pink concoction, all the while keeping her eyes on her host. "Your housekeeper was right. You are a nice man."

"That just goes to show how trusting you are. Actually, I'm an axe murderer."

"Peter Pan? An axe murderer? I hardly think so."

When they finished their meal, Tina insisted on placing their dishes in the dishwasher before allowing Hank to lead her into the living room.

"Sit, Ryan," he told the big dog, who was following at their heels.

Tina smiled as she watched Ryan immediately obey his master. "Good dog."

"I told Faynola to bring our coffee in here." He motioned toward the deep mauve damask sofa, waiting for her to be seated before dropping down beside her.

After Tina took a few sips of her coffee, she took stock of their surroundings. Everything in the room was elegant, from the silk-knotted drapery cords to the lighted, professionally framed artwork on the walls. "What a beautiful room. I assume Sheila did the decorating in here too?"

Hank smiled proudly. "Uh-huh, she did the whole house, all except the fourth bedroom. She didn't have time to do it before—" He stopped midsentence and gazed toward the window.

"I'm so sorry, Hank. I wish there was something I could do to take away the pain."

He let out a long, slow sigh. "It's better now. Honest it is. It's just that I haven't talked with anyone about it for so long—"

"And here I am, asking all sorts of questions."

Tina's heart was touched just thinking about the kind of love Hank must've had for his wife.

"I think seeing you again has brought back all the old memories." Hank gave her a wistful smile. "You know, I really have dealt with this loss. A long time ago. Sometimes, though, I still get a little sad."

"Of course you do. It's perfectly understandable that you'd be a little sad from time to time. It sounds as though the two of you had a wonderful marriage."

He nodded. "We did."

"You mentioned you'd nearly married again?"

He leaned back into the sofa and spread his arms wide across the back, crossing his ankles and staring at the ceiling. "Yep, I did. I met this really special woman. Glorianna Kane. She'd lost her husband, who was a real scoundrel by the way, in a tragic accidental shooting."

"Was she from around here?"

"No, but you may remember her aunt Anna. She owned that big quilt shop downtown, across from where the cruise ships dock."

"The Bear Paw? Of course I remember her. Anna was a nice lady. In fact, I worked in her shop one summer as a cashier. She was a terrific employer."

"Well," he went on, "Glorianna is her niece. Anna passed away a few years ago and left everything to her. I handled the legal part of it. She was from Kansas City."

"But you didn't marry her?"

Hank pursed his lips and shook his head. "Nope. My best friend married her. Took her right out from under my nose at the altar."

Tina's jaw dropped. "You're kidding, right?"

"Nope, Trapper—"

"Not the Trapper Timberwolf we went to school with!"

"Yep. One and the same."

"But he was always such a nice guy. What happened to him?"

Faynola brought in the tray with more coffee. Hank motioned to her to place it on the table, then waited for her to leave the room before continuing. "Trapper was—and still is—a nice guy."

"But surely he's not your best friend anymore!"

"Yep, believe it or not, he is." Hank slapped his knee and laughed aloud. "Actually, I was the best man at their wedding."

"No!" Tina gave him an incredulous stare. "If you were, I'd say you were the best man, in more ways than one."

Hank laughed, as he filled her cup and handed it to her, before filling his own. "The two of them belonged together. I knew it right from the start, but I was too stubborn to admit it. I'm sure now, looking back, I was only kidding myself when I thought Glorianna could forget her love for Trapper and love me." He blew into the steaming hot liquid, his gaze never leaving her face. "You know, losing her nearly killed me, but I loved her enough to want to see her happy. Trapper was the man for her. I finally admitted it, despite my feelings for her."

Tina lifted her own cup in a mock salute. "To you, Hank Gordon. You are truly an amazing man."

His hand went up between them as he shook his head. "Nothing amazing about it. I just came face to face with the facts, was smart enough to accept them, and probably saved all of us a whole bunch of grief. Too many folks find out they've made a mistake after it's too late. I was lucky enough to find out first."

"Do you—"

"Still love her?" He stared off in space, as if asking himself that same question.

"Nope, not anymore. I can honestly say I'm over it. Sometimes I wonder if much of what I thought was love for Glorianna was really loneliness. Maybe I was in love with the idea of being in love again. Who knows?"

Tina bristled at the thought of someone treating Hank so callously. "I can't imagine a woman doing something like that to a fine man like you. I'm surprised you'll have anything to do with either of them. Sounds to me like you'd be better off without them."

Hank quickly turned to face her, a frown deeply etched on his forehead. "Don't say that, Tink. She never meant to hurt me. Glorianna is one of the finest women I've ever known."

"Doesn't sound like it to me!" *But who am I to judge?* she asked herself. *With my lousy track record?*

"Well, she is, and I want you to meet her. I'm sure you two'll really hit it off." His face softened. "She's a lot like you."

"Oh?" Tina grimaced. "I'm not sure I'm glad to hear those words."

"It was a compliment, believe me. You'll see, when you meet her. Glorianna is a very special person, and you'll love her kids."

Tina's brows raised. "She and Trapper have children?"

Hank grinned as he pointed to a framed photograph on the mantel. "Oh, yes. Todd was seven when she came to Alaska. Then little Emily Anna was born on their wedding night, and—"

"On their wedding night?" Tina leaned back into the sofa, her hand going to her forehead. "What kind of a woman is she anyway? And Trapper? I can't believe he'd get a woman pregnant and then not marry her until time for their baby to be born!"

❧

"Whoa, there. You're judging them too harshly. Let me explain." Hank rose and walked to the fireplace, fetched the photo, and placed it in her hands. "Glorianna's husband died in an accident. Not long after that, she was notified she'd inherited her aunt's quilt shop here in Juneau, and she moved up here. That's when she met Trapper."

"And you?"

"Yes, and she met me. The attorney who took care of all the paperwork for her works for my firm."

"And you fell in love with her. So how did Trapper get into the picture?"

"Actually, he came into the picture first, way ahead of me, and things were going pretty well for the two of them. But when Glorianna found out she was pregnant, he had a bit of trouble—"

"He had a bit of trouble?" Tina turned her head away and shoved the photo towards Hank. "What a creep!"

"No, you've got it all wrong." Hank shook his head vigorously. "Trapper wasn't the baby's father. Her deceased husband was!"

"Whew, that's a relief. For a minute there I thought old Trapper'd been ready to desert the woman when he found out he was going to be a daddy. This sounds like one of the TV soaps!"

"No, he'd never do anything like that. But the news did come as a shock to him. He took off in that seaplane of his to do some big job up in Fairbanks and was gone for a number of weeks. That's when I came into the picture, as you so delicately put it."

Tina gave him a sideways grin. "So? Who came on to whom?"

Hank flinched. "It wasn't like that, Tink. I went to Glorianna's place as her attorney and ended up fixing a leaky pipe."

"That's a new approach."

"It wasn't meant to be an approach. You might remember the Calhouns. They're clients of mine now, and they'd asked me to dinner. So, knowing Glorianna didn't know many folks in town and hadn't had a chance to get out much since she'd arrived, after I fixed the pipe, I invited her to go with me. She accepted, and we had a lovely evening. So it was only natural that I invite her out again. One thing led to another and, voilà! I was in love!"

"But was she?"

Her question hit him hard right in the heart. Had he only kidded himself into thinking Glorianna had been in love with him? Because he'd so desperately wanted a wife and family? "Looking back, I know now it was only wishful thinking on my part. After all, you said it yourself, I'm a good guy."

"You are, and she'd have been lucky to have married you. I hope Trapper is living up to her expectations. You had to have been a hard act to follow."

Hank lowered himself onto the sofa beside her and took the photo from her hands, staring at each smiling face as he remembered the day that was to have been his wedding day. "Trapper finally came to his senses. He did the only thing he could think of to stop the wedding. He snatched my bride away from me at the altar."

"You're kidding, right? Things like that only happen in romance novels."

"Oh, it happened all right. He burst into the church, grabbed her up in his arms, and took off with her in that souped-up pickup of his. It all happened so fast, everyone just stood there watching. Me included."

"Did you go after her?"

"Yes, once I realized what was happening. But it was too late. In my heart I knew he'd done the right thing. I just didn't want to admit it to anyone."

Tina let out a long breath of air. "Okay, so he captured your bride, but you were kidding me about being the best man at their wedding, weren't you? After what they'd put you through?"

"I was shocked when Trapper asked me. I wanted to deck him."

"Why didn't you? You had every right."

Hank's finger traced the fluted edge of the lovely frame. "I guess God intervened. Somehow, the hurt and embarrassment I'd felt seemed to melt away when Trapper apologized for what he'd done. His intention hadn't been to hurt me. It'd been to claim the woman he loved." Hank shrugged. "I was just in the way. Couldn't be mad at a guy forever for that."

"What about her? She could've stopped him, refused to go with him."

"Oh, she struggled. We all saw her do that. Kicking and hitting at him when he scooped her up. We could still hear her screaming as they drove off."

"But his persuasive charms must've won out. She married him," she said with disgust.

"Persuasive charms? I'm not so sure that was it at all. It was their love, Tink. A love so strong, it compelled them both to go against the world to be together."

Tina leaned into Hank and stared at the picture. "What about the baby? Was it really born on their wedding night?"

Hank grinned. "Yep, she sure was, and that little Emily Anna had to be the prettiest little girl ever born."

She smiled up into his face. "She's adorable."

"Trapper and Glorianna have two kids of their own." He pointed to the handsome young man seated on Trapper's lap. "This is Chip. He's about four now. Emily Anna, of course. Here's Todd, their oldest. And this—" He paused, grinned, and pointed to the baby being held by the attractive woman seated beside Trapper who had to be Glorianna, "is the newest addition."

Tina braced her hand against the sofa and raised herself to Hank's level, planting a kiss on his cheek. "What an old softie you are. You're still the same lovable Hank I knew as a child. I just wish there was some way I could take away the pain you've suffered. First you lost your wife. Then Glorianna. You deserve better, Hank. So much better."

His arm circled her shoulders, and he pulled her close. "I think better just arrived. You're here."

Chapter 3

H ank inserted the key in the lock the next morning, with a backward look. "You sure you want to fix up this old place?"

Tina let out a giggle and shrugged. "Too late to turn back now. Gram is counting on me. Guess I've got my work cut out for me."

The two grinned at one another as the old door creaked open. "Better let me go in first, in case there're any ghosts milling around in there."

"Or worse yet—bats!" Tina nodded, then followed close at his heels, brushing aside a spider's web with a shudder.

"And things that go bump in the night?"

"Those too! Whew, this place really smells musty." She placed her box of cleaning supplies on a table, moved quickly to the big plate-glass window, and flung open the drapes, setting loose a cloud of dust. "I think I could grow plants in here. There must be a quarter inch of dust accumulation."

Hank blinked and fanned a palm before his face, faking a cough. "If you're going to work in here you'd better wear a dust mask. I've got some in my workshop I can let you have. That stuff is really hard on your lungs."

She grabbed at his arm. "Don't worry about me. I'll be fine, and I promise to wear a mask."

He punched a switch on the wall, and the room was instantly flooded with a garish light from the overhead fixture. "You've already had the power turned on?"

"Actually, it was never off. Gram was afraid the pipes would freeze, so she's been paying the fuel and electric bills."

"Tink, it's been several years since your grandmother was home!"

"I know, but you know Gram. She was determined that, one day, she'd return. I tried to talk her into selling the place, but you remember how headstrong she could be. She's as stubborn as they come. It was her money, so there wasn't much I could do about it."

Hank followed Tina into the kitchen, watching with interest as she turned on both faucets in the old white porcelain sink and a combination of both water and air rumbled out in spurts. How was she ever going to get the place in shape as quickly as she'd planned? To him, it looked like a monumental job. "Don't tell me she paid the water bills too."

"Yep, good thing too. I needed it to get started with my cleaning." She pulled a faded dish towel from a drawer, dampened it, and began wiping off the countertop, turning the dust to mud. "I went shopping yesterday and bought those cleaning supplies. Oh, and I've had the phone turned on. I didn't want to be here alone without a phone."

While she opened cupboard doors and checked shelves and drawers, Hank turned up the thermostat on the furnace, made sure the refrigerator was running, and checked out the burners and the oven. "Other than being dusty, things seem to be in good shape," he told her, brushing his hands together.

"I'll have to take down the curtains and wash the windows. And the linoleum needs a good coat of wax. And the cabinets need new shelf paper, and I'd like to paint the walls and put up a new border around the ceiling. Maybe some yellow sunflowers. Gram always liked sunflowers. And—"

"Whoa!" Hank spun her around to face him, his hands gently clamping her shoulders. "I thought you were just going to clean the place up, I didn't know you were planning an entire remodeling job."

"It's for Gram, Hank."

Her face took on a serious air, and he was sure she was blinking back tears. He wished he hadn't teased her about her exuberance for the old house.

"She deserves the best, and I'm going to do what I can to make it happen for her."

"And I'm going to help you," he told her, planting a kiss on her forehead before rubbing his hands together expectantly.

"I can't ask you to do that. You've got a law practice to take care of, not to mention your personal life. I'm sure I can hire someone to help me."

"Look, Tink, I try to keep my work load down to eight-to-five weekdays, so I'm available to help you every evening and all weekend. Besides, I could use the exercise. You'll be doing me a big favor if you'll let me help you."

"No, it's asking too much. You've already helped me by inviting me to stay at your house until I get this place in shape. I'll never be able to repay you, as it is."

"Yes, you can. You can go to church with me tomorrow morning."

"I–I don't know, Hank. I haven't been to church in a long time. I'm not sure God would even recognize me."

"I'll remind Him who you are. Say yes. You go to church with me, and I'll help you with the house. Can't beat a deal like that, can you?"

"Well—when you put it that way. I–I guess—"

"Okay, it's a done deal." Hank pulled off his coat and hung it over the back of a kitchen chair, then reached out his hand to assist her with her jacket. "I'm here to stay, Tink. Now where do we start?"

❧

Tina slipped out of her jacket, all the time eyeing the man who had come to her rescue so many times. How she'd dreaded coming to Juneau again. The thought of staying in a cheap motel and working on the house by herself had nearly kept her from fulfilling her grandmother's last request. But then she'd run into Hank and all of that had changed. She was staying in his beautiful home, and he was volunteering to help her with the renovation. "How can I be so lucky?"

"Hey, kiddo, I'm the lucky one. I've got you back in my life."

They wandered from room to room, taking stock and making a list of the paint, scrapers, nails, screws, tools, and the other things they'd need for the job. At noon he drove to a nearby deli and brought back sandwiches, chips, and drinks, while Tina cleaned up the bathroom as best she could, putting out the new towels and washcloths and a fresh bar of soap she'd bought the day before.

The two settled themselves on the sofa, after pulling off the old sheets Gram had spread over it before leaving her beloved Juneau, ready to enjoy their impromptu lunch and good conversation. Both jumped when the phone began to ring.

Tina made a mad dash for it. "Hello."

"No. Not now. I'll call you back. I'm sorry. You'll have to wait. Just be patient. I'll phone you tonight. Good-bye."

"I forgot you'd had the phone turned on," he said, looking curious.

"Oh, I'd nearly forgotten too. It was some man from the lumberyard."

He frowned. "Lumberyard? I thought they closed at six. You said you'd call him back tonight."

Her brows lifted. "Oh? Did I say tonight? I meant tomorrow."

Her answer didn't seem to satisfy Hank, but she was glad he didn't ask any more questions.

"Remember those wonderful sandwiches your mom used to make for us?" Tina asked as she popped a potato chip into her mouth. "She'd load them up with slices of ham and cheese and lettuce. Umm, those were the best sandwiches I'd ever eaten. We didn't have sandwiches like that at our house. We barely had food of any kind."

"I also remember how much you loved her brownies."

"I always made a pig out of myself, didn't I?"

"I wasn't going to say that, but now that you've brought it up—"

Tina swatted at his arm. "As I recall you did a pretty good job on those brownies yourself!"

"We sure had fun, didn't we?"

"We sure did."

"Even this house brings back memories. I can remember walking you here after school. Remember that tire swing?"

Tina jumped to her feet and rushed to the window, pulling the curtain aside and peering out. "It's gone!"

"The rope probably rotted years ago."

She let the curtain fall back in place with a sigh. "Probably. I was hoping it was still there. I loved that swing."

"Me too. I always planned to put one up when I had kids. Guess that'll never happen now."

The faraway look in his eyes spoke worlds, and it ripped at Tina's heart. "You'd have been a wonderful father, Hank."

"I like to think so. My dad was a great role model."

"My folks were lousy role models. I always wanted to be like your mom. She was the best. I know you miss her. And your dad too."

Hank checked the thermostat, lowering the setting a few degrees now that the house had begun to warm up, then, once again, took his place on the sofa. "I do miss them."

Tina pulled an old photo album from a shelf by the fireplace and blew the dust from its cover. "Wanna take a trip down memory lane with me? I'll bet our picture is in here."

Hank nodded and patted the seat beside him.

Carefully opening the brittle cover, Tina let out a giggle. "That's me! The day I was born."

"You sure were a scrawny little thing. But cute," he added quickly.

She gave him a frown, then looking back at the album, squealed with delight. "Look, here I am on my first birthday, eating a piece of birthday cake!"

He leaned in for a better look. "You sure you're eating that cake? Looks more to me like you were mashing it into your face. What's the matter? Couldn't you find your mouth?"

Ignoring his teasing remark, she flipped to the next page. "Oh, Hank, that's you!" Her finger pointed to a chubby little boy sitting in a sand pile, playing with a red toy fire engine.

"Me? You really think that's me?"

"I know it's you. I'd recognize that smile anywhere."

Hank grinned. "Who's that pretty little girl with the doll?"

"Me, you silly. I was pretty then, wasn't I?"

"Not as pretty as you are now, Tink."

She smiled up at him. "No wonder you were always my favorite boy." She flipped another page. "There's your mom!

I didn't know Gram took her picture."

"Me either. She looks happy there."

"Oh, Hank, look! Gram saved my first report card." She carefully lifted the yellowed folded piece of paper and peeked inside. "All A's."

"With grades like that, you should've gone on to college."

Her fingers pressed shut the card's cover as she stared off in space, reminded of less happy times. "I never planned to go to college, especially after my dad died. Mom had left me, and my grandmother sure couldn't afford to send me. All I could think about was graduating from high school and getting out of Juneau and away from the bad memories. You know, Hank, I always thought my mom and dad's six pack of beer meant more to them than I did. It seemed I was always in their way. I'm sure they both wished I'd never been born."

"Don't even think that!" Hank brushed a lock of hair from her forehead. "I knew you had it rough at home, but I really don't remember you complaining that much about it. Not even when I asked you about the bruises you always seemed to have on your arms and legs."

"What good would complaining do?" She shrugged. "I learned to live with it, as best I could. That seemed to be my only choice in life. At least until I was out on my own."

"How did the time get away from us? It seemed one moment we were kids playing in a sandbox, and the next minute we were seniors, graduating from high school. And look at us now. What happened, Tink?"

A feeling of melancholia swept over her. A heaviness that was indescribable. What a mess she'd made of her life. Nothing had turned out like she'd planned. What happened to all those dreams, those visions of success? "I don't know, Hank. I honestly don't know."

She closed the album and placed it back where it belonged, but in so doing noticed a big cardboard box wedged into the bottom shelf of the bookcase. A box she couldn't remember ever seeing before. Stooping, she gave it a few tugs. It finally dislodged, and she was able to carry it to the coffee table.

Hank watched with interest. "Whatcha got there?"

"Probably more pictures."

There were two long strips of packing tape holding the lid in place. He pulled out his pocketknife and easily sliced through them before lifting the lid and setting it to one side.

Tina's fingers sifted through the hundreds of snapshots. "I have no idea who most of these folks are. Probably distant relatives. Oh, look. Here's my mom and dad's wedding picture!" She held it out for him to see. "They looked happy then, didn't they? Too bad they had to change. I rarely saw either my mom or my dad ever smiling like that. Most of the time they were either fighting or dead drunk."

Hank took the picture but remained silent.

"Oh, and here's a picture of Tippy, your dog. Remember how he'd fetch the newspaper for your dad?"

Hank reached for the picture. "I sure do. He was a great dog. He died of old age when I was off at college. I'm glad I wasn't here at the time. Mom said he had a pretty rough time of it at the last. I'd rather remember him as the feisty, active dog he was most of his life. I dread the day I lose Ryan."

"And here's one of our old house! I can't believe it was this small. A living room, one bedroom, a tiny kitchen, and a bathroom that barely held the bathtub.

My condo in Chicago is a little bigger than this, and it's in the low-rent district. Of course I have to walk up three flights of stairs to get to it."

Hank laughed, then took the picture and stared at it for a long moment before putting it back in the box.

Tina rummaged her fingers through the myriad of photos, finally pulling a large flat box from the very bottom.

"What's that?" Hank asked as she untied the ribbon and lifted the lid. "More pictures?"

Her broad smile said it was something good, something familiar. "Valentines!" she told him excitedly as she pulled several handmade cards from the top of the pile and fanned them out across the table top.

Hank picked one up, read it silently, then handed it to her. "From one of your many admirers."

Tina read the verse. "From Charles Pickering. Funny, I don't remember Charles Pickering at all."

"I do. He was that skinny little kid who wore thick glasses. I think he sat behind me in arithmetic."

She lifted another valentine from the pile. "This one is from Caroline, my best friend."

Hank snickered as he took it from her. "I thought I was your best friend."

"She was my best girlfriend," Tina said, correcting herself. "And here's one from Mrs. Lindsey, our teacher. She was nice, wasn't she?"

"She sure was. She gave me A's when I deserved B's."

"Did not!"

"Did too!"

"Did not. You were one of the smartest boys in the class."

"You'd better say that. Isn't there a valentine in there from me? I always gave you a valentine."

Tina filtered through the stack of cards, calling out each sender's name as she shifted each one to the bottom of the pile. One of the very last ones was the one she was seeking. A beautiful heart, cut from red construction paper and trimmed with white paper flowers and white hand-cut hearts. Each one pasted on a bit askew, but nonetheless pretty. She smiled when she saw the handwriting. It was definitely that of a third-grade boy. "Oh, I like this one," she said waving it before him with a teasing smile. "Let me read it to you."

Hank covered his face with his hand. "That one looks very familiar. Mine. Right?"

"All I'm going to say is that this guy was a real poet." She began to read, exaggerating each word, enunciating it carefully, smiling at him at every pause. " 'Tink is pretty. Tink is smart. I'll love you forever. Here is my heart. Be My Valentine.' And it's signed 'Peter Pan.' "

Hank listened, remembering how he'd struggled to come up with words that rhymed. Poetry had never been his best talent, but he'd tried. "I meant it, you know," he said shyly.

"That I was pretty? And smart?"

He took her hand in his and gazed into her eyes. "Of course, but I really loved you. Or at least I thought it was love. My mom kidded me and told me it was puppy love."

She reached up and tenderly stroked his cheek. "And I loved you too. Actually, you're the reason I've never married. I've compared all men to you, and none of them ever measured up. You spoiled me, Peter Pan. You were perfect."

"Me, perfect? Hardly." Hank was sure he was blushing, something he hadn't done in a long time.

"You were to me."

He kissed the tip of her nose. "Ah, but you were young and impressionable. I still can't believe some big, handsome, intelligent man hasn't swept you off your feet and whisked you off to the altar."

"Not yet," she said softly, the smile disappearing from her face. "Not yet."

As Tina gathered the valentines from the table, Hank carefully folded the red heart in half and slipped it into his jacket pocket, along with the handmade envelope, unobserved, before rising and rubbing his hands together briskly. "We, my lady, had better get to work if you're going to have this place ready for your grandmother."

"Yes, sir!" She gave him a half salute before sliding the lid onto the box and wedging it back into the bookcase shelf.

Tina moaned and opened one eye as the buzzer sounded on the alarm clock on her nightstand. Every muscle in her body ached. Why she and Hank had worked at cleaning up Gram's house until ten she'd never know. But she had to admit, they'd made great headway. She glanced at the clock. Eight o'clock. That gave her an hour to shower, wash and dry her hair, and get dressed for the middle service at Hank's church. She'd been dead tired when they'd gotten home from Gram's and had gone right to bed. Why had she ever agreed to go with him?

A slight rap on the door made her throw back the covers and reach for her robe.

"Tina?" a male voice said in a whisper. "Time to get up."

One look at the mirror, and she knew there was no way she was going to open that door. "I'm up," she whispered back, her face pressed against the door. "Give me an hour, okay? I want to shower and wash my hair."

"You sleep okay?"

"Oh yes, much better than I did at that motel, thanks to you and your wonderful hospitality."

"I'll tell Faynola to have breakfast on the table about nine. We need to leave for church by nine-thirty."

She was about to tell him she'd changed her mind and would be working at the house all day, instead of going to church with him.

"Tina?"

"Yes."

"I'm glad you're going to church with me this morning."

"Ah—yeah, me too. Just don't expect me to make a habit of it."

❧

Hank sneaked a peek at his companion as they stood side by side, singing and sharing a hymnal. She was every bit as beautiful as she'd been the day she'd graduated from high school, perhaps even more beautiful. Funny, he'd never really thought of her as beautiful back then. She was his good friend. The one he could count on to stand by him when he needed a helping hand, or encouragement. The one who'd cheered him on at football games, even when he'd fumbled the ball. The one who'd nominated him for class president, then had run his campaign. His buddy. His confidante. Nothing more.

When they sat down, he casually took her hand in his and gave it a slight squeeze. The smile she shot up at him melted his heart, and he had to admit, he hadn't had feelings like that since he'd spent time with Glorianna Kane. Nearly every day since his wife had died and he'd lost Glorianna, he'd asked God to bring another woman into his life, the woman of His choosing. Someone to share his home, his joys, his ups, his downs, his life, and all that he had. But God hadn't seen fit to answer, and he'd almost begun to think he'd be spending the rest of his life alone. Could Tina be that person? That one special woman God had for him? She'd come into his life so suddenly, so unexpectedly. They had much in common, and Tina would be a wonderful wife. He shook his head to clear his thoughts. But no matter how hard he tried, he couldn't get his mind off the lovely woman sitting beside him.

❧

Tina smiled up at Hank when he took her hand in his. It was like old times again. When she was five and learning to roller skate, she'd fallen down, hard, and Hank had come skating over quickly, concerned about her and offering his hand to help her up.

Then when she was in the ninth grade and tumbled down a flight of stairs at their school and all the other kids stood laughing at her clumsiness, it was Hank who told them all to shut up and reached out his hand to her. When she'd worn a borrowed dress to the junior prom because her mother couldn't, and wouldn't, buy her a new one, and one of the snooty girls had made fun of it, calling it ugly and old-fashioned, it was Hank, the most popular boy in school, who wiped away her tears and told her she was the prettiest girl there.

Hank had always been there for her. Dear, sweet, even-keel Hank. It was hard to imagine a woman, any woman, preferring another man to him. She'd never tell him, but all through high school she'd had fantasies about being Hank's girlfriend. But he'd never thought of her in any way except that of a friend. Now here she was with him again, staying in his home, working side by side with him at Gram's house, sitting next to him in church, and it felt good. Familiar. Cozy.

"I hope you'll come again next Sunday," Hank told her as he ushered her out to the foyer, nodding to friends and acquaintances, stopping now and then to shake hands and introduce Tina to his friends on the way to his SUV.

"Maybe. I have to admit I did enjoy the service." She gave him a slight nudge with her elbow. "I'd forgotten what a nice bass voice you have."

"You did pretty good harmonizing with me too. Remember how we used to sing that silly song about Old Aunt Jemima and the swimming hole? I learned it at Cub Scout camp and taught it to you."

Tina grinned. "Of course I remember it. We sang it often enough. It drove your mom crazy!"

"She was only teasing when she complained. She really liked it."

"Your mom was a good sport. She liked anything you did, and she was always nice to me. So was your dad."

"Yeah, my folks were tops. Even as a kid I knew it."

As he opened her door, a tall, good-looking bearded man hurried across the parking lot toward them. "Hey, Hank!"

Hank turned, then stuck out his right hand to the man who took it with a vigorous shake. "Hi, Claude. How goes it?"

"Fine, but I have a quick legal question for you, if you've got a minute."

"It'll only take a minute," Hank told to Tina. "Okay?"

She nodded as he opened the car door and motioned her inside. She crawled in, waited until he'd closed the door, then sank back in her seat. Good old Hank. I wonder how many other lawyers would take their personal time, on a Sunday morning, to dole out free legal advice?

With her window closed against the cold morning air, she couldn't hear what they were saying. But from all appearances, Hank was doing most of the talking. No doubt giving the man the legal help he was seeking. As she watched him smile and gesture with his hands, she saw not the stable, dependable, professional man he had become, but the handsome boy with whom she'd grown up. The boy she'd loved all her life. The boy she still loved. But it was too late. Even if Hank could ever feel the same way about her as she felt about him, it was too late. Much, much too late.

"Nice guy," he said as he opened the door and slid beneath the steering wheel. "I should've introduced you to him."

"I thought nice guys made appointments with their attorney at their office to ask for legal advice, instead of asking for freebies in a parking lot."

Hank's face took on a scowl. "He's not only a client, he's a good friend, Tink. He'd never take advantage of me. If I had a question about a minor plumbing problem, I'm sure he wouldn't expect me to arrange a house call, even though he owns the plumbing company I usually do business with." The scowl turned to a slight smile as he inserted the key in the ignition and the car roared to attention. "Besides, he's a brother in Christ. We're buds!"

"Ouch. Should have kept my mouth shut, but remember, Hank, I've lived in Chicago a number of years. There you pay for everything you get. There's no such thing as free advice."

He released the brake and pulled the lever into the drive position, and the car moved slowly into the line of traffic waiting to exit the parking lot. "Juneau has changed since you've been gone, that's for sure. But it's still pretty laid back, and folks around here are still low key. Don't ever hesitate to ask for help when you need it. Most folks are more than willing to run to your rescue."

She gave his arm a playful jab. "I've noticed."

After discussing several options for lunch, the two of them decided on Hank's favorite restaurant, The Grizzly Bear. Though the parking lot was crowded, they soon found an empty slot, and he easily maneuvered the SUV into it. Hank took Tina's hand as they walked toward the door.

A pleasant-faced woman met them at the entrance, a stack of menus in her hand. She rushed to throw her arms around Hank's neck. "Hank! Where've you been keepin' yourself? Me and Dyami was just talkin' about you the other night."

"Just been busy, Emily." He turned to Tina, once again taking her hand in his. "I want you to meet an old friend. In fact," he said, pausing, "you might remember Tina. She went to school with Trapper and me. She worked for awhile as a cashier in Anna's shop." Then turning to Tina, he said, "Tina, this is Emily. She owns The Grizzly Bear."

The woman cocked her head and smiled. "Surely this isn't that little girl who used to live down the street from you. The one who wore the long pigtails?"

Tina stuck out her hand. "It's me."

"Quit hugging my mother," a deep male voice ordered as a handsome, bearded man moved quickly past the woman and extended one hand toward Hank.

Hank took the man's hand, giving it a firm shake. "Hey, guy. I wondered if you'd be here today."

The man looked slightly familiar to Tina, although it was hard to tell with that heavy head of black hair and the well-waxed handlebar mustache. It seemed everywhere she went with Hank, a multitude of friends and close acquaintances managed to appear out of nowhere.

"This has to be Tina. Remember me?" the man asked, a friendly smile peeking out from beneath the mustache. "I'm Trapper. Trapper Timberwolf."

Chapter 4

She had a sudden urge to strike out at the man who'd hurt Hank so badly. *How dare he call himself a friend?* "Trapper. Of course I remember you. I just didn't recognize you at first," she said coolly. "Hank's told me all about you."

Trapper withdrew his hand quickly, his smile disappearing. "Oh, oh. I think I know what you mean."

Hank jumped between the pair. "Tink, I told you things were fine between Trapper and me now."

"He's right, Tina. Thanks to Hank's understanding and his willingness to forgive, which—" He paused, and she was sure the look he was wearing was one of guilt. "I was going to say, which was more than I think I could have ever done. He was willing to forgive me for probably inflicting the worst hurt possible on him."

"Only because I knew all along Glorianna was really in love with you, old buddy," Hank inserted, smiling, his hand still on his friend's shoulder. "I have to admit, it was only through God's help and a lot of prayer. What I really wanted to do was deck you and take my girl back, but I knew I'd only be fooling myself. You and Glorianna belong together."

"Did I hear my name?" an attractive woman asked as she wiggled her way in between the two men.

Hank slipped an arm about her waist and pulled her close, giving her a kiss on her cheek.

But before he could introduce her, Tina blurted out, "You must be Glorianna, the woman who hurt Hank so badly."

Glorianna stopped smiling. So did Trapper. And so did Hank.

"How could you do such a thing?"

"Look," Trapper said, his deep voice a mere whisper as he looked around at the other restaurant patrons standing near them, "why don't the two of you join us for lunch? We can continue our conversation there, instead of here in the lobby."

Eat with you? Tina wanted to shout out at the man. *Why would I want to spend any time with you and that woman? What you did to Hank was unforgivable! But she kept her peace, not wanting to further embarrass Hank.* She hoped he'd tell Trapper no, and they could either find another table or go to another restaurant.

"We'd love to have lunch with you and Glorianna," Hank said as he moved to Tina's side, his arm circling her waist. "Are the kids here?"

"Nope. Glori's mother and dad are here visiting for the week. They insisted the two of us have a nice, peaceful, kidless lunch today. I think they're fixing hot dogs at home."

"Too bad," Hank said as the four of them moved toward the table, with Trapper's mother in the lead. "I wanted Tink to meet them."

Tina could feel her anger rising, and she had to bite her lower lip to keep from saying things she felt needed to be said. *Are these people all mad? When someone hurts you, you don't just forgive them and go on with life, pretending things are all rosy and hunky-dory. Hank, how can you be so congenial with these people?*

"Trapper, let's put Glorianna here, next to Tink," Hank told his friend as he pulled out Tina's chair. "I want them to get acquainted."

Tina gave Hank a glare, hoping he would get the message that she didn't want to get to know Glorianna. There was no way she could ever be friends with the woman, but Hank only smiled back. She considered faking a headache or rushing to the ladies' room on the pretense of becoming violently ill, wishing she were any place but sitting in the foursome at that table.

"Oh yes," Glorianna said as she slipped into the chair. "I do hope we can be friends. When Hank came over the other day and told us you were in town, well, we just thought it was wonderful. He was so happy he ran into you when he was returning that nightgown Trapper bought for me."

Trapper sat down and folded his long legs under the table. "Boy, was he ever. I was afraid I was imposing on him, asking him to exchange that gown for a smaller one, but he sure didn't see it that way. He even thanked me for asking him to do it when he told me about meeting you in the department store."

"I couldn't believe it was really Tink. It'd been years since I'd heard from her," Hank explained as he handed her a menu.

"Tink?" Glorianna muffled a giggle. "You call her Tink?"

"Long story. But yes, I've called her Tink since we were toddlers. She was a very special part of my growing-up years. My best friend," Hank explained.

"You're moving back to Juneau?" Trapper asked, picking up his menu.

Still miffed, Tina struggled to speak without letting her anger show, not for their sakes, but for Hank's. "Yes. My grandmother and I. I put her in a nursing home here in Juneau when we arrived. I go visit her at least once a day."

"Hank said—" Glorianna began, her gaze fastened on Tina. "He said your grandmother is dying? I'm so sorry!"

Despite her feelings of resentment, Tina found herself mellowing with each moment. Glorianna's concern for her grandmother seemed so sincere. So real. "Yes, the doctor says she may last six months, but it's doubtful. Her desire was to come back to Juneau. To die at home in the old house she and my grandfather shared for nearly fifty years."

"And you're getting her house ready?" Trapper asked with a smile that, too, seemed sincere and filled with concern. "I know Hank is helping you, but I'd be glad to help too. I'm gone most of the week on my job, but I'm free on weekends, and—"

"No, thank you," Tina said quickly. The idea of spending more time with these people did not set well with her at all. "Hank and I are managing, and the work is coming along quite nicely."

Hank grinned. "Actually, I think we're even a bit ahead of where we thought we'd be when we first drafted out the renovation plans. But if we need you, I'll call you," he told Trapper, as he folded his menu and placed it on the table in front of him.

"That goes for me too, Tina." Glorianna warmly touched Tina's arm with the tips of her fingers. "With my folks here to look after the kids, I could help you this week. Maybe wash windows? Or clean out cupboards? I'd be glad to help in any way I can."

Am I in la-la land? Can all this nicey-nice stuff really be happening? Tina wondered as she looked at the three. *How can they ignore the awful thing that happened between them? Is this all an act? I'd think Hank would want to rip their heads off!*

"No. Thanks for your offer," she answered without enthusiasm, mustering up a weak smile, "but there really isn't anything for you to do right now."

"Maybe she could help you paint that hallway," Hank inserted.

Tina wanted to strangle him. "I'm sure you're much too busy. Didn't Hank say you inherited Anna's quilt shop? The Bear Paw?"

"She used to work for your aunt," Hank explained quickly, his gaze flitting to Tina, then back to Glorianna.

"Yes, I still own the shop. But once little Emily Anna was born, I knew being home with her like I'd been with my oldest son, Todd, was the most important thing in my life. As quickly as I could, I more or less phased myself out of it. Oh, I still keep a close watch on it and lend a helping hand now and then and teach a few classes. But Jackie Reid, the woman who managed the shop for Anna, pretty much runs things. She's made it possible for me to be right where I want to be—at home with my children."

I wish this woman wasn't so likable, Tina thought as she listened to her words. *She's not at all what I expected. Glorianna has values and is certainly not trying to make her mark in the world.*

The waiter arrived, took their order, then brought their dinner salads. Without preamble, each reached for one another's hand and Hank prayed.

"You've never married?" Trapper asked after the "amen."

Tina picked up her fork, wondering what other things Hank had told them about her. It seemed they knew much more about her than she did them. "No. Came close a few times, but realized I was more in love with love than I was with the man. I backed off before things got that far." She wanted to add, *You two should have backed off too, rather than hurt a fine man like Hank,* but kept her silence.

The three stole quick glances at one another, and she knew her words had made them uncomfortable. If they hit the mark, so much the better.

"Well, I guess that's to your credit," Trapper finally said, twirling his fork in his salad without meeting her eyes. "Mistakes are hard to unravel. There are consequences."

Tina nodded. "Yes, there certainly are."

"Look," Trapper said, putting down his fork and wiping at his mouth with his napkin, frustration showing on his face. "Let's just say it and get it over, instead of pussyfooting around. I, for one, would like to clear the air." He turned his full attention to Tina. "What I did to Hank was horrible. I admit it. If he'd done the same thing to me—well, I'm not sure what I would have done. I was stupid, Tina. I loved Glori right from the first day I met her. I knew it. She knew it. My parents knew it. But I was too stubborn to admit it to myself. And like an idiot, I was afraid to commit to her, knowing that commitment would change my life forever, and I liked my life exactly as it was. Or so I thought I did, until I nearly lost her to Hank."

Tina cast a quick look Hank's way, feeling like a spotlight was being focused on her, and she didn't like the feeling. But Hank sat quietly nibbling on his salad.

"Please try to forgive us, Tina," Glorianna said gently, after exchanging an adoring smile with her husband. "The last thing either of us wanted to do was hurt Hank. And don't blame Trapper. It was my fault. I loved Trapper, but I knew once he found out I was pregnant with my deceased husband's child, he would run the other way, and that's exactly what he did. Kind, understanding Hank showed up at my door when I needed someone in my life. I'd lost Trapper. I was new to Alaska. I was trying to run a business with no business experience, and there was Hank. Strong, intelligent, smart, witty Hank. But it wasn't like you think. I honestly cared for Hank. I still do! But in a different way than I did for Trapper. If I'd had any idea Trapper wanted to marry me, I would never have accepted Hank's proposal. I was as appalled as anyone when he burst into the church and gathered me up in his arms and carried me off. I fought him—"

"She sure did!" Trapper added, in his wife's defense. "I had the scratches and bruises to prove it."

"Someday," Glorianna told her, "you'll meet that special someone, and you'll want so much to spend the rest of your life with him, you'll do everything you can to make it happen. Then I think you'll understand a little better about our situation and why we behaved the way we did. You can't imagine how miserable we were about what we'd done to Hank."

Hank laid down his fork. "It's true, Tink. I was furious at first. When I caught up with them I was ready to kill Trapper. Well, not kill him, but I was going to maim him for life! But the minute I saw the two of them together, with Trapper holding Glorianna in his arms, her still in her wedding gown, I knew it was I who was wrong. Not them. I'd taken her from him when she'd been her most vulnerable. She was his. It was I, not Trapper, who stole the bride from her beloved."

"You're much too generous," Tina said, still chafing at the ordeal her friend had gone through.

Hank took her hand and squeezed it hard, his eyes penetrating hers. "Give it up, Tink. I have. Long ago. You were my best friend from the time we were in diapers, right up through high school. These two, along with you, are my best friends now. I don't want to give up any of the three of you. I know, if you give them half a chance, you'll learn to love them as much as I do. Please. Won't you try? For my sake?"

Although tiring because of the work they were doing, the next few days were some of the happiest days Hank had known in a long time, working side by side with Tina, listening to the ring of her laughter, and exchanging smiles as they kidded one another.

Sometimes, as he sat at his desk trying to keep focused on the work he was doing for his clients, he found himself watching the clock. Looking forward to the evening when he would be with Tina. Scraping off old wallpaper, stripping layers of paint from the doors and woodwork, reputtying drafty windows, cleaning rust stains from the bathtub and lavatory, and the myriad of other chores that needed to be done to make Gram's house livable. He'd offered to lend her enough money to have the work done, since Tina's grandmother's money would probably be enough to pay for only the supplies and not much of the labor. But Tina wouldn't hear of it, saying her grandmother preferred to keep everything debt free.

Secretly, he was glad when she'd said no. If someone else was doing the work, there wouldn't be a reason for the two of them to spend evenings and weekends together. And besides, it made him feel good to actually do some physical labor. It sure beat spending big bucks to join a health club. Although he'd never had difficulty sleeping nights, now he was asleep the minute his head hit the pillow. Sometimes he was so tired after a day at the office and a night working at Gram's, he even considered forgoing his nightly shower.

Tina was hard at work, steaming the last bit of wallpaper in the back bedroom, when Hank arrived with a big bag of Chinese take-out for supper, and didn't even hear him come in. He placed the sack in the kitchen, then slipped up behind her, wrapping his arms about her waist. "You really ought to keep that front door locked. Anyone could come in here and snatch you up!"

She turned off the steamer and spun around in his arms, facing him, her face just a breath away. It was all Hank could do to keep from kissing her. "Looks to me like someone just did," she said with a grin, making no attempt to escape his grasp, her finger tapping the tip of his nose.

Hank could feel his heartbeat quicken as he gazed into her eyes. *Hold it, boy. Take your time. She's given you no indication she wants anything more than your friendship. You don't want to get hurt again. Make sure this relationship is going somewhere before you make any advances.* Reluctantly, he loosened his grasp and backed away.

"Seriously, Tink, you need to be more careful. Juneau is a nice town, but like all major cities, it has its problems too. Please keep the door locked when I'm not here. And remember, you've got guys you don't even know working up on that roof this week."

"You're an old worrywart," she told him as she flipped the switch on the steamer and turned back toward the wall. "But I will."

He leaned over and pulled the plug from the receptacle. "Soup's on. Time to quit and have a little supper. Why don't you go wash up while I put things on the table? I'll bet you haven't eaten all day."

She grinned and pulled a wadded-up candy bar wrapper from her pocket and held it up before him. "Yes, I did. After I got back from visiting my grandmother. See!"

"Oh, terrific. Nourishing food." He grinned as she turned and tossed the wrapper into the big trash box in the middle of the floor.

After a wink, she disappeared into the bathroom. He had to laugh at her appearance. She looked nothing like the attractively dressed woman who went to church with him on Sundays. Her jeans had holes in the knees, her shirt had the pocket nearly ripped off, her tennies had paint spattered on them, she wore no makeup, and her hair was pulled back in a tight ponytail. But to Hank, she was still one of the most beautiful women he'd ever seen. What had happened to that average-looking little girl with whom he'd grown up? The one with the perpetually skinned knees and dirty face. The tomboy who could climb trees nearly as fast as he could. The one who carried frogs around in her pocket.

One thing was certain. That girl had changed. Outwardly, at least. Inside, he had a feeling she was the same caring, compassionate Tink he'd always known.

Hank pulled two clean plates and some silverware from the cupboard, added ice to two glasses, filled them with soft drink, and waited for Tina before sitting down. In minutes, she bounced into the kitchen wearing a clean shirt, the paint spatters gone from her face, except for one tiny spot on her forehead. Hank smiled at the transformation as the tip of his finger gently flicked off the offending blob of paint.

She giggled and swatted at his hand. "I tried! But one of our next projects had better be getting that new mirror up in the bathroom. Kinda hard to wash your face by feel."

His finger slid beneath her chin, lifting her face to his. "It looked kinda cute.

I should've left it there."

"You!" She brushed his hand away and plopped into a chair, sighing. "I'm tired. You get to sit in that plush office all day, letting your secretary do the work, while I'm here slaving away."

"Hey, tomorrow is Saturday. My time's coming. Tomorrow you can sit in the chair and watch me work. You deserve a break."

She reached for an egg roll but drew her hand back quickly. "Guess you'll want to pray before we eat."

"Well, He has provided our food. Don't you think we ought to thank Him for it?"

"I guess. But if He provided it and you went after it, I'd better be grateful to both of you!"

Hank couldn't conceal his smile as he reached across the table and took both her hands in his, lifting his face heavenward. "Thanks, Lord, for this food we are about to eat. Thank You for the strength and desire You've given Tink as she's set about on this monumental task of getting her grandmother's house ready for her. And thank You most of all for bringing Tink back into my life. Amen."

For only a brief moment, Hank thought he detected a tear in Tina's eye. It had to be because he'd mentioned her grandmother's illness, but he hoped it was more than that. From all appearances, it seemed to him Tink had turned her back on God. As a Christian, Hank was concerned for her. Although he had to admit at times he, too, had thought God had deserted him. Especially in the dark of the night, when his life had become unbearably stressful because of Sheila's cancer. Sometimes instead of turning to God, he'd given up to despair and shaken his fist at Him. Challenging Him to spare her life, if He was real, and truly a God of love. God hadn't seen fit to do that. Instead, He'd taken his precious wife from him. Other times, he'd felt God's presence and known He was in control. That taking Sheila was part of His overall plan. That even though he could see no valuable purpose in it, through prayer and God's Word, he'd been able to face it all and praise God instead of blaming Him. Now, looking back, he wondered how he could have ever doubted God and His wisdom.

"Hank."

He suddenly realized he was still holding on to both of Tina's hands and she was smiling that little mischievous smile at him across the table. "Sorry. Guess my mind wandered."

Her smile disappeared. "From the look on your face, it must've wandered to something unpleasant. Want to talk about it?"

"I–I was thinking about Sheila."

Tina pulled her hands from his and opened the little carton of sweet and sour pork, forked out a few pieces, then pushed the container toward him. "I wish I'd known her."

Hank absentmindedly took a few pieces from the carton. "Me too. She was a real lady."

She opened the box of Chinese food and placed two of the egg rolls on her plate before handing the little box to him. "I know you loved her, but somehow I can't see you living the rest of your life alone."

"At first, I thought I'd never be able to even consider having another woman in my life, but time changes that perspective. You get lonely. You see couples holding hands, walking in the park with their kids, and your heart aches to have a wife and children of your own. You work at your job and make good money doing it, but for what?"

"I'm sorry things didn't work out with Glorianna."

He opened the lid on the carton of niu ju chin jow and pushed it across the table. "But what about you? At least I've had a wife I adored. How come you've never married?" He forced a grin. "And don't say it was because you compared all men to me. I don't believe that for one minute."

Tina dabbed the paper napkin at her lips as she smiled and leaned back in her chair. "I've dated a number of men, Hank. I've honestly tried to find the right man, but I'm afraid I've been a lousy judge of character. The guys I thought were decent turned into long-armed monsters. You have no idea what a woman is expected to do in return for a nice dinner and a movie these days. To put it plain and simple—I preferred not to have the hassle."

"Good for you." Hank smiled, then gave her an incredulous look. "Surely you're kidding me about the guys you've met."

"Nope, I'm not kidding. You've never lived in a place like Chicago. Men are different there, at least the men I met. After having a few of my first dates turn into a battle, I soon learned to just say no and not take any chances. I found the easiest way to avoid a wrestling match was to avoid dating altogether. Sad, isn't it, that you can't trust most men."

"So you've never found that one special man?"

"The women there are different too," she went on, ignoring his question. "Oh, not all of them, of course, but most of them seem to accept the fact that they're going to have to—" She paused, as if not sure how much explanation was needed.

"I get the picture."

Tina's face brightened. "Let's drop this subject and talk about more pleasant things."

"Like?"

"Like—what do you do for fun? When you're not helping damsels in distress remodel their grandmother's homes, that is. Surely you have interests other than lawyering."

"Lawyering?" A smile tilted his lips. "Is that a word?"

"It is in my dictionary."

He became thoughtful. "What other interests do I have? Well, let me see. Occasionally I fly up into the bush with Trapper and help him with his ministry to the bush people."

Her eyes opened wide as her jaw dropped. "Trapper is a missionary?"

"His main job is flying his seaplane for a number of major clients who have him on retainer. The rest of the time, he's a self-supporting missionary. He takes medicines and supplies to the people, that sort of thing. He and another missionary friend of his, a doctor. Sometimes Glorianna and the children go along. She takes fabric and teaches the women to make little things she can sell in her shop, to give them some badly needed money."

"It isn't hard for you to spend time with them? After what they did to you?"

"No, not at all! I wish you'd believe me," he said emphatically. "I love them both, and I love their children. I'm happy they include me in their lives."

"Hank Gordon. You're one in a million. Why didn't I meet someone like you, instead of all those Neanderthals? If I had, I might not—"

Hank waited a moment for her to finish her sentence, but when she didn't, he flashed her a smile, shrugged, and tore open one of the two fortune cookies that came with his order. He unfolded the tiny piece of paper and, reading to himself, tried to conceal the smile that threatened to erupt. *The love you have been searching for may be right under your nose.*

Eagerly, Tina unfolded hers and read aloud with a laugh, " 'Confucius say, man who live in glass house shouldn't run around in holey underwear.' " She turned to Hank. "What does yours say?"

Hank fumbled for words as he folded the tiny piece of paper and carefully slipped it into his pocket, saying the first thing that popped into his head. "Some coincidence, huh? It says the same thing as yours."

"Yeah, some coincidence," she said casually, as she began to clear the table. "I love those fortune cookies. It's amazing how many times their sayings are right on target."

Remembering the words printed on the one he'd slipped into his pocket, Hank asked, "You don't really believe in that sort of stuff, do you?"

She stacked his plate on top of hers before picking up their glasses, chop sticks, and plastic forks. "No, of course not! But you have to admit they're fun to read."

Hank fingered the tiny slip of paper in his pocket. "Yeah. Fun."

"I'll put these dishes in the sink and wash them later. I want to finish painting that trim around the pantry door before I clean up my brush. Then I want to start taking everything out of the kitchen cupboards and sort out what we'll keep and what we'll throw away."

Hank gathered up the little paper cartons and tossed them into the large trash can. "Sounds good. I'm going to work on that loose board on the front porch." He picked up his tool pouch and strapped it about his waist before slipping on his jacket and gloves. "Holler if you need me."

She nodded. "I will."

He located the loose board, then remembered he'd left his bag of nails on the table in the front hall. He pushed open the front door and found Tina hovered over the telephone, her back to him, speaking softly to someone on the other end. He picked up the nail bag and was backing out the door, when suddenly she began to speak more loudly and he caught her words.

"No! Don't! Not now. I'm not ready! I don't care. Listen to me. The time is not right. I want to get Gram's house ready first."

Hank stared at her. She seemed agitated. No, not agitated, angry. But why? And to whom was she speaking? She barely knew anyone in Juneau, especially not well enough to talk to them in such a terse manner. He stood silently, debating whether he should withdraw or offer to help with whatever was wrong. But Tina seemed to sense his presence and turned quickly toward him, giving him no choice. The look on her face was like that of a child who'd been caught doing something forbidden.

"I'll talk to you later," she said curtly into the phone before hanging it in its cradle.

"Anything wrong?" Hank asked with concern, not wanting to embarrass her by letting her know he'd overheard her conversation.

"No," she said, taking on a smile, "just a telemarketer. Makes you wonder how they got this number."

From the way she turned away from him and started fumbling with her hair, he knew she'd prefer to keep whatever that conversation was about to herself, and he wasn't about to press. He held up the bag. "Forgot my nails."

"And I'd better get back to the cupboards."

Hank watched as she moved into the kitchen. Something wasn't right with Tina. But what? This was the second time he'd caught her talking angrily to someone on the phone, and she'd made light of it both times. But from the look on her face, whoever was on the other end of that phone was saying something that upset her. What was Tink keeping from him?

❧

Tina held her breath as she walked away. It wasn't right to keep this from Hank, but what choice did she have? He'd never understand. And she certainly didn't want any lectures!

No, I'm doing the right thing. Hank is a reasonable man. I can explain things to him later, just not now. I should never have taken him up on his offer to stay at his home. If I'd said no and hadn't accepted his offer to help me fix up Gram's house, he would never have had to find out. Things would have gone as planned, and no one would have been hurt. But no. I'm as vulnerable to Hank now as I was in high school. I couldn't resist the chance to be around him again. To be a part of his life. Even if just for a little while. Dumb! Dumb! Dumb! She rinsed the dishes and put them in the sink, barely aware of what she was doing.

"That didn't take long."

Still wrapped up in her thoughts, Hank's voice startled her as he came into the room, and she dropped a glass on the floor, shattering it over the discolored linoleum, and she began to cry.

He maneuvered quickly through the broken glass and wrapped her in his arms. "Don't cry, Tink. I'm sorry. I thought you heard me come in the front door."

"I—I'm sorry, the glass, I mean—it was my fault—I—"

"Your fault? Who's blaming you? And what difference does it make? It was an accident. If anyone's at fault, it's me. But who cares? It was just an old jelly glass. You can probably buy them at the thrift store for a dime apiece. It's certainly not worth crying over." He rested his chin in her hair.

It felt so good to be close to him. For a moment she forgot all the reasons she shouldn't be in his arms. "I'm sorry," she told him, her voice a near whisper. "I guess all of this remodeling is getting to me."

"You've taken on a big task and are doing far more than originally planned. We can still hire someone to come in here and finish this, if you're not up to it."

She lifted watery eyes to his, a tear running down her cheek. "It's what I'm doing to your life that upsets me, Hank. You haven't had a minute to yourself since I arrived."

His thumb brushed away the tear. "Have you heard me complaining? Having you come back to Juneau is the best thing that's happened to me in a long time. I'm afraid, since losing Glorianna, I've dug a hole for myself. Except for the happy times I've spent with Trapper's family, it seems all I've done is work. Or sit at home nights and watch ball games on TV. Oh, Sundays I go to church, but that's about it. But now with you here, my life has a purpose, and I'm loving every minute of it."

"Y—you're sure?" she asked between sniffles. "You're not just saying that to make me feel better?"

"Cross my heart. There's no place I'd rather be than right here, helping you get this place ready for your grandmother. Honest."

"Well—"

"It's your call. Do we get busy and finish fixing this place, or do we call a contractor and his crew of professionals to finish it faster than the two of us can? I'll still put up the money, if you want to get it done in a hurry."

"No, I can't let you do that. I've done a lot of strange things in my life, but going into debt isn't one of them. I won't use your money."

"You won't be in debt. I won't even charge you any interest, and you can pay me back when you can. There's no hurry."

"But I'd be indebted to you. Is that so much different?"

He doubled up his fist and touched a gentle blow to her chin. "For one, I volunteered; you didn't twist my arm. Two, I told you I need the exercise, so you're doing me a healthy favor. And three, I want to be here. I enjoy working with my hands, and being with you is the bright spot of my day. Until you came, I'd been pretty much stuck in a rut. If there's any indebtedness, it's on my part. You've made a new man out of me, and I like the feeling."

Her tear-stained face brightened as she looked up into his eyes. "Bet you think I'm a big baby."

"No, not a big baby. You're a caring woman with a lot of responsibility on her shoulders. Your job, your grandmother, undertaking this renovation. And from the looks of it, you've carried all that responsibility alone. You deserve a good cry."

"Thanks." She pushed away from his grasp and wiped her eyes on the tail of her paint-stained shirt. "I'm glad you understand. Some people think I'm crazy to come back up here, even for a while."

"I can't imagine anyone saying that about what you're doing. You've got a good heart, Tink. You always have had. I can't say I'm the least bit surprised by what you're doing for your grandmother." He didn't ask, but he wondered who those folks were she was speaking about. They didn't sound like the kind of friends Tina would have, and she no longer had parents to criticize her actions.

"Thanks, Hank. Your support is important to me."

"How was your grandmother feeling today when you visited her?"

"You know Gram. She let on like she was fine, but the nurse told me she'd had a terrible night. But she's happy to be back in Juneau and continues to smile." With one more quick wipe at her eyes, she backed off and began fidgeting with the broken handle on one of the cabinets. "I'd better remember to get another handle next time we go to the lumberyard."

Hank watched her with great interest. He was growing fonder of Tink each day, but her mood swings troubled him. One minute she was flitting around the old house, smiling and singing. The next, she was distant, spacey, as if somehow there was an invisible wedge between them, and it unnerved him. At first he'd assumed her melancholia was simply shyness. After all, it'd been years since they'd seen one another. Other times, it seemed her body was in Juneau, but her mind was somewhere else. Then there were the mysterious phone calls. Not one time had she ever told him who was on the other end. What was going on in Tina Taylor's life? And why did she choose to hide it from him?

Hank tried to put the out-of-character episodes from his mind, blaming them on Tina's weariness from the overwhelming job she'd undertaken. From the beginning, he'd been going out of his way to do things to make her happy.

Bringing flowers unexpectedly. Buying her favorite candy. Treating her to hot fudge sundaes after a long day of working at the house. Each time, her rewarding smile would make it all worthwhile. But then he'd overhear her on the phone or hear her crying long after the lights had all been turned out and she'd gone to bed, and he'd feel so helpless. *Tink, what is going on with you?*

Saturday afternoon, as the two of them were working at the house, there was a rap on the door. Hank had just entered the living room in search of his coffee cup when he heard it. "I'll get it," he hollered out to Tina, who was putting the final piece of shelf liner in one of the newly painted kitchen cabinets.

Ryan rushed to the closed door and sniffed at it, a low growl rumbling through his chest. Hank pushed him aside and pulled open the door, expecting to see a friend from church who'd come to check on their progress or one of the neighbors coming by to introduce themselves. But the tall, slim, long-haired, bearded man, clothed head-to-toe in black leather, a skull attached to a long silver chain dangling from his ear, was definitely neither of those. "Yes?" Hank said apprehensively, glad Tina had thought to engage the lock on the storm door. "Is there something I can do for you?"

"Tina here?" the stranger asked, looking past him as he spat on the newly scrubbed front porch.

Hank's eyes widened. "Tina? Ah—sure—she's here."

"Who is it, Hank?" Tina called out from the kitchen.

Hank stared at the man, unable to believe Tina would have anything to do with someone of his sort. "Does Tina know you?"

The man hitched up his leather pants with a gloved hand and grinned at Hank, revealing two shiny gold front teeth. "She sure does. Me and her is engaged. We're gonna be married!"

272

Chapter 5

Tina came into the living room, a dish towel in her hands. "Who was it?"

"I—ah—" Words seemed to fail Hank as he continued to stare at the man. Knowing from the startled look on Hank's face something was radically wrong, Tina hurried to the door. Her heart felt as though it'd dropped into her shoes as her eyes locked with the caller's. "Lucky? Wh–what are you doing here?" The last person she expected to see, or wanted to see, at her door at such an inopportune moment was Lucky Wheeler.

The man smiled toward Tina and reached for the door handle. "Aw, my little sweetie, you really didn't want me to stay away, did you?"

Tina turned quickly toward Hank, who appeared immobilized, his face ashen, his gaze darting from Tina to the man and back again, as if he was in a state of shock. "Hank, this is Lucky, Lucky Wheeler."

"I told you I'd let you know when the time was right for you to come!" she said sharply, turning to face the man. She couldn't keep the raw edge from her voice. Why would Lucky forge on ahead when he knew she wasn't ready for him yet? "You should have listened to me."

"But I missed you, baby," he said, tugging his collar up about his neck. "Aren't you gonna to let me in? It's cold out here. I ain't used to this Alaskan air. Come on, unlock the door."

Hank, finally seeming to find his voice, grabbed Tina's wrist as she reached for the little lever to unlock the door. "You—you really know this man?"

She nodded, her heart aching for deceiving Hank, after all he'd done for her. Why hadn't she gone ahead and told him about Lucky right at the start? Looking back, she'd been stupid to even think she could keep the two of them from meeting one another. "Yes," she stammered, "I know him."

Hank looked as if he was about to explode. "Surely he's not telling the truth! This has got to be some kind of joke! You aren't really planning to marry this man, are you?"

Tina sucked in a fresh breath of air, floundering for the right words to say to help soften the blow Hank had just been delivered. "Nearly," she said quietly, avoiding his eyes. "I haven't said yes yet."

"Surely you're not serious, Tink!" Hank grabbed her by the shoulders, ignoring the man at the door. "You haven't said a word about a boyfriend!"

"Well, I am her boyfriend, and a cold one at that!" The impatient man gave

273

several hard yanks on the door handle. "Are you guys gonna open this door and let me in? I already let the taxi go, and it's a long walk back into town."

Hank stepped back out of the way, releasing Tina, and said rather harshly, "I think you'd better open the storm door."

She pushed past him, released the lock, and Lucky thrust his long body through the opening, slamming the door shut behind him. "Whew, I thought Chicago was cold! Got any hot coffee in this place?"

Tina cast a quick glance at Hank, then back to Lucky. "Yes, in the kitchen. I just made a pot."

Ryan sniffed at the man's heavy black leather boots.

With a sudden move, Lucky landed a swift kick to the dog's head, sending him sprawling and yelping in pain.

"Hey, there!" Hank hollered as he quickly bent over the dog. "What was that for?"

"Don't like dogs. Never have," the man said arrogantly, as if his dislike for dogs gave him the right to mistreat them. "He shouldn't have been sniffin' around me like that."

Hank sent a questioning look toward Tina, but remained silent.

"You shouldn't have done that, Lucky!" Inside, she was seething at his uncalled-for behavior. His actions only made it harder for her to explain his presence to Hank. "Come on, I'll get your coffee," she told him as she made her way to the kitchen, leaving Hank still bent over Ryan.

Lucky tugged off his black leather gloves and rubbed his hands together briskly as he followed her, seemingly unconcerned about the damage he may have inflicted upon the dog.

Tina took a cup from the cupboard, filled it to the brim with steaming hot coffee, and handed it to him. "Why, Lucky? Why did you have to come now? I told you to wait!"

"I missed you, babe. I thought I'd come on and help you with your grandma's house." He took a big swig, then smacked his lips together loudly. "Mm, mm, good coffee."

"But I told you to wait."

"Because of Lover Boy?" He gestured toward the doorway.

She glanced toward the living room, then answered in an almost whisper through gritted teeth. "No, he's not the reason. I wanted to have the house ready first. I thought we'd agreed you'd stay in Chicago until I told you to come."

He gave her a reproving look. "You didn't tell him about me, did you?"

She shook her head. "No. The time never seemed right. But if I'd known you wouldn't listen to me and were planning to come on ahead—"

Hank appeared in the doorway, his face still an ashen white. "Any more of that coffee left?"

Tina forced a smile, although the last thing she felt like doing was smiling. "Sure, let me pour you a cup. How's Ryan?"

"Okay, I hope. I put him in the bedroom and shut the door."

"Come over here and have a chair," Lucky ordered, as he eyed Hank suspiciously. "You and me need to get acquainted."

Hank seated himself next to the man and took the cup from Tina's hands.

"Guess Tina didn't tell you about me," Lucky said boastfully, with a near sneer. "Why am I not surprised?"

"No, I guess she didn't."

"I wanted to, Hank. Honest I did," Tina said defensively, wishing this whole scenario could have been avoided, and if the two men had to meet, it would have been under better circumstances. "It's just—I mean—we were so busy with the house—and—"

"You should've told me, Tink. You shouldn't have kept this from me."

Knowing he was right, but hating to admit it, even to herself, she poured herself a cup of coffee, then dropped into a chair between the two men. "Yes, I should have. I owe you both an apology."

"Well, mine will have to wait." Lucky stood quickly to his feet. "Where's your bathroom?"

Tina gestured toward the hallway. "Second door on your left."

"You're sure that mutt's locked in?"

Hank's retort was icy cold. "Yes, I made sure he was safely locked in, so he wouldn't get kicked again."

Lucky threw back his head with a laugh that set Tina's teeth on edge. It was as though he deliberately wanted to cause trouble for her, and she couldn't understand why. Unless he was miffed because she hadn't told Hank about their relationship.

She waited until she heard the bathroom door close, then leaned toward Hank. How could she ever make him understand? "I wouldn't blame you if you never forgave me. I should've told you about Lucky."

"You mean about Lucky and you, don't you?"

She could tell by his tone her deception had hurt him deeply. "Yes, about Lucky and me. But it's not what you think—"

"You mean he's lying about the two of you being engaged?"

Her fingertips rubbed at her forehead, at the beginnings of a whopper of a headache. "Yes. I mean no. I mean—it was never settled. Lucky thinks we're going to be married, but I've never actually said yes or no."

"But you must've given him some indication." He glanced down the hallway before continuing. "I distinctly remember asking you if you'd ever had a special man in your life."

"You did ask me, but I never answered you."

"Look, Tink. I don't know anything about that man, but I can tell you one thing, he'd better not kick my dog again!"

The sudden sound of the toilet flushing, the running of water, and the bathroom door opening caused their conversation to come to an abrupt stop.

"Hey, Hank," Lucky said as casually as if he were talking to an old friend. "I hear Tina's been staying at your house. Got another empty bed?"

Now Tina's jaw dropped. "Lucky!"

"Well, does he?" he asked, turning to her with raised brows.

"You'll have to get a motel," Tina shot back, shocked at Lucky's audacity. "Or sleep on the floor here. We could put down a few blankets. I got rid of the old broken-down mattress. Since I haven't gotten around to papering Gram's room, I haven't bought a new one yet."

"Well, since I ain't got no money to pop for a motel room and I sure ain't gonna sleep on no floor, guess I'll have to stay over at old Hank's place with the two of you." Lucky plopped back down in the chair and stuck out his empty cup. "At least until I get me a job. Motels are expensive."

"I'll pay for the motel," Tina said, knowing the money she'd set aside to live on until the house was ready for occupancy was dwindling every day. This was an expense she hadn't planned on. If she'd known Lucky was going to pull this stunt, she would've kept Gram's old bed instead of giving it to the rescue mission.

"No, it's okay. Lucky can stay at my house. No sense paying for a motel. I've got plenty of room." Hank swallowed hard, then added, "I'm sure the two of you'll want to be together."

Tina's mouth tightened. After what Lucky had done to Ryan, Hank was willing to open his home to him? Unbelievable!

"Okay," Lucky said, setting his empty cup back down on the table. "Then it's settled. I don't know about the two of you, but I'm bushed. Can we call it a day now? I need me a couple of beers and a bed real bad, and in that order. It's been a long day."

"Oh?" Hank asked, picking up Lucky's cup and carrying it and his own cup to the sink. "What time did you leave Chicago?"

Lucky let out a loud snort. "Time? Or day?"

Hank frowned. "Time or day? What do you mean?"

"Well, I left Chicago four days ago. Got into Seattle late yesterday. Flew from there this morning."

"Surely you didn't ride your Harley all the way to Seattle! You hitchhiked, didn't you?" Tina asked, eyeing the man as she poured the remainder of her coffee into the sink.

"You bet. Would've hitched from Seattle here too, but since that weren't possible, I grabbed me a flight. Took nearly everything I had in my pocket to pay for it," he explained, adding a few cuss words for emphasis. "And here I am!"

Hank pushed his empty chair up close to the table and stepped aside. "So you are."

The ride to Hank's house would have been silent if it hadn't been for Lucky's constant chatter as he filled them in on each of the drivers and rigs he'd hitched with on his way to Seattle. Tink hung on the man's every word, even though he was using words Hank would just as soon never be used in a lady's presence. *What's with this woman? She's not acting at all like the Tink I thought I knew.*

Hank sighed with relief when the car finally came to a stop inside his garage. The three of them piled out.

"Hey, Hank old boy, you got yourself quite a spread here. Guess bein' a lawyer, you took some big old rich guys for a cleanin'. No wonder you lawyers have such a bad name."

Hank fought the desire to bounce back with a remark about guys who can't even afford a plane ticket, but decided nothing would be gained by exchanging snide words with the man. "It's not exactly a spread, as you call it, but I like it."

"That wasn't a very nice thing to say, Lucky, after Hank was good enough to invite you to stay at his home," Tina called back over her shoulder as she stepped into the large mudroom just off the kitchen.

Invite? Hank set his jaw. *I didn't invite him. He invited himself! I just agreed for your sake!*

"What is it they say about lawyers?" Lucky asked with a chuckle as he followed at Tina's heels. "Deep down, they're pretty nice guys? About six feet deep down."

Hank's blood boiled as Lucky's laugh boomed out.

Tina turned and gave the rude man a chafing look. "Lucky, stop it! That remark was uncalled for!"

"Hey, I didn't give lawyers a bad rap. They gave it to themselves by takin' a big cut of everybody's money."

"I'm afraid you don't know much about me, Mr. Wheeler," Hank began, for some unknown reason feeling he needed to defend himself. "I would never take advantage of a client."

Lucky whirled around to face him with a mocking scowl. "You expect me to believe that one? How about them big fees you charge? This house must've set you back a pretty penny."

"I only charge the going rate. And much of my work is pro bono."

Lucky gave him a blank stare. "What's that mean?"

"It means," Tina inserted, with a tug at his arm, "Hank does free work for those who can't afford to pay him."

"You've got to be kiddin'," he told Hank, pulling away from her grasp and adding a few more cuss words. "There ain't nuthin' in this world that's free.

Somebody must give you a kickback under the table, right?"

"No!" Hank answered firmly, closing the door behind him before taking off his coat. "No kickbacks. I like doing it. It's my way of giving back to the community, and I look at it as a service to God."

Lucky's hands went to his hips. "Don't tell me you're one of those God freaks!"

Tina tugged on his arm again. "Lucky. Let it rest!"

"It's okay, Tink."

"No, it's not okay," she said with a stomp of her foot. "We're guests in your home. We have no right to talk to you like that!"

Lucky slipped an arm about her waist. "We? You got a frog in your pocket, honey?"

"You," Tina corrected with a targeted punch of her forefinger to his chest, "are being just plain rude!"

The repugnant man glared at her. "You should've told this man about us, Tina. What's the matter? Ashamed of me because I don't wear designer suits like your boyfriend?"

"Hank's been very good to me, and he's not my boyfriend!" she shot back in an almost scream.

"Been kinda cozy, I'll bet, with just the two of you alone in this big house!" Lucky shot back. "I'd like to have been a little mouse and watched!"

"I—I'm sorry to interrupt." Faynola appeared in the mudroom doorway with Ryan at her side. "It's the phone for you, Mr. Gordon. It's Mr. Timberwolf. He's calling from Anchorage."

Hank turned to Lucky, his face filled with anger. "That remark was ridiculous and totally improper, Mr. Wheeler, and as long as you're in my home, I'd prefer you refrain from using swear words. I have to get the phone, but believe me, we'll discuss your rude comment later. And keep your distance from my dog! This is his home too."

Lucky gave a snort, then, in a mimicking, falsetto voice, said to Hank's back as he left the room, "But believe me, we'll discuss your rude comment later."

❧

"Enough, Lucky!" Tina gave him an exasperated look. "For your information, the two of us have not been staying alone in this house. Faynola is Hank's full-time housekeeper." Lucky's degrading mocking made her want to slap him.

"Oh, but what happens after the lights go out at night?"

Tina had had enough. "Just when I think you've changed, you pull a trick like this! I wish—"

"You wish I'd never come and interrupted your tea party?"

She blinked hard and pressed her lips together, trying to remember the good things about the man. "I was about to say, I wish you'd grow up and behave like a gentleman."

"Mr. Gordon said you'd be staying in the guest room," Faynola said, keeping her distance from the two. "I've put fresh towels on the foot of the bed. If you need anything else—"

"Thank you, Faynola." Tina forced back her anger and smiled at the woman. "Dinner will be on the table at six."

"Hey, Fannie, how about a big, juicy steak?" Lucky asked, licking his lips. "I ain't had a nice steak in a long time."

"And you're not having one tonight!" Tina said angrily. "You'll have whatever Faynola is preparing!"

Lucky shrugged. "Well then, maybe we can have steak tomorrow night. How about it, Farina?"

"Her name is Faynola, Lucky."

"I'll take the steaks out of the freezer in the morning and marinate them for dinner," the housekeeper said, backing away. "Tonight we're having fresh salmon."

"Not one word!" Tina cautioned as Lucky's nose wrinkled up. "You're a guest in this house. It's about time you began to behave as one."

"You've sure gotten high and mighty since you left Chicago."

"Not high and mighty, Lucky. It's just that I'd almost forgotten how nice the folks in Alaska can be. Things are different here, and if you're going to stay, you'll have to change your ways, or you'll never fit in."

"Who says I want to fit in?"

Hank hurried back into the room and pulled his jacket off the hook. "Well, it looks like you two are going to have to eat dinner alone. Trapper is stuck in Anchorage, and the Boy Scout Father and Son Banquet is tonight. He's asked me to stand in for him and go with Todd."

"This another one of your bongo bongo things?" Lucky asked with a deriding laugh.

"It's pro bono," Hank said quietly, but his eyes had fire in them. "And no, I'm doing this as a favor for a friend. I hate to run off and leave—"

"We'll be fine," Tina inserted quickly, almost relieved the two men wouldn't have an opportunity to finish the conversation they'd started. "Enjoy your evening with Todd."

"I will. I know Mr. Wheeler is eager to get a good night's rest, so I'll see you two in the morning. If you need anything, just ask Faynola."

Lucky grinned. "Lead me to the fridge. Right now, all I need is a couple of ice cold beers!"

"Sorry, pal," Hank called back over his shoulder. "No beer in this house. Period!"

❧

"Where'd you disappear to?" Tina stared at Lucky with a scowl as he came back into the room. "Where did you get that beer? You know what Hank said! There was to be no beer in his house, and he meant it!"

"I was a mite thirsty, so while you and Farina was gettin' supper on the table, I walked to that gas place down the street and bought me a six-pack. Don't get your feathers all riled up. I won't let him see them!" he told her as he placed two cans on the table.

"I wondered why you'd left the room. I couldn't imagine what'd happened to you. Now I know!" She glared at him as she pointed a finger in his face. She wanted to throttle him for going against Hank's wishes like that. "Take those cans and the other four to the garage, and put it in that big trash barrel. You cannot bring that stuff into Hank's house!" she stated firmly, hoping her message was coming through loud and clear. But she knew from the look on his face, it wasn't going to be that easy to get him to get rid of that vile stuff.

He sat back down at the table. "Well, la-de-da! Excuse me, Miss Prissy! Who named you queen? I'll take them to the trash when I finish with them."

Tina ignored his remark, and they ate in silence. Finally, she placed her napkin on the table. "For a man who turned up his nose when he heard we were having fresh salmon for dinner, you sure cleaned up your plate. How many servings have you had?"

Lucky reached for another dinner roll, his fifth. "I was hungry, that's all."

"Oh? You didn't like the salmon?"

"Sure wasn't as good as a nice, thick, juicy steak." He slathered butter over his roll, dropping a blob on the tablecloth. "But I'm sure lookin' forward to that steak tomorrow night."

"This isn't a restaurant. You can't tell Faynola to—"

"Hey, she offered."

"Only because you put her on the spot. And that's another thing. We can't expect Hank to furnish our meals, as well as our housing. He's been nice enough to allow us to stay here, and—"

He shoved a big hunk of roll into his mouth. "He's been feeding you every night, hasn't he?"

She nodded, wishing he'd chew with his mouth closed. "Yes, he has, but you're here now. That makes a big difference. One extra person was asking a lot. Two is ridiculous."

He reached across the table, taking the remains of Tina's roll from her plate. "Why? That Farina woman has to fix his supper. All she has to do is add another potato to the pot and put a few more of them green things in the salad bowl."

"Her name is Faynola, not Farina. It'd be nice if you'd be courteous enough to at least call her by her right name."

"Well, hoop-de-do! How'm I supposed to remember?"

"Both of us staying here is an imposition on Hank's magnanimous generosity and hospitality."

"Oh, using more hoity-toity words on me, huh?"

She bit at her lower lip and gave him a harsh stare. "You know very well what I mean."

"Yeah, I know what you mean." His fist hit the table. "You wish I'd never come. I'm not good enough for your rich friends."

She forced her face to soften a bit. "It's not that, Lucky. I haven't seen Hank in years, yet he's been good enough to allow me to stay in his home and even offered to help me get Gram's house ready. If it weren't for him—"

"If it weren't for him, I'd have probably heard from you more often."

She didn't like the accusing tone of his voice. She'd called him as often as she could.

"That's one reason I came on ahead. I didn't like the way you'd always cut me off on the phone when that guy came into the room. I had a feeling you hadn't told him about me, and I'd like to know why." His voice was loud and brash. "I am your boyfriend, or have you forgotten?"

She put a finger to her lips. "Remember, Lucky, we're not alone. Faynola is in the kitchen. I don't want her to overhear us. You know she'll go right to Hank with our words."

"So? Let her! What're we sayin' old Hank shouldn't hear?"

Tina clenched her fists. "Let's just let it drop. Okay?" She stood to her feet and began gathering up their plates.

"Whatcha doin' that for? Let that maid do it!"

Angry at his words, she snatched the napkin out from beneath his elbow, nearly tipping over his beer. "She is not a maid. She's a housekeeper."

"Same thing in my book. She's gettin' paid to do that kind of stuff."

"But not for two additional people! I certainly don't expect her to wait on me, and neither should you." She spun around and headed for the kitchen.

"Aren't we gonna have cake or pie?" he called after her.

"You defy Hank's wishes, and then you have the nerve to ask about dessert? Look! Either I'm not making myself clear, or you're just plain stupid! No beer in Hank's house! I mean that, Lucky. If you can't abide by the rules, you're out of here!"

Lucky lifted his palms toward her. "Okay! Okay! I hear ya."

"Good! Because that's the way it's going to be. None of that stuff on the Gordon premises! Ever!"

He nodded, then began to rummage around in his right pocket, then the left. "Got any money, Tina? I'm a bit short."

She glared at him, her patience with him nearly exhausted. "Did you quit your job again?"

"Not exactly."

"What's that mean? You were working at the garage and getting paid pretty good for someone with no experience as a mechanic. What happened?"

Lucky's fingers stroked at his untamed beard. "I sorta got fired."

"Fired? You got fired? Again? Do you realize how long I had to talk to convince that man to hire you? How could you? After I'd worked so hard to help you find that job."

"He accused me of stealing."

"Did you steal from him?"

"Not exactly."

"How could you not exactly steal? Either you did, or you didn't!"

"I only borrowed a few of his old tools. If he'd needed them I'd-a brought them back. I'm sure his insurance would've replaced them."

Tina couldn't believe what she was hearing. Glen Coven had been kind enough to give Lucky a chance, and this is the way he repaid him—by stealing his tools!

"Besides, the work was too hard. That man expected me to crawl under those trucks and lay on my back on that creeper thing. My arms got tired, havin' to reach up all day."

"Other men do hard work like that. I'd think a body builder who spends as much time at the gym as you do could handle it with no trouble at all. If he wanted to work. That's your problem, Lucky. You don't want to work!"

"Sure I do. I'm gonna find me a job here in Juneau, right after I help you get that house ready for your grandma."

"Good, I'm glad to hear it, but I really don't need your help on the house. I think it'd be best if you go ahead and get you a job now. I'm running low on funds. I won't be able to give you money much longer."

Lucky groaned. "Aw, Tina. I need a break. I'll get a job later."

"No, you'd better get it now. I'm going to ask Hank to help you find a job. He seems to know everyone in Juneau."

"Is it all right if I finish clearing the table, Miss Tina?"

Tina whirled around to find Faynola standing behind her and wondered just how much she'd heard. Probably most of it. "Fine," she said, her voice changing quickly from one of anger to appreciation. "We're finished, and the dinner was delicious. Thank you."

"Yeah, Fantasia," Lucky inserted, "it wasn't half bad."

The two stood silently as Faynola placed the things on her tray. "May I get you anything else?"

"I was just tellin' Tina, I could sure go for a big piece of pie. Got any?"

"Lucky!"

Faynola gave the man a gentle smile. "As a matter of fact, I baked an apple pie this afternoon. It's Mr. Gordon's favorite. I was going to wait until he got home to cut it."

Tina could almost see Lucky's mouth watering.

"Well, cut it now!" he told the woman as he grabbed her arm and nearly dragged her toward the kitchen. "Got any ice cream to go with it?"

Tina stood aghast at his rude behavior. She had to get him out of Hank's home as fast as she could. If she could get Lucky to help her, maybe she could get the house ready to have the carpet laid sooner than expected. *Dreamer. Lucky has only one speed when it comes to work. Slow!*

"Miss Tina, may I offer you a slice?" Faynola asked, as she placed a large wedge of pie on a plate, topped it with two generous scoops of ice cream, and handed it to the man.

"Thank you, Faynola," she answered, narrowing her eyes and shaking her head with disgust at Lucky, who'd already begun to devour the pie. "I think I'll wait and have mine when Hank gets home. I want to hear all about the banquet."

For some reason, Lucky's loud chewing and bad manners were really getting to her. Was it because she'd been away from him for several weeks? Those things had bothered her before, but nothing like they did now. Could it be because she'd been spending so much time with Hank? A real gentleman? Or was Lucky deliberately trying to annoy her?

She watched as Faynola busied herself at the sink, rinsing dishes and loading them into the dishwasher. Tina knew the woman felt uncomfortable hearing their bantering and let the subject drop. "Well, I've got some paperwork to do. I'm going to my room," she told them with a yawn. "Let me know when Hank gets home."

"Maybe you can take a short nap so you'll be all rested up for Peter Pan when he gets back," Lucky said with a snarl, chomping on his last bite of pie. He turned to Faynola, who was still working at the sink, her back to him. "Hey, Farina, did you know Tina and Peter Pan was sweet on each other when they was kids?"

"That's not true!" Tina shouted at the man, her patience wearing thin. "He was my best friend! That's all!"

Faynola stared at the two of them. "Who is Peter Pan?"

"Hank," Lucky answered simply, with a devious grin.

Tina moved toward him angrily, accidentally knocking over the beer can.

"Now see what you've gone and done!" He jumped to his feet, brushing the splatters of beer from his leather vest with the palms of his hand. "I hope you're proud of yourself, Miss High and Mighty!"

Faynola hurriedly handed a dish towel to Lucky, then began dropping more towels onto the table and the floor, before bending to blot up the spills.

"No," Tina told her, stooping down beside her and taking the wet towels from her hands, "I'll do it. It was my fault. Let me clean it up."

"I don't—"

"I know you don't mind, Faynola, but you work too hard as it is. You're not going to clean up my messes."

"What a waste of good beer," Lucky said, blotting at his wet clothing, "and look what you've done to my vest!"

Tina couldn't remember a time she'd been more furious. The stench of the spilled beer was nearly making her sick to her stomach. But she bit her tongue and kept control of the comment that nearly forced its way out of her mouth. "It'll dry," she said, willing herself to sound calm.

They all turned as the outside door opened and in stepped Hank.

Hank stared at the three of them. Tina on her hands and knees wiping up the floor. Lucky with stains on his leather vest. And Faynola looking as if she'd seen a ghost. "What's going on here?"

"Not much, Hank old boy," Lucky explained in an almost jovial manner. "Little spill, that's all. Tina did it."

Hank frowned as he stooped and took the wet towels from Tina's hands. "Looks more like a flood, I'd say."

"I'm so sorry, Mr. Gordon." Faynola took the towels from her employer. "It was all my fault."

Tina stood quickly to her feet. "I'm the one who knocked that can off the table, not you."

Hank stepped in and positioned himself between the three. "Look, I don't care whose fault it was. That beer should not have been in this house in the first place!"

He turned toward Lucky, angry and frustrated with the man. "I thought I'd made myself clear. I don't want that stuff anywhere around, and I'd better not find it here again! I mean it! Got it?"

Lucky gave him a smirk and turned away.

Hank gave him an I-mean-business look. "Let's just drop it."

Without turning back, Lucky gave him a grunt.

Restraining himself, Hank turned to Faynola. "Get me that yellow plastic bucket from the garage, and I'll clean this floor up for you. You have no business getting down on your knees with your arthritis. Tina, take those wet towels into the laundry room and start the washer. You'll find the detergent on the shelf." He turned to face Lucky. "It's late, and you've been up since dawn. Why don't you take a nice hot shower and go on to bed? I'm sure Tina wants to get an early start on her grandmother's house tomorrow, and she could sure use your help. It's been a long day for all of us. You ladies go on to bed. I'll finish up here and turn out the lights."

After saying a quick good night, the women moved in the direction they'd been told.

Lucky hiked up his pants and stood his ground. "Tryin' to get rid of me, huh?"

Hank gave the man a blank stare. "Get rid of you? Is there some reason I should get rid of you?"

"Me gettin' here kinda messed up your playhouse, didn't it?"

Hank frowned. "Look, Lucky. You and I don't seem to speak the same language. You'll have to explain yourself."

"You think I don't know what's been going on since Tina got here? With you two livin' here in this house."

"I don't know what you think has been going on, but believe me, nothing has. Tina is a beautiful woman, and I enjoy her company, but—"

Lucky harrumphed. "You don't expect me to believe that, do you? I know what goes on in a man's mind when he's with a purty woman, and it sure ain't friendship."

"Look," Hank said evenly, trying to control his emotions, "you don't know me, but you do know Tina. She wouldn't even consider staying at my house until she found out my housekeeper lived here full-time."

"So you're tellin' me you never even tried to come on to Tina?"

For the first time in his life, other than the day Trapper had carried his bride away, Hank wanted to bust someone in the nose. He drew in a deep breath and clenched his fists at his sides, willing them to stay there. "That's exactly what I'm telling you. I'd never put Tina in a compromising position."

"What's the matter with you?"

"Nothing's the matter with me." Hank stood up straight and tall, nose to nose with the man who seemed to bring out the worst in him. "I'm a man who loves God and respects women, and I'm proud of it."

Lucky stepped back and stared at him.

Hank drew in a deep breath and sent up a quick prayer for help. "I need to make you understand a few things. I'm a born-again Christian, which means I've confessed my sins and accepted Jesus Christ as my Savior, and—"

"You?" Lucky gave him a sardonic grin. "Mr. Goody-goody Hank Gordon, a sinner? Ya wouldn't kid me now, would ya? I can't imagine you doin' nothin' that'd be called sin. Ain't you always been a Sunday school boy? I'll bet them teachers just loved you. You was so good."

Hank struggled to keep his cool. "Yes, I was—and am—a sinner. We're all sinners. Mere mortals. I'm a sinner saved by God's grace."

Lucky gave him a puzzled look. "Whatcha mean? Was and am? I thought you was perfect."

"No, far from perfect, but I try to follow the standards God has set in His Word. But even at that, I sin. Pretty often, despite my desire to live for Him. But I go to Him in prayer daily and ask Him to forgive me. He's promised in His Word He will."

"Like how do you sin? Ya don't drink beer. Ya don't swear. Ya don't rob banks!" His face took on that same sardonic smile. "And ya claim ya ain't been tryin' to make claims on my woman. What do you do to sin?"

"Well, those things you mentioned are sins, but there are other sins too. The kind of sins folks do every day. Anger, lying, cheating, impatience, selfishness, that sort of thing. But the greatest sin of all is turning your back on God. Refusing to believe He is God and letting Him rule and reign in your life. Constantly seeking His will."

"That don't sound like much fun! Who'd want to be a Christian if you gotta live a dull life like that? Sounds to me like bein' one of them so-called Christians is for sissies. Not red-blooded men like me! I kinda like bein' a sinner."

"Well, that's a decision each person has to make for themselves. But hear me, Lucky. If you ever want to talk about it, I'm here. Nothing would make me happier than to open God's Word and share it with you."

"Well, I'll just keep that in mind. But don't hold your breath till I get there."

Hank leaned toward Lucky and zeroed in close. "One more thing. I told you absolutely no beer in this house. I don't know where you got those cans or if you have any more. But if you do, I'd suggest you immediately put it in the trash container out in the garage. I will not—I repeat—I will not have it in my home. Is that clear? If I ever find you have brought beer into this house again, I'll have to ask you to leave." He grabbed the man's wrist and leaned even closer. "Maybe you think because I'm a Christian I'll let you get by with it again. But believe me I won't. It's because I am a Christian that I'm being so firm about this."

Lucky pulled away from his grasp and rubbed at his wrist. "Okay, man. Okay. You don't have to get so all-fired mean about it. I hear ya!"

❧

"I started the washer, Hank," Tina said as she came rushing back into the room.

"I'd better go help Faynola find the bucket." Hank disappeared into the mudroom, leaving the two of them in the kitchen.

"I'm sorry for losing my temper," Tina began, "but you simply cannot talk about Hank that way. He's a good man."

"Good for what? Makin' advances on my woman when I'm not around?"

She let out a sigh. It'd been a wearing day, and her energy had been all spent. "Let's get something straight right now. I am not your woman. I don't belong to anyone."

"You belong to me, or have you forgotten?"

His possessive words skyrocketed her anger to the overflow level. "No, I haven't forgotten! I owe you, Lucky, but you do not own me. There's a big difference."

"You mean because I haven't put a ring on your finger?"

"No, a ring has nothing to do with it. I'll never be owned by anyone. Ownership means control, and I'll never be controlled. I'm a human being. I know I've gotten far away from God, but I well remember the things I learned in Sunday school and church. I'm as important to God as anyone who has lived, lives now, or ever will live."

"I thought the man upstairs said men were more important than women—that you females were supposed to obey us males." He finished his statement with a haughty laugh that set her teeth on edge. "That man knew what he was talkin' about. If that woman hadn't disobeyed her husband in the garden, all us men'd be livin' on easy street, eatin' grapes and wearin' palm leaves."

Despite her anger, Tina had to laugh inwardly at Lucky's warped knowledge of the Scripture. "She didn't disobey her husband, Lucky. She disobeyed God. And by the way, it wasn't palm leaves, it was fig leaves, and we don't even know that for sure."

"You two discussing the Bible?" Hank asked with a perplexed look as he came in with the yellow bucket and began to fill it at the sink.

"Oh, yeah. Talkin' about the Bible is one of my favorite pastimes, right, Tina?"

The smile left her face. "I'm going to bed." With that, she turned and left the two men alone.

Lucky let out a big yawn and stretched his arms open wide. "Me too. I sure hope Farina makes a big breakfast. I'm—"

"Not tomorrow," Hank told him as he lifted the bucket from the sink and lowered it to the floor, before stooping down beside it. "Her knees have been bothering her. I think it's the change in weather. I told her to sleep in. She has a doctor's appointment tomorrow afternoon. There are a number of dry cereals in the cabinet, fresh milk and juice in the refrigerator, and a few bagels in the bread keeper. We're all on our own in the morning. I'm going in to the office about six to get some extra work done. I'll probably be out of here long before the two of you are up. Help yourself to whatever you need."

Lucky listened but appeared not to comprehend what Hank was telling him. "You mean we gotta fix our own breakfast?"

"If you want to eat," Hank replied as he wrung out a rag and began mopping up the floor with a circular motion. "Or maybe you can talk Tina into cooking something for you, but don't count on that either. She usually goes by to see her grandmother before going to the house. I doubt she'll be interested in doing any cooking before she goes."

Tina came into the kitchen, wearing no makeup and dressed in her pajamas and robe. "I forgot a glass of water," she told them as she went to the cupboard, pulled out a glass, and filled it at the sink.

Lucky puckered up his face. "Old Hank says Farina can't cook breakfast in the mornin'. Her knees hurt. You gonna cook for me?"

She gave him a vacant stare. "Lucky, didn't you tell me one time you used to work at a lunch counter? As a fry cook?"

He nodded. "Yeah, a long time ago, but I never liked it."

"Well, if you're hungry in the morning, I suggest you pull out your culinary skills and cook your own breakfast. But you'd better do it early because you're going to have to not only cook your own breakfast, you're going to have to clean up after yourself. We're not going off and leaving a mess for Faynola."

"But you used to cook for me sometimes," he told her with puppy dog eyes, "when we was livin' in Chicago."

"That was when circumstances prevented you from taking care of yourself. If you want a simple glass of juice, a cup of coffee, and a bowl of cereal, I'll be happy to pour the juice for you and put your glass, cup, bowl, and spoon in the dishwasher when you're finished, but more than that, you're on your own. But whatever you do, you'll have to do it early. I'm always out of here by seven-thirty at the latest." She turned to go but he caught her arm.

Hank wanted to add his two cents' worth, but kept quiet as he watched, proud of Tina for making a stand and refusing to cater to the man's whims.

"How you gonna get there? Hank's leavin' early to go to his office, so he can't take us."

"He's letting me drive his pickup truck."

Lucky gestured toward Hank. "Oh? You give her some old wreck to drive while you tool around town in that flashy SUV? Some guy you are!"

Tina gave him an incredulous glare. "For your information, the pickup I'm driving is less than six months old, and it's nearly as flashy as the SUV!"

"You're trying to tell me this man lets you live in his house, eat his food, drive his new pickup, and he helps you with the remodeling—all because he's a good guy?"

"Yes, exactly."

"Or is it because you let him—"

Tina turned and walked away before he could finish his sentence.

Chapter 6

It was seven-twenty when Lucky staggered into the kitchen the next morning, his long, dark hair a tangled mess, lines etched into his face. "You mean Farina's really not gonna fix breakfast?"

"Faynola is an old woman. Did you forget what Hank said about her knees? You've got ten minutes. The coffee is hot, and you can stick a bagel in the toaster to take with you."

"How come you're bein' so mean to me?"

She lowered the paper she was reading a bit more and peered at him, her eyes squinted, and she frowned. "Because you're acting like a spoiled child, that's why! To think you brought that beer in the house after Hank had warned you about it! That really upsets me!"

"I'll bet old Hankie boy isn't as innocent as he lets on. Come on, tell me the truth." Lucky's eyes narrowed as he leaned toward her. "You and I both know there's more goin' on between you two."

Her chin jutted out. "I can't believe you'd say such a thing! Don't you know me better than that?"

"I know you ain't let me do more'n kiss you!"

She pointed to her left hand. "I don't intend to let anyone do more than kiss me until there's a ring on my finger."

His tone mellowed. "Aw, baby, I said I'd get you a ring."

"With what, Lucky? You still owe a bundle on your Harley. You were living with a buddy because your landlord threw you out, and—"

"I tried to get you to let me move in with you so—"

"I may have wandered far from God, but I still have principles. I refuse to let any man move in with me! For any reason—until I'm wearing a wedding ring!"

"You know it's that Hank guy's fault. He bugs me, him and that mangy dog of his, and he's messin' with your head, and you don't even know it."

"Messing with my head? What's that supposed to mean?"

Lucky ripped open the bread wrapper and stuck two pieces of whole wheat bread in the toaster. "You live here in this fine house for a few weeks, and you forget all about our life in Chicago. Don't you miss all the places we used to go together? The good times we used to have?"

She shook her head sadly as she folded the newspaper in half and placed it on the empty chair beside her with a grunt, still wearing a scowl. "You mean going to the midnight movie because the tickets were cheaper then and taking our own popcorn because we couldn't afford the theater's prices? Or do you mean going to those motorcycle rallies? Getting hit on by a bunch of rowdy drunks? Or maybe visiting your cousin at the local jail? Yeah, those were fun times all right."

"You sure had me fooled. I thought you liked doing those things with me," he shot back, his voice loud and accusing as he yanked open the refrigerator door.

"I never did like those things, Lucky." Realizing their voices were getting louder with each come-back, she took a deep breath before continuing, her voice an almost whisper. "I only did them because of you. Because of what you—"

He put up a hand. "You don't have to remind me."

"Two minutes," Tina said in a controlled manner, wanting to put an end to their exchange of words and looking at the wall clock. "The pickup is leaving in two minutes. You'd better get a hurry on, or you'll get left behind." She stood to her feet and picked up her cup and spoon.

Fifteen minutes later, they entered the house on Ocean View Boulevard.

❧

Hank had a hard time keeping his mind on his work. After much persuasion, when he'd phoned Faynola, she'd reluctantly filled him in on the tense conversation she'd overheard between Tina and Lucky.

Why? Hank asked himself over and over. *Why would Tink put up with the man? How could she put up with him? None of it makes any sense. Not only is Lucky not Tina's type, he's downright rude! Surely Tink's tastes and standards haven't lowered that much since she left Juneau. But—she has been living in Chicago all this time, and from the sounds of it, in a not-too-nice neighborhood. Perhaps she's gotten used to having men like Lucky around her all the time. She said she hadn't gone to church in years, which is where she should have been if she wanted to find a good, solid man who loves God.*

He shuffled a few papers on his desk and stacked them up neatly, barely aware of what he was doing. Maybe she wasn't interested in a good, solid man who loved God. The thought made him shudder. If only she'd talk to him about Lucky, explain what she saw in the man. He glanced at the sleek chrome desk clock one of his grateful clients had given him when he'd won a difficult case. Ten o'clock.

He picked up the phone and dialed, hoping Lucky wouldn't be the one to answer. He had to talk to her. To make sure she was okay. He was concerned about her being alone with that man, although why it concerned him, he didn't know. No telling how many times she'd been alone with that character when they were in Chicago. Still, she was in Juneau now, and he felt the need to protect her.

He became more concerned with each ring, finally hanging up after he'd counted to twelve. Next he phoned Faynola.

"No, Mr. Gordon. I haven't heard a word from them. Like I told you when you called, they left about seven-thirty."

He thanked Faynola after asking her to let him know if they returned home, then stared at the phone. Where could they be? Next he phoned the nursing home, but they hadn't been there. Surely they hadn't gone to the lumberyard. He'd made sure they had all the supplies they'd be needing for their current projects.

He jumped when his secretary entered the room, his mind on the people who should be at the house on Ocean View Boulevard.

"Sorry to interrupt, Hank," she told him as she placed a call slip on his desk. "Jean Carter just phoned. Her car won't start. She won't be able to make her ten-thirty appointment."

Hank stood quickly to his feet with a smile. "No problem. I need to be away for a couple of hours anyway."

The woman's eyes rounded, and she seemed surprised by his words. "But what about that brief you wanted me to type up for you? I thought you were in a hurry to get it—"

Hank patted her shoulder as he grabbed his coat from the rack and raced past her. "I'll have it for you sometime this afternoon."

On the way to Tina's house, he redialed her number on his cell phone. Still no answer.

❦

Tina frowned at Lucky. "The least you could do is help me with this. You're taller than I am. It'd be easier for you to reach. I've already done most of the others."

Lucky shook his head. "I think it's better if I hold onto the ladder for you, to steady it."

Tina shrugged. "Whatever."

"I don't know why you wanna wash those stupid windows anyway. It's cold out here."

She squeezed the trigger on the bottle of window cleaner before pulling a fresh rag from her jacket pocket. "I know, but this is the first time the sun has been shining all week. I wanted to take advantage of its warmth on the glass." She ran the rag in a circular motion over the window pane until it sparkled before starting back down the ladder.

"Can we quit now?"

She sent an exasperated look toward him as her foot touched the ground. "I still have the east window to do, but I guess this is enough for today."

The sound of a car pulling into the driveway caught her attention. "Wonder who that is? Can't be Hank; it's too early for him to come by on his lunch hour."

"Why haven't you been answering your phone?" Hank yelled out as he rounded the corner of the house and rushed toward them. "I've been calling for nearly an hour."

She gave him a puzzled look as she gestured toward the clean windows. "I've been up there on the ladder. I wanted to take advantage of the sunshine."

"You could have let me know!"

She let out a chuckle as her eyes filled with mock amusement. "Let you know that I was going outside to wash windows? Whatever for?"

"Yeah," Lucky chimed in with a deriding smirk. "Who do you think you are? Her keeper?"

Hank blushed and fumbled for words. "Ah, no—it's just—well, when I—the phone rang—"

Tina's gloved hand reached out and patted his cheek. "Thanks, Hank, for being concerned about me, but—"

"But she don't need you. I'm here to take care of her," Lucky inserted quickly, stepping between the pair, standing with the toes of their shoes nearly touching.

What's with these guys? Tina lifted her hands in despair. "What is this? You two haven't said a pleasant word to each other since—"

"He always starts it!" Lucky's finger shot out accusingly.

"I do not," Hank responded defensively.

"Whoa! Enough." Tina stomped her foot and tugged at each grown man's sleeve. "I feel like I'm back in the third grade, with you two bickering like this." She turned to Lucky and ordered, "Go into the house and start sanding on that back bedroom door."

Lucky gave her an unpleasant snort but did as she'd instructed, grumbling beneath his breath all the way to the back door.

Once he was out of sight and she heard the door slam, she turned to Hank, both hands on her hips. "Now for you! What's with you, Hank? I know it's asking a lot of you to let Lucky and me both stay at your house, but you're the one who invited us. I would never—"

"Surely you know I only invited him because of you. I didn't want you to leave! I like having you stay at my house."

"I–I like being there too."

Hank stepped forward and took her hands in his. "Why Lucky, Tink?"

She looked away, avoiding his kind eyes. "I don't know what you mean."

His forefinger slipped beneath her chin, tilting her head upward, causing her to face him. "He's not the man for you. I think we both know that, but for the life of me, I can't figure out what kind of hold he has on you. I know you don't love—"

"Could—could we talk about this later?"

"Hey," Lucky called loudly, as he stood holding the back door open. "Keep your hands off my woman!"

Tina backed quickly away from Hank and headed toward the house. "Are you coming in?"

"No, guess not. I'd better get back to the office if I'm going to be able to get away at five and come and help you. Or maybe with Lucky here, you don't need me."

Tina turned around slowly. "Oh, Hank, Lucky could never take your place."

He grinned shyly. "That's what I was hoping."

"And besides, I think he's starting that new job tomorrow at a car wash."

❧

Hank moved toward the bed with a smile. "Hi, Mrs. Taylor. How are you feeling this morning?"

Harriett Taylor reached out a trembling hand. "Oh, Hank. Come and sit by me. These old eyes of mine can't see you very well."

He pulled up a chair and sat down, taking her frail hand in his. It seemed to him she was even more fragile than she'd been the last time he'd visited her. "Tina's coming by later. I haven't seen you for a day or two. I hope you aren't too disappointed it's just me."

"I'm probably the envy of all the ladies here at the nursing home, having a handsome man come to visit me. Of course I'm not disappointed. You've always been very special to me."

"Tina's really working hard on your house. You should see the things she's getting done. In no time at all she'll be able to take you home."

She gave him a little smile. "From what my granddaughter tells me, you're doing a lot of the work. How can I ever thank you?"

"By taking care of yourself. That's all."

Her face became serious. "I'm so glad you're spending time with Tina. She told me Lucky was here. That man has never been good for her. I try to stay out of her business. But when you're as old as I am, and you love someone, it's hard to keep quiet."

He patted her hand. "All we can really do, Mrs. Taylor, is pray."

"I'm praying she'll forget all about that awful man and start paying more attention to you."

He weighed his words carefully before answering, finally saying, "Me too."

❧

The next evening, Hank showed up at Tina's at exactly five-thirty, his arms loaded with carryout food, which Lucky began to devour the moment he came in the door. Lucky started eating even before Hank had time to thank the Lord, and afterward parked himself on a kitchen chair and watched television on the little set her grandmother had kept, while Tina and Hank worked on the house.

"Well, that's it," Tina said with a smile, as she brushed her palms together. "I think we're finally ready for the carpet installation."

Hank stood back and admired their work. "Yep, soon as they get that carpet down I'll nail the baseboards in place, and you'll be ready for the furniture."

She stood on tiptoe and kissed his cheek. "Only because of you. I could never have done this without you. Gram will be so pleased. I told her we were nearly finished."

Hank looked over her shoulder through the kitchen door and, seeing Lucky engrossed in a movie, seized the opportunity and threw his arms about Tina, pulling her to him and kissing her sweet mouth. He'd longed to kiss her since the day she'd come back into his life. He was surprised when she didn't struggle to free herself. "Oh, Tink," he said softly into her ear when he finally, reluctantly, ended their kiss. "Do you have any idea how much I've wanted to kiss you?"

"I—I—"

His lips sought hers again, cutting off her words. This time he felt her arms circle his neck as she leaned into him and kissed him back. "Hank, oh, Hank."

"Hey, Tina, bring me some of those peanut butter cookies!" Lucky called out when a commercial blared from the TV.

Hank propelled himself quickly past Tina and into the kitchen. "She's not your servant, Lucky! That woman has been working hard all day." Hank paused. "If you were half a man, you'd be doing the heavy work instead of watching her do it!"

The look on Lucky's face as he jumped to his feet should've prepared Hank for what was to come, but it didn't. He was not at all ready for the blow of the man's fist on his chin and the blood that gushed forth from his lip.

Tina sprang forward and set herself up as a barricade between them, screaming for Lucky to stop. But Lucky only pushed her aside and followed up with a second blow that hit Hank squarely in the gut, knocking the wind out of him and leaving him gasping for air.

Instinctively, Hank's survival mechanism kicked into gear. He sucked in a deep breath, clenched his fists, and plowed into Lucky, hitting him first on the cheek, then the shoulder, then the stomach.

Lucky reeled a bit, seemed to regroup, then doubled up a fist and struck out again, this time landing it on Tina as she once again stepped in between them, his ring biting into her face.

She screamed and fell backward into Hank's arms, blood running down her cheek and flowing onto her sweatshirt.

"Look what you've done to her!"

"Your fault as much as mine," Lucky retorted angrily. "I thought you Christians were supposed to turn the other cheek."

"Is that what you were counting on?" Hank snapped back as he glared at the man. "Hurry up! Get one of those new dish towels out of that drawer next to the sink. Wet it down with cool water, wring it out, and bring it to me. Now!" Hank ordered as he protectively pulled Tina close, not about to let the repulsive man get an inch nearer to his precious Tink. "Hurry up! I'm taking her to the hospital. This cheek'll probably need stitches, thanks to you!"

"I'll take her. She's my—"

"What are you going to pay the hospital with? Empty beer cans?" After pressing the wet towel to Tina's cheek, Hank scooped her up in his arms and headed for the door. "Do you think you can turn off the lights and lock up? Or is that asking too much?"

Lucky shrugged. "Okay, you take her."

Hank pushed past the man without so much as a look back, his only concern for Tina.

As he glanced at the shaking woman sitting in the SUV, so close beside him, her head resting on his shoulder, her shirt soaked with blood, a cold wet towel pressed to her cheek, love for her filled his heart. Surely this episode would cause Tina to see Lucky for what he was. A loser. A real loser.

"Hank."

"Yes."

"Don't be mad at Lucky. You don't know him like I do. He's not as bad as he seems."

Hank slipped an arm about her shoulders and kissed the top of her head. "He's not the man for you, Tink."

"I don't have any choice. I have to marry Lucky," she whispered softly as she pressed the towel to her face.

Hank stiffened at her words. "You're not—"

Chapter 7

Pregnant? No!" Tina said emphatically, pulling away slightly and lifting her face to his with a groan. "How could you ask me such a thing?"

"Look, Tink, I'm sorry to have even considered something like that, but for the life of me I can't think of one good reason you'd even consider marrying that man!"

"I wish you hadn't hit him."

"Me hit him? He started it. What was I supposed to do? Stand there and let him use me as a punching bag?" A faint smile curled at his lips as he remembered his fracas with Lucky, totally amazed by how quickly things had happened and how he'd automatically responded. He'd never hit another man in his entire life. Not even Trapper when he'd taken Glorianna from him on his wedding day. Yet he'd held his own with Lucky. His lip and chin were sore, and his stomach felt like he'd run into a brick wall. But other than that, and a few feelings of guilt, he felt fine.

"Maybe it'd be best if Lucky and I moved out of your house. We could—"

"No! I won't hear of it." The idea made Hank ill. If Tina moved out he wouldn't have an excuse to be around her, not with her allegiance to Lucky. He couldn't let that happen. Not yet, anyway. And he certainly didn't want them staying in Harriett Taylor's house alone. "You two better stay in my home until the carpet is laid and the furniture delivered."

When they arrived at the hospital, Hank parked next to the emergency room door, disregarding the no parking sign. As he'd suspected, the cheek required stitches, but only two small ones. He cringed and felt the pain right along with her as he watched the doctor work the curved needle through her delicate skin, feeling guilty and knowing he was partially responsible for her injury.

Two hours later, after he'd made sure Tina was resting comfortably, he knelt beside his bed, unsure what to say to God. After thanking Him for all the blessings He'd bestowed upon him by bringing Tina back into his life, he decided it was time to get serious. *Lord, I've actually had a fistfight,* he confessed. *Me. Hank Gordon. The man who has always abhorred violence of any kind. I've let that man bring out the worst in me and I'm not very proud of it!*

He gulped hard, then continued. "God," he asked aloud this time, with a glance upward as he let out a deep sigh. "Was Lucky right? Was I, as a Christian, supposed to turn my cheek after he'd hit me and let him use it as a target? Is that really what you meant in Your Word?"

He waited, but no answer came from heaven. No thunderbolts jagged their way to earth. No lightning ripped across the sky. But in his heart, Hank was sure his Lord understood why he'd done what he'd done.

Since there were no sounds of stirring in either Tina's or Lucky's room the next morning, Hank decided to forgo breakfast at home and instructed Faynola to let them sleep in and not awaken them early, as Tina had requested. She'd been sure she'd feel like working at the house that day, but Hank knew better and had advised her to take the day off and spend it with her grandmother, resting and recouping from her injury.

He wheeled into the convenience store parking lot, selected two raised doughnuts and a cup of coffee from the deli section, and proceeded to the cash register.

"That'll be two-seventy-seven," the clerk told him.

Hank reached into his pocket for his billfold, only to find it empty. He was sure when he'd bought gas there had still been two twenty-dollar bills left in that billfold. He fumbled around in his pocket for change and, by using a combination of quarters, dimes, nickels and two pennies, came up with the amount. *I know I had two twenties,* he reasoned to himself as he climbed into the SUV and headed for his office.

He phoned home at ten. "How is Tina?" he asked when Faynola answered on the first ring.

"I looked in on her a bit ago. She's still sleeping," the old woman whispered into the phone. "But that man is gone. He left in your pickup about an hour ago."

Hank frowned. "Lucky has my pickup? Was he driving it to the car wash and leaving Tina stranded there without transportation?"

"Sorry, Mr. Gordon. He didn't say. Just told me to fix him some sausage, eggs, and pancakes, ate them, and left."

"He told you to fix him breakfast?"

"Yes, sir, and—"

"Faynola, you do not have to take orders from that man. Don't let him walk all over you like that!"

"But he's your guest. I would never—"

"He's only a guest because of Tina. I do not want you going out of your way for him. I mean that, Faynola! I'm your boss, not Lucky. You do what I say!"

The phone was silent for a moment, and Hank thought perhaps the connection had failed or he'd upset her with his strong words.

"I—" Silence again. "I hate to have to tell you this, but last night, when I got up about four o'clock to get a drink of water, I saw Mr. Wheeler standing by the front hall table. I wondered what he was doing up at that time, so I watched him. He was taking some money out of a billfold. You'd left your billfold on that table."

Hank could feel his blood pressure rising. *That explains the missing twenties.* "I'll take care of it, Faynola. Thanks for telling me, but I doubt he was taking money out of my billfold. Just keep an eye on Tina for me, please. And don't say anything to her about this. I don't want to upset her."

"Mr. Gordon, that's not all."

"Oh no. There's more? Why am I not surprised? What else?"

"After I saw him take the money out of the billfold, I kept an eye on him. He—he went into your office. I don't know what he was doing in there. I'd planned to tell you this first thing this morning, but you left much earlier than I'd expected."

Hank couldn't remember a time he'd been so angry, but he kept his voice as even as possible. "Did he see you?"

"No, sir."

"Thank you, Faynola. I'll take care of it, and remember, not a word about this to Tina."

Struggling to keep his anger at bay, Hank glanced at his bruised fist, then dialed Tina's phone number at the house, thinking maybe Lucky was there. But even after waiting while the phone rang twenty-three times, no one answered. He no longer had to wonder what had happened to the missing forty dollars, but where was Lucky? Or more importantly, where was the truck? And if he'd found his lockbox in the office, how much more money had the man taken?

At eleven Hank drove by Tina's house, and seeing no truck in the drive, headed on home. Tina was sitting at the kitchen table watching Faynola peel carrots for their evening meal and gave him a lopsided smile as he entered. The small bandage on her face did little to cover the blue and purplish bruise on her cheek. "You were right," she told him as he sat down beside her and folded her hand in his, "I do feel kinda lousy today. Those pain pills the doctor gave me made me drowsy. I decided to take the day off as you recommended. I called Gram, and we had a nice visit, but I never got to the nursing home."

"I'm sorry you didn't get to see Harriett, but I'm glad you're resting. You've been working way too hard. We'll see how you feel tomorrow."

"He took your truck."

"I know. Faynola told me. Do you have any idea where he was going?"

She shook her head. "No, I didn't even know he was taking it. He's asked to borrow it before, but I've never let him."

"Well," Hank said, forcing a smile, "don't worry about it. He probably had a good reason." *Yeah, forty, and about another thousand dollars' worth of good reasons, if he took everything I had in the lockbox.* "I have a feeling you've been giving him money. Have you?"

"Ah—some. But I'm beginning to reach the bottom of my savings account, so I haven't been able to give him much lately. He's really been down on his luck lately."

"Yeah, so I've heard a dozen times from him. I've tried to help the man, but he's left every job I've gotten him. Isn't it about time he started looking for one on his own? Started accepting some responsibility for himself? Maybe that's where he is now. He sure hasn't been much help on the house."

The tip of her finger idly traced the pattern on the tablecloth. "He got fired from the car wash job. He says he's been scanning the newspaper for openings, but, so far, he hasn't been interested in any of them, or they've informed him he doesn't have the necessary skills. I told him maybe if he went to apply for them in person, rather than over the phone, it might help."

Not the way he looks, with that long, dangling earring and that smart mouth of his! "Tina, from what you've told me, money has been in short supply for you. How can you just hand your hard-earned wages over to an able-bodied man like Lucky? Don't you realize you're only encouraging his laziness?"

"Please don't talk about him that way, Hank. You don't know how much he means to me."

"No, I guess I don't," he said, rising with a shake of his head. "I have a lunch appointment with a client. I only stopped by to see how you were doing." He bent and kissed her good cheek. "See you about five-thirty."

It was nearly eight-thirty that evening before Lucky showed up with Hank's pickup. Hank had been waiting for him, but decided to confront him alone later, for Tina's sake. He'd already checked the lockbox. The man had picked the lock and taken the money. Hank fully intended to call the sheriff, but his thoughts went to Tina. Would she believe Lucky was a thief? Faynola hadn't actually seen him open the lockbox.

He waited until the man entered the house, then checked out his pickup, making sure there hadn't been any dents or damage inflicted on it since he'd last seen it. From the outside, it looked fine. But inside was another story. Empty beer cans, candy bar and chewing gum wrappers, and greasy French fries were strewn about the cab, on the seat, as well as on the floor, and the ashtray was filled with cigarette butts. The stench nearly got to Hank as he backed away and slammed the door. This would be the last time that ungrateful man took his truck. He'd see to that! He'd lent it to Tina, not Lucky, and he was going to make sure both his houseguests knew it. He only hoped Tina would understand.

All day, Tina had been seething at Lucky's audacity. "Tell me where you've been!" she demanded as he sauntered into the house, as if he didn't have a care in the world.

"I'd say it's nobody's business where I've been," he snorted back angrily, as he shoved past her toward the kitchen. "I'm a grown man, or have you forgotten?"

She followed close at his heels. "It became my business when you took

299

Hank's truck without permission."

"And there's the little question of the forty bucks missing from my wallet and a little over a thousand dollars from my lockbox!" Hank inserted irately as he came in from the garage and joined them in the wide hallway.

Lucky stopped midstride with a menacing glare, first at one and then the other. "What is this? Stack-it-on-Lucky day?"

Tina's mouth gaped. "You stole money from Hank's wallet and his lockbox? Then took his truck without permission? After all he's done for you? How dare you? You're nothing but a common thief!"

"Oh?" Lucky's brows lifted, then lowered into a frown as deep lines folded into his forehead. "You believe what that man says? How do you know he didn't make all this up to make me look bad?"

"You don't deserve this good woman," Hank said, stepping in front of Tina protectively, his face mere inches from his rival's. "You know good and well you took that money. Faynola saw you with my wallet. Are you accusing her of lying too?"

"Sure, she'd lie. She works for you, don't she?"

"But she'd never lie for me. The best thing you could do for Tina is to get lost. I'd half hoped you wouldn't show up at all. It'd be worth losing my pickup truck and the money, just to get you out of her life! I'd even treat you to a one-way airline ticket back to Chicago!"

Lucky's fist shot out again. But this time, Hank was ready for him and blocked it by grabbing the man's arm and quickly twisting it up behind his back, a defensive move he'd seen in old movies. But Lucky responded with a counter move Hank hadn't expected and sent him reeling backward into the wall, knocking two framed pictures from their moorings and sending them crashing to the floor.

"Now see what you've done!" Tina flew into Lucky, her anger soaring, her doubled-up fists crashing against his chest. "After Hank has put up with all your foolishness and even helped you get those jobs!"

"You're taking his side? Against me? I'm the man you're going to marry. Not him!" Lucky grabbed both her wrists and held her at arm's length, his eyes narrowed, his face gnarled into a threatening scowl. "He hasn't done a thing for me, Tina. It's all been for you! Don't you see? Everything that man has done has been to keep you from me! He's crazy about you!"

Tina stopped struggling and glared at him. "That's a rotten thing to say! Hank and I are just good friends, or at least we were until you pulled this trick! Now he probably hates me for bringing you into his life!" Tina yelled back at him.

Lucky looked over his shoulder at Hank. "Tell her! Be man enough to admit it!"

Hank seemed to grope for words. "If I have any feelings for Tink, I've kept them to myself, out of deference to you. Not because of anything worthwhile I've seen in you, Lucky, but because of what Tina seems to see in you. But I will admit, I do not think you are the right man for her!"

"It's really none of your business, Mr. Know-it-all! You're just jealous because she's mine!"

"I don't belong to anyone!" Tina screamed, her face belying her frustration. "Apologize to Hank now, Lucky! I mean it! And you're going to give back every cent you've stolen from him!"

"Oh, yeah? Says who?" With that, Lucky released her and headed down the hall toward his room, banging his fists into the walls as he went. "Satan will turn into a snowman before I apologize to that man!"

Hank bit back his anger, gently took Tina by the arm, and led her into the kitchen, where Faynola stood waiting, ready to spoon out the beef stew she'd prepared. "Let's forget about him for now. Okay?"

She nodded, brushing back a tear. "I'm so sorry—"

"You needn't be. It wasn't your fault."

"But it was," she said, dropping into the chair he'd pulled out from the table. "I brought him here."

The loud slamming of the front door, then the roar of Hank's truck starting, brought them both to their feet. But by the time they reached the front porch, the truck was speeding down the street, with Lucky at the wheel.

"I'm going to call the sheriff and have that man arrested!" Hank shouted, angrily shaking his fist, as he stood staring at the pickup.

Tina grabbed his wrist, her eyes pleading. "No, please! Don't cause him any trouble. I'm sure he'll bring it back."

Hank couldn't believe what he was hearing. "Look, Tink! This man turned up unexpectedly on my doorstep and invited himself to stay in my home. He brought beer into the house against my wishes. Made more work for Faynola. Tried to assault me. Twice! Stole my money. Took my truck without asking. Not to mention how disrespectfully he treats you! And you're asking me not to call the sheriff? Come on. Get serious!"

"Please, Hank," she whispered softly as she gazed up at him, her eyes filled with tears, her tone imploring. "I'm begging you. Don't call the sheriff! You don't know the things Lucky's gone through. He's had a pretty rough life."

There was something about the way she asked him that seemed to melt his resolve, despite his anger. "He doesn't deserve you, you know! Why do you put up with that man? Do you have any idea what you're asking?"

He was disappointed when Tina ignored his question and simply repeated, "Please don't call the sheriff. For me?"

Hank allowed his face to soften some. "Okay, I won't call—this time. But I'm tired of putting up with him, Tink! You'd better keep him in line, and I want that money back. If he doesn't return it, all of it, I will call the sheriff! We can't let Lucky continue to get by with such things!"

"M—maybe I can repay you, if you'll—"

301

"No!" he fairly shouted at her. "Don't even think it! I want it from him!"

Once they were back in the house and he was alone in his study, he phoned a lawyer friend in Chicago who worked closely with the district attorney's office. "Yeah, Lucky Wheeler," he said in a low voice to the man on the other end. "I'm almost certain the guy's got a record. See what you can find out."

Chapter 8

Despite her concern about Lucky's whereabouts, the next two days were the happiest Tina had ever spent as she and Hank put the finishing touches on the house.

"Do you think he went back to Chicago?" she asked Hank, as he placed a new log on the fire that evening. "It's been two days since he left."

"I don't know. I hope so. But that would mean he either abandoned my pickup or sold it. He sure couldn't drive it out of Juneau. My guess is that he conned one of the seaplane pilots to take him to Anchorage or Vancouver."

"I thought I knew the man so well. I feel responsible for—"

"Look, I'm not going to let him ruin our evening. Let's put Lucky out of our minds, if just for a few hours. Okay?"

Tina dropped to the floor and leaned back against the newly upholstered sofa and wrapped her arms about her legs. "What did you mean when you used the word *if?*"

Hank grabbed the iron poker from the hearth and stirred up the coals before sitting down beside her. "When I used the word *if?* When did I use it? I don't know what you mean."

"The night Lucky left. You said, 'If you had any feelings for me.' I just wondered what *if* meant. That's all."

"Oh, that word," he answered with a shy grin.

She scooted a bit closer to him, cocked her head a bit, and looked up into his eyes with an impish smile. "Yes, that word."

Hank stared into the fire for a long moment before responding to her poignant question. "Tink," he began slowly, "when you showed up in that department store that day, I–I—"

She gave a slight nudge to his ribs with her elbow. "Yes?"

"It—it was like you were a gift from God. I even thanked the Lord for sending you to me. I was so sure you were the answer to my prayers. I wouldn't admit this to anyone but you, but I've been pretty lonely these past few years. I haven't had anyone special in my life since—"

"Since Sheila—and Glorianna?"

He nodded.

"I thought maybe you and I could get together again, but when I met Lucky—"

"I guess you were surprised—"

"Worse than surprised, Tink. Shocked is a better word."

"I know I should have told you about him, but I honestly didn't think the two of you would ever meet. He wasn't supposed to come until after I called him. Then I met you at Beck's, moved into your house, and you began helping me, and—"

He shifted slightly to face her. "Why, Tink? Why Lucky? You two are nothing alike. How could you even consider marrying him? The man's not only obnoxious, he's a thief!"

Tina shuddered and began to weep uncontrollably. She no longer felt like smiling. "Oh, Hank, it's such a long story. I hardly know where to begin, but I—I guess I—I need to tell you the whole thing. You've been so kind, you deserve to know."

"Take your time. Begin anywhere you like."

Staring into the fire, her mind going back to that dreadful night and all of its ramifications, she began. She hated to have to repeat her awful ordeal. "I was penniless when I decided it was time to leave Juneau. I had to get away and start making it on my own. I borrowed five hundred dollars from Gram, plus enough money to get a plane ticket to Chicago, and—"

"Why Chicago? Why not Los Angeles? Or maybe Dallas?"

"Because I'd heard the jobs were plentiful in Chicago, and they paid pretty good too. I couldn't find an affordable apartment and ended up staying at the Rescue Mission for a couple of weeks. The people there were really nice. They helped me find a job and a place to live with a couple who worked second shift at a factory. They needed a baby-sitter to stay nights with their three children. In return, they gave me a place to stay and food to eat. I don't know what I would've done without them."

"Poor Tink. I never knew."

She could almost feel his compassion as his fingers entwined with hers. "I—I lived with them for nearly a year, saving every penny I could. I finally moved into a tiny apartment right next to the El, I read about the job with Beesom Parts, applied for it, and went to work in the sales department answering phones."

He nodded. "I've heard about them. Good solid company."

She smiled through her tears. "Yes, they are. And they've been good to me. From the phone job, I was promoted to the mailroom as assistant to the manager. I stayed there for about four years, taking business management courses at night at the local junior college. By the time I graduated, my company was just beginning to move its catalog onto the Internet, and I applied for a job on the design team. To my surprise, I got it. I've been there ever since, only now I'm the senior design technologist and have become part of the distribution management team."

"I'm very proud of you," Hank said, beaming with enthusiasm for her accomplishments. "It sounds like you've worked very hard to get to that position."

"I have," she agreed, wishing she could end the story there, on a high note.

"I didn't mean to interrupt. Go on with your story."

She sucked in a deep breath, knowing the rest of her tale was going to be much harder to tell. "About six years ago, after Gram fell and broke her hip, she admitted she could no longer take care of herself and needed to go into a care home. I couldn't bear the thought and invited her to leave Juneau, come to Chicago, and move in with me, so I could look after her."

"And she did?"

"Yes, but she refused to sell her house. She always said she wanted to die in her own home, like Grandpa did."

"I always liked your grandpa. Too bad he died so young."

"I know. Gram really misses him."

"So things worked out well for both of you, huh?"

She smiled. "Oh yes. Gram's been a delight to have around. We've had some great times together. She rarely complains about anything. Living together has been the best thing that could've happened to both of us."

"What did she think when you began dating Lucky?"

Her face sobered. "She never liked Lucky, but she—" Her words fell off. "Gram was always telling me I should find some nice guy and get out and enjoy life. She hated it that I spent all my free time at her side. I tried to tell her I didn't really care about dating and loved being with her, but I don't think she ever believed me. Besides, I really never met anyone I'd want to get serious with."

"Before you started dating Lucky?"

"No, Hank. It wasn't like that with Lucky and me."

Hank shrugged. "Then how was it?"

Her hand rose to cup her cheek, which was now healing nicely. "About six months ago, Gram had two bad spells with her heart. They really scared me. The second one put her in the hospital for a number of days, and her doctor said she needed someone to look after her around the clock. That's when they discovered the cancer, when they were running some routine tests on her. Her heart is terribly weak too."

"Oh, Tink, that's much like it was with Sheila. What an ordeal this has been for both of you."

"It was a real shock-a-roo all right. I located a nursing home about eight blocks from where I live and moved her there. Each night as I got off work, I'd take the El to the care home, made sure she ate her dinner, and visited with her a little bit. Sometimes we'd watch a show on TV together, and then I'd walk home."

Hank's brow lifted. "Wasn't that a little dangerous? Walking home by yourself?"

She nodded, rather than answering his question, needing time to regroup before going on. "I–I was always careful, and I tried to get home before eight. But one evening we were having so much fun, laughing and talking about Gram's childhood, I lost track of time and it was nearly nine before I left. I decided to take the bus, but it whizzed by just as I walked out the door. Rather than wait thirty minutes for the next one, I decided to walk. I'd lived in Chicago all those years and nothing had ever happened to me. I thought I'd be fine. It was only eight blocks. I guess I'd gotten a little cocky."

She almost hoped Hank would say something, get up to add another log to the fire, make some comment that would delay her story. Anything, but he didn't. He just sat silently holding her hand.

"It was dark by the time I left. I took off down the sidewalk, looking both ways, listening for footsteps behind me, keeping an eye on anyone approaching me, but everything seemed fine. I was just two blocks from my apartment and feeling pretty confident, when I reached an alley between two tall apartment buildings. Suddenly, out of nowhere, two motorcycles came roaring down the street and turned into the alley, stopping right in front of me. I panicked. I didn't know whether to try to run around them or scream or what."

Hank's grip tightened on her hand. "You had to have been terrified!"

She took a couple of deep breaths before continuing. Just relating the events made her stomach ache. "Before I could do anything, one of the men jumped off his cycle and grabbed me and pulled me into the alley behind a Dumpster."

"What about the other man?" he prodded softly.

"He—he parked his cycle and came and stood by us, watching and laughing at me as I struggled, sneeringly flashing his knife at me. The man holding me actually told me what he was going to do to me."

"Tink! Oh, Tink! No!" Hank said with a gasp.

"I—I tried to talk him out of it, but the more I begged the tighter he held me. He smelled awful, Hank! I'll never forget that smell. Like rotting meat. I begged the other guy to help me, but he only laughed in my face and said he'd take his turn with me when his buddy got finished."

"Did they—"

"Let me go on. Hopefully then you'll understand." *This is so hard to talk about.* "I thought I was a goner. I wanted to die. If I could've gotten that man's knife away from him, I think I would have plunged it into my own heart rather than face what I knew was about to happen to me."

Pausing to look into his eyes, she saw her own fear reflected back at her. "As he pulled my coat off and ripped my blouse, I heard the sounds of another motorcycle. I was afraid it was a third man, and I was terrified! But the man on this third motorcycle was coming to my rescue. Later, I learned he'd heard me scream. Anyway, he roared right in beside us and leaped off his cycle, right on top of the man who'd ripped my blouse, and began beating on him with his fists."

Hank's eyes widened as he listened. "Not Lucky—"

"Yes, it was Lucky."

"What about the other man? The one who—"

"That man tried to pull Lucky off, but he kept right on beating the man on top of me, yelling for me to run. Finally, I succeeded in getting out from under them. I wanted to run like he'd told me, but I couldn't just leave him there, fighting off the two men alone. It was as if I was glued to the spot. I just stood and screamed, hoping someone would hear me and call the police."

"Did anyone come?"

"No. Lucky kicked the second man in the groin, and he really got mad. He stabbed that knife into Lucky's back. I watched that wretched man as he pulled it back out. There was blood all over it. Then, with his foot, he flipped Lucky over on his back and stabbed him again, this time in his stomach. I've never seen so much blood. When he lifted the knife a third time, I realized I'd better get out of there fast before they came after me."

"What did you do?"

"I ran across the street into a liquor store and asked the clerk to call the police. Then stood there in the window, trembling in fear, as I watched the first man kick Lucky in the head with the toe of his big, heavy boot before they climbed back onto their motorcycles and sped off." She went limp as her hands covered her face. "He did it for me, Hank. And he didn't even know me."

❧

Hank couldn't believe what he was hearing. Lucky, the foul, uncouth man who'd been living in his house, eating his food, taking his truck, stealing his money, using his Lord's name in vain. That Lucky had put his life on the line for a stranger? Amazing!

"He nearly died. I rode with him in the ambulance to the emergency room. The doctors and nurses on duty just shook their heads when they saw him and realized how much blood he'd lost. I even heard one of the doctors tell a nurse that Lucky wouldn't make it through the night."

"But obviously, he did," Hank replied thoughtfully, running each detail over in his mind, thinking how heroic it was for Lucky to come to Tink's rescue.

"They took him to surgery to try to repair the damage. It took almost all night. The police came to the hospital and asked all kinds of questions. The rape counselors came and questioned me, telling me how fortunate I was to have had someone come to help me like he did. I didn't even get to talk to Lucky for two days, and even then, he was too weak to respond. I learned from a friend of his, who'd seen the story on the news, that Lucky had lost his job and was without any kind of insurance, so of course I offered to pay his hospital bill."

"It must have run in the thousands, considering the surgeries and special care he probably needed!" Hank said, letting out a low whistle.

Tina let out a sigh. "It did. I'll probably be paying on it the rest of my life."

"Whew, I hadn't realized things had been that rough for you. You poor kid, I'm beginning to see why you tolerate that man."

"I'm making good money now, and I'm thankful for my job. If it weren't for those doctor and hospital bills, I'd actually be able to live fairly comfortably."

Hank stretched his long legs out in front of him and gazed at the fire that would soon go out, if he didn't add another log. "He doesn't help with the bills?"

"No. He keeps saying he's going to, but he's been laid off a couple of times this year, and then he's had to quit a couple of jobs because of his injuries. He's not allowed to lift anything over thirty pounds. But I don't mind. I owe it to him. If it weren't for me, he'd never have been hurt like he was."

"I think I'm beginning to get the picture. You're convinced you owe that man your life, and you're willing to spend the rest of that life making it up to him, right?"

"Yes, I hadn't thought of it exactly that way, but yes, I do owe him my life. But please, don't say anything to him about this. He asked me not to tell you. He claims he's not a hero."

No, he'd rather I'd think you were madly in love with him! Hank stood to his feet, pulled a new log from the bin, and added it to the smoldering fire. "When did you decide to marry him, Tink?"

She looked up at him with such sad eyes he wanted to grab her and kiss her, to make all the hurts go away.

"It was his idea. I haven't exactly said yes."

"But you must have implied it." He hoped the disappointment in his heart wasn't revealed in his voice.

"I've never actually told him I was going to marry him, not really," she murmured softly. "I—I don't love him, not like I think a wife should love the man she's going to spend the rest of her life with."

"I knew it!" Hank said almost victoriously, slapping his palms together as he paced back and forth across the room. "I knew you didn't love him. Oh, Tink. I was so afraid—"

"But—I owe Lucky—"

He stopped pacing. "You can't marry a man you don't love. Don't you see? You'd be nothing but miserable being tied to him in that way. You'd both be miserable."

"You may be right, but I do owe him, and he wants to marry me." She covered her face with her hands, and he was sure she was crying. "I'm sorry, but this is so hard to talk about."

"And I'm sorry to put you through this, but I need to know. Make me understand." Hank could see just repeating the whole sordid experience was putting her through torture, but he had to know exactly where this fierce loyalty she had for Lucky was coming from and why she'd been willing to dedicate the rest of her life to the man.

"You don't know Lucky like I do. He can be so sweet. Sometimes, he says that—"

"Sweet?" Hank asked aloud with a grimace, stunned by her words. *Not the*

Lucky who followed you to Juneau! The Lucky I know seems to be taking advantage of a tragic situation, and milking it for all it's worth. "Look, Tink," he said, trying to soften his words, when what he really wanted to do was grab her by both arms and try to shake some sense into her. The woman seemed blind where Lucky was concerned. Always ready to stand up for him and his callous ways. "I can understand your loyalty and wanting to somehow pay him back for what he did. But marriage? No! You can't do it. You can't give your entire life to him because of one good deed."

She stared at him, her brows lifted. "A good deed? It was far more than a good deed, and he needs me. He put his own life in danger for me! All of his friends talk about how much he's changed since the two of us have been together."

"I'd hate to have seen what he was like before this so-called change!" Hank said with a grunt.

"Oh, I have to admit, at first, even though I knew what would've happened to me if he hadn't come along, I was afraid of him. He—he was everything my grandmother had warned me about." She blinked hard and looked away as she swallowed at a sob. "Wh–when he came roaring into that alley, I actually thought he was those horrid men's leader."

Hank dropped back down beside her and brushed a lock of hair from her forehead. "You poor, poor baby. I can't even imagine how frightened you must've been. I didn't mean to snap at you."

"It's impossible to put into words, especially when they—"

"Shh." Hank put a finger to her lips. The pain in her voice was almost more than he could stand. For a moment he, too, felt obligated to Lucky, knowing what would've happened to his Tink if the man hadn't come along and intervened. He touched a palm to her cheek and gently lowered her head onto his shoulder. "It's okay. You're safe now. It's over."

"Sometimes, when he lets his temper get the best of him, I have to admit I'm still a bit afraid of him," Tina said, lifting her gaze to his, finally. "But I'm sure he'd never hurt me."

"Are you trying to convince me? Or yourself?" he prodded softly, as his finger touched the adhesive bandage where the doctor had placed the two tiny stitches.

"Lucky says it'd be cheaper if we were married," she went on, ignoring his question. "We'd both be staying in my apartment, instead of paying for two places."

Hank gave her a dubious look. "You'd marry the man because it's cheaper to live together? That's hardly a good reason."

"Hank! Because of his injuries it's been impossible for him to keep a job, and I can't afford to keep paying his rent too."

"You're paying his rent?" Hank couldn't believe what he was hearing. "Tink, no wonder you're having money problems! Surely the man was paying his own way before he met you! Why not now?"

"I'm sure he was, but you saw what happened when you got him those jobs here in Juneau. He had to quit the very first day because he couldn't handle the work. It was too hard for him with his physical condition, a condition he suffered coming to help me!"

"Come on, Tink, get real! Face up to it. The man lied to you! I haven't wanted to say anything about it, but I've talked to his employers. He either quit because he didn't like the work, or he got in a fight with a customer or one of the other men on the crew. His physical ability had nothing to do with it!"

She reeled back in surprise. "But he said—"

"From my vantage point, I'd say he's lied to you a number of times. Did you actually hear his doctors say he shouldn't lift over thirty pounds or do physical labor?"

"Well, no." She hung her head and fiddled with a loose thread on the hem of her shirt. "Not really. He told me that's what they'd said."

Hank shrugged and leaned back against the sofa, locking his hands behind his head. "I rest my case."

"Tink," Hank began again, purposely keeping his voice soft and gentle, not wanting to offend her with his next question. "Think about your wedding night. Could—could you, as his wife, give yourself wholly to him?"

She began to weep. "Th–that's the reason I haven't s–said yes to L–Lucky. I–I don't th–think I c–could."

For some unknown reason, a comment he'd heard on the evening news years ago popped into Hank's mind. When the newscaster had chided Wayne Gretzky, the well-known ice hockey player, in an after-game interview, for missing so many shots with the puck, he'd reminded the man, "You'll always miss 100 percent of the shots you don't take."

This may be my only shot, Hank told himself as he mustered up his courage, *and I'm going to take it!* He bent and kissed Tina on her cheek, then whispered in her ear, "Could you give yourself wholly to me, if the two of us were married?"

Chapter 9

Tina felt her body go rigid. *What did Hank ask?* Had she misunderstood his words?

"Well, could you?"

Through her tears she forced a smile. "Wh–what kind of a qu–question is that?"

"Just curious," he said, looking as if he wished he'd never asked it.

She relaxed and smiled to herself through her tears as Hank blushed. "You in the marrying market, Mr. Gordon? I thought you said you were afraid of falling in love again."

He gave her a sheepish grin as he brushed away her tears with the pad of his thumb. "I'm not afraid of falling in love, Tink. It's the landing that scares me!"

"I know. I guess in some ways I'm like that too, although I've never felt true love for someone like you have. It's the idea of committing yourself to one person for the rest of your life that terrifies me. I always told myself when I stood at that altar and said I do, I would mean it. I would make those vows with the intent of staying with that one person until death do us part."

"But you're willing to commit to Lucky!"

"I said I felt I owed him my life, but I still haven't said yes to his marriage proposal. I just can't bring myself to do it. Not yet. But I can't put that decision off indefinitely. Bringing Gram back here and remodeling her house has just delayed it." Tina leaned her head onto his shoulder with a heavy sigh. "I just wish I loved Lucky like—"

"Like?"

In her heart she wanted to say "You," but instead she said, "Like a wife should."

❧

Hank nuzzled his chin in her hair. *Oh, dear God, why? Why did you let Tink back into my life? I didn't need this. Not after losing my precious Sheila and then Glorianna. There for a while I thought You'd sent Tink as the answer to my prayers. You know how I've longed to have a wife to share my life. She and I were getting along so well, having so much fun together, working side by side on her grandmother's house. Then Lucky appeared out of nowhere, staking his claims on her, taking her away from me, and I'm losing her, just like the others.*

"Hank?"

He pulled his thoughts together quickly. "Yes?"

"Tell me what it's like to be in love. Really in love, like you were with Sheila."

Hank sniffed at the sweet fragrance of Tina's hair. "Well, it's hard to describe that kind of love to someone else. At first you find yourself wanting to be around that person every minute." *Like I've wanted to be around you.* "You want to do nice things for them." *Like helping you work on your grandmother's house.* "You go out of your way to make sure they're content and happy." *Like I do when I worry about you and try to make sure things are going okay in your life.* "You find yourself thinking about them every moment you're apart." *I can't get my work done at the office for thinking about you.* "You try to provide for any needs they may have." *I've wanted you to stay in my home rather than a boring old motel room, and I certainly wanted to make sure you ate proper meals and got a good, restful night's sleep!*

She nudged him in the ribs with her elbow. "Your description sounds like a mom with a new baby, not the kind of love I'm talking about," she told him in a teasing manner. "I'm talking about a love between a man and a woman."

Hank reassessed his words, amused at her reaction. "Umm, I guess in many ways, the love of a mother for her newborn child is much the same. She'd lay down her life for that child." He flinched and wished he hadn't uttered those words. That was exactly what Lucky had done for her! "I–I mean—" he stammered, wishing he could withdraw his statement and begin afresh. "I–I mean, she's given birth to that child, and in some ways, it's still a part of her own body." *That made a lot of sense, stupid!* he told himself angrily. "She—ah—"

"Lucky did that for me," she interjected quietly.

Hank wiped his hand across his eyes. *You big oaf, you're only making his case stronger. Think before you speak!* "Yes, I know he did," he said, being careful not to add more brownie points to his adversary's score. "But it's not the same. Oh, not that those things aren't valid, they are. But there's more to it than laying down your life for that person. Soldiers do it for people they've never even met when they take up arms and go to the battlefield. Firemen do it. Policemen do it too. Sometimes living with that person is the hard part. You know, once you're married, things change. Dating and saying I do are two different things."

"Different? How?"

"Well, all the time Sheila and I were dating, she looked like the perfect woman. I mean, her makeup was perfect, every hair was in place, she was always dressed beautifully. She said the right things, did the right things." Hank smiled and let out a chuckle. "And anytime I was with her, I made sure I was clean shaven, wore my best clothes, kept my hair cut like she liked it, took her to places she liked, even though I'd rather have gone someplace else. But—" He snickered.

"But what?" she asked, gazing up into his eyes.

"Well," he continued after adjusting his position a bit, "the honeymoon was perfect. We made over each other like we were a couple of lovesick teenagers. But once we got back to Juneau, things changed. For both of us."

"Changed? How?"

He grinned. "I'll never forget that first night after we got home. I was too tired to shower, so I just pulled out the old T-shirt I normally slept in and crawled into bed as soon as Sheila disappeared into the bathroom. Then ten minutes later she came out, looking like an escapee from a horror movie, with some weird-looking blue thing tied around her head and thick pink cream slathered all over her face. All I could see were two round holes where her eyes had been. I nearly screamed out in fright!"

Tina laughed. "Sure you did."

"Well, actually I wasn't scared, but I was sure shocked. This was not the woman I'd dated. Instead of that pretty pink nightgown she'd worn on our honeymoon, she was wearing a long-sleeved flannel thing that hung clear to the floor. I took one look at her and wondered if I was going to have to face this same monster each night of our life."

"Well," Tina said, nudging him again, "from the sounds of it, you didn't look much better. An old T-shirt? Come on. And I'll bet you didn't even shave before you went to bed. That after-five shadow of yours probably wasn't too appealing to her either. Did you shave on your honeymoon every night?"

Hank nodded slightly, hating to admit the truth. "Yeah, I did."

"Okay, go on. What else changed?"

"Lots of things. I was a struggling attorney at the time, just out of law school, and we really had to budget. I complained to Sheila constantly about her spending. I remember one time I even hit the roof because she'd bought drapes for our little apartment without asking me. We had a doozy of an argument and didn't speak to each other for days."

"I'll bet she had her complaints too. I doubt you were Mr. Perfect."

"Oh, yeah, and she let me know about them. 'Hank, don't leave your dirty socks on the floor. Hank, put the lid down on the toilet. Hank, wipe your feet before you come in the house. Hank, you play the radio too loud. Hank, don't use so much salt.' On and on and on. But I deserved all of it. I'd lived alone too long, I guess. I didn't realize those things were important to her. Just like she didn't realize how important my dog was to me. Or why I spent so much time tinkering with our old car. Or why I turned out the lights every time I left a room, or how leaving the lid off the toothpaste just didn't seem important to me. And neither did the tiny spots I left on the mirror when I used dental floss. That's all part of being married, Tink. I know each of these are only little things, but they're reality. Two lives trying to mesh together. They're the bits and pieces that take the bloom off the rose. Divorces occur because of the little things that get on people's nerves, their personal idiosyncrasies. I know. As an attorney I'm confronted with it every day as I try to help people weed out their assets after a divorce. Problem is, like it says in God's Word, we can't see the beam in our own eye. We never see our own problems. Only the other person's."

He waited, but Tina didn't respond. She just looked as though she was pondering his words, and he hoped he was getting through to her.

"It's even difficult for a couple to have an ideal marriage when they both love God, but it sure helps. A marriage happens, and suddenly you have someone else in your life to consider, and it's not easy, even if you love them. Especially if you've been living alone for a long time."

She eyed him suspiciously. "If marriage is so bad, would you ever want to do it again?"

"We're not talking about me, Tink." He shifted uncomfortably, not ready to answer her question, a question he'd deliberated on many times since having her back in his life. "And besides, I didn't say marriage was bad. I merely said things are different when you're dating than when you're married. It's not all fun and games. It's monthly bills, responsibilities, putting up with one another's faults and weird little habits—that sort of mundane stuff."

"What if another woman came along and swept you off your feet? Would you be willing to have another try at it?"

She'd put him on the spot and asked the one question he wouldn't even attempt to answer. He loved having Tina back in his life, and he wished he didn't have to constantly compete with Lucky for her attention, but marriage? As much as he thought he wanted another woman to share his life, was he actually ready to take another walk down the aisle to the altar? To take another chance on losing a woman he loved? "I'm—I'm not exactly sure," he finally said.

Tina eyed him for a moment, as if she wasn't sure what to say next, then stood to her feet, yawned, and, stretching out first one arm and then the other, said, "I'm beat. Let's call it a night."

Later, long after the house was silent, Hank knelt beside his bed, folding his hands in prayer and searching his heart before his heavenly Father. *God, I think I love Tink, but at this point in my life, I'm not sure what love really is. I did a lousy job of explaining it to her.* Remembering their conversation brought a smile to his lips. *I enjoy being with Tink, hearing her laughter, sharing her sorrows about her grandmother, helping her at the house, having her sit by my side in church on Sunday mornings—but—is it because I love her? Or because I've been alone so long and she's the first woman who has paid any real attention to me since I lost Glorianna? Could it be only friendship I'm feeling for her? Or is it the real thing? I've always heard loneliness does strange things to people. Am I reacting out of loneliness? Is this the reason Tina so willingly let Lucky into her life?*

He took a deep breath, letting it out slowly. *Oh, Lord, I don't know what I feel, but I sure don't want to make any more mistakes. Keep me from making a fool out of myself. Help me, please. Give me wisdom and discernment. When it comes to women, I'm at a total loss.*

Early the next morning, long before Hank's alarm clock was set to go off, Lucky loudly wheeled the missing truck into Hank's driveway, hitting the trash can with a loud bang. Hank, Tina, and Faynola all came running from their bedrooms, wrapping their robes about themselves and hurrying to the door.

"You'd better stay in your room, Faynola. This could get ugly."

The woman nodded and scurried away.

Hank flung the door open just as Lucky reached for the knob.

"Well, howdy, folks," he said with a toothy grin, swinging the set of keys on his finger as if nothing had ever happened. "Breakfast ready?"

Tina rushed up to him and banged into his chest with her fists, her face red with anger. "How dare you show up here and even think of breakfast after what you've done, stealing from Hank, taking his truck like that, and disappearing?"

Hank's fists doubled at his sides, not because he was ready to strike out at the man, but because he was trying to control his anger. "If it weren't for Tina begging me not to call the sheriff, you'd be in jail right now," he snarled at the arrogant man.

"Aw, I wasn't worried. I knew she'd talk you out of it." Lucky flung one of his arms about Tina and pulled her close as she struggled to keep her distance. "My little sugar babe loves me. She'd never let you call the sheriff, would you, honey?"

It was all Hank could do to keep from wringing the man's neck and holding him until the sheriff could come and arrest him. "My truck better be in one piece," he said in a low monotone, forcing himself to hold back his wrath.

With a snort followed by a belly laugh, Lucky let loose his grasp on Tina. "Your truck was okay 'til I hit that trash can someone left sittin' in the driveway."

"Give me the keys," Tina demanded, holding out her hand and standing toe to toe with the man, her eyes filled with rage. "Now."

Lucky's face sobered. "Ah, Tina, honey, don't be so testy. I was just havin' me some fun, out meetin' some of these Alaskan Eskimos. I'm tired of workin' all the time."

This time Hank had to bite his tongue, hard, to keep from reminding Lucky who had actually done all the work on the house and who had quit his job.

"I should've called the sheriff myself," she told Lucky as he held the keys just out of her reach, her patience with the man at a final end.

"Aw, babe. I was just teasin' you. I was really out lookin' for another job. I'd never—"

"Lucky, don't lie to me! You didn't quit those other jobs because you couldn't do the work! You got fired! Hank told me!"

Lucky whirled around and faced Hank with fire in his eyes. "He's the one who lied!"

Hank met his hard stare with one of his own as he grabbed the phone and poised a finger over the keypad. "Shall we call one of your ex-bosses? Let him tell Tina why he fired you?"

"Are you calling me a liar?"

Tina cringed at the word, suddenly aware life was repeating itself. Her father had been a liar and a cheat, claiming others did him wrong, never able to hold a job, or even wanting to. How many times had they gone without food because he wouldn't get out and provide for his family instead of lying on the couch all day, guzzling his beer? Her parents' marriage had been a rotten one. Both her mom and dad had been miserable. When they weren't drunk, they were fighting or passed out on the couch. Did she want the same kind of marriage? Is that what life would be like married to Lucky?

"I'm the one who called you a liar," she shouted back at him. "Leave Hank out of this!"

"Leave him out of it? He's the one who's turned you against me!"

"If anyone turned me against you, it's you yourself! Not Hank!" she shot back, her heart racing with anger at herself for how foolish she'd been. For the first time since that fateful night when he'd come to her rescue, she was seeing the real Lucky. How could she have been so blind? He had been using her! Just like Hank had said.

Lucky whirled around and jerked his shirt up, exposing his bare back. "See that, Tina! That's what I got when I took those guys on for you. I nearly died savin' you! And this is the thanks I get for it?" He swung around and, with his thumbs pushing the waistband of his jeans down a couple inches, revealed a second scar, this one causing a deep indentation on his belly. "Old Hank ever put his life in danger for you like I did?" he shouted, leaning toward her.

"I would, if necessary!" Hank responded, without hesitation.

Lucky tugged his jeans back into place and gave Hank a mocking sneer. "Don't believe him, Tina, he's lying! He wouldn't do it."

Tina turned her head away, the sight of the deep scars bringing back the horrible remembrances of the night she'd worked hard to forget.

Hank grabbed a manila envelope from the desk drawer and pulled out a handful of official-looking papers, holding them out to Lucky. "Oh? And I suppose the Chicago police department is lying too."

Tina jerked the papers from Hank's hands and shuffled through them. "What are these?"

"Just a few police reports on some of Lucky's shenanigans. I got them from a friend of mine in the Chicago D.A.'s office."

"Lies, nothing but lies," Lucky shouted back in his defense, but the look on his face said otherwise, as arrogance turned to fear. "They're all against me. I never did none of that stuff."

Tina's jaw dropped as she read aloud from the first paper. "You have a police record?"

Chapter 10

When Lucky didn't answer she read on. "And you've been in prison? For armed robbery?" Her heart pounded against her chest as she thought of all the times she'd been alone with the deceitful man.

"I was framed," he said simply, with a sideways glance toward Hank. "The witnesses lied. Somebody paid them off."

Tina dropped down into a chair with a gasp as she flipped through the handful of papers. "You've been married! You told me you've always been single, and you've—"

"Three times!" Hank interjected, stepping up close to Tina, "and he's still married to his last wife."

Tina sucked in a deep breath and let it out slowly, shaking her head sadly and feeling like the most gullible person on the planet. "Oh, Lucky, I trusted you. You should never have lied to me like you did. And to think I was ready to marry you and spend the rest of my life trying to make it up to you for what you did for me."

"Keep reading, Tink," Hank prodded in a firm voice.

Tina blinked back the tears filling her eyes. She'd believed everything Lucky had ever told her, and he'd done nothing but lie to her.

"He's been arrested for domestic violence too. Several times. He beat one of his wives so badly she ended up in the hospital and had to have emergency surgery!" Hank said, pointing to the paper. "If you'd married him, his next victim could've been you."

Suddenly Tina's anger turned toward Hank. "You've known this and you didn't tell me?"

"The fax came in late last night," he explained quickly. "You were already in bed. I was going to tell you first thing this morning, but then that man came roaring into the driveway, waking us all up, and I didn't get a chance. I'd never keep something this serious from you, Tink. Surely you know that."

"He's jealous. He's always been out to get me, babe. Come on back to Chicago with me. Let's get outta this screwy place. You and me don't belong here."

"You can't be serious! After what I've just learned about you, you think I'd go with you? Marry you?"

Lucky spun around, his eyes menacing and dangerous, the lines deeply set in his forehead, his fists clenched. After rambling off a bunch of obscenities at

318

Hank, he added, "You're the cause of this. Me and her was doin' fine, until you came along. I oughta—"

Hank stood up to his full height, looking as if he was ready to do battle. "I'd think twice before swinging those fists of yours," he said coolly. "Remember, I'm the guy who is going to file charges on you for the theft of the money you took from my desk and stealing my pickup. Add that to the other things you're wanted for, plus leaving the state of Illinois without permission when you're still on parole—"

Tina's hand flew to her mouth. "You're on parole?"

"He sure is. And he's wanted for questioning on a burglary that happened the day before he left Chicago to come to Juneau." Hank walked quickly to the phone and picked up the receiver. "I'd say once I call the sheriff and let them know where you are, they'll come after you with lights flashing and sirens screaming, and you'll be heading back to prison."

Without warning, Lucky sprinted forward and grabbed Hank's robe, pushing him into the wall, his nose mere inches from Hank's face. "I'm gonna get you, Mr. Lawyer. You and Tina! High and mighty people like you make me sick. If it weren't for you bein' so nosy and lookin' for any excuse you could find to take her away from me, nobody would've known I was in Juneau. Now because of you I'm on the run again." He jabbed an elbow hard into Hank's ribs.

"No, you're not going to blame me for this," Hank said resolutely, his voice showing no sign of fear, his hand still clutching the phone. "You did this to yourself."

"I don't get mad, Hank old boy, I get even!" Lucky said through gritted teeth, as his elbow made another quick jab into Hank's ribs. "You'd better watch your backside! Both of you!"

Tina propelled herself into the man, one hand flailing at him furiously, the other still holding onto the papers. "Leave Hank alone! He's only trying to protect me!"

Lucky released his grip on his adversary's robe and grabbed Tina's wrist. "I put my life on the line for you, and this is the thanks I get?"

Hank reached toward Lucky, but Tina waved him off. This was between Lucky and herself. It was up to her to get things settled.

"I do owe you, Lucky," she said, gulping hard. "If it weren't for you fighting those men off that night—" Her voice quavered a bit, but she went on. "When I saw how badly you were hurt, I vowed I'd spend the rest of my life making it up to you." Her emotions were about to get the better of her, but she hung on. "I would have. Even though I didn't love you, I was planning on marrying you. And—"

"Until he came along," Lucky shot in between her words. He grabbed the papers from her hand, wadded them up, threw them on the floor at her feet, then pointed a long bony finger toward Hank. "This rich lawyer made you forget all about old Lucky and the beating he took to save you from being raped—or worse!"

319

She cast a quick glance at Hank. "Being with Hank only made me see what real love could be. I'd never experienced that before. Can't you see, Lucky? Even if I'd married you, the truth about your prison record would have come out eventually, not to mention the fact that you are on parole and wanted for questioning and still have a wife! What kind of a life would that have been for either of us?"

Lucky's hold on her wrist increased, and she wanted to scream out in pain.

"You're no better than he is," he snapped, with squinted eyes and flaring nostrils. "I risked my life and what did you give me in return? The boot, that's what! When you ran into your old boyfriend! Suddenly what old Lucky had done wasn't so important to you!"

"No, that's not it at all," Tina countered. "You're a criminal, a liar, and a cheat, and still married!"

"Yeah? Well, that's the way I see it! To me, you and old Hank here are two of a kind, and I'm gonna—"

Hank stepped in between the two, squarely facing up to Lucky. "Yeah? And exactly what are you gonna do?"

"Like I said, I don't get mad, Hank old boy, I get even. I swear I will. I'm not going to spend another day in prison." Lucky stepped back a couple of steps, pulled a knife from his pocket, and released the long, shiny blade with a loud snap. "You file a complaint on me, and I'll kill you." He waved the knife menacingly through the air, its tip nearly touching Tina's chin. "Both of you!"

The malicious man turned on his heels and raced out the front door, leaving the pair gaping after him.

Hank threw his arms about Tina and pulled her close, his hand stroking her back protectively as the sound of his pickup starting and the squealing of tires told them Lucky had, once again, taken his truck.

"Now what?" Tina asked as she rested her head against him, her heart tensing with fear against his strong chest. "Do you think he meant wh—what he said?"

Hank placed a gentle kiss on her forehead before releasing her and grabbing the phone. "I'm sure of it. I'm going to call the sheriff."

She watched as he dialed the number, knowing it had to be done, despite Lucky's threat. Lucky was a menace to society. He'd been involved in armed robbery, and he'd served time in prison. It was only a matter of time before he was found.

❧

Hank watched Tina as he spoke to the sheriff. He couldn't even begin to imagine the turmoil she must be experiencing at that moment, and he almost felt guilty for putting her through it. He'd had his suspicions about the man from the first moment they'd met. Tina had looked at Lucky through rose-colored glasses, seeing only his good points and his willingness to help her when she'd needed it.

When he finished his conversation, he placed the phone back in its cradle and turned to her, his expression somber. "Pack your bags. We're going away for a few days."

She looked up at him with the round, confused eyes of a child. "Why? Where are we going, and what about Gram?"

"She'll be safe. It's not her he's after. You can phone her and tell her where you are." The last thing he wanted to do was frighten her even further, but she had to know. "Did you read the last page of that fax I gave you? About Lucky? The notes my friend at the D.A.'s office added?"

She shook her head. "I didn't have time."

"He said Lucky was considered armed and dangerous and a real threat to society. That all precaution should be taken by anyone around him, especially those trying to arrest him."

Tina scrubbed a hand across her face. "Oh, Hank. What did I get you into?"

"You didn't get me into anything. I knew Lucky was trouble the minute I met him. I could've walked away then, but I didn't. I got myself into this with my eyes wide open. Don't blame yourself."

"I–I wish I'd been that perceptive."

He took her hand in his and lifted it to his lips. "You only saw in him what he wanted you to see. It wasn't your fault. Any woman in your shoes would have felt the same obligation." He smiled at her, hoping to somehow relieve her fear. "Hey, if he'd done that for me, I would have felt the same way."

"But he's threatened you. Both of us! I'm so afraid—"

"That's the very reason we're getting out of here for a few days, to give them time to find him. He can't get far. They'll get him soon, then we can come back home."

"But what if he talks one of the seaplane pilots into taking him to Anchorage or Vancouver or some other place? Like you thought he might have done before?"

What she was saying was, indeed, a possibility, one he hadn't wanted to voice. "Let's let the sheriff worry about it. They know what to do. I'm going to take you where he won't find us, just to be on the safe side. Although I doubt his threats to kill us were real," he said, trying to sound as if he believed it.

"But what if they were—"

Hank put a finger to her lips. "Go pack. We'll take Faynola and Ryan with us. I have a place where we'll be safe."

Thirty minutes later, the SUV backed out of the driveway with Hank at the wheel, Tina by his side, Faynola in the seat behind them, and the big Siberian husky in the back, with his nose pressed up against the rear glass.

❧

Tina caught a glimpse of Hank's strong face in the rearview mirror. How thankful she was for him. If she hadn't run into him in the department store that day, her life might have turned out very differently. She shuddered at the thought.

What if she'd married Lucky, only to find out later he was still married? And had served time in prison? Had been arrested for domestic violence? And was even on parole? The thoughts made her stomach clench, and she thought she was going to be sick. But seeing Hank seated beside her, knowing he was doing all he could to protect her, set her mind at ease.

"Where are we going?" she asked, as they finally turned off the highway and onto a narrow winding road, covered over with a dense growth of trees.

"A friend of mine has a cabin up here." Hank gave her a wink. "Lucky won't be able to find us. We'll be safe."

She leaned her head against the headrest, linked her fingers together over her chest, and closed her eyes. "Good. I don't want to see you get hurt."

Hank let out a chuckle. "Me, get hurt? You don't think I can take care of myself? And you?"

She winced. "Not if Lucky has a gun."

He reached an open palm to her, and she slipped a hand into it. "Don't you realize, Tink, I wasn't kidding when I said I, too, would give my life to protect you?"

The words hit her right in the heart. Hank meant what he said! He would give his life to protect her.

"Did you hear me?" he prodded softly when she didn't make a comment. "That's what true love is all about, Tink. Loving the other person so much, their life is more valuable to you than your own. It's the kind of love between a man and a woman God speaks about in His Word. Not the kind of love Lucky said he had for you. His kind demanded retribution."

Tina pondered what he said. "But—you don't love me like—"

Hank gave her hand a squeeze. "Yeah? Who said?"

"What about groceries?" Faynola called out from the backseat, unknowingly interrupting their conversation.

Hank let loose of Tina's hand and turned slightly in the seat to face her. "All taken care of. While you two were packing, I called the caretaker, and by the time we arrive he should have everything we'll need all stocked up. He and his wife promised to have the furnace turned up and a roaring fire in the fireplace."

❧

"Whose cabin is this?" Tina asked, as the two of them lingered over Faynola's coffee the next morning at the little table in the crude kitchen.

"Belongs to one of my clients. He's always after me to use it. I thought this was the appropriate time. Most folks don't even know it's here."

"The perfect place for hiding out?" Her lips curled into a slight smile. "Just what we need."

"Or a place to relax for a few days," Hank countered, taking on a smile of his own. "How about a hike in the woods? Pretty country out there."

Tina nodded. Her insecurities of yesterday seemed to have faded somewhat with the good night's sleep. "Sure. I'd love it."

The two pulled on their heavy coats and boots and started up a path someone had made through the trees. It was a beautiful cloudless day, a perfect Alaskan day, the kind written about in travel brochures, picturing a late season snow.

"Why, Hank?" Tina asked him thirty minutes later as they came to a slight clearing.

Hank brushed the freshly fallen snow off a roughly hewn seat with his glove, sat down, and motioned her to sit beside him. "Why, what?"

"Why would you do all of this for me? I'm sure you have much too much work piled up in your office to take time off to watch over me."

He brushed a lock of hair from her forehead, then took her hand in his, his gloved thumb working gently over her knuckles. "Because you and your safety are important to me."

"But you haven't seen me since we were teenagers. It's been years."

He scooted a bit closer to her. "Don't laugh, but I've been asking myself the same thing. There's just something about you that brings out the hero in me, I guess. I like the feeling."

"I'm not worth it," Tina confessed, as she pulled her collar up about her neck. "You shouldn't be putting yourself in jeopardy to protect me. I'm a nobody."

"Of course you're worth it. Whatever makes you say such a thing?"

Tina sat silently for a moment. "You're so—so godly."

"Godly? Me?" Hank sat up straight. "I'm far from godly, although I'd like to be."

"Don't tease me, Hank. You know what I mean. Everything you do is right. Has meaning. You're—perfect."

"Oh, Tink, I'm far from perfect, believe me. You don't know what goes on in my head."

"Like what?"

Hank looked pensive. "Like the anger I felt the day Lucky kicked Ryan. Or when I found out he'd stolen that money from my desk. Or the way I wanted to punch his lights out when he treated you like he did. Oh, I'm far from perfect!"

"But—" She paused. "Wasn't all that what they call justifiable anger?"

He grinned. "Now you sound like a lawyer."

"Well, wasn't it?"

"Umm, I guess you could say so, but that doesn't make it right. I should've let God take care of it, instead of wanting to handle things my own way."

"See, that's what I mean. You're godly!"

He gave her hand a squeeze. "Tina, being godly isn't being a good person. Being godly means living by God's standards, with Him at the helm of your life. As Master of all you do, think, and are. Does that make sense?"

She gave him a slight nod. "Sorta. I remember hearing things like that when you and I attended Sunday school and church when we were kids. But that's been so long ago, I've forgotten most of what I learned. I hadn't been to church in years, until I came back to Juneau and started attending with you. Gram tried to talk to me many times about God, but I wouldn't listen. I–I thought she was being old-fashioned."

"It's never too late in God's sight."

"I'm not worthy of His love. I've turned my back on Him for so long. He's probably forgotten all about the little girl who used to pray to Him every night."

"He never forgets, and He's always waiting with open arms. A relationship with us is what He longs for most, but we have to invite Him into our lives. He won't barge in uninvited. And we have to confess our need of Him." Hank released her hand and slipped an arm about her shoulders. "As I recall, a skinny little girl with long pigtails went to the altar the same night I did and asked God to take charge of her life. Do you remember that?"

She leaned her head onto his shoulder. "Yes, I remember, and I meant it then, but—"

"Just tell Him you're sorry, Tink. Don't you know in Isaiah 49 He says He has engraved you on the palms of His hands? He's never forgotten you. Ask Him to move in and take up residence in your heart again. Put Him first in your life."

Watery eyes lifted to his. "And everything will be rosy?"

Hank laughed. "No, not rosy, but you'll have Him to turn to when things aren't rosy. He's always there to listen. His will, although at times we wonder about it, is always best for us."

She thought long and hard about his words. In her heart, she knew he was right, but was she ready to take such a step and commit her life to God? At this moment, He seemed so far away. "Let me think about it," she told Hank as she rose and pulled him up with her. "I'm not quite ready."

Hank felt his heart clench. Tink had been so close to saying yes to God. He could feel it. If only he had the right words to make her understand. If only he was as godly as she thought he was. *Lord,* he prayed as he walked along close beside her, his heart filled with both sympathy and love, *if this is the woman You would have me spend the rest of my life with, now that Lucky is out of the picture, give me a sign. Somehow, let me know. I don't want to make any mistakes, for Tink's sake as well as mine.*

He'd barely gotten the words out of his mouth when a large tree fell across their path and a frightened Tina literally leaped into his arms. Hank smiled to himself. *Was that You, God?*

324

Chapter 11

I don't know when I've enjoyed myself this much," Tina confessed as Hank squatted down in front of her, with Ryan at his side, and snapped the clasp on her cross-country ski boots. "I'd nearly forgotten how much I loved Alaska."

"Kinda gets in your blood, living here. I've traveled to most of the touristy spots of the world, but there's no place like Alaska. I don't think I could live anywhere else." He snapped the other clasp and pointed to one of the mountaintops barely peeking over the trees. "I love this country. Have you ever seen a more beautiful place?"

Tina shielded her eyes from the morning sun and watched as an eagle soared high above them. "No, I wish I'd never left."

"You had good reason." He stood and stretched his arms wide, taking in a deep breath of the morning air. "I don't know how you stood living at home as long as you did."

"Maybe I should never have left. Maybe if I'd stayed—"

"Tink, you did all you could. You have no reason to feel guilty."

She knotted her scarf tighter about her neck. "But maybe if I'd been more patient with him, Dad wouldn't have—"

"It was his choice, Tink. You could've been an angelic child, and he still would have taken his own life. If not then, sometime."

She stood silently as the eagle landed on the very tip of a tall tree, wondering at the magnificence of the mighty bird.

Hank couldn't keep his gaze off Tina. The rosy glow on her cheeks, brought on by the chilly Alaskan air, made her all the more beautiful. "Hard to tell why he did what he did. I guess people do it to avoid the realities of life."

"I don't think they ever loved me. Not really." She lowered her eyes. "I hate to admit it, but I was ashamed of them. When we had programs at school, I actually hoped they wouldn't show up, so the other kids wouldn't know I had drunks for parents. Wasn't that terrible of me?"

"No, I understand. I was there, remember? I saw the empty beer cans and wine bottles piled up on your front porch. Not to mention the dozens of liquor bottles and cans strewn about the yard. Living in that situation would embarrass any kid. I know you did what you could to make that place look presentable. You literally raised yourself, Tink. If their brains weren't fried, they'd have been very proud of you."

"That's no excuse. I should've been there for them. Maybe I was the problem. Maybe they never wanted kids. Maybe it'd have been better for everyone if I'd never been born."

He grabbed her arm. "Don't say such a thing. Of course they wanted you."

"We don't know that. They never told me they loved me, not once, and never treated me like your parents treated you!"

Hank had no answer. He knew firsthand what Tina was saying was the truth. He'd seen her father hit her for no reason at all. He'd seen her mother so drunk she couldn't even hold a hairbrush to Tina's head. He remembered the wrinkled clothes she'd worn to school because her mother wouldn't iron them for her. "My mom sure loved you."

She smiled. "Yes, I know. If it weren't for her and the way she took me under her wing and for my grandmother, well—I wouldn't have had any idea what a real loving mother should be like. I loved your mother too, and I'll always be grateful to her for being kind to a little ragamuffin like me."

"You were the daughter she wanted and never had. God only allowed them to have one child. Me!" Hank told her with a laugh as he pointed to his chest with his forefinger.

"You? Get serious, Hank. You were the delight of both your father and mother. You have no idea how lucky you were to be born to them. When I have children, I—" She stopped midsentence. "Maybe God won't let me have children. I know I'd be a lousy mother."

Hank slipped his arm about her shoulders. "Of course He will. He knows your heart, Tink. He knows what you've gone through."

"Do you think I was so hungry for love, I mistook Lucky's attention for the real thing?"

He had to examine his own motives before answering. "Maybe."

Tina pulled away from him and snatched up her ski poles. "Enough of this kind of talk. Let's get going!"

Hank watched as she took off across the clearing, and his heart went out to her. *Is what I feel for you sympathy or love?* Then lifting his eyes heavenward, he sent up a prayer. *Please, God. Send me another sign. Like I said, I sure don't want to make any mistakes.*

Supper was ready and on the table when the two came in from their day in the snow, and Faynola met them at the door. "You two are sunburned! Didn't you wear that sunscreen I found in the cupboard?"

Hank pulled off his stocking cap, then his coat. "Oops, I forgot. It's still in my pocket."

"You had sunscreen in your pocket?" Tina asked, hanging her coat on the hook next to his. "Why didn't you tell me? I would've used it. My nose is a bit sore already."

Hank touched the tip of her nose with his finger. "Because I think you look cute all pink like that."

"You'd better look in a mirror, Hank Gordon. You look like a raccoon with those big circles around your eyes!"

Faynola shook her head. "Will you two quit your bantering and come to the table? Things are getting cold."

After supper, Tina helped her clear the table and wash up the dishes before slipping into her nightgown, robe, and slippers. Hank had already had his shower and was sitting on the floor in front of the fireplace when she joined him. "Did you call your grandmother again?"

"Yes, she said she was fine and sends her love. I didn't give her many details. No sense in worrying her."

"It's been a good day, hasn't it?" he asked as she snuggled up close to him.

She nodded and leaned her head on his shoulder. "Umm, it's been a wonderful day."

"What'll we do tomorrow?"

She appeared thoughtful. "If we have to stay here tomorrow, how about building a snowman?"

He smiled and rested his head against hers. "I think there's an old fisherman's hat in the closet we can put on him, and I saw an old broom in the shed when I got the ski poles out."

"Maybe Faynola will let me have a carrot for his nose."

"We can put my muffler around his neck."

"You two sound like a couple of little kids," Faynola told them as she entered the room, her presence causing them to suddenly pull apart. "I'm going on to bed, but first I wanted to ask you, Mr. Gordon: Have you heard anything from the sheriff?"

Hank's boyish expression disappeared. "I'm glad my friend leaves his phone connected. I called the sheriff again, right after we got in tonight. Looks like we're going to be here for at least another day. They haven't found any trace of him, but—" He paused with a quick look toward Tina.

"What, Hank? Tell me."

"Someone robbed a convenience store about midnight last night, and the description the clerk gave them fits Lucky to a tee. Even the surveillance camera shot looked like him, even though the man had a stocking cap pulled down low on his forehead. Though I doubt he's out of money."

Tina let out her breath slowly. "Oh, Hank, no."

"Anyway, so far, other than him meeting their description, there's no sign of him. No one actually saw the vehicle he was in. He must've parked it out back. My guess is he stole another truck. They're still checking. But they're pretty sure Lucky was the guy on the videotape."

Tina swallowed hard. "And I'm the one who brought him into all your lives."

"You can't feel that way, Miss Tina. It's not your fault," Faynola assured her, patting her arm. "No one blames you."

"She's right, Tink. You're not to blame at all. You only tried to help Lucky. You had no idea things would turn out like this."

Faynola yawned. "Well, good night. I'm going to go to my room and read. Let me know if you need anything."

Hank smiled at Tina. "We'll be fine, Faynola." When the pleasant woman was out of earshot, he added, "I love that woman, but three's a crowd."

She rested her head on his shoulder, and they sat staring into the fire, simply enjoying one another's company. It seemed to Hank nothing needed to be said. Just being together like that was enough. When the clock chimed ten, they said good night and went to their rooms.

As Hank knelt by his bed and folded his hands, he pursed his lips and shook his head. "I should've kissed her!"

He phoned his office early the next morning and discovered there were some important papers he needed to sign for one of his most prestigious clients. "I hate to leave you two by yourselves, but I think it'd be safer if I drove into town alone. What I have to do at the office will only take about fifteen minutes, and I'll head right back. You have the phone. If you need anything you can call the caretaker, but I doubt it'll be necessary. There's no way Lucky could know where we are, and I think his threats were nothing more than blowing smoke. He only wanted to frighten us."

"Oh, Hank, do you have to go?" Tina asked as she followed him to the door.

"Yep, but I'll be back quick as a wink. You'll hardly know I'm gone. I'm leaving Ryan here. Keep him in the cabin with you."

❧

As promised, Hank was back in only a couple of hours, bearing two large shopping bags. One for Tina and one for Faynola. "You have to open them at the same time," he told them with a sly grin.

The two women giggled as each watched the other and, at the exact same time, pulled open the tops of their bags.

"Mr. Gordon!" Faynola shrieked as she pulled out a soft, fuzzy teddy bear dressed in overalls, with a big red bandana tied about his neck. "I love him." She hugged the bear tightly to her with a giggle. "I haven't had a teddy bear since I was six. Thank you so much!"

Tina took her time taking out her gift, although her hand had gone into the bag at the same time as Faynola's hand had reached into hers. "I like to prolong my surprises," she told Hank as she continued to feel around in the bag. "It's not a teddy bear, I can tell by his ears. It's not a duck, I can tell by his feet—"

"Open the bag!" Hank told her with an expectant boyish grin.

She ripped open the bag and pulled out another fuzzy stuffed animal. "A raccoon!" she squealed with delight. "And he looks just like you!"

"I figured you'd say that." Hank's face mirrored his joy at her reaction to the unexpected gift. "Do you like it? I stopped the SUV at the truck stop for gas, and they had these silly little stuffed animals. I couldn't resist getting them for you girls, being you're stuck up here at the cabin. I thought they might cheer you up."

"Oh, thank you, Mr. Gordon," Faynola said, still hugging the bear close to her. "I'm going to put him on my bed right now."

Tina waited until the woman was out of sight, then walked over to Hank and put her arms about his neck. "You old softie. That was so sweet of you. I'll keep him always. In fact, I'm going to name him Peter Pan, after the sweetest boy I've ever known."

The last words Hank had uttered before he'd gone to bed came to his remembrance. *I should've kissed her.* He wrapped his arms about her and pulled her close. Then taking his time, he planted a kiss in her hair, then on her cheek, on her nose, and then his kisses trailed slowly to her mouth. At first, barely touching her lips, then, rubbing his lips softly against hers until he could take it no longer, he kissed her like he'd longed to kiss her since that first day in the department store.

When their lips finally parted, he felt Tina melt into his arms as he held her tightly against his chest, never wanting this moment to end. "Oh, Tink. Tink. Tink. Do you know how long I've wanted to do that?"

She gazed dreamily up into his eyes. "Do what?"

He reared back slightly with a frown. "Kiss you like that!"

"Like what?" she asked, with big innocent eyes that tore at his heart strings and made him want to claim her as his own.

"You don't remember?" he asked, nuzzling his cheek against hers.

She smiled up at him with a mischievous smile that made his heart do a flip. "No, I don't remember. I guess you'll have to do it again."

Hank swallowed hard. "Happy to oblige."

"I thought we were going to build a snowman," Tina said softly as he pressed his lips against hers.

"Later."

It was nearly three by the time the two began gathering the snow into a mound for their snowman. They giggled and teased each other, occasionally tossing an ill-aimed snowball at one another. The sound of their laughter echoed in the hills around them, even bringing Faynola, with Ryan at her side, to the window to wave at them every now and then.

"Bet you can't find me," Tink told Hank as she shoved a handful of snow down his collar and took off on a run. "Close your eyes and count to fifteen before you come after me!"

He counted out loud, then took off through the trees after her. He tried to follow her tracks, but the fresh snow had fallen in mounds, making it difficult to tell which were tracks and which were the unusual formations caused by the snow falling from the tree branches. "Tink!" he called out loudly, once he'd decided perhaps he'd gone the wrong way. "Where are you?"

But no one answered, and he began to worry. What if Lucky had found them? Found her?

"Tink!" he called even louder. "This isn't funny! Where are you?"

Still no answer. He listened carefully, but there wasn't a sound, not even a rustling of the wind in the trees.

"Tink!" he yelled again, this time cupping his hands to his mouth. "Come out this instant! I mean it!"

"What a sore loser!" a lilting voice answered from somewhere behind him. "You barely gave me time to hide."

He turned quickly to find Tina perched on top of the shed, a mere fifteen feet from him. One hand went to his chest, while his other hand covered his mouth, his heart racing with relief.

"Help me down," she told him with a coy smile. "I won!"

Without a word, he went to the shed and lifted his arms to her. She slipped down into them easily.

"I was so scared," Hank admitted as he pulled her close and cradled her to him. "I thought Lucky had taken you from me."

Tina leaned into his strength. "Oh, Hank, I never meant to worry you. It was only a game. Like we played when we were kids."

"I know," he said, pulling her even tighter against him. "I thought I'd lost you. I won't leave you again until Lucky is caught and behind bars. I should never have driven into town to sign those papers. Nothing is more important to me than you. I–I—" He swallowed hard. Why was it so difficult to say it? "I–I–I love you."

Tina gasped. "You love me?" But she soon shook her head and pushed away. "Don't toy with me, Hank. Please."

Despite her protests, he pulled her close again. "I'm not toying with you. I–I know now—I do love you." He smiled as he remembered asking God for a second sign. "I only hope that someday you can love me too."

"I've loved you since we were four, Hank Gordon. There's never been anyone else. Not really. Aside from what I feel for you, the feelings I had for Lucky were the closest things I'd ever felt for a man. I'd tried to convince myself it was love, but all the time, deep down inside, I knew it was only gratitude. Not the kind of love I wanted. I was deluding myself. But what I'm feeling for you has to be that kind of love. You've asked nothing of me, even though you, too, said you were willing to die for me. I owe you nothing, but if necessary, I know I would lay down my life for you. I can't imagine anyone doing that unless they truly loved the person. That's why I was so confused about Lucky. I'm still not sure of his motives."

Hank's lips sought hers, and he found them cold from the chill of the Alaskan day, but filled with warmth and love for him, and he knew this was the woman God had sent to be his mate. But one thing remained a problem between them. Tina had still not given her life over to his Lord. Hank knew the two of them could not have sweet fellowship, as husband and wife, until she did. *Oh, God,* he called out from deep within his heart, desperately needing God's guidance. *You've given me two signs already. But would You plant this kind of love in my heart for a woman who doesn't love You? I need another sign. Just to be sure.*

"Hank?" she whispered against his kiss. "Tell me more about how God sent His Son to die for us."

Hank quickly sent up a thank-you prayer before spending the next hour with his Bible, going over God's plan of salvation with the woman he loved.

"Supper's ready," Faynola called out to the two sitting on the sofa in front of a blazing fire.

Hank closed his Bible and took Tina's hand in his. "You have no idea how happy you've made me, by asking me to explain the Scriptures to you, Tink."

She smiled up at him as his arm encircled her waist, and they walked into the little kitchen. "I'm glad I've made things right with God. I never meant to separate myself from Him. It just happened."

"Made your favorite, Mr. Gordon," Faynola told him as she placed a big square of lasagna on his plate.

Hank's eyes lit up. "Don't ever let anyone steal you away from me, Faynola."

"No way, Mr. G. I like working for you. I was just telling Mr. Bojangles this afternoon what a kind, considerate man you are."

Hank frowned. "Who is Mr. Bojangles?"

"My teddy bear!" she answered, with a snicker. "The one you gave me!"

They all had a good laugh.

"I'm going to phone the sheriff again, right after supper," Hank told them, as Faynola placed another square of lasagna onto his plate. "I don't like the idea of that man being out there without us knowing where he is, and you need to get back to your grandmother."

Tina nodded. "Me either. I'm so afraid he'll try to make good on his threats, and I'm worried about Gram."

A sudden noise made them all jump.

"It's him!" Hank shouted, knocking his chair over as he leaped to his feet. "I recognize the sound of my truck. You ladies stay here! Keep Ryan with you. I'm going—"

But before he could get out of the room, the sound of shattering glass penetrated the house, causing them all to back away from the archway between the

331

living room and the kitchen. Glass shards shot through the room like bullets, and a rock hit the wall opposite the glass panel by the front door.

"Get down!" Hank ordered as he shoved the women toward the kitchen table. "Under there, and don't come out until I tell you."

"But where—"

Hank gave Tina a look that told her there wasn't time to ask questions. "His quarrel is with me. Stay put!"

As Hank started into the living room, Lucky began pounding on the door, shouting obscenities, and using God's name in vain.

"Get out of here, Wheeler!" Hank shouted at him, as he hurriedly crossed the room, small pieces of glass crunching beneath his shoes. "No one wants you here, and we don't want any more trouble. Do yourself a favor and leave!"

"Don'tcha wan yur truck back?" Lucky yelled out, his words slurring.

Hank could tell by his voice he'd been drinking, which, he knew, made the man even more dangerous. "No, take it with you and go."

"You and me has a score to settle," Lucky yelled back, slurring his words even more.

"Not as far as I'm concerned. Now get out of here." Hank checked to make sure the door was locked, then leaned his back against it.

He waited for an answer, but Lucky didn't make another sound. *Where is he?* Hank asked himself. *And is he armed?* He shot a glance at the gun cabinet. He hadn't let Tina know, but he'd checked it that first night, after she'd gone to bed, making sure there was plenty of ammunition. In case he needed it to defend the three of them.

"Lucky?" he called out.

No answer.

He looked toward the kitchen door and could barely make out the two women crouched beneath the table, but was relieved to see them there, especially with Ryan at their side.

Had Lucky decided to go around to the back door? The one off the kitchen? Was it locked? He couldn't take a chance on leaving his position. So in as loud a voice as he dared, he called to Tina, telling her to make sure the door was locked. He watched as she moved out from under the table, his heart pounding with fear for her safety, until he saw her return and slip back down beside Faynola, whose eyes were as round and large as the saucers she'd used at their dinner table.

"Lucky," he called more loudly, once he was satisfied Tina was safely back under cover. "Answer me! What do you want?"

Still no answer.

Then he heard the truck start and the tires squeal, as Lucky backed out and turned into the narrow drive leading down to the main road. The man was gone.

"You can come out now," Hank called out to Tina and Faynola.

The two women warily joined him in the living room, Ryan at their side, both of them trembling and shaken from the experience.

"What did he want?" Tina asked as she melted into his open arms.

"He never said. I couldn't get him to answer. All he said was he had a score to settle with me. Those were his last words. And he was dead drunk. Men don't think straight when they've got alcohol under their belt. I don't like this at all."

"How did he find us?" Tina asked, clutching tightly to his arm.

"Must've seen me in town and followed me out here. I thought I was being careful. I circled around a bit before heading back to the cabin."

"Now what?" Faynola asked with a shaky voice as she hung onto Ryan's collar.

"Now he knows where we are. I think we'd better head back into town. Fast. I'm calling the sheriff. You ladies get whatever you need to take with you. We'll leave the rest here and come back for it later. I want to be out of here in no more than five minutes."

The women did as they were told, but when Hank picked up the phone there was no dial tone.

The phone was dead.

Chapter 11

Hank stared into the receiver. *Lucky must've cut the phone line on the outside of the house! Too bad my cell phone won't work here in the mountains.* Not wanting to worry Tina and Faynola, he placed the phone back in the receiver and hurried to retrieve his briefcase and the few things he wanted to take with him before turning down the thermostat on the furnace and securing the screen in front of the smoldering fire. He hurried into the little attached garage and found an odd-shaped piece of plywood and a few nails and a hammer. The plywood wasn't perfect, but it was large enough to cover the narrow window panel Lucky had broken out.

"We're ready," the two women said, as they rushed breathlessly back into the little living room, each with a stuffed animal and a small bag in their hands.

Hank motioned them out, then pulled the door shut behind him, making sure it was locked before leading the way to the SUV. But when they reached the vehicle, the sight that greeted them made them all gasp. The windshield was shattered. Lucky had bashed it in with a big rock.

"Oh no," Hank said, as he moved closer for a better look. "He's slashed all four tires too!"

Tina dropped her bag and buried her face in her hands. "Oh, Hank. It's all because of me."

Faynola wrapped her arm about Tina. "Don't worry, Miss Tina. The sheriff is probably on his way right now. He'll take us back to town."

Hank bit at his lip. "I'm afraid the sheriff isn't coming. Lucky cut the phone line."

Now it was Faynola's turn to cry. It broke Hank's heart as he watched the two women huddled together, wrapped in each other's arms, trying to comfort one another.

"We'd better get back in the cabin," he told them, trying to keep his voice from betraying his fear for their safety. Once they were inside, he sent them into the kitchen to put the coffee pot on. He used that task to keep them busy while he pulled several guns from the gun cabinet and loaded them with ammunition. For all he knew, Lucky could've parked the truck and walked back in. He might even be hiding behind a tree or the shed or in the dense foliage, watching them.

"Guns?" Tina asked him, as she came back into the room, carrying two cups of coffee, the cups chattering on their saucers as she carried them with unsteady hands that betrayed her fear.

"I'm sorry, Tink. I know you're afraid of guns, but I have no choice. I don't think Lucky would follow through with his threats, but you—" He stopped and let her finish the sentence for herself. He was sure by now she knew all too well what Lucky was capable of doing. He took a cup from her and forced a smile he hoped appeared confident. "Just a precaution, that's all."

"I–I—know."

After turning on the outside floodlights, he asked Faynola to stay in the kitchen and watch for any movement at the back of the house. Hank shoved the couch across the room and took up a position in front of one of the larger windows. He wanted to keep vigil and have a panoramic view of the front entrance and the road. Unless Lucky walked back in through the woods, he'd have to come this way.

Tina settled in close beside him, fear etched on her face. "If I'd known all those things about Lucky, I would never have gotten anywhere near him, no matter what he'd done for me."

Hank placed the rifle across his knees and slipped his arm about her shoulders. "I've been thinking about that. You know, Lucky had to have had some good in him to stop that night when he saw you were in trouble. Too bad the good part didn't win out over the bad."

"Do—do you think God could forgive someone like Lucky? After all he's done?"

Hank's arm tightened about her. "Of course He could, Tink. In fact, sometimes it's easier for a man to realize he's a sinner when he has a record like Lucky does, than when he's just an ordinary Joe going to work to support his family every day."

Tina smiled and rested her head on his shoulder. "Good. Maybe someday Lucky will get right with God, like I have."

The long, dark hours of the Alaskan night dragged on and on, with no sign of the frightful man. About midnight, Hank sent the women on to bed, promising to keep vigil. He knew it would be difficult for them to sleep, but with Lucky on the loose, no telling what might happen, and he wanted them to be rested. He also knew, although Tina had been concerned that he might fall asleep, there was no way sleep could overtake him as long as his Tina was in danger.

She joined him at the window at six the next morning, urging him to get some sleep while she kept watch. "Please, Hank. I'll awaken you if I see anything."

He'd barely gotten to sleep when she caught sight of a red pickup edging its way slowly up the road. With panic seizing her, she shook Hank. "A truck's coming, but it's not the same color as your truck! Do you think Lucky has stolen another one?"

He jumped to attention, fully awake, and grabbed up the rifle. But his frown and the determined set of his jaw disappeared quickly as a smile broke across his unshaven face. "It's Trapper!"

"Trapper? Are you sure? Why would he be coming up here?"

"I'd know that truck anywhere!" Hank said as he stood the rifle against the wall and rushed toward the door. "I helped him put that rack on to hold his kayak."

By the time the truck came to a stop in the driveway, Hank had donned his coat and was out the front door. "Hey, am I glad to see you! What're you doing up here?"

"Got worried about you," Trapper answered, as he exited the truck and the two men shook hands. "Your secretary called me late last night and said she'd been trying to reach you for hours, but the operator kept telling her the phone was out of order. I figured I'd run up here and check on you. Good thing you told me where you were going."

Tina rushed out of the house and threw her arms about Trapper's neck. "Oh, Trapper, God must've sent you!"

The man did a double take. "God sent me? What do you mean?"

"Come on in, and I'll tell you all about it," Hank told him as he took his friend's arm and ushered him toward the cabin. "Tink's right. God had to have sent you."

A little over an hour and a half later, after the four of them, along with Ryan, had wedged themselves into Trapper's truck, the little group arrived back in Juneau, safe and sound.

"We got him less than an hour ago," the sheriff told them as he met them in the outer office. "The guy's got nerve. One of my men spotted your pickup parked in back of your house. Would you believe the drunken idiot was actually asleep in your bed? Looked like he'd broken in through the kitchen. Pretty dumb, huh? Leaving the truck exposed like that."

Hank offered a slight grin. "Yeah, pretty dumb. But at least you caught him, and we can all go back to our lives, without having to worry about him and his threats. He probably figured he was safe, with the three of us stuck up there at the cabin without a phone."

"What'll happen to Lucky now?" Tina asked, holding tightly to Hank's hand.

"I'm not exactly sure yet. He'll have to answer to us for what he's done here in Juneau. Then I imagine they'll send someone from Chicago to pick him up and take him back there. Looks like he's going to be locked away for a long time."

Hank extended his right hand. "Thanks, Sheriff."

"Need a ride home?"

Hank shook his head. "No, thanks. I think Trapper'll take us."

Trapper smiled. "No problem. That's what friends are for."

Tina stood on tiptoe and kissed Trapper's cheek. "You have no idea how much I appreciate you checking on us like you did."

"Don't thank me. God made me come. He wouldn't let me sleep, just kept me thinking about you two, until I got out of bed and drove up there."

"God leads in strange ways sometimes," Hank said, remembering the three signs he was sure had come from God when he'd asked for them. "Let's go home."

❧

Tina grinned as Hank doused his pancake with maple syrup. "I'm going to go see Gram this morning and get her things all packed up, in preparation for her move. After that, I'm putting up the Christmas tree and decorating it. My next project will be to cook supper for you, Hank!"

Faynola placed another pancake on Tina's plate. "Oh? Taking over my job, are you?"

Tina's fingers grasped the woman's arm. "Oh no, Faynola. I could never do that. I couldn't compete with you."

The woman smiled down at her. "I'm glad you've come back into Mr. Gordon's life, Miss Tina. I've watched you two find each other. It's been more romantic than any romance novel I've ever read, and I've had a front row seat. You two belong together. I could've told you that the first week you came to stay here at the house."

"You should've told me," Tina said, with a childlike glance toward Hank. "It would've saved us all a lot of time and grief. I guess I'm a slow learner."

"You had reason to be," Hank told her with a wink at his housekeeper as he forked another bite. "Lucky had a pretty tight hold on you."

Tina smiled at both of them. "That's all over now. I'm free."

❧

"Isn't that the most beautiful tree you've ever seen?" Tina asked Hank after dinner, as they sat locked in each other's arms on the sofa, staring at the hundreds of tiny twinkling lights wrapped around the plump evergreen.

"Uh-huh," Hank answered in barely a whisper, turning to look at the lovely woman next to him. "But what I'm seeing is more beautiful than any old Christmas tree."

She swatted at him playfully. "Keep those words coming, Peter Pan. A girl can never hear too many compliments."

"I mean every one of them."

"Guess what else I got done today?"

He brought her fingers to his lips and kissed the tips of them, one at a time. "What?"

"I got my computer all set up and even made contact with my office. I was afraid they'd think I was never going to get back to work, but they assured me things have been a bit slow. I think they only said it to make me feel better. Anyway, I told them I was bringing Gram home and would be ready to get back to work, full-time, by Monday. I can't believe they've been as understanding as they have."

"I can. I'll bet you're a terrific employee."

She smiled appreciatively. "I try."

"I did something today too. I rented a hospital bed for your grandmother, from that medical supply house downtown. I'm sure she'll be more comfortable on it than on a regular bed."

Tina straightened. "But they're so expensive! I wanted to rent one for her, but—"

"My treat. Don't give it another thought. They're delivering it the first thing tomorrow. We'll call it one of her Christmas presents."

"Oh, Hank. Are you sure you're not my guardian angel, instead of a mere mortal man?"

"Quite sure," Hank told her with a mischievous grin, as he tilted her chin and stared into her eyes. "No angel could feel about you like I do. It's a privilege given only to us mortals."

Early the next morning, the couple stood at Harriett Taylor's bedside at the nursing home, holding hands. "We're here to take you home, Gram," Tina told the frail woman. Her dream was finally coming true. She was taking Gram to the house on Ocean View Boulevard, fulfilling her wish.

Her grandmother wept openly as she extended a delicate hand covered with huge brown spots. "I—I can't begin to t—tell you how much this m—means to me. You've m—made this old woman very happy."

"I know, Gram. That's why I wanted to do it." Tina took hold of the small hand and gave it a squeeze. "But I couldn't have done it without Hank. I can't tell you all he's done for me. And the work he's put in on your house!"

"Don't listen to her, Mrs. Taylor," Hank said modestly. "She's exaggerating. Besides, we've both loved every minute of getting your house ready." He gave the old woman a wink. "It gave me a good excuse to be around your granddaughter."

The woman leaned back into her pillow, her free hand going to her heart. "Praise God, I'm so glad Lucky is out of your life, Tina. As grateful as I was to that man for what he did for you that night, I never liked him. Or trusted him. He was not the man I'd asked God to give you." She cast a quick glance toward Hank. "But I have a feeling He's answering my prayers."

Tina felt Hank's hand on her shoulder. "He did, Gram. He sent Hank back into my life. Through him, and his patience with me, I've come back to God. I've given my life over to Him and accepted Christ as my Savior."

Mrs. Taylor closed her eyes. "Oh, you dear ones. I'm so happy. Now I can die in peace. God has answered my prayer, even above and beyond what I ever dreamed. I know Hank is a fine man. He'd have to be—he's a Gordon. He's proven that by the way he's taken care of you while you've been in Juneau. I was so relieved when you phoned and said you were staying at his house. I loved his parents." A tear rolled down her wrinkled cheek. "I—I—just wish my son would have been—"

Tina leaned over and pressed her face against the old woman's. "You did all you could, Gram. Dad and Mom were just not cut out to be parents. Their bottle of liquor was more important to them than I was. In one of his messages, our pastor here in Juneau said all a parent can do is try to raise a child the way God would have you raise them, but the final decision rests with them. You did your best. Daddy just chose to live differently than you'd taught him. So did Mom. They both knew better. They just didn't care."

"I'm so thankful Hank's parents were good to you. Heaven only knows what your life would've been like without their influence."

"Me too," Tina agreed as she stroked her grandmother's forehead. "Hank has arranged for an ambulance. We're here to take you home, Gram."

❧

The smile on Gram's face when Hank carried her into the little house on Ocean View Boulevard made every bit of their work worthwhile. "Welcome home, Gram," Tina said, pulling the old double wedding ring quilt over the frail body before bending down to kiss her grandmother's cheek.

Hank's heart filled with awe at Tina's dedication to the tiny, nearly helpless woman in the bed. He wished he could take away all the hurts Tina had suffered at the hands of both her parents and Lucky. Not much in her life had gone right, yet she'd managed to land a decent job, work hard, get promoted, and never forget her allegiance to the one person who'd loved her all those years. Harriett Taylor.

"Thank You, God," the slight woman said softly, as she folded her hands. "Thank You for hearing this old woman's prayers. I'm finally home." With that, she closed her eyes and fell fast asleep.

Tina placed a kiss on the tip of her finger, then transferred it to her grandmother, barely touching the wrinkled forehead, before smiling up at Hank, her eyes filled with grateful tears. "Yes, she's finally home, and just in time for Christmas. Thanks to you."

❧

"Good morning. Tina Taylor. How may I help you?"

Hank leaned back in his desk chair and smiled into the phone. "Hey, what a cheery voice. You have a great phone presence."

"Hi, Hank."

"So? How's it feel to be back to work again?"

"Wonderful! I'd almost forgotten how it is to be an important, viable part of the Beesom Parts team. Not much happening at the main office because of the holiday, but I've been on the phone and the Internet most of the morning, getting back into the swing of things."

"How's Harriett doing?" he asked, doodling oddly shaped hearts on a scratch pad as he talked.

"Doing better than I was afraid she might after her first night home. I was afraid she'd be exhausted. But she had a good night's rest and ate a big breakfast. Now she's watching her soap operas on TV," she told him with a giggle. "She got hooked on them at the care home. She said that's all they did all day."

"Well, at least those soaps keep her busy so you can do your work. Faynola made up a big pot of venison stew, so you won't have to cook tonight. I know it's not a very fancy dinner for Christmas Eve, but I thought your grandmother might enjoy it. The two of us, and Ryan, will be there about six."

"I know Gram likes venison stew. She's told me many times how she used to make it for my grandfather. You're too good to me, Hank. I'm glad you're bringing Faynola and Ryan. I want Gram to meet them."

"Get used to me being good to you, kiddo. This is just the beginning. See you around six."

By six o'clock, Tina had helped her grandmother bathe and dress in a fresh gown. She'd had her own shower, and the two of them were ready and waiting expectantly when Hank and Faynola arrived, laden down with the boxes of food Faynola had packed. He smiled at the two of them, as Ryan bounded in past him. "How are my favorite ladies?"

Harriett Taylor lifted her head from the pillow and reached out a hand. "Hank. Dear, dear Hank. What a sweet man you are. Just seeing that handsome face of yours makes this old lady feel young again. And that beautiful dog must be Ryan. Tina told me all about him."

Hank put the boxes on a chair, moved quickly to the bed, and kissed her cheek. "Aw, careful there, you'll give me a big head."

Tina had already placed a card table next to the hospital bed, covered it with a bright red tablecloth, placed a colorful candle and candle ring on it, and set it for three with her grandmother's lovely white dishes and monogrammed silverware. Then she'd taken a red napkin and added the same white dishes and silverware to her grandmother's tray. After giving Ryan one of the venison bones to keep him busy while they had their meal, Faynola helped Tina put the rest of the things on the table, and the four enjoyed a hearty dinner.

Once things had been cleaned up and put away, Faynola pulled a chair close to the old woman's bed, and the two ladies prepared for a good visit, while Hank and Tina moved into the living room and Hank built a fire in the fireplace. Once the logs had taken hold and begun to burn, he lowered himself to the floor and wrapped his arms about Tina. For long minutes they sat there, warming themselves by the fire, staring at the bright lights of the Christmas tree. It seemed conversation was no longer necessary between them. Just being together was enough.

Tina nestled in close to him, loving the manly scent of his clothing, his hair, his aftershave. Lucky had never smelled pleasant like that. He'd always smelled of leather and the grease from his cycle. She wondered how she'd ever tolerated it. Just the thought of it now made her cringe.

"It's hard to believe Christmas is already here," Hank finally said. "I'm glad we're spending it together. Without Lucky."

Tina nodded dreamily. "Me too."

Finally, at ten, Faynola came into the room with Ryan trailing along beside her, telling them she'd gotten Harriett ready for bed and tucked in for the night, and the old woman was fast asleep. She busied herself tidying up the room and pulling her coat from the hall closet, giving the couple time to say their good nights in privacy.

Hank gave Tina one final kiss, then pulled himself away, motioning Ryan toward the door. "See you tomorrow morning."

❧

Hank and Faynola arrived at nine Christmas morning with a partially cooked turkey and all the fixings for a grand meal.

He found Tina all showered, her hair curled up like he'd never seen it before, and she was wearing a pretty red dress. As she and Faynola went into the kitchen to finish preparing Christmas dinner, Hank went into Harriett's room to spend some time with her.

"Would you read my Bible to me?" she asked as she gestured to the big old family Bible Tina had placed on her bedside table. "I'd love to hear the Christmas story from the second chapter of Luke. These old eyes can't focus on the words any longer."

Hank nodded, opened the Bible, and with a smile began to read, taking note of all the comments Harriett had penned into the margins. Tina's parents might have been losers, but praise God, she had a concerned grandmother who loved God and had prayed for her all these years.

After a marvelous Christmas dinner, Hank carried Harriett into the living room and lovingly laid her on the sofa on top of the quilt Tina had spread out for her, placing a pillow beneath her head. The old woman's eyes filled with tears as she looked upon the colorfully lit Christmas tree, filled with the ornaments she'd collected over her many years. "This is the best Christmas ever," she told them, blinking hard. "I never thought I'd actually make it home again, but you two have made it happen, and I am so grateful."

"I have presents for my three best girls," Hank added, moving to the base of the tree and picking up three beautifully gift-wrapped packages. He handed a gift to each one with a flourish of his hand.

"You first," he told Harriett.

"But I didn't get you anything," she said sadly.

"Yes, you did. You gave me the best present. Your granddaughter."

She gave him a quick smile as she pulled the ribbons from the box and opened it. Inside was a lovely pink bed jacket with matching pink slippers. "Thank you, Hank. They're perfect."

"You next," he told Faynola.

She grinned and pulled off the ribbons from her gift. "Oh, Hank, blue, my favorite color." She held up a snuggly soft chenille robe with matching slippers. "How did you know my size?"

"Easy. Peeked in your closet when you weren't looking." He turned to Tina. "Now you," he told her, holding out her gift.

"I can't," she told him, her heart touched with his generosity. "You've done so much for me already."

"Open it, Tink. Please."

She dabbed at her eyes with her sleeve and began to pull the ribbons and the paper from the small box. She let out a gasp as she pulled out a second box, a small velvet one, and lifted the lid. "Oh, Hank. A diamond watch! You shouldn't have. It's much too expensive!"

"Nothing is too expensive for you, Tink." He took the little box from her hand and removed the watch. "Here, let me put it on you."

She held out her arm. He opened the clasp, slipped the dainty watchband over her wrist, and pressed the catch until it closed with a snap. "Now you won't have to keep asking me what time it is."

"But you—"

He put a finger to her lips. "No more. I wanted you to have it. I just hope you like it."

Tina stared at the tiny gold face circled by a ring of diamonds. "It's the most beautiful watch I've ever seen. I'll cherish it always."

"It's not nearly as beautiful as the woman I bought it for."

She backed away quickly. "I have a present for you too. But it's nothing like the one you gave me. I'm almost embarrassed to give it to you."

"Whatever it is, it'll be special because it came from you."

She hurried to the closet and brought back a flat, rectangular box, wrapped in brown wrapping paper and tied with hemp twine. Attached to the twine were three hand-carved wooden stars and a tiny little card made from parchment paper, with *To my Peter Pan, with love,* Tink hand lettered in green ink. "It's not much, but I hope you'll like it," she said apologetically, as she placed it in his lap.

Hank read the little card, then fingered the beautifully hand-carved stars, turning them over and over in his hand. "Where did you get these? I've never seen anything like them."

She gave him a bashful look. "I—I carved them. With that old pocket knife I found at Gram's. I used to carve a little bit when I was a kid, when I'd hide in the woods behind our house to avoid my father's beatings. Sometimes, when I was especially frightened, I'd be there for hours. Carving helped to pass the time."

"I'll keep them always," Hank said, carefully removing the stars from the twine and slipping them into his shirt pocket. "Just because you made them for me." He pulled the twine from the package, then the paper. "Oh, Tink! This is wonderful! Who did it?" He held up a framed hand-sketched picture of his parents for Faynola and Harriett to see. "Did someone locally do this for you? It looks exactly like them!"

"I—I did it," she answered softly, hanging her head. "I sketched it from a photograph I found in that album in your living room bookcase. I know how much you loved them."

Hank's eyes widened. "You did this? I didn't know you were so talented. Tink, this is as good as any professional artist would've done! I'm amazed."

"You're just saying that to make me feel good."

He moved quickly to her side and pulled her into his arms again, tilting her face up to his. "No, I'm saying it because I mean it! There isn't another gift you could have given me, at any price, that would have pleased me more. Oh, Tink, thank you. Merry Christmas, sweetheart." He bent his head and tenderly kissed her lips. "Your grandmother is right! This is the best Christmas ever. And just the first of many, if I have my way about it."

Wrapping her arms about his neck, Tina returned his kiss. "Merry Christmas, you wonderful, thoughtful man."

Later that night, after placing the precious picture of his parents on his nightstand, Hank knelt by his bed and thanked the Lord for the many blessings He'd bestowed upon him, especially for sending Tina back to him. *And Lord, thank You most of all for speaking to her heart and making her see her need of, once again, having a relationship with You. You've answered my prayers, abundantly above what I asked.*

❧

New Year's Day passed by quickly, and so did the first two weeks of January. Each day, Tina and Hank watched as Harriett Taylor's strength waned. The doctor came to the house often to check on her, since she was much too weak to get out of bed. Each time, he warned Tina and Hank to be prepared for her passing. It could come at any time.

During the evening of January the twentieth, Harriett called Hank and Tina to her side. "Hank," she said in a voice so faint he had to kneel next to her just to hear her. "Please, would you pray for me? I'm ready now. I want to go home, to my heavenly home. Would you ask God to take me? I'm so tired, and the medicine no longer takes away the pain."

Hank nodded, and after kissing the old woman's cheek, he took both her hands in his and bowed his head. "God, You know how much Tink and I love Harriett and how hard it is for us to even think of losing her. But her heart and her body are giving out on her, Lord, and she's ready to—to come to You."

Tina watched as he swallowed hard and pressed his eyelids tightly together, knowing how difficult it must be for him, and loving him for doing what her grandmother had asked.

"We thank You that we were able to get her house ready in time to bring her home for Christmas," he went on, "and for the weeks we've had with her since then. But now she says she's ready to go to her heavenly home. She's—she's asked me to—" Slowly, he looked into Harriett Taylor's aged face, his tears flowing unashamedly. "I'm sorry. I can't say it. I just can't."

A feeble hand came to rest on his shoulder, as the woman motioned him near and spoke with great effort in a faint whisper. "It's okay. God knows what I asked you to do. Thank you, Hank, you're a good man."

Harriett slipped away quietly in the middle of the night, a smile on her face that only her Lord could have put there.

"I don't know what I'm going to do without her, Hank," Tina told him between sobs as she watched them take her grandmother away. "She was the only link I had to my past. The only living relative I knew about. Now I'm all alone."

"No, Tink, not alone. I'm here. I love you, and I'll never leave you. We need to be grateful for the time we've had with her."

Tina threw her arms about his waist and held on tight.

"At least your grandmother got her final wish. She died at home."

❧

The funeral was held on the twenty-third at Hank's church. As Tina stood by him, singing the songs her grandmother had requested, she thought about all the pain the woman had gone through with her son, Tina's father. Her precious, sweet grandmother had suffered so much, yet she'd never turned away from her Lord. How was she ever going to get along without that saintly woman? The only blood relative who'd ever truly loved her?

"Harriett Taylor loved God," the minister was saying. "And she loved her granddaughter, Tina Taylor. Many of you knew Harriett when she lived in Juneau a number of years ago and are here because you've lost an old friend. Many of you didn't have the privilege of knowing her and are here because you've come to love Tina in the short time she's been with us here in this church. Harriett Taylor will be missed, but do not mourn as those mourn who have no hope. Harriett Taylor is in the arms of her Lord, as she'd asked. No more will she endure the pain inflicted on her by her mortal body. This is a day for rejoicing!"

Tina glanced around at the many people gathered in the church, her church family now. Trapper, Glorianna, their children, Faynola, and dozens of others.

Just the sight of them made her heart glad. Although she would miss her grandmother and life would never be the same without her, she knew the minister was right. It was a day for rejoicing. Her grandmother was in heaven with her grandfather. She smiled up at Hank through tears of happiness and tightened her grip on his arm. "Thanks, Hank, for helping me fulfill my grandmother's dream. I could never have completed it in time without you."

His hand cupped hers. "No thanks needed, Tink. I did it because I wanted to. And I'm here to stay. You can count on it. Others might've failed you, but I'll never let you down, I promise."

She leaned into him. "Do you realize her last wish, to die at home, is what brought us together?"

"I sure do, and I'll always be grateful to her."

Hank spent long days at his office, catching up on the things he'd left undone when he'd come to Tina's rescue. Evenings and weekends, the two were inseparable. Spending their time together in front of the fireplace, listening to CDs, reading from the Bible, and enjoying one another's company. Hank could barely wait to get to the house on Ocean View Boulevard at the end of the day.

"I rarely see you anymore," Faynola complained to him one evening in mid-February, as he rushed in to shower and change clothes before going to spend the evening with Tina.

Hank grinned. "You should be glad. You don't have to cook for me."

"I like cooking for you." She watched as he flitted around the room nervously. "What's the matter with you? Did you lose something?"

His smile broadened. "Nope, just have things on my mind."

All through dinner, Tina kept her gaze on Hank. For some reason, tonight he wasn't himself. He seemed fidgety. Nervous. She wondered if he was having misgivings about what she thought was their budding relationship. She was happier than she'd ever been, but did Hank share her happiness? Maybe he wished he'd never gotten involved with her topsy-turvy life. But hadn't he promised her he was there to stay? Finally, she could stand it no longer and decided to confront him. "Is anything wrong? Have I done something to upset you?"

He shook his head and, with a mischievous grin, took her by the hand and led her to the sofa in front of the fireplace. He sat down and pulled her onto his lap. "Know what day this is?"

She gave him a coy grin. "February fourteenth?"

He nodded. "Valentine's Day."

She pulled away from him slightly, took a large white envelope from the top drawer of the end table, and handed it to him. "Happy Valentine's Day, Hank. You thought I forgot, didn't you?"

He opened the envelope and pulled out a valentine, showing two people sitting on a couch in front of a blazing fireplace, hugging each other. He gave her a wink and read the words aloud. " 'Some folks may like to go to Paris. Some might like to go to Rome. Some might like to visit the pyramids. Me? I'd rather be right here at home. With you! I love you, Peter Pan. Tinker Bell.' " He bent and kissed her cheek. "Thanks, Tink. I hope you mean those words."

"I do mean them," she said, tenderly stroking his cheek. "I love our times here in front of the fireplace. And I love you."

"Now you," he said, reaching under the toss pillow and pulling out a crumpled white envelope. It looked as if it had been run over by a Mack truck.

She frowned. Why would he give her something in such pitiful condition? She tried to appear not to notice and pulled open the flap. What she found inside made her heart sing with joy. It wasn't the lovely, lacy, expensive Valentine she'd expected to receive from Hank. It was a homemade one, created from red and white construction paper by a third-grader many years ago. Filled with excitement, she pulled it from the envelope and pressed it to her breast. "Oh, Hank, I love it. I thought you'd thrown it away."

"Read it," he told her, his face quirked into a smile.

With a song in her heart, she wiped the tears of joy from her eyes and read it aloud with great emotion. " 'Tink is pretty. Tink is smart. I'll love you forever. Here is my heart. Be my Valentine.' And it's signed 'Peter Pan.' " She threw her arms about his neck and planted kisses all over his face. "Oh, Hank, I love you too!"

He pushed her away. Surprised, she stared up into his face, wondering if she'd misunderstood his card.

"Will you?" he asked, as he reached into his jacket pocket and pulled out a small white box tied with a red satin ribbon. "Be my Valentine? Every day of our lives and not just on Valentine's Day?"

Too filled with emotion to do anything but nod, she took the box from the man she loved and hurriedly untied the ribbon, hoping it contained what she thought it did, but fearing it didn't.

Hank's hand reached out and covered hers. "You have to answer me first. Will you?"

She leaned into him, the box still in her hand, half opened. "Of course I will! Oh, Hank, I love you so much it hurts. I think I always have. I can't even find words to express my love for you."

He gave her a satisfied grin. "Okay, then. Open your gift."

With trembling fingers, she yanked off the ribbon, then the paper, and opened the little white velvet box inside. Her palm went to her mouth as she let out a loud gasp. "Oh, Hank, it's beautiful!"

He took the lovely pear-shaped diamond solitaire from the bed of velvet and slipped it onto her finger. "Will you marry me, Tink? Be my Valentine forever?"

"Oh yes. Forever and ever and ever and ever. I love you, Peter Pan!"

Hank swept her up in his arms. "We've wasted way too much time. I want us to get married as soon as possible."

"Me too. I want so much to be your wife."

He became serious. "Remember the question I asked you? About your wedding night, if you married Lucky?"

Tina well remembered his words. Those words were what caused her to question her loyalty to Lucky and made her see what her life would have been like if she'd married him. "You asked if I could wholly give myself to you if the two of us ever married. I'll never forget that question as long as I live. I nearly went into shock!"

"What's your answer, Tink?"

"Oh yes, my dearest. Yes, yes, yes! I can hardly wait. I know now loving you is going to be the sweetest experience of my life."

Hank brushed his lips across hers. "You mean the sweetest experience of our lives."

"The sweetest experience of our lives!" she said, correcting herself, then added with an excited giggle, "Would it be too soon if we set the wedding for three weeks from today?"

The church was packed with friends and neighbors. The pastor was standing at the altar. The groom was there, and so was the best man. Everything was in readiness for the wedding of Hank Gordon and Tina Taylor, except for one thing.

The bride was missing.

Chapter 13

Hank stared at the closed double doors at the back of the chapel. *Where is Tink?* He glanced at his watch. *The ceremony was to have started fifteen minutes ago.* Was history repeating itself? Was he going to be left at the altar again?

"Don't worry, Hank," Trapper said, patting his shoulder reassuringly. "She probably got delayed in traffic."

Hank's brows lifted. "In Juneau? On a Saturday? Not likely."

"Maybe she had a flat tire. Maybe the—"

"Maybe she decided not to marry me after all!" Hank said with a slightly angry tinge to his voice. "Is this déjà vu?"

"No, and don't you even think it. That woman loves you."

Hank yanked the bow tie from his neck. "Yeah? Then where is she?"

Trapper clutched his friend's arm. "Give her a few more minutes."

"Do you think we should dismiss the audience?" the pastor prodded gently, as if not wanting to upset the already upset bridegroom even more. "It's beginning to look like she isn't going to make it. Surely she would've phoned the church by now if she'd had a problem getting here."

Hank lifted his hands in exasperation. "Yeah, send them home, or let them stay and eat the cake. I don't care. I'm leaving!" With that, he rushed down the aisle and out of the church. His face filled with anger, his heart ached with grief. He searched the parking lot for signs of her car and, finding none, headed the SUV for the house on Ocean View Boulevard. Seeing Tina's car still parked in the driveway, he pulled to a sudden stop behind hers and pulled out the house key she'd given him. He was determined to rush in, have it out with her, and ask for his ring back. He'd spent big bucks on that ring, and if she wasn't going to marry him, the least she could do was return it.

But the house was empty.

When he called out her name, she didn't answer. He checked each room. Her wedding gown was hanging in her bedroom, her veil lay neatly spread out across the bed, her hose and satin slippers lay on the chest. He pulled open the closet doors, expecting to find her clothing gone, but everything was in its place. Where was Tink? Why hadn't she gotten dressed and come to the church as planned? If she'd planned to leave and not go through with the wedding, why hadn't she at least left a note? None of it made any sense.

With a heavy heart, filled with both disappointment and rage, he drove the SUV across town to his home. Faynola met him at the door. "That friend of yours in Chicago just called. I think he said he was a district attorney. He wants you to call him immediately! He said it's urgent! I tried to call you on your cell phone, but you must've turned it off."

"Did he say what he wanted?" Hank asked as he quickly looked up the number and dialed the phone.

"No, but from the sound of his voice, it must be something important!"

The man answered on the first ring. "Hank! Man, am I glad to hear your voice. We've got trouble here. I just learned that guy you asked me about, that Lucky Wheeler? They were transferring him to another prison, and the van got hit by a bus. Some of the passengers were injured, and in the confusion, he walked away. He's been on the loose for four days now, and so far they don't have a clue as to his whereabouts. I thought you should know, in case he tries to come back to Alaska, which is doubtful. We think he's still in the Chicago area."

Hank went numb. *Lucky escaped? Could that have anything to do with Tina's disappearance?* Frantic, he phoned the sheriff.

"I'll get out another APB right away," the man told him. "You don't think he'd come all the way from Chicago to Alaska again, do you?"

"I hope not, but you never know. He made some pretty serious threats, and Tina didn't show up for our wedding today. I'm worried."

"Oh, Hank. I'm sorry. Do you have any idea where she might be?"

He lowered himself onto the desk chair. "No, I just hope—"

"Let us know if we can do anything to help. Maybe it was only wedding jitters. I hear that happens to brides once in a while. They just take off without telling anyone, to think things over."

Hank thanked the man, then leaned his head against the wall. He had no idea where to begin to search for Tina. He wasn't even sure he wanted to, not if she'd deliberately left him standing at the altar, the laughingstock of all their friends. Yet what if she was in danger? What if Lucky had come back to Juneau? He dropped to his knees by the chair and pled with God to help him find his Tink. He had to at least know she was safe.

Each time the phone rang, Hank darted to answer it, but each time, it was well-meaning friends asking about Tina. He checked with the sheriff one last time about two in the morning and finally fell asleep on the sofa, exhausted, the phone by his side.

When it rang at four a.m. he grabbed it up quickly, expecting to hear the sheriff's voice, but the voice on the other end was definitely not the sheriff's. He could barely hear what the person was saying and nearly hung up, thinking it was a prank call.

"Who is this? Speak up," he told the caller angrily, resenting being awakened at that hour for nothing.

"Hank, it's me—me. Tina," a faint voice said. "Lucky c—came to the house and f—forced me to go w—with him."

Hank clutched the phone tightly. He could tell she was crying. "Where are you?"

"At y—your friend's c—cabin."

Thank God my friend had the phone line repaired. "Why, Tink? Why did he take you there? Did he say?"

"To keep me from marrying you. He wanted to ruin our wedding. He—he said it was to get e—even with us."

"Has he hurt you?"

"No, he hasn't hurt me, b—but he's been drinking h—heavily. I'm so a—afraid of him. I'm afraid he might—"

"Where is he now?"

"H—he finally passed out. He's a—asleep on the couch, but he has the k—keys to the old car he's d—driving in his pocket. I c—can't get to them, and I'm a—afraid to start walking. I—I don't know what to do. He—he has a gun."

Hank jumped to his feet and began pacing back and forth, as far as the phone cord would allow, running his fingers through his hair nervously. *God, what do I tell her? I'm nearly an hour away from her.*

"Hank, I'm s—sorry about our wedding," she said softly into the phone, and he could tell she was still crying. "You kn—know I'd—"

He stopped pacing. "Listen to me, and do exactly what I say," he told her, hoping his plan would work. "Can you see the gun?"

"Yes, it's lying on the s—sofa beside him. But I'm a—afraid of g—guns, and I could never sh—shoot anyone!"

"I know, sweetie. Walk carefully over to the sofa, pick up that gun, then open the outside kitchen door and leave it standing wide open."

"Y—you want me to leave the c—cabin?"

"No, you'd freeze out there. But if Lucky wakes up and sees the door open, he'll think you've left and go after you."

"Then wh—what shall I do?"

"Take the gun with you, go into that upstairs closet, and cover yourself with blankets, pillows, anything you can find. He probably won't even think to look for you in the cabin. Don't come out for any reason until I get there. Do you understand?"

"Yes," she said, faintly between sobs. "I'll o—open the back door, then take the g—gun upstairs with me and h—hide in the closet until you get here. But h—hurry, Hank. I'm scared."

"Pray, sweetheart. You're not alone. God is with you." He pressed the phone tightly to his ear, not wanting to miss one word. "Tink."

"Yes?"

"If he should come upstairs and find you, you know you might have to shoot him, don't you? To defend yourself."

"I could never sh—shoot anyone!"

"We'll pray it won't come to that, but Lucky is a desperate man, and he's drunk. He's liable to do anything. I just want you to be prepared. I'm coming for you, my love."

"Oh, Hank. H—hurry, please hurry!"

"I'm on my way."

Hank phoned the sheriff, then leaped into the SUV and drove at breakneck speeds, pressing the accelerator to the floor. He had to get to Tink before Lucky woke up. "God, please protect her," he cried out as his hands gripped the steering wheel. "I'm sorry I ever doubted her. I should've known better. Please, God, please comfort her, and keep her safe until I get there!"

It seemed to take forever before he reached the narrow road leading up to the cabin.

❧

Tina lay covered beneath a pile of blankets and pillows on the floor of the closet, holding her breath and praying. *God, please! I've turned my life over to You, and I'm trusting You to keep me safe until Hank gets here. Don't let Lucky find me, I beg you! And keep Hank safe. Lucky hates him and would like nothing better than to harm him.* She held her breath and lay motionless, her heart pounding so loudly she was afraid Lucky might hear it.

His drunken voice suddenly boomed out angrily, echoing through the cabin. "Tina! Where are you? You can't hide from me!"

Fear gripped her heart. *What if he comes up those stairs and finds me?* She listened, hoping he'd discover the open kitchen door and go in search of her as Hank had said he would.

"Oh, so you've taken out on foot, have ya?" she heard Lucky yell out, then the slamming of a door, and she breathed a bit easier. Hopefully, he'd taken the bait. *I've got to do exactly as Hank told me and not come out until he comes for me. Lucky may still be down there.*

❧

As the SUV approached the house, Hank could see several marked cars in the driveway and breathed a sigh of relief. The sheriff and some other officers had arrived ahead of him, just as he'd hoped. He leaped out of his vehicle and hurried toward the three officers standing by one of the cars.

"We got him," the sheriff called out. "The idiot was wandering around in the trees. He was so drunk he could hardly stand up. He didn't even put up a fight."

"Where's Tina?" Hank asked frantically, not even glancing at the man secured in the back of the sheriff's car. She was his only concern.

"Don't know, Hank," he said, sadly shaking his head. "We've asked him, but all he would say was she left while he was asleep. He was pretty upset because he couldn't find her. I've got two men searching the woods for her now. Wish I could tell you more."

Hank smiled. "I think I know where she is." With that, he darted up the steps of the cabin, taking them two at a time, and bolted through the door, calling out her name.

❧

Tina pushed back the blankets, quilts, and pillows at the sound of his voice and rushed from the closet, throwing herself into his arms as they met at the head of the stairs. *Praise God!* Her Hank had come, and she was safe!

The feelings of love she felt as she pressed herself against him overwhelmed her. "Oh, Hank, I missed our wedding," she said sadly. "Can you ever forgive me?"

Hank brushed aside a tear and held her close. "Oh, Tink, if anyone needs to ask forgiveness, it's me. When you didn't show up at the church, I thought you'd decided not to marry me after all, and I was furious!"

Her hand rose to stroke his cheek. "Never, my love. I'd never leave you like that. I love you too much to hurt you."

"And I love you, Tink." He buried his face in her hair. "I prayed for God to protect you, and He did. We have much to be thankful for."

She snuggled her face against his broad chest, drinking in his masculine fragrance. "I prayed he'd protect you! I was afraid you'd confront Lucky. He was so drunk, and he might have had another gun in that old car—"

"Shh!" He put his fingers to her lips. "Everything's okay now. The sheriff is probably already on his way back to town, with Lucky locked in the backseat. He won't bother us again. They'll make sure he's locked up tight this time."

"And we can get married? As we'd planned?"

Hank pulled her close. "Oh yes, my precious, as soon as possible! Only this time, you're not getting out of my sight on our wedding day."

A grin formed on her tear-stained face. "Don't you know it's bad luck for the groom to see the bride on their wedding day?"

Hank threw back his head and let loose with a loud belly laugh. "Bad luck, Tink? I don't think any piece of bad luck could be worse than what we've gone through already!"

Chapter 14

Well, old buddy," Trapper whispered in Hank's ear as they stood at the front of the church a second time, waiting for the music to begin. "Here we are again."

Hank fingered his bow tie. "Yeah, I sure hope things go right this time. My batting average is at rock bottom when it comes to weddings."

Trapper rested his hand on his friend's shoulder. "Don't worry. Glorianna's with her. She won't let her get away this time."

Hank let out a big sigh. "I sure hope you're right. I couldn't stand being left at the altar again."

❧

"You look beautiful," Glorianna told Tina as she straightened her veil for her. "I can hardly wait to see the look on Hank's face when you walk down that aisle toward him."

Tina turned to smile at the woman she'd come to love almost as much as a sister. "I really love him, Glorianna. I just hope I can make him as happy as you've made Trapper."

"Don't worry, you will. You two were made for each other. I love Hank like a brother, but he and I were never destined to be together. It was always Trapper I loved. I think, deep down, Hank and I both knew that from the beginning."

Tina slipped her arm about Glorianna's shoulders. "I realize that now, but at first I hated you for what you two had done to Hank. Now I realize you and Trapper did the best thing for everyone, and I love you both for having the courage to do it." The two women embraced, but separated quickly as the music sounded.

"Are you ready?" Glorianna asked, her face aglow with happiness for her new friend. "It's time to start down that aisle. I've had strict orders from both Hank and Trapper to make sure you didn't get away."

Tina took one step toward the door, then panicked, her hands going to her throat. "My necklace? Where is it?"

Glorianna gasped. "I don't think you were wearing a necklace when you got here."

"I don't remember putting it on," Tina said, nearly in tears as she fingered her bare neck. "Are you sure I wasn't wearing it?"

"Pretty sure. Could it be in your bag?"

Tina turned quickly, eyeing the small bag she'd brought with her. "I don't think so. At least, I don't remember putting it in there. Oh, where is it? My brain has been so scattered all day!"

"Hold on, I'll check." Glorianna carefully stepped over the long satin train and grabbed up the bag, quickly searching its contents. "It's not in here!"

"What am I going to do? My beautiful heart-shaped necklace. I have to wear it!" Tina blinked hard and dabbed at her eyes.

"Be careful. You're going to mess up your makeup." Glorianna pulled a tissue from the box on the vanity and handed it to her. "You're the bride. Everyone will be looking at you, not me. You can wear my necklace."

"You don't understand! Hank bought that necklace for me to wear at our wedding! He made such a big deal of it! He said if we ever had a daughter, she'd be able to wear it at her wedding. He wanted it to become a family heirloom, and I've lost it! He'll be so disappointed if I'm not wearing it!"

Glorianna put a consoling hand on Tina's arm. "Take it from me, sweetie, as beautiful as you look in that gown, he'll never even notice."

"I hope you're right." Tina dabbed at her eyes, again, trying to calm down. She'd just have to explain to Hank later that she'd misplaced the necklace. Surely he'd understand.

"The organist has already played the bridal song once. We'd better get out there, or Hank and Trapper will come looking for us."

Tina nodded. "I'm ready, I guess."

Glorianna knelt to pick up the train again, and as she did, she let out a second gasp. "There's a velvet box on the floor under the table!"

"That's it! That's my necklace!"

a◆

"Where is she?" Hank turned to Trapper as the bridal song ended, and the organist played the introduction for the second time.

Trapper shrugged. "Got me!"

Hank tugged at his cummerbund, his eyes pinned on the double doors. "Think she's changed her mind?" he asked in a half whisper.

"Be patient, old man. Maybe she got her veil caught in her zipper or a run in her stocking. Who knows about women? As long as I've been married to Glori, I still don't know what makes her tick."

Hank bit at his lip. *Come on, Tink. Don't disappoint me again! Not a second time!*

Finally, the double doors parted and Glorianna appeared, in a pink silk organza gown and carrying pink carnations. When she reached the front of the church, Tina appeared in the open doorway, in a long flowing bridal gown of white satin and beaded silk organza, and she was wearing the diamond heart-shaped necklace Hank had given her.

Hank caught his breath. He couldn't take his eyes off his bride as she moved slowly toward him. She was a vision of loveliness. Her smile told Hank everything was going to be fine this time. *Surely no man has ever loved a woman more than I love Tink.* He wanted to run down the aisle, sweep her up in his arms, and carry her to the altar, but he restrained himself and waited.

"Down, boy," Trapper said over his shoulder with a snicker.

Hank laughed nervously, then licked at his dry lips. *Hurry, Tink, hurry! I've waited so long for this minute.*

When she joined him at the altar, he couldn't resist and slipped an arm about her waist, pulling her close to him, kissing her lips right on top of her veil. "I love you, Tinker Bell."

She smiled up into his face. "I love you too, Peter Pan."

The pastor cleared his throat loudly, and the audience laughed. "Are you two ready to get on with the vows, or shall I just pronounce you husband and wife and get it over with?"

Hank looked up at him with a broad grin. "No, sir, let's do this up right. I've got an arm around her now, and she can't get away. Take as long as you like."

The Baby Quilt

Chapter 1

Jackie Reid's eyes misted over as she stared at the vast array of hand-quilting thread lining the shelves of The Bear Paw Quilt Shop. So many colors from which to choose, so many varieties. Trying to keep her emotions in check, she picked up a spool and rotated it in her fingers. She'd spent weeks planning her project, and now she was ready to begin. The color had to be just right. Blue might be nice since—

"Is that for the new block of the month you're designing for the class?"

She spun around quickly, one hand going to her chest, her heart pounding with guilt, not about to share her thoughts. "I—I didn't know you were here."

Glorianna Timberwolf wrapped an arm about her employee's shoulder and gave it a gentle squeeze. "No wonder! You seemed to be a million miles away. Whatever were you thinking about?"

"Ah—I—ah—was—wondering—if I needed to order more thread, that's all." Jackie donned a fake smile, hoping Glorianna hadn't noticed the tear that had nearly slipped down her cheek. It seemed she wore her emotions on her sleeve these days. She couldn't help it. This time of year always sent her into an emotional tailspin. Especially now that she was getting older. Her biological clock's gentle ticking seemed to clang more loudly each year.

The woman tugged on her arm. "You work too hard and spend way too much time in this shop. Tina and I are going to lunch at The Grizzly Bear, and we want you to come with us."

Her fingers trembling, Jackie hastily put the spool back in its place and stared at the quilt shop's owner. It was hard to think of Glorianna Timberwolf as her boss. Despite their original differences, over time she had become a close friend. "I—I really shouldn't. I have to get next week's schedule posted, and our supply of batting is running low. We need to rearrange the pattern area and change the displays in the windows—"

Glorianna held her palms up with a playful scowl. "Stop! You're making me dizzy. You, Jackie Reid, need to get out more often. Just the other day, Tina and I were talking about you, and—"

"Did I hear my name?" The voice came from somewhere on the other side of a huge quilt display. Both Jackie and Glorianna turned as a lovely, dark-haired woman peeked around the corner, then sauntered toward them. "Glorianna's right. What you need is a man in your life!"

Oh, no. Not that subject again. Jackie steeled herself against the words she knew would follow Tina's pronouncement. Someone was always trying to match her up with one of the local Alaskan men here in Juneau. Why couldn't they understand? There simply wasn't room for a man in her life. Now or ever. At least, not since she'd dated Trapper Timberwolf years ago, long before he met and married Glorianna. Jackie and Trapper's relationship had been more platonic than serious.

Glorianna nodded. "I agree. I was just telling Jackie she works too hard. She needs to take a break and have lunch with us."

"Look," Jackie said, forcing another smile while trying to maneuver herself inconspicuously away from the thread counter. "I appreciate your offer, but—"

Glorianna planted her hands on her hips. "Hey, I'm the boss, remember? I do own this shop. I think I should have some say around here, even if you are the shop's manager." She pointed in the direction of the back room. "Now get your coat, and let's get out of here before some customer tries to lure you away from us."

"Yeah," Tina chimed in, moving to stand by Glorianna. "We need to have some serious girl talk."

Jackie's smile disappeared. "Please, not the we-have-just-the-right-man-for-you thing again." Even though she knew their hearts were in the right place, she wished they'd leave her alone to live her life the way she wanted to live it. *Who am I kidding? My life is nothing like I want it!*

"Aw, sweetie." Glorianna linked her arm through Jackie's. "You deserve some happiness. You have so much to offer. You're beautiful. You have a great sense of humor. You're intelligent."

"Boring. Too demanding. Uninteresting," Jackie added with a shrug. "Besides, I am happy. I love working here at The Bear Paw."

Tina leaned close and shook her finger in Jackie's face. "Hey, who do you think you're talking to? Glorianna and I know you, Jackie. Probably better than anyone else in your life does. No one should have to depend on a job to provide happiness. And, not only that, you're selling yourself way too short. You're far from boring or any of those other things you mentioned. It's just that you've been out of circulation way too long. You need to get out of that apartment of yours and do things. Meet new people. Try new adventures. I can't believe a beautiful woman like you has never married again. Many other widows do."

"I can't believe it, either. She's right, you know," Glorianna added as she nudged Jackie toward the back room.

Jackie forced herself to grin. "What can I say? The right man has never come along. Besides, being single has its good points."

"Yeah, you're only saying that because you've been a widow so long you've forgotten. There's nothing like sharing your life with the one you love, is there, Tina?"

"That's right. I can't imagine life without Hank." Tina grinned at Jackie.

"Get your coat. We're going to lunch, and you're coming with us."

Jackie cast a quick backward glance toward the thread counter. "You win. Okay. Give me a sec."

In less than a minute she was back, purse in hand, and tugging on her coat. Glorianna and Tina, still engrossed in conversation, nodded and headed for the door. Jackie waved toward one of the clerks to let her know she was leaving, then rushed to join them.

Sam Mulvaney's feet were tired, and he'd had about as much of the crowd as he could take for one day. He'd never expected the Dallas helicopter show to be this big. If he didn't find an empty chair soon, he might have to resort to sitting on the floor of the big exhibition hall. Finally spotting one way off in the corner, he hurriedly made his way toward it, hoping someone else wouldn't get there first.

"This chair taken?" he asked the man seated next to it.

"Nope. The guy who was here said he was leaving. Looks like it's yours."

Sam dropped into the chair, placed his briefcase on the floor, then stuck his long legs out in front of him. "I thought I was pretty physically fit, but I'm sure not used to this much walking. My dogs are killing me."

The man turned slightly toward him with a chuckle. "Yeah, mine, too, although I hate to admit it."

"You a pilot?"

His seat companion grinned. "Yep. You?"

Sam nodded. "Sure am. Learned to fly these babies in the army. Been out a year, and I'm still trying to decide what I want to be when I grow up."

"Career military?"

"Yep. Retired after twenty years of service. You ever in the military?"

The man shook his head as the corners of his mouth lifted in a smile that could barely be seen through his thick beard. "Naw, though I considered it at one time. Things weren't goin' so well in my life, and I thought I needed to make a drastic change."

"Being in the military is a drastic change until you get used to it." Sam grinned, shifted his position in the seat, and stuck out his hand. "I'm Sam Mulvaney."

The bearded man took his hand and shook it vigorously. "Trapper. Trapper Timberwolf. Nice to meet you, Sam."

"Umm, Timberwolf. That's an unusual name. Don't think I've ever run into a Timberwolf before. Not even in the army, and believe me, I've heard some unusual names. Where you from?"

Trapper's thumb and forefinger smoothed his dark mustache. "Alaska. Juneau, to be exact. There're a few Timberwolfs up there. None I'm related to, other than my dad and mom."

Sam reared back, his brows raised. "Alaska? Now that's one place I've always wanted to go. I bet it's beautiful up there."

The man's face lit up. "Oh, yes. It's God's country. There's no place like it. You need to visit sometime."

"Yeah, I'd like to," Sam said slowly, trying to remember if he'd ever known anyone who had actually lived in Alaska. "You said you were a pilot. I guess since you're at this Helicopter Association International Show, you must fly a helicopter."

Trapper shook his head. "Nope. I fly a seaplane. A six-passenger de Havilland DHC 2 Beaver."

"Hey, I learned to fly seaplanes when I was stationed at the Fort Lewis, Washington, army base. A Cessna 185 Skywagon. I sure enjoyed flying those things. Sweet model. I've never flown one as big as the de Havilland Beaver." Sam leaned back and crossed his ankles, his feet feeling much better now that he'd taken a load off them. "I've heard seaplanes are as common as those big, old mosquitoes you have in Alaska. Is that true?"

Trapper huffed. "I have to admit our Alaskan mosquitoes deserve every bad comment you've heard about them. They're huge! But, yes. What you've heard is true. Seaplanes are about as common as mosquitoes. But up there we really need them. They're a necessity."

Sam paused, thinking over the stranger's words. "You own your own plane, or do you work for someone?"

Trapper smiled proudly. "It's mine. I formed my own company a number of years ago, but I'm looking to expand. God has been good to me, and I have more seaplane business than one man can handle."

Startled by his words, Sam stared at Trapper. Most of the men he knew didn't go around talking about God the way his new acquaintance did. They used His name in a derogatory way. He'd done the same thing himself, though he wasn't proud of it.

"I'm thankful, of course, that people want to work with me," Trapper went on, "but it does present a problem. I can't be in two places at once. I'm losing business I wish I could keep."

Sam frowned. "I'd think with that many seaplanes in the area it'd be a simple matter to hire a pilot to work with you."

"Ah, but that would mean buying another seaplane. At this point I'm not sure a purchase like that would be wise. For two reasons. Number one: Seaplanes aren't cheap. Number two: I'm pretty picky. I would never hire just any old pilot. He'd have to be not only highly qualified as a pilot, but I'd hope he would share my values."

"I don't get it." Sam extended his hands, palms up. "Why are you here at the helicopter show if your business is flying seaplanes?"

"Because I've decided, instead of adding another seaplane, it might be smarter if I got me a helicopter. I'm sure you know, although it seems a lot of folks don't, that Juneau is only accessible by air or sea. So big trucks and cranes are hard to come by. More and more, as in the other states, heavy-duty helicopters are being used to carry equipment to sites and lower it into place. I've done quite a bit of research, and I'm convinced I could more than double my business the first year with a helicopter. So," he said, gesturing toward only a small portion of the mammoth display that covered acres of ground, "I came down here to check them out."

"Well, you came to the right place." Sam let his gaze wander across the crowded hall. "If you have any questions, this is the place to get answers. Seen anything yet that might work for you?"

"Maybe. I'm going to have me another look tomorrow." Trapper stood, stretching first one arm, then the other, before bending and picking up his briefcase. "But right now I'm goin' back to the hotel, have me a big, juicy steak in the lobby restaurant, then head for my room, where I can sit in the comfort of an easy chair and read all those brochures I picked up."

Sam stood, too. "Sounds like a great idea. I've had about all I can take for one day." He picked up his own briefcase. "Where you staying?"

Trapper laughed. "The closest place I could find. The Hyatt Regency over on Reunion Boulevard. At least they're providing HAI shuttles from here to the hotel—if you can get one, with this crowd."

"Hey, that's where I'm staying. Wanna share a cab?"

"Sure, but only if you're interested in having a steak with me."

Sam nodded as the two men made their way through the throng toward the exit doors. "Sounds good to me. I haven't made any plans for dinner."

"Air!" Trapper said as he burst through the outside doors. He sucked in a big gulp and looked toward the sky. "I'm not used to being cooped up in a building all day. Give me the wide open spaces of Alaska any day."

"Sure like to see that country of yours sometime. I love winter sports. Skiing, hiking, skating, all that kind of stuff," Sam remarked as they motioned to the bellman for a cab. "Maybe someday I'll take one of those cruises I hear about on TV."

"Those cruises are nice, and I can't knock them, because the biggest share of my wife's business comes from them, but you only see a small part of our beautiful country that way."

Sam's interest piqued, he asked, "Oh? What type of business does your wife have?"

The bellman blew his whistle, and a cab pulled up in front of the pair. As soon as the two men were settled and headed for the hotel, Trapper answered Sam's question. "She owns The Bear Paw Quilt Shop. Her building faces the pier where all the cruise ships dock. When those babies unload, that whole area becomes wall-to-wall people. Those cruisers love to shop, and they flock to The Bear Paw. When the ships are in port, you can hardly move through the aisles."

"I didn't know that many women in the world made quilts. I thought it was nearly a lost art," Sam commented, thinking how little he knew of civilians' lives.

Trapper chuckled. "Far from it. You'd be surprised how many people quilt or would like to learn how. And," he said, smiling as if the shop were his instead of his wife's, "she carries a big line of gift items. Real high-quality stuff. She also carries some items made by the bush country people. I pick them up for her when I fly there to deliver medicines and other supplies those folks need. Her customers love the handmade items, and it gives the bush people some much-needed money. They have so little of this world's goods."

Sam was puzzled. "If they don't have much money, how can they afford to pay you to fly those things in to them? Isn't that expensive?"

"Pay me?" Trapper let loose a robust laugh. "They don't pay me! I volunteer to deliver it to them, and I usually spend the rest of the day helping them in any way I can. Sometimes several days."

To Sam, that arrangement didn't make sense. This Trapper fellow seemed like a savvy businessman. Why would he take his precious time, put hours on his plane, and do it for free? "Surely they pay for the things you bring them and your expenses!"

"Nope. Not a penny. For any of it."

Now Sam was really confused. "But why would you do such a thing?" He could see a big grin break out across his new acquaintance's face, even with his heavy mustache and full beard.

Trapper put a hand on Sam's shoulder and looked him eye-to-eye. "For the Lord, man. For the Lord!"

The cab came to a sudden stop. They'd reached the hotel. "That'll be thirty-five dollars," the cabbie said, turning in his seat to face them.

❧

"Sure glad I ran into you," Trapper told Sam as he reached for his water glass. "I was dreading eating alone."

"I know what you mean." Sam glanced around the restaurant. "Looks like we were lucky to get a table. This place is packed."

Trapper laughed. "Sounds like an oxymoron, doesn't it? Eating alone in a crowd."

The two enjoyed a pleasant exchange of conversation until their meal arrived, consisting of huge steaks, baked potatoes slathered with butter and sour cream, green salads, and a basket filled with freshly baked rolls, hot from the oven.

"Umm, do those ever smell good." Sam picked up his knife as he eyed the roll basket.

"Mind if I pray?"

Sam's gaze immediately went to this stranger with whom he'd agreed to have dinner. He slowly placed the knife back on the edge of his plate. "Ah, sure. Go ahead." After watching Trapper lower his head and close his eyes, Sam lowered his but kept his eyes open, hoping those seated around them wouldn't think they were a couple of religious freaks.

"Lord," Trapper began, "I want to thank You for this food You've provided, for Your bountiful blessings, and for Sam. You're so good to us, Father, and we praise Your name. Amen."

Sam felt the corners of his mouth turn up as his gaze met Trapper's. "Doesn't seem to make any sense to thank God for the food when you're the guy who's gonna pay for it."

Trapper returned his smile, picked up his napkin, and spread it across his lap. "Ah, but He also provides my good health, which makes it possible for me to work every day. He guided me to the seaplane I should buy when I went into business. And He sends clients my way, which enables me to pay for my dinner!"

Sam let out a snicker. "I get the point. How long you been into this God thing?" As soon as he asked, Sam wished he could take his question back, realizing some folks might be offended by his flippant attitude.

"Not long enough," Trapper answered, his smile never fading as he reached for a roll. "Once, a long time ago, I was close to the Lord, then my fiancée walked out on me and I turned my back on Him. Not a very smart move for someone who calls himself a Christian."

"I'm sorry—I didn't mean to pry." Again Sam wished he could take back his words. Their meal had started out so pleasantly, and he'd ruined it with his stupid remarks. "I had no right to ask you such a personal question."

Trapper took a bite of his roll, then picked up his knife and fork, poising them over his steak before looking up. "No problem. I don't mind talking about it, if you don't mind listening."

"I never know when to keep my big mouth shut. Thinking before speaking has never been one of my virtues," Sam said with a nervous laugh, still feeling guilty for his lack of acumen.

Trapper inserted the fork into his steak and used the knife to slice off a bite, then waved it in the air. "God has a way of waking a person up. That's what He did with me. Thanks to Him, I got my life back on track, and I wouldn't trade the life I have now for anything. He knew what was best for me. Once I turned control back over to Him, everything fell into place."

Sam mulled over his words. Thinking back over his own life, he wondered how different it might have been if he'd let God take control, instead of making the foolish decisions he'd made on his own.

"More coffee, gentlemen?"

Sam nodded and pushed his cup toward the waiter. Trapper did the same.

"Umm, you can't beat the aroma of a good hot cup of coffee." Sam lifted the cup and took a big whiff.

"You got that right. My wife, Glorianna, always has a big, insulated canteen waiting for me when I leave for the day. I'd hate to think how many cups of this stuff I've drunk in my lifetime."

"Does she like Alaska as much as you do?"

Trapper took a slow sip before answering. "Yes, although it took her awhile to adjust. She's originally from Kansas, but she's a true Alaskan now. You'd never be able to get her to move away."

With a smile, Sam peered at him over the rim of his cup. "Sounds like you have the perfect setup."

Trapper nodded as he placed his cup back in the saucer. "About as perfect as a man can have, I reckon. I think I'll be happy doing just what I'm doing until my dying day." He chortled. "Or until arthritis makes it impossible for me to climb up into my plane!"

Sam sobered. "Wish I could say I loved my job. This past year, ever since I got out of the army, I've been working for a guy who runs a helicopter ferrying service. Although I love the flying part, most of my days are spent transporting businessmen from one place to another. Some to attend meetings, others to look over their vast cattle ranches from the air, some to horse shows, and some just because they're bored. To them I'm only the man who sits in the pilot's seat making sure they have a safe, pleasant flight to whatever destination they've decided they want to go. Most of the time they don't even bother to say hello or goodbye. Maybe, once in a while, one of them will give me a tip, like you'd give a bellhop for delivering your luggage to your room, but that's about it. Kinda makes a guy feel as if he isn't worth much. Know what I mean?"

"Yeah, I think I do." Trapper took another roll from the basket and tore it apart, placing one half on his plate before picking up his butter knife. "They should show some respect for you, considering all the training and hours of flying it took for you to get where you are."

Sam nodded. "Tell that to those pompous corporate execs. They think I'm nothing but a servant."

"There's nothing wrong with being a servant. But even a servant deserves respect," Trapper said with a wink before he popped another piece of the roll into his mouth.

"Well, this job sure didn't gain me any respect! I miss the excitement of my old army days and the missions I flew. I guess I should've stayed in."

"It's too bad they treat you that way, but in God's sight every man has the same value. He plays no favorites."

Sam felt himself fidgeting in his seat. Should he tell Trapper the whole story or keep it to himself? After all, he'd probably never see the man again. What difference did it make?

"Sam? You okay? You seem preoccupied about something."

"I—ah, I don't know why you'd care, or be interested in knowing, but I did something this week. Something I hadn't planned on doing. At least not yet."

Trapper tilted his head and raised a brow. "Oh? From the look on your face, I take it whatever it was, was none too pleasant."

"You're right. It wasn't, but it was for the best. I caught my boss and his secretary in a rather—what shall I say?—precarious situation? The guy has a beautiful, loving wife and four precious children! It made me so mad to think he could do such a thing that I roared into his office and quit." Sam snapped his fingers loudly. "Just like that. I told him I could never work for someone like him and look him in the face every day."

Trapper's brows rose. "Good for you. Men like that need to know they can't get away with cheating on their spouses."

Sam let out a long, slow sigh. "But that means I don't have a job."

"Sometimes a man's gotta do what a man's gotta do. I think you did the right thing. I know I couldn't work with a man knowing he'd take his marriage vows that lightly. I admire you for what you did. Not many men would've taken a stand like that."

"Well, I don't regret it, but it kinda threw my life into chaos. I've had a couple of other offers, but I'm not ready to make up my mind yet. I've even tossed around the idea of forming my own company. I have a little money saved up and some my folks left me. That's why I'm here now."

"Well, timing is everything. Maybe this is your time."

"Yeah, maybe." Sam took his last sip of coffee, placed his napkin on the table, and leaned back in the chair. "I'm stuffed. That was one good steak."

"I agree." Trapper wiped at his mouth with his napkin, then placed it beside his plate. "It's been a good, but tiring, day. I'm gonna look over my notes and the brochures I picked up at the show, then hit the sack."

Sam pulled a few bills from his wallet and placed them on the table. "You going back tomorrow?"

Trapper nodded, then reached into his own wallet. "Yeah, I want to take another look at a couple of models and maybe talk to a few representatives. I have some questions I need answered."

"So you've pretty well decided to add a helicopter to your business?"

"Seems the Lord is leading me in that direction. Now all I need to do is settle on which helicopter will be best for my purposes and find me a pilot."

Sam stood and pushed his chair close to the table. "Well, you've come to the right place. The helicopter show is—"

Trapper jumped quickly to his feet and grabbed onto Sam's arm, his eyes widening. "How about you?"

Sam frowned. "How about me? What do you mean?"

"You interested in moving to Alaska?"

Chapter 2

M e?" Trapper motioned to their empty chairs. "Sit back down. We've got some talking to do."

Sam lowered himself slowly. "About what?"

"I'll have to pray about it, of course, but I've been thinking about the way the two of us met. You know, with God nothing is pure happenstance. You're bummed out with your job and have admitted you need a change in your life. I've decided to buy a helicopter for my business, and I'll need a good pilot. One with lots of experience. Especially one who is also a seaplane pilot. I think you might be my man!"

The eager look on Trapper's face sent Sam's mind reeling. "Me?"

Trapper leaned across the table. "Yes, you. You've said you'd like to see Alaska, and—"

"I said I'd like to visit Alaska." Sam shook his head. "I never said I'd like to move there."

"Ah, but that's only because you don't know what Alaska is like. You'd love it there, man. The air is like no other place, and the mountains are beautiful. You already told me you like winter sports. Think about it!"

Sam leaned back and crossed his arms over his chest. "I—I don't know. It does sound interesting, and you're right. I would like to try something new."

Trapper pulled one of his business cards from his wallet and handed it to Sam. "Like I said, I have to pray about this, but I have this feeling in my gut. I think God wants us to work together. Why don't you come along with me tomorrow when I talk to some of the reps? I'd like your opinion. I'm interested in that Bell 206 L III. It'll lift up to twenty-four-hundred pounds or carry six passengers. That baby is supposed to be a real workhorse. I've been looking at a used one up in Juneau that may be just what I need. Maybe you can give me some insight."

Sam stared at the man. That very morning when he'd stood in front of the mirror shaving, he'd told himself he needed a change. Something challenging. Moving to Alaska would certainly be new and challenging, no doubt about it. "Ah—sure. I'll go with you. I'd intended to go tomorrow anyway."

Once again Trapper stood, this time extending his hand. "We have a busy day ahead of us, Sam. We'd better get some sleep. Meet me here in the restaurant about seven. We'll have breakfast before we go."

Sam nodded. "Sure, seven it is."

Jackie sat staring at the small stack of fabrics she'd brought to her apartment above the quilt shop, arranging and rearranging the colors but never able to come to a decision. Finally, she pushed the fabric aside with a sigh of frustration. Surely there was more to life than this! Oh, she loved her job and loved working for Glorianna, but wasn't it about time she began to think about her future? Was she planning to work in a quilt shop for the rest of her productive years? Then what? What would she do when she reached retirement age? Move into one of those assisted-living places and spend her days playing cards, listening to soap operas, and looking forward to Bingo? She shuddered at the idea. *With no one to care if I live or die?*

She wandered to the window, pushed aside the curtain, and gazed out onto Gastineau Channel. A seaplane was moving slowly across the water toward the docks, leaving a long V-shaped trail behind it. How nice it would be to glide across the water and take off into the clear, blue Alaskan sky, leaving her troubles and cares behind her. She'd gone with Glorianna and Trapper on one of their trips to the bush country, and the excitement and pleasant memories had stayed with her. The feeling of exhilaration she'd experienced at lift-off was like no other feeling she'd ever had. It was as if she were suddenly free—free from all of earth's claims on her. It was a euphoria she couldn't explain. She pressed her forehead to the glass and watched until the little plane taxied up to the dock and came to a stop. What a mess she'd made of her life. If only she could turn back the clock.

"What you need is a man in your life!" That's what Glorianna said, and so had Tina. *But what do they know about my needs?* A tear rolled down her cheek and dropped onto the windowsill. *They don't even know the real Jackie Reid. No one does. No one knows the ache in my heart. No one will ever understand the pain I feel. The empty spot that can never be filled. It's a part of me I'll always keep hidden.*

Sam was waiting for Trapper the next morning at a table in the far corner of the restaurant. Although the two of them weren't to meet until seven, he'd been a full half hour early. He'd lain awake most of the night, thinking over the events of the past week. Exactly one week ago, at about this very same time, he'd gone into the office of K and K Helicopters to check on his upcoming assignments—something he did routinely. That's when he'd found his boss and the secretary together. He'd wanted to deck the guy, but he hadn't. And now he almost wished he had! But what had he done instead? Quit! Right there on the spot. Now here he was, seven days later, unemployed and considering a move to Alaska, of all places!

"Good morning!"

Sam stood quickly, thrusting his hand out to grip Trapper's. "Hello, Trapper." After they were seated and the waitress had filled Trapper's coffee cup and refilled Sam's, the two men perused their menus, both deciding on the breakfast sampler.

"I hope you slept well," Trapper said as he placed his napkin in his lap, then carefully took a sip of the steaming hot coffee.

Sam picked up his cup and stared into it. "Not exactly."

"Oh?" Trapper's brows raised.

Sam offered a weak smile. "I couldn't get our conversation off my mind, about me moving to Alaska and joining your company."

"I thought about it a lot, too, Sam, and I prayed about it. Both last night and again this morning."

"Oh? Did God tell you anything?"

Trapper placed his cup back in the saucer and anchored his elbows on the table, steepling his fingers. "I think He did! I definitely feel Him leading us together, Sam. I don't know exactly how or why yet, but—"

"I thought of nothing else all night. I feel the same way. Almost as if I'm being drawn to Alaska." Sam bent and reached into his briefcase, pulling out a folder. "Look these over, Trapper. The day I quit my job, not knowing what I was going to do, I updated my resumé."

Trapper scrubbed his mouth with his napkin, reached across the table, and took the folder. "Hey, this is just what I needed. Sure glad you brought it with you."

Sam watched as Trapper read over each paper, occasionally looking up with a smile, sometimes even adding a satisfied-sounding, "Uh-huh."

Finally, with a shake of his head, Trapper closed the folder and handed it back to him. "I'd say that's a pretty impressive resumé. In fact, you may be overqualified for my purposes. I doubt I'll be able to pay you what you're worth and still buy that helicopter. I had no idea you had such extensive training, although I have to admit you're exactly the man I'd want to hire if I could afford you."

Sam grinned. "I thought you said your God was leading us together. Are you saying He made a mistake?"

"You got me on that one! No, I know He doesn't make any mistakes, but let's get real. I can't afford you. K and K was paying you some pretty big bucks. You could get a job most anywhere with your credentials."

Sam became serious. "Look, Trapper. Like I said, I was awake most of the night, turning this thing over and over in my mind. Yes, you're right. With my credentials and years of experience, I can probably get a job almost anywhere in the nation. And, I'll be honest, I never once considered Alaska. But being with you and seeing the way your face shows pride when you talk about it, I've come to the conclusion Alaska might be a place I'd like to live."

"But, Sam, I can't pay you what you're worth. Not and buy a helicopter too."

"Bear with me, Trapper. Hear me out."

"Hope you men are hungry," the waitress said as she placed a big breakfast sampler platter in front of each one. "I'll be right back with your biscuits and gravy."

Trapper squared the platter in front of him. "Wow! I had no idea it'd be this big!"

"Me, either, but it sure looks good." Sam sent a smile Trapper's way. "I guess you'll want to thank your God for this, right?"

"Sure do. Do you mind?"

"Nope. Go right ahead."

This time Sam not only bowed his head while Trapper prayed, but he also closed his eyes.

"Here ya are. Biscuits and gravy. Anything else?" the waitress asked as she eyed each man.

"I think we're taken care of, but keep that coffeepot handy," Sam told her with a wink, motioning to his half-empty cup.

"Hey, this ham's pretty good." Trapper gestured toward the big slice of honey-cured ham on his plate.

Sam sliced off a small bite, forked it, then stared at it. The ham might be good, but he had other things on his mind. "As I was saying, I've given this a great deal of thought. About six hours' worth, when I should've been sleeping."

Trapper chortled as he buttered his biscuit.

"Do you remember when I said I'd even considered starting my own business? And I had a little money put back?"

"Sure, I remember."

Sam smiled, then went on. "Look, Trapper—I know how much that model Bell helicopter you're interested in costs. Even used, one will probably go for big bucks. Being in the army for twenty years I had very few expenses, and because of some earlier unpleasant experiences in my life I'd rather not go into, I've been pretty frugal with my money. Not only have I been able to save and invest wisely; as an only child I inherited everything my parents had when they passed away."

Trapper's eyes narrowed. "Are you saying you want to invest in my business?"

Sam sat up straight and tall and looked Trapper in the eye. "I want to be your partner."

❧

"Glorianna, it was the most amazing thing," Trapper told his wife as he sat on the edge of the bed and pulled off his shoes and socks. "I nearly didn't even go to Dallas, but I couldn't get that helicopter convention off my mind. It was as if God was pushing me there. Then meeting Sam like I did was the real clincher. I mean, thousands of people were in that huge convention center, and who comes and sits right beside me? Sam!"

Glorianna sat down beside him and began to massage his shoulders. "But a partner? Are you sure you want to do this? You barely know the man!"

"Umm, that feels good." He turned slightly toward her. "Think about it, sweetheart. If someone had come and applied for the job as pilot, I would've looked over his resumé, visited with him for maybe an hour or so, made a few phone calls to check him out, and, if I liked the guy, probably hired him. Sam not only had his impressive resumé with him, but he has way more credentials than anyone I know, and the two of us did spend nearly two days together!" He reached up and cupped his wife's hand before giving it a reassuring squeeze. "Trust me, Glori. I know what I'm doing. Only God could have led us together the way He did."

"What if he doesn't like Alaska?"

Trapper huffed. "He loves outdoor sports, and he loves flying. Put that together with beautiful scenery, the wide open spaces—and what's not to like? I think the guy'll love it!" He lifted his shoulder a bit. "Ah—right there. That's it."

Glorianna's fingers moved to the spot he indicated.

"Doesn't his wife have a say in all this? Surely he's married."

"Married?" Trapper shrugged. "Don't know. I never asked him, and he never said."

She gave his shoulder a slight slap. "You never asked? You may have an irate wife on your hands, you know. Not many women appreciate their husbands coming home from a convention and telling them they're moving to Alaska!"

"Guess we'll find out soon enough. He'll be here tomorrow afternoon. I made arrangements for Sam to fly in from Vancouver with one of my clients in his King Air. He's meeting Sam there first thing in the morning."

His wife's jaw dropped as her eyes widened. "That soon?"

"Yep. I wanted him to take a look at that used Bell helicopter I'm thinking about buying before I sign the final papers. The guy really knows his stuff, Glori. He's exactly the kind of pilot I need. Even flies seaplanes." He pulled his change from his pocket, placed it on the bureau, and headed for the bathroom. "I thought we might have a little welcome-to-Alaska dinner for him at Mom's restaurant. Let him get a good taste of Mom's Alaskan salmon. Maybe Tina and Hank Gordon will come along."

She followed him and sat on the edge of the tub while he brushed his teeth. "You really think God sent this man to you?"

Trapper pulled the brush from his mouth and gave her a frothy grin. "I've been praying about this for a long time, Glori. I'm convinced Sam is the answer to my prayers."

She gave his image in the mirror a wistful look. "I sure hope you're right. Taking on a partner is a major step."

Trapper rinsed his mouth and dried it on the towel, then, with a smile, bent and kissed Glorianna on the lips. "I know. I nearly lost you by hesitating and not making up my mind. Remember? Dumb me. I even let you and Hank get as far as the altar before I realized how stupid I'd been. I still can't believe I had the guts to snatch you away from him on your wedding day! I felt much better after he and Tina met each other again and he married her."

"I can't believe it, either. I'm surprised Hank will still speak to either of us after what we did to him."

"Only by the grace of God, Glori. Hank is one in a million. Maybe more. I don't know anyone who would've been willing to forgive us like that man. He's a real inspiration. That's why I want Sam to meet him. From our conversations in Dallas, although the man has principles, I doubt Sam's a Christian. Hank will be a good influence on him."

Glorianna frowned as she stood and wrapped her arms around her husband's waist. "As will you, my darling. You're my idea of a fine Christian man." She gave him a squeeze. "Even if you did purloin Hank's bride away before we could say 'I do.'"

He whirled around in her arms and quickly planted a kiss on her cheek before pulling back with a quizzical stare. "Purloin? Is that what I did?"

She giggled. "I remember my mother singing that old song when I was a kid. It said something about 'purloining my true love away.' Isn't that what you did? Purloined me away from Hank?"

He threw back his head with a laugh. "So now I'm a purloiner. I guess I'll have to look that up in the dictionary."

Glori's expression sobered. "I hope you've made the right decision, Trapper, about taking on this Sam fellow. Because if you haven't—"

"I know I have. You'll think so, too, once you've met him." He gently kissed her cheek again. "I've already called Mom and made seven o'clock reservations for our welcome dinner. Now do you want to call Tina, or do you want me to call Hank?"

≈

Sam took one final look at the crudely drawn map Trapper had given him, glanced at the sign, then turned into the parking lot of The Grizzly Bear Restaurant. *Nice place. Wow! Look at all these cars. I'll bet I'm in for a terrific meal.* He switched off the key, checked to make sure his wallet was in his back pocket, and climbed out of the rental car. He shut the door and, with a glance at his watch that told him he was nearly twenty minutes early, headed across the parking lot toward the entrance. *So far, everything Trapper told me about Alaska is true. I think I'm gonna like living here.*

His mind was so caught up with his thoughts that he barely noticed the woman who was also walking toward The Grizzly Bear's entrance, only a few feet ahead of him. That is, until she gave a slight glance back over her shoulder and he caught her profile.

"Jackie?" Sam's mind raced. Were his eyes playing tricks on him? "Is that you?"

Without responding, the woman stopped walking and stood motionless, her back still toward him.

He stared at her, unsure how he should approach her or if he even wanted to. Cautiously, he moved a few steps forward, almost hoping he'd made a mistake and it wasn't her. After all, how many five-foot-five, dark-haired, attractively dressed women could there be in Alaska? Probably thousands and thousands.

Positive he'd made a mistake, he caught up with her and was ready to apologize, when she turned to face him.

Chapter 3

S—am? Is—is that really you?"

Sam couldn't move. *Not Jackie. Not here in Juneau.*

"Wh–what are you doing in Alaska?"

He gaped at her. "I'm—I'm moving here," he finally said, as visions of the woman he once knew so well flooded his mind.

She bowed her head as her hand went to her chest, and she let out a long, slow sigh. "This can't be happening."

Sam fumbled for words. "Surely you don't live here."

Jackie nodded, her gaze still directed toward the ground. "Yes. Juneau has been my home since—" She stopped midsentence.

Sam could have finished that sentence for her. He was sure he knew what she was going to say next. "Why Juneau? You never even mentioned wanting to visit Alaska."

"Strange situations sometimes mean strange resolutions."

The two stood staring at one another for what seemed like an eternity to Sam. Jackie fingered the gold chain about her neck. "Did you get married again?"

He shook his head. "No. How about you?"

"No."

He leaned a bit closer. "Isn't that the gold chain I gave you for your birthday?"

She nodded and turned away. "Yes. I rarely take it off."

"I'm surprised you still have it."

"You said you were moving here," Jackie finally said, still not looking him in the face. "Maybe it'd be best if you changed your mind."

Sam shoved his hands into his pockets and wiggled the toe of his boot in the dirt of the unpaved parking lot. "Too late. I've already made an agreement."

Jackie brushed a tear from her eye. "Oh, Sam. Please don't move to Juneau. This is my home now. I've had the same job for a number of years. I don't want to leave. I assume you're still a pilot. Surely you can find work elsewhere. Please make this easy on both of us and leave."

Her words tore at him and made him more uncomfortable than he'd been in a long time. "I already told you. I can't. Someone is counting on me."

She lifted misty eyes to his. "Juneau is a fairly small city, Sam. I've—I've—"

He frowned. "You've what?"

"I didn't want to have to explain my past or the reason our marriage failed, so when I applied for my job I told everyone I was a widow. That my husband had died in a hunting accident. With you here—"

"With me here you're afraid everyone will find out you've lied?"

She nodded.

"Why would you tell them something like that, Jackie? Surely you knew it would catch up with you eventually."

"No, I didn't think it would. Juneau is miles away from the life I once lived. I never expected someone from my past to show up here. Especially you! And I couldn't stand the idea of calling myself a divorcée. It was like admitting to a failure."

Sam shrugged. "I don't get it."

She took in a deep breath and exhaled it slowly. "Look, Sam. I arrived here with very little job experience, and jobs for people like me with a limited education were hard to come by. I'd done a little quilting when I was in 4H, so when I saw a help-wanted sign in the window of—"

Sam's palm hit his forehead, and he let out a gasp. "The Bear Paw Quilt Shop?"

Jackie stared at him, her mouth gaping once again. "How did you know that's what I was going to say?"

Sam let out a sigh as he laid his hand on Jackie's shoulder. "You're not going to believe this. Talk about coincidence. The man I signed the agreement with to become his partner is Trapper Timberwolf."

Sam felt Jackie reel beneath his grasp, and for a moment, he thought she was going to faint.

Jackie's hands went to cover her face as she began to weep openly. "Once again, you've ruined my life. Oh, Sam, why, of all places in this world, did you have to pick Juneau?"

In some ways, Sam wanted to pull her into his arms and comfort her. In other ways, he wanted to turn his back on her and remind her she was the one who had done the ruining, not him. Instead, he stood awkwardly, his hands dangling at his sides, doing nothing but watch her sob.

"I'll—I'll have to le–leave now. Th–there is no w–way Glorianna will k–keep me on as her ma–manager when she f–finds out my life has been no–nothing but a l–lie."

A silent rage swept over him. "I hate to remind you, Jackie, but your lies are what got you into the trouble in the first place. I would've thought you'd learned your lesson."

Without warning she struck out at him, her fist landing on his chest. "I did not lie to you! I don't know how many times I have to tell you that!"

He grabbed her wrist and held on tight, hoping to avoid another onslaught, his anger with his ex-wife about to get the better of him. "You expect me to believe that? When you just told me how you've lied to your boss and everyone who knows you since you arrived in Juneau? Give me a break, Jackie. Your life has been one constant lie, and we both know it!"

"I did not lie to you, Sam!"

He stared into her mascara-stained eyes, watching the tears roll down her cheeks. Then, in a controlled voice, he said, "Let's not get into that. We both know there's no solution."

She nodded and lowered her eyes.

"Here." He pulled a freshly laundered handkerchief from his pocket and handed it to her. "You've got that black eye stuff messed up."

He watched as she pulled a compact from her purse and wiped at her eyes. He hated to admit it, but she was as beautiful as he remembered her. If anything, she was even more beautiful. *Jackie in Juneau. Unbelievable.*

Still sniffling, she gave him a weak smile. "Talk about irony. Glorianna failed to give me his name, but she invited me here tonight to help them welcome Trapper's new business partner. The last person I expected his new partner to be—was you."

"I'm sorry, Jackie. If I'd had any idea—"

"You couldn't have known."

"I guess not."

She blinked her eyes several times. "I'll turn in my resignation tomorrow, before they have a chance to fire me."

The look on her face was so pitiful, it made him feel like a heel. "No, I'll try to break my agreement with Trapper. It'll be easier for me to leave than you."

She put a hand on his arm. "No, I got myself into this mess. I'll leave. I'll tell them I've had another job offer."

Sam looked down at her with a raised brow. "Another lie?"

"If that's what it takes. But you have to promise me you won't tell them what you know about me. I can't face the idea of Glorianna knowing she's had a liar working for her, managing her shop, even baby-sitting her children. She's been like a sister to me. I can't hurt her that way."

He shook his head. "No, Jackie. I won't let you quit your job. You're already established here. I'm not. Surely there's a way we can get around this."

"How?"

Thoughts raced through his mind. Sure, she'd lied to him, but she'd gone off and made a decent life for herself. Did he have the right to take that away from her? But what about his commitment to Trapper? His partnership with Trapper was the kind of thing he'd hoped for all his life. Was he willing to give it all up because of Jackie's lies?

"I have no other choice, Sam. I have to leave."

He took her hand in his and held it gently. "Look. Either way, I'm going to have to lie to Trapper. If you leave, I'll have to lie to keep Glorianna from finding out why you've lied to her, and I'll be lying by not letting them know the two of us knew one another before I got here. If I leave, I'll have to lie to Trapper about the reason I'm trying to break our agreement. I can't win either way."

"I'm—I'm sorry. It seems I'm always the cause of problems in your life, when I really don't mean to be."

He shook his head sympathetically. "Okay. Here's my offer. We'll both stay, and for now we'll pretend we've never known one another. We'll be the strangers they expect us to be. I don't like this any more than you do, but I can't ruin your life over it."

She brushed away another tear and looked up at him. Sam felt as if he were looking into the face of a naughty, repentant child.

"But be forewarned, Jackie. Our deception may be discovered when we least expect it. A word, or a look, or a slipup, and it's all over. Those have a way of coming out. If that happens, you have to promise me you'll come clean with the Timberwolfs and accept the full responsibility for our lying. Is that a deal?"

"Oh, Sam. Do you mean it? You'd do that for me?"

He felt her hand cover his, and old feelings of protectiveness wafted over him, but he tried to shove them aside. "Not for you, Jackie. I'm doing this for the Timberwolfs and for me. I'm being selfish in all of this. I don't want to give up this partnership, and Trapper is counting on me. I hope you and I will be seeing very little of each other, and we can make this thing work."

"You don't know how much I appreciate this, Sam. I know how opposed you are to lies of any kind. You've always made that clear. I promise if our deception is ever discovered, I'll take full responsibility."

Sam leaned toward her and touched the tip of her nose. "If you're going to have dinner with the Timberwolfs, I suggest you go on into the ladies' room and freshen up. I'll wait a minute before I come in. We don't want anyone seeing us together. Remember," he added with a half-smile as he backed away, "act casual when we're introduced, and don't let your face give you away."

"Thanks, Sam."

Sam watched as she walked away. Except for the tearstains on her face, she was as beautiful as the day he'd married her.

❧

"Hey, guy," Trapper said, rising. "I was beginning to wonder if you were gonna show up. Did you have any trouble finding the place?"

Sam reached out and shook Trapper's hand. "A little. I missed a turn." *There goes lie number one!*

"Oh? I guess I'm not as good a map drawer as I thought I was." He turned and gestured to those seated at the table. "Gang, this is the man I've been telling you about. My new partner and friend, Sam Mulvaney."

Sam grinned as he looked into four friendly faces.

"Sam, this is my wife, Glorianna."

"Nice to meet you, Sam. Trapper's told me all about you. Welcome to Alaska."

Sam reached out his hand. "You're every bit as pretty as Trapper said."

Trapper laughed. "And she's mine. Don't forget it." He turned to the couple seated to Glorianna's right. "These folks are our best friends, Tina and Hank Gordon."

"Ah, the Gordons. Trapper has mentioned you a number of times. I've looked forward to meeting you both."

Trapper waved his hand toward one of the two empty chairs at the table. "Sit down. Take a load off."

"Are you married, Sam?" Tina asked as soon as he was seated.

Sam grimaced. "Married? No. My wife and I divorced a long time ago."

"Well, she made it!" Trapper said with a broad smile, rising again as Jackie approached the table. "Jackie, come and meet my new business partner, Sam Mulvaney."

"Nice to meet you, Sam."

Jackie's hand was shaking as she extended it toward him. Although no one else at the table probably noticed, Sam did.

As Sam rose, he cradled her hand in his and looked into her eyes, and flashes of other, more pleasant, times surfaced from his memory. "Hello, Jackie." He pulled out her chair, waited until she was seated, then lowered himself into his own chair as he'd done hundreds of times over their married life.

"Jackie has managed my quilt shop for years, Sam," Glorianna explained. "If it weren't for her and her wonderful management and people skills, I wouldn't be able to be a full-time mom."

"So this here's Sam!" A tall, slender woman with a raspy voice who looked much like Trapper approached the table, flanked by an equally tall man. "I'm Emily, the mother of that fuzzy-faced man you've taken on as partner. And this here's Dyami, Trapper's father. Welcome to Juneau."

Sam rose and smiled at the pair, amazed by the resemblance. "Nice to meet you both."

"Sit down—sit down," Emily told him as she fluttered her hands toward his chair. "I've got some nice baked salmon waitin' in the kitchen. Your waiter will be here in a minute with your drinks." She and Dyami waved, then scurried off to chat with the restaurant full of customers.

Trapper laughed as he gestured toward his parents. "Guess you can tell who's the talker in our family. Dad doesn't get a chance to say much."

"I like them," Sam said with a grin. It was hard to keep his eyes off Jackie as she sat next to him, and he wondered if the two of them had made the right decision. Would they be able to carry their deception off as they'd planned, or would it backfire in their faces?

Trapper gave his glass a clink with his knife. "Let's hold hands and thank God for our food."

Sam took hold of Glorianna's hand, then reached for Jackie's. How many years had it been since he'd held her hand? When was the last time? He bowed his head and listened as Trapper talked to God, much like one would talk to a friend, and he almost envied him.

"It's a treat to have Jackie here with us tonight," Glorianna said after Trapper's "amen." "I'm afraid she devotes most of her time to my shop." She sent a glance toward Tina that Sam didn't understand.

"I enjoy working at The Bear Paw, Glorianna. You know that."

His gaze went from one woman to the other as the waiter placed their water glasses on the table.

"I know you do, and it pleases me." Glorianna turned her attention back to Sam. "Tina and I have both been telling Jackie she needs to get out more often. Have a little fun. Just because a woman is a widow is no reason for her to quit living."

॰

Jackie nearly choked on her water. She swallowed hard as she set her glass on the table. It was all she could do to keep from looking at Sam, but she knew she didn't dare.

Trapper shook his head. "You'll have to forgive these ladies, Sam. Glori and Tina are like a couple of old magpies when they get together. Always fluttering over one thing or another. Tryin' to fix things that ain't broke."

Glorianna slapped playfully at Trapper's hand. "Well, if Sam is going to be part of our little group, he'll have to get used to it."

"If you got any skeletons in your closet, Sam, you'd better come clean about them now. These girls won't be happy 'til they know every little thing about you." He gestured toward Jackie. "Isn't that right, Jackie?"

She nodded. "Yes, but only because they care about people."

Hank grinned as he took Tina's hand in his. "That they do. If anyone has a problem, these two are the ones to come to. Sometimes, when some of my clients have marital problems, I almost tell them my wife and Glorianna can help them better than I can. As an attorney I can solve their legal problems. But when it comes to personal problems, these two are better, by far, than any counselor I know of."

Trapper leaned to one side as the waiter placed his salad on the table. "Hear that, Sam? But I guess since you don't have a wife, you won't be needing their services."

Sam nodded with a slight grin. "No, I guess I won't."

Jackie shifted nervously in her seat. *Perhaps if Glorianna and Tina had been around to counsel Sam and me, we may have stayed together. Stayed together? What am I thinking? No one could've helped us, not with the way Sam felt about me.*

They finished their salads, then devoured fresh salmon, baked potatoes, green snow peas, and the wonderful bear claw rolls for which The Grizzly Bear was famous.

"Anyone for pie?" Trapper asked when their empty plates had been removed from the table.

Almost in unison, five people shook their heads.

"Well, it's been a good night." Trapper looked around the table. "Good food, old friends, and a new acquaintance who is making a new life for himself here in our beloved Juneau. Welcome, Sam."

Jackie began to relax. Dinner was nearly over, and neither she nor Sam had said or done anything that would indicate they'd ever known each other.

The group bid one another good-bye, promising to have dinner together again soon.

"Where you parked, Jackie?" Glorianna asked as they all exited the restaurant.

Jackie gestured to the far end of the parking lot, pointing toward her sports car.

Trapper pulled his car keys out of his pocket. "How about you, Sam?"

"I'm out that way, too."

Glorianna smiled at the pair. "Good, then you can walk Jackie to her car. We're parked around at the side, right next to Hank's car."

"I don't need anyone to walk me to my car. I'll be—"

Sam stepped forward and slipped his hand into the crook of her arm. "I'll be happy to."

"Good." Glorianna grabbed Trapper's arm and leaned into him as they turned away. "Thanks, Sam."

"Glad to have you with us, Sam." Tina and Hank gave everyone a wave and headed off toward their own car.

"Thanks. It's nice to be here."

Jackie tried to pull her arm away, but Sam held on. "They can't see us now. You can quit pretending."

Sam let out a slight chuckle. "Quit pretending I'm a gentleman? I don't want you walking across this parking lot by yourself."

She stopped, pulling her arm away and firmly planting her hands on her hips. "I've gotten along without you all these years, Sam Mulvaney! Don't start pretending you care about me now!"

He grabbed onto her arm again and gently pushed her in the direction of her car as she struggled to free herself. "Hey, kiddo! From this evening on, our lives are going to be nothing but one big pretense, thanks to you and your lies! You want to call this whole thing off?"

She quit fighting him and let herself relax. "You know I can't do that."

"Then start acting like this is the first time we've met, and let me walk you to your car."

They walked along silently until they reached her car. She pulled her keys from her purse, unlocked the door, and crawled in as Sam stood watching her every move.

"Thanks," she said, forcing a slight smile in his direction.

He pulled a pad from his pocket and scribbled something on it before folding it up and handing it to her; then he gave her a mock salute and headed for his rental car.

As he walked away, she unfolded the paper and read it.

Chapter 4

Jackie stared at the note.

I'm staying at Grandma's Feather Bed Motel. Look up the number in the phone book and give me a call tomorrow. I think we need to talk.

Her gaze followed him across the parking lot. *Sam. My Sam. The love of my life. Oh, he's a bit heavier, and he has a few crinkles at the corners of his eyes, but he's still the handsome man I married when I was eighteen and fresh out of high school.*

She folded the little paper and stuck it in the outside pocket on her purse, pulled the gearshift into reverse, and backed out of her place with one final glance his way. He waved as she pulled out of the lot and onto the street. *Oh, Sam, why did you have to come to Juneau?*

Her apartment above the quilt shop was dark when she pulled into the parking spot marked Manager. Looking around, she grabbed her purse, got out of the car, and moved quickly up the outside stairway. Why hadn't she thought to turn on a lamp before she'd gone to dinner? She hated coming back to a dark apartment. Well, too late to think about that now. Besides, she had other things on her mind.

Like Sam.

Once inside, she made sure to lock the door behind her, turn on a lamp in the kitchen—the one she usually left on all night—and made her way to her bedroom. After a quick shower, she slipped into her pajamas, then took her purse, pulled out Sam's note, and reread it. *I'm staying at Grandma's Feather Bed Motel. Look up the number in the phone book and give me a call tomorrow. I think we need to talk.*

"About what, Sam? What else could we have to talk about?" she asked aloud, the words nearly lodging in her throat as she remembered happier times. Picnics in the park. Rowing on the lake. Holding hands in a movie. Sharing a banana split. Funny how the memory of those insignificant little things stood out above all the rest.

She remembered how she'd argued with her parents when she'd told them she and Sam wanted to get married. "You're way too young," her father had said. "It'll never last!" And it hadn't! Her father had been right—but not for the reasons he'd listed. It hadn't been money or boredom or any of the other things he'd said. If any of those things had been the trouble, perhaps they could've worked things out. Reached a compromise. Her father had been right about one thing. They hadn't known each other as well as they should have. They'd barely discussed the thing that would become the major obstacle in their marriage.

Her cheeks wet with tears, Jackie pulled out a large white box from beneath her bed and set it down beside her. She stared at the lid for a long time before removing it and pulling out six pristine white, hand-quilted blocks, the ones she'd started less than three weeks ago as a memorial to the beloved child she'd lost. "Only six more, Sammy." Her hands trembled as she sorted through the little stack, fingering each one lovingly. "Six more, then I'll add the sashings and borders, and it'll be finished."

She clutched the blocks to her bosom, patting them much like she would a crying baby to comfort it. "I love you, Sammy, my precious baby."

Rocking her body back and forth as she sat on the edge of the bed, she began to hum a lullaby. The windup clock on her nightstand ticked loudly, keeping time with her rhythm.

Finally, she placed the blocks back in the box one at a time, stacking them neatly and smoothing them out with her fingertips. *I'm glad I decided to make this baby quilt for you, Sammy. No one will ever know how I grieved at your death. Somehow just working on it and putting the tiny stitches into it helps lessen my pain.*

From a plastic bag, she pulled a square of white fabric with a quilting pattern traced onto it, along with a piece of batting she'd precut and another square of fabric. This square was also white but printed with tiny flowers. She sandwiched them together with the blue and white one on the bottom and pinned them securely with small safety pins before carefully slipping a silver thimble onto her finger. Taking a threaded needle from her pincushion, she began to quilt.

Unable to think about sleep, she quilted the entire block before placing it back in the box and attaching a long, handwritten note to it. As she lay in the darkness of her room, she thought of Sam.

~❧

Sam tossed and turned. He was dead tired. It'd been a long flight from his home in Memphis to Vancouver; then he had flown with Trapper's client all the way to Juneau. Was that what was keeping him awake? Was he simply too tired to sleep?

Come on, Sam, old boy. You know the trip wasn't that tiring. After all, you slept nearly ten hours in that nice Vancouver hotel after your plane landed. And the trip in that King Air sure didn't take any work or put any stress on your body. Be honest. Seeing Jackie again after all these years is what did it.

He flipped onto his side and buried his face in the pillow. He'd thought he'd gotten that woman out of his system, but who was he kidding? Wasn't she the reason he'd never married again? Hardly ever dated?

He had to admit, even though he'd been shocked when he'd noticed her crossing that parking lot and believed he never wanted to lay eyes on her again, the old vibes were still there. Maybe being in the same city, especially one the size of Juneau, wouldn't work out as well as they'd thought it would. He doubled his fist and rammed it into the pillow. *I hate all this lying! I'm not sure I can live with it.*

Jackie stared at the phone the next morning. She lifted the receiver and slowly held it to her ear, her finger poised idly over the numeric keys. Finally, she dialed.

"I'm glad you called. We need to talk."

Just the sound of his voice twanged at her heartstrings. "Why, Sam? Are you having second thoughts about our arrangement?"

"I'd rather discuss this face-to-face. Why don't you come to my motel about seven? It's out on Mendenhall Loop Road. Just off Glacier Highway, out near the airport. Park in the lot on the west side and come in through that entrance. My room is at the head of the stairs. Number six. I'll order room service for dinner, and we can talk there."

She clutched the phone tightly. "Do—do you think that's wise? Under the circumstances?"

"You have a better idea?"

Her brain raced. With a population of only thirty-one thousand, Juneau didn't have many places you could go without running into someone you knew. "No, th—the motel will be fine."

The day seemed to drag by. Jackie buzzed through her everyday, routine tasks, but her mind was elsewhere. Even the staff noticed, and several of them asked if she was feeling well. She smiled and told them she was fine.

"Hey, whatcha think about my new partner?" Trapper asked Jackie when he and Glorianna came into the shop late in the afternoon. "Nice guy, huh?"

"More than nice, I'd say." Glorianna gave her a teasing smile. "Just about your age, too, and he's single."

"He seemed nice enough." Jackie hoped her words sounded casual. "I'm sure he's an excellent pilot. Didn't you say he'd learned to fly in the army?"

Trapper frowned. "Did I say that?"

Oh, no! Jackie flinched inwardly. Maybe Trapper hadn't mentioned that when they'd all had dinner. How would she know otherwise? Had she already goofed? "Maybe I just assumed it—since so many pilots have received their training that way," she added, trying to cover up for any mistake she might have made. She hated deceiving these people who had been so good to her, but what choice did she have?

"Well, I'm glad he's here." Glorianna slipped her arm into Trapper's. "Let's hope his being here will take some of the stress off my wonderful husband, and he'll be home more often. The children and I miss him when he's gone." She gave Jackie a wink as the pair turned to leave. "Maybe you can show Sam around town. I'm sure he'd appreciate it."

Jackie sent her a please-don't-try-to-be-a-matchmaker look she knew Glorianna would understand.

After closing up the shop, she pulled her car into the motel parking lot at the appointed time. She took a quick glance in the rearview mirror, then warily made her way toward Sam's room, holding her breath with each step.

"Anyone see you?" he asked as he opened the door and motioned her inside.

"No, I don't think so." She glanced around the cozy room. "Nice. Do they really have feather beds?"

He gave her a shy grin. "Yes."

Jackie pulled off her jacket, then seated herself in one of the two wing-backed chairs. "Are you having second thoughts, Sam? Is that why you wanted to talk?"

"I barely slept a wink last night. I hate lying to these decent people."

She leaned back in the chair with a deep sigh. "I know. I hate it, too."

"Trapper and I went to look at that helicopter this morning. The one we're planning on buying for our business. It's exactly what we need, the price is right, and since the guy who owns it is in a financial bind, he's ready to deal." He sat down in the chair opposite her and leaned forward, his elbows resting on his knees. "One problem. We have to give him an answer by tomorrow, or he's going to fly it to Seattle and try to sell it there. I have to be mighty sure this thing is going to work out before I invest my life's savings in this deal."

"Are you—are you saying—?"

"I'm saying I'm still having qualms about this charade you and I are participating in."

Her heart pounded furiously. "So one or the other of us has to leave Juneau?"

His gaze went to the floor as he rubbed at his forehead. "I don't know, Jackie. I honestly don't know. I don't want to leave and let Trapper down, but I don't want you to have to leave, either. After all, you were here first."

She stared at him, wishing she had an answer that would be perfect for both of them. He'd hurt her once, hurt her terribly. So much that she'd even considered ending her life, but she had no desire to hurt him back. She had loved him too much at one time to do that. "Oh, Sam. I'm so sorry. The chance to fulfill your lifelong dream, and I'm the one to mess things up." She reached out and placed her hand on his wrist. It felt good to touch him again. Even in this tense situation, her flesh tingled. "You stay. I'll go."

His hand cupped hers, and her heart soared. "No. This is your home. If we can't work things out, I'll go."

She lifted misty eyes to his. "Don't go, Sam. I can't bear the idea of your disappearing out of my life again. I've missed you, Sam. I know you think lying comes easily for me, but it doesn't. But if lying will make it possible for both of us to stay in Juneau, then lying seems to be our only choice."

"I've missed you, too, Jackie. I tried to find you a number of times, to make sure you were all right. But no one seemed to know where you'd gone, or if they did, they weren't telling. I couldn't stay married to you, not after what you'd done, but that didn't mean I was no longer interested in how you were."

She wanted so much to explain that she hadn't done what he'd thought she had, but what good would it do? Hadn't she already told him a hundred times? Maybe more? He wouldn't believe her then; why should he believe her now? Especially when she was telling him she was willing to lie just to keep her job?

Sam pulled his hand away and extended an open palm. "I'm willing to do whatever it takes so we can both stay. Are you?"

She examined her heart. Of course she would. She'd do anything to keep Sam in her life now that they were able to be civil to one another again. Those last few weeks they'd been together had been miserable. His accusations had hurt her so deeply she hadn't been sure she'd ever recover. Their bitter divorce had been the final blow. She'd never forget the look on Sam's face as he'd walked out of the judge's chambers, his eyes filled with bitterness and hatred. A shudder coursed through her just thinking about it. "Yes, Sam. I'm willing. I'll do whatever it takes."

A knock on the door brought a quick end to their conversation. "Room service," a voice called out.

Although the meal wasn't the best they'd ever had, they both enjoyed it. They talked about old times, the mutual friends they'd had, Sam's final days in the army—everything but the baby.

"I'll walk you out," Sam said when she finally stood to leave.

"No, someone might see us. Can you imagine what Trapper and Glorianna would think if someone told them they had seen us coming out of a motel together?"

He held her jacket out for her. "Yeah, I guess you're right. Go on out, and I'll come downstairs in a minute or two and wander out to my car, as if I'm getting something out of the trunk. At least I have to make sure you get safely to your car."

"No one has checked on my safety for years, Sam. It's not necessary."

The corners of his mouth turned up slightly. "I'm here now, Jackie."

She gave him a guarded smile. "I know."

As she moved toward the door, he suddenly bent down and kissed her cheek. "I'm glad you were able to create a new life for yourself, and I want you to know I wish you well."

She nodded and tried to hold back her tears as she rushed into the hall and down the stairs, the feel of Sam's kiss on her cheek ripping at her heart.

Although it was after nine by the time she showered and dressed for bed, she pulled a new block from the box, threaded a new needle, and began to quilt, letting both her joy and frustration flow through her fingertips as she took each tiny stitch.

Something she'd never expected had happened. Sam was back in her life.

The sudden ringing of the phone made her jump, and she pierced her finger with the needle. Grabbing a scrap of fabric, she blotted at the blood as she picked up the phone. It was Glorianna.

"Hi, Jackie. I hope I'm not calling too late. I tried you several times earlier, but you must've been out. Trapper and I have invited Sam to attend church with us in the morning. Tina and Hank will be there, too. Could I talk you into going with us?"

"I–I don't think so, but thanks for the invitation."

"Oh, come on. I think you'll really like this man once you get to know him. Tina and I have decided he's the perfect man for you. He's good-looking, single, and a real gentleman. It's time—"

Jackie pressed her eyelids together tightly. "I'm sure he's all those things, but—"

Glorianna laughed. "Do you realize, in all these years, you've never once accepted an invitation to attend church with me? We'd love to have you come with us, Jackie. Please say yes."

"Well, when you put it that way—" Jackie answered, feeling trapped but not wanting to admit it.

"Fine. Trapper and I will pick you up at nine-thirty. I'm so glad you're coming with us. We'll all have lunch together—"

"You never said anything about lunch," Jackie countered, remembering how awkward their dinner together had been.

"You have to eat, Jackie. It's only an innocent lunch. See you in the morning." Before Jackie could add a further argument, Glorianna hung up.

"What are you doing here?" Jackie's jaw dropped and her eyes widened when Sam appeared at her door the next morning. "I was expecting the Timberwolfs."

He shrugged. "I got a call from Trapper. He asked if I'd pick you up. What could I say?"

She sucked in a breath of air, not at all sure she was prepared for this, as she grabbed her purse and closed the door behind her.

The Timberwolfs and the Gordons were waiting for them in the church's welcome center. After warm words of greeting and a friendly wave from Emily and Dyami, they all made their way into the sanctuary, with Sam scooting in next to Jackie. He left a bit of space between them, for which she was glad. All went well until the worship leader asked everyone to move a little closer to their neighbors to make room for others who were looking for seating in the overcrowded sanctuary, and she felt Sam slide toward her.

She didn't know most of the music, and she was sure Sam didn't, either, since the two of them had rarely attended church during the time they were married; but she thoroughly enjoyed the congregational singing. She'd forgotten what a mellow baritone voice Sam had, and she kept remembering how he used to sing in the shower.

It was hard to sit that close to him, their shoulders touching. She could feel his warmth radiating through the flimsiness of her sleeve. Occasionally, she would slip a sideways glance at his strong profile, and her heart would flutter. Sam Mulvaney. She'd never expected to see him again, and here he was sitting beside her.

Once the six friends were all gathered around the table at The Grizzly Bear, Trapper asked God's blessing on their food. Jackie sneaked a peek at Sam just before the "amen" and was surprised to find him with his head bowed and his eyes closed.

"What did you think of the pastor's message? That man really knows God's Word," Trapper said when the conversation started up again.

Hank nodded as he reached for the basket of rolls. "Can you believe the way he explained those parables? I don't think I'll ever forget that illustration he used about the prodigal son." Then, turning his attention toward Sam, he asked, "What church did you attend in Memphis, Sam?"

Sam shot Jackie a nervous glance. "I—ah—really didn't have time for church."

Tina's brows raised. "Surely you didn't work seven days a week!"

"Now, Sweetie, don't go giving Sam a hard time," Hank inserted with a reassuring smile toward Sam. "Some guys do work seven days a week. I know I did when I was in college, and I still had trouble paying my bills!"

"Whew! I'm glad that's over," Jackie whispered to Sam as they made their way out of the restaurant and toward his car. "I don't know about you, but I was pretty uncomfortable."

Sam nodded. "Yeah, me, too. It was bad enough worrying if they were going to ask us something we'd have to lie about; but then they started talking about the preacher's message, and Hank asked me about going to church. I don't like this one bit, and I don't enjoy talking about that God stuff. I'm so afraid I'll say the wrong thing or mention something I shouldn't, or my face will give me away when I'm lying."

"I feel the same way; only I've been living like this for the past seventeen years. I've lied so long, I've nearly forgotten what real truth is." She wished she hadn't said that. It almost sounded like a confession.

"Oh, great! A flat tire!" Sam said with disgust as he squatted and glared at the back wheel. "I thought they were supposed to keep good tires on these rental cars."

Jackie leaned over him and stared at the offensive tire. "Do you want me to call someone to—?"

"I can change it myself," he half-snapped as he rose and inserted the key in the car's cargo compartment. "Just stay back out of my way."

She watched silently as he yanked off his jacket, despite the chilliness of the day, and struggled to pull the jack loose.

"You'd think those engineers would come up with a better way than this to attach a jack! It's obvious they've never had to change a flat tire."

"Ah—maybe you should undo that thingamajig," she said warily as she peered over his shoulder.

He stopped fumbling and looked up at her. "What thingamajig?"

She moved past him and touched a shiny, round metal strip. "That one."

He gave her a look of exasperation as he twisted the metal strip to one side and slid the jack free. "Dumb way to do it, if you ask me."

She swallowed a giggle but didn't respond.

"Now where'd they put the handle?" he asked, still holding the jack while shoving a toolbox, a bag of rags, and a shovel to one side.

Men! Jackie leaned over and pulled a metal bar from along the side of the cargo area's wall. "This it?"

Sam nodded his head, a deep frown cutting into his forehead. "Thanks."

But as he inserted the metal bar into the side of the jack, it was at once obvious the two pieces weren't meant to go together. "Can you believe it? Someone put the wrong size handle in here!"

She watched anxiously as his jaw tightened, afraid he might explode from frustration at any minute. "I could call—"

"No! I'll figure something out. Just be patient!"

Okay, buster, you're on your own!

He adjusted his position as he stared at the jack, as if by willing it he could make the handle somehow fit.

Jackie pulled her collar up around her neck, trying to ward off the slight wind. "Ha–have you ever worked a jack like this one before?"

"Course I have," he said in a monotone without turning to face her.

"Maybe someone in the restaurant has a jack they could loan you."

This time he didn't turn his head; he just stared at the tire. "I said I'd figure something out."

He stood, glaring at the jack, then the handle, then the jack again. She could almost hear the wheels of his brain churning.

Typical male response.

Finally, he leaned into the trunk again, this time pulling a small roll of tape of some sort from the toolbox. "Aha! Maybe I can make this work." He snapped off a short length of tape and wound it around the handle, wrapping it as tightly as he could. But when he tried to slip it into the jack's opening it was too thick.

He gave her a macho man look as he pulled out his pocketknife and began to whittle tiny pieces from the tape.

"Hey, man. Need some help?" a young man who looked to be in his mid-teens asked as he drove slowly by in a beat-up old car that looked like a refugee from a junkyard.

Sam donned a carefree smile and waved him on. "No, thanks. I've got every-thing under control."

The kid smiled back at him, turned his stereo on full blast, and drove off.

"Why didn't you ask him if he had a jack?" Jackie asked, her patience wear-ing thin.

" 'Cause I'm gonna make this thing work!" he snarled back, the pleasant expression he'd given the young man now history. "Wait in the car. No sense in you standing out here in the cold."

With one final push, he shoved the metal handle into the jack's opening. "Got it!" His face beamed victoriously.

He slipped the jack into its proper position under the car's frame and began to pump away with the handle, the car rising ever so slightly with each down-ward motion.

"See—I told you I'd do it," he told her, turning to her with a typically male smile as he gave the handle one more stroke. But he'd no more than uttered the words when the metal handle unexpectedly slipped from its hole.

Jackie screamed as she watched Sam's hand, still holding the handle, crash into the jack's heavy metal base.

He grabbed his injured hand and held it to him as he struggled to stand. Blood flowed from the fresh wound on the back of his hand.

Intuitively, she grabbed the silk scarf from her neck and wrapped it around his hand as he stood groaning and leaning against the side of the car.

"Is it broken?" she asked with concern.

"How should I know?" he spat out between groans as he bent over and cra-dled one hand in the other.

"We need to get you to a doctor," she said, trying to reach his hand to see what damage may have been done to it.

He tilted his head back and squinted his eyes tightly together. "We don't have transportation, or have you forgotten?"

"I'll see if there's a first aid kit in the glove compartment," she said, for lack of another solution, as she crawled into the car.

"They wouldn't put a first aid kit in a rental car!" he shot back at her.

She crawled out of the car with a smile. "Maybe not, but they might put one of these in there," she told him, holding up a fairly good-sized vinyl bag. "It was under the front seat."

His face still scrunched up with pain, he asked, "What is it?"

She moved quickly beside him and opened the bag so he could see its con-tents. "I'd say it's a small air compressor. Looks to me like one of those thingies that hooks up to the cigarette lighter."

Sam stared at the bag. "Guess I got all riled up for nothing."

"Happens in the best of families," she told him, still worried about his hand

and trying to muffle her amusement. "Now, if you'll talk me through this, we'll get this tire pumped up and get you to the hospital. That hand looks like it could use a couple of stitches."

She located a small package of tissues in the car's console and placed a handful against the gaping cut on his hand. Ignoring his protests, she wrapped the blood-soaked scarf around the tissues to hold them in place. Then, taking the little compressor from the bag, she smiled up at him. "You gonna tell me how to work this thing?"

She followed his instructions as she hooked the compressor from the lighter socket to the tire valve, and soon the air was flowing through the line and the tire was inflating.

"Not too much," Sam cautioned. "There—I'd say that's about enough. That should hold it until I can change it."

She shook her head. "No, until you can get it to someone else who can change it. From the looks of that hand you're not going to be changing any tires for a few days." She crawled into the driver's seat and motioned him inside. "I'm taking you to the hospital."

It was nearly two hours before Jackie pulled Sam's car into the parking place in front of her apartment.

"I'm sure glad you didn't break any bones," she told him sympathetically as she shoved the gearshift into the park position. "The way your weight went flying onto that hand, I was afraid you'd be walking out of that emergency room wearing a cast."

He stared at the bandage. "Yeah, me too, and I'm thankful it wasn't my left hand. I'm not ambidextrous like some left-handed people are. I'm a total lefty."

She grinned. "I remember."

He reached into his jacket pocket with his free hand and pulled out a small plastic bag containing her bloodstained scarf. "The nurse put it in there. Guess I owe you a new one."

"Actually, you gave me this one. For Christmas the first year we were married." She took the bag from him and slipped it into her coat pocket. "I only wear it for special occasions. I—I was hoping maybe you'd remember it."

He shrugged and smiled awkwardly. "Afraid I don't."

"It's a man thing." She reached for the door handle, then gave him a smile. "Only women remember things like that."

"I owe you more than a scarf." His face took on a sheepish grin. "Thanks for being patient with me today. You know, about the tire. I guess I behaved pretty badly."

"Not too bad. Considering."

"Jackie."

"Yeah?"

"Remember that time you warned me about driving over that rocky road near our apartment and I did it anyway?"

She dipped her head and gave him a sideways smile. "Uh-huh, I remember."

"I do some pretty stupid things, don't I?"

"Umm, no more than most of us do, I guess. We've all done our share of stupid things." She pulled her coat about her and slipped out of the driver's seat. "Sure you don't want me to drive you back to the motel?"

He opened his door and crawled out, cradling his hand. "Naw, I can drive with one hand."

As they passed one another, Sam reached out and pulled her to him.

Startled, she stared up into his face, not sure what was going to happen next.

He cuffed her playfully under her chin. "You're a real trooper, Jackie Mulvaney."

She gave his arm a slight slap. "Jackie Reid, remember? Make sure you don't slip up and call me that in front of Trapper or Glorianna!"

He grasped onto her arm and leaned into her face, his warm breath falling upon her cool cheeks. "You'll always be Jackie Mulvaney to me."

She caught her breath as he moved closer, and when his lips touched hers, she felt herself yanked back to a time nearly twenty years ago. A time when she and Sam had been so in love they couldn't bear to be separated for more than an hour. She leaned against him, enjoying the sweetness of his kiss, reveling in their nearness.

Sam. Her Sam.

As his kiss intensified, she melted into him, and for that brief moment, she was his again, and it felt wonderful.

"Thanks for putting up with me today," he whispered against her lips. "Sorry for my bad manners."

"I was glad I was there for you."

He kissed her once more, then pulled away with a grin. "Yeah, me, too. I'd better get out of here."

She dipped her head and gave him a shy smile. "Please be careful driving."

He nodded as he crawled into his car. "I'm always careful."

When the phone rang in her apartment at nine that evening, Jackie assumed it was one of the staff calling in sick and took her time answering.

"Hi, it's me."

She recognized the voice immediately. It was Sam.

"I've thought long and hard about this, Jackie. Kissing you was a mistake. I got carried away, and I apologize. I've been thinking a lot about things since I got back to the motel. After our uncomfortable lunch with the Timberwolfs and the Gordons today, I've come to a decision, and I doubt you'll like it."

Her heart dropped with a thud.

"Tomorrow's the day Trapper and I are supposed to either accept or refuse the man's offer on that helicopter. I hate to go back on my word, but I have to get out of here before things go any further. I can't keep all this lying up, Jackie. It's against everything I've ever believed in."

Jackie felt her herself go weak, and she grabbed onto the chair beside the phone. "Wh–why? I thought we—"

"I'm not a liar, Jackie. I'd like to help you out, but I can't do it. I've wrestled this thing back and forth since that first night. My mind's made up. There's nothing else to talk about. Your secret's safe. I won't tell Trapper about you."

A click, and the phone went dead.

Jackie couldn't move. His words had pinned her hand to the chair. *Sam, oh, Sam.*

Eventually, she made her way into the bedroom and collapsed face-first across her bed. "God," she cried out, beating the lovely, double-wedding-ring quilt with her fists as tears gushed forth, "if—if You're r–real, and Y–You're a God of lo–love like the pa–pastor said this morning, ho–how could You let our ba–baby die? And how co–could you let S–Sam come back into my li–life again? You know how much I lo–love him. How mu–much I've always loved h–him. Now he's wa–walking out on me a–again. The pa–pain is more than I can be–bear!"

After she'd cried herself out, she pulled the seventh block from the box, removed the note she'd pinned to it, and added a few more lines, telling her precious Sammy his father had changed his mind and was going back to Memphis.

❧

Trapper grinned from his seat behind his desk as Sam entered. "Morning, Sam. Well, this is our big day! By the way, how's that hand doing? I heard about it from Glorianna. Guess she'd talked to Jackie."

"Doin' okay, I guess. Still pretty sore." Sam walked slowly across the little room, his face somber, as he pulled a folded paper from his jacket pocket and placed it on the desk before his new friend. "I hate to do this to you, Trapper, but our deal's off. I know it's not even official yet, since we haven't signed a legal contract spelling out the conditions, but I'm dissolving our partnership."

Frowning, Trapper stood, unfolded the paper, and read it silently. "This is some sort of joke, right?"

Sam shook his head. "No. No joke. I'm going back to Memphis. I have a reservation booked on the next flight out."

Trapper dropped back down in his chair and stared at him. "I thought you were as happy about this deal as I was. Did something happen to change your mind?"

Okay, Sam. Go ahead. Tell another lie. What's one more going to hurt? "I've decided I don't like Alaska after all. After hearing the local folks talk about those long Alaskan nights, I'm afraid I'd get claustrophobia."

Trapper's fingers worked at his beard. "But—you knew all about that before you came, and honest, those long nights aren't that bad. You get used to them."

Sam's good fist clenched at his side. "This place is too isolated for me. I'd go stir-crazy. Nope. My mind's made up. I can't stay."

"I'll be honest, Sam. I'm completely baffled. I knew, I just knew, the Lord had brought us together. You were an answer to prayer, Sam."

"Well," Sam said, backing toward the door, anxious to get out of Trapper's sight as quickly as possible, before he broke down and told him about Jackie, "maybe you only thought He did. Sorry to disappoint you, but I'm outta here. I've got a plane to catch."

"If you change your—"

"Sorry, but I won't. Please give my regrets to your wife, and tell Tina and Hank good-bye for me." With that, Sam closed the door and hurried to the rental car.

❧

Still dressed in her pajamas, with her eyes swollen and red from crying most of the night, Jackie sat staring out the window of her second-floor apartment. Earlier she'd phoned one of the ladies on the staff and told her she wasn't feeling well but would try to be in later in the day. Every bone in her body ached, and her head was killing her. In less than a week's time, her life had become a mess, and she didn't care if she lived or died.

She ignored the slight rap on the door, thinking it was probably her neighbor, an elderly woman who occasionally brought over fresh cinnamon rolls. But when she heard Sam's voice calling out her name, she rushed to the door and flung it open. "Did you change your mind? Are you staying?"

He stepped in and closed the door behind him.

Chapter 5

No, I'm afraid not. I can't stay in Alaska, Jackie. I think we both know that. I've already given Trapper my resignation."

"I–I was afraid of that."

He shifted uncomfortably, fingering his bandage. "I've never been much for believing in God and praying and all that stuff, as you well know. But sitting in that church yesterday morning I felt God's presence. Just looking at that beautiful stained glass window made me feel guilty. It was bad enough that I was lying to Trapper and Glorianna and the others, but to God?" He moved to the sofa and sat down, patting the seat beside him. "I know if I stay Trapper'll expect me to go to church with them. I don't think I could handle that a second time."

"Telling him must've been difficult."

"I felt like an idiot. I couldn't give the man a single valid reason for walking out on him."

Realizing she was still in her pajamas, Jackie quickly pulled her robe from the chair where she'd left it the night before and slipped it on before sitting down beside him. "I know what you're saying. I felt the same way. It was as if God was shaking His finger at me."

"Well, I just came by to tell you if you ever need me, you can reach me at this number." He pulled one of his old business cards from his pocket and handed it to her.

She stared at it. "You're going back to Memphis?"

He nodded. "Yeah. Aside from the years you and I lived together and my years in army housing, it's the only home I've known."

"Was Trapper angry when you told him?"

"No, but I almost wish he had been. I'd have felt better if he'd punched my lights out like I deserved." He shifted in his seat again. "You know what he said? He said he'd been sure God had sent me to him. Can you believe that?"

She nodded thoughtfully. "Yes. Knowing Trapper, I can believe it. He never does anything, no matter how insignificant it is, without praying about it first. He's a remarkable man."

"That he is, and I'm one big louse for deceiving him."

"You want some coffee? I could sure use some."

He glanced at his watch. "Sure. I've got a couple of hours before I have to head to the airport." He gave her a slight grin. "While you're in the kitchen, you might want to do something with your hair."

She felt herself blushing. She must look frightful! All that crying, and she hadn't even brushed her teeth yet, let alone combed her hair. "I had a rough night," she said simply.

When she came back five minutes later with two steaming cups of coffee in her hands, she had applied a touch of makeup to her face, her hair was combed, and she was wearing a dab of lipstick. If Sam was leaving, she didn't want him to remember her the way she had looked when he'd arrived at her apartment.

"Here you go," she said, smiling as she handed him his cup. "I'm glad you came by."

"Me too." He sucked in a deep whiff of the rich, dark coffee and exhaled slowly. "You and I've had a pretty tumultuous life, haven't we?"

She nodded as she stared into her cup. "Good word for it. Tumultuous. But we had some good times too." She watched as Sam blew into his cup, then took a slow sip. "I loved those good times."

"Yeah. Too bad they had to end."

She felt herself tense up. "You ended them, Sam. Not me. I never wanted the divorce. It was your idea. I loved you. I loved our life together."

He frowned over the rim of his cup. "I ended it? I think you have a lapse of memory. As I recall—"

She quickly set her cup on the coffee table with a kerplunk. "Why can't you believe me? I wanted that baby as much as you did!"

He banged his cup down beside hers. "Can't you stop lying, even for a moment? I remember very distinctly when I told you on our fourth wedding anniversary that I thought it was time we had a baby. And what did you say? You said, 'No, I don't want children!' Isn't that right?"

Her insides began to churn as her own anger flared. "I was twenty-three at the time! We hadn't even discussed when we'd start our family! And you were in the army! We had no idea when you might be sent off to some faraway place, if I'd get to go with you or if I'd be left at home—waiting and hoping you'd return safely! Having a baby was the furthest thing from my mind. I'd never even been around a baby. How did I know if I'd be a good mother? Or if I'd end up leaving my child with a baby-sitter most of the time like my mother did with me? I wouldn't wish that on any child! And, besides, I wanted to go to college and make something of myself. There wasn't room in our lives for a baby. At least not then!"

His eyes flashed as his thumb went to his chest. "You didn't need to go to college! I was supporting you! Me! The breadwinner of the family!"

"On army pay? Hey, don't forget I was a military brat myself!"

He leaned back on the sofa and, with a grunt of frustration, locked his hands behind his head. "I'll never forget the look on your face when that doctor said you were pregnant."

Annoyed, she shifted her weight from one foot to another. "Okay," she said, willing her voice to sound calm. "I admit it. I was upset. No, I was worse than upset. I was furious with you. I thought you'd tricked me because you wanted a baby, and you knew I wasn't ready."

"I didn't trick you, Jackie. I mean it. I hope you believe me."

She pointed a finger in his face, her anger rising with each breath. "You have the nerve to ask me to believe you, when you wouldn't believe me?"

"You didn't want that baby, and you know it!" he shot back. "Why don't you just admit it?"

"I did want our baby!" She drew a stuttering breath. "Ho—how many times do I have to tell you? Oh, not at first! I'll admit that, but—"

He spun around, his chin jutting out defiantly. "You wanted an abortion, and you got it! You didn't care what I wanted! I would've taken that baby and gladly raised it alone if necessary, but you—"

She jumped to her feet and leaned over him, firmly planting her hands on her hips. "I didn't get an abortion! How many times do I have to tell you? If you hadn't stormed off and taken that long assignment in Germany so readily, you would've been there with me, and you would've known!"

"You grumbled the entire three months before I left on that assignment to Germany!"

"Of course I grumbled. I felt lousy! I was sick to my stomach every day; my feet and hands were swelling! You knew I was miserable, but did you stay home? Tell the army your wife was having trouble with her pregnancy? No! You headed off to Germany with your flyboy friends! Flying those helicopters of yours was more important to you than your pregnant wife! I was alone, Sam. I needed you there with me!"

"Having a baby is a perfectly normal event. A lot of army wives go through their pregnancies with their husbands overseas. You were young and healthy. You didn't need me by your side every moment!" Sam rose and began to pace about the room. "That assignment meant more money. Something we needed very badly, or have you forgotten all the furniture and appliances we went in debt to buy?"

"I begged you to stay. You knew I was frightened. This was my first baby, and I was all alone. How do you think that made me feel? You were the one who begged me to have your baby, and you left me!" She plopped back down on the sofa, her head in her hands. Why couldn't he understand? Why didn't he believe her? The look on his face told her he was no more ready to believe her now than he had been then.

"I admit I wasn't ready to have a baby before that. But when I had my fifth month checkup and saw that tiny figure on the ultrasound screen, I wanted to shout for joy. I had no idea you could see things like that." She felt herself smiling at the remembrance. "I'd even heard our baby's heartbeat. Call it a natural maternal instinct or just plain loving it because it was a product of our love—whatever the reason, I suddenly knew I wanted that baby to live and be healthy."

He whirled around to face her. "You expect me to believe your melodramatics? Admit it, Jackie! You got rid of our baby! I made it easy for you, didn't I? Taking off for Germany like I did. If I had been there—maybe I could've talked you out of it. Or at least made you promise to have it and let me raise it."

Her eyes widened. "I wish you had been there. Maybe if you'd seen the agony and pain I suffered, you'd understand. That doctor tried to save our baby. He did everything he could. I hoped and prayed our little boy would make it!"

Sam covered his face with his hands. "It was a boy? I had a son?"

"Yes. A boy," she answered softly. The grief written on his face as he withdrew his hands tore at her heart.

He lifted his head slowly, his look of grief suddenly changing to a look of anger once more. "You did away with my son?"

"No!" She stomped her foot. "I didn't! The doctor said that many times, when there was a problem like I—"

"Problem? I know more about your problem than you think I do. I haven't told you this because a wife of one of the guys in my unit told it to me in confidence. It's the main reason I have a hard time believing you, Jackie."

Her eyes widened. "What? What could she have told you? I'd like to know."

"She said you asked her if she knew any doctors who'd quietly perform an abortion since you didn't want to go to the army doctor." He turned and headed for the door, his eyes menacing as one hand rested on the knob, his bandaged hand pointing at her accusingly. "Are you going to tell me that never happened and his wife was lying about it? What reason could she have?"

Jackie hung her head with shame at even remembering she'd done such a thing. "No, I'm not denying it. I did ask that woman about a doctor, but that was only a few days after you left for Germany, long before I heard our baby's heartbeat and the doctor did the ultrasound. I—I was upset about you leaving me."

"That's what you say now, but that's not the way I heard it!"

"Maybe the woman forgot when it was I asked her." She grabbed onto his arm. "I am telling you the truth, Sam!"

"The truth? You've told so many lies, Jackie, that I doubt you even remember what the truth is." He jerked his arm away. "I should've had my head examined for even thinking I could stay in the same city with you!"

He yanked the door open and stood glaring at her.

The tension in the room nearly crackled, and the hatred she saw in his eyes made her want to vomit. She grabbed onto his arm. "If only you'd talked to the doctor on duty at the hospital emergency room! He would've told you—"

"The emergency doctor at some little rinky-dink neighborhood hospital? If it happened like you said it did, which I doubt, why didn't you call the army

OB-GYN? Answer me that!"

"Sam! I tried to explain that. I was frightened when I started hemorrhaging. All I could think about was getting to someone who could help me. The hospital was much closer than the doctor's office. I was scared, Sam! Surely you can understand that. I wanted my baby to live as much as you did!"

He yanked his arm from her grasp and stepped through the door. "Good story, but I don't believe a word of it."

She flinched as the door slammed hard behind him. The sound of screeching tires told her Sam was out of her life. This time for good.

❧

"Oh, Jackie, you'll never believe what happened!"

Jackie looked up from the ledger and fiddled with the tea bag in her cup, hoping Glorianna wouldn't notice how upset she was.

Glorianna leaned forward and let out a slight gasp. "What happened? Your eyes are all red!"

"I—I changed contact cleaner. The new stuff must've irritated my eyes." *Another lie. Where is this all going to end?*

"Well, you better let your optometrist take a look at you. Your eyes are really puffy."

Jackie nodded. "I will."

"Well, as I was saying," Glorianna went on, "you'll never believe what happened. That nice Sam Mulvaney—he walked right into Trapper's office yesterday and quit! Resigned! He gave him some flimsy excuse about Alaska's darkness and isolation. Trapper was shocked. He was sure God had led him to that man."

Jackie glanced down at the floor awkwardly. "I—I'm sorry to hear that. I know Trapper was counting on him."

Glorianna rolled a chair up beside her and sat down, still talking about Sam. "Tina and I were so excited when we met Sam. We were sure he was the perfect man for you. When we saw the two of you sitting together in church, well, we both just knew you were made for each other. Sam seemed to be one of the nicest men I've ever met. Trapper even mentioned he thought you two would make the perfect couple, and he's usually a great judge of character."

Jackie wanted to clamp her hands over her ears to block out Glorianna's words. If only she knew—

"He was such a kind and thoughtful man. I was positive he would sweep you off your feet the way Trapper did me, and you two would live happily ever after. Of course, Sam never did say he was a Christian, and that's very important if you want to have a happy marriage."

Glorianna gazed off into space. "I'm sure you remember how far Trapper and I were from the Lord when we met. I was pregnant with my deceased husband's baby, and when Trapper learned that, I figured he'd be gone forever. He wasn't sure he even wanted children, especially another man's child. But God intervened. He wanted us together. If two people love each other and are committed to Him, Jackie, they can work out almost anything. Trapper and I are living proof of that."

Jackie well remembered Trapper and Glorianna's courtship. At one time, she'd even deluded herself into thinking perhaps Trapper was interested in her. *Maybe if Sam and I had gone to church and become Christians and made more of an effort to understand each other's feelings, we could've made it. What was it the pastor said Sunday? That we must confess our sins and ask for God's forgiveness?*

Glorianna was so caught up in her one-way conversation that she didn't seem to notice Jackie wasn't making any comment. "I don't know how anyone can get along without the Lord in their life."

"But—what if you haven't committed any really big sins?"

Glorianna rested her hand on Jackie's shoulder. "Oh, sweetie, the Bible says all have sinned. That means everyone. You, me, Trapper, even that nice Sam Mulvaney!"

"So you're saying if I don't confess my sins and ask God to forgive me and turn my life over to Him, I won't go to heaven?"

"Oh, Jackie. I didn't say it. God did."

Jackie closed the ledger and folded her hands on top of it. "Someday I might want to do that, but not now. I'm not ready. I have too many other things on my mind."

Glorianna gave her a smile as she patted her shoulder affectionately. "God's always ready to listen, but don't wait too long. I'm here, if you ever want to talk."

I really don't want to discuss this now. "Look, Glorianna. I appreciate it that you're concerned about me, but you'll have to excuse me. Some new merchandise arrived this morning, and I need to go over the invoices."

Jackie left work earlier than usual and trudged her way up the steps to her apartment. She opened a can of vegetable soup, heated it in the microwave, and carried it into her living room. After eating less than half of it, she picked up the remote and turned on the TV, flipping from channel to channel without seeing what was on.

She gave up and turned it off. She carried her bowl back into the kitchen, dumped the uneaten soup into the garbage, and placed the bowl and spoon in the dishwasher. As she moved to the coffeemaker, she remembered the last time she'd used it. When she'd made coffee for Sam. Rubbing her eyes with her sleeve, she filled her cup and carried it into her bedroom, then placed it on the edge of her bed, staring at the blank wall.

Finally, she picked up the new quilting magazine that had come in the morning mail, leafed through it quickly, then tossed it onto the bed. *Oh, Sam, if only I hadn't been so childish and you hadn't been so determined.*

She moved robotically into the bathroom, brushed her teeth, and readied for bed. Why did life have to be so hard?

Oh, Sammy, my precious, precious Sammy. I did want you! You do know that, don't you? I don't know if babies go to heaven, but I hope you can hear me.

Heaven! Panic seized her. *If I don't ask God to forgive my sins, does that mean I won't go to heaven?* The thought terrified her. What if Glorianna was right? What if the only way someone could be sure she was going to heaven was the way Glorianna had explained it?

Wearily she dragged herself into bed, still entertaining thoughts of Sam. *I'll always love your father, Sammy, no matter what.*

Jackie struggled to get through each day, putting on her mask, laughing when she didn't feel like laughing, going through the usual routine of managing the shop, but every waking moment was filled with thoughts of Sam. Was he back in Memphis? Working at his old job? Did he ever think about her? Had her words made any impression on him? Would she ever see him again?

Some days she picked up the little card he'd given her and nearly dialed his number in Memphis, if only to hear his voice. But, remembering how eager he was to get away from her, she hadn't been able to do it.

The following week was no better. Finally, after realizing she had practically nothing in the apartment to eat and not wanting to go out to a restaurant alone, Jackie drove to the grocery store. She grabbed a cart and began pushing it down the aisle, grabbing things willy-nilly off the shelves, unconcerned about their fat or calorie content or if they were things she'd even eat. She just wanted to finish her shopping and get back to the sanctity of her apartment and away from the world. But as she was nearing the last corner, ready to head for the checkout counter, she heard someone on the other side of the rack asking a clerk to help him find the Swiss cheese.

Sam?

Chapter 6

Could it be?

No, surely not.

Her heart racing, she rounded the corner and met him face-to-face. "Sam?"

He gave her a sheepish grin. "Yeah, it's me. I'm back."

"But—but why? I thought you were leaving for good."

"I was." He pulled a large, plastic-wrapped hunk of Swiss cheese from the shelf. "Long story. But to make it short, Trapper phoned and begged me to come back. He said he knew the reasons I gave him for leaving didn't hold water; but whatever it was, it was my business, and he promised not to pry into my life."

"But—what about the helicopter you two were going to buy?"

He shrugged. "Seems the guy with the helicopter reconsidered when we didn't make him an offer. Apparently, he'd made some unwise business decisions and had gotten himself in a financial bind. He's offered to let us have a lease option instead, and we're going to pay him a monthly lease fee, which can be broken at any time. If we decide we want to buy that helicopter, all of our lease money will apply to the purchase price. That means no money up front, except the monthly fee. Trapper suggested we give our partnership another try, so I've agreed to stay for a few months and fly the helicopter for him, at least until he can find another pilot. If things don't work out, he's agreed I can walk away with no questions asked and no obligation. How could I refuse such an offer after the man has been so understanding? Especially since, this way, I won't have to tell him my real reason for leaving."

"You really think it'll work?"

He shrugged again. "I'll be gone 90 percent of the time, so it looks like you and I won't be seeing much of each other." He glanced around but, not finding anyone close enough to overhear their conversation, continued. "I probably should've called you first and told you I was coming back. But after the way we parted, I—"

She held up her hand between them. "Don't. I'd rather not talk about it. Just promise me you'll keep our secret—that's all I ask."

"Think we can treat each other civilly?" He gave her that half-grin, the one that always made her smile. "The last thing I want is to cause you any trouble. Honest."

"I'm sure we can, if we set our minds to it." She lowered her gaze, avoiding his eyes. "At least we can try."

"I'm sure the best way to handle this is to act natural, like two people who've just met and are becoming good friends. Trying to avoid one another will probably give us away quicker than anything. Let's just go with the flow and let things happen."

She nodded. "I'm sure you're right. I'll try."

He grinned. "We'll both try."

"I'm glad you're back, Sam." She felt his hand rest on her arm, and the old tingle returned.

"Yeah, so am I."

"Your hand doing okay?"

He held it out for her to see. "It's fine now."

"See you around," she said, biting back her jagged emotions.

"Yeah." Sam tossed a box of crackers in his basket before moving on down the aisle. "See you around."

Jackie leaned on the shopping cart's handle and watched him go.

Once again, Sam was back in her life, and she wasn't sure whether to cry or shout for joy.

Putting the groceries away seemed to take forever. With so much turmoil going on in her life, she'd neglected the mundane things and had to wash the refrigerator shelves and drawers before she could place anything in them. She hadn't started the dishwasher in nearly a week, even though she'd loaded it daily with dirty dishes, and the laundry had piled up with her barely even noticing it. She set about cleaning everything until the kitchen sparkled. Not that she cared, but it gave her something to do, something to keep her mind off Sam and his unexpected return.

"So the lies will have to continue," she said aloud as she flipped the light switch to the off position and headed for her bedroom. She filled the tub, added a small vial of bubble bath, and climbed in, resting her head on the little plastic pillow suction-cupped to the tub's back. The warm water felt good, soothing, just what she needed. *Relax, Jackie. Relax. You're too uptight.* She closed her eyes, but even doing that didn't block out Sam's face.

After a good soak, she climbed out of the tub, toweled off, and pulled on a clean nightgown. She gazed into the mirror as she brushed her hair, tilting her head first one way, then the other. *What does Sam see when he looks at me? Does he see me as the young bride he married?* She huffed. Not likely. *He probably sees me as a liar and a cheat, and he'd be right.*

She wandered aimlessly into her bedroom and turned on the lamp as the clock chimed nine. Before Sam had shown up in Alaska, she'd been busy every second. Working long hours at the shop each day, teaching quilting classes at night, attending an aerobics class, and taking part in a number of community activities. Now there seemed to be no purpose in her life. Each day was the same as the day before. Where were those challenges, those accomplishments? What had she become?

She went to the only thing that seemed to bring her solace and satisfaction these days. Sammy's quilt.

~

"You have to come, Jackie. It's a welcome-back dinner for Sam. You're part of the six musketeers! It wouldn't be the same without you, and guess who else will be there?"

Jackie froze. *Not another surprise. No more matchmaking attempts, please.*

"The Silverbows! Dr. Buck and his wife, Victoria. You remember them. You met them when you flew up to the bush with us. Buck had some business to take care of here in Juneau, so Victoria came along. Since Buck is a pilot, too, I'm sure the men will have a lot to talk about. That'll give us women a chance for a little girl talk."

Jackie tried to remain calm. "I—I don't know—"

"It's only dinner." Glorianna grabbed hold of her arm, her eyes shining with enthusiasm. "Please! For me and Trapper? He's so excited to have Sam back. But be careful! Trapper said none of us is to mention anything to Sam about the reasons he left. Whatever they were, it's his own personal business."

Jackie remembered Sam's words. *I think the best way to handle this is to act natural. Like two people who've just met and are becoming friends.* "Sure. I—I'd love to come. What time should I be there?"

~

Sam smiled at the group gathered around the table at The Grizzly Bear. "It was nice of you to welcome me back like this. I haven't had many friends in my life. Oh, I had buddies in the army, but none of us was ever in the same place for very long. Seems I'm always saying hello and good-bye to someone."

Trapper lifted his water glass. "To good friends."

Everyone followed his lead and added, "Hear, hear!"

"I'd like to propose a toast." Hank rose and, with a broad smile, placed a loving hand on Tina's shoulder. "We have good news, too. We're having a baby!"

Jackie shot a quick glance toward Sam, knowing how difficult it would be for her to be around Tina and a new baby after losing her Sammy. For a brief second, she caught Sam staring back at her.

"Wow! I'd say that is good news," Trapper said with almost as much excitement in his voice as if he and Glorianna were going to be the proud, new parents. "No one could make better parents than the two of you. That baby is mighty lucky."

"This baby is a gift from God." Tina smiled at her husband as she splayed her hand across her stomach. "We were beginning to wonder if it'd ever happen, but God is faithful, and our baby is developing nicely."

"Now if she can just get over the morning sickness," Hank chimed in, beaming at his wife. "I'm finally gonna be a daddy! Can you believe it?"

"Do you have children?" Victoria asked Sam.

Jackie was sure her heart stopped beating as all eyes turned toward her former husband.

He huffed. "No, I'm afraid I'm not that lucky. I envy all of you. I've always wanted children."

Jackie felt bile rise in her throat. She was glad no one asked her that same question. She could never have answered without crying.

"Well, it's been nice to meet you, Sam." Victoria smiled at him across the table. "I want you to know you're working with a fine man." She gave her husband's ribs a playful nudge. "Trapper is almost as fine a man as my Buck!"

"Hey, I'll take that as a compliment." Trapper gave Victoria a grin. "I'll bet those kids of yours have grown since we've seen them. I know ours sure have. That little Emily Anna of ours is about as purty as they come. You'll see when we all get home tonight. I'm glad we finally talked you into staying with us instead of going to a motel. Wish you didn't have to rush off so soon. Sure you can't stay on a few days?"

Buck placed his napkin on the table and leaned back in his chair. "Nope. Duty calls. I've got a couple of boxes of medicine I need to get up to the bush people before bad weather sets in, and Tori wants to pick up the gift items the bushwomen have been making to sell in her shop." He smiled at Sam as he nodded toward his wife. "I've always called my wife Tori."

"You're quiet tonight, Jackie," Glorianna inserted when there was a lull in the conversation.

Jackie forced a smile. "I'm just enjoying being here with you. Like Sam, I haven't had many true friends in my life, only acquaintances. That is, until I moved here to Juneau."

"See, Glorianna—that's exactly what I was telling you," Tina interjected with a pleasant grin. "Jackie and Sam probably have far more in common than they realize."

Glorianna gave Tina a be quiet frown. "Ti—na."

Trapper shot his wife a slight wink. "I'll bet the Silverbows are ready to hit the sack, honey. They had a long flight today. We'd better let them get to bed."

"Not that long a trip." Buck snickered. "Only about 550 miles. Anchorage isn't that far from Juneau."

Trapper pointed an accusing finger in the man's direction. "Then you have no excuse for not visiting us more often."

Buck pointed his finger back at Trapper. "I think that works both ways. You need to come and visit us."

"Well, now that Sam is here, maybe Trapper and Glorianna will be able to get away once in a while," Hank added.

Trapper rose and spread his arms wide. "I make a motion we call it a night!"

Sam stood quickly. "Again, I want to express my appreciation to all of you for welcoming me back like you have. You've made this man very happy."

Jackie's heart swelled with pride. Sam was such a gentleman. She knew how much Victoria's question had upset him, but he'd handled it with finesse. She also knew how much it had hurt him to walk out on Trapper as he had, and she vowed that, no matter what it would take to keep Sam in Juneau, she'd do it. No words or accusations, no matter how unfounded they were, could kill her love for him.

Glorianna bustled into the shop several days later, all excited. "Guess what! I've signed a contract with one of those quilting machine companies. We're going to sell them here at The Bear Paw!"

Jackie listened with rapt attention. For well over two years she'd been pushing for this, and she was as excited as Glorianna. *Maybe this new project will help me keep my mind off Sam.*

"And you're going to Seattle to take the training!" Glorianna went on without missing a beat. "You'll be there three days. I already called and made plane reservations for you for seven fifteen tomorrow morning. You'll be staying at the WestCoast Grand Hotel on Fifth Avenue. The class begins the next day. Can you get ready that fast?"

Jackie's eyes widened as the words whizzed past. "Leave in the morning? Why so soon?"

"They're not holding another class for six weeks." Glorianna leaned across the counter, her fingertips touching Jackie's hand. "Oh, Jackie, please say you can make it. I'm so anxious to start offering these machines for sale at The Bear Paw. Maybe we can even teach some classes on machine quilting."

"Well—but what about—?"

"Don't you worry about a thing. I'll help out here while you're gone. You'll only be a phone call away if we run into any problems we can't handle without you. It'll do you good to get away for a few days. Come on. Say yes."

She's right. I could use a change of scenery. My life's been pretty grueling lately, even though I haven't seen Sam since his welcome-back dinner. "Okay. I'll do it!"

It was nearly six-thirty the next morning when Jackie rushed breathlessly into the airport. She gave the woman her name, checked her bag, and, with her boarding pass in hand, headed for the crowded waiting area near the gate.

"Hi. I was beginning to wonder if you were going to make it."

She knew who it was before she turned around. "Sam? What're you doing here? I thought you'd probably flown up to Fairbanks with Trapper."

He stood and pointed to two empty chairs, motioning her toward them. "Naw. I didn't go. He wanted me to check out that helicopter we're going to lease and see if it needed any repairs or modifications before we took delivery."

She was puzzled by his words. "Isn't that helicopter in Juneau? What are you doing here in the airport waiting area? Are you meeting someone?"

"Nope, going to Seattle with you." He gave her a mischievous grin.

If he'd told her he was on his way to Mars, he couldn't have stunned her more. "But why?"

"Since Trapper's up in Fairbanks on that job, he won't be home for a couple of days. Seems one of his major clients called Glorianna and wanted him to hop on a plane to Seattle and pick up some parts they needed for some big machine they operate. Since he wasn't available, she asked me to go. We should be in Seattle in about four hours. I'll be able to pick up the parts and catch the last plane back tonight."

When their flight was called, Sam reached for Jackie's carry-on bag, but she grabbed it up herself. When they boarded the plane, she was relieved to learn Sam's seat was a good four rows behind hers. She allowed him to put her bag in the overhead compartment, said thank you, and sat down, buckling her seat belt. As soon as they were airborne and the seat-belt sign had been turned off, she tilted her seat back and closed her eyes.

"Sure nice no one took this seat next to you," Sam said as he sat down beside her. "The flight attendant said it was okay if I moved up here with you."

Unnerved by the way their shoulders were touching, she scooted toward the window. "Ah—sure—"

He seemed to sense her uneasiness. "I can move back, if you'd rather."

She shook her head. "No, I—I can use the company."

"Now," he said, swiveling in the seat, "tell me all about this quilting machine thing Glorianna is so excited about."

She explained what the machine could do and why it would be a good, solid, saleable item for the shop, with Sam hanging on her every word, occasionally asking a question. It was nice to be able to talk to him without an argument.

When the plane landed in Seattle, Sam grabbed her bag from the overhead compartment and ushered her into the terminal. "Well, since I don't have a suitcase to pick up, I guess this is where we separate. I'm heading on over to that parts company. Have a good time in Seattle."

She thanked him for carrying her bag, told him good-bye, and headed toward baggage claim. Sitting by him on the flight hadn't been uncomfortable at all. They'd actually had a pleasant conversation. Maybe pulling off this deception wasn't going to be as hard as they'd feared.

She checked into the hotel, ate a quick sandwich in the little café across the street, and, having the rest of the day to do whatever she pleased, took a cab to Pike Place Market and wandered through its many unique shops.

It was nearly seven when she finally got back to her hotel room. After putting her shopping bags in the closet, she picked up the room service menu.

Do I really want to eat in my room, or should I go downstairs to the elegant restaurant I noticed when I checked in?

The restaurant won out.

After Jackie was seated at a table near the spectacular fountain in the center of the room, she began to scan the menu.

"Hey, got room for one more?" Sam asked as he slipped into the chair opposite her.

"Sam! I thought you were flying back to Juneau tonight!"

He motioned to the waiter to bring him a menu. "So did I! Seems some of the parts I was supposed to pick up aren't ready yet. Some mix-up thing with the settings on the machines, and they're having to make them all over again. So," he said, closing the menu and laying it on the table, "I'm stuck here for a couple of days 'til they get things corrected and crank those parts out. I had to run out and buy myself a couple of shirts and some toiletries since I didn't bring a bag with me."

"How did you know I was here?"

He let out a chuckle. "I didn't! When I phoned Glorianna to see what I should do, she told me to check into this hotel and wait. I guess this is the hotel she and Trapper always use when they're in Seattle."

Although the thought upset her, Jackie couldn't hold back her grin. "You do see what they're doing, don't you?"

Sam looked perplexed. "Doing? I guess not. What do you mean?"

She let out a girlish snicker. "They're trying to get us together!"

His brows lifted as his hand went to his chest. "You and me?"

She closed her menu and leaned forward. "You haven't heard the whole story. Before Glorianna arrived in Juneau, Trapper and I—well, let's just say we were good friends. He was the first man since you who had shown any real interest in me. I took it the wrong way. So when Glorianna appeared on the scene and those two started spending time together, I actually resented her, and I guess I was pretty obvious about it. Kinda standoffish, if you know what I mean. I had the idea that if she hadn't arrived in Juneau, maybe my relationship with Trapper might have blossomed into something. Then, when Trapper and Glorianna broke up and he went to Fairbanks on a job, she and Hank Gordon became an item, and eventually, she agreed to marry Hank and accepted his engagement ring."

He gave her a surprised look. "Trapper never told me any of this. Hank and Glorianna were actually going to get married?"

"They would have, too, if Trapper hadn't come to his senses and rushed into the church as the ceremony began and snatched Glorianna away. It was the talk of the town for months. In time, Hank forgave Trapper, and they became good friends. Then, a number of years later, Tina came to Alaska, and the rest is history."

Sam's brows were raised as he shook his head. "Wow! I had no idea. I can't imagine Trapper doing anything that bold. He must've really loved Glorianna to do such an unorthodox thing. Wow!"

"I was lonely, Sam, and Trapper was such a nice man and a real gentleman. Oh, all we ever did was go to a couple of movies, but I really enjoyed his company, probably because he reminded me a lot of you."

Sam scratched his head. "No reason you shouldn't have dated Trapper. You and I had been divorced for a long time. Actually, I was surprised when you told me you'd never remarried. But what's that got to do with me and you?"

She laid her menu on the table and folded her hands. "Don't you see? That's the reason Glorianna is trying to turn us into a couple. After Trapper and Glorianna were married, she and I became good friends. I think she always felt a little sorry for me. Maybe she thought if she hadn't shown up, Trapper and I might have gotten together. As soon as she and I became friends, she started encouraging me to get out and date and find a good man. Then Tina came to Juneau, and she and Hank ended up getting married. Ever since then, those two women have tried to match me up with every eligible bachelor they know."

"Are you ready to order?" the waiter asked politely as he suddenly appeared at their table. "Or would you prefer I come back a bit later?"

Jackie quickly gathered her thoughts. "I'll have the petite steak, medium well, baked potato, and green beans. And iced tea, please."

"No coffee?" Sam asked with a grin.

She giggled. "Coffee and iced tea. I'm thirsty."

Sam took both their menus and handed them to the man. "Make mine the same, but give me the rib eye. And coffee."

"So did they?" he asked as the waiter moved away.

She gave him a blank stare.

"Did Glorianna and Tina have any success trying to match you up with those guys?"

She tilted her head back with a laugh. "No! But they did try."

"And now they're at it again, huh, with me?"

"They mean well, Sam. Didn't you ever wonder why I was invited to your welcome dinner and to church and those other places? I felt like a fifth wheel. I knew what they were doing, but what was I to do? Refuse my boss's invitations?"

He sipped at his water, peering at her over the rim of the glass. "I'm glad you didn't refuse. It may've been weeks before I discovered you were in Juneau if you hadn't come to The Grizzly Bear that first night."

"Well, all I'm saying is you should be prepared. Those ladies are a determined pair. I think they enjoy being matchmakers!" She smiled up at the waiter as he placed their dinner salads before them.

Sam appeared thoughtful. "Well, we are both red-blooded, unmarried people. We must've been a good match at one time. We got married, didn't we? Maybe we'd look less suspicious if we played along."

His words surprised her. "You mean it?"

He shrugged. "Sure. Why not? Sure beats trying to ignore each other."

Their conversation came to a halt as the waiter refilled their water glasses.

"The Timberwolfs and the Gordons really are nice people, aren't they?" Sam finally asked when they'd exhausted the matchmaking subject. "Except sometimes I wish Trapper would quit pestering me about becoming a Christian. I'm not convinced his way is the only way to get into heaven."

"I know. Glorianna does that to me too. I've always thought if you were a good person and didn't do anything to hurt anyone, you'd automatically go to heaven when you died. But that's not what she says, and sometimes it worries me." Jackie cut a crisp slice of cucumber in half and popped it into her mouth.

"Well, I agree with you, to a point. I do think you have to be a good person, but I also think you have to do some good deeds. You know, help people, give money to the poor, give your old clothes to Salvation Army, maybe help build homes for the poor, that sort of stuff. Things like Trapper does."

"But that's not why he does them."

Sam shook his head as he reached for the basket of rolls. "He says he does those things because he's a Christian, not because they're going to get him into heaven. I've heard Hank say the same thing. Did you know Hank gives hours and hours of free attorney time to people who can't afford to hire him? He says it's his service to God."

"And that's not all," Jackie added, placing a nicely browned roll on her bread plate. "Hank goes along with Trapper some of the time and helps the bush people. Tina and Glorianna do, too."

He forked a bright red cherry tomato and twirled it in the air. "Amazing. They all have plenty of things to keep them busy, without doing that for free."

"Dr. Silverbow does the same thing. He flies his seaplane into the bush country several times a month, takes medicines he pays for himself, and doctors anyone who needs him. All for free. He even pays for the plane's gas!"

"Be careful—these plates are hot." The waiter carefully placed their dinners before them, then poured each a cup of coffee.

"Umm, these look great." Sam grinned with enthusiasm as he picked up his knife and fork and sliced off a piece of the juicy steak. "I guess we don't have to pray since Trapper isn't here."

Jackie nodded. "Guess not."

They enjoyed their steaks in near silence. Finally, she asked, "Do you think small children go to heaven? They're really not old enough to make that kind of decision for themselves."

He blotted his mouth with his napkin and cocked his head. "Hmm. I don't know. I'd think they would." Sam gave her a frown. "Did you think about that before you—?"

Jackie gritted her teeth. "I didn't—"

"Keep your voice down," he said in a mere whisper before glancing around to see if those seated at the nearby tables were listening to their conversation.

She glared at him, her voice now trembling with anger. "If you say one more word about me—"

He reached across the table and grabbed her hand, giving it a consoling squeeze. "Maybe we'd better let this subject drop."

Few words passed between them as they finished their meal.

Sam walked her to her room, taking the key from her hand and opening the door for her. "Thanks for letting me join you for dinner."

She felt as awkward as a sophomore on her first date. "I—I've always hated eating alone."

"Look," he said, lifting her chin and tilting her face up close to his, "I'm really sorry for that smart remark I made at dinner." His lips grazed her cheek. "I—I won't lie to you. I still don't believe you. But rather than acting like friends, I'd like for us to be real friends, especially if we're both going to continue living in Juneau."

Her heart pounded furiously. His closeness and his warm breath on her cheek were almost more than she could bear. Was he going to kiss her? *Oh, Sam, it's been so long since you've kissed me and held me in your arms.* "I—I'd like that, too."

"Maybe it'd be best," he whispered against her cheek, "if we avoided even a mention of our baby."

Chapter 7

Chaffed by his words, she drew her head back quickly. "Avoid talking about our baby? How can you avoid talking about something that was so precious but ruined your life?"

"I'm sorry, Jackie, but it seems even the mention of that baby sets us against one another. Is that the way you want it?"

"Of course that's not the way I want it, but how can I forget him?" In some ways, Sam was right. What good would arguing do? He hadn't been there when it happened; she'd been alone, and there was nothing she could do to convince him of the truth. *What I want is for you to believe me!*

"I don't expect you to forget about him, but—"

She held up her hand between them. "For the sake of peace between us and so we won't arouse suspicion, I'll try"—she bit back feelings of anguish and despair as she drew in a deep breath and finished her sentence—"I'll try to keep my emotions under control."

"Good. That's all I ask. I know you believe otherwise, but I really want us to get along." With a hint of a smile, he pulled his pen and a piece of paper from his pocket. "Give me the address where you'll be attending your class and the time you'll be finished. I'll pick you up, and we'll make a night of it."

Surprised and pleased by his request, she scribbled the information on the paper and handed it to him.

"See you tomorrow," he said, tucking it into his pocket before bending to plant a quick kiss on her cheek. "Get a good night's sleep."

Jackie leaned against the door until she heard the elevator doors close; then, her hands trembling, she hurried to her suitcase and pulled out a sealed plastic bag containing scissors, a needle and thread, a thimble, and the tenth block.

❧

Sam got off on the twelfth floor and walked briskly toward his room. He'd been so close to pulling Jackie into his arms and kissing her, instead of giving her that quick peck on her cheek. *You idiot! That would've been one of the stupidest moves you've ever made. Things are no different now than they were seventeen years ago.*

❧

Sam was already waiting in the hall when Jackie rushed out of her class the next afternoon.

"Well, did you learn anything?" He gave her a smile that was both warm and teasing.

She patted the hefty user's manual resting on her arm. "Everything is controlled by computer now. You wouldn't believe what these machines can do."

"I hope you're not on overload. I have a great evening planned."

She brightened. "Oh? Where are we going?"

Sam gave her a boyish grin. "You'll see."

"Wow!" Jackie said thirty minutes later as she and Sam stepped off the elevator and onto the observation deck of Seattle's famous Space Needle. "What a view! How high are we?"

"The visitor's book said six hundred five feet. From here you're supposed to see not only all of Seattle but Puget Sound, Mount Rainier, and the Cascade and Olympic Mountains."

Jackie pointed off in the distance. "Oh, look! Isn't that Smith Tower down there? I think I heard someone mention it in our class today."

Sam shrugged. "Got me!"

They wandered around the deck, pausing now and then to gaze through the telescopic viewers that were available to the public, trying to locate the points of interest listed on the signs posted at each viewer.

"Hungry?" Sam asked finally, after glancing at his watch. "I made reservations for six-thirty."

She gazed up at him, still in awe of their surroundings. "Reservations? Where?"

He took her hand and led her down the stairway to SkyCity, the elegant revolving restaurant one flight down. In no time, they were seated at one of the intimate tables for two flanking the outer glass wall. The excitement she felt brought back memories of their early days together when just having a hamburger was a special occasion.

"Oh, Sam, what a wonderful place! I've always wanted to come here."

"I've heard the food is pretty good." He picked up his menu.

"We have an excellent special tonight," the waiter said as he brought their water glasses.

Sam closed his menu. "Why don't you just bring us whatever you recommend?"

The man smiled. "Excellent choice, sir."

"That's kind of risky, don't you think?" Jackie asked with a snicker as the man scurried away.

Sam arched a brow and grinned. "Guess we'll find out when our food arrives. Now," he said, his smile broadening, "close your eyes and hold out your hands."

She gave him a coquettish smile. "Why?"

He waggled a finger at her. "Just do it, okay? Humor the old guy."

She did as she was told and felt something soft and silky fall onto her palms.

"Okay, you can look now."

She let out a gasp of pleasure as she stared at the lovely, floral silk scarf. "Oh, Sam! It's beautiful!"

"To replace the one I ruined." He ducked his head shyly. "Remember?" He held up his hand and pointed to the healing scar.

"You didn't have to do this. I was able to rinse the blood out of the other one. But I love it." She held it to her cheek, enjoying its luxurious feel against her skin. "It—it's gorgeous. The most beautiful scarf I've ever seen and, I'm sure, very expensive."

"It looked like you. All soft and feminine and pink. I knew it was the right one the minute the salesclerk showed it to me."

She struggled to hold back tears. Before Sam had come back in her life, she hadn't cried in years. Now it seemed everything made her cry. Some days with joy. Some days from pain. Today was one of those joyful days. "Thank you, Sam," she said, reaching over to pat his cheek. "I'll keep it always."

"For an appetizer," the uniformed man said as he returned to the table, "we'll start with a sampler of prawns, grilled chicken, and grilled pineapple, served with two dipping sauces—a spicy chili sauce for the prawns and pineapple, and a curry peanut sauce for the chicken. Piled high in the middle of this is a nice Asian slaw."

"This is splendid," Jackie said as she forked up a piece of the grilled pineapple. "I can hardly wait to taste the rest of our meal."

After the waiter cleared away their dishes, he appeared with their next course. "Now we'll have a Caesar salad and lobster bisque," he said as proudly as if he'd prepared them himself. "Enjoy."

As the restaurant rotated back to face Puget Sound, the magical hour Sam had hoped for arrived, as pink and orange hues tinged with purple crept across the western sky. He had to smile as he watched Jackie's face. He was glad he'd brought her to this place.

"I–I feel like I'm floating in space," she said dreamily as she stared at the spectacular remains of the magnificent sunset.

"And now here are our entrées," the waiter said with a flourish of his hand as he lifted the beautifully garnished plates from his tray and ceremoniously placed them before them. "Northwest Salmon Wellington with pesto and lemon cream for the lady and a broiled New York Strip loin for the gentleman."

"I'm stuffed," Sam said, leaning back in his chair once their meal had been nearly consumed.

"What is that?" Jackie placed her fork on her plate and pointed to something another waiter was serving at a nearby table. "It looks like mounds of ice cream in a fish bowl, with dry ice steaming around it."

"Beats me!"

When the waiter arrived, Sam asked him about it.

415

"It's called a Mount Rainier, sir, and it's always met with screams of delight. Would you and the lady like one for dessert or perhaps a lemon tart?"

"I think not," Sam said after a quick glance toward Jackie. "Maybe another time."

"Oh, look," Jackie said, leaning toward the window once the table had been cleared. "The lights are coming on all over the city. What a spectacular view!"

Sam nodded as he presented his credit card and signed the ticket. "I'd like to take one last look from the observation deck before we go. How about you?" He loved the way her face lit up when she was excited.

"Sure."

They made their way once again to the stairs and climbed back up to the deck. With the warmth of the day's sun gone, the night air was chilly. Sam slipped his arm around Jackie's waist and pulled her close, nestling his chin in her hair as they stood gazing at the sparkling jewels of the city lights below them. "This is nice, isn't it?"

"Uh-huh," she answered dreamily as she leaned against him. "Very nice."

"Think you can put up with me tomorrow night?"

She gave him a lopsided grin. "Uh-huh. Why?"

Sam brushed his lips gently against hers as he whispered, "I'd like to take you to dinner again."

It was nearly eleven before he turned out the light and climbed into his bed. He hadn't had such a good time in years. As he pulled the covers over his head, he asked himself one question: How could he hate a woman and love her so much at the same time?

Sam met Jackie after her class again the next day with a plan to spend the entire evening together. It was a plan she accepted readily.

"I thought we'd have a leisurely dinner in the hotel tonight," he told her as they drove through the streets of Seattle toward Fifth Avenue. "That okay with you?"

She nodded. "Yeah, great. It's been a really stressful day. My head is swimming with information. It'll be nice to have an early dinner and relax, but I do need to do some studying later. Since tomorrow is our last session, they're giving us a test. I want to pass with flying colors."

❧

The Terrace Garden was crowded, but the maitre d' led them to a small table for two in a far-off corner. They opted for seafood, the waiter's recommendation, then waited with anticipation as they discussed the possibilities of his choice.

"You're wearing your scarf," Sam said proudly, leaning forward as he reached out to touch the filmy silk.

"Yes, I love it. It's beautiful." As her fingers rose to stroke its softness, their hands touched.

He caught her hand in his and pulled it to his lips, kissing it gently as his gaze locked with hers. "Not as beautiful as you. You're still a knockout."

She found herself speechless and could only smile back.

"You've grown even more beautiful with the years, Jackie," he added, kissing her hand again.

Her heart came to a dull, thudding stop as she gazed into his eyes, and she was his captive. She'd always be his captive, no matter how far apart they might be.

"I still can't believe you haven't remarried, Jackie," he said in an almost-whisper as he gazed at her intently, still holding her hand.

"I've never found anyone I'd want to marry. What about you?"

He turned loose of her hand and stared off in space. "I guess I could say the same thing. I dated a few women, but none of them more than once or twice. There just weren't any sparks. It seemed like a waste of time and money."

"I'm sorry I nearly ruined your plans, Sam."

Sam gave her a confused stare. "Plans? What plans?"

She gazed at her water glass. "You know. About moving to Alaska and becoming Trapper's partner."

"I have to admit I was sure shocked when I saw you walking across that parking lot."

She offered a slight sideways grin. "I was shocked, too. I thought I was hidden away so no one would find me."

By the time they finished their dinners, they'd discussed the city and its landmarks, the weather, the Seattle Seahawks, and a number of other fairly innocuous things, each avoiding the one topic that always sent them into an argument and caused bitter words—the baby.

"Thanks, Sam. This has been a nice, relaxing evening," Jackie told him when they reached her door. "I guess we won't be seeing one another again until we're back in Juneau."

Sam grinned. "Oh, yes, we will. I picked up the parts this afternoon. They got them ready sooner than expected. I'll be going back on your flight tomorrow."

Jackie's heart played hopscotch. Being with Sam the past two days had resurrected old feelings of love. A love that had no future, a love she tried to deny still existed.

"I've really enjoyed being with you here in Seattle, Jackie." He took her key from her hand and inserted it into the lock, pushing the door open before handing it back to her.

She slipped the key into her purse and stood awkwardly staring at him. This was the man who, at one time, she had loved more than life itself. "I–I've had a good time, too." She froze as he took her hand, linked his fingers with hers, and leaned close.

"I've wanted to kiss you, you know," he whispered softly as he lessened the space between them, his face just inches from hers. "I've been fighting the impulse since that first night."

"I–I'm not so sure that would be a good idea." *But I wish you'd try.*

"Why? We're two single adults."

She dipped her head, avoiding his eyes. "We're two divorced, single adults."

He slid a finger beneath her chin, drawing her face up to his. "Precisely."

She stood motionless. Why was he taunting her like this? They both knew there was no future for them. He'd made that clear years ago. Wasn't it futile to pretend anything else?

A chill rushed down her spine as he edged closer and closer. She felt her lips moving toward his, and she couldn't stop them. Suddenly, his mouth claimed hers, and they fell into an embrace.

Try as she may, she couldn't pull away. Although he'd hurt her more than she'd ever been hurt in her life, she still loved him and wanted to stay in his arms forever. This was where she belonged. No man could ever take Sam's place in her heart or her life.

Sam kissed her again, and this time she melted into his arms willingly, loving the feel of his lips and the way his arms enfolded her. For just this moment, nothing else mattered.

"I didn't think I'd ever see you again," he said in a mere whisper when their kiss ended, the gentle expression in his eyes caressing her face. "I've missed you, Jackie."

His warm breath falling across her cheeks sent ripples down her spine. "I–I've missed you, too, Sam."

Finally, she asked, her voice low and husky, "Does this mean you believe me now?"

He pushed away slightly with a pained look. "I wish it was that simple. I'll admit I'm attracted to you, Jackie. I–I've never stopped loving you, but no matter how hard I've tried, I can't forgive you for what you did. Kissing you like that was—well, it was an idiotic idea. I shouldn't have done it."

"But I—"

He held up his hands and backed quickly into the hall. "I'm sorry. It was a mistake. I let my feelings for you cloud my judgment. I should have had better control."

"Sam, it's been over seventeen years now!" Jackie grabbed onto his arm and fought against tears as his words grabbed her heart and ripped it to shreds. "Perhaps it's time we tried to put the past behind us."

"I wish I could do that. I've really tried. But I couldn't do it then, and I can't do it now." As he took hold of her arm and stared into her face, she could see the sadness in his eyes. "If only you'd continued with your pregnancy and had the baby. Let me raise it. But, no, you took matters into your own hands. Against my wishes."

"I didn't, Sam. I didn't!"

With a final look of hopelessness and exasperation, Sam walked away, leaving her in the open doorway.

She leaned against the door, crushed, feeling almost as bad as she had when Sam left her all those years ago. She'd been a fool even to consider there might be a chance for them to get back together. *You should have known better!*

Since she'd received no more communication from Sam, Jackie rode to the airport alone the next afternoon. She'd been almost glad he hadn't been in the lobby when she'd checked out after her final training session. She couldn't stand another confrontation. Already on board by the time he came onto the plane, she pretended to be reading her magazine as he walked by. The flight seemed to go on forever. By the time they reached Juneau, she was a bundle of nerves. *Now what?* How would they ever be able to go on with their deception, considering what had happened between them in Seattle?

Instead of going directly to the baggage claim area and taking a chance on running into Sam since he'd be picking up the big bag of parts, she stopped at the airport snack bar and ordered a cup of coffee, hoping it would calm her down. By the time she claimed her bag, he was nowhere in sight.

"Did you and Sam spend any time together while you were in Seattle?" Glorianna asked the next morning as she came into the shop.

Jackie turned her back toward her boss and busied herself straightening up the notions counter. "Aren't you more interested in hearing about the school you sent me to?"

"Well, of course, I want to hear about that. I just thought, since the two of you were staying in the same hotel, perhaps you—"

Jackie whirled around. "I wish you'd give up trying to match me up with Sam!"

"What's the matter, Jackie? It's not like you to snap at me like that. You know I meant no harm."

She rubbed at her forehead. "I—I'm sorry. I'm just tired—that's all. It was pretty late by the time I got back to my apartment last night. Even though I learned a lot, and I'm excited to tell you all about it, the school was pretty intense."

"Of course you're tired. How thoughtless of me. Why don't you take the rest of the day off? The shop's not that busy, and we can talk about your training session tomorrow."

Grateful for her understanding, Jackie smiled appreciatively. "Thanks, Glorianna. I have quite a few things in my notebook I want to go over with you. Doing it tomorrow will give me a chance to get everything organized first."

Taking her boss's advice, Jackie made her way up the outside stairway to her apartment. She unpacked the rest of her suitcase, did a couple of loads of laundry, cleaned the bathrooms, dusted and ran the sweeper, and mixed up a casserole for supper. It seemed cleaning and doing household chores always made her feel better and took her mind off things. When the casserole was done, she ate her supper in silence, placed the few dishes in the dishwasher, then picked up a romance novel she'd been intending to read. But when on the first few pages the hero and heroine had an argument and separated, she closed the book. "Too much like real life," she said as she placed it back on her nightstand and pulled the little plastic bag from the box beneath her bed where she'd placed it when she'd come home.

Oh, Sammy, what a mess we've all made of our lives.

She worked, painstakingly applying each stitch until she finished the tenth block. As she reached for her notepad and a pen, she felt a nagging tug at her heart.

Sam! My dear, beloved Sam. Why did you have to come to Juneau?

❦

Sam sat at the counter in the little café down the road from Grandma's Feather Bed, chomping on a raw carrot stick. How could he have been so foolish? He should never have kissed Jackie. That was a stupid thing to do, even if she did look so kissable, standing in that doorway, her big blue eyes focused on him, her lips beckoning him to taste them. He picked up another carrot stick and idly dipped it into the small pile of salt he'd sprinkled onto his plate. *You idiot, you're as in love with that woman now as you were the day you married her. Why don't you admit it? There'll never be another woman for you, and you know it.*

"Hey, I tried to call you at the motel. They said you might be over here."

Startled, Sam swiveled on the stool and rested an elbow on the diner's counter. "When did you get back?"

Trapper sat down beside him and took a menu from the rack. "About an hour ago. I was on my way home from the airport. But since Glorianna had left the kids with Mom and Dad so she could attend a scrapbook party some friend of hers was having, I decided to see if you wanted to grab a bite of supper with me."

"Well, I'm about finished, but I'll sit with you while you eat. Then maybe we can have a slice of pie."

Trapper placed his order, then asked, "How'd the Seattle trip go? I hear you had to wait around for those parts."

Sam nodded. "Yep, nearly three days. Big waste of time."

Trapper grinned. "Oh? I heard you and Jackie were staying at the same hotel. You mean you didn't invite that pretty little gal out to dinner?"

"Yeah, we had dinner a couple of times," Sam answered, picking up his empty coffee cup and trying to sound casual.

"She's a good woman, Sam. You could do a whole lot worse. I figured the two of you would hit it off real good."

"I don't think it'd be wise to lead some woman on right now. I have too many things going on in my life. I'm not even sure I'll be staying in Alaska."

Trapper frowned at him over the rim of his cup. "I don't like the sound of that."

"Oh, I haven't made any new decisions. We haven't even taken delivery on that helicopter. So far I like Alaska, even more than I thought I would. I just mean there's still a slight possibility things won't work out. I don't want to get attached to some woman, then go off and leave her. That's all."

Trapper nodded as he held out his cup to the waitress. "How come you never remarried? A good-looking guy like you should have his pick of women."

Because I never found another woman I could love the way I love Jackie! "I don't know. Just never did."

"You gonna spend the rest of your life alone, Sam? Somehow, when I first met you, I had you figured as a family man—married with a bunch of little kids. I was really surprised when you told me you'd been divorced. You and your wife missed the best part of life by not having children."

"Tell me about it." The words slipped out of his mouth before he could stop them.

Trapper's brows lifted. "Your wife didn't want kids?"

Sam shook his head sadly. "Nope, not even after four years of marriage."

"But you did?"

"Yeah, real bad."

"Usually it's the other way around."

The waitress brought Trapper's hamburger and fries.

He sprinkled salt on them, then doused them with ketchup. "Something on your mind you want to talk about, Sam? I get the feeling you've been holding back on me. Seems like it's been gnawing on you ever since you got here."

"I guess we all have our problems."

"Glorianna noticed it too. At first I told her I thought you were just uncomfortable because of the way she and Tina were trying to match you up with Jackie, but—well, now, I think it's more than that."

If only you knew, Trapper. Sam stared into his cup. "I guess when I realized that matchmaking thing was going on, it did make me uncomfortable. But I thought I was keeping it to myself. Guess I didn't do a very good job."

"I think Jackie was as uncomfortable as you were. I've never seen that girl so fidgety. I've asked Glorianna to back off and leave you guys alone."

"No need. I think Jackie and I understand each other fairly well. We've talked about it some."

"Good. I'd hate to have the two of you at odds with each other." Trapper bit into his burger, then wiped his mouth with his napkin. "I hope you two can be friends."

Sam flinched. After the way he and Jackie had parted, he doubted she'd ever want to speak to him again. "I hope so too."

"You're both important to Glorianna and me."

Sam waved a carrot stick in his direction. "Trapper, can I ask you a question?"

Trapper nodded. "Sure. Ask away."

"I've been thinking about some of the things that preacher of yours said. I remember coming home late when I was in high school and finding my daddy on his knees, praying. I always hated that sight. In my eyes it made him look like a wimp. My mama was always after me to attend church with them. Do you think they're in heaven?"

Trapper placed his napkin on the counter and began to stroke his beard. "Well, it isn't mine to say. Depends. Some people play at Christianity. I'm not saying your folks did that. Only God knows for sure. Like the pastor said, God made the rules. It's up to us to decide if we want to follow them. From the sounds of it, your folks probably did."

"So—if I want to see them again, I have to play by the rules. Is that what you're saying?"

"Exactly. So many people turn their backs on God's Son, Sam. Don't be one of them."

Sam thought long and hard about Trapper's words and about Jackie as he lay in bed that night. He loved her. There was no use denying it any longer, but he could never live with her as husband and wife, not after what she'd done. But he could stay in Alaska and keep watch over her. At least that way he'd be able to be around her, see her, and know she was safe.

If only she'd carried our baby to term—

Jackie clutched the phone in both hands. "I don't mean to be rude, Glorianna, but I just don't want to go to church with you."

"Why? You said you enjoyed going with us the last time."

"If you must know, it's Sam."

Glorianna let out a little gasp. "Sam? Has he said anything out of the way or done something to offend you?"

"No, nothing like that," she was quick to say, lest Glorianna get the wrong idea. "It's—well, I know you and Tina mean well, but it's embarrassing to have your friends try to fix you up with a man." There. That sounded like as good an excuse as any.

"I'm sorry, Jackie. That's what Trapper told me. I think Sam feels the same way you do. It's just that Tina and I were so sure you two were made for each other. We meant no harm. Please say you'll come. You don't have to sit next to him. I'll make sure you sit on the opposite end of the pew from Sam. Please. I really want you to come."

Jackie squiggled her lips. "Okay, but I am not going to The Grizzly Bear with you for lunch, and I don't want you to try to pressure me."

"I promise."

The Timberwolfs, the Gordons, and Sam were already seated when Jackie arrived at church the next morning. She checked to see where he was seated, then headed down the opposite aisle, scooting in next to Glorianna, who welcomed her with a warm smile.

As usual, she enjoyed the congregational singing and the special music, but when the pastor announced his message was to be on the sin of lying, Jackie wished she hadn't come.

"Lying is a sin, no matter what the reason," the pastor was saying. "God hates lies," he added as his eyes slowly scanned the congregation. "Even those little white lies we tell so easily."

Jackie fidgeted in her seat, checking her watch often, wishing the service would end so she could get out of there. *Is Sam having the same pangs of guilt?*

"Lies are but one of the sins we commit against God," the pastor went on. "We need to confess those sins and ask His forgiveness."

As soon as the congregation was dismissed, Jackie said a quick good-bye and hurried out of the sanctuary, ignoring Sam.

Late that afternoon in the privacy of her apartment, she pulled out the study sheet that had been tucked into the church bulletin and carried it to the kitchen table. She also carried the Bible that Anna, Glorianna's mother who had owned the shop before Glorianna had come to Alaska, had given her the first week she'd gone to work at the quilt shop. She looked up the reference in the Book of Proverbs and read aloud, " 'Lying lips are abomination to the Lord: but they that deal truly are his delight." *If God hates lying lips, He must really be upset with me!* The words rang in her ears like a bell that refused to stop pealing. *I'm not only lying; I'm living a lie!*

She closed the Bible and rested her head on its cover, her tears flowing. She didn't know how long she sat there or that she'd fallen asleep; but when she woke up, the apartment was dark.

Feeling totally spent, she wandered into her bedroom and prepared for bed. But, as she lay there, wide awake, her thoughts went to Sammy and the little quilt she was making in his memory. Feeling much too restless to sleep, she turned on the lamp, pulled the eleventh block from the box, and began to quilt.

The next evening, when she heard a knock on the door, she knew, even before she opened it, that it was Sam.

Chapter 8

Sam pushed his way into the room without being invited. "I've come to a decision, Jackie. I'm going to tell Trapper about us. I'm sick and tired of all this lying. As I sat in that church yesterday and heard the pastor's words, I knew he was talking directly to me!"

"I know. I felt the same way, but please, Sam, not yet. I know the truth must come out, but I need a little time. Once you've told them, I'll have to leave Juneau and start a new life someplace else. Glorianna is as honest as anyone I've ever known, and she'll never allow me to continue to work in her shop once she finds out what a liar I've been."

He gave a dejected shrug. "That's exactly the way I expect Trapper to respond. Looks like we'll both be out of a job."

"Give me a few days, okay? I'll get my affairs in order and pack my things. As soon as they're told, I'll take the next plane out of Juneau." She put a hand on his arm and gazed up into his eyes. "Please, Sam. This is the last thing I'll ever ask of you. I just need time."

Sam took a deep breath and let it out slowly. "Okay, but one more week is the limit. Either you tell them, or I'm going to. I can't go on like this anymore."

She watched as he moved out the door without even saying good-bye. As she readied for bed, she pulled block number eleven from the box.

The next day was miserable as Jackie began to wrap up her affairs. She worked untiringly on the shop's books, made sure there would be adequate inventory when she left, wrote farewell notes to leave behind for the staff, and wrote out checks for her end-of-the-month bills. After that, she stopped by the bank, closed out her personal account, and drew out her savings.

When Trapper's mother came into the shop, Jackie spoke to her but scurried off instead of visiting with her as she usually did, her mind on a dozen other things that needed to be taken care of before she could leave Juneau and the home she loved.

How shall I tell them? Should I call everyone together and blurt it out? Or tell Glorianna, then the others, one by one? Or let her tell them? Maybe I should just vanish and leave a note behind.

When she heard a knock on the door that evening, she hurriedly put the box she'd been packing behind the sofa.

"You can't fool me, Jackie," Emily Timberwolf said as she bustled in past her.

"I can always tell when a woman's not feeling well. Especially one I know as well as I know you. You coming down with a cold?"

"I—I'm not sure. Maybe." *Another lie. How easily I tell them now.*

"I've brought you some soup, and I want you to sit down this minute and eat it while it's hot," the kindly woman told her as she grabbed hold of her arm and led her to the table.

"I—I—" The words wouldn't come.

Emily quickly pulled up a chair and sat down beside her, slipping her arm about her shoulders. "What is it, child? You can tell Emily anything. I'd never betray your confidence."

Jackie ached to tell someone. Keeping secrets from those she cared about had taken their toll on her. Could Emily be trusted? "You—you don't know me, Emily," she said, trying to hold back her tears. "Not really."

The woman pulled Jackie's head onto her shoulder, patting her back as one would pat a crying baby. "Then tell me about yourself, Jackie. Tell Emily what's bothering you."

"I'm—I'm not who you think I am."

"Why don't you tell me all about it?"

Jackie sucked in a fresh breath of air. "I've been living a lie, Emily, and it's been tearing at my gut. I can't sleep. I can't eat. I'm miserable."

"You want to tell me about your lie?" Emily prodded softly, still patting her back.

"I—I can't. Not yet."

"I only thought it might help to get it off your chest and talk about it. The Lord knows about your lie, Jackie. Do you want me to pray with you about it?"

Tears pooled in her eyes, making it hard to see. "I—I don't think God wants to hear from me. I've never—you know—confessed my sins and asked His forgiveness, like the pastor said."

Emily shrugged. "You can do it right now, if you want."

Jackie gave her a surprised look. "Here? In my apartment? I don't have to be in the church?"

Trapper's mother gave her a gentle, understanding smile that went straight to her heart. "God doesn't care where you are when you ask for His forgiveness, honey. He just wants to hear from you."

"I—I don't know how."

Emily took her hand, and the two of them knelt beside the sofa. "You don't need to confess your sins out loud if you don't want to, sweetie. He already knows what they are. Just confess them in your heart. He'll hear you. You know, God loved us so much He sent His only Son to die on the cross, Jackie, for your sins and mine."

Jackie listened carefully as Emily answered each of her questions; then, still kneeling beside the sofa, she silently poured out her heart to God.

"And please, God," she added aloud after confessing her sins and asking forgiveness, "take over my life. I've made such a mess of things. I'm Yours, Lord."

"Now that wasn't so hard, was it?" Emily asked as she stroked Jackie's hair. "God created us to love and serve Him, but He wants us to do it of our own free will. Once we've turned our lives over to Him, He'll never leave us or forsake us."

Feeling a new sense of lightness and freedom, Jackie rose, then helped the older woman to her feet. "Thanks, Emily. You've always been like a mother to me. I've often wished I could be like you."

"You're a lovely young woman. Any mother would be proud to call you her daughter."

Any, except mine. "If you don't mind, I'd like to be the one to tell the others about my decision to accept the Lord."

Emily gave her hand a squeeze as her wrinkled face smiled. "I won't say a word."

They talked a bit more; then Emily kissed her cheek, took her soup pan, and departed. Jackie waved, then shut the door. She'd finally asked the Lord to come into her heart, but the lie was still there, waiting for her to confess it to those she loved. *Oh, God, give me the strength to do what's right.*

A smile crept across her face. Now she had God to turn to, and as Emily had said, He'd promised never to leave her or forsake her.

Jackie glanced at the clock and, deciding it wasn't too late, phoned Sam and asked him to come over. "I have something important to tell you."

"Can't this wait? I'm packing. Trapper and I are flying up to Skagway. I'll be back in a couple of days."

"This is important, Sam. Please. I need to see you before you leave."

While she waited, she worked on the eleventh block.

❧

All the way to her apartment, Sam pondered her words. What could be so important that she'd ask him to come over again so soon? He could think of only one reason. She'd changed her mind about telling everyone they'd been husband and wife and leaving Juneau.

"I've confessed my sins and asked God's forgiveness, and He's forgiven me!" she blurted out the minute she opened the door. "I've given my life over to Him!"

Sam did a double take. Jackie's whole demeanor was different. "When? How?"

She told him about Emily's visit and how she'd prayed with her.

"Did you tell—?"

"No! I didn't have to. She told me I could confess my sins in my heart, that God knew what they were. I didn't have to say them out loud." She grabbed onto his hand and pulled him to the sofa. "You don't know what a burden He lifted from my shoulders. It—it was as if He was right here, telling me everything would be all right, if I trusted my life to Him."

"I–I don't know why you're telling me."

"Because I want to get my life straightened out with you too, Sam. I've sinned against you, and I'm asking for your forgiveness."

"You—you—"

"No! I didn't abort our baby. I was only a kid, Sam, when you told me you wanted me to get pregnant. I'd never been around children. It wasn't that I was opposed to having children—ever—just not then. Not until we were both ready, but you wouldn't see my side of it. You wouldn't even listen."

He felt himself frowning. "Are you saying it was all my fault?"

She reached out and touched his arm. "No. I'm not blaming you. All I'm saying is the timing was wrong. I admit when I found out I was pregnant I considered having an abortion. Several friends of mine had gotten rid of their babies that way, and knowing how I felt, that I wasn't ready yet, they encouraged me to go through with it. It sounded like a quick way out."

"How easily you were influenced," he snapped. But instead of snapping back as she'd always done, Jackie remained calm.

"Do you remember that last day we were together? Before you left for Germany?"

He nodded.

"Your parting words to me were not—'I love you, Jackie,' or 'Take care of yourself, Jackie.' They were—'If you don't go through with this pregnancy, I'll leave you and get a divorce.' "

She blinked, and he knew she was trying not to cry.

"I was so hurt I wanted to get rid of that baby just to spite you, but I couldn't do it. Not yet, anyway. I continued going to the doctor, stayed on the diet he gave me, exercised, read the books for expectant mothers—all of it—and with each thing I became more involved. Then something happened."

Sam was sure she was going to confess to changing her mind and having the abortion, and a horrible ache consumed his whole body. He wasn't sure he could take hearing those vile words come from her mouth.

"Our baby moved! I felt it, Sam, and it was the most wonderful experience of my life. I so wanted to share that precious moment with you, but you were off in Germany, flying that helicopter. I was always jealous of that helicopter. You seemed to care more for flying than you did for me."

His own eyes misted over. He'd never realized that before.

She smiled, and it was one of the sweetest smiles he'd ever seen on her face.

"By then, I was twenty-one weeks into my pregnancy. The doctor said I should have an ultrasound procedure, to make sure things were going okay since I'd been doing a little spotting."

Her words were convincing, and for a moment, he was almost tempted to believe her story. But how easily she lied. Perhaps she'd made up this whole scenario as a cover-up. No! He wouldn't be taken in by her sweet demeanor. He wouldn't be swayed with her elaborate story about feeling the baby move and the ultrasound. Had she made all this up hoping he'd take her back? Support her now that she wasn't going to have a job?

"I don't believe you any more now than I did all those years ago. How gullible do you think I am? Did you think you could sway me with that story about that doctor telling you our baby was a boy? Come on, Jackie. I wasn't born yesterday. I did the right thing when I walked out on you."

Jackie bowed her head and mumbled to herself, and for a minute, he almost thought she was praying. Probably that story about confessing her sins was all a lie, too.

"I've heard enough. I'm getting out of here." He made his way quickly to the door. "Six days, Jackie. That's all you've got! Not a day more!"

"Sam!" she called out as she rushed to the door after him. "You need to do it, too! Confess your sins and ask God for forgiveness!"

His thumb rammed into his chest as his chin jutted out and his eyes narrowed. "Me? I'm not the one who aborted our baby. God may have forgiven you if you really asked Him to as you said you did, but I can't forgive you. I wanted that baby, and you got rid of him! Like a piece of unwanted trash."

He yanked the door shut and ran down the stairs, two at a time, eager to put as much distance between him and Jackie as possible.

❧

Jackie stood leaning against the cool metal of the door for a long time, pressing her head against its surface. Her attempt to ask for Sam's forgiveness had been futile. Not that she'd expected him to pull her into his arms, kiss her, and tell her he believed her, but she had hoped that, at least, he'd forgive her for ever considering ending her pregnancy. Her mind went back to that awful day when she'd lost Sammy. How she'd needed Sam to be with her. She'd been so alone. Only that emergency room doctor and nurse knew how she'd suffered and the agony she felt when she lost her little boy.

Eventually, she backed away from the door, locked it, and headed for her bedroom to finish the eleventh block and write her note to Sammy.

❧

Sam sat behind the steering wheel of the rental car, staring at Jackie's apartment until the lights went out in her living room. The sincerity he'd seen in her eyes ripped at his heart. Could she have been telling the truth after all? He shook his head to clear it. Of course she wasn't telling the truth! She'd been talking about having an abortion right up to the day he'd left for Germany. He'd warned her. She knew what would happen if she went through with it. She'd made up that story about having a miscarriage to cover up her guilt.

And what about the thing she'd told him about confessing her sins to God? Did she think if she confessed them her guilt would disappear and she could go on with life as if nothing had happened?

She had some nerve, telling him he needed to confess his sins too. He wasn't a sinner. Well, he was living a lie right along with her, but that wasn't his fault. It was hers. He'd never done anything bad. He'd donated his time to help coach a Little League team when he'd been stationed in Washington. He never cheated on his taxes. He always behaved himself with women. What did he have to confess?

But, even as he tried to convince himself he wasn't a sinner, Trapper's words came flooding over him, and he couldn't get them out of his mind. "God made the rules. It's up to us to decide if we want to follow them."

"Not now, God. Not now."

≈

Jackie arose early the next morning and sorted through the things she'd be taking with her and the things she'd leave behind, placing them in piles until she could get some packing boxes. The shipping costs would be outrageous, but some things she couldn't bear to leave behind, things that meant a great deal to her. It would be worth the extra expense to keep them. Although Sam had said he'd give her a week to come clean with everyone, after thinking things over, she'd decided it would be best for everyone if she got it over with as soon as possible. It made no sense to delay it.

She worked like a madwoman at the shop, organizing shelves, setting up new displays, anything she could think of that would leave the shop in the best condition possible when the day arrived that she had to leave. She owed that much to Glorianna. Just the thought of telling her best friend in all the world that she had lied and was walking away from her made her sick to her stomach.

She was desperate now to finish the hand-quilting on the little blocks. Although tired from her busy day, after supper she began work on the twelfth block. She smiled as she placed each tiny stitch, comforted by the knowledge she was no longer in control of her life. God was. How sweet it was to commune with Him now that she'd made her peace with Him. She found herself pouring out her heart to Him, telling Him things she'd never think of telling another living soul. What a joy it was to know now that someday she'd be in heaven. If only Sam could be there with her.

The next day was much the same as the day before, with Jackie making sure she'd tied her loose ends in readiness for her departure. That evening she carried the box containing the blocks into the living room, tuned the radio to her favorite station, and worked with perseverance until she'd finished the twelfth block, sewing in her love with each stitch. Working on the quilt brought her great joy and a happiness she knew had to come from God. She even took time to write and attach the final love note to Sammy.

Jackie arrived at the shop way ahead of the staff the next morning. There were things she wanted to do without an audience. By the time the other employees arrived, she was in her office working on the final additions to the books, bringing every entry as up to date as possible. It'd been an excellent year for the shop. The books showed the profit margin had risen dramatically because of some of the new programs and classes she'd implemented. At least, as far as the shop was concerned, she could hold her head high. *Too bad I can't say the same thing about my personal life!*

Later that day she phoned Glorianna, Tina, and Emily and invited them and their husbands to her apartment the next evening for dessert, saying she had some things to tell them. She was excited about the first thing, and it would be easy to tell, that she'd accepted the Lord; but the second one, confessing her lies, was going to be extremely difficult. She wanted to invite Sam, too, but she feared his being there might make things more awkward for her and for them. No, she was the one who'd not only lied to them but convinced Sam to go along with her lies against his better judgment. She alone was the one who should tell them. Though each of the women quizzed her as to the purpose of her invitation, she held strong and kept her silence.

That evening, Jackie flitted around her apartment, cleaning and moving anything into the back bedroom that would give even a hint of her plans to leave. Once everything was in place, she took her shower and climbed into bed. She pulled the box of quilt blocks up beside her, taking them out one by one to admire them, then fanning them out across the bed. As she stared at the intricate patterns she'd quilted onto each block, quiet tears slipped down her cheeks. All twelve blocks were so beautiful, each with its own intricate pattern, and attached to each one was her love note to Sammy. She could assemble them into a quilt later by adding the sashings and borders. It'd been important to her that she have all twelve completed before she left Alaska, and she had accomplished her goal. She'd worked on many quilts since joining the staff of The Bear Paw Quilt Shop, but none of them held the meaning of this one. She'd quilted her very heart and soul into these blocks.

Once she'd put the stack back in the box, she picked up the Bible from her nightstand and read until nearly midnight. Then, kneeling by her bed, eyes closed, hands folded, she prayed. *God, I know You've forgiven me for my sins, and I praise You for that, but I wonder if even You can get me out of this mess I've made for myself. I've not only destroyed any future I might have had here in Alaska with my lies, but I've destroyed Sam's job as well. I want to do the right thing, and I need Your help.* As she crawled into bed, a sweet peace came over her, and she slept more soundly than she had in weeks, despite the turmoil going on in her life.

Although several of the staff raised questioning brows the next day when

Jackie praised them for their work and thanked them for their cooperation with her, no one questioned her motives. Since this was the final day she'd spend in the shop, she couldn't resist letting them know how important they had become to her.

When all the employees had left for the day and she was alone in the shop, she gathered up the last box of her personal belongings. She stood gazing at the array of lovely quilts mounted on the walls, the colorful rows and rows of fabric and all the other things she'd grown to love since coming to work seventeen years ago at The Bear Paw. Finally pulling herself away, she moved through the stockroom and out the heavy steel door, locking it securely behind her before climbing the steps to her apartment. She had one hour to prepare for her invited guests.

After Jackie freshened up, she arranged the little cakes she'd bought at the bakery on a lovely cut-glass tray and placed it on the table next to the bouquet of fresh flowers she'd picked up at the florist. She switched on the coffeepot, added silverware, napkins, plates, cups, and saucers to the table, then stood back to give the room one final check. Everything was ready.

Glorianna, Trapper, Tina, Hank, Emily, and Dyami arrived right on time, each one smiling at her as she took their coats and hung them in the hall closet.

"Hey, where's Sam?" Dyami asked, rubbing his hands together and looking around.

"I–I didn't invite him."

"I figured you'd invite him, too," Trapper said with a raised brow. "He's in town. We got back from Skagway this afternoon. Want me to call him?"

Jackie shook her head. "No. I purposely didn't invite him."

Although brows raised and everyone seemed surprised by her words, no one made any further comment.

"Please," Jackie said, gesturing toward the dessert table in hopes of changing the conversation, "help yourselves. I have plenty of everything."

Once everyone had been served and seated on the sofa and chairs she'd arranged in a half circle, Jackie moved to stand in front of them, her heart racing, her palms sweaty. Other than facing Sam after she'd lost the baby, this was the hardest thing she'd ever had to do.

"Okay, out with it," Glorianna said, looking somewhat worried. "Please don't tell me someone has made you a better offer and you're quitting your job."

Emily gave Glorianna a knowing grin. "If her news is what I think it is, you'll be happy to hear it!"

Glorianna planted her hands on her hips with a playful smile toward her mother-in-law. "She's told you, and she hasn't told me? I thought I was Jackie's best friend!"

"Emily's right. Part of my news is good, and it's one of the reasons I called all of you here tonight." Jackie tried to push the bad news to the back of her mind and gave them a joyous smile of victory. "Emily came to see me the other night. After we talked and she explained a few things to me, I accepted the Lord as my Savior!"

Glorianna and Tina rushed to her side, congratulating her and hugging her so tightly it was hard for her to breathe.

"That's the best news I've heard in a long time," Trapper said, his own joy radiating from his bearded face.

"Tina and I have been praying for you every day," Hank added, grinning.

Jackie smiled at each one in the circle. These people had been her family. They'd encouraged her, come to her aid whenever she'd needed them. "I–I know I should've done it a long time ago, but I was trying to make things too hard. When sweet Emily made me see how simple God's plan really is and convinced me He could love someone like me, I had no other choice but to ask Him to take over my life."

"Well, I'm glad you invited us all here. This is a cause for celebration." Trapper rose and moved to the table, refilling his cup and picking up another little cake. "Anyone else for a refill?"

Once everyone had refilled their cups and added another cake to their plates, they seated themselves again, and Jackie stood before them. The lump in her throat was nearly gagging her to silence, and she wondered if she'd be able to get the words out—words she'd rehearsed so carefully all day.

"Please, everyone. I–I have something else to tell you. Some–something that must be said."

Chapter 9

All chatter stopped as six people gave her their full attention. She was sure her voice reflected the panic going on inside her.

"What I'm about to tell you will shock you, but I'm hoping you'll hear me out." She clenched her fists at her sides and drew in a deep breath.

"I've lied to everyone from the first day I walked into The Bear Paw and applied for a job. I told everyone I was a widow and that my husband died in a hunting accident. He didn't. He divorced me."

"You've lied to me all this time, Jackie? Why? I don't understand."

"It started out with my lie to Anna when she hired me. She mentioned that the girl whose place I would be taking had been divorced during the time she worked at The Bear Paw, and Anna had been very upset by it and had expressed her feelings to the girl. That was the reason the girl had quit. I knew, right then, if she found out I had just gone through a divorce she wouldn't hire me, so I told her I was a widow. I needed that job. By the time you inherited the quilt shop from Anna, the lie had become a solid part of my life. There was no way for me to unravel it. I knew I had to live with it. You were as adamant as Anna about divorce. I knew I couldn't tell you, either."

"You're right concerning Anna's feelings about divorce," Emily said with a sympathetic smile toward Jackie. "She was almost glad when that girl left. She had strong feelings about those who broke their marriage vows, and she made no bones about expressing those feelings openly and at every opportunity."

"There's more," Jackie said, holding up her hand. "Please let me finish."

Glorianna nodded and settled back in her chair.

"My husband was nearly four years older than me. We married right after I graduated from high school, and he joined the army." She paused, remembering that happy time. "Everything was great the first three years. I loved him with all my heart, and I think he loved me the same way. Then—"

Trapper stood and gave her a compassionate smile. "Jackie, you really don't have to tell us this. It's obvious you're very emotional about your marriage and the divorce, but your business is your business."

"No, it's not. All of you deserve to know, especially Glorianna. Oh, I know she'll never be able to trust me to work at the shop again, now that I've told you the truth and she knows she's had a divorced liar working for her; but the time has come that I have to make things right. Not only with you six, but with God."

She motioned Trapper back down to his seat. "Please, Trapper. I have to tell you the complete story. You'll see why later."

Although he seemed reluctant, Trapper settled back in the chair and waited.

"I'd been working at a fast-food place trying to get enough money saved so I could go to college. Then one day, out of the blue, my husband came home from a training trip and told me he wanted us to have a baby as soon as possible. Just like that. We'd never even discussed when we'd start a family, just that someday we would! I'd always talked about wanting to go to college and making something of myself. I was from a poor, uneducated family, and I was determined to have a career." As she grabbed onto the back of Emily's chair for support, she felt the woman's hand cup over hers, and Jackie gave Emily a smile.

"I was furious with him. I tried to explain to him that I hadn't even thought of having children yet and how badly I wanted to have a career, but he was adamant. He said if I loved him I'd give him a baby, and he accused me of being selfish."

She looked around and found six faces staring at her. She couldn't help but wonder what was going on in their minds.

"We argued about it nearly every day, but neither of us would give in. My girl-friends sided with me and told me I had every right to have a career. After all, he did! His army buddies sided with him, many of them saying they'd insisted their wives give up any idea of having a career to become mothers. Oh, I think we both still loved one another. I know I loved him, and we expressed our love often, but that didn't stop the fighting over the issue." She paused to gather her thoughts. *Be honest. Tell them the whole story, exactly as it happened. No lies. No excuses.*

"Then the thing I least expected happened. The base doctor told me I was pregnant. I was furious, but my husband was ecstatic. He rushed out and began buying all sorts of baby things, spending money we didn't have, for the baby I didn't want. I–I told him—" She stopped midsentence. How could she say the words?

"I–I told him—I was going to have an—an abortion."

A unified gasp came from the group, and Jackie could tell by their expressions her declaration had shocked them beyond belief.

"Needless to say, he was livid. He swore at me and called me terrible names and said if I went through with it I would be a murderer! I tried to explain my feelings to him, but he wouldn't listen. Two of my girlfriends, who hadn't wanted children but whose husbands had, had gone through abortions, one twice, and they encouraged me to stand up to him. They told me to remind him this was my body, not his, that we were talking about. The decision should be mine."

She paused and thought her words over carefully before going on.

"I hated being pregnant. I couldn't keep anything down and had to quit my job, which infuriated me. I struggled along for nearly three more months, knowing if I was to have an abortion it'd have to be soon. He went to every doctor's appointment with me and acted like a sappy new father, asking the poor doctor all sorts of questions. I didn't want him to go, but he insisted. Then, a couple of weeks after my fourth month checkup, he came home all excited because the army was sending him on a special mission to Germany. My first thought was that with him gone it'd be easier to arrange an abortion. I'd gained way too much weight, my hands and feet were swollen, and even my nose had gotten bigger. All I could think about was getting rid of that baby and getting back to my normal self and how mad I was at my husband for leaving me alone at a time like this."

Even though no one voiced a comment, she could tell from their expressions that her friends were in shock, and she could almost hear their thoughts. *Jackie? This Jackie they'd known so well? Never!*

"The day my husband left, we had the worst fight of all. It went on most of the day while he was packing. His final words to me as he left the house, knowing it would be at least two months before he got back, were 'If you do anything to get rid of that baby while I'm gone, I'll divorce you!' and I had no doubt he meant it. But his threats didn't matter. I was so arrogant and immature I'd already decided what I did with that baby was my business, not his. I–I fully intended to get rid of it, but a few weeks later, something happened that I hadn't counted on. I was sitting in a chair watching TV when I felt something. A movement in my stomach. As I rubbed my hand over the spot, I felt it again. I can't begin to tell you what a sensation that was. For the first time, I realized that thing in my stomach, the thing I wanted to rid myself of, wasn't a thing at all. It was a live human being! I sat in awe as my baby moved! My baby!"

Jackie cast a quick glance toward Glorianna and found the woman's eyes as round as saucers.

"I called and excitedly told the base doctor the next morning about the movement, and you know what he said? 'That little one wanted his mommy to know he was doing fine.' I called my girlfriends and told them I'd decided against the abortion. They told me I was a fool, but I didn't care. I went to my appointment that next week, and when I heard my baby's heartbeat I broke down and cried. I was so happy. Because I was still spotting, the doctor wanted to do an ultrasound immediately, to make sure everything was okay."

Tina's hand spread across her stomach. "Oh, Jackie, what an ordeal for both of you."

"Wh–when"—Jackie gulped in a breath of air as she felt a tear roll down her cheek—"wh–when I actually saw my baby on that screen, I screamed out with joy and wondered how I could ever have considered getting rid of our precious baby. The doctor told me our baby was a boy. I was so happy."

She paused to catch another breath. "But the doctor's face told me something was wrong. When I asked him about it, he said the next few weeks would be critical and mentioned something about low-lying placenta previa, which I didn't understand. He said I'd have to stay in bed and be very careful. By that time, I wanted that baby so bad, I would've gone to the moon if the doctor had asked me."

"Did you tell your husband?" Tina asked timidly, as if she was afraid her question might upset Jackie.

"I wanted to. I hadn't heard from him since he'd left, which kind of surprised me. But, I guess, knowing the way I felt, he figured it'd be best to leave me alone. He knew my mind had been made up, and I suppose he figured he'd done everything he could to stop me from going through with the abortion. I tried to call him at the base. I was so happy, and I wanted him to be happy, too. I even called his commander. He said my husband was out on maneuvers and couldn't be reached, unless it was an emergency."

She paused long enough to take a sip of her cold coffee, then went on. "I contacted a few of his buddies that evening and told them to have him call me if they heard from him, but he never did."

"But things went along okay?" Glorianna asked, leaning forward, a tender look on her face now.

"Actually, I felt better than I had in months. I was no longer sick to my stomach, and the swelling in my feet and hands had stopped. My neighbor, bless her heart, did my grocery shopping and cooked me a few meals. I was marking the days off on the calendar until my son would arrive and I could hold him in my arms. I was so sure things between my husband and me would return to normal once he learned I was as excited as he was about the birth of our precious baby."

"Was he?" Emily asked, her eyes wide.

"I never had a chance to find out. The day before my next doctor's appointment, I began to hemorrhage. Terrified, I grabbed my car keys and headed for the hospital."

Am I telling them more than they need to know? she wondered as she regrouped her thoughts, her misty gaze flitting from one person to the next.

"I ran into the emergency room screaming for someone to help me, but there was nothing they could do." She fought to hold back her tears, but the memory was too much. "Our baby was stillborn, which the doctor said meant if there hadn't been any trouble, he was old enough that he could have survived outside the womb."

Glorianna rushed to her side and cradled her in her arms. "Oh, Jackie—I'm so sorry. I had no idea, and to think you were all alone when it happened."

"I–I've never felt so all alone. I needed my husband there with me."

The room took on an eerie silence.

After Glorianna went back to her chair and Jackie regained her composure, she continued. "They kept me overnight, I think because I was so despondent. One of the social workers came to talk to me about losing my baby; then she drove me home in her car while a friend of hers followed in my car. Two days later, my husband got back from his mission."

"He had to be upset by your baby's death, but he must've been glad to hear you'd had a change of heart," Trapper said, leaning forward.

"He didn't believe I'd miscarried. He was outraged when I tried to tell him our baby's death hadn't been my fault. He accused me of lying, saying I'd been responsible for our baby's death. His words hurt, but after the way I'd been so insistent about not wanting a baby, I couldn't blame him. He—He—"

Even after all this time, Jackie found it hard to say the words. Finally, she blurted out hysterically, "He accused me of killing my own baby, then walked right out that door and went to a divorce lawyer. I never even had a chance to tell him how I'd felt our baby move and heard the heartbeat and watched it on the ultrasound screen. He didn't even know our baby was a boy."

The room was silent as all of them kept their eyes fixed on her. Jackie pulled a paper napkin from the table and dabbed at her eyes before going on.

"The day the divorce became final, I left town. I took the first bus heading out and ended up in Denver. I checked into a motel, not sure where I would go from there or what to do with my life." She hung her head, her words barely audible. "I–I even considered suicide."

When no one spoke, she swallowed hard and began again.

"Th–there was an ad in the Denver paper, advertising a cruise to Alaska. I took some of the settlement money from the divorce and booked the trip. Two weeks later, when the ship anchored in Juneau, I got off with the other passengers, intending to spend the day visiting the shops and aimlessly wandering the streets. Eventually, I ended up at The Bear Paw. When I saw a help-wanted sign in the window, I went in and applied. And, as you know, Anna hired me, and I've been here ever since."

"But I don't understand, Jackie," Glorianna said, shaking her head. "Why are you telling us this now? Why didn't you leave your past in the past and keep your lies buried? We may never have found out, if you hadn't told us. Why resurrect old memories now?"

"Did you ever hear from your husband again?" Tina asked, ignoring Glorianna's question.

"Not until recently. I'd cut all ties with my past and didn't expect to hear from him ever again. I supposed he'd married someone else and, by now, had a houseful of the kids he'd wanted."

"You've heard from him?" Hank asked as he slipped his arm about his wife and pulled her close. "I can't imagine any husband being that cruel."

Jackie weighed her words carefully. Her intent wasn't to make Sam look bad. "Yes, I've heard from him, but please don't judge him too harshly. You have to remember how badly he wanted that baby. I was the one who said I was going to get an abortion. Of course he was going to be upset. I can see that now. At the time, I felt he was being ridiculous. I was the one who listened to my friends' bad advice. We were both wrong."

"Does he want to make things right? Is that why you've heard from him?"

Jackie shook her head sadly. "No, Glorianna. I wish that was the reason. He didn't have any idea I was in Juneau, until the two of us ended up at the same place at the same time. He's the reason I've never married or been interested in dating another man. I still love him and always will."

"How does he feel about you?"

"Oh, Tina, I have no idea. He still says he could never live with me after I purposely lost our baby, so I assume he no longer has any feelings for me. I've tried to tell him the truth—that although I did everything the doctor told me, I miscarried—but he won't even discuss it. He doesn't believe a word I say."

"I'd like to meet that guy," Trapper said, shaking his head. "Having a baby should be the decision of both the husband and the wife. No man has a right to dictate to his wife, especially when it involves her body. Is he still here in Juneau?"

Jackie nodded. "Yes, Trapper. It's Sam."

Chapter 10

Trapper leaped to his feet. "Sam? Sam Mulvaney? Surely not! Is this some kind of a joke?"

The overwhelming silence in the room was deafening.

Jackie shook her head sadly while trying to keep her emotions in check. "No, no joke. Sam is my ex-husband, my baby's father."

"But I'm the one who talked him into coming here!" Trapper reasoned aloud. "He told me he'd been divorced, but he never mentioned a baby."

Tina's hand went to her mouth. "And to think Glorianna and I tried to match the two of you up! We thought you were perfect for one another."

"I'm still confused." Trapper rubbed at his forehead. "If what you're telling us is true, and I have no reason to believe it's anything but the truth, that means Sam has been deceiving us too. But why?"

"Don't blame Sam. I asked him to lie for me," Jackie confessed. "He didn't want to; in fact, he refused. But I knew when Glorianna found out I'd been lying about my past she wouldn't let me keep working at the shop. So when I ran into Sam in the parking lot the first night he came to Alaska—"

"That's the first time you'd seen him since your divorce?"

Jackie gave Tina a weak smile. "Yes, that's the reason we were both a bit late. We had a long talk before we came into The Grizzly Bear. After much persuasion, I was able to convince Sam to keep my secret, but he made me promise, if the truth ever came out, I would take full responsibility. That's what I'm trying to do now."

Hank shook his head. "I can't believe it. Sam Mulvaney."

"That's why he later resigned and headed back to Memphis," Jackie explained. "He couldn't stand deceiving you, Trapper."

Glorianna flinched. "And I arranged for the two of you to be booked on the same flight to Seattle and have reservations at the same hotel."

"You had no idea, Glorianna. You meant well. In fact, Sam and I talked about the matchmaking you and Tina were trying to do."

"No wonder you didn't invite Sam to be here tonight," Dyami said, picking up his cup and refilling it.

"So I'm leaving Alaska. I have reservations on a late afternoon flight tomorrow." She turned to Glorianna. "I've done the best I could to make sure the shop is in order. You'll find all the book work up to date, and I've made sure all the supplies are ordered. I'll leave the shop keys, as well as the keys to my apartment, on the table when I leave."

"Maybe we'd better talk about this—"

Jackie shook her head. "No, Glorianna. I know how important honesty is to you in everything. You'd never be able to trust me again, knowing how I've lied to you." Then turning to the others she said, "I want all of you to know how much you've meant to me. I love each one of you and hope you can find it in your heart, someday, to forgive me."

"Is—is Sam going with you?" Trapper asked.

She gave him a nervous laugh. "No, I'm afraid where I go and what I do is the last thing Sam is interested in. He's made it perfectly clear he wants nothing more to do with me."

"Then he's staying?" Glorianna asked.

Jackie shrugged. "I doubt it. He's convinced Trapper won't want a liar as a partner, but I'm sure he'll let you know." She moved from one to another, giving them each a guarded hug. "Please pray for me, and be assured I'll be praying for you. Accepting the Lord was worth coming to Alaska. Now, if you'll excuse me, I have some things to finish up if I'm going to make my flight tomorrow."

Her six guests filed out without a word, each wearing a stunned expression that broke her heart. After locking the door behind them, Jackie washed and dried the dishes, making sure each one was put in its place. She was determined to leave the apartment as clean as she'd found it when she'd moved in.

Exhausted from the experience of having to confess her lies, after praying and thanking God for giving her the strength to tell them the truth, Jackie fell into bed, worn out both physically and mentally.

After a night of tossing and turning, she crawled out of bed at five. Although most of her things were already packed, she still had much to do. She scurried around the apartment—dusting, running the sweeper, cleaning windows and mirrors—and carried a few boxes and an odd assortment of things that needed to be boxed into the living room and placed them on the floor. By nine o'clock, she had nearly everything in order. Gathering a few large boxes from the quilt shop storeroom to hold the things she'd decided to ship was the only task that remained. *I can't do that!* she realized suddenly. *Do I really want to go into that storeroom and take a chance on running into some of the staff and having to explain my reasons for leaving?* Then she remembered the Dumpsters out behind the big grocery store down past the courthouse. *They probably have exactly what I need.*

She shoved a few of the smaller boxes to one side, picked up her purse and keys, and quickly made her way down the stairs to her car.

❧

Sam sat eyeing the phone. He'd told Jackie he'd give her one week and if she didn't tell Glorianna and Trapper the truth by then, he was going to tell them. Surely she'd alert him before she admitted to them her life had been a lie.

He glanced at his watch. *I'm going that way. Maybe I'll stop by the quilt shop and ask her if she's decided when she's going to tell them. She's probably there by now.*

"No, she's not here yet," one of the clerks told him when he entered through the back way. "That's funny, too, because she's always the first one here. I hope she's not sick."

Sam excused himself and raced up the outside stairway, taking two steps at a time. He knocked, but when she didn't respond he tried the door. Finding it standing slightly ajar, he ventured in, calling out her name. Boxes were piled near the door and some by her chair. Others that looked as if they were ready to be packed sat on the sofa, the chairs, and the coffee table. No doubt about it—Jackie was preparing to leave Juneau.

Noticing the red light was glowing on the coffeepot, he took a cup from the cupboard and filled it, picked up one of the little cakes sitting on a plate in the middle of the table, then sat down in the recliner to wait for her return. She must have planned to come back soon since the coffeepot was still turned on and the door was unlocked. Maybe she was visiting with a neighbor or had run to the store for something.

Sam sipped the hot coffee slowly, listening carefully for any sounds of her return. He pulled a magazine from the wastebasket sitting next to the chair and leafed through it. Finding nothing of interest, he leaned to put it back where he'd found it when he noticed a white box sitting on the floor near his feet. Deciding it was probably some quilting thing Jackie was working on, and having nothing better to do, he pulled out the little stack of blocks and placed them on his knee. He gazed at the intricate, hand-quilted design on the top one and was amazed at the evenness of the stitches and how tiny they were. The woman was a masterful quilter, no doubt about it.

As he started to place it back on the pile, he noticed a note pinned to the back. Carefully he unpinned the paper, unfolded it, and began to read: *Dear Sammy, I don't know why I'm writing this, except to say I love you and to remind you—you are in my thoughts day and night.*

Sam's brows rose. "I thought she told me she never had a serious boyfriend. Who is Sammy?" he asked aloud.

His interest piqued, he picked up the second block.

Sammy, my dear, facing up to the fact that you were gone was the hardest thing I've ever had to do. I'm making this quilt for you, Sammy. Of course you'll never see it, but I'm making it as a token of my love. Don't think too harshly of me. Please.

He picked up the third block and quickly flipped it over. "Another note?"

My precious one. I wish you were here with me. I'm miserable without you. I want so much to hold you in my arms and kiss your sweet face. I cry as I go to bed each night, wishing I could hug you to me.

441

"He left her? When? And why is she making a quilt for someone who must've walked out on her?"

He removed the pin from the fourth block, being careful not to tear the paper. *My beloved one. I miss you desperately. If only I could hold you and kiss your dear face. You're constantly on my mind. Where are you now, Sweetheart? In a better place? A place filled with love and sunshine? I long to be with you.*

Sam stared at the note. "Who is this Sammy character?" He pinned the notes back where they belonged and pulled out the next block, noting it too was hand-quilted with beautiful, even stitches. As he suspected, a note was pinned to it as well.

I pulled out your pictures today. You looked so handsome in that cap. Just looking at it made me smile. The day those pictures were taken will be etched into my memory forever, especially the one taken of us in the rocking chair.

He hurriedly grabbed up the sixth block. *I have your birthday circled on the calendar, my love. Every year on your special day I buy a little cake and light a candle. If only I could spend those days with you. The pain of losing you never goes away.*

Sam scratched his head. More confused by her words than ever, he replaced the pin and picked up the seventh block. "Who is this guy?"

He pricked his finger as he struggled with the tiny safety pin. After grabbing his handkerchief and blotting his finger, he read the note.

Sammy, my love, my precious one. Today something unexpected happened. I ran into Sam! Yes, Sam. He's in Alaska. I wanted to talk to him about you, but I couldn't. He'd never understand, and I didn't want to argue. I've made a new life for myself here. I don't want it spoiled. He made it quite clear years ago he wanted nothing to do with me, and it broke my heart. I've decided this quilt will be my tribute to you, Sammy, darling. I wish I could give it to you.

"This doesn't make any sense. Why would she mention me, and why is she making a quilt as a tribute to him? Did he die in a car accident or from some disease?" He read on out of sheer curiosity.

If only Sam had believed me, dear Sammy, perhaps things would have turned out differently. I've heard stress does strange things to your body, and I was certainly under a great deal of stress when I was carrying you. Oh, I admit I didn't want you when your daddy first talked about having a baby. But the day I felt you move—well, it was a miracle, Sammy. All of a sudden I saw you as a real baby, and I shouted out with joy. I wish Sam could've been there with us. It was an awesome experience.

Sam let out a gasp, and his hands began to tremble. "Sammy was our baby?" He stared at the words. "How can that be?"

Then the doctor let me listen to your heartbeat, and I've never felt such happiness. My baby! The day he did the ultrasound was the most exciting day of my life. I actually got to see you! Not everyone would have thought so, but to me you were beautiful. I decided at that very moment to name you Sammy, after your father. If only Sam had been there with me, my joy would have been complete. I tried to phone him, to tell him about you, but he was on that mission to Germany and couldn't be reached. Oh, Sammy, I loved him so much. If only your father had loved me enough to trust me and believe me.

Sam stared at the paper, his hands still shaking. Had Jackie been telling him the truth?

I'm so afraid you experienced pain. I keep thinking there must've been something I could've done differently, even though I know now I couldn't. It's just that I'm your mommy, Sammy, and I was supposed to take care of you. There was nothing I could do but lie there and watch it happen and know I couldn't stop it. I tried so hard to do the right things for you from the day I felt you move inside me. I ate healthy foods, exercised, everything I knew to do; but it wasn't good enough. I wanted to protect you, to keep you safe—to give you the best start in life I could. Where did I fail you, my precious one? My darling child? Sam clutched the note to his chest as his eyes filled with tears. "Oh, Jackie, if you were telling me the truth, I've done you a terrible injustice."

He took a deep breath and read on. *I'm so sad tonight, Sammy. Your father decided he couldn't keep lying to everyone. He's going to resign from his partnership with Trapper and go back to Memphis. Although his being here has made my life difficult, I didn't want him to go. I still love him. I always will.*

Sam buried his head in his hands. "Oh, Jackie, how could I have treated you like that? I loved you, too!"

The eighth block tore at his heart. *Oh, Sammy, guess what! Your father is back in Juneau. Although he's been gone only a few days, I've missed him terribly. Today he almost treated me like I was human. We've reached an agreement. We're going to try to be friends. Maybe he's finally beginning to realize I've told him the truth all along!*

Sam smiled as he remembered that day. Jackie had never looked more beautiful as she'd grinned at him over her shopping cart. He'd never admit it to her, but in his heart, although he knew it was impossible, he had wished their relationship could be more than just friends.

"Oh, Jackie, it seems since we've found each other again, our lives have been nothing but a roller coaster of emotions. I'm sorry for taking you on this crazy ride going nowhere."

He pulled the next block from the stack and unpinned its note.

It's late, and I'm tired; but before going to bed I had to write and tell you how much I love you. Sometimes I dream of holding you and kissing your sweet face, only to wake up and find I'm alone in my room. It's hard for me to realize you've been gone this long. Life has been hard without you, Sammy. Very hard. I only wish your father would accept the truth.

Glorianna told me some disturbing things a few days ago. She said if I don't confess my sins and ask God to forgive them, I can't go to heaven. I can't get her words out of my head. I guess I'm going to have to read the Bible for myself. If you were here with me, perhaps we could read it together. It makes me sad I was never able to read those sweet little children's storybooks to you at bedtime. I love you, baby.

Sam swallowed hard and rubbed at his eyes, the words blurring on the paper. Trapper had told him the same thing Glorianna had told Jackie. Could God really be that judgmental?

Oh, Sammy, your father kissed me, the note on the tenth block said. *Although later he said it'd been a mistake. But I knew better. He wanted to kiss me. I could tell. Could he still have feelings for me? Unfortunately, we got into another argument afterward, and we ended up coming back from Seattle separately. I'm so confused by his actions. He admitted he is still drawn to me. Why can't he believe me? If only he'd talked to the doctor, checked the emergency room records; then he'd have known I was telling the truth.*

Sam stared at the paper, then smacked the side of his head with his palm. Why hadn't he bothered to check the hospital records? "Why? Because I was too stubborn, that's why! I was so sure she'd done what she'd threatened to do that I wouldn't even listen to her." His gaze went back to the paper, and he reread the words: *If only he'd talked to the doctor, checked the emergency room records; then he'd have known I was telling the truth.*

He stared at the words, rereading them again. "Why didn't I listen to her? Give her a chance to prove she was telling the truth after all? I never once considered what she was going through. She was young, naïve, with no desire to have a baby at that time, and I insisted on it. Having a baby should've been our decision, not just mine. How could I have been so selfish?"

He sat for a long time, staring at the wall, remembering the many arguments they'd had—most of them started by him. "If only I had a chance to go back, how differently I'd do things."

With a deep sigh, he unpinned the note from the eleventh block.

Oh, Sammy, I saw your father today. We all went to church, but I made sure to sit on the opposite end of the pew. The words the pastor read from the Bible about lying lips really got to me. I'm sure God is upset with me. It seems my life is built on nothing but lies.

But something good came of it, my dear one. Thinking I was sick, dear Emily Timberwolf came to see me and brought me some soup. She's such a kind and caring woman. She told me, straight out, I needed to get my life right with God—that God wanted to forgive my sins—that He was a God of love. And, Sammy, guess what! I did it! Right here in this very apartment. I can't begin to tell you of the sweet peace that came over me. Now I know I'll be in heaven someday. If only Sam could be there with me.

Sam gulped hard as his fingers rubbed at his eyes and the words on the paper blurred. His heart raced as he tried to catch his breath. "Emily Timberwolf? She must've told Jackie the same thing Trapper told me. That God wants to forgive my sins, but first I have to admit I'm a sinner." He shook his head sadly. "Who did I think I was kidding? I am a sinner. If I'd done nothing worse in my life than what I've done to Jackie, the woman who at one time I loved more than life itself, I'm sure God would see me as a terrible sinner! Oh, God, what have I done? What have I done?"

He leaned back in the chair, trying to gather some semblance of composure, his gut tied in knots. *If only Sam could be there with me.* Her words rang in his ears. "After all I've done to her, she still wants us to be together." Finally, he lifted the note and continued to read.

I was so happy knowing God loved me and could forgive me, but my joy soon turned to sadness, Sammy. Your father came to me and said he couldn't go on with our lying. I tried to tell him I'd gotten my life straightened out with God and He'd forgiven me, but he didn't seem to care. He was more interested in the ultimatum he was giving me.

Sam paused and blotted at his eyes with his sleeve.

Either I tell Trapper and Glorianna, or he will. He's right. I know he is. This lying is killing me, too. He's given me a few days to get things ready to leave before I have to tell them. After that, I'll be flying out of Juneau and away from the friends I love. But at least I won't have to keep living a lie. Oh, Sammy, if only you'd lived, our little family might be together now, and none of this lying would have happened.

Carefully, Sam repinned the paper to the back of the eleventh block, again taking note of the tiny stitches his ex-wife had lovingly added, each one perfectly in line with the one before it. He could almost see her sweet face as she painstakingly wove the needle in and out of the fabric.

The sound of a car's engine sent him quickly to the window, but it was only the next-door neighbor. He refilled his coffee cup and stood staring at the white box for a long time before he got up the courage to sit back down and pick up the last block, knowing how upset Jackie would be if she knew he was delving into her personal items like this. It was obvious she had never intended for anyone but her to see the blocks or read the notes she had penned to her son.

Finally, he settled back down in the chair, looked over the block, and unpinned its note.

Quilting this twelfth block and writing this note, my dear baby, has brought back bittersweet memories. I'm so thankful, even though the doctor was afraid to let me see you, that he finally agreed and allowed me to hold you close to my heart and kiss you good-bye. Other than the day I said "I do" to your father, those were the most precious moments of my life.

You looked so sweet as you lay in my arms, swaddled in that pale blue blanket with that funny little hat on your head as the nurse took our picture. I've cherished those little pictures, Sammy. Those first few years I kept them locked away in my diary. Just the sight of them made me burst uncontrollably into tears. But things have changed since that awful time of my life. I've grown up, Sammy. I've matured. Now I love to hold your pictures next to my heart and remember your sweet little innocent face. Someday maybe I'll be able to look at the picture my friend took of your tiny gravestone.

Gravestone! The word yanked Sam back to reality. He leaned his head against the back of the chair and closed his eyes. "My son is buried somewhere in the cold, cold ground, and I don't even know where?"

I was hoping one day, her note went on, *your father would want to see the pictures I've saved.*

"Why should she want to show them to me after the hurt I've caused her? I failed my wife when she needed me most." His head swirled. "Dear God, what You must think of me, too. How could either You or Jackie ever forgive me?" he cried aloud.

Trapper's words penetrated his thoughts. "So many people turn their backs on God's Son, Sam. Don't be one of them."

Sam lifted his tear-filled eyes heavenward. "But I am one of them, God! I've not only turned my back on Your Son, but I've turned my back on my own son as well and on my wife, too. Can You ever forgive me? Can Jackie ever forgive me?"

As Sam stared upward, he remembered one of the Scripture verses about forgiveness he'd heard at Trapper's church—that if you confess your sins and ask forgiveness, God will do it.

"Can it be that simple, Lord?" he asked out loud, his voice low and wavering. "If I do as Your Word says, can I know for sure I'm going to heaven?"

Another verse from the Bible filled his mind as clearly as if the pastor were standing beside him now, reading it to him. " 'Whosoever believeth in him should not perish, but have everlasting life.' " *I want to go to heaven, God. Surely, if You said it, it's true.* He longed to have that same peace Jackie spoke about when she'd told him her good news.

Pulling a handkerchief from his hip pocket, he wiped it across his eyes before glancing at the wall clock. He'd been there for nearly forty-five minutes. Where was Jackie?

He paced about the room, trying to imagine the gamut of emotions Jackie must have felt as she worked on those quilt blocks and wrote her notes to her baby. Their baby. Finally, he moved back to the chair, picked up the last note again, and read the rest of the words.

I'm sad today, my precious Sammy. Your father said some very cruel things to me before he left for Skagway. If only he'd been there when I miscarried you and witnessed my sorrow, he'd know I could never harm you. I'm afraid he'll go to his grave believing I ended your life willingly. I've turned this all over to God now, baby. It's in His hands. No matter what happens or how much Sam's dreadful accusations hurt me, I'll always love your father. And I'll always love you.

With all my love, Mama.

The paper fell to the floor as Sam thrust his head into his hands and wept. "Oh, God," he cried out from the depths of his soul, "I've sinned against You so many times in so many ways. Please, please forgive me for ever denying I'm a sinner." He dropped to his knees and spread his arms open wide, lifting his face upward. "Forgive me, I pray. I believe what You said in the Bible. I'm asking You to come into my heart and cleanse it. I'm not worthy of Your love, but I beg You to hear me now. Take me, God. I'm giving myself totally to You. I've made such a mess of my life. Only You can straighten it out."

Sam froze at the sound of the door opening behind him. He'd been so caught up in communing with God that he hadn't heard someone coming up the outside stairway. He cast a hurried, concerned glance at the pile of quilt blocks he'd left on the floor.

"Sam? What are you doing here?" Jackie glared at him as she pushed the door closed behind her, shutting out the cold morning chill.

Chapter 11

Her words hung in the air like icicles from a roof, unanswered, as Sam stared at her. "I—I—" His gaze went to the paper lying on the floor at his feet.

Jackie followed his gaze, then gasped as she quickly bent to retrieve the paper. "You—you've been—"

He nodded. "Yes, I know I had no right, but—"

"How could you? These letters are to my son! Surely they were of no interest to you! Did you have to spoil the one thing I had left? How dare you invade my privacy?"

Sam struggled for the right words. "Th—the door. It was standing slightly open."

"No, I distinctly remember turning the lock." She gathered up the quilt blocks, placed the note on top of them, and stuffed them hurriedly into the white box.

He stood, his hands dangling idly at his sides, like a penitent child who'd run out of excuses for his errant behavior. "I—I know you don't believe me, Jackie, but the door was standing open. You know I don't have a key."

A bit of the harsh anger disappeared from her face as she eyed the door and gave him an exasperated look. "I do have to tug on it sometimes to get the lock to engage, but that's no excuse for you to come in here uninvited. This is my home, or at least it is until I leave for the airport this afternoon."

She snatched the box from the floor, placed it on the sofa, and plopped down beside it, carefully replacing the lid. "I hope you didn't—"

Sam found it difficult to get his feet to move as he stood awkwardly by the chair. "I did, Jackie," he confessed, his eyes once more glazing over with tears. "I—I read them all."

She bowed her head and buried her face in her hands. "Oh, Sam. Wh—why did you have to co—come barging back into my li—life?"

He wanted so much to take her in his arms, comfort her, tell her how sorry he was, but why would she let him? So far everything he'd done since he'd come to Juneau had either blown up in his face or hurt Jackie. All because he'd been too stubborn to accept the truth. Cautiously, he moved the last few steps separating them and knelt before her, pulling her hands away from her face and taking them into his. "I'm sorry, Jackie, for everything. I—I want you to know that."

Tenderly, he kissed her fingertips one by one as he stared up into her lovely face, tears now rolling down his cheeks unashamedly. "I've sinned against you by not believing you. You were my wife! The one person in this world I loved the most and should trust the most. How could I not believe you?"

Jackie eyed him suspiciously. "I–I don't understand."

His finger pointed to the white box. "I–I read all about it, sweetheart. How you'd decided to go through with the abortion, despite my warning." He gulped hard, barely able to say the words. "Ho–how you changed your mind when you felt our baby move inside you."

"Sam, I know you don't believe I could have a change of heart over something that sounds so simple, but"—she leaned her head back and stared at the ceiling before going on—"to me, our baby moving like that was a miracle!"

"I–I should have been there with you."

She blinked and said in a mere whisper, "Yes, you should have. You missed a wonderful experience."

"I know, and I'll never forgive myself. I could've turned down that assignment, but I was furious with you. You were determined to go through with the abortion, and I didn't want to be around when you did it. It seemed I was the only one who wanted that baby."

Her breath hitched. "I–I wanted him too, Sam. When I felt that first movement and realized my baby was alive in me—well, all I can say is, in that moment, I became that child's mother. Me. Jackie Mulvaney."

Those two words sent daggers into his heart. Jackie Mulvaney. His wife. The one he'd promised to love, honor, and cherish. He'd vowed to protect her. From whom? If she needed protection from anyone, it was from him, her own husband!

Unsure how to proceed, Sam slowly slipped his arms about her waist and, when she didn't protest, pulled her close. "I am so sorry, Jackie, so sorry! Although I don't deserve it, I'm asking your forgiveness. Please, sweetheart, can you find it in your heart to forgive me?"

She leaned forward with a heavy sigh, and their foreheads touched. "Forgive you for what, Sam? For the many times you accused me of killing our baby? For you coming to Alaska and ruining the life I had here with the only true friends I've ever known?" Her voice was shaky and raw with emotion.

To his dying day Sam would remember the anguish in her voice. "Yes," he answered, trying to keep his own emotions under control. "Both of those and a whole lot more. I know I don't have the right to ask for forgiveness, but I'm begging you, sweetheart, please—try to find it in your heart to forgive me."

She drew back a bit and gave him a puzzled look. "Why do you keep calling me 'sweetheart'? I don't understand, Sam. Is this another one of your mixed signals?"

She seemed vulnerable, almost childlike herself, and suddenly, Sam's heart overflowed with love for this woman. A love he'd deigned to forget for the past seventeen years. "It's—it's because—I love you, Jackie. I always have. I guess that's why it hurt so much when you said you were going to do away with our baby. It was like you wanted to get rid of a part of me too."

Her entire being shuddered at his remark. "No! It wasn't that way at all! I"—she bowed her head shyly—"I loved you. You were my life."

"You were my life too. I wanted us to have that baby as a symbol of our love, the two of us made into one. It nearly killed me when you—"

She put a quick finger to his lips. "Don't say it, Sam. Please."

"I know now you could never have had an abortion. Those sweet letters you wrote to our Sammy were—"

"You did read them!"

"Yes, every word. I told you I did. But only because I had to know the truth." He shifted on his heels and pulled her close. "I wish I could do something to make up for all the pain I've caused you. I'm so sorry."

The tenderness and compassion she could see in his eyes touched her deeply. Her voice a mere whisper, she told him, "All I've ever wanted was for you to believe me."

He took one of her hands and folded it in his. "I do believe you, dearest. I've been such a fool."

Dare she believe him? Dare she trust her heart?

"God has forgiven me, Jackie, and I'm asking you to do the same thing. I want to start the rest of my life with a clean slate. Can you find it—?"

She raised her eyes and met his gaze head-on. "You did? You really asked for God's forgiveness? You're not just saying that?"

He brought up his hands to capture her face. "Yes. Just like you did when Emily came to see you and like Trapper had told me. The pastor's words when he read those Scripture verses had etched a place in my heart, and I couldn't forget them. I am going to spend eternity in heaven with you, Jackie. I know that now."

"Oh, Sam, you have no idea how happy that makes me. Of course I can forgive you."

Without warning, he stood and swung her up in his arms as his lips claimed hers in the sweetest kiss she'd ever experienced. She trembled against him, her tears wetting his shirt as she clung to him.

Jackie felt her heart racing. Sam. The love of her life. The only man she'd ever loved, and she was in his arms once again. "I wish you could've seen him, Sam," she murmured, her face pressed tightly against his strong chest.

Sam pulled her even closer. "Tell me about him. I—I need to know. I want to hear everything."

She drew in a deep breath. "Are you sure? Some of it's not very pretty."

He placed a gentle kiss on her forehead. "I'm sure."

Jackie breathed a quick prayer to God, asking Him for strength, then began her story. "I went for my regular visits to the doctor. Although most things seemed to be coming along okay, he was concerned because I was still spotting and carrying my placenta a bit low. But he told me it usually moved into place by itself. I guess you'd been gone about a month or so when I felt movement in my stomach. I knew right then it was our baby."

She looked up at him. "Oh, Sam, I can't begin to tell you what a feeling that was. By the time I went for my next checkup, he was moving all over the place. Because of my spotting and since my mother'd had high-risk pregnancies, the doctor decided to do an ultrasound. I didn't know what that was, but when I saw our baby moving around on that screen I shouted so loud I'm sure I scared the nurse out of her wits. Then the doctor asked if I wanted to know if it was a boy or a girl! Of course I answered yes. Well, it took a little bit of time; but finally Sammy moved into position, and we could tell he was a boy. I told the doctor I was going to name him Samuel Nathan Mulvaney, after you, Sam."

"I know." Sam gulped hard, his eyes blinking rapidly, tears rolling down his cheeks. "I read it in one of your notes."

In all the years she'd known him, she'd never seen him cry. He'd been too proud of his tough guy, macho man image to let his emotions get the better of him. She used to think it was from all the training he'd received in the army and from being around other military men with the same attitude.

"I can't begin to tell you how happy I was. I tried to phone the base in Germany, but you were on assignment. I wanted so much to share this wonderful experience with you. The doctor had even printed out Sammy's ultrasound picture so I could send it to you."

Sam nuzzled his chin in her hair. "Oh, Jackie. I'm so sorry."

She forced herself to continue. "I'd felt pretty good, but I suddenly began to feel tired. I'd put on quite a bit of weight, and I attributed it to that. Then I started spotting more heavily. When I called the doctor's office, they said spotting was fairly common and told me to come in the next morning." She paused. "I was scared, Sam, but aside from my so-called friends I had no one else to talk to."

"And I couldn't be reached."

She nodded. "Exactly. The spotting did slow down a bit, but then as I got out of bed at nearly dawn I began to hemorrhage. The sight of all that blood terrified me. All I could think about was getting help."

"And you drove yourself to the hospital instead of calling an ambulance or going to the doctor's office?"

"Yes, and since you've read my notes, you know what happened. I—I—"

He put a finger to her lips. "Shh, don't say it."

"I never dreamt the pain would be so severe. I thought I was dying, but I didn't care. All I could think about was that precious baby. I'd have gone through anything to keep him alive."

His warm breath struck her cheeks as he rested his forehead against hers.

"I–I didn't know—"

"They tried desperately to save him, Sam, but they—they couldn't."

Sam cupped her face between his hands and stroked her cheeks with his thumbs. "Oh, Jackie. Dear, sweet Jackie."

She drew a deep breath through numb lips. "Although he only weighed three pounds and two ounces, he was beautiful, Sam."

She smiled, the memory as fresh as if it were yesterday. "The doctor advised against my seeing him, but I had to do it. I had to! Finally, he agreed. I watched as the nurse cleaned up our baby and swaddled him. She even put a funny little hat on his head, like they do all newborns."

"Was he—did he—"

"He was perfectly formed. Ten teensy fingers and ten teensy toes, and his little face was like that of an angel." She let out a nervous giggle as she remembered how the little hat had nearly swallowed up his tiny head. "The nurse got her Polaroid camera and took pictures of him. Then she let me sit in the rocking chair and hold him, and she got pictures of the two of us."

Even through her tears, she could see Sam's lower lip quiver.

"Do—do you still have those pictures?"

"Yes, but I've packed them away in preparation for leaving Juneau."

"I'd like to see them."

Her heart pounded erratically at his words. "I was hoping, one day, you would. I even have the tiny little identification bracelet the hospital made for him, and I've framed his precious little foot and handprints."

Blinking, Sam rubbed the bridge of his nose with his thumb and forefinger. "I–I wish I'd been there with you. You shouldn't have had to go through that alone. We—were a family."

Jackie swallowed at the lump in her throat. "Our son would've been seventeen now, Sam, probably finishing up his junior year of high school."

Sam slipped his arm across her shoulders and rested his head against hers. "You think he would've been the star quarterback for his school's football team, as I was?"

She responded with a slight chuckle and reached a hand up to touch his cheek. "I'm sure of it. And he'd have driven all the girls crazy with his good looks."

She felt his chest rise and fall.

"I wish I could've seen him."

"He looked like he was sleeping, Sam. I kissed him and told him how much we had both wanted him to live, and I told him I'd named him Sammy, after you."

He drew in an audible breath and sent her a self-deprecating look. "I let you both down. Then, like a self-righteous fool, I came home from Germany and accused you of killing our baby. How you must've hated me."

"Your words only hurt me because I loved you so much."

Sam rose and began to pace about the room, his steps short and uneven, his hands flailing wildly through the air. "And I killed that love."

Suddenly, she was moving toward him, as if being drawn by a magnet. She flung her arms about his waist and hugged him tightly, resting her head against his strong back. "Don't you see, Sam? Nothing you could do could kill my love for you. Not even that! I loved you then. I love you now." Her words tumbled out before she could stop them.

Sam spun around in her arms and stared down at her. "You mean it? You still love me? After all—"

She touched a finger to his lips. "Yes. I'll always love you."

"Do—do you think there's even the slightest chance for us?"

She leaned into him, enjoying their closeness as she pressed her face to his shoulder. "Do you?"

He slid a finger beneath her chin, lifting her face to his, his still-youthful eyes blazing with a passion she'd thought had long ago been lost. "I'd give anything to have you back as my wife."

Jackie's eyes filled with fresh tears as she gave him a coy smile. "Anything?" She watched as his lips moved slowly toward hers and he hovered tantalizingly close. She felt the same old flutter of excitement she'd felt on their wedding day when they'd enjoyed their first kiss as husband and wife.

"Anything," he whispered against her lips. "Jackie, will you marry me all over again? Be my wife?"

Chapter 12

"Ma—marry you?"

She stared at him with startled exhilaration. Never had she expected to hear those words again from Sam.

"Will you, Jackie? I know I have no right to ask, not after the way I've behaved, but you said you'd forgive me and—"

She couldn't contain her smile. It was her decision now. He'd been the one to end their marriage the first time. Now, all these years later, it was up to her to decide if that marriage could be rekindled. But one thing still bothered her. She looked longingly into his face. "Oh, Sam, I want desperately to say yes, but I–I don't know. The doctor never said for sure—but I may not be able to give you children. I don't even know if I'd ever be able to carry a baby to full term—" She slowly lifted her eyes to meet his. "And I'm over forty now."

A hint of a grin tilted the corners of his mouth. "Hey, kiddo, we're both over forty now. As much as I'd like to have had children, that's the last thing I'm concerned about now." He gave a boyish shrug. "But if it happens, it happens!"

Slowly she placed her hand in his and smiled up at him as old feelings of love surrounded her heart. "Then, yes, Sam, my answer is yes!"

He wrapped his arms about her so tightly she found it difficult to draw in a breath as she gazed into his eyes.

"I don't have much to offer you, Jackie. As soon as I see Trapper, I'll be out of a job. I don't own any property. I don't even have a rented apartment back in Memphis to offer you. I'm sure many men could lay much more at your feet, if you'd let them. But I promise to love, honor, and cherish you for the rest of our lives."

Jackie's vision became fuzzy as she looked into his handsome face, the face that had haunted her dreams for the past seventeen years. Could this, too, be a dream? Would she wake up in her bed, only to find she was alone in her dark, empty room? She wanted to freeze this moment in time, to remember it forever.

"Being with you, spending the rest of our years together—that's all I ask. You're the only man I've ever loved or wanted as my husband. I'm sure God designed us to be together. Only He could have performed a miracle and brought us both to Juneau like this."

His misty gaze never left her face. "I don't deserve you, sweetheart, but with God's help I know we can make it. I want to be the kind of man God wants me to be. A man like Trapper. I want to be the husband you deserve."

His words flowed over her like a crystal river, blanketing her, engulfing her, bathing her with the love she desired. She watched as a slow smile crept across his face, and despite any misgivings she might have had, she knew she could trust this man with her very life.

He pulled her forward and cradled her to him as his warm lips planted tiny kisses at her temple, her eyelids, then the tip of her nose. She clung to him as if he were her lifeline, her hands splaying across his back, her fingers fanning out across his broad, muscled shoulders.

"I love you, Jackie Mulvaney," he whispered, his words feathering her ear.

His close proximity played havoc with her senses. She could feel her heart beating in time with his, and it was a delicious feeling. Her whole body shivered as he lowered his mouth onto hers, and she melted into his arms, absorbing his masculine scent. Gone were all the thoughts of getting her things packed in time to catch her afternoon flight out of Juneau. Gone were the feelings of hurt and disappointment she'd felt for over seventeen years. Nothing else occupied her thoughts but her love for this man, the joy of being in his arms once again and the anticipation of becoming his wife, as she returned his kisses.

Finally, Sam pulled away slightly, his arms still circling her waist as he gazed into her eyes. "We'd better hurry if we're going to fly out of here today."

She gave him a startled look. "Y–you're going with me? Now?"

"Yes, it's the only way." He motioned toward the empty boxes she'd brought back from the supermarket. "Go ahead with your packing. I'm going to tell Trapper we're leaving."

"He already knows, Sam. I should've told you earlier. I invited Trapper and Glorianna, his parents, and the Gordons over last night. They know the whole story."

Sam rubbed at his forehead and let out a heavy sigh. "I'm sure they think I'm nothing but a scoundrel now that they know about Sammy and that I was your husband."

"My intent wasn't to make you look bad, Sam. I explained it was my fault for being so insistent about having an abortion."

A slow smile of understanding crept across his face. "I know that, sweetie. I'd expect that from you. They deserved to know the truth. I'm leaving Trapper in a bind, but now that he knows why, I'm sure he'll understand. I do want to let him know I've gotten my life straightened out with God. That man has been praying for me."

"He's a fine man. He'll be glad to hear it."

Sam gave her a quick peck on the cheek. "Facing him is going to be hard, but I can't put it off. I'm going to see him now; then I'll head over to Grandma's Feather Bed, throw my things in my suitcase, and call the airport for reservations.

I'll be back as quick as I can."

He kissed her once more, then pulled on his jacket and headed for the door, reminding her again, "I love you!"

∂

Jackie hurried to the window and watched as Sam slid into the rental car, started the engine, and headed off toward the Timberwolf house. Everything had happened so fast, so unexpectedly. She'd crawled out of bed that very morning, brokenhearted, despondent, and feeling as if her life were coming to an end. But, thanks to God, that was not to be. Sam was back in her life for good, and she would soon become his wife.

After putting a CD in the player, she flitted around the house, humming to the music as she placed things in each box, sealing it with packing tape, and labeling its contents. When she was finished, she danced into the kitchen, whirling and pirouetting and singing along with the lead singer on the CD, her joy bubbling over uncontrollably. She'd just poured herself a glass of juice when she heard a knock on the door.

Sam's back!

Jackie opened the door and gasped. It was Sam all right, but he had an entire entourage with him.

He gave her a lopsided grin as he gestured toward the little group, and they all moved inside. "I tried to talk them out of it, but they insisted on coming."

"It was Trapper's idea," Glorianna said proudly, holding onto her husband's arm.

"Yeah," Hank chimed in, reaching for Tina's hand. "He said friends needed to rally around each other in a time of need, and we are your friends, Jackie, both yours and Sam's."

Tina giggled as she rubbed her slightly rounded tummy. "This little guy is gonna need an uncle Sam and an auntie Jackie."

Jackie frowned. What were they saying?

Emily moved quickly to her side and wrapped an arm about her shoulders. "You didn't think you were gonna get away from us that easily, did you?" She motioned to her husband, who was standing silently by the door. "Come on over here, Dyami. Tell this girl how much she means to us."

The elder man shuffled across the floor and took Jackie's hand in his, patting it in a fatherly way. "We love you, girl. God loves you, too. Don't ever forget it."

Jackie smiled at each one through her tears. "I love all of you, but—why are you here?"

Sam pulled her from Emily and into his arms. "They want us to stay, sweetheart, both of us. Glorianna wants you to stay on as the manager of her shop, and Trapper still wants me as his business partner. Can you believe it?"

Six people encircled them, their arms entwined with one another's.

"It's unanimous," Trapper said, speaking for all six. "We want you both to stay. I've got big plans, and they include Sam and that helicopter we want to buy."

Sam grinned. "Yeah. Mulvaney-Timberwolf Aviation."

"How about Timberwolf-Mulvaney Aviation?" Trapper shot back, an exaggerated smile peeking through his heavy mustache and beard.

Sam uttered a playful snort. "I can live with that."

Trapper's face took on a seriousness Jackie had rarely seen on him. "What you did, Jackie—lying to us all these years—was wrong. But, considering the circumstances, I think all of us understand and have accepted it. You were covering up a painful part of your life. A part you wanted to put behind you. We couldn't fault you for that. Most of us have things in our lives we'd prefer to forget."

Glorianna gave her a sweet smile. "You could've told me, Jackie, once we became friends. I'd have been disappointed, but I wouldn't have thought any less of you. I could tell that first day I met you there was something troubling about you, a leave-me-alone type of attitude that bothered me. I knew you resented me because of Trapper, but it was more than that. I didn't know what, but that's hindsight, isn't it? Please know we all love you, honey, and want both you and Sam to stay. The Bear Paw's customers would never forgive me if I let you get away."

Trapper's smile returned. "Besides, you have God to turn to now. Sam tells me he's accepted the Lord, too. Nothing could please us more. Glorianna and I have been praying for both of you." He nodded toward his parents. "Mom and Dad have, too."

"So have Tina and I," Hank added. "You two are very special to us."

"Buck and Victoria Silverbow have had you on their prayer list too," Trapper interjected. "I can't wait to tell them the two of you have not only accepted the Lord, but you're back together. Only God could have worked that one out."

Jackie found herself speechless. Yesterday she'd felt rejected and alone. Now Sam was back in her life, and so were her friends. God was truly good.

Sam gave her a loving squeeze as his smile broadened. "What's the answer, sweetheart? It's up to you. Glorianna says we can stay right here in this apartment, if you like. Or we can get our own house. I'll be happy living anywhere, as long as I'm sharing that home with you."

"Stay," Tina said, reaching a hand across the circle. "Please. It wouldn't be the same without you."

"Yeah, stay. I need those big bucks you and Trapper are going to pay me for being the Mulvaney-Timberwolf"—Hank paused and gave them a big grin—"or the Timberwolf-Mulvaney attorney. Whichever name you decide on."

Still finding it hard to speak, her heart running over with love for these wonderful friends, Jackie looked from one kind face to the next, then back to Sam. "Let's stay!"

"Up a couple of inches," Jackie told Sam a month later as he held the little quilt against their bedroom wall. "Now over just a bit."

"Here?" he asked, after making the slight adjustment. "Make sure this is where you want it before I drill the holes in the wall."

She backed up a couple of steps and squinted her eyes. "It's perfect."

Sam took a pencil from his pocket and made two small marks on the wall, then lowered the quilt. "Honey, are you sure seeing this quilt on the wall every day won't make you sad? It holds a lot of memories."

She carefully took the little blue and white quilt from his hands and held it out to admire. "How could it make me sad? I made it as a memorial to our son. To Sammy."

Sam stepped up behind her and wrapped his arms about her, nestling his chin in her hair. "I'm glad you made it, but I'm really happy you wrote those sweet notes to him. If I hadn't come to your apartment that morning and found your door unlocked and barged my way in, I might never have seen those quilt blocks or the notes, and I would've lost you. You could've flown out of Juneau, and I'd never have found you again."

"It was God's doing, Sam. I'm sure of it. The last thing I wanted was for you to find those quilt blocks. I'd been so careful to keep them hidden under my bed all the time I was working on them. They were between Sammy and me, and no one else. Especially not you."

"I hadn't planned to come to your apartment that morning. I didn't even know you'd already told everyone about our lies. But I woke up early and couldn't go back to sleep. All I could think about were the awful things I'd said to you before I left for Skagway. I didn't want you to leave without at least telling you I was sorry."

He spun her around in his arms and captured her face between his palms, his blue eyes reaching into the very center of her heart. "And when I knocked and you didn't answer, I nearly turned away and started down the stairs, but something deep within me told me to check the door. I did and found it standing open just a crack. I hadn't even noticed it when I'd knocked. I knew you'd be upset if I went in while you were gone, but I had to see you. We'd already parted bitterly once. I couldn't let that happen again."

"Oh, Sam, what if you'd gone on that morning, before I got back home?" Just the thought struck panic to her heart.

"But I didn't, sweetheart. I know now it was God speaking to me, making me stay. He wants us together, Jackie. I think He created us for each other."

"I think so, too." Jackie stood on tiptoe and planted a kiss on her husband's lips.

His hand caressed her cheek. "You were the most beautiful bride I've ever seen. Even more beautiful than you were the first time I married you!"

She was sure she was blushing. "I was amazed at how many of our new

Christian friends were at our wedding. I think the whole church was there."

He nodded. "I'm glad the Silverbows were able to make it. They're nice folks. I'm sure we'll get better acquainted with them when I begin to do those wonderful missionary flights into the bush with Trapper and Hank."

Jackie gave him a teasing smile. "You'd do those things for free?"

A hint of amusement quirked at his lips. "For free for God!"

"I made this little quilt for our son, Sam," she said dreamily as she pulled away and let her fingers trace the intricate stitching on one of the quilt's blocks. "I only wish I could have wrapped it about him."

Sam pulled her into his arms again and cradled her head against his chest. "I know, sweetheart. I do, too."

She tilted her head up a little, regarding him thoughtfully as she clung to the little quilt. "I never want us to forget about Sammy. This little quilt will always serve as a reminder of him. He was a part of us, Sam, and we were a part of him. As you said, my dear husband, this baby quilt is a symbol of our love."

Sam kissed her cheek, then pulled away and pointed toward the wall where he'd made the pencil marks. "Sure that's where you want me to hang it?"

She nodded as she gazed at her husband. "Absolutely sure."

She watched lovingly as he headed toward the shed to get the drill. She and Sam were together again.

This time for keeps.

A Letter to Our Readers

Dear Readers:

In order that we might better contribute to your reading enjoyment, we would appreciate your taking a few minutes to respond to the following questions. When completed, please return to the following: Fiction Editor, Barbour Publishing, Inc., P.O. Box 719, Uhrichsville, OH 44683.

1. Did you enjoy reading *Alaskan Midnight?*
   ❑ Very much—I would like to see more books like this.
   ❑ Moderately—I would have enjoyed it more if _____
   _____
   _____

2. What influenced your decision to purchase this book?
   (Check those that apply.)
   ❑ Cover   ❑ Back cover copy   ❑ Title   ❑ Price
   ❑ Friends   ❑ Publicity   ❑ Other

3. Which story was your favorite?
   ❑ *Northern Exposure*   ❑ *Be My Valentine*
   ❑ *Hand Quilted with Love*   ❑ *The Baby Quilt*

4. Please check your age range:
   ❑ Under 18   ❑ 18–24   ❑ 25–34
   ❑ 35–45   ❑ 46–55   ❑ Over 55

5. How many hours per week do you read? _____

Name _____

Occupation _____

Address _____

City _____ State _____ Zip _____

E-mail _____

If you enjoyed

Alaskan
MIDNIGHT

then read:

❀

Georgia

LOVE IS JUST PEACHY IN
FOUR COMPLETE NOVELS

Heaven's Child by Gina Fields
On Wings of Song by Brenda Knight Graham
Restore the Joy by Sara Mitchell
A Match Made in Heaven by Kathleen Yapp

HEARTSONG ♥ PRESENTS

Love Stories
Are Rated G!

That's for godly, gratifying, and of course, great! If you love a thrilling love story but don't appreciate the sordidness of some popular paperback romances, **Heartsong Presents** is for you. In fact, **Heartsong Presents** is the premiere inspirational romance book club featuring love stories where Christian faith is the primary ingredient in a marriage relationship.

Sign up today to receive your first set of four, never-before-published Christian romances. Send no money now; you will receive a bill with the first shipment. You may cancel at any time without obligation, and if you aren't completely satisfied with any selection, you may return the books for an immediate refund!

Imagine. . .four new romances every four weeks—two historical, two contemporary—with men and women like you who long to meet the one God has chosen as the love of their lives. . .all for the low price of $10.99 postpaid.

To join, simply complete the coupon below and mail to the address provided. **Heartsong Presents** romances are rated G for another reason: They'll arrive Godspeed!

YES!   Sign me up for Hearts♥ng!